W9-CAE-122

DATE DUE

The
Black Book
of Secrets

The

BLACK BOOK
of SECRETS

F. E. HIGGINS

FEIWEL AND FRIENDS · NEW YORK

A FEIWEL AND FRIENDS BOOK
An Imprint of Holtzbrinck Publishers

Library of Congress Cataloging-in-Publication Data Available Upon Request

ISBN-13: 978-0-312-36844-9
ISBN-10: 0-312-36844-5

First published in the United Kingdom by Macmillan Children's Books, a
division of Pan Macmillan

Cover and title page art © 2007 by Greg Ruth
Cover design by Rich Deas
Book design by Susan Walsh

The text type was set in Monotype Pastonchi, originally designed in 1927 by
Francesco Pastonchi and Eduardo Cotti.

First U.S. Edition: October 2007

10 9 8 7 6 5 4 3 2 1

www.feiwelandfriends.com

For Beatrix

Non mihi, non tibi, sed nobis

A Note from the Author

I came across Joe Zabbidou's Black Book of Secrets and Ludlow Fitch's memoirs in a rather curious manner. They were tightly rolled up and concealed within the hollow of a wooden leg. How I came to be in possession of the leg is unimportant right now. What matters is the story the documents tell.

Unfortunately neither Joe's Black Book nor Ludlow's memoirs survived the centuries intact, and when I unrolled them, it was obvious that they had suffered damage. Not only were the pages brittle and water-stained, but much of what I had was also illegible. The fragments and extracts are reproduced here exactly as they were written. I corrected Ludlow's spelling—it really was quite dreadful—but I did no more than that. As for the parts that are

missing, what else could I do but draw upon my imagination to fill the gaps? I pieced the story together in the way I thought best. I like to think I stayed as close to the truth as I could with the few facts I had. I do not claim to be the author of this story, merely the person who has tried to reveal it to the world.

—*F. E. Higgins*
England

The
Black Book
of Secrets

CHAPTER ONE

Fragment from
The Memoirs of Ludlow Fitch

When I opened my eyes I knew that nothing in my miserable life prior to that moment could possibly be as bad as what was about to happen. I was lying on the cold earthen floor of a basement room lit by a single candle, no more than an hour's burning left. Instruments of a medical nature hung from hooks in the beams. Dark stains on the floor suggested blood. But it was the chair against the opposite wall that fully confirmed my suspicions. Thick leather straps attached to the arms and the legs were there for one purpose only: to hold down an unwilling patient. Ma and Pa were standing over me.

"'E's awake," crowed Ma excitedly.

Pa dragged me to my feet. He had me in an iron grip, my arm wrenched up behind my back. Ma held me by the hair. I looked from one to the other. Their grinning faces were only inches away from mine. I knew I should not look to them to save me.

Another man, concealed until now in the shadows, stepped forward and took me by the chin. He forced open my mouth and ran a blackened, foul-tasting finger around my gums.

"How much?" asked Pa, drooling with anticipation.

"Not bad," said the man. "Thrupence apiece. Maybe twelve in all."

"It's a deal," said Pa. "Who needs teeth anyway?"

"Someone, I hope," replied the man dryly. "I sell 'em for a living."

And they laughed, all three, Ma and Pa and Barton Gumbroot, the notorious tooth surgeon of Old Goat's Alley.

Once the money for my teeth was agreed with Barton, they moved quickly. Together they dragged me over to the surgeon's chair. I kicked and shouted and spat and bit; I wasn't going to make it easy for them. I knew how Barton Gumbroot made his living, preying on the poor, pulling their teeth, paying them pennies and selling them for ten times as much. I was racked with fear. I had no protection. I was going to feel it all. Every single nerve-stabbing twinge.

They came close to succeeding in their evil quest. Ma was struggling with a buckle around my ankle, her hands shaking from the previous day's drinking, while Pa was trying to hold me down. Barton Gumbroot, that loathsome monster, was just hovering with his gleaming tooth-pull, snapping it open and shut, open and shut, tittering and salivating. I believe to this day his greatest pleasure in life was inflicting pain on others. So much so that he couldn't wait any longer, and before I knew it I could feel the cold metal of his instrument of torture clamped around a front tooth. He braced himself with his leg on my chest and began to pull. I cannot describe to you the pain that shot through my skull, my brain, and every nerve end in my body. It felt as if my whole head were being wrenched off. The tooth moved slightly in my jaw and another white-hot shooting pain exploded behind my eyes. All the while Ma and Pa laughed like maniacs.

Rage swelled in me like a mountainous wave. I heard a roar worthy of a jungle beast and I was taken over by seething fury. With my free leg I kicked Pa hard and sharp in the stomach and he collapsed on the floor. Barton, caught by surprise, let go of the tooth-pull, and I grabbed it and walloped him around the side of the head. I unstrapped my other leg and jumped down. Pa was groaning on the floor, Barton was leaning against the wall holding his head, and Ma cowered in the corner.

"Don't hit me, Ludlow," she begged. "Don't hit me."

I will not deny I was tempted, but this was my one chance to escape. Pa was almost on his feet again. I dropped the tooth-pull and in a matter of seconds I was out of the door, up the steps, and running down the alley. I could hear Ma screaming and Pa shouting and cursing. Every time I looked back all I could see were Pa's snarling face and Barton's hooked tooth-pull glinting in the yellow gaslight.

As I ran I tried to think where to go. They knew so many

of my hiding places. I decided on Mr. Jellico's, but when I reached his shop the place was in darkness and the blind was down. I hammered on the window and shouted his name, but there was no reply. I cursed my bad luck. I knew if Mr. Jellico was gone at this time of night he might not be back for days. But knowing this was little help in my current predicament.

So where to now? The bridge over the River Foedus and the Nimble Finger Inn. Betty Peggotty, the landlady, might help me. I ran out of the alley and onto the street, but they were already waiting for me.

"There 'e is," screeched Ma, and the chase was on again. They surprised me, Pa especially, with their stamina. I had not thought they would last so long. For at least a half-mile they chased me down the uncobbled narrow alleys and the filthy streets, tripping over bodies and avoiding snatching hands, all the way to the river. Every time I looked back they seemed to be closer. I knew what would happen if they caught me again. The ache in my bleeding jaw was all the proof I needed.

By the time I staggered onto the bridge I was barely able to hold myself upright. Halfway across I saw a carriage outside the Nimble Finger. Just as its wheels began to turn, I clambered on the back, hanging on for my life. As the carriage pulled away the last thing I remember is the sight of Ma sinking to her knees. She was screaming at me from the riverbank, and the monster, Barton Gumbroot, was shaking his fist in rage.

My name is Ludlow Fitch. Along with countless others, I had the great misfortune to be born in the City, a stinking place undeserving of a name. And I would have died there if it had not been for Ma and Pa. They saved me, though it was not their intention, when they delivered me, their only son, into the hands of Barton Gumbroot. This act of betrayal was possibly the greatest single piece of luck I ever had. Ma and Pa's diabolic plan brought about the end of one existence and the beginning of another: my life with Joe Zabbidou.

CHAPTER TWO

FRAGMENT FROM
THE MEMOIRS OF LUDLOW FITCH

I didn't know at the time, but I had hitched a ride on a carriage that belonged to, and contained, a Mr. Jeremiah Ratchet. We rattled along for hours, he inside snoring like a bellows, so loud I could hear it above the clatter of the wheels over the ruts, while outside I was clinging to the carriage like an organ-grinder's monkey. The weather worsened and it started to snow. The road narrowed and the potholes became larger, deeper, and more frequent. The driver had no thought for passenger comfort. If it wasn't for the fact that my hands were frozen in position I might well have fallen off. Despite this, and my churning innards (I suffer terribly from travel sickness), toward the end of the journey I was dozing. The carriage began to climb a steep hill, and finally we reached the place that was to be my home for the near future, the mountain village of Pagus Parvus.

Under any other circumstances I would not have chosen to come to Pagus Parvus, but at the time of traveling my

destination was out of my hands. At last the carriage stopped outside a large house and the driver climbed down. I heard him rap on the carriage door.

"Mr. Ratchet," he called. "Mr. Ratchet."

But there was no reply, so he went to the house and rang for the maid. A young girl came out looking none too pleased. The driver called her Polly. Together they dragged the man up the steps, accompanied by much snoring (his) and grunting (theirs) and hauled him inside. I took the opportunity to jump down and sneak a look in the cab, wherein I found a leather purse, a fringed printed silk scarf, and a pair of gloves. I wrapped the scarf around my neck and slipped the gloves over my numb fingers. The purse contained only a few pennies but it was a start. I got out and saw the young girl standing in the doorway looking straight at me. There was a slight smile on her face and her eyes held mine for a long second. I heard the driver coming back and knew it was time to go. I could have gone either way, up the slope or down, but for some unknown reason I chose to climb.

The hill was treacherous. As I climbed I heard the church bell strike four. Although it was no longer snowing, the wind was sharp as a knife and I knew I needed shelter. Despite the hour, and the lack of streetlights, I could see well enough where I was going. It was not the moon that lit my way, for she was only a sliver, but all the lights ablaze behind the windows. It seemed that I was not the only one still awake in this village.

I stopped at an empty building at the top of the hill. It stood alone in the shadow of the church, desolate and separated from the other houses and shops by an alley. I was looking for a way in when I heard approaching footsteps in the snow. I ducked into the alley and waited. A man, hunched over, came carefully down the hill. He was carrying a large wooden spade over his shoulder and he was mumbling to himself. He passed right by me, looking neither to his left nor his right, and crossed over the road.

As he melted into the night another figure appeared. To this day I remember the man emerging from the gloom as if by magic. I watched him climbing steadily toward me. He took long strides and covered the distance quickly. He had a limp, his right step was heavier than his left, and one footprint was deeper than the other.

I believe I was the first person to see Joe Zabbidou and I know I was the last. Was it just coincidence that had us both arrive here together? I suspect other powers were at work. Unlike me, he wasn't fleeing. He had a purpose, but he kept it well hidden.

CHAPTER THREE

Arrival

It was not easy to describe Joe Zabbidou accurately. His age was impossible to determine. He was neither stout nor thin, but perhaps narrow. And he was tall, which was a distinct disadvantage in Pagus Parvus. The village dated from times when people were at least six inches shorter and all dwellings were built accordingly. In fact, the place had been constructed during the years of the "Great Wood Shortage." The king at the time issued a decree that every effort must be made to save wood, with the result that doors and windows were made smaller and narrower than was usual and ceilings were particularly low.

Joe was suitably dressed for the weather, though unheedful of the current fashion for the high-collared coat. Instead he wore a cloak of muted green, fastened with silver toggles, that fell to his ankles. The cloak itself was of the finest Jocastar wool. The Jocastar—an animal akin to a sheep but with longer, more delicate legs and finer features—lived high up

in the mountains of the northern hemisphere. Once a year, September time, it molted, and only the most agile climbers dared venture up into the thin air to collect its wool. The cloak was lined with the softest fur in existence, chinchilla.

On his feet Joe wore a pair of black leather boots, highly polished, upon which sat the beautifully pressed cuffs of his mauve trousers. Around his neck was wrapped a silk scarf, and a fur hat shaped like a cooking pot was pulled down tightly over his ears. It could not fully contain his hair, and more than a few silver strands curled out from underneath.

With every step Joe took, a set of keys hooked to his belt jingled tunefully against his thigh. In his right hand he carried a rather battered leather satchel straining at the seams, and in his left a damp drawstring bag from which there emanated an intermittent croaking.

Quickly, silently, Joe climbed the steep high street until he reached the last building on the left. It was an empty shop. Beyond it was a walled graveyard, the village boundary, within which stood the church. Then the road stretched away into a gray nothingness. Snow had drifted into the shop doorway and gathered in the corners of the flyblown windows. The paintwork was peeling and an old sign in the shape of a hat creaked above the door in the biting wind. Joe took a moment to survey the street down to the bottom of the hill. It was the early hours of the morning, but yellow oil lamps and candles glowed behind many a curtain and shutter, and more than once he saw the silhouette of a person

cross back and forth in front of a window. A smile broke across his face.

"This is the place," he said and let himself in.

The shop itself was quite tiny. The distance between the display window and the counter was no more than three paces. Joe went behind the counter and opened the solid door that led into a back room. A tiny window on the far wall allowed the dusty moon-glow to lighten the gloom. The furniture was sparse and worn: two ladderback chairs and a table, a small stove, and a narrow bed pushed up against the wall. In contrast the fireplace was huge. At least six feet across and nearly three deep, it took up almost the whole of one wall. On either side of the hearth sat a faded uphol-stered armchair. It was not much, but it would do.

In the depths of the night, Joe busied himself settling in. He turned up the wick and lit the lamp on the table. He un-wound his scarf, took off his hat and unfastened his cloak, and put them on the bed. Then he opened his satchel, and as a silent observer peered through the window, Joe emptied it out onto the table. The onlooker never moved, though his already huge dark eyes widened impossibly as Joe pulled out clothes, shoes, a collection of trinkets and baubles, some rather fine jewelry, two loaves, a bottle of stout, another bottle (dark-glassed and unlabeled), four timepieces (with gold chains), a brass hurricane lamp, a rectangular glass tank with a vented lid, a large black book, a quill and bottle of ink, and a polished mahogany wooden leg. The satchel was deceptively spacious.

Deftly Joe fixed the tank together, then took his drawstring bag and loosened the tie. He set it down gently on the table and a second later a frog, a rather spectacular specimen of mixed hue and intelligent expression, emerged daintily from its folds. Very carefully Joe picked it up and placed it inside the tank, whereupon the creature blinked lazily and munched thoughtfully on some dried insects.

As Joe dropped another bug into the tank he stiffened almost imperceptibly. Without a backward glance he left the room, the eyes at the window still following him curiously. But they didn't see him slip out into the street. No human ear heard him tiptoe around the back of the shop, where he pounced upon the figure at the window and held him up to the light by the scruff of his scrawny neck.

"Why are you spying on me?" asked Joe in the sort of voice that demanded an answer without delay.

Joe had the boy in such a grip that he was half choking on his collar and his feet were barely touching the ground. He tried to speak, but fear and shock had rendered him unable. He could only open and close his mouth like a fish out of water. Joe gave him a shake and repeated the question, though less harshly this time. When he still received no answer he let the young lad fall to the snow in a crumpled, pathetic heap.

"Hmm." Joe took a long, hard look at the boy. He truly was a pale and sorry figure, undersized, undernourished, and shivering so hard you could almost hear his bones rattle. His

eyes were striking, though, dark green with flecks of yellow, and set in a ring of shadow. His skin matched the snow in tone and temperature. Joe sighed and pulled him to his feet.

"And you are?" he asked.

"Fitch," said the boy. "Ludlow Fitch."

CHAPTER FOUR

Poetry and Pawnbrokers

Ludlow sat at the table shivering in silence while Joe tended the fire. A blackened kettle hung over the flame and every so often Joe stirred its contents.

"Would you like some soup?"

Ludlow nodded and Joe ladled the thick mixture into two bowls and set them down. The boy gulped his noisily in spilling, overfull spoonfuls.

"Where have you come from?"

Ludlow wiped soup from his chin and managed to whisper. "From the City."

"I see. And do you wish to go back?"

He shook his head violently.

"I cannot blame you. In my experience the City is a rotten, diseased place full of the very worst of humanity. The lowest of the low."

Ludlow nodded again and drank at the same time, with the result that the soup dripped onto his gray shirt collar.

Without hesitation, he put the stained cloth in his mouth and sucked out the juices. Joe watched unsmiling, but with amusement in his eyes.

"And what did you do in the City?"

Ludlow put down the bowl. The warming soup had brought life back to his frozen limbs. "All sorts, really," he said evasively, but then, under Joe's intense gaze, he continued, "though mainly I picked pockets."

"Your honesty is refreshing, Ludlow, but I doubt there'd be much of that sort of work here," said Joe dryly. "This is a small village. There's little to take."

"I can always find something," said Ludlow proudly.

"I believe you could." Joe laughed, looking at the boy thoughtfully. "Tell me, have you any other talents?"

"I run fast and curl up so tight I can hide in the smallest places."

Whether this impressed Joe or not, it was difficult to tell. "Useful, I'm sure," he said, "but what of schooling? Can you write and read?"

"Of course I can," said Ludlow as if Joe was a fool to suggest otherwise.

If Joe was surprised he did not show it. "Then let me see your skill." He rummaged through the pile on the table, then handed Ludlow a quill, a pot of ink, and a piece of paper.

Ludlow thought for a moment, then wrote slowly in his plain, spidery hand, the tip of his tongue sticking out of the corner of his mouth:

A Pome

The rabit dose be a gentel creture

Its furr is soft, its tale is wite

Under the sun a gras eater

In a burro it doth sleep the nighte.

Joe stroked his chin to conceal his smile. "Who was it taught you to spell? Your parents?"

Ludlow snorted at the very suggestion. "My parents care not for the written word, nor for me. I was taught by Mr. Lembart Jellico, a pawnbroker in the City."

"Lembart Jellico?" repeated Joe. "How very interesting."

"Do you know him?" asked Ludlow, but Joe was busy looking for another sheet of paper.

"Write this," he said and dictated a couple of sentences, which Ludlow wrote carefully before handing back the paper to be examined.

"Two *b*'s in Zabbidou," said Joe, "but you weren't to know that."

He stood back and took a long, hard look at the boy. He resembled so many City boys, dirty and skinny. He certainly smelled like one. His clothes were barely functional (apart from the scarf and gloves, which were of a much higher quality), and he had a distrustful face that gave away the wretchedness of his past existence. He was bruised and his mouth was very swollen, but there was a spark of intelligence—and something else—in those dark eyes.

"I have a job for you if you want it."

Ludlow's eyes narrowed. "Does it pay?"

Joe yawned. "Let's discuss that tomorrow. Now it is time to sleep."

He threw Ludlow his cloak and the boy curled up in the space beside the fire. He had never felt such soft fur before, and it wrapped itself around his legs almost of its own accord. Ludlow watched through half-closed eyes as Joe stretched out on the bed opposite, his legs not quite fully extended, and began to snore. When he was certain that Joe was asleep, Ludlow pulled out the purse he had stolen from the carriage and hid it behind a loose brick in the wall. Then he took the paper and read it once again.

My name is Joe Zabidou. I am the Secret Pawnbroker.

A secret pawnbroker? thought Ludlow. *What sort of job is that?* But he did not ponder the question for very long before drifting off into a sleep full of wild dreams that made his heart race.

CHAPTER FIVE

FRAGMENT FROM
THE MEMOIRS OF LUDLOW FITCH

I hadn't meant to tell Joe I was a pickpocket and I don't know why I told him the truth. As for pawnbrokers, naturally I knew what they were. I'd been in and out of their shops enough times when I lived in the City. Whatever Ma and Pa managed to steal and had no use for, they pawned. Or they sent me to do it. There were plenty of pawnshops, practically one on every corner, and they were open all hours. They were busiest after the weekend, when everyone had spent their wages on drink or lost them at the card table. By midmorning on Mondays a pawnshop window was quite a sight, believe me. People brought in every sort of thing: shirts, old shoes, pipes, crockery, anything that might fetch even a ha'penny.

The pawnbroker, however, wouldn't take just anything. And the money he paid wasn't good at all, but when people grumbled that he was cheating he would say, "I'm not a charity. Take it or leave it."

And usually they took what he offered because they had

no choice. Of course, you could always buy back what you pledged, but you had to pay more. That's how a pawnbroker made his money, getting rich from the poor.

But Lembart Jellico wasn't like the others. For a start, he was hidden away down a narrow lane off Pledge Street. You would only know he was there if you knew he was there, if you see what I mean. I found him because I was looking for somewhere to hide from Ma and Pa. The entrance to the lane was so narrow I had to go in sideways. When I looked up I could see only a thin sliver of the smoky city sky. Mr. Jellico's shop was at the end of the lane, and at first I thought it was shut, but when I pressed my nose against the door it swung inward. The pawnbroker was standing behind the counter, but he didn't see me. He looked as if he was in a daydream.

I coughed.

"Sorry," said the man, blinking. "How can I help you, young lad?" he asked. Those were the first kind words I had heard all day. I gave him what I had, a ring I had taken from a lady's finger (a particular skill of mine, to mesmerize unfortunate passersby with my sorrowful gaze while relieving them of the burden of their jewels). Mr. Jellico's eyebrows arched when he saw it.

"Your mother's, I suppose?" he said, but he didn't push me for an answer.

Mr. Jellico looked as poor as his customers. He wore clothes that people had never come back to claim (and he couldn't sell). His skin was white, starved of the sun, and had

a slight shine to it, like wet pastry. His long fingernails were usually black and his lined face was covered in gray stubble. There was always a drip at the end of his nose and occasionally he wiped it away with a red handkerchief that he kept in his waistcoat pocket. That day he gave me a shilling for the ring, so I came back the next day with more spoils and received another. After that I returned as often as I could.

I don't know if Mr. Jellico made any money. His shop was rarely busy, the window was dirty, and there was never much on display. Once I saw a loaf of bread on the shelf.

"Young lass," said Mr. Jellico when I asked him about it. "She swapped the bread for a pot so she could boil a ham. She'll be back tomorrow with the pot and she'll take the bread, a little harder maybe, but it will soften in water."

Such were the strange arrangements between pawnbroker and customer!

I don't know why Mr. Jellico showed me such kindness, why he chose to feel sorry for me over the hundreds of other lads roaming the perilous streets. Whatever the reason, I wasn't complaining. I told him what Ma and Pa were like, how they treated me, how little they cared for me. Many times when it was too cold to stay out, and I was too afraid to return home, he let me warm myself by his fire and gave me tea and bread. He taught me the alphabet and numbers and let me practice writing on the back of old pawn tickets. He showed me books and made me copy out page after page until he was satisfied with my handwriting. It has been remarked that my style is a

little formal. I blame this on the texts from which I learned. Their authors were of a serious nature, writing of wars and history and great thinkers. There was little room for humor.

In return for this learning I carried out certain chores for Mr. Jellico. At first I wrote out the price tags for the window, but as my writing improved he let me log the pledges and monies in his record book. Occasionally the door would open and we would have a customer. Mr. Jellico enjoyed talking and would detain them in conversation for quite some time before taking their pledge and paying them.

I spent many hours in the back of the shop engaged in such tasks, and Ma and Pa never knew. I saw no reason to tell them about Mr. Jellico; they would only have demanded that I steal something from him. I had the opportunity, many times, but although I would not hesitate to cheat my parents out of a few shillings, I could not betray Mr. Jellico.

I would have gone to him every day if I could, but he wasn't always there. The first time I found the shop closed I thought he must have packed up and left. I was surprised that he hadn't said goodbye, even though it was the sort of thing I had come to expect from people. Then a few days later he came back. He didn't say where he had been and I didn't ask. I was just glad to see him.

This went on for almost five months until the night I fled the City. As I lay in the fireplace that first night at Joe Zabbidou's I had only one regret, that I had left without saying goodbye to Lembart Jellico. There was little chance I would see him again.

So when Joe said that he was a pawnbroker I was pleased. He seemed different from Mr. Jellico and I knew that Pagus Parvus was nothing like the City, but I felt safe. I thought I knew what to expect. But of course I didn't know then what a Secret Pawnbroker was.

A Grand Opening

Pagus Parvus was indeed very different from the City. It was a small village clinging for its life to the side of a steep mountain in a country that has changed its name over and over and in a time that is a distant memory for most. It comprised one cobbled high street lined on either side with a mixture of houses and shops built in the style that was popular around the time of the great fire in the famous city of London. The first and second floors (and in the case of the home of wealthy Jeremiah Ratchet the third and fourth floors) overhung the pavement. In fact, sometimes the upper levels stuck so far out that they restricted the sunlight. The windows themselves were small with leaded panes, and dark timbers ran in parallel lines on the outside walls. The buildings were all at strange and rather worrying angles, each having slid slightly down the hill over the years and sunk a little into the earth. There was no doubt that if just one collapsed it would take all the others with it.

The village was overlooked by the church, an ancient building mostly frequented these days when someone was born or died. Entry into this life and exit from it were deemed noteworthy occasions, but for most villagers the intervening existence did not require regular church attendance. On the whole this suited the Reverend Stirling Oliphaunt very well. He didn't seek out his flock; he preferred them to make their own way.

Besides, the hill really was unusually steep.

Despite this, and the snow, by midmorning the next day a small crowd had already gathered outside Ludlow's new home. Even before the sun had fully risen behind the clouds, a rumor was circulating that the old hat shop had a new occupant. One by one the villagers puffed and panted their way up the hill to see for themselves. The murky windows were now clean and transparent, although the varying thickness of the glass distorted the display somewhat, and the people pressed their faces up against the panes, eager to see what was on show.

"Is it a junk shop?" asked one man. A reasonable question under the circumstances, for the contents of the satchel, excepting the food and drink, had been priced with a tag and placed in the window. The wooden leg was propped in the corner, but there was no indication of its cost.

"It's animals," said another.

Joe's frog was clearly visible, sitting in its tank on the counter. In the daylight it was quite remarkable in appearance: Its glistening skin was a patchwork of vibrant reds,

greens, and yellows. It was most unlike any frog that lived in the soupy ponds of Pagus Parvus. Its feet were not webbed; instead they were more like long-fingered hands with knobbly joints and toes, which would have made swimming quite tricky.

As if on cue, Joe's face appeared in the window. He was holding a sign, which he placed carefully at the bottom of the display. It read:

Joe Zabbidou ⟶ Pawnbroker

The villagers nodded to one another, not necessarily in approval, more as if to say "I told you so," even though they hadn't. Joe then emerged with a ladder that he propped against the wall over the door. He climbed confidently to the top and unhooked the old hat-shaped sign. He fixed to the pole the universal symbol of the pawnbroker: three polished golden orbs stuck together in the shape of a triangle. They swung on their chain in a lazy arc, glinting in the low winter sun.

"Is the frog for sale?" someone asked.

"I'm afraid not," said Joe solemnly. "She is my companion."

This admission amused the crowd greatly and their titters created a cloud of breath around their heads.

"'Ow much for the leg?" asked another. Joe smiled benevolently, descended the ladder with remarkable speed, and stood before the crowd.

"Aha," he exclaimed. "The leg. Now there's a tale."

"A tail?" queried a youngster known less for his wit than for his inquisitive nature, while beside him his two brothers sniggered.

"A tale indeed," said Joe. "But one for another day." There were sighs of disappointment and Joe cleared his throat and raised his hand.

"Ladies and gentlemen, my name is Joe Zabbidou," he announced, pronouncing the "J" with a sort of shooshing noise so it sounded more like "sh." "And I am here to serve you. I stand under the sign of the three golden orbs because I am a pawnbroker, a respectable profession in existence for centuries, of Italian origin, I believe. I give you my guarantee"—here he placed his right hand on his heart and cast his eyes heavenward—"that I will pay a fair price for your goods and take a fair fee when you choose to redeem them. All items accepted: linen and shoes, jewelry and watches—"

"Wooden legs," shouted out a voice.

Joe disregarded this interruption and continued smoothly.

"You have my word. You will not be cheated by Joe Zabbidou."

For a moment there was silence, and then generous applause. Joe took a bow and smiled at his audience. "Thank you," he said as they came forward to shake his hand. "You're very kind."

Inside Ludlow jerked awake from a dream in which he was being pricked with a thousand tiny needles. He sat up to find that the fire had been revived and one of the logs was spitting, sending burning sparks onto his cheeks. Joe was nowhere to be seen, but there was bread and milk on the table, and a jug of beer, and Ludlow realized that he was very hungry. He drank some frothy milk and ate a thick slice of warm bread. He sat back, satisfied, but not for long. Hearing the commotion outside, he went to the door to have a look.

Joe was still shaking hands with the villagers. When he saw Ludlow he nodded in the direction of the crowd, who were milling around, loath to leave this object of curiosity. Joe's arrival was an exciting event for Pagus Parvians. Few strangers ever came to their village.

And a pity they don't, thought Joe as he scanned the eager faces in front of him. There was that hook nose again and again, those close-set narrow eyes, the crooked smiles, each in a different combination on a different countenance.

This place could do with some new blood, he thought. Then out loud to Ludlow he said, "Quite a welcome, eh, Ludlow?"

He turned back to his audience and continued to greet them while Ludlow wondered idly if any had a pocket worth picking.

CHAPTER SEVEN

The Morning After

Halfway down the street, Jeremiah Ratchet was suffering from his escapades of the night before. He had woken with a pounding headache and a raw stomach.

"Cheap ale," he grumbled. "I don't know why I drink in that foul, stinking City."

But of course he did know. He went there because he didn't trust the tavern owners in Pagus Parvus to serve him a decent quart. The one time he had gone into the Pickled Trout at the bottom of the hill he couldn't quite rid himself of the suspicion that the landlord, Benjamin Tup, had spat in his ale. But the accusation didn't go down very well. Besides, he despised the other drinkers, most of whom were in his debt. Jeremiah was happy to take their money but he preferred not to drink with them. And the feeling was mutual.

So Jeremiah went instead to the City, where he sought entertainment in the Nimble Finger Inn on the bridge over the River Foedus. There he drank wine and beer, smoked fat

cigars, and played cards until the early hours with a motley bunch of fellows: thieves and gamblers, resurrectionists, and undoubtedly a murderer or two. Although he would never admit it, he felt quite at home in the Nimble Finger.

Jeremiah groaned again when he remembered he had lost a considerable sum of money at the card table.

There's nothing for it, he thought. *The rents'll have to go up.*

Jeremiah liked simple solutions to problems, and rent increases seemed to solve most of his. He did not care about the trouble this caused his tenants. He turned over in bed, but his attempts to sleep again were thwarted by the foul air that wafted up from under the blankets.

Too many onions, he thought as he flung back the curtain and swung his legs over the side. He squinted in the daylight and only then became aware of the noise out on the street. He stumbled and belched his way over to the window to see crowds of people making their way up the hill.

"Polly!" he shouted. "Polly!"

"Yes, sir," she answered, jumping to her feet, for she was only over by the hearth stoking the fire and thinking about the boy with the green eyes she had seen the night before.

"What's all this noise? A man can't sleep with the racket."

"I believe that the hat shop has been occupied, sir."

"By a hatter?" Jeremiah loved to wear a hat, the higher the better. He felt it was a physical measure of his importance. It also gave him the appearance of being taller, for what he didn't lack in overbearing pomposity he lacked in inches.

"I don't know, sir. There's a rumor it's a pet shop."

"A pet shop!" Jeremiah spluttered. "Who can afford the luxury of pets in this place?"

The thought of a single one of his tenants owning a pet was too much for Jeremiah. Although he loved to indulge himself in all sorts of extravagances, it galled him to think that others might, too. So, in a fit of pique, he dressed and staggered up the hill, red-faced and nauseous, last night's alcohol seeping through his enlarged pores. He shoved his hands deep in his pockets and pulled his collar around his neck. His mood had not improved when Polly reported that she had failed to find his gloves, scarf, and purse.

"Blasted coachman," swore Jeremiah as he trudged through the snow. "Thieving, lying hound. Deserves to be whipped."

Polly waited for her master to go some way up the hill before throwing on her own tatty red cloak and following at a safe distance. Jeremiah arrived at the shop just in time to hear Joe's speech, after which he made his presence known (though his neighbors had already caught his odor and moved away).

CHAPTER EIGHT

I stayed in the doorway while Joe stood on the pavement, and I watched as each person approached him. He took whichever hand they offered and enclosed it in his own. At the same time he leaned forward and said something. Whatever it was, it made the women smile and the men straighten up and inflate their chests. I couldn't resist a grin, though I didn't quite know why.

While Joe was still busy shaking hands, a minor commotion started up at the back of the crowd. I stuck my head out a little farther and saw a bulbous man, his face glistening with sweat, pushing his way to the front. The people parted reluctantly to allow his passage. He stood in the snow in a manner that suggested he was supported solely by his own self-importance. He cocked his large head to one side to squint at the golden orbs with a yellowing eye.

There was something very unpleasant about the man: His

bulk was offensive, his stance was aggressive. I was not inclined to make myself known to him, so I stayed where I was.

I suspect Joe had already noticed him but had chosen to ignore him. Eventually, after the man had positioned himself only a matter of feet away and coughed loudly three times, Joe acknowledged his presence and introduced himself.

"Joe Zabbidou," he said, holding out his hand.

The man stared at Joe as if he were a snail on his shoe.

"Ratchet," he said finally, refusing to shake. "Jeremiah Ratchet. Local businessman. I own most of this village."

When I heard the name my ears pricked up. So this was Jeremiah Ratchet, the man who had inadvertently brought me to Pagus Parvus and at the same time brought about a change in my fortunes. His rather grand statement was greeted with quiet snorts of derision from the crowd, even a hiss, and his wide forehead creased in an angry frown. He put his hands on his hips and sniffed, in the manner of a rooting hog. If I had been in that crowd, I would have pinched his purse before he could blink. He was the sort of man who deserved to have his pocket picked. Then again, I thought, as I tried to conceal a smirk, I already had it.

The two men faced each other, Joe's steady gaze taking Ratchet in. Everything about Jeremiah smelled of money: from his perfumed hair to his dark, woolen, three-quarter-length coat; from his mustard-colored breeches right down to the shiny leather of his riding boots. Unfortunately nothing about him smelled of good taste.

"Listen here, Mr. Cabbagehead, or whatever you call yourself. You'll get no business here. You're not needed. These people own nothing of any worth." Jeremiah laughed meanly and puffed out his chest even more. "I should know; most of them owe me back rent."

"We shall see," said Joe, recoiling slightly. Jeremiah's breath was quite pungent. "I have always found in the past that most people benefit from my help."

"Help?" queried Jeremiah. "I don't think we need your sort of help. I help people 'round here. If they need money they know whom to ask. You'll find I provide for the village. You'll pack your bags soon enough."

He turned sharply, satisfied that Joe had been well and truly put in the picture, and strode away with a sort of wide-legged gait that became more ridiculous as he gathered speed.

"Jeremiah Ratchet," I heard Joe say softly, "I think our paths will cross again."

Somehow Jeremiah's presence had cast a sort of gloom over the crowd, and in twos and threes they set off down the hill, holding on to each other for support. Only one person lingered, a young girl. I thought I knew her face but couldn't place it until she was almost right in front of me.

"Hello again," she said softly. It was Polly, Jeremiah's maid.

"Hello," I replied, but though I racked my brain I could

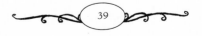

think of nothing more interesting to say, so we just faced each other in silence. She looked cold and tired. Her knuckles were red, she wore no gloves, and her fingertips were blue.

"I'd better be off," she said finally. "Ratchet'd be angry if he knew I was talking to you." That said, she turned around and skipped away. I felt a little sorry for her, with her stick legs and red nose. I couldn't imagine Jeremiah Ratchet was the most favorable of masters.

Joe was leaning casually on the ladder, watching us, but suddenly he looked away. I followed his gaze and saw for a second time the small hunched figure with a shovel on his shoulder. He had been right at the back during the whole show, his craggy face expressionless. Now he was going in the opposite direction to everyone else, toward the church. Joe watched him go through the gates, then beckoned to me.

"Hurry," he said and strode off in the wake of the crooked stranger. I pulled the door closed and a little thrill of excitement made me shiver all over.

CHAPTER NINE

Obadiah Strang

An ancient graveyard surrounded the church, and the slope was such that it was impossible to dig a grave without one side being higher than the other. Fortunately for its occupants, Obadiah Strang, the gravedigger, was very good at his job and took great pains to ensure that the floor of each grave was level, so the poor dead soul in the coffin could achieve peace on his back and not on his side. Whenever there was a funeral the mourners were constantly on the move, shifting from one foot to the other as they tried to stand up straight. Only mountain goats that wandered in from time to time seemed at ease, able as they were to keep their balance at any angle. The graveyard must have seemed like a home away from home. Not only that, the grass was particularly rich.

Joe stepped through the rusting church gates, closely followed by Ludlow, and stopped to listen. The rhythmic sound of shoveling came to him on the wind, and when he looked

down the slope between the headstones he saw Obadiah Strang hard at work digging a hole.

Stooped even as a youngster, Obadiah had finally reached the age that his bent back had always suggested. He looked like a man who dug holes for a living, and over the years his hands had fixed themselves into the shape of the handle of his shovel. He had great difficulty picking up small objects but was thankful that his clawed fingers could comfortably hold a bottle of ale.

Obadiah continued with his task for quite some time before he noticed that he had company. He clambered out with the aid of a small ladder and stuck his shovel into the pile of earth with some force. Sweat congealed in his eyebrows and he wiped his forehead with the back of his hand, leaving a dark smear. It was not easy to dig a six-foot-deep hole in the winter.

Joe greeted him with a warm handshake. "I saw you at the shop," he explained.

"Ah," said Obadiah gruffly, "you're the pawnbroker. Well, I'll tell you now, you'll get no business from me. I've little more than the clothes I stand up in."

He looked suspiciously at Ludlow, who was hanging back behind a sinking headstone. He didn't like the look of the boy one bit. He wouldn't trust him as far as he could throw him, and that would be quite some distance, seeing as there wasn't a pick of meat on his scrawny bones. Besides, Obadiah never trusted people who didn't blink, and Ludlow's stare was quite unnerving.

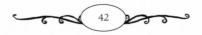

"And who's this?"

"My assistant," said Joe smoothly, pulling him forward.

Ludlow smiled and put out his hand, albeit hesitantly. Obadiah ignored it.

"Assistant? You pay an assistant? You pawnbrokers are all the same. You claim poverty but live otherwise." He picked up his shovel, but Joe took him by the arm.

"Wait."

"What do you want from me?" said Obadiah impatiently. "I'm busy."

Joe stared hard into Obadiah's tired eyes. Obadiah wanted to look away, but for some reason he couldn't. His ears filled with a soft noise, like the sea on a rocky shore, and he felt his knees tremble. His fingertips were starting to tingle. Ludlow watched in surprise as the gruff old man seemed to soften and relax.

"You look like a man with a story to tell," said Joe slowly. "Why not come up to the shop tonight? At midnight. No one need know."

Obadiah struggled to get the words out. "Perhaps I will," he said, "perhaps I won't."

"Until then," replied Joe, as if his invitation had been accepted, and he blinked, breaking the spell, whereupon Obadiah had to steady himself on his shovel.

CHAPTER TEN

FRAGMENT FROM
THE MEMOIRS OF LUDLOW FITCH

I didn't really understand what had happened in the graveyard. I knew that some sort of arrangement had been arrived at, but its exact nature escaped me. As we left the church grounds I suddenly had the feeling that we were being watched. Out of the corner of my eye, I saw a figure observing us from behind a tree. From his dress I presumed him to be the local vicar. I nudged Joe. He had seen him, too, and he nodded a greeting, whereupon the reverend became very flustered, turned tail, and fled into the church.

Outside the shop the pavement was empty apart from three young boys who ran away as soon as they saw Joe. He laughed as they skidded down the hill. Once inside we went through to the back and sat by the fire. After a few minutes, when Joe showed no sign of talking to me but all the signs of a man on the verge of a snooze, I asked him about my job.

"Your job?" he replied with a large yawn. "I'll tell you later. For the moment just wake me if we have any customers."

And that was it.

I went into the shop and leaned my elbows on the counter, contemplating my situation. The frog watched me for a minute or two and then turned away. Although I had always earned a living, I had never had a job before. I hadn't exactly been raised on the straight and narrow. Pa and Ma together were as big a pair of crooks as ever breathed the Lord's air. They made their living from thievery and I had little choice but to follow in their footsteps, even before I could walk. I was a small baby, and stayed slight. At the age of eighteen months Pa took to carrying me around in a bread basket on the top of his head. He covered me with a few stale loaves. I still remember the terrible swaying from side to side and the fright that kept me rigid. To this day I cannot travel in any moving vehicle without feeling sick.

When the opportunity presented itself Pa would say out of the corner of his mouth, "Lud, me lad," and that was the sign for me to reach out and pinch the hat, and sometimes the wig, of an innocent passing gentleman. Imagine the poor fellow's surprise as his head was bared, leaving him open not only to embarrassment but also to the ravages of the elements. Of course, by the time he looked for the culprits we had long since disappeared into the crowd.

This caper brought in a pleasing sum, since wigs and hats fetched good prices, but inevitably the time came when I could no longer fit into the bread basket. Ma suggested that I be sold to a chimney sweep. My skinny frame more than suited the narrow, angled chimneys. By then I was beginning

to understand that when my parents looked at me with their glassy eyes, they saw not a son and heir but a convenient source of income to support their gin habit. The life of a chimney sweep was harsh and short, and I was supremely grateful when Pa decided I could earn more for them if I learned to pick pockets. Thus, with the minimum of training (spurred on by his belt), I was sent out onto the streets on the understanding that I was not to return without at least six shillings a day for the tavern.

I had little trouble earning this, and any extra I kept for myself. I seemed to have a natural bent for such work: My fingers were nimble, my tread light, and my expression innocent. Sometimes I was a little careless and my victims would feel my fingers in their pocket, but I had only to hold their gaze for a moment to convince them that it was not I who had filched their purse or wallet. If I looked at Ma that way she used to cuff me around the side of the head and hiss, "Don't look at me with those saucer eyes. It don't work on your old ma."

But, you know, I think it did and that was precisely why she got so angry.

She could cuff me only if she caught me, and most days I avoided her and Pa like the plague. When I had earned enough, usually by noon, and needed to warm up, I went to Mr. Jellico's. I couldn't go home even if I wanted to, for Ma and Pa had rented out the room during the day to night workers on the river.

It wasn't such a bad life, not at first, and I didn't know any

other way. I had heard you were supposed to love your parents, but I don't think that is what I felt for them. Some kind of loyalty perhaps, a blood tie, but not love. But once their desire for gin consumed them, my life became unbearable. It didn't matter how much they had, they wanted more. Eventually, whatever I brought home wasn't enough. I suppose that's when they came up with their fiendish plan. I should have known they were up to something. They had started smiling at me.

I shivered when I recalled the desperate chase of the previous night. I could still feel Pa's hand on my shoulder and Ma's screeching voice rang in my head. And then there was Barton Gumbroot's glinting instrument of torture. I couldn't bear to think of it. How strange that I was so far away from it all now.

Joe was still snoring, so I took the opportunity to examine the goods in the shop window. The jewelry was bright and pretty; the hurricane lamp was polished and looked in working order. The timepieces were wound and ticking. Without a second thought I put two in my pocket, but almost immediately a sharp tap on the window made me jump. Polly was right outside. She waved and I wondered how long she had been there watching me. I went out to see her. The snow was packed down where the crowd had been earlier, and she stood carefully on its icy surface.

"It's quiet today," I said.

"Same as usual," she replied.

It was midmorning and my ears listened out for the clash-

ing cries of street sellers shouting their wares, the traveling musicians with their fiddles, the ballad singers, the clatter of cattle hooves on the cobbles on the way to the slaughter-house, the hissing of the knife grinder's wheel, the rows and fights that broke out on every street corner. But this was not the City, and Pagus Parvus was almost silent. I heard a laugh or two and the blacksmith's hammer but little else.

"Do you want to come in?"

"Can I see the frog?" she asked.

The frog was watching us when we went in. She really was a marvelous creature, her skin bright and glistening like a damp rock. There was no sound from the back room, so I carefully lifted the lid and reached into the tank. The frog seemed a little agitated as I tried to coax her with a bug, and she retreated to the far corner.

"Are you sure you should?" asked Polly nervously.

"Why shouldn't—"

"Don't touch the frog," barked a voice behind me, and I jumped back immediately. Joe was practically next to me and I hadn't heard a sound. An icy blast came in from the open door before Polly slammed it shut on her way out.

"I only wanted to show—"

Joe came forward and replaced the lid, pushing it down firmly. "You mustn't touch her," he said sternly. "Until you gain her trust she only allows me to handle her. Do you understand?"

I nodded and the awkward silence was broken by the sound of the door again and the hesitant inquiry of our first

customer, an elderly lady wearing a monocle in her left eye. She frowned unevenly to keep it in place.

"Mr. Zabbidou? I have an item to pledge."

Joe smiled broadly.

"A lovely piece," he said. "Look, Ludlow, a chamber pot."

CHAPTER ELEVEN

A Midnight Visitor

"Wake up," hissed Joe, shaking Ludlow's arm. "He's here."

Ludlow sat up slowly and listened as the church bell struck midnight. He shivered. The fire had died down and he could see his breath. Joe put a small log on the glowing embers and lit the lamp. He placed two glasses on the mantelpiece along with a dark brown bottle, and then he went to the table and laid his black book in front of the chair.

"Sit here," said Joe to Ludlow. "Stay very quiet, and when I give you a sign, write down everything you hear in the book. I've marked the page."

Ludlow shook off his doziness and sat at the table. He picked up the book and examined it. It was old, but well kept, thick and just too weighty to hold in one hand. On the leather cover in gold leaf were the words, *Verba Volant Scripta Manent.*

In the bottom right-hand corner were the initials *JZ* in large, decorative gold lettering. A piece of red ribbon marked

the new page and a quill lay waiting in the crease. The white pages seemed to glow in the half-light, and Ludlow couldn't help but run his fingers over their smooth surface. He quickly flicked through the preceding pages; they were written with a heavy hand and crackled when he touched them. Ludlow had not been told not to pry, but he had the distinct feeling that Joe would disapprove if he did. Quietly he put the black book back down as he found it, open to the clean page.

Outside the pawnshop Obadiah Strang stood on the pavement wringing his gnarled hands. He wanted to knock but he was afraid. Perhaps the dead didn't scare him, but sometimes the living did. Losing his nerve, he turned around and was about to retreat down the hill when the door opened behind him.

"Obadiah, my dear chap," said Joe warmly, stepping into the street and taking the man by the arm, "I've been expecting you."

Once more, under Joe's penetrating gaze, all resistance deserted Obadiah and he allowed himself to be led into the back room and placed gently on the chair by the fire. Ludlow sat without moving, a little nervous, watching everything closely. Obadiah pushed his knuckles into the soft arm of the chair and Ludlow winced as they cracked loudly.

"Will you have a drink with me?" asked Joe. "Something special?"

Obadiah grunted and Joe poured two drinks from the

bottle, handing one to Obadiah. He took his own and sat down opposite the gravedigger.

"Good health," he toasted.

Obadiah took a tentative sip from his glass, and then another longer one. Spirits were not his usual tipple and he'd never tasted one of this caliber. He savored the sensation of warmth as the alcohol ran down the back of his throat. Feeling his knotted shoulders relaxing, he leaned back into the chair.

"Why am I here?" he asked. This wasn't what he planned to say, but it was what came out.

"Because you need help," replied Joe.

"And you can help me?"

Joe nodded and leaned over. "When I look at you, Obadiah, I see a man who has a secret. A secret that is such a burden it threatens to engulf you. It keeps you awake at night and gnaws at your guts every day." He leaned even closer. "It doesn't have to be like that."

Obadiah's eyes were shining. A small tear squeezed from the corner of one and ran down the lines that scored his cheek.

"What can I do?" he whispered desperately.

Joe's voice was soothing and full of promise. "Pawn your secret and free yourself of its terrible burden."

"Pawn it?" Obadiah was a little bemused from the drink, and from Joe's eyes and his soft voice. His head felt as if it were slowly sinking underwater.

"You mean you will buy my secret? But why?"

"It's my business," said Joe. "I am a pawnbroker."

Obadiah shook his head slowly and his brow creased with confusion. "But if I pawn it, then must I claim it back? If I don't, you will have the right to sell it. And if you sell it, then it is no longer a secret." Obadiah liked to make life easy by thinking in a simple and logical fashion.

"Ah," exclaimed Joe. "I think you will find my terms quite agreeable. If you wish to reclaim your secret, then you pay what you took plus a little extra. If not, then I will keep the secret for you for as long as you want, a lifetime if that is your wish. In fact, if you never reclaim it, I will hold it until you are in the grave and beyond, and then I doubt you would care so much."

"Well, I s'pose that sounds fair, Mr. Zabbidou."

Joe smiled. "Let us get started. I am anxious to set a mind at ease."

He nodded discreetly to Ludlow, who realized this was his cue. With a shaking hand he raised the quill and dipped it in the ink. He held the quill poised over the pristine page.

"And you swear you won't tell?" asked Obadiah, quivering.

Joe shook his head solemnly. "Never," he said. "On my life."

"Then hear this and maybe you can help. God knows, no one else can."

For the next hour the only sound in the room was Obadiah's trembling voice and the soft scratching of a nib on paper.

Ludlow's work had begun.

CHAPTER TWELVE

EXTRACT FROM
THE BLACK BOOK OF SECRETS

The Gravedigger's Confession

My name is Obadiah Strang and I have a terrible secret. It haunts my every waking hour, and at night when I finally manage to sleep it takes over my dreams.

I might only be a humble gravedigger but I am proud of it. I have never cheated anyone: They get six feet, no more, no less. I have always led a simple life. I need very little and I ask for nothing. I was a contented man until some months ago when I fell afoul of my landlord, Jeremiah Ratchet.

It had been a difficult week, short on gravedigging and even shorter on tips. When rent day came around I didn't have it. No doubt you already know of Jeremiah Ratchet. He is a hated man in these parts, and I feared what he would do to me. But he surprised me and suggested that I pay double the next week. Like a fool I accepted his offer. But when rent day came again he claimed that I owed him eighteen shillings, not twelve.

"Six shillings' interest on the loan," he explained with an oily smile.

Of course, I didn't have the extra money, and a week later the debt had increased again. I paid what I could and tried to reason with him, but Jeremiah Ratchet must have a hole where his heart should be. After four weeks I owed so much I could never hope to pay.

That was his intention all along.

"I have a suggestion," he said the next time he came over, "a way for you to work off your debt."

Although I distrusted the man by now, I had no choice but to listen.

"I need you to do a job for me, something eminently suited to your skills. I will provide the tools."

Then he explained to me his despicable plan and I flew into a rage and threw him out. He stood on the path and called back to me. "If you will not do it, then I will evict you. You know where I am if you change your mind. I'll give you a week to think it over."

That night I cursed myself again and again for getting myself into debt to the monster. By the time the sun rose I knew that I had no choice. I sent for Ratchet and he came to the cottage to explain what I had to do. He handed me my only tool: a wooden spade.

"Quieter than a metal one," said Jeremiah. "Anyone in this business knows that."

And what a business, the business of bodysnatching.

That night, some time after one, I went to the churchyard

with a heavy heart. How I hated myself for what I was about to do. I knew the grave in question. Hadn't I dug it myself the previous day and watched the coffin lowered into it that very afternoon? And now here I was digging it up again. With every spadeful of dirt I thought of that scoundrel Ratchet. His wealth was made off the backs of the poor. He must have half the village in his debt.

It was raining now and the moon hid herself behind the clouds, ashamed to witness what I was doing. The wind whipped around my head. Water streamed off my hat. The cold froze my hands. The dark clay was sticky with water. It took a supreme effort to raise the shovel; it released only with a loud sucking noise as if the earth herself had come alive and was trying to pull it, and me with it, into the bowels of hell below.

As the earth piled up on the side my sweat mingled with the driving rain. In my chest my heart pounded like a blacksmith's hammer. At last I hit wood. I dropped to my knees and scraped the coffin clean with my hands. The lid was held down by a single nail at each corner. I forced the edge of the spade underneath and began to lever it up. The wood splintered and cracked and split. "Sweet Lord, forgive me," I muttered and crossed myself as a bolt of lightning ripped the sky apart. In its fiery light I gazed down on the poor soul within.

He wasn't a rich man, I could tell from the quality of the finish on the box and the cheap fittings, but who was in these parts? Rich or poor, like us all, he ended up in the dirt. He was young, though, and his handsome face was un-

marked by the accident that had killed him—he had fallen under the wheels of a cart. His pale hands were laid across his chest and his ashen face was peaceful. His earthly worries were over. Mine had just begun.

I hesitated only a second, then took the poor chap by the shoulders and dragged him out of the coffin and up onto the side of the grave. I looked up at the heavens and I swore that this was the first and last time I would do this. I thought that, the soul gone, a body would be lighter, relieved of the burden of life, but I felt as if I were lifting a dead horse. I dragged him across the grass between the headstones to the church gates, where Jeremiah had said there would be someone waiting.

I saw them. Two men dressed in black, their faces and heads hidden beneath hoods. Without a word they took the body and threw it onto the back of their cart between barrels of ale. They covered it with straw and then took off.

I waited until I could no longer hear the horses' hooves before returning to fill in the grave. I worked like a man possessed, shoveling with the energy of a demon, and when it was finally done I went home.

I woke the next day convinced I had dreamed it all, but there by the fireplace was the wooden shovel. I could hardly bear to look upon myself in the mirror. Whatever my reason for doing it, I was still no better than a common body-snatcher. Resurrectionists, they liked to call themselves, but to give a person a fancy name don't change his nature. Doubtless the corpse was now far away, likely as not in the City, under the knife of a surgeon in the anatomy school

and all in the interest of science. At least that's what the doctors said. They paid good money for bodies, and Jeremiah was lining his pockets with it, but never had I thought I would be involved in such a grisly, sinful business.

Jeremiah came knocking that night.

"My men say you did a good job."

It was not a compliment I wished to accept.

"And where are the valuables?" he asked me.

"Valuables? What are you talking about? Isn't it enough that I unburied a body for you? Now you want more?"

He shrugged. "I have it on good authority that that young man was buried with a silver timepiece and a gold ring. Belonged to his father. Strange custom, to bury what could be sold for cash."

I could hardly believe what I was hearing. Ratchet wanted me to be a thief for him as well as a bodysnatcher.

"I did what you asked," I said. "The debt is paid."

He shook his head.

"I think not, Mr. Strang. After all, you owe quite a considerable sum and you haven't collected the valuables. Next time you will have to be more careful."

"Next time?"

I didn't dare to argue anymore, for then I saw what a fix I was in. The penalty for grave robbing was prison at the very least, but only if you were lucky enough to survive the lynching by the dead man's relatives.

That was over six months ago, and Jeremiah has called on me again and again to do his dirty work. I don't like to think

how many bodies I have unearthed. All I know is if I am
caught, Jeremiah will not be the one to suffer.

That man enjoys the fruits of my wickedness and I can do
nothing about it. I lie awake until the small hours, tortured
by my actions. I am betraying the trust of the villagers, a
trust I have built up all my life. If they knew they would
string me up as soon as they got hold of me.

Jeremiah Ratchet. How I detest that man. If I thought I
could get away with it, I'd take a swing at his big, fat head
with my shovel. ✳

Ludlow hesitated at that last sentence, but he had been instructed to write everything he heard, so he did. He stole a
look at Obadiah, who was as ashen-faced as the very corpses
he unearthed. Then he put down his quill, laid a sheet of
blotting paper between the pages, and closed the book. Obadiah sat back in the chair, exhausted, and covered his face
with his hands.

"You've got to help me, Mr. Zabbidou. I'm a broken man,
unworthy of life."

Joe laid his hand firmly on Obadiah's knee.

"Rid yourself of those murderous thoughts," he said.
"They will only eat at your soul. There is a natural justice in
this world. Perhaps it is not as swift as we should like, but
believe me, Jeremiah Ratchet will feel its force. Now, go
home and you will sleep, and you will not dream."

Obadiah sighed deeply.

"You know, Mr. Zabbidou, I believe you might be right."
He stood up to go, but Joe held him back.

"Your payment, as agreed." Joe handed him a leather bag
of coins and Obadiah's eyes widened when he felt its weight.

"I'm most grateful to you, Mr. Zabbidou," said Obadiah.
"I can make good use of this."

"And so you should," replied Joe, shaking his hand
warmly. "So you should."

"And what of Jeremiah?" he ventured nervously.

Joe merely blinked once slowly. "Be patient, Mr. Strang.
Be patient."

CHAPTER THIRTEEN

FRAGMENT FROM
THE MEMOIRS OF LUDLOW FITCH

Thus ended my first long day with Joe Zabbidou. It was after two when Obadiah left, and Joe stood at the door and watched him go down the hill and into his cottage. He waited until the lights were extinguished and the place was in complete darkness before coming back in and locking up. I stayed at the table staring blankly at the closed book, my mind spinning at what I had just heard. Now I understood. *It's a book of secrets,* I thought, *and Joe is the Secret Pawnbroker.*

It was difficult to believe that Joe had allowed me to touch such a book, let alone write in it. How I desired to throw it open and read it from cover to cover! What other tales of desperation and despair would I find in there?

I could hear Joe moving around in the shop and talking to the frog. Quickly I opened the book, flicking from page to page, and I read the opening lines of one confession after another:

> *My name is Eleanor Hardy and I cannot live with my lies any longer . . .*
> *My name is George Catchpole and I have a most shameful secret . . .*
> *My name is Oscar Carpue. In a fit of mindless rage, gripped by madness, I . . .*

That was all I managed to read before Joe came whistling back into the room. I snapped the book shut and jumped awkwardly to my feet, knocking over the chair.

"Let us see how you have done," he said, ignoring my confusion and taking the book from the table. I watched nervously as he examined what I had written.

"Excellent work, boy," he said, placing the red ribbon on the next clean page and closing the book. "I doubt I could have done better myself."

A sudden burning flushed my cheeks. I was not used to praise. To cover my embarrassment I pointed to the golden words on the cover.

"What language is this?"

Joe's face lit up. "Ah, Latin," he said. "The language of precision. What is spoken flies, what is written never dies. Remember those words, Ludlow. People believe what they read, whatever the truth of it."

Joe held up the book and spoke quietly. "The stories we

have in here are very precious to their owners and, as a result, of monetary value to others. They have confided in me, confessing their deepest secrets, and it is my duty to protect them. Wherever I go, there is a criminal element, loyal to no one, who would pay well for this and use it for financial gain or worse. But these confessions have been trusted to us, Ludlow, and we must not speak of them outside this room."

Joe did not seem to be including me among those criminals. But just then my hand felt something cold in my pocket and my heart skipped a beat. The timepieces. I still had them. He must not have noticed they had gone. I resolved to return them as soon as possible.

I nodded solemnly. "I can keep a secret," I said.

"I believe you think you can, Ludlow. But I also know what it is to be human. Temptation is a curse to all men."

"I can do it," I said firmly. "Just give me the chance."

For a moment I thought he might say no, but he laughed and said, "What is life if you don't take a chance now and again? I knew a fellow once who only made decisions on the toss of a coin. Should he get up or stay in bed? He tossed a coin. Should he eat or should he not? He tossed a coin. He lived thus for nearly two years until he was struck down by illness. So he tossed a coin to decide whether or not to send for the physician and the coin said yes."

"And he was cured?"

"Well, unfortunately for him, the physician was not the best. His diagnosis was somewhat awry and the medicine he gave was rather too strong, so the poor chap died the next day."

I didn't understand what Joe was trying to tell me.

"You see, Ludlow," he explained, "life is a gamble whatever way you play it. Now, where were we?" He patted the Black Book of Secrets and his tone became more serious. "Of course, if you are to work for me, there are a few things you need to know. First, we always start on a clean page. I make it a rule to go forward, never to go back." He smiled knowingly and stared into my eyes. He knew I had looked in the book.

"And second, when we are finished we must keep it somewhere safe from prying eyes."

I watched as he put the book in no more safe a place than under his mattress. Was this some sort of test? Was he tempting me to steal it?

As I continued to stare he asked me a curious question.

"Do you believe in luck, Ludlow?"

I had thought about this more than once in my life. "I believe some people are luckier than others. Such as those who are not born in the City."

Joe laughed. "Ah yes," he said, "a most unfortunate birthplace. Most born there die there. But you have managed to leave."

"Then I must be lucky."

He shrugged. "Perhaps it is not just luck. Maybe it was Destiny herself brought you here to me."

"Destiny? More like my own two feet!" Then I asked him, "Which do you believe in, luck or Destiny?"

Joe considered for a moment before replying, "We make our own luck, Ludlow, by our actions and our state of mind.

As such you control your own fate. Only one thing is certain: None of us can escape the grave."

Then he surprised me further by handing me a shilling. Although it was unexpected, I took it.

"For a job well done. Add it to the other coins in your purse," he said and winked.

We went to bed soon after that. When I heard Joe's snoring I felt in the crevice behind the brick for my purse and dropped in the shilling. Then I settled down again, wrapped up in the cloak. Sleep evaded me, for my mind was restless. I turned over and thought of Obadiah and Jeremiah Ratchet. Poor Obadiah, he was right to be disgusted at himself; grave robbers and bodysnatchers were considered below contempt. What a cruel irony, for a gravedigger to have to unbury the dead. As I pitied the gravedigger, my contempt grew for Ratchet. He might have brought me to the village, but that was more luck than design.

An hour passed and still I was awake. My mind was thick with confusion. I knew that had Ma and Pa been here they would not have thought twice about hitting Joe over the head and taking the Black Book of Secrets. As for the bottle on the mantel, that would have been downed long ago.

They would have expected no less of me. My instincts— to lie, to steal, to cheat—were bred into me practically from birth. But here, in Pagus Parvus with Joe, they seemed wrong.

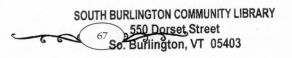

I lay in an agony of indecision. My conscience tried to stop me but, I am ashamed to admit, despite Joe's kindness to me and his warning, I gave in. How could I be expected not to do what had come naturally to me my whole life?

Carefully I eased the book out from under his mattress and tucked it in the crook of my arm. I wrapped the cloak around me and crept through to the shop. The frog watched me with accusing eyes and I could hear Joe's deep and noisy breathing. I was surprised to find that the door to the street was unlocked. I pulled it open and stepped outside. It had all been so easy. Not a floorboard had squeaked, not a hinge had creaked. Snow was falling lightly and a glow fell on the street from the lights in the windows. Like last night, most of Pagus Parvus was still awake. If I went now I could go down that hill and never be seen again.

Suddenly I felt the timepieces jarring against my leg and I stopped. I laughed quietly at my own stupidity. What was I thinking? It was the middle of the night, the middle of winter. Behind me was a warm bed and food and someone who seemed to care for me; ahead of me was nothing but white snow and bitter cold.

I hurried inside and placed the timepieces back in the window. With a shaking hand I slipped the Black Book back under the mattress, willing Joe not to wake, and crept over to the

fireplace. As I curled up beside the orange coals I chastised myself.

It was hard to believe that only a day or so ago I had been in the foul City, living the precarious life of a common thief and facing at the hands of my own parents a terrible betrayal. Yet here I was now earning a living, and one more mysterious and exciting than I could ever have imagined. "Ludlow," I said to myself, "you are a fool."

I looked at Joe, fast asleep, and I knew whatever happened tomorrow, and the next day and the next, I never wanted to go back to the City. I might have to live with my past, but here, with Joe, I had a future.

CHAPTER FOURTEEN

Of Frogs and Legs

Ludlow woke the next morning to the smell of warm bread. Joe was standing in front of the fire toasting the heels of a loaf on the end of the poker.

"Just in time," he said, as Ludlow emerged from his nook. "Did you sleep well? I was a little disturbed myself."

"Well enough," mumbled Ludlow, yawning.

Joe dropped the toast onto a plate and sat down at the table. "I forgot to lock the door last night. We could have been murdered in our beds."

Ludlow's cheeks burned as hot as the toast.

Joe continued smoothly. "So, now you've had a chance to think it over, will you stay? It's not a difficult job. You would be a great help to me."

"I should like to stay," said Ludlow. "Very much."

"Then it is settled. Time for breakfast."

In the City, Ludlow's breakfast might have been a moldy crust or hard porridge. In Pagus Parvus, in the back room of the Secret Pawnbroker's, it was a veritable feast. The table was laden with toasted bread, boiled hen's eggs, thick slices of pink ham, a slab of golden butter, and two jugs, one of beer, the other of fresh milk. There was even cutlery, but Ludlow did not let this slow him down and he ate as if he were a condemned man. Joe looked on, marveling at the boy's appetite as Ludlow gulped down a second cup of milk, then eyed the pork pie that sat in the middle of the table.

"The butcher dropped it off this morning," said Joe. "And the baker brought the bread by. Such hospitality."

"Maybe they just want you to buy more of their old junk," muttered Ludlow.

Joe took another large bite of toast and washed it down with a mouthful of beer. He dabbed at his chin with a napkin that lay across his knees. Ludlow had not seen such gentility before, and self-consciously he wiped his mouth with his sleeve. Then for once he waited until he had swallowed before speaking.

"You know," he said, "I feel sorry for Obadiah. I think he is a good man."

"Being good isn't always enough," Joe said.

"I suppose you've heard many stories like his?"

Joe nodded. "And many far worse. But that is little comfort to the poor man. He is right to be scared. If he is caught, then he will certainly be put in prison or hanged from the nearest tree."

"And Jeremiah? What about his part?"

Joe frowned. "He would deny everything. After all, what proof is there that Jeremiah is connected? It is a poor man's word against a rich man's. The verdict is as good as decided already. I fear Jeremiah has such a grip on this village that no one here would dare accuse him, let alone try to convict him."

"Do you think the money is enough?"

"For now," said Joe. "He will be able to pay his rent at least. But I wonder what else Jeremiah has up his sleeve."

"Perhaps we can help him in other ways," said Ludlow.

Joe shook his head. "No, no. I must not interfere in the course of things. Our job is to keep secrets. Once it is in the book, the matter is closed. In fact, we should not even be speaking of it now."

"So is there nothing we can do?"

But Joe was silent.

Business came in fits and starts all day and by closing time Joe's display benefited from the addition of a flower vase in the Grecian style, a pair of leather suspenders with silver clips (one missing), a sturdy pair of scuffed boots (only slightly down at heel), and a set of decorative brass buttons. The chamber pot sat in the corner next to the wooden leg. Toward the end of the afternoon Ludlow was rearranging the buttons in the window when he became aware that he had an audience. Three boys stood outside—the same three who had been in the crowd when Joe had first introduced himself—their heights descending from right to left. They pressed their faces against the window, but they appeared to be shy about coming in. Joe went to the door.

"May I help you young fellows?" he asked and fixed them with his stare.

The youngest proved to be the bravest. "We have nothing to pawn," he said, "but we want to see the frog."

Joe laughed. "But of course, come in," and the three piled in, the youngest pushed to the back now that the invitation was extended.

They were the Sourdough (to rhyme with "enough") brothers, sons of the bakers, Ruby and Elias. They went up to the tank and looked in awe at the colorful creature, which repaid their interest by promptly turning its back to them.

"What's it called?" asked the middle one of the three.

"She," corrected Joe. "Her name is Saluki."

"What does she eat?"

Joe showed them the bags of sticky, writhing worms and shiny-cased bugs that Saluki ate. He allowed them to drop the tasty tidbits into the tank through a hatch in the lid.

"Can I hold her?" This time it was the youngest who spoke.

"May I," corrected Joe. "I know that you *can*. After all, it is not difficult to hold a frog. What you seek is my permission."

"May I?" asked the boy, twitching with frustration.

"No." This request was made again and again on each subsequent visit (the Sourdough brothers came daily), and although Joe agreed that the boys had to be admired for their optimism and persistence, he always refused on the grounds that Saluki was not the sort of frog that liked to be held.

"Would she jump away?"

"She's a tree frog," replied Joe. "More of a climber than a jumper."

"Where did you get her?"

A dreamy look came into Joe's eyes. He hooked his thumbs in his waistcoat pockets and rocked back and forth on his heels.

"She comes from a land on the other side of the world, where the earth curves to the south and there are all sorts of creatures that you couldn't even begin to imagine."

"Did you catch her?"

"She was a gift," he said, "from an old man to a young lad, such as yourselves."

The Sourdoughs tittered.

"Yes, even I was young once," said Joe.

Joe had a tale for the boys almost every day they came up to the shop. He mesmerized them with stories of the far-away lands he had visited, where the mountains spewed fire and molten rock; of the forests where the trees were so tall that it was always cold night on the forest floor and yet their leaves were burned by the sun. He spoke of ships and cities

that lay together on the bottom of the ocean, of the frozen wastes where the sun never set. But there was one thing he never told them about, no matter how hard they pleaded, no matter how urgently they begged.

"Tell us about the wooden leg," they implored.

But Joe always shook his head. "Not today," he would say. "Perhaps tomorrow."

CHAPTER FIFTEEN

Wagging Tongues

Polly would have liked to spend as much time in the shop as the Sourdoughs, but while Elias and Ruby were happy for Joe to entertain their boys, Jeremiah was not so lenient and Polly's visits were shorter and less frequent. She and Ludlow still enjoyed their brief chats over the counter, although actually it was more a case of Ludlow listening and Polly talking, for once she got started it was no easy task to stop her. "I don't know what it is about this place," she giggled more than once, "but every time I come in here my tongue just runs away with itself."

Ludlow liked to listen. He was curious about the village and its inhabitants, Jeremiah in particular, and Polly was more than happy to tell him about the goings-on in the large house down the hill.

She told him of Jeremiah's habits (generally bad) and tempers (the same) and unreasonable demands (many and often). Ludlow soon realized that life had not treated Polly well.

She was bright but suffered the disadvantage of little education. In those days ambition wasn't as free and easy as it is today, and although Polly was far from satisfied with her lot she
was resigned to it. Her parents had died when she was only a
baby; Lily Weaver, the local seamstress, had taken her in. Lily
taught her to sew, and indeed Polly showed some skill, but
Lily quickly realized there wasn't enough work in the village
for the two of them, and soon Polly became nothing more
than an extra mouth to feed. Fortunately, or rather unfortunately for Polly, it was about that time Jeremiah Ratchet
made it known that he was in need of a maid. So Polly had
wrapped up her few belongings in an old spotted linen cloth,
tied it to a stick, and walked across the road to Jeremiah's,
where she had lived and worked for the last six years.

"It's not as bad as you might think," said Polly. "As long as
I do what I'm supposed to then he can't complain over-
much." But Polly always looked tired and hungry and Ludlow almost felt guilty that he worked for Joe, Jeremiah's
complete opposite.

"It was better when Stanton Cleaver was around," Polly
told him one day.

"Stanton Cleaver?" asked Ludlow.

"The butcher's father. When I first came to Jeremiah's, he
and Stanton used to eat together nearly every night of the
week. It gave me some peace."

"What happened to him?" asked Ludlow.

"He had a bad heart, at least that's what Dr. Mouldered

said, and he died very suddenly. They buried him so quickly no one even saw the body. Everyone thought Stanton was a great man, but I'm not so sure. He treated Horatio, his son, really badly. Anyway, after Stanton died Jeremiah didn't have any more friends in the village, so he started gambling in the City. He's still at it, and I never know if he's going to come in late or early, but whatever the time, he's always drunk." She sighed. "I don't understand why you left the City to come to this place, stuck out here in the middle of nowhere. Was it really that bad?"

"It's much worse than I told you," said Ludlow grimly. "You'd hate it, Poll. It's full of all sorts of nastiness."

"Some people say that you left the City because you committed a crime," said Polly. "They think you're on the run."

Ludlow frowned. "Let them think what they want."

"And what about Joe?" she persisted. "Where did he come from?"

Ludlow shrugged. The few times he had asked, Joe had avoided the question very successfully. Ludlow did not actually know very much about his new master. Even in the exotic stories he told to the Sourdough brothers Joe somehow managed to give little away.

"Anyway," said Polly with a grin, "no matter. He's got Jeremiah in a proper lather. You should hear how he curses the pair of you. One day he really will explode!"

Whatever Jeremiah Ratchet thought of Joe and Ludlow, the villagers made good use of the pawnshop. True, they owned little of any great value, but unlike most pawnbrokers, Joe took everything he was offered, even the most ridiculous and worthless items—a moth-eaten, slightly moldy stuffed cat being one such example—and paid good money as he promised. Ludlow could not imagine even Lembart Jellico accepting such a pledge.

As most customers came in wheezing after climbing the hill, Joe instructed that a chair be set by the door, and it was gratefully received. Ludlow watched them from behind the counter, gasping and coughing and complaining. Eventually the noise would subside and they would come over to show whatever sorry item they had brought. Joe would hold it up to the light and turn it this way and that. Sometimes (but very rarely) he would take out his jeweler's glass and examine the object close-up. All the while the customer stood by hardly breathing, fists closed and white-knuckled, hoping that Joe would take the useless object. He did of course, and they were all grateful, immensely so, and thanked Joe profusely. Often that was the end of business and they would back out of the door still saying thank you. But sometimes the person hung on, hopping from one foot to the other, pretending to be interested in Saluki.

Eventually Joe would turn around and ask quite innocently, "Is there anything else?" The hint of a smile danced at the corners of his mouth.

Invariably they would talk about Jeremiah Ratchet.

"You must be a brave fellow, Mr. Zabbidou. There's not many would stand up to Jeremiah."

They were referring to that first day when Joe had dared to disagree with Mr. Ratchet. It had made a great impression upon the villagers.

Joe's response was always the same. "I simply stated the truth."

"He's thrown another family out on the streets, you know," they would continue, undeterred by Joe's apparent indifference. "At least, he had those brutes do it for him. They wear masks over their faces so we don't know who they are. And for the sake of a few pennies' rent, Mr. Zabbidou. It's not right."

If they expected Joe to do something about it, they were disappointed. He merely shook his head sadly.

"A terrible business," he said. "A truly terrible business."

CHAPTER SIXTEEN

Fragment from
The Memoirs of Ludlow Fitch

The City was gray from dirt and disease; Pagus Parvus existed in a gray light that was cast by clouds that never seemed to go away. I soon learned the weather in the region varied little from what I had experienced the night I arrived. Sitting as it was on the exposed side of a mountain, covered in snow eight months out of twelve and rained on for the other four, Pagus Parvus was not popular with outsiders, and those who lived there left it rarely. Although rumors had reached them of a vehicle that moved by itself, they had not yet seen one of these great iron beasts, and the parallel tracks it rode on were not coming in the direction of Pagus Parvus. If given a choice Pagus Parvians preferred to travel by horse and carriage, but that was a privilege of the few, so mainly they were on foot.

If it had not been for Joe there was little to keep me here, but still I began to think of it as home. My days as a pickpocket were long over and I was glad not to have to

thieve anymore. I continued to wear Jeremiah's gloves and scarf, however. It was worth it to see how he stared whenever we met.

At night, after supper, we would sit by the fire and talk. We discussed many things but seldom reached any conclusions. Joe was a man of few expressions; his face rarely gave anything away, although he became quite animated when we talked about Saluki. That frog was treated like a queen. Joe fed her the finest bugs and snails and worms and the Sourdough boys were up almost every day just to fuss over her.

We also talked about Jeremiah Ratchet. Whenever the shop bell rang I had taken to guessing whether it would be a pledge or merely another complaint about Jeremiah. The blustering buffoon had practically the whole village beholden to him. He seemed to spend his days either threatening to evict his tenants or sending his masked men to do just that. Every time I heard his name I became more and more frustrated that no one in the village seemed willing, or able, to challenge him.

"Why do you think the villagers tell you so much about Jeremiah Ratchet?" I asked Joe.

"Because they are impatient."

It was a typically brief reply. Sometimes conversations with Joe were like riddles.

"Jeremiah," he continued, "is a heavy burden for a small place like this."

"Then why don't they do something? There are enough of them."

Joe shook his head. "Jeremiah is a cunning fellow. Each person is so caught up with his own predicament that he cannot see true strength is in the crowd. To overthrow Jeremiah they must work together, but he has them divided and held hostage to their fears. They believe he has informers in the village."

"Surely the villagers wouldn't betray each other?"

"No doubt they are forced to," said Joe. "And because they cannot trust each other they are unwilling to plot against Jeremiah in case he finds out. They talk to me because I am a stranger and Jeremiah has no hold over me. In their desperation they think I might save them from that scoundrel."

"And will you?" I asked. Silently I willed Joe to take him on.

"However bad the situation, I cannot change the course of things," he replied, and would not be drawn on the subject any further.

I cannot count the number of times Joe said this. It always left me wondering: Was he suggesting that he knew the course of things? And although he maintained that he was unwilling to bring about change, his very presence had already had a noticeable effect on the villagers. After all, he had come to Pagus Parvus a stranger, opened his shop, and in a matter of days he had gained the respect and admiration of all around him. We were all drawn to him, like the moths that fluttered noisily outside the lighted windows at night. Some people make their presence known with loud voices or grand gestures, but Joe didn't have to do that. He was a soft-spoken

man who didn't waste words. But you could just feel when he was near.

As for how Joe made a living, well, that was a complete mystery to me. After all, what sort of business was it to give money away? How else could you explain what he was doing? The window display was growing daily, but although he paid for many items, I rarely saw him sell anything.

And then there was the Black Book of Secrets. Pagus Parvians were quick to take advantage of the service he offered, and at midnight Joe was handing out bags of coins to all and sundry. There were many secrets in Pagus Parvus. During the day the place seemed nothing more than what it was, a small mountain village. It was only in the hours of darkness that it became obvious all was not well. All those wakeful nights I spent looking down the hill, I knew that behind the windows each glowing lamp, each flickering candle, told a tale. Shadows moved across the curtains, silhouettes paced in the dark, pressing their knuckles against their foreheads in frustration and guilt.

Joe listened intently to every tale of woe, and regardless of the confession, he never passed judgment. I know he paid well, but I did not know upon what basis Joe calculated a secret's value. I did ask him once where his money came from and he simply replied, "Inheritance," and made it clear the conversation was over.

Elias Sourdough came up one night from the bakery and admitted that he had been cutting the flour with alum and chalk. That was worth four shillings. When Lily Weaver came

by and said she had been cheating her customers out of cloth by using a short measure, he gave her seven. Even Polly paid us a visit, sneaking out of Ratchet's house late one night to admit to stealing his cutlery. Joe, and I, knew this already. Polly had pawned a knife and fork only two days previously, but it wasn't until she was gone that we noticed Jeremiah's initials on each piece. I had to admire Polly's cheekiness. She knew we couldn't put them in the window (though wouldn't I have loved to have seen Jeremiah's face at the sight of his own cutlery on display). Instead Joe used them for his dinner.

Each night Joe stoked up the fire and set the bottle of liquor and two glasses on the mantel and I took the Black Book from its hiding place and filled the inkwell. Then we sat and waited, he in his chair by the fire and I in mine at the table. There was hardly a night went by without a knock on the door as the church bell struck twelve. I played my part. As the villagers gave their confessions, I sat in the shadows and wrote it all down, word for word.

Sometimes it was hard not to shout out at what I was hearing. Every so often I would sneak a look at Joe sitting by the fire resting his elbows on the arms of the chair, his fingers slightly touching. His face was like a blank page, whatever was said. Very occasionally he would bend back his forefingers for a split second, make circles in the air with the tips and then bring them back together again. But not once did his expression change.

CHAPTER SEVENTEEN

Horatio Cleaver

"He's a murderer," hissed the oldest Sourdough. "He takes his chopper in the middle of the night and goes hunting for fresh meat. Man meat."

"And he puts it in his pies," added the middle brother, while the third, the youngest, began to whimper.

The three boys stood outside the butcher's window watching as he sharpened his knives. They loved the scrape of the blade on metal and to see the sparks that flew around his head.

"If you know this," asked the youngest tremulously, "how come he's not in jail with all the other murderers?"

His brothers poured scorn on this ridiculous suggestion.

"There's no proof, stupid. You can't put a man in prison without proof."

"And the proof is in the pies," said the other. "By the time the murder is discovered, it's too late."

"Yeah, cos they've been eaten!" shrieked the pair in unison.

As for Horatio Cleaver, the subject of this slander, as soon as he saw their wet noses against the window he roared at them and ran to the door and shook his knives violently in their direction.

"Get your filthy noses off my p-p-panes," he shouted.

The trio ran away screaming and laughing, tripping and skidding down the icy hill with their arms flailing.

Ludlow and Joe arrived just in time to see the Sourdough boys disappearing in the distance. Horatio was still standing at the door of his shop, his fists clenched, when he noticed them. They were a strange sight. Joe stood out from the crowd and not only on account of his unusual height. He strode with a confidence, despite his limp, that was both disarming and enviable. Even people who had lived in the village all their lives could not negotiate the steep icy slope with such ease. Ludlow was always a few steps behind, no higher than Joe's elbow, trotting to keep up.

Horatio quickly slipped back inside behind the counter. Joe stood for some moments looking in the window, eyeing the butcher's wares. Today he had for sale a selection of "Prok Peyes," a "Brayse of Fessants," best "Lam Clutets," and "Hole Pukled Chikins." Horatio had not often seen the inside of a schoolhouse.

"I won't be long," said Joe, and he went in, leaving Ludlow outside, where he stood and watched.

As a butcher, Horatio Cleaver was far from the best, but he was the only one the village had so people made do. His father, Stanton Cleaver, had been renowned near and far for his meat-carving skills and was remembered fondly by all his customers. He could butcher a whole cow, head to tail, in under three minutes, a feat he performed annually to wild applause at the county fair. Who could forget the sight of Stanton holding up the Butcher's Cup to deafening cheers, his white apron sodden with blood and his hands stained pink?

Horatio certainly couldn't and, unfortunately, he was never likely to take his father's place on that stand. He was reminded of this fact every day when he heard the disappointed sighs of his customers and the "tut-tuts" as he hacked at their joints and their chops. But they always took the rather roughly hewn cuts of meat he handed them, for if they got more than they asked for, they certainly paid less than it was worth. Horatio had never been good with numbers and the complex relationship between weight and price was one he hadn't quite managed to grasp.

And if it wasn't the customers sending him scornful looks it was Stanton himself, for painted on the wall behind the counter was a life-size portrait of the man complete with a boning knife in his hand and a sneer on his face. Horatio could feel his eyes boring into the back of his head and he grew nervous and stammered—a legacy of his time serving his father. It was only on his p's, however, and most noticeable when he was nervous or his temper was roused.

Stanton was not an easy man to forget. Despite the fact that he had been in the grave nearly five years, he had a long reach. Late at night Horatio would wake, gasping for breath as if the master butcher's hands were around his neck, suffocating him. Horatio had not had a happy apprenticeship, and his father had often been driven to violence by his son's poor butchering skills.

Horatio had started in the shop as soon as he could reach the counter, and over the years the young butcher had begun to take on the appearance of the meat with which he worked all day. He had gradually become more solid in the body, rather like a bull, and his thick, hairless forearms were shaped like two shanks of lamb. His skin was the color of hung meat, a sort of creamy blue, and of similar texture. His face was long and his nostrils flared and his brown eyes surveyed his surroundings with mild interest. The tips of his fingers were thick and blunted; for a man who made his living working with knives he was surprisingly careless.

Horatio wiped his bloodied palms on his graying striped apron and greeted Joe with a pleasant "Good afternoon" and a nervous smile. He nodded in the direction of the fleeing children.

"I should make sausages out of them," he joked, the blades of his knives glittering in the lamplight. Outside Ludlow shuddered at the sight.

Joe laughed politely. "Let me introduce myself," he said. "I am Joe Zabbidou—"

"The p-p-pawnbroker," interrupted Horatio.

Joe responded with a small bow.

"You're up in the old milliner's shop. I hope you do better than Betty P-p-peggotty."

Joe raised his left eyebrow quizzically.

"She made hats," continued Horatio, blowing on his huge red hands. The temperature in the shop was only marginally higher than outside. "Very expensive, mind. P-p-peacock p-p-plumes, ostrich feathers, silk flowers, and all that sort of thing. Not to my taste. Too fancy. Me, I like a p-p-plain hat." He touched his white butcher's cap proudly and left specks of gristle on the brim.

"So I see."

"She couldn't make any money so she went to the City, to run an alehouse, I believe." He secured a piece of pork to the counter with the heel of his hand and hacked at it absentmindedly with a knife.

"Wrong location, see. Too far up that cursed hill. No one goes up that end these days unless they're laid out in a box. Even then they have to be p-p-pulled up. Takes six horses. And the noise of that coffin on the cobbles! Would wake the dead." He stopped, knife in midair, to laugh at his own joke.

"They come up to me," said Joe.

"So I've heard. Well, maybe you'll have more luck than she did."

"Jeremiah Ratchet thinks not."

Horatio spat with contempt into the sawdust.

"Didn't take him long to stick his oar in."

"He said he was a businessman."

"P-p-pah!" exclaimed Horatio. "That slimy toad. I'll wager he's made a deal or two with the devil in his time. He lives off the backs of the p-p-poor. Lending money, then taking all they have when they can't p-p-pay it back. Throwing them out of their homes for the sake of a few days' rent. He'll bleed this village dry. No wonder he got on so well with my father; they were cut from the same cloth."

He brought down his knife with a tremendous crash, sending a huge pork chop spiraling into the air and over the counter. Joe caught it with lightning speed.

He looked straight into the butcher's sad eyes and though Horatio wanted to look away, for some reason he couldn't. His ears filled with a soft noise, like wind through trees, and he felt his legs go weak. His deadened fingertips seemed to have developed pins and needles.

"You sound like a man who needs to get something off his chest," said Joe quietly. "Come up to the shop tonight. Maybe I can help."

"I doubt it," replied Horatio slowly, mesmerized by Joe's gaze.

Joe was insistent. "After midnight, so no one knows."

"Perhaps."

"Excellent," said Joe, smiling broadly and breaking the spell. "Until then."

"What about my p-p-pork chop?"

"I'll have it for my supper," said Joe. "I'll pay you later, when you come up."

The church bell sounded midnight as Horatio pulled his coat closer and raised his fist to the door. The pale half-moon watched quietly as he dithered, in two minds whether to knock. He hadn't meant to come and he didn't really understand why he was here, but as midnight approached his restless feet had taken him out of the door and up the hill. How could this stranger help him? In fact, how did this stranger even know he needed help? He remembered how Joe had looked at him. Had he sucked his thoughts out of his head?

Horatio raised his fist, but before he could strike the wood Joe opened the door.

"Horatio, come in," he said warmly. "We've been expecting you."

He led the silent butcher into the back room, where the fire was blazing. Horatio lowered his sturdy frame into the offered chair and frowned as it creaked alarmingly. Joe handed him a glass of the golden liquid and he took a long draught, then another. His cheeks flushed and his eyes shone.

"A powerful drop," he said and drained his glass.

"I believe you have a secret you'd like to pawn," prompted Joe.

Horatio's eyebrows met in a quizzical frown. "What do you mean?"

"It is what I do," explained Joe. "I buy secrets."

Horatio considered the proposal for a short moment. "Then buy this," he said.

Ludlow was already settled at the table, the Black Book open before him, and Horatio began.

CHAPTER EIGHTEEN

Extract from
The Black Book of Secrets

The Butcher's Confession

My name is Horatio Cleaver and I have a dreadful confession.
Guilt has driven me to the brink of madness. I cannot sleep. Instead I pace the floor until dawn, going over and over in my head what I have done. I desire only one thing: to be freed of my terrible burden.

I know people think I am a fool, both as a man and as a butcher. I lack the talent that my father, Stanton, had and I am the first to admit it. He was a true master of his trade. His skill with a cleaver was unrivaled and he won every butcher's competition in the county for his speed and precision. They called him Lightning Stan. To Pagus Parvians he was the greatest hero since Mick MacMuckle, the one-armed blacksmith who could shoe a horse blindfolded.

To me he was a beast.

When my mother was alive I was spared the worst of his

excesses, but she died, still a young woman, and I was left at his mercy. He was a sly fellow, you see. To the villagers he was a cheerful chap, always ready to flatter the ladies and joke with the gentlemen. But away from the counter, out the back in the cold store, he was a different man. He was a monster. He beat me every day with anything he could get his hands on: pigs' legs, rump steaks, even chickens with their feathers still on. All the time he told me I should be grateful to him for teaching me his trade.

"Nobody else would have you," he said and I began to believe him.

I was so nervous that I made even more mistakes and he became angrier. He laughed at my spelling, yet wouldn't allow me any schooling; he mocked my stammer, knowing that only made it worse. As for my work, I did my best but I'm no carver—I'm all fingers and thumbs, what's left of them. As punishment, or for a joke, he would lock me in the ice store until my hands were so stiff I couldn't bend them around a knife.

My life was miserable. At night I slept on the sawdust behind the counter while he snoozed upstairs in front of a warm fire with a glass of whisky. I wanted to run away, but he had me so scared I couldn't think straight. So I suffered the lashing of tongue and belt, and inside I seethed like a mountain about to explode.

And then there was Jeremiah Ratchet. My father saw in Jeremiah a kindred spirit—namely a glutton with an insatiable appetite for money—and the two would sit by the fire in the room above the shop well into the early hours sipping ale and brandy while I waited on their every whim.

"P-p-pour us another, p-p-please, Horatio," Jeremiah would say mockingly and the two would burst into throaty laughter. Or, "Remind me, Horatio, how much is your lamb?"

"Twelve p-p-pennies a p-p-pound."

One day Jeremiah came in laughing. "I see you have a new product," he said, pointing to a sign in the window, a sign I had written. To my shame it read: "Micemeat Peyes—three pense eech."

"Micemeat pies?" bellowed my father, grabbing a chicken, his face puce with rage.

That night I realized I had nothing left to lose. The time had come to fight back. They say revenge is a dish best eaten cold. I served it up hot and steaming.

The next evening my father sat down as usual to a hearty meal of potatoes and pie, one of my own creations, and Jeremiah joined him as he often did. To see these men at the table was repulsive in the extreme. They ate as if they had only hours to live. Barely was one mouthful masticated before another was crammed in. Gravy dribbled down their chins, piecrust clung to their greasy cheeks, and their napkins were spotted with food.

I watched, fascinated and repelled at the same time, as they tucked in. For they had just eaten a very special pie. Micemeat indeed!

The next morning I woke to the sound of agonized screams from upstairs. I found my father groaning and writhing on the bed. His face was covered in pus-filled boils, sweat ran from his brow, and his breathing was rapid and painful. He was clutching at his stomach and every so often he would let out a screech of pain. I called for Dr. Mouldered, but by the time he arrived it was clear to us all that my father was on the verge of death.

Mouldered seemed perplexed. "Well, although I think it is probably a malfunction of the heart, I am a little puzzled by the boils. How peculiar. Has Mr. Cleaver been bitten by a rat?"

I could feel my own face burning and my heart racing. Whatever his illness, it wasn't from a rat bite, more likely from biting a rat. Possibly the one I had served up to him in the pie the night before. Or maybe it was another of my ingredients. The recipe was simple: If it was dead it went in— hair, fur, paws, claws, and all. There was a minced mouse, two fistfuls of hard-back beetles, plump bluebottles, and juicy purple worms, not forgetting the toad I found on the road squashed by a cartwheel.

I watched my father for a day and a night, and all the time he moaned in agony I berated myself for my stupidity. I had only wanted to punish him. I didn't want him to die.

But die he did.

He exhaled his last breath as I stood over him. And what did I feel? Everything: remorse, guilt, rage—and relief. I closed his eyes, covered him up, and went for Dr. Mouldered.

"Heart attack," he said wearily without even opening his bag and left almost immediately.

Of course, the villagers mourned his passing.

"What shall we do without Stanton?" they cried. "Who shall represent us in the county competition?"

"I could try," I said once and they looked at me as if I were a piece of gristle in a cheap pie.

Well, with my father gone my life should have taken a turn for the better. But I hadn't reckoned on the guilt that would consume me, or on Jeremiah Ratchet.

A few days later he paid me a visit. I hadn't seen him since the night of the fatal meal. He was as white as a leaf starved of the sun and his bloodshot eyes were sunken into his dry flesh.

"I have a bone to pick with you," he said sternly. "Or should I say foot?" He held out his hand and there on his palm was a tiny but unmistakable rat's big toe.

"I found it between my teeth," he said. "After that pie you served us, the one that made me sick as a pig for the last three days. The same pie that killed your father. I see you buried him quick enough."

My heart froze in my chest but I managed to stammer, "Mr. Ratchet, what do you mean? If the p-p-pie killed my father then how come you are still alive and well?"

Ratchet narrowed his eyes. "Obviously I didn't eat the rest of the poisoned rat."

He leaned over the counter so I could smell his sour breath.

"I'll be keeping an eye on you," he said.

And he left, but not before helping himself to a couple of fine steaks and a piece of mutton, although he ignored the pies. And because I didn't stop him Jeremiah knew that he was right.

What a cruel and fickle mistress Fate is: to kill one and yet to leave the other to torture me. Ratchet comes every week and takes what he pleases: a goose or two, a pheasant, a piece of beef. How long will that satisfy him? What will happen to me if he tells? I know what I did was wrong, but must I suffer on its account for the rest of my life? Is there no respite from this agony?

I am not a man without a conscience, I am deeply ashamed of what I have done, but I don't know how much longer I can endure this torture. I have not slept through the night since the day my father was buried. ✳

Ludlow put down his quill, laid a sheet of blotting paper between the pages, and closed the book.

"I can give you respite," said Joe, and he looked into Horatio's troubled eyes. "Your secret is safe in the book now, I swear to you."

Horatio sighed deeply and the lines on his brow slowly disappeared. His eyes brightened and he yawned widely.

"I feel better already." He stood up, but hesitated to take the coins that Joe offered, a substantial amount.

"Mr. Zabbidou, I feel it is I who should be paying you!"

Joe shook his head. "Not at all, Mr. Cleaver. It is a fair exchange."

"Very well," said Horatio and made his way to the door, where he stopped for a moment. "I swore I would never bake a rodent pie again, but I cannot deny there are days when I am tempted. Every time Jeremiah Ratchet comes in, striding about as if he owns the place, flaunting his posh clothes and smelling like a perfumery, wouldn't I like to give him one more special."

"The day will come when you will not have to suffer that man any longer," said Joe. "Ratchet'll get what's coming to him. Just be patient."

Joe took Horatio to the door and Ludlow sat silently at the table. Horatio's story had reminded him of things he wished to forget. Ludlow knew what it was like to have a violent father. What bad luck for Horatio to be born to such a man. But did that mean he had been destined from birth to murder him?

Joe watched as Horatio made his way back to the butcher's. He waited until he saw him go into his shop and the light go out upstairs. He smiled. Horatio was going to sleep tonight. But there were others who wouldn't.

CHAPTER NINETEEN

A Disturbed Night

While Joe was listening to the woes of the villagers, halfway down the hill Jeremiah Ratchet lay wide awake in his bed. Prior to Joe's arrival, it was rare to see a light on after midnight in Jeremiah's house. A man with no conscience often sleeps soundly, and Jeremiah would snore hour after hour (keeping Polly awake up in her attic bedroom), blissfully untroubled by the fact that he was the chief cause of insomnia in Pagus Parvus.

Now Jeremiah spent his nights tossing and turning. He called for Polly at ungodly hours, requesting a warm drink or a book to read or fresh hot embers for his bed warmer. But nothing worked. Sleep would not come.

Jeremiah Ratchet lived right in the middle of the street in a house that was five times the size of those he rented out to his unfortunate tenants. He had spent many years filling it with all sorts of treasures, but in the end the effect was similar to his clothing: loud and difficult to miss, and not a pleasant sight. The house had seven bedrooms (though he had never entertained an overnight guest), a marvelous dining room served by a large kitchen (most nights he ate alone), and room for five servants in the attic (his innate meanness meant he kept only two: Polly and a boy to look after his horses, but he slept in the hay).

Jeremiah used to take great pleasure from wandering the musty, shadowy corridors with his hands clasped smugly behind his back. He contemplated the portraits on the stairs: seven generations of Ratchets watching him with cold eyes and curled lips. He admired the shine on his silver and reveled in the luxury of his imported rugs—hand-tied by carpet weavers in an African desert. Sometimes when he dug his fingers into the pile he imagined he could feel the grains of sand under his nails. In fact, it wasn't his imagination. Polly's cleaning left much to be desired.

But this was all before Joe Zabbidou arrived.

Joe had rattled Jeremiah from that very first morning. Although he had not gone up to the shop since then, not in daylight at any rate, Ratchet knew what was in the window. Polly had been instructed to pay regular visits—although not to enter the shop—and she described the display to him in great detail.

"Chipped chamber pots and old boots!" exclaimed Jeremiah. "How can a man make money in such a way? He must be a fool!"

For generations, the Ratchet family in Pagus Parvus had profited from the poor unfortunates in the village. By stealth,

force, and inherited duplicity Jeremiah had continued the tradition. He had acquired ownership of cottages and land, which he rented out to the villagers at rates that could only be described as criminal. He evicted them periodically, to show them he meant business, and then allowed them back on the understanding that they owed him even more rent. Obadiah was not the only one who had made the mistake of falling into debt to him, and in this way Jeremiah's fortune grew.

In his own mind it was all down to his skill as a business-man. Of course, it is easy to be a skilled businessman when there is no competition, but Jeremiah was beginning to real-ize that Joe might be the rival he had never had. Unfortu-nately for Jeremiah, he did not own Joe's shop, a fact that caused him immense irritation. What galled him even more than that was Joe's apparent wealth. He had convinced him-self that it was Joe's money that afforded him his elevated status, especially as he was so generous with it, and that it couldn't last. Two weeks after the pawnbroker first opened up Jeremiah was surprised to find that Joe's shop was still in business, and judging by the number of people who passed Jeremiah's house on their way up the hill, Joe's foolish trade in chamber pots and old boots was thriving.

Jeremiah was further irked when Obadiah Strang had come up to him in the street with a queer look on his face.

"Now, Obadiah," Jeremiah had said impatiently, "I hope you aren't going to try to get out of this week's rent again. I told you—"

"Here," said Obadiah triumphantly, "take this." He thrust a leather bag toward Jeremiah, who took it and opened it curiously. It was full of coins.

"It's all there," said Obadiah. "Now my debt is paid."

The gravedigger walked away with head held high and Jeremiah stood in the snow, mouth agape. As the passersby began to snigger at him he turned and hurried home. Polly came up from the kitchen and met him in the hall.

"Someone left this for you," she said. She was holding the wooden spade. Jeremiah snorted and pushed past her and went into the study. He slammed the door so hard the windows rattled.

Obadiah wasn't the only one to have suddenly come into money. At least three other debtors had paid up. "Where are they getting it from?" Jeremiah asked himself, and the only answer he could think of was Joe Zabbidou. Jeremiah's temper was now even shorter, and Polly and the stable boy bore the brunt of it. He had never considered that any of them would pay their debts. If business continued in this manner Jeremiah was going to have to find other ways of making money.

Recently he had heard there was profit to be made from selling teeth, both false and real. Ironically, the rich suffered with tooth rot more than the poor. Doubtless their sweeter, more exotic diet was to blame, unlike the coarse fare of their poorer counterparts. Well-off ladies and gentlemen would pay handsomely for a set of real teeth to fill their gaps, not least because it was an obvious show of wealth. Jeremiah

wondered if he could take advantage of this business opportunity. Last time he was in the Nimble Finger he had heard mention of a certain Barton Gumbroot who knew more about these things. Mentally he made a note to meet with him next time he was in the City.

For now, though, he had to deal with the pawnbroker. Every time he thought of Joe, that string bean of a character whose hair defied description, he could feel his teeth clamping together and a headache starting at the base of his neck. As for the boy, his skinny, short-legged attendant who went with him everywhere, he seemed a sly little devil. He wore a scarf and gloves that looked suspiciously like his own, the ones Jeremiah was certain the coach driver had stolen. And those big dark eyes. Jeremiah had never once managed to hold Ludlow's gaze. He always had to look away.

Ever since their first meeting a creeping sense of dissatisfaction had wormed its way into Jeremiah's veins. Now when he walked down the street the villagers looked at him sideways and it unnerved him. His ears were filled with the sound of laughter, though the faces around him were grim. There was a change in the village. It was in the very air he breathed. He could feel it in his bones and it made him shiver. And he knew that it was something to do with the pawnbroker.

It didn't take Jeremiah long to notice Joe's nocturnal visitors. Now what was that all about? Lying awake in the middle of the night, Jeremiah tossed and turned in his foreign-made four-poster bed. The slightest noise seemed to

be magnified tenfold as he listened for the footsteps passing under his window. He had tried to ignore them, burying his face in the mattress, but he couldn't stand the smell of his own breath and had to come up for air. He sat up and frowned and talked to himself and drummed his fingers on the counterpane until he heard the soft crunch of the snow outside on the pavement. Then he would jump from his bed and race to the window. He could see the dark figures going up to Joe's, but he couldn't make out who they were. Whatever it was they were up to, it could only mean more trouble for him. In his nightshirt Jeremiah shook his clenched fist at them and pounded the floor in a fury.

"This man must be stopped," he shouted into the night.

CHAPTER TWENTY

FRAGMENT FROM
THE MEMOIRS OF LUDLOW FITCH

If Joe was a source of interest to the villagers, then I was equally a source of interest to the younger members—namely Polly and the Sourdoughs. I'd not had friends before, and where I came from, people's only loyalty was to money. But the Sourdough boys weren't like that. They were good company and made me laugh and I liked them. Except perhaps for the oldest. I always had the feeling that I couldn't quite trust him. You never really knew what he was thinking.

Polly, however, was less interested in Saluki and more interested in stories from my past. "Tell me about the City," she urged. "I want to know everything."

So I told her: about the dark, enclosed streets with the houses so close together that the sun could never break through; about the broken pavements littered with rotting food, dead animals, dogs, and putrefying rats; about the pools of rancid water and the swarms of flies that hovered in clouds above the surface. I told her about the people, sitting

in the gutter and begging for money to go into the taverns, or lying drunk, thrown out of the same; and I told her about the unbearable coldness of the winter, when people and animals died and froze where they lay.

Through all of this flows the River Foedus, her slow-moving waters thick as soup. Lord but she lives up to her name; her unrelenting stench hangs over the City like a shroud. She is not to be trusted. I have seen her shiver to shrug off the ships tied at the piers, causing them to rock violently from side to side, their creaking and groaning of protest mingling with the frightened shouts of the oarsmen and passengers on the small ferries crossing her broad back. All fear her murky waters. Few are known to have survived such a noxious dipping. And once she has them the Foedus does not surrender her victims quickly. She drags them under and sucks the life out of them, before disgorging them days later bloated with lethal gases and bug-eyed, ready to explode.

The Foedus splits the City in half and divides the people in two. The rich live on her north bank, the poor on the south. One bridge alone spans her back. Perhaps once it had a name but now it is known simply as the Bridge. It is lined on either side with taverns and inns and hostels of the vilest kind, and in these dark and smoky dens of vice all men, whether from the north or the south, are equal: They fight, they gamble, they drink, they murder. I, too, have been in the Nimble Finger Inn, the tavern so beloved of Jeremiah Ratchet and Ma and Pa.

And in a city whose lifeblood is crime, there is also punishment to stem its flow. It's an ill wind that blows no good, and although I hate to say it now, I made a good living then out of the misdeeds of others, especially on a Wednesday: hanging day at Gallows Corner.

A hanging was as good as a holiday. The crowds enjoyed the spectacle almost as much as the poor fellow on the gibbet detested it. The prisoner would arrive on the back of a cart, having been taken from Irongate Prison and driven down Melancholy Lane to the gallows. He would have been in a sorry state when the journey began, but by the end he was wretched. It was common for the onlookers to pelt the cart with whatever came to hand as it passed: rotten fruit and vegetables from the gutters, occasionally a dead cat. I never once threw even a potato peeling at any of those poor devils. Who was to say it wouldn't be me next week?

The crowd cheered as the criminal was led up the steps and the noose was placed around his (or as often as not, her) neck. Now I turned away, not least because this was prime pickpocketing time. When the crowd stood fixated on the ghastly scene unfolding before them I moved among them, taking whatever I could get my hands on. I heard the trapdoor open and the crossbeam creak as the weight fell. And as the crowd roared I sneaked away before anyone noticed that their purse was gone.

Polly lapped up every word. "One day I will go there," she said, her eyes shining. And no matter what I said I couldn't persuade her otherwise.

Although I told Polly many things I didn't tell her about Ma and Pa. I didn't tell her how they robbed me and whipped me or why I really left the City. And I never once said what they had tried to do to me and how it came back to me at night in my dreams. Always my father's face looming above mine and his hands around my neck, or were mine around his?

I could never forgive Ma and Pa for what they did, but I was also grateful to them. Pickpockets, regardless of their age, were treated harshly by the courts. If Ma and Pa hadn't chased me from the City, I know sooner or later the noose would have been around my neck and my lifeless body would have been hanging from those gallows.

CHAPTER TWENTY,ONE

Stirling Oliphaunt

As the days wore on more and more villagers were bene-fiting not only from Joe's generous payments for their pawned goods, but also from his midnight trade. Although they didn't talk about their good fortune, it was obvious that something was afoot. Without a doubt Joe was the breath of fresh air the village had needed for a long, long time. The place seemed brighter somehow, as if the buildings them-selves had released a huge sigh and relaxed back to allow the light in. One morning the whole street was brought to a standstill when the clouds parted for a minute or two and blue sky was seen in between.

"It's a miracle," declared Ruby Sourdough. Of course, the clouds came over again and the blue sky was gone, but it was enough to know that it did exist.

Whether this was a miracle or not, the one person in the village who was actually qualified to make such a statement was still in bed and missed the historic event.

The Reverend Stirling Oliphaunt.

For twenty years Stirling Oliphaunt had looked at himself in the mirror every morning (usually not far off noon) and congratulated himself on his posting to Pagus Parvus. A man of his ilk couldn't have asked for a better job—his ilk being that of a lazy, slovenly boor whose purported belief in higher powers furnished him with an easy living. When he had arrived in the village two decades ago he had stood at the gates to the church and cast a bushy-browed, fat-rimmed eye down the hill.

This is what I have been waiting for, he thought. *That hill must be forty degrees, if not more.*

In those days the villagers were a little more inclined to listen to the word of the Lord, so much to Stirling's disappointment, for nearly eight months he was forced to preach a sermon every Sunday. His distinct monotone and the repetitive nature of his subject (the devil, the Dark Side, hell, fire, brimstone, and all related issues) ensured that he addressed an ever-dwindling audience. Eventually, as was his desire, it dwindled to none. Henceforth Stirling passed his days restfully, enjoying fine wines and good food at the church's expense and generally doing as he wished, which was very little. He still thought of God. There had to be one, for how else could a man be blessed with such good fortune?

Now Stirling was more than a little disconcerted by the events of the past few weeks. From his exalted position at the top of the hill, he had not failed to notice the increase in pedestrian traffic. At first he thought the villagers might be

coming to him, expecting a service of some kind, and he breathed a sigh of relief when he realized that Joe Zabbidou was the draw.

Stirling had grown used to a life of ease with little interruption and certainly no demands from his flock. When Jeremiah had approached him with the body-snatching business plan Stirling saw no reason to stand in his way, and he was handsomely rewarded with gifts from Jeremiah's wine cellar. This might not strike you as characteristic of Jeremiah until you consider that he drank most of his donations when he came to see Stirling on Thursdays.

Stirling had seen Joe Zabbidou, and his young assistant, that first morning in the graveyard, but he was not inclined to welcome formally the new members of his congregation. Later Polly, who came up every day to cook and clean by arrangement with Jeremiah, told him that the hat shop had a new owner.

"A hatter?" asked the reverend.

"No, a pawnbroker."

"A pawnbroker?"

Polly didn't reply. Stirling had a tendency to turn statement to question—it helped enormously when you didn't have any answers. He had developed the habit in a previous parish where the locals were an inquisitive bunch who enjoyed lively theological debate and were determined that Stirling should enjoy it, too.

"A pawnbroker?" he repeated. He considered briefly how this might affect his position in the village and concluded

that it wouldn't affect him at all. In fact, he didn't think Joe's arrival would have much of an effect on anyone. He was surprised, therefore, at the level of animosity Jeremiah Ratchet felt toward the newcomer.

It was late afternoon and the reverend was dozing in a chair when he was brought rapidly back to wakefulness by a tremendous thumping at the door. Polly was there to open it, but she was elbowed out of the way as Jeremiah strode past her into the drawing room.

"Jeremiah?" said Stirling. "A pleasure, I'm sure. Is it Thursday already?"

"It's Tuesday, but I have an important matter to discuss with you."

"Is it about Obadiah and the bodies?"

"Not Obadiah. That blasted pawnbroker."

Stirling roused himself to an upright position.

"Mr. Sobbi—whatever his name is? Isn't he a harmless chap?"

"Harmless!" spluttered Jeremiah. "Harmless! The man is the devil incarnate."

Exhausted by his outburst, and the trip up the hill, Jeremiah fell into the chair opposite the reverend. Polly handed him a drink, topped off Stirling's, and then made herself scarce. It did not do to stay in the same room as that pair. She much preferred to listen from outside the door.

Jeremiah finished his glass in one gulp. He reached over to the table and took the decanter and set it on the hearth beside him.

"Stirling," he announced, "that pawnbroker is very bad for business. In particular, my business. He has filled his window with the greatest collection of junk you have ever seen, and not only that, he has paid for it."

"How is this a problem?" Stirling was trying to sound interested, but he had the beginnings of a headache and was overcome by the urge to yawn.

"His payments are so wildly out of keeping with the true value of the pledges that I fear soon *all* the villagers will be able to pay off their debts."

"I see," said Stirling.

"And if people aren't in debt to me how then do I make money?" continued Jeremiah, and to emphasize his point fully he leaned over and gave Stirling a poke with his fat forefinger. "You have got to do something. My livelihood depends on it."

Now Stirling was awake. "Me? Do something? What can I do?"

"You must convince those peasants that Joe Zabbidou is the devil's spawn."

"The devil's pawn? But is this true?" Stirling had never before thought he might have to deal with the devil's pawn.

"Pawn, spawn," said Jeremiah with intense irritation. "What's the truth got to do with it? This is business. They are to have no further doings with him upon pain of death."

"I'm not sure," said Stirling cautiously.

"Just do it," snapped Jeremiah.

CHAPTER TWENTY TWO

Stirling Makes a Stand

"Good people of Pagus Parvus," began Stirling, "I beseech of you to listen to me."

Beseech of? he thought in a sudden panic. *Is that right?* No matter, it would do. There was no one here who was an expert in the complexities of the English language. His voice quavered audibly and his hands shook. He wished he had taken a second shot of whisky to steady his nerves. It had been years since he had addressed a crowd, and certainly never in such uncomfortable surroundings. It was snowing lightly and he was standing on a box in the middle of the main street, just north of Jeremiah's house. He had thought it a good spot. He cleared his throat and raised his voice.

"For I tell you now, I have been visited by an angel in the night."

Until this point his audience had consisted of three mortals, namely the Sourdough boys armed and ready with snowballs. Everyone else, once they had established who he

was, had walked around him, so much so that his podium was already circled by a ring of footprints in the trampled-down snow. It was only when he said the word *angel* that people stopped to listen. These heavenly creatures appealed greatly to their starved imaginations. Soon there was a small crowd gathered before him, their red-nosed faces looking up at him expectantly.

"An angel?" inquired one.

"Yes, an angel."

"You sure about that, Stirling?" shouted Horatio. "Maybe it was a visitation from the bottle. Too much port can have that effect."

The reverend reddened and carried on. "A great angel came from the clouds and roused me from my bed."

"What did this angel say?" mocked Horatio, making no attempt to disguise his disbelief.

"He said, 'Stirling, you must tell the people of Pagus Parvus to beware, for the devil has come among you and he is tricking you with his wiles and his filthy lucre.'"

"'Wiles and filthy lucre'?" laughed Elias Sourdough. "What language does he speak? Is this angel from a foreign country?"

"Money," said Stirling impatiently. "The devil is among us and luring us with his money."

"There's only one devil in this town and we don't see his money," said Job Wright, the blacksmith, and he pointed in the direction of Jeremiah's house. At the same moment the upstairs curtain twitched, and Stirling wondered if perhaps he should have gone a little farther up the hill.

"Not Mr. Ratchet," he hissed, then raised his voice, "but Joe Zabbidou, the Devil's Pawnbroker." He said this with great feeling, at the same time shaking his clenched fist at the sky. There were gasps all around and Stirling realized that finally he had their full attention. Unwilling to lose this advantage, he hurried along.

"Joe Zabbidou has come to us without warning, appearing from nowhere in the night, to entice you all into his shop with his fancy goods."

Ludlow, who was watching all this from Horatio's doorway, raised his eyebrow. "Fancy goods? A chipped chamber pot. Hardly."

"What does he intend to do with us?" asked Lily Weaver.

"What does he intend to do with us?" repeated Stirling out of habit.

He had not anticipated this question when he had been preparing his speech. He had not thought that he might be challenged. He couldn't recall such a thing when he was in church; granted, most people were asleep then.

The silence was deafening.

"Erm, well, let me see, ah yes, once he has lured you he will take you over to his side, the Dark Side."

Unfortunately for Stirling, this was where he lost his tenuous hold on the audience. Pagus Parvians did not consider the Dark Side in any way threatening. They had not forgotten those long Sunday sermons from years ago when the reverend bored them half to death droning on about the very same subject. They began to shuffle their feet and talk to

their neighbor or walk away. Desperately Stirling tried to re-capture the moment. Jeremiah had promised him a case of the best port.

"If you go over to the Dark Side, then you will be lost for-ever and will burn in the fires of hell."

"At least we'd be warm," shouted Obadiah, and the crowd laughed.

"Do not jest about the Devil," warned Stirling, in a final at-tempt to hold them. "You never know when he is listening."

"Hang about, Reverend," said Ruby Sourdough. "Here comes the beast himself. Why don't we ask him about this Dark Side?"

Joe was indeed coming down the street at his usual jaunty pace. He had the grip of a mountain goat. Right now one or two of the villagers were wondering whether his shoes did indeed conceal those telltale cloven feet.

"'Morning, all," he called and smiled. "Did I hear some-one mention my name?"

Although Stirling was not being taken seriously, it did seem to some a rather curious coincidence that Joe had turned up at this particular moment.

"'Ere, listen to this, Mr. Zabbidoof," said the youngest Sourdough, at the front of the crowd. "Stirling says yore the Devil come 'ere to burn us all in 'ell."

Stirling protested immediately. It had never been his in-tention to actually confront Beelzebub, merely to slander him in his absence. "I didn't say that," he protested hurriedly. "It is a sin to tell a lie, lad."

"Yes 'e did," said Elias Sourdough to Joe. " 'E said you were gonna loor us wiv your tricks and wiles."

Joe smiled. "I have no tricks. You know what I am, a pawn-broker. Have I ever pretended or acted otherwise? As for wiles, you are welcome to come and look for them. Perhaps they are in the window?"

At that everyone burst into raucous laughter. Stirling scowled, picked up his box, and slunk away.

CHAPTER TWENTY-THREE

FRAGMENT FROM
THE MEMOIRS OF LUDLOW FITCH

Stirling's performance in the street was the talk of the villagers for three whole days. As far as they were concerned, the reverend's humiliation was just one more in the eye for Mr. Ratchet (who had watched the entire scene from his window, barely concealed behind the curtain) and another victory for Mr. Zabbidou. The battle lines might as well have been drawn in the snow.

There was no disputing Pagus Parvus had given Joe a warm welcome. It could be measured almost from the moment he defied Jeremiah Ratchet. This initial enthusiasm had not waned—just the opposite—it had increased immensely. Now at the very sight of him the villagers behaved as if he were royalty. I swear upon my evil pa that I witnessed more than once some fellow kneeling before him. Poor Joe, he could not go from one end of the street to the other without being stopped a dozen times by well-wishers, inquiring after his health and his business and even Saluki.

Joe was always polite. His manner was consistently warm and friendly, but I could tell that this adulation was beginning to trouble him.

"I did not come here to be venerated," he mumbled.

As I lay during long sleepless nights the same question turned over in my mind: "What did you come here for?" I knew by now that things were not, and could not be, as simple as they appeared. A man arrives out of nowhere in an isolated village and hands over money from a bottomless source for worthless objects and secrets. It didn't make sense to me, but whenever I tried to ask Joe about his past he refused to engage and immediately talked about something else.

I wondered whether Joe's aversion to all the attention was modesty, and I paid little notice to his discomfort. While he tried to avoid the limelight, I bathed in his reflected glory. When I walked the streets of the City I was nobody: In Pagus Parvus I was prince to Joe's king. Of course, Joe was the one they wanted to talk to, his was the hand they wished to shake, but they spoke to me, too, if only to say good morning. It made me smile. If they had ever seen me in the City they would have crossed to the other side of the road.

Perhaps it was the fact that the village was so isolated that made Joe (and me) even more special. But, special or not, I had a feeling that as long as Jeremiah Ratchet was in Pagus Parvus it wasn't going to be enough.

Our days were always busy. I had my jobs to do and Joe had his, but we were never rushed. Being in the shop sometimes felt like being in another world where everything happened at half speed. I never saw Joe make a hurried movement; there was no urgency to his life, but, for all that, it was difficult to shake off the feeling that we were waiting for something to happen.

In the late afternoon, when it was quiet and Polly and the Sourdoughs would have been and gone, we would both sit by the fire and enjoy the warmth and the comfort it brought. At such times I couldn't imagine ever returning to the City.

"I'm never going back," I said to Joe one night.

"Never say never," Joe replied quickly. "All things change."

Certainly my fortunes had changed. In my eyes Joe was the father I had always wished for. I had new clothes that he had given me. As for my rags, we both enjoyed watching them burn on the fire that night. At least once a fortnight I relaxed in front of the fire in a huge tin tub filled to the brim with hot water, and every day we had two decent meals. The Pagus Parvians had proved most hospitable and hardly a day passed without some sort of food parcel being left on the doorstep: rabbits, pigeons, sparrows (a delicacy in these parts, marvelous stuffed with onion and allium) and occasionally a whole chicken from the butcher's.

"Bribes." Joe laughed. "They think if they feed me I will change my mind." He didn't, but he still threw the meat in the pot.

As the harsh memories of my previous life faded, my mind started to play strange tricks on me. I began to worry that life was too good. Surely a boy such as I, with my past and the crimes I had committed, deserved punishment, not reward?

Joe tried to reassure me. "It's common enough to think like that," he said, "to feel unworthy of good fortune, but have you forgotten what I said to you about luck?"

"You said we make our own luck."

"Exactly. You made yours by coming here. Now you work hard and you deserve what you have."

"But I never intended to come here," I insisted. "It was chance that Ratchet's carriage was outside the Nimble Finger."

"But it was you who chose Jeremiah's carriage."

"What if I had gone down the hill instead of up? I might have worked with Job Wright shoeing horses. Then you would have taken on one of the Sourdough boys when they came up to see the frog."

"That is a possibility," said Joe, "but the Sourdough boys can barely read or write."

"I can only do that because I went to Mr. Jellico."

"But you sought him out."

And so it would go on, in circles, until one evening Joe asked, "Are you happy here?"

"Yes."

"And if you could go back in time, to the City, what would you change?"

"I don't know," I said. "If I had done something different then I might never have met you."

"Exactly," said Joe with finality. "Everything that happened to you, bad or otherwise, ultimately brought you here."

There the conversation ended because the shop door opened and someone called for service. Joe always woke at the sound of the door, no matter how deeply asleep he seemed, but in case he didn't Saluki gave a violent belch whenever she heard someone approaching. I felt it was a warning.

For a frog, Saluki was good company. When I had the chance I liked to feed her, to watch her tongue shoot out across the length of the tank, and almost too quick to see, the bug or grub or insect would be gone. I had not taken the lid off the tank again since that first day. Joe had forbidden me to do so and I didn't want to touch her. Occasionally he took her out and held her in the palm of his hand. He would stroke her back with such gentleness, and she would burp softly and seem to glow. I hadn't forgotten what he had said about gaining her trust, and I hoped that one day I would.

I remember those days in the shop well, warm and cozy away from the cold outside world. But of course the outside world still came knocking at the door. The villagers were obviously grateful for everything Joe had done for them, and gradually, one by one, they were freeing themselves from Jeremiah's iron grip. But their previous desperation was now replaced by anger—that Jeremiah had treated them so badly

for so long, that he had taken so much from them, that he had kept them living in fear. As each managed to pay Jeremiah back the money they owed, they wished to pay him back in other ways, too.

One night we had a visit from the local physician, Dr. Samuel Mouldered. I wasn't surprised. After all, Joe had sought him out the previous day, as he did all his midnight customers, and invited him up. Like most, he had an interesting tale to tell.

Samuel Mouldered was a rather morbid man with a permanently gloomy expression on his face, so his patients never knew if they were to live or die. They may have been alarmed to discover that often the doctor did not know, either. You see, Mouldered wasn't a doctor at all, just a convincing quack who was on the run from a posse of duped customers who had discovered that his miracle cure was little more than boiled nettles and corked wine.

Pagus Parvus was an ideal hiding place for such a man. To be fair, Mouldered was quite harmless. Since coming to the village some ten years ago he had practiced medicine on the premise that most illnesses burned themselves out over the course of seven days. Thus he prescribed his miracle cure (now a more palatable mixture of honey and beer) for a week's duration, and on the whole he achieved quite remarkable results. As for death itself, no one ever questioned the unusually high occurrence of heart attacks in the area. They trusted the doctor and his diagnoses.

Samuel Mouldered's greatest fear was that Jeremiah would discover his secret.

"I cannot promise that Jeremiah will never find out," Joe had said, "but he will not hear it from us. You have my word."

Joe held the door open, but Mouldered seemed reluctant to go.

"The man is a monster," he declared. "For years we have suffered at his hands. The villagers want revenge. I know they hope you will help them."

"What can I do?" asked Joe quietly. "I am merely a pawn-broker."

"That's not what they think," muttered the doctor as he stepped into the street. Joe merely shrugged and handed Dr. Mouldered a purse of coins.

"*Vincit qui patitur,*" called Joe after him, but he was already out of earshot.

I looked at him.

"Who waits, wins."

I listened to Dr. Mouldered's confession, writing it all down as was my duty, but I was uneasy. I asked Joe again if he didn't think we should do something.

"People's lives might be in danger," I said. "Dr. Mouldered doesn't know what he is doing."

Joe was adamant. "He's not doing any harm. And there is no one else in the village who would do his job."

I protested some more and Joe had to remind me that we were in the business of keeping secrets.

"How long do you think we would last if we gave away this information? The business would be in ruins."

The business, I thought. *What business?* We certainly weren't making a profit. Surely the money had to run out eventually and what would happen then? But I had slipped into this way of life so easily and I couldn't bear the thought that it might change, so I kept my doubts to myself because, whether or not I understood what was going on, I was unwilling to do anything that might upset Joe.

CHAPTER TWENTY FOUR

Jeremiah Has a Plan

Jeremiah Ratchet was close to his wits' end. He had had just about enough of Joe Zabbidou's apparent disregard for his standing in the community. His business, his lifestyle, his pleasures were all in jeopardy because of that man. He could hardly bring himself to say Joe's name and even then he could only spit it, usually accompanied by a shower of brown, stringy saliva and crumbs. Jeremiah liked to mull things over at dinner.

Jeremiah rarely ate in his magnificent dining room and usually took his meals in the study with a dinner tray on his lap. It was a room of generous proportions, though badly lit, and shelved from floor to ceiling. Each shelf was packed tightly, bowing under the weight of an extensive array of books. Jeremiah was a collector. He loved to have things, sometimes for no other reason than that. He was not much of a reader, mind; he found the concentration required quite a strain on his head. As a rule he only kept books that he thought would impress others or increase in price. As a result the titles tended to be obscure and either full of facts that he didn't understand or plots that he couldn't fathom. Jeremiah was a fine example of the sort of person who knew the cost of everything but the value of nothing.

In his study Jeremiah bit into a mouthful of lamb and chewed thoughtfully on Joe Zabbidou. The man was a complete menace. Earlier that day Job Wright had come up to Jeremiah outside the baker's and presented him with a purse of money that covered over half his debt. Then, after lunch, Polly told Jeremiah about the pair of horseshoes she had seen in the pawnbroker's window, and Jeremiah knew that once again Joe Zabbidou had been at work.

"They're lovely and shiny," Polly had said innocently. "I should imagine Joe paid very good money for them." She left the room quickly and Jeremiah was certain he heard her sniggering all the way to the kitchen.

"I should have thrown him out that very first day," he said ruefully. "I left it too late." But even Jeremiah suspected that it would never have been that easy.

Jeremiah realized, of course, that his tenants' sudden ability to pay was directly linked to the display in the pawnbroker's window. He reckoned, however, that Joe could not possibly finance everyone's debt and that sooner or later he would be out of business and then everything would be back

to normal. But Joe did not operate within the usual constraints of commerce.

Jeremiah shook his head slowly. "How can a man thrive when he pays a small fortune for worthless junk?" he asked himself every day. And every day he waited for Polly to come back from the Reverend Stirling's so he could hear the latest report on the shop window. And every day it plunged him deeper into depression. How it had pained him to call upon Stirling for help when he had proved to be little better than useless.

"What shall I do?" moaned Jeremiah as he saw his income dwindling further, for once all the arrears were paid, he couldn't possibly survive on rent alone.

He still had money in the bank, inherited from his father, but it had been greatly depleted over the years by his frequent gambling. Jeremiah's high living had a price. He owed money to his tailor and his hat maker, to his wig maker and his boot maker, and he preferred not to think of the debts that were mounting at the card table.

There was blackmail, of course. Since he had unearthed Horatio's little secret there had been no shortage of fresh meat in his kitchen. And until recently he had been making good money from Obadiah and the grave robbing. Unfortunately, as far as grave robbing was concerned, things weren't looking too good at present, and not only Joe was to blame. Jeremiah's bodysnatchers (who also doubled up as bailiffs during the day when Jeremiah needed help with

an eviction) had brought him the bad news a couple of nights ago.

"The anatomists in the City don't want the old bodies no more," said one of the bodysnatchers. "They want fresh young ones."

Jeremiah groaned. "Don't they understand? There aren't any young corpses in Pagus Parvus."

"It doesn't have to be a problem," said the other man carefully.

"How do you mean?" asked Jeremiah.

The wily pair exchanged knowing glances, which was not easy through their black face masks, and burst into throaty laughter. "Well, let's just say there's a young lad up the hill, in the old hat shop, would make a nice specimen."

"Ludlow?" asked Jeremiah. "But he's alive and kicking."

"The fresher the better," said the first.

For a fleeting moment Jeremiah actually considered just what they were suggesting. Many times he had wished never to have to meet Ludlow's knowing gaze again, but as a solution to his problems, out-and-out murder was a little extreme even for Jeremiah.

"No, no," said Jeremiah hurriedly. "I'm sure that won't be necessary. There must be another way. What about teeth?"

"Teeth?"

"I heard you can sell them," began Jeremiah, but the two men just laughed. "Oh, never mind," he ended despondently.

The men shrugged in unison. "Then there's nothing else

we can do for you. Give us our money and we'll trouble you no more."

And that had been that.

Jeremiah set aside his plate, the meal only half eaten, and slouched back into his chair. He had no appetite. He was too depressed to look at his books, not even *The Loneliness of the High Mountain Shepherd*—his all-time favorite, on account of the fact that shepherds tended to have a limited vocabulary and to tell a simple story.

If Joe stayed in the village and continued as he had done up until now, Jeremiah knew that it could only mean more trouble for him. He was going to have to take matters into his own hands.

"Pagus Parvus is not big enough for the two of us," he declared to the shadows. "One of us will have to go."

Feeling very sorry for himself, he trudged upstairs and prepared for bed. He couldn't resist looking out of the window. By now it was an obsession. He could see the pawnbroker's shop at the top of the hill and the smoke that curled out of the chimney every night into the early hours.

"What is he doing up there?" he asked himself for the hundredth time.

Jeremiah was still no nearer to finding out why the pawnbroker received visitors well into the night, and he lacked the imagination to come up with an explanation on his own. He

had heard someone say that Joe was giving advice, but he could discover no more. He asked Polly many times if she knew what it was all about, but she just looked at him blankly.

If only I could find out, thought Jeremiah, *then perhaps I might be able to do something*. But whatever nighttime trade was going on at the pawnbroker's, no one would talk about it. So Jeremiah drew his own conclusions and decided that it was all part of Joe's plot against him. Having concluded thus, he was even more desperate to know the truth. One morning, therefore, when the oldest Sourdough dropped off the bread, Jeremiah was waiting for him outside the kitchen door and grabbed him by the scruff of the neck.

"I want you to do a little job for me," Ratchet muttered.

"Does it pay?" asked the boy.

Jeremiah laughed and the poor lad was treated to a panoramic view of the inside of his mouth. That mottled tongue, the fleshy uvula, those stained teeth, the meat and piecrust from the previous night still wedged firmly between them.

"I'll tell you what you'll get if you don't do it," he hissed. "I'll tell your father that I found you sneaking around my kitchen looking for something to steal. Something like this," and with a sleight of hand that would have surprised even Joe, Jeremiah somehow managed to take a silver candlestick out of the boy's pocket, upon which trick the poor chap burst into tears.

Jeremiah released his hold. "Just do what I say," he growled, "and you'll be no worse off. You must find out what's going on at the pawnbroker's."

The lad hesitated, but the threat of his father was enough. He really had no choice. It took him a week, standing hour after hour in the freezing cold at midnight around the back of the pawnbroker's shop. And every night it was the same. He heard the crunch of snow and the knock at the door. He watched as Joe handed his visitor a drink and sat him by the fire. In the corner he could see Ludlow writing furiously in a large black book. He could not hear what was being said, but he guessed quite quickly what was in the leather bags that Joe handed over at the end of the meeting. Eventually he decided he had learned as much as he was going to (he was also becoming increasingly afraid that Joe had seen him), and duly presented himself in Jeremiah's study.

"So?" asked Jeremiah eagerly. "What did you find out?"

"They talk to Joe and Ludlow writes down what they say in a big black book."

"And that's it?" It wasn't at all what Jeremiah expected.

The boy nodded. "Whatever they're telling him, it's worth money. Joe pays them, bags of it. Dr. Mouldered was there the other night. I couldn't quite hear what he was saying, but his face looked as if it might be important. And I know my own father has been up there."

So did Jeremiah. Elias Sourdough had paid him nearly all his back rent.

"And what of the frog?" asked Jeremiah in desperation. He couldn't see how any of this was going to help him.

"She's called Saluki. Joe treats her like she's something special. He won't let anyone touch her, but sometimes she

sits in his hand. I reckon she might be worth a few shillings. I've never seen anything like her."

Jeremiah was perplexed. As he lay in bed that night thinking over what he had been told, it gradually dawned on him that, in fact, the Sourdough boy had given him exactly what he needed to know.

"The book," he said out loud and sat bolt upright. "The book holds the answer."

Jeremiah's mind was racing. Whatever was in that book, Joe was prepared to pay handsomely for it. It made sense then that if Joe somehow lost the book, or perhaps it was taken from him, then he would also pay handsomely to retrieve it. Or, better than that, perhaps he would agree to leave Pagus Parvus *and* pay up in order to get the book back. With Joe gone, all Jeremiah's problems would be solved. Jeremiah's excitement mounted. What a fine revenge he could exact for all the trouble Joe had caused him. But there was one small flaw in the plan.

How do I get the book in the first place? he wondered. But just before sunrise he had the answer. The time had come for Jeremiah Ratchet to pay Joe Zabbidou a visit.

CHAPTER TWENTY-FIVE

The Cat's Away

Ludlow stirred. A log split on the fire beside him and a new flame burst from its heart. He welcomed the warmth. Joe had long since reclaimed his cloak.

"One day you will have a cloak such as this, Ludlow," he had said, "but it must be earned. Jocastar wool does not come cheap."

Joe had not left him lacking. In the place of the cloak he had given Ludlow a large cushion stuffed with straw and two rough but clean-smelling blankets. Every night Ludlow curled up on the cushion and covered himself right up to his ears with the blankets.

But sleep did not come easy, and when he did sleep his vivid dreams caused him to twitch and mutter. More often than not he woke in a sweat after some strange dream about one of the villagers. Jeremiah, smelling so badly that Ludlow would wrinkle his nose as he slept; Obadiah, always in a hole, always digging; Horatio mixing the ingredients for one of his vile pies. The confessions of the Pagus Parvians would haunt him until the dream would turn into a nightmare. The villagers would recede into a sort of fog and his father's face would suddenly appear above him. His hands would reach out of the mist and tighten around Ludlow's neck until everything went black. Then he would wake up violently and leave his bed to look out of the window down the street until he was driven back by the cold.

Every morning Joe would ask, "How did you sleep?" and every morning Ludlow gave the same reply, "Well, very well indeed." Joe would raise a skeptical eyebrow but he never said more.

One morning, after a particularly bad night, when Ludlow had been shaken awake five times by the hands throttling him, Joe announced he was to be away for a few days.

"You needn't open the shop if you prefer," he said. "The weather feels quite stormy. I doubt there'd be much customers."

Ludlow, although he wanted to appear willing, protested only feebly. He liked the thought of having the place to himself for a while.

"When will you be back?" he asked as Joe stepped out into the street.

"When my business is done."

Ludlow could sense there was little point pursuing the matter, and he watched as his employer limped off up the hill past the graveyard. Joe was right. The skies were ominously dark today and the cobbles were buried under a fresh

snowfall. There was little other life in the street, but it was only five o'clock in the morning. As soon as Joe was out of sight Ludlow closed the door and promptly jumped onto Joe's bed and went back to sleep.

When he woke some hours later he thought for a moment that he had slept right through the day and into the night. In fact, it was midafternoon, but it was uncommonly dark and cold. Outside a screaming wind buffeted the walls and windows; inside snow had fallen down the chimney and was gathering on the hearth. The fire had practically gone out and Ludlow knew that he must revive it. When he had finally brought it back to life and had a kettle hanging over the flame he went through to the shop and stood at the door. His view of the street was somewhat obscured, for the village was in the grip of a snowstorm the like of which he had never seen before. The three golden orbs were blowing wildly in the wind and snow was piling up in every corner and doorway. He could see no more than a few feet down the street.

What about Joe? he thought. He could only hope he had found shelter before the storm. Then a flash of red in the white flurries caught his eye. Someone was outside.

"Oh, Lord," muttered Ludlow. "It's Polly." He opened the door and it was snatched out of his hand by the wind. Huge flakes stung his face and he was half blinded by the driving snow.

"Polly!" he shouted. "Polly!"

Polly was almost close enough to touch but she couldn't hear him over the whine of the wind. Ludlow didn't stop to

think and he stepped out into the full force of the storm. He grabbed Polly by the arm and pulled her toward him. Her white face lit up under her hood and together the two of them leaned into the wind and collapsed inside the shop. The door slammed shut behind them.

"What were you doing out there?" cried Ludlow.

Polly answered in short breathless gasps. "I was—coming back—from Stirling Oliphaunt's." She was shivering violently, her nose bright red with the cold. "He doesn't care—about the weather—he still wants me to clean for him."

Ludlow shook his head in disbelief. "You could die out there. You're freezing. Come through and have some soup. The fire's lit. You can stay until the weather clears."

Polly hesitated. She had only been behind the counter once, the night when she confessed to various petty crimes, mainly relating to Jeremiah Ratchet and her pilfering of small knickknacks from his house. Although she felt that she deserved them, and she needed the money, equally she had felt the need to confess.

"Where is he?" she asked, looking around nervously. Polly couldn't help feeling a little scared of Joe Zabbidou, and she was always afraid of what she might say if he looked at her with his cool gray eyes.

Ludlow shook his head. "He's away. I'm in charge."

Polly relaxed a little and followed Ludlow through to the fire, where she stood close enough to be singed but not quite close enough to catch alight. "Mr. Ratchet would kill me if he knew I was in here with you." She laughed. "He don't mind

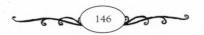

me spying for him, but he said not to fratter—fratter-something with the two of you."

"Fraternize?" asked Ludlow.

"That's the word."

"What do you mean, spying?" interrupted Ludlow. "So is that why you come?"

"Of course not," said Polly indignantly. "But it gives me a good excuse. Your Mr. Zabbidou has Mr. Ratchet tearing his hair out. Jeremiah wants so badly to know what goes on up here that he's told me to look in the window every day and tell him what I see."

"And what is that?" asked Ludlow stiffly.

"Junk," she replied.

"And?"

She saw the look on Ludlow's face and added quickly, "I don't tell him nothing else. Not even about the book."

"Maybe Jeremiah should come up one night," said Ludlow.

"Ooh, yes, I bet he has a secret or two." Polly moved a little away from the fire and looked directly at Ludlow. "Do you?"

Ludlow frowned. "Me? No. What do you mean?"

"Don't get your pants in a pickle," Polly teased. "I was only asking. I suppose you don't need to sell your secrets, with what Joe pays you."

"Hmm," said Ludlow, thinking of a way to change the subject.

"I told a lie or two when I was up here," said Polly suddenly.

"When Joe said he paid for secrets, I reckoned the worser the secret was, the more money he'd give me." Quickly she put her hand to her mouth and shook her head, annoyed with herself. "I don't know why I told you that. I don't want you to think badly of me." Then she laughed. "Stop looking at me like that, it makes my tongue loose!"

She looked around again, more slowly this time. "So, where is it then?"

"What?" Ludlow wished Polly would stop asking him so many questions.

"The book of secrets. The one you write in."

"It's hidden," he said quickly, but his eyes flicked to Joe's bed before he could help himself. Polly saw and in an instant dived for it. Ludlow lurched toward her but he was too slow. Polly stuck her hand under the mattress and grabbed the Black Book. She pulled it out, jumped onto the bed, and held it out of Ludlow's reach.

"Let's have a look then," she said mischievously, waving it above her head. "There must be some interesting tales in here."

"No," said Ludlow desperately, "it's forbidden. Joe says so."

Polly laughed. "Joe's not here, in case you hadn't noticed. What harm would it do?"

"No," said Ludlow, but with less conviction. After all, it wasn't as if Polly was suggesting something he hadn't already thought of.

"I promised Joe," he said weakly.

"Joe wouldn't know," said Polly slowly. "And you must have heard most of these secrets already."

"Only the ones from Pagus Parvus."

"Then let's look at the others, from before Pagus Parvus, in a place where we don't know anyone. How could that be wrong?"

Ludlow could see how it made sense, probably because he wanted it to. He sat on the bed feeling a crippling twinge of guilt, but ignored it. This was the first time he had been left alone with the Black Book of Secrets, and already he was about to betray Joe. But if he was honest with himself, he wanted to read the stories as much as Polly did.

"I suppose we could look at the beginning."

Polly nodded eagerly. "The very first story, the oldest."

"All right," said Ludlow firmly. "But no more."

"Of course," said Polly. "Here you are then," she said, handing Ludlow the book.

"I thought *you* wanted to do it," said Ludlow, putting his hands behind his back as if by not actually touching the book he wouldn't be part of the betrayal.

"But I can't read, stupid," said Polly matter-of-factly. "We don't all have your fine education."

Ludlow sighed, and unable to hold off any longer, he took the heavy book from Polly's hands. Feeling slightly sick, he slowly opened the cover, smoothed down the very first page, and began.

CHAPTER TWENTY SIX

EXTRACT FROM
THE BLACK BOOK OF SECRETS

The Coffin Maker's Confession

My name is Septimus Stern and I have an odious secret. It has followed me for nearly twenty years. Wherever I go I know it is there, like a shadow, waiting to pounce on me when I least expect it, to torture me for another night, to make me hate myself even more than I do already.

I am a prisoner of my own mind and you, Mr. Zabbidou, are my last hope of release.

I am a coffin maker by trade, and a fine one at that. Over the years my reputation spread far and wide across the country and I was never short of work. It might seem strange to you that I make my living from the misery of others, but I am not a sentimental man, Mr. Zabbidou. I believe I provide a service to those in need, regardless of the circumstances, and I earn my reward.

Very early one morning, in late autumn, a stranger came

into my workshop. He claimed to be a physician and insisted that I call him Dr. Sturgeon.

"A patient of mine has just died," he said mournfully, "and I need a coffin."

He seemed a little nervous, but that was not unusual. I said that was the business I was in and I was sure I could help him out.

"I have been assured you are a fine coffin maker," he continued. "I want you to do something special for me."

Again, I thought nothing of this request. I presumed he meant that I should line the box in a luxurious material, silk perhaps, or maybe use a more expensive wood. Sometimes I was asked to fit gold or silver handles and plates. All this I had done before and I told him so, but he shook his head.

"No, that is not what I want. You see, you may recall the case recently where a young man was buried while still alive. I hasten to say it was not I who pronounced him dead. You can imagine the distress this caused the family when they subsequently discovered that he had attempted to break free from the coffin and was unable."

I said to Dr. Sturgeon that indeed I did recall the case in question, for I had provided the coffin. The dead man had been placed in the family tomb and a month later, following the death of another family member, they opened the tomb to find the coffin on its side on the floor. They opened the lid, but of course it was too late then. Their son was quite decayed, though it was still clear to see that his hands were

no longer by his sides and, by all accounts, his mouth was open in an expression of excruciating despair.

"I wish to ensure the same tragedy cannot happen again."

I thought this a sensible notion and listened as he outlined his idea for a coffin with a mechanism that allowed air to circulate around it in case the deceased should ever wake up. We agreed on a price, and as speed was of the essence, I started work straight away. It was not a complicated design, requiring little more than a pipe connected to the coffin that should reach the surface to allow air in (the doctor insisted this should be concealed—"It might upset the vicar," he explained), and I completed it late that night. I delivered it myself the next day to the address given, a grand country manor, some hours' horse ride away. The doctor himself opened the door.

"Welcome," he said. "The master is a little indisposed at present. He has asked that I deal with this business."

He beckoned me in and we passed an open door and when I glanced within I saw a man, whom I presumed to be the master, sitting very still in a chair by the window. He was pale and old and looked quite ill. The doctor inspected the coffin thoroughly and asked many questions as to its reliability. Finally, when he was reassured that it would operate efficiently, we carried it down into the cellar.

"It is the master's wife who has died," he said. "She lies in the cellar where it is cool."

"How did she meet her end?" I asked as we struggled with the awkward burden.

"An ague," he said and was no more forthcoming than that.

Finally we reached the bottom. The temperature was considerably lower than upstairs and I saw the lady lying stretched out on a table. She looked pale but peaceful, and contrary to my expectations, there were no signs of sickness. I don't know what it was about the whole affair, but suddenly my suspicions were aroused. She looked so tranquil it was difficult to believe that she was dead, but certainly there were no signs of life. There was a strange smell in the room which at the time I attributed to the dampness.

"Tragic," I murmured.

"It is indeed," replied the doctor, and despite the coolness I saw that he was sweating. He stroked the dead lady's hand with unequaled tenderness and it disturbed me to see how he looked upon her. After all, she was not his wife.

"So young and beautiful," he said. "The vicar is coming over this afternoon and she shall be buried in the family plot."

Once we had deposited the coffin the doctor seemed anxious to show me to the door. "I think perhaps you should delay no longer," he urged. "The weather is turning and the day is wearing on. I should not like to think of you on that road at night. It is notorious for highwaymen."

I inferred from his tone that I had outstayed my welcome, and so I took off there and then. I did not feel that the weather was any worse than that morning, in fact it seemed better, but I was pleased to be gone from the place. I had been well rewarded for my work, but it left me with a nag-

ging doubt that something was not right. For days afterward
I could not rid my nostrils of the smell in the cellar.

Some months later by chance I happened to travel to that
same region again. An impulse made me take the fork in the
road that led to the manor, and I stopped at the gates. They
were locked, but through the bars I could see that the house
was closed up and the gardens were overgrown. There was a
notice on the pillar that the property was up for sale and to
contact the agents Messrs. Cruickshank and Butterworth in
the next town. As that was my intended destination, I paid a
visit to their offices to inquire as to the whereabouts of the
owner. I spoke to Mr. Cruickshank, a most affable gentleman, who answered my many inquiries comprehensively.

"Strange affair," he said. "First the wife dies and then the
master. Only the son left. He inherited the lot. He's gone
abroad and left instructions for us to dispose of the property on his behalf. Should make him a small fortune."

"Son?" I queried.

"Aye, a doctor."

"How did the old man die?" I asked.

"Now that's an even queerer tale. The night after the wife
was buried the doctor heard screaming from his father's
room. He ran in and found his father half dead in his bed,
purple in the face, hardly able to move apparently, barely
able to speak. He told the doctor that he had woken to see
his dead wife kneeling over him with her hands around his
throat, strangling him. He died soon after. The shock killed
him—he had a feeble constitution and his heart couldn't

take it. I feel sorry for the son. The poor chap lost a father and a stepmother in one go."

"You mean the dead woman wasn't his mother?"

Mr. Cruickshank shook his head. "His real mother died when he was but a lad and his father married again. She was the prettiest lady I ever did see, though nearly forty years his junior. Don't know what she saw in him myself."

I thanked Mr. Cruickshank for his time and went on my way, but I was even more unsettled than before. My curiosity had been satisfied but my suspicions had not been allayed. As had been my intention all along, I paid a visit to the apothecary to purchase a cough remedy. When I entered the shop I was halted in my tracks by a potent and unmistakable smell. The very same smell I had noticed in the cellar at the manor. When he heard the bell the apothecary came out to see me.

"What is that smell?" I asked without delay.

"Ah," he said conspiratorially, "it is my very own special sleep remedy. Highly effective, very powerful. It sends a person into a deep sleep and once asleep they look quite lifeless and cannot feel pain. I believe the surgeons in the hospitals might find it useful in operations."

"Tell me," I said with a quickening heart, "do you know a Dr. Sturgeon?"

"One of my best customers," he said proudly. "He swore the remedy was the best and only cure for his insomnia."

I took my cough linctus and started for home with a heavy heart. Now I knew the truth of the deception into which I

had been unwittingly dragged. What a convoluted plot. Only the most devilish of minds could have dreamed it up. After all, how can you try a ghost for murder?

You see, Mr. Zabbidou, I believe the young doctor administered the apothecary's potion to his father's wife and tricked his father into believing she had died. Then, with the aid of my coffin, he buried her. While underground she could still breathe, so when the potion wore off and he unearthed her later that night, she was sufficiently alive to appear at her husband's bedside and to half strangle him, knowing that his heart was feeble. So not only did the doctor inherit his estate but also his young wife. Doubtless now the two of them are enjoying the fruits of their wickedness in a far-off country.

I cannot forgive myself for the part I played. You're the only person in the world who knows this, Mr. Zabbidou. I hate to think that anyone else should ever find out what I did. They say you are a man of your word and I believe them. Now I think I can sleep. ✳

CHAPTER TWENTY-SEVEN

FRAGMENT FROM
THE MEMOIRS OF LUDLOW FITCH

After I finished reading the coffin maker's secret we both looked at
each other guiltily.

"Poor beggar," said Polly quietly. "It wasn't even his fault."

"There's a little bit more," I said. "Right at the bottom of
the page."

"What does it say?"

"*Quae nocent docent.*"

Polly looked blank.

"I think it must be Latin."

"Latin?"

"It's another language. Joe uses it sometimes. He says you
can say more with fewer words. He likes that."

"Well, you'd better not ask him what it means," said Polly
quickly, "or he'll know you've been snooping."

I said nothing. I couldn't help feeling Joe would know anyway. I closed the book and put it away.

"I don't want to hear anymore," said Polly and I was glad.

So we sat and waited for the storm to ease. Just the two of us, in front of the fire drinking soup and wrapped in blankets to keep warm. I think we both knew we were wrong to read the book, but Polly tried to shrug it off with a laugh.

"He'll never know," she said, trying to convince herself. "Don't fret so much."

By early evening the wind had died down and the snow had eased. Polly stood up and stretched. "I'll be off," she said. "Mr. Ratchet'll be looking for his supper." Before she went she looked at me nervously.

"You won't tell him, will you, Ludlow?"

I shook my head. "If he finds out, I'll say it was just me."

She grinned. "He'll forgive you. Just stare at him with your big green eyes."

Somehow I didn't think that trick would work on Joe.

Four days later, although the worst of the storm was over, it was still dark and wintry and very cold. I kept the shop locked up. The hours passed slowly. I fed Saluki and swept the floor and dusted the display. I had plenty of time to think about what Polly and I had done, and by the fourth day I had managed to convince myself that I need not have worried. After all, no one had come to any harm. We didn't do it out of malice, just curiosity. At the back of my mind was the nagging doubt that Joe had set a trap for me, and although it hurt me to think that he didn't trust me, it was

worse to know that he was right. But did that make it fair? Was there any person out there strong enough to resist looking?

The night before his return I was nearly asleep by the fire when I thought I heard a noise outside. By the time I opened the door onto the street there was no one there, only footprints under the window, large footprints. I knew who had made them, not from their size but from the smell that lingered in the air. A Jeremiah Ratchet smell.

On the fifth morning Saluki set up a tremendous croaking and a few seconds later someone began rattling at the door. "Ludlow," called a voice, "let me in."

It was Joe. I was very pleased to have him back and I only hoped that I could hide my guilty feelings. He came in, looked the place over, and clapped me on the back.

"Good to see you kept the shop in order in my absence," he said. I had made sure that everything was in its place.

"There was a terrible storm," I said before I could stop myself. "Polly came by and sat with me for a while." I hadn't meant to tell him that, but when Joe looked at me in a certain way I just had to say what was on my mind. I stared at the floor. I didn't want to reveal any more of my thoughts.

"I know," he replied.

"You know?" Had he read my mind?

"I've just seen her in the street, going to the butcher's. She told me all about it."

My heart shuddered. I hoped that was all Polly had said.

"Anyone come knocking?" Joe asked.

I shook my head. "I think Ratchet was sniffing around, though."

"Shouldn't surprise me. He's an inquisitive fellow. He's certainly not the first to spy at the window."

Joe didn't just mean me. I remembered when Dr. Mouldered came up, Joe told me afterward he was certain someone had been outside. But right now I was interested in Ratchet. "Why don't you do something about him" I urged. "Is it really so unreasonable of the villagers to ask?"

Joe sighed. "You must be patient, Ludlow."

"Why? What are we waiting for? Do you know what's ahead?"

This seemed to amuse him. "Have you seen my crystal ball?" he asked. "If you have, I should very much like to know where it is." He was half laughing, but then he became serious again.

"I am no seer, Ludlow, believe me. If I was, do you think I would be doing this?" He gestured around the room.

I wasn't going to let him off the hook this time. "What exactly are you doing, Joe? Who are you? Why did you come here?"

He leaned back on the counter and stretched his long legs out in front of him. "I am just an old man, Ludlow, trying to help those in need."

"But the book, the money. You give all the time. What do you get back?"

"It doesn't have to be about taking. Don't you think it's enough to give? Why should I expect anything in return?"

I was beginning to understand, but it was not easy. I suppose I was still a thief at heart. My whole life in the City had been about taking for myself and taking care of myself.

"You've seen their faces," Joe continued. "You know how they feel when they come at midnight and how they feel when they leave. Why should I want more than that?"

"But they want more," I said.

"And that, Ludlow, is precisely my problem." He turned on his heel and went into the back room. I followed him. He pulled the Black Book out from under the mattress and stood by his bed looking around.

"I've been thinking," he said, "perhaps we should put the book somewhere else."

I couldn't imagine where. The room was hardly big enough for a choice of hiding places.

"Aha," he exclaimed after a few moments. "I have just the place. You can look after it." He swooped down and slid it under my cushion.

I was quite taken aback and struggled not to show it. "Do you think it will be safe?"

"In your hands?" said Joe with a wink. "I'm sure of it. And now, speaking of books, there is a volume I wish to have. Come with me."

And so we went to see Perigoe Leafbinder.

CHAPTER TWENTY EIGHT

Perigoe Leafbinder

Perigoe Leafbinder had been in the book business for over thirty years, as she liked to remind anyone who came into her shop, and if a book had been printed, she knew about it. Perigoe made a reasonable living but not necessarily from the locals (despite there being little else to do in the dark evenings but read, few had acquired the skill). She operated a very efficient delivery service, by means of a horse and trap, to the north side of the City, where lived the rich and idle, who bought books purely to demonstrate their style and intellectual superiority. Perigoe had learned early that it was not difficult to make money out of other people's vanity.

She was a small woman, almost a dwarf, with a pinched face and a rather crooked smile. In recent months her left eye had developed an irritating twitch, which increased when she was nervous, a state she was in most of the time, with the result that she was constantly winking. Her flared nostrils supported a pair of round spectacles, almost as if they had been designed for the purpose. They made the arms of her spectacles redundant, for they never fell off even when she bent over. Since her husband's death some three years previously Perigoe had taken to wearing black almost exclusively and, given her size and apparel, was often difficult to see in the dim light. She took great pleasure in emerging from dark corners and tapping browsers on the back, making them jump.

Joe entered the shop, leaving Ludlow outside, and stood for some minutes in the silence surveying his surroundings. He had to stoop somewhat and when he took off his hat his wild hair brushed the oak beams that traversed the ceiling. The walls were shelved and freestanding bookcases stood close together in parallel lines across the floor. Joe walked between them, running his long fingers across the dark spines of the books. There seemed no particular order to the place: Novels sat beside scientific works, art beside mathematics, antiquarian volumes beside new.

Perigoe appeared as if from nowhere and poked him with a wizened forefinger.

"Mr. Zabbidou, I believe." Her voice was almost inaudible. Perigoe always spoke as if she thought someone was eavesdropping.

"Indeed I am," replied Joe. "A pleasure to meet you, Mrs. Leafbinder." He took her bloodless hand in his and kissed it with great ceremony.

Perigoe allowed her hand to linger, remembering for an instant a time when she might have blushed at such a gesture.

"How may I help you?" she asked and winked three times.

"I seek a book," said Joe, "about animals, amphibians in particular, by S. E. Salter. I was hoping that you might possess such a volume."

"Well, I believe I do," said Perigoe and glided across the floor, almost as if she were not in possession of feet, to find it. She returned quickly and handed a book to Joe, a slim volume with a hard cover and color plates. He held it firmly between thumb and forefinger and looked her deep in the eyes. Perigoe found it difficult to avert her gaze.

"I thought you might wish to share a drink with me," he suggested. "Tonight, perhaps?"

Perigoe nodded slowly and her eyelid flapped like a sheet in the wind. She wanted to look away but for some reason she was unable. Soft music filled her head, like early-morning birdsong, and her bony fingertips were beginning to prickle as if she had been stung by nettles.

"At midnight?"

Perigoe nodded again.

"Until then," said Joe, breaking the spell, and he went to the door. He held up the book.

"How much do I owe you?"

Perigoe's heart was fluttering like a trapped moth and she had to steady herself on a shelf. "There's no charge," she whispered.

Joe reached for the doorknob as a dark shadow on the other side filled the frame. He could hear the sound of heavy breathing and moments later Jeremiah Ratchet burst

in like an overfermented bottle of ale popping its cork. When he saw Joe he snorted scornfully. Joe merely stepped back to allow him entrance, tipped his hat in greeting, and slipped out without a backward glance.

As they made their way back to the shop Ludlow wondered what business Jeremiah had with Perigoe. Surely he was not a man of letters. Ludlow tried to read the title of the book Joe now held, something about amphibians, but it was obscured by the folds of his cloak.

To the outsider, compared with most others in the village Perigoe Leafbinder had a good life. She ran a successful business and did not want for money. She had enjoyed her married life, and now she was equally satisfied with widowhood. But still she stood under the three golden orbs at midnight. Like so many of her fellow Pagus Parvians, she harbored a ruinous secret that would not leave her be. She raised her arm in the light of the expectant three-quarter moon.

Joe opened the door before she could knock.

"Mrs. Leafbinder," he said, "I've been expecting you."

Perigoe glided in silently and Joe led her to the back room.

"So what is it you do up here late at night?" she asked and her eyelid twitched rapidly.

"I buy secrets."

Perigoe adjusted her spectacles nervously as she considered what he had just said. Finally she said, "I have a secret I'd like to sell. Will you take it?"

"But of course," replied Joe and handed her a glass. "I am sure that any secret of yours would be of the highest quality and worth a good sum of money."

Perigoe blushed and winked twice, took a small sip of the syrupy liquid, and began.

CHAPTER TWENTY-NINE

Extract from
THE BLACK BOOK OF SECRETS

The Bookseller's Confession

My name is Perigoe Leafbinder and I have a wretched admission.

The Leafbinders have been in the business of books for nearly two centuries, and I am proud to carry on the tradition. I have spent thirty years of my life in this shop and God willing I should like to spend another thirty, but if I cannot free my tortured mind I doubt I'll see out another year.

There is in existence a book of which three copies are considered immensely valuable. The story itself is not of any great interest or literary worth, merely the simple tale of a mountain shepherd. What makes the book sought after is the fact that the thirteenth line on the thirteenth page is printed backward. No one knows how this happened; some believe the printer was in league with Beelzebub and the words were turned during one of his devilish ceremonies.

Others say the letters were reversed by a flash of lightning from heaven, a sign of approval from the greatest shepherd of them all, the Lord himself. Or maybe it was the printer's young apprentice—he liked a drink and enjoyed a joke. Whatever the reason, out of the two hundred printed copies of the book this mistake occurs only in three.

The whereabouts of two of the three misprinted books is known: One is in a museum in a foreign city, the other is with the family of the shepherd who wrote the tale. They live with their sheep on the mountains and are rarely seen. They have kept it for generations and refuse to sell it at any price. They say that money is of no value to them. The third book had been missing for almost two hundred years. It was thought to no longer exist.

To possess this volume would bring instant fame and wealth and I, like many others, have dreamed for years of finding it, but in vain.

Some months ago I was in my shop when I heard the bell and I saw a frail old woman making her way slowly between the bookcases. She walked stiffly with the aid of two walking sticks. Her left elbow was held tightly against her side, making her slow progress even more painful, and I could see at once that she concealed something beneath her cloak.

I stepped out into her path and greeted her and I led her into the office, where she leaned her sticks against the desk. It was nearly six and I was looking forward to closing up and retiring for the day. In an effort to hurry things along I inquired rather brusquely, "Madam, how may I help you?"

She eyed me with suspicion, and asked, "Do you buy books?"

I nodded.

"What would you say this is worth?"

She took a tatty volume in maroon leather from beneath her cloak and proffered it across the table. She seemed unwilling to let it out of her grasp and I had to tug with some strength to relieve her of it. She kept her little black eyes on me all the time.

I examined the novel, rather carelessly at first, for I felt it could not be of much value. The leather cover was stained and worn, the title was illegible, and it looked as if it had been quite badly treated.

But when I opened it I was quite unprepared for what I saw. There on the title page were the words:

"*The Loneliness of the High Mountain Shepherd* by Arthur Wolman."

My heart lurched in my chest. Could this be the missing third copy? The old lady's eyes were boring into me all the time as I carried out my examination. Casually I turned the pages. They were brown with age and mold and some were stuck together. I reached page thirteen and I was close to apoplexy when I read it. The thirteenth line was reversed.

.yadnuS a no peehs ym raehs ot deḳil I

"Hmm," I mused as if of two minds about something. And indeed I was. Imagine, in my hands I held a book that

could bring me acclaim and riches, but only then did I realize I could not afford to buy it. In my dreams I had never
considered how I would pay for it; I had only ever thought
that somehow the book would be mine.

I reasoned that I had two choices. I could pretend the
book was worthless and offer the old lady a token amount of
money, or I could tell her the truth and then she would go
away and sell it to someone who could pay.

The question was: Did she know the value of the book? I
could feel droplets of sweat on my forehead and it took all
my concentration to stop my hands from shaking. Her eyes
were like needles in my skin.

"Well?" she said rather testily.

My answer sealed my miserable fate.

"It is an interesting volume," I said slowly, "but it is not
particularly valuable." Those words set me on a path from
which there was no return.

She looked disappointed and for one brief instance I allowed myself to hope. Could it be possible she was ignorant
of its true worth?

"But," I said, trying to reassure her, "it just so happens
that I have a customer who has an interest in this author, so
I should be glad to give you ten shillings for it. I am sure you
agree that is a generous offer, considering its rather poor
condition."

I smiled, charitably, I thought. The old lady smiled back,
in a mean-mouthed, tight-lipped sort of way.

Then she opened those thin lips and hissed, "You filthy

liar. You low-down cheat. Do you think I am a fool? That because I walk with sticks I have feathers in my head?"

I had been found out. I stood up and tried to placate her growing fury.

"Perhaps I made a mistake. Let me look again." But it was too late. I was beyond redemption.

"This book is worth many times what you have just offered me and yet you choose to insult me. You are nothing but a crook. Give it back to me."

She reached across the table and snatched at the book and all I could think was that my dream was being taken with it.

"I will take this elsewhere," she said, still tugging. "To someone with integrity."

"I'm sorry," I cried, close to tears. "A moment's weakness. After all, I am only human. I can be tempted." I was still holding on to the book. I couldn't bear to let it go.

"Pshaw," she spat. "I have heard enough."

We struggled across the desktop. First she would hold sway, then I, until finally I gave one mighty wrench and the book came free. The old lady fell backward and I watched in horror as her head cracked on the arm of the chair and she crashed to the floor in a crumpled pile of skin and bone. I ran to her and dropped to my knees at her side, leaning close to see if she was still breathing.

She hissed in my ear, *"yadnuS a no peehs ym raehs ot dekil I,"* and then expired, her final breath fogging my spectacles.

"Oh, Lord above," I muttered. "Now what do I do?" It was

not usual for a customer to die in the shop and I was unsure of the correct procedure. And while I dithered the voice of the Devil, surely it could only be he, piped up in my ear.

"Take the book," he whispered. "Take the book. Who will know?"

I should like to say that I argued, that I engaged in a debate about the immoral nature of his suggestion, but that would be untrue. Instead I picked it up from where I had dropped it and stuffed it behind Gibbon's *Decline and Fall* on a high shelf above the desk. When I turned around I was startled to see Jeremiah Ratchet standing in the open doorway. I had no idea how long he had been there.

"My dear Perigoe," he asked, "what on this miserable earth are you doing?"

"She has died in my shop," I wailed. "She just collapsed."

"So I see," he said.

Dr. Mouldered arrived and Ratchet stood to one side eyeing the scene. His presence made me feel distinctly uncomfortable.

"Heart attack," pronounced Mouldered after the briefest of examinations. Ratchet gave one of his loud snorts and Mouldered closed his bag and hurried away. To my intense relief the undertakers arrived not long after, the body was removed, and Jeremiah left.

That night after dark I came up with a plan. I wanted to sell the book but I had to be careful. I couldn't be sure who else knew the old lady owned it. I had heard of someone in the City who would pay me a good price for such a book and

who could be trusted not to reveal my identity. Of course, there would be no celebrity, no fame, but it was a small sacrifice. If I went now, I could be back before dawn and no one would be the wiser. I hid the book in my cloak and stepped outside straight into Jeremiah Ratchet.

"My dear Perigoe," he said in that loathsome way of his, "I wonder what business has you leaving Pagus Parvus at this time of night."

"My own business," I replied sharply. "Now step away and allow me to pass."

He stayed where he was. "I have been thinking over the events of this evening: the death of that poor unfortunate woman, the book . . ."

"The book?"

"There is a price for keeping secrets," he said.

His tone frightened me. "What you are suggesting, Mr. Ratchet?"

"I think that you are on your way to the City to dispose of the book, the very one you stole from the old lady this afternoon, for a rather large sum of money that you will keep all to yourself."

"There is no book, Mr. Ratchet."

"Well," said Jeremiah, "then we have a problem. You see, if you do not find the book, which I know is here, then I will be forced to tell the magistrate that I witnessed that woman's death at your hands. The penalty is hanging, you know, for murder."

"Murder?"

"I saw everything," said Jeremiah. "I watched you attack that old lady and then push her to the ground, only to wrest the book from her dying hand."

"That is not how it happened," I protested, but Jeremiah merely laughed.

"Consider what I have said carefully, Mrs. Leafbinder. I am sure you will come 'round to my way of thinking."

I am ashamed to say that I cursed the duplicitous scoundrel for a full minute, but I knew when I was beaten.

"Tell me what you want, Mr. Ratchet," I said finally.

"It's quite simple, my dear. I wish to have the pick of your shelves whenever I choose and a small payment, shall we say five shillings, on a weekly basis."

"And what of the book?"

He pretended to give the matter some consideration. "Well, I could take it to the City, of course, but I think I shall wait. Perhaps after a few years I will sell it for its full value. Meanwhile, if you would be so kind as to hand it over, I shall keep it safe."

What a heartless, sadistic man stood in front of me. I had no choice but to take his terms. I knew Ratchet would not hesitate to go straight to the magistrate, who I did not doubt could be persuaded with money to believe anything Ratchet wanted, and I would be hanged for murder.

"I'll be back on Friday for my fee," he said and went off with the precious book under his arm.

Needless to state, he has been as good as his word. Every Friday he collects his money and takes whatever else he

pleases. As for *The Loneliness of the High Mountain Shepherd*, I lie in bed every night and curse my greed and stupidity a thousand times. Meanwhile Jeremiah is bringing my business to its knees.

I cannot change what I have done, Mr. Zabbidou, and I am sorry for it. All I want is to sleep again, to forget. ✳

Ludlow put down his quill, laid a sheet of blotting paper between the pages, and closed the book.

Joe took Perigoe's cold hand.

"You will sleep," he said, "now your secret is safe."

"But what of Ratchet?" asked Perigoe, a tremor in her voice. "He still has the book."

"Be patient, Perigoe. He will pay for what he has done. That is all I can say. Now, take this"—he handed her a bag of coins—"and go home to get some rest."

Joe watched as Perigoe walked back to the bookshop. He saw her go in and waited for the lights to go out. Then he went to bed, smiling. Joe Zabbidou had no trouble sleeping.

CHAPTER THIRTY

FRAGMENT FROM
THE MEMOIRS OF LUDLOW FITCH

Perigoe's secret was the last one I wrote in the Black Book. The morning after her visit Joe sent me out for some bread. I greeted the bakers as usual, but their response was icy. Elias served me in silence and his eyes were shooting daggers. The oldest boy, who was behind the counter, couldn't even look at me. I bade them goodbye and left, wondering what I had done to offend them. As I stepped out of the door I saw the other two Sourdough brothers across the street. Usually they liked to walk with me, but today they ran away and watched from farther down the hill. One of them threw a snowball. It hit the side of my head and stung sharply. When I put my hand to the wound it came away bloody and I saw a small stone lying at my feet.

Suddenly the window above me opened and the next second a pail of freezing, dirty water drenched me from head to foot. "That's right," came a jeering voice. "Get back up the

hill to your devil friend. We don't want you around here." It was Ruby.

I broke into a run and raced back up to the shop, bursting through the door. I slammed it behind me and threw across the bolt.

"What happened?" asked Joe, noticing the blood on my face.

"I'm not sure," I said, "but Elias wouldn't talk to me and Ruby threw a pail of water on my head."

Joe looked puzzled. "For what reason?"

"I don't know," I spluttered. "All I wanted was a loaf of bread."

I peeled off my cloak and hung it in front of the fire. Joe was sitting, leaning forward with his hands clasped under his chin. I shook my dripping head and drops of water turned to steam on the burning logs.

"Did you know this was going to happen?" I asked. "Is it because of Jeremiah?"

"I don't know about Jeremiah," said Joe slowly, "but I must say I expected something like this."

"Why?"

"Because there is a fine line between gratitude and resentment. Everyone is happy to accept my money—they smile and say thank you, and go away and forget how badly off they were before I arrived. Then they come back looking for more."

I was surprised at the bitterness in his voice. This wasn't the Joe I knew, who harbored no resentment, no ill-feeling,

who took it all in his stride. It unsettled me to see this side to him.

"You sound as if this has happened before," I said.

"It has, but usually I know why."

"Well, whatever the reason, I think it's unfair," I began, but at the same time Saluki suddenly started to croak loudly in the shop and the peace and quiet of the morning was violently interrupted by the sound of a riotous altercation in the street.

Joe leaped up and ran to the door. I followed him, and together we hurried down the hill. The sight that greeted us, were it not for the seriousness of it, would have been quite ridiculous and more suited to the theater. Jeremiah Ratchet and Horatio Cleaver were arguing, actually grappling with each other, in the middle of the road. And the cause of their disagreement? A turkey.

Joe's eyes sparkled. "It has begun," he said.

As we approached the fray it became apparent what was going on.

"You'll not take any more of my meat, you thieving windbag!" shouted Horatio, and the onlookers cheered. It seemed that the whole village had come out to watch: the Sourdoughs, Perigoe, Obadiah, Benjamin Tup, Job Wright, Lily Weaver, Dr. Mouldered, Polly, and even a few faces that were unfamiliar to me.

Ratchet said nothing, just planted his feet more firmly on the ground and pulled with all his might. He held the turkey's legs, Horatio had its head, and the poor dead creature was

near torn in two. Jeremiah was purple with the effort and Horatio's cheeks were a similar shade.

The men were well matched: both stout and solid on the ground. Horatio was slightly taller, but whether this was an advantage or not on the icy road was debatable. The air was filled with cursing and swearing, spit and clouds of breath.

"It's my turkey!" shouted Jeremiah. "You owe me, Horatio."

With one huge tug he managed to unbalance the butcher, who let go of the bird rather than fall over. Jeremiah, of course, fell instead, and to have the turkey was no consolation for his loss of dignity as he spun on the ice three times before coming to a stop at Joe's feet.

The crowd cheered and laughed and clapped as Jeremiah struggled to stand. Only Joe held out his hand to help, but Jeremiah ignored it and took off home, still holding the limp bird.

"Good riddance," shouted Elias Sourdough.

Jeremiah didn't look back. I was surprised. He was not the sort of man to let someone else have the last word.

Horatio came up to Joe in a state of great excitement about what he had just done. I had never thought to see this quiet man so elated.

"Did you see that, Joe?" He was breathing heavily and he was shaking. "I stood up to him. I told him he could take no more of my meat. Just like you said."

He seemed to have forgotten that Jeremiah had the turkey.

He waited for Joe to answer, to pat him on the back, to

congratulate him, but Joe said nothing. His face turned from gray to white and, for an instant only, anger flared in his eyes.

"I didn't say that," he muttered. "I didn't say that at all."

Job Wright, the blacksmith, stepped forward and his mouth was curled in a snarl.

"So," he said, and his voice was brimming with sarcasm, "you've finally come to help us."

"Ratchet's time will come," said Joe simply. "All you have to do is wait. For now, can't you all be happy that your fortunes have changed?"

"But how long must we wait?" asked Obadiah. "You told me Jeremiah would feel the force of your justice."

Horatio looked toward the crowd. "And he told me he'd give him what was coming to him."

Then it was Perigoe's turn. "I've been to him, too," she said as loudly as she could, "and he said he'd make Jeremiah pay."

"That's what he told me," came another voice.

"And me," said someone else. "But I thought I was the only one!"

"What are you talking about?" asked another and his neighbor (who had recently sold his own secret) immediately turned to him and began to tell him all about Joe's midnight confessional and the Black Book.

Suddenly everyone was talking at once as they realized exactly how many of their fellow villagers had secretly visited Joe Zabbidou at the stroke of twelve. Those who had been personally invited to the back room now felt cheated that it wasn't an exclusive service—Joe really did know how

to make people feel special—and those who hadn't been invited felt cheated that they had not been considered worthy of the service. Whatever the individual's circumstances, the disgruntled crowd, who only moments ago were laughing at Jeremiah, turned united to Joe Zabbidou and fixed him with an icy glare. I looked at them all, their faces glowing in the cold, their narrow eyes focused on Joe. My palms were damp with cold sweat. These were no longer friendly faces and I was frightened.

Job Wright stood with his legs apart and his powerful arms crossed against his chest. In the absence of any other volunteer, he appeared to have taken on the role of village spokesman.

"So, Mr. Zabbidou, what have you to say to that?"

The chattering stopped instantly. Seconds passed and the silence strained at its seams and threatened to explode. I could see the muscles in Joe's jaw clenching and unclenching and he spoke through gritted teeth.

"I said none of those things. You have twisted my words, words I offered to comfort you."

"Then what exactly did you say?" challenged the blacksmith.

"I said to be patient." Joe looked around the scornful faces before settling on Perigoe and Horatio and Obadiah, who stood together in a nervous huddle. "Is that not the truth?"

At first no one answered.

Then Horatio nodded, shamefaced. "I think maybe you did say that," he said quietly.

Perigoe and Obadiah reddened and nodded, too, but Job wasn't so easily appeased.

"What is this nonsense?" he snorted loudly, slamming his fist into his open palm. "First you promise to help and now, when we ask for that help, you hide behind words. You are no better than Jeremiah Ratchet himself. In fact, you are worse. He at least does what he says."

He turned around and addressed the mesmerized onlookers. Job had them hanging on his every word in a way Stirling Oliphaunt would never have been able. I could hardly believe how he had changed. He, too, had been in at midnight, like the rest of them, and taken the money and peace of mind gladly, but now he seemed intent on leading the village against us.

"Jeremiah Ratchet must be punished for what he has done to us," Job declared. "We've waited long enough. We started without Joe Zabbidou and we'll finish without him."

"Hear! Hear!" said a voice from the back, and a deep rumble of approval rolled through the crowd.

"You don't understand," said Joe, trying to make himself heard above the discontented mutterings. But he was wasting his time. No one was listening to him anymore. All eyes were on Job. Now I was really scared, for me and for Joe. I could feel how angry they were. I wanted to shout at them, to tell them to listen, but no sound came from my mouth.

Job turned to Joe. "You come here," he sneered. "You take our secrets and make false promises. Tell us, what are you going to do with those secrets? How many of us are in your debt?"

"I paid you for your secrets," insisted Joe. "I kept my side of the bargain."

Job pounced. "Aha, so it is about money. And is it not true you paid so much that even if we wanted them back, we couldn't afford them?"

"It was a fair exchange," shouted Joe, by now weary and exasperated. "I never expected the money back." Everyone was talking at once. "You know it is my business."

Job came right up to him until their noses were almost touching.

"Business?" he laughed. "At last we are getting to the truth. Jeremiah Ratchet says he is a businessman. I see you two are no different."

He turned and addressed the restless throng. "Maybe we are going after the wrong man. Maybe Jeremiah Ratchet and our good friend Joe Zabbidou here are in this together!"

I looked at the enraged faces before us and it was hard to believe that these were the same people who had once welcomed Joe with open arms. I could hear the words *liar* and *cheat* and I was incensed. I took a step forward, thinking I might be able to protect him, but Joe held me back.

"It is not like that," he said. "I have told you no lies. I never promis—"

But Joe couldn't finish because the crowd had turned against him. They began to boo and hiss.

Joe stood there in a daze, his arms hanging loosely by his sides. People began to pelt him with snow and gravel and anything they could find. I grabbed his hand and dragged him

away. I knew we were in danger out here in the open. I looked back only once and to my dismay I saw Jeremiah Ratchet standing on his doorstep. His arms were folded across his chest and when he caught my eye he opened his mouth and began to laugh.

I locked up the shop and pulled down the blinds. We stayed inside for the rest of the day. I couldn't believe what had happened and I paced between the rooms, going over and over it in my head.

"How could they do this to you? After everything you've done for them."

Joe sat calmly by the fire. He heard my rantings but didn't reply. He hardly said a word the entire afternoon, but I could tell that his mind was working furiously. What was he planning? Revenge on the village or revenge on Jeremiah? Surely it had to be one or the other. In my heart, though, I knew it was neither. Revenge was not Joe's way.

Joe seemed to be talking to himself, reassuring himself that he had done nothing wrong. "I have always paid a fair price," he muttered. "When the deal is done, it is done and no one owes anyone. But still for these people it's not enough. They accused me of making false promises."

"They misunderstood you," I said.

He looked up at me. "I promised nothing. Jeremiah has no hold over me, but that doesn't mean I can do anything

about him." His face was screwed into a deep frown and his eyebrows were almost touching. "There are rules and I must obey them."

"Rules? What rules?" I asked. But Joe was talking to himself again.

"I gave them money, far more than they deserved, and I told them to be patient. That is all. It is hardly a commitment. But now they treat me as if I have betrayed them. Why must it be in human nature to hear one thing but to believe that it is another?"

"Because we want things to get better," I said. "Otherwise, we would all give up."

Joe closed his eyes. "*Dum spiro, spero*," he said. "While I breathe, I hope."

CHAPTER THIRTY ONE

The Reluctant Messenger

Down at the Pickled Trout Benjamin Tup was struggling to cope with his customers' demands. He had never had to deal with a full tavern before and tonight the place was heaving with the villagers, some of whom, such as Perigoe Leafbinder, had never even been over the threshold. They sat and stood and leaned and perched on every available surface in a tight circle, somehow managing at the same time to hold on to a mug or a jug of ale. Job Wright was the only one who was reasonably comfortable, having taken center stage on a rickety, ale-stained table.

"Fellow villagers," he boomed to the excited and slightly tipsy crowd, "I say the time has come to take back what is rightfully ours. You all saw Horatio this afternoon, a braver man I have never seen. The way he held on to that turkey is something I will not forget for the rest of my years."

Horatio blushed at the praise and staggered under the

slapping hands that rained down on his back. He covered his ears as deafening cheers rattled his brain.

"But this is only the beginning," continued Job. "All this time we thought it was Jeremiah who was the source of our misfortune. But now we know, he is merely the lackey of Joe Zabbidou. Stirling was right, Joe is the Devil and he is playing his evil games with us. Is there any one of us here who can say we are not in his debt?"

"We all owe him," they shouted back. "Each and every one of us."

"He had us fooled," said Job grimly. "But it's not too late. We can still stop him."

Only one voice dissented and that belonged to Polly. She jumped up on the table and stood in front of Job. The villagers were surprised into an uneasy silence.

"Don't listen to this," she urged. "It's not Joe we have to worry about. It's Jeremiah. Joe helped you all. Why are you doing this to him?"

Some of the villagers, the more sober among them, murmured that Polly had a point.

"The girl's right," said Lily Weaver. "Shouldn't we deal with Jeremiah first?"

Elias Sourdough then climbed up onto the table, which now shook alarmingly. "No," he said. "It's Joe needs sorting. And if you want proof, listen to this." He reached into his pocket and took out a piece of paper and read from it.

"If you wont to keepe yore seecret leve five shilins at the churche gattes tonite and I'll say nuffin."

The crowd gasped.

"Yes," said Elias, "a blackmail letter, left secretly in my shop, no doubt by Ludlow, and written by none other than Joe Zabbidou. And this is only the beginning. Who will be blackmailed next?"

The villagers needed no more convincing, and outside the tavern, hidden in the shadows, with his ear pressed up against the window, Jeremiah Ratchet also heard what Elias had to say. As he listened an ugly, wet-lipped smirk spread across his fleshy cheeks. Now he knew everything.

Polly's heart sank. *I've got to tell Ludlow,* she thought, creeping out of the tavern and darting away up the hill. She rapped loudly on the pawnbroker's door until Ludlow finally let her in and brought her through to the back room. Polly stood uncomfortably in front of the fire, twitching and wringing her hands. Her face was pale and she licked her lips nervously.

"What can I do for you, my dear?" asked Joe evenly.

"There's something I've got to tell you." Her voice was barely above a whisper. "Something I think you should know."

In the corner Ludlow paled. What could she mean? *Don't tell him what we did,* he urged her silently.

"I want to help you." She was almost apologetic, and then the words tumbled out all over each other. "I'm here to warn you. I think you are in danger. Since the turkey fight everyone's been in the Pickled Trout. They're all so angry. I've heard some awful threats. Something dreadful is going to happen, I just know it."

"To me or to Ratchet?" murmured Joe.

The answer was clear in Polly's eyes. "Now that everyone knows what you do at midnight, they're all talking about the Black Book. They think you used magic to charm their secrets out of them."

"Magic?" Joe raised his eyebrows in mild surprise.

"Obadiah said you gave him an enchanted potion to loosen his tongue."

Joe's eyes widened. "What pyretic brains these people have. It's nothing more than brandy, to calm their nerves."

"Job says you paid all that money so they'd always be in your debt. He says you're trying to take over from Jeremiah Ratchet."

"He's just a troublemaker," tutted Joe dismissively. "So the villagers have taken a dislike to me because I paid them too much? This is madness."

"They judge you by the standards they know, and all they know is Jeremiah Ratchet. You promised things—"

"No," he interrupted sharply. He never promised.

Polly corrected herself. "They *believe* you promised them help but now you've fallen back on your word, like Ratchet." She paused for a second. "And then there was the letter."

"Letter?" Joe and Ludlow spoke in unison.

Polly shifted uncomfortably. "I didn't believe it until Elias Sourdough showed it to everyone in the tavern. He read it out. It's a blackmail letter. He says it's from you. It says you want five shillings at the church gates tonight to keep quiet about his secret."

"So that's why they wouldn't talk to me," exclaimed Ludlow.

"They think I wrote a blackmail letter? For five shillings?" Joe laughed in utter amazement. "They believe I have started to threaten them?"

"Yes," said Polly hurriedly. "And if you want to win back their trust then you have to show that you're on their side. Before they do something terrible."

"Whose side do they think I am on?"

She didn't answer, just nodded down the hill.

"Tell me," said Joe in a voice that was strangely flat, "how do I prove otherwise? What would they have me do with Jeremiah?"

"Maybe you could give the potion—I mean brandy—to Jeremiah."

"And if I do? What then?"

Polly looked a little embarrassed. "Under the influence of the brandy, he is bound to admit to a terrible crime and then you can blackmail him back."

I snorted loudly. Joe would never do something as underhanded as that.

"This is beyond belief!" thundered Joe. "Blackmail is not my business."

"I'm sorry, Mr. Zabbidou," said Polly quickly, shrinking back against the fireplace. "I'm only trying to help. Everyone's so angry with you. I just thought you should know."

"What of Jeremiah?" asked Joe suddenly. "What does he know of this?"

Polly shook her head. "I don't know. Maybe nothing. But

I'm sure he's up to something, too. He had one of the Sour-dough boys in his study the other day. I just wish I knew why."

Joe shook his head wearily and leaned against the mantel. "How it saddens me to see how quickly men turn against each other."

Polly looked desperately at Ludlow. "Please be careful," she said and then she was gone.

CHAPTER THIRTY-TWO

Fragment from
The Memoirs of Ludlow Fitch

After Polly left Joe took out the brandy and two glasses and set them on the mantel. Then he sat down heavily and closed his eyes. "Now we must wait," he said.

"Are you expecting someone?"

"Perhaps."

"Should I fetch the book?"

"Not yet."

I sat at the table. What else could I do? I was trembling, I had been all day, and my mouth was dry. I heard the church bell ring every hour. Midnight came and went, and all outside was still. My lids became heavy and I rested my head on the table and began to doze and then to dream. I was running for my life. I knew there was someone behind me but I couldn't see who it was. Every time I looked back I was blinded by a glinting light that came out of the darkness. My lungs were screaming and my legs were leaden. I tried to

call out but I couldn't open my mouth. Pa emerged from the mist again and threw me to the ground and started to choke me. I could hear Ma and someone else running toward us, their footsteps pounding like hammers.

I woke, shaking and with my heart racing, but the hammering continued. Someone was banging on the door. Joe was already in the shop. I knew who it was. There was only one man in Pagus Parvus who would feel the need to make his presence known in such a heavy-handed fashion.

Jeremiah Ratchet.

I ran through and saw Jeremiah's huge silhouette blocking out the light from the moon. His fist was raised ready to come down again, but Joe was already there and opened the door so quickly that Jeremiah fell in.

"Hurrumph," he snorted, predictably, as he steadied himself.

"Ah, Mr. Ratchet, what a pleasant surprise."

Jeremiah planted his feet firmly on the shop floor and took a good look around as if he was claiming the territory for his own. He saw the frog and for a second the two creatures eyed each other with interest, though Saluki's waned first. Then he pushed his way past and went into the back room. Joe went after him. I slipped in and sat at the table and shrank against the wall, trying to hide in the shadows.

Jeremiah stood at the fire warming the seat of his pants. He folded his arms and wrinkled his nose, as if the place had a bad smell. Joe poured a couple of brandies, large and

small, and handed the large one to his visitor. Jeremiah drank it in a single gulp.

"Mr. Zabbidou," he said, "I'll come straight to the point. I am not the type to mince words. I believe in saying what's what."

"And that is?" Joe was strangely calm, but my stomach was turning over and over.

"You had me foxed for a while, but I've worked it out now. I know your game."

He waited for Joe to respond, a smug smile across his cheeks as if he expected praise.

"My game?"

"I'll not deny it, you've caused me and my business no end of trouble. At first I thought you were plotting against me. I've seen the comings and goings in the middle of the night. The villagers thought you were some sort of hero, but I couldn't understand why. To me you were just a nuisance. But now I know what you do and I'm here because I want you to help me."

He seemed nervous and droplets of sweat oozed from his hairline. He dabbed at them with his handkerchief.

"What?" I exclaimed before I could stop myself. I looked at Joe. "You don't believe this, do you?"

Joe signaled to me to be quiet. "How can I help, Mr. Ratchet?"

Jeremiah sighed deeply and sat down heavily, wedging his quivering posterior into the armchair. Then to my astonishment he began to sob. It was not a pleasant sight.

"I wish to unburden myself of a terrible secret," he mumbled through his tears. "I didn't know whom else to turn to. You are the only one who can help."

I could hardly contain myself. Ratchet wanting to confess? Ratchet sobbing? This had to be some sort of trick. But Joe carried on as if this behavior were completely normal.

"And how can I do that?" asked Joe kindly.

Jeremiah looked out through his chubby fingers. "With the book," he said. "The Black Book of Secrets."

I shook my head in disgust. Jeremiah Ratchet did not deserve even a drop of ink in that book. I was about to say as much, but Joe spoke before me.

"A wise decision," he said. "Ludlow, fetch the book, please."

I was paralyzed with confusion. Joe was going along with this charade. He was going to buy Ratchet's secret. Why? To blackmail him, like Polly said? Surely Joe would never do anything like that!

"The book, Ludlow," repeated Joe pointedly.

With dragging feet I went to fetch it, aware of Ratchet's eyes on me all the time. I pulled the book out from under my cushion and was about to lay it on the table when, with a loud sucking noise, Jeremiah launched himself from his chair and came right at me. The speed of his approach was surprising, his bulk gave him great momentum, and I put up my hands to shield myself. Jeremiah threw himself against me and with a violent shove sent me crashing into the table. Out of the corner of my eye I saw the book spin

off toward the ceiling, its pages flapping and turning, and then a huge swollen hand reached up and snatched it from midair.

Jeremiah Ratchet was in possession of the Black Book of Secrets.

CHAPTER THIRTY-THREE

FRAGMENT FROM
THE MEMOIRS OF LUDLOW FITCH

*There ensued a rather comical scene. Jeremiah had the advan-*tages of surprise and weight, but these were countered by the brandy he had consumed. Joe was light on his feet and was the faster of the two. With speed that defied the laws of physics, Joe leaped over the back of his chair, displaying the grace and agility of a young gazelle. In two strides he was at Jeremiah's side and he whipped the book from his sweaty clutches. Jeremiah cursed and lurched like a drunken elephant from one side of the room to the other, while Joe merely sidestepped his clumsy attempts to grab it back. I watched uselessly from the floor where I had fallen, severely winded, after sustaining the impact of Jeremiah's full weight.

The entire display lasted no longer than a minute. Jeremiah was forced to give up and slid down the wall to sit in a most undignified fashion with his legs splayed and his mouth wide open. His face was bright red, his eyes were bulging, and his lungs rattled with every drawn breath.

Joe stood over him, his clothes disheveled and his hair wilder than ever. His spidery shadow danced gleefully on the wall. I dragged myself up and joined him.

"I must protest at your behavior, Mr. Ratchet," scolded Joe. "It is not what I would expect from a man of your standing."

Jeremiah struggled to his feet.

"Listen, Mr. Zabbidou," he said and all pretense of sobbing and remorse was gone. "You don't seem to understand. You're finished in this place. The villagers are coming to get you. You'll be run out of here. But before you go, I want the book. And what I want I get."

I laughed. Poor Ratchet. He was the one who didn't understand. Joe would never give up the book.

"Absolutely not," said Joe. "The book is confidential and I will never surrender it."

"Ah now, Zabbidou," persisted Jeremiah, and Joe winced with distaste at this familiarity, "don't be like that. What use is the book to you anymore? Why take it with you when I can have it and make good use of it? We're both businessmen, Zabbidou. To keep it would be nothing short of spiteful."

"Exactly what would you do with it, Mr. Ratchet?" asked Joe.

Jeremiah looked surprised. "Blackmail, of course. Only I'd make a better job of it than you. Five shillings at the church gate? Not very sophisticated, if you don't mind my saying."

I stood openmouthed at the sheer cheek of the man.

"Joe didn't write that letter," I began, but Joe motioned with his hand for me to be quiet.

"Under the circumstances, Mr. Ratchet," he said, "I do not feel I can take your pledge. I think it is time for you to go."

Jeremiah surprised us both and held up his hands in surrender. "As you wish," he said and made his way meekly into the shop. I watched from the doorway as Jeremiah stopped at Saluki's tank and placed his hands on the lid. Now what was he going to do?

"Give me the book," he hissed at Joe through his yellow teeth, "or I will kill your precious frog."

"I'm warning you," said Joe quietly. "Do not touch the frog. She does not like it."

" 'She does not like it,' " mimicked Jeremiah like a petulant child. "Give me the book and it won't matter."

"Don't touch the frog." Joe's voice was menacing.

"Ha!" shouted Jeremiah and he flung the lid away, reached in, and grabbed Saluki with both hands.

"No!" shouted Joe, but it was too late.

Jeremiah yelped and dropped her. Saluki landed on the floor with a soft thud and sat very still, looking a little dazed.

"I think it bit me," Jeremiah said, his eyes wide with surprise and confusion. "I think it bit me." Undeterred and desperate, he picked up the tank and raised it above his head.

"Give me the damned book or the frog gets it."

Joe, and Saluki, looked at him sadly. "Believe me," said Joe, stepping into the shop, "it won't do you any good." And

at that he handed the Black Book of Secrets to Jeremiah Ratchet.

Jeremiah's eyes shone as he snatched the book with a triumphant crow. "I'll be the judge of that."

Without another word he stomped out and slammed the door. Gracefully and precisely, Saluki climbed up the counter and back into her tank. Joe replaced the lid and dropped in a couple of bugs and the frog chewed them as if nothing had happened. And it was strange, I never thought a frog could look satisfied, but at that moment I swear Saluki did. Her colors glowed with a vibrancy that near lit up the room and her bright eyes seemed to say, "You were warned, Ratchet. You were warned."

CHAPTER THIRTY-FOUR

Departure

Jeremiah Ratchet was gripped by intense glee. He longed to skip, but the icy road permitted only a short-stepped, cautious haste. So instead he punched the air with his fist and let out an audible "Ha! Ha!" into the night.

He was distinctly pleased with himself. He had guessed quite rightly that the Black Book was the key. To possess it now almost made up for his earlier humiliation at the hands of Horatio and the turkey. And, of course, if it hadn't been for that altercation, he would never have found out exactly what was in the book. After he had gone home with the turkey he had watched the crowd, and Joe and Ludlow, from his window. He had heard it all, every single word. What fools they were, those villagers, to trust their secrets to Joe Zabbidou. And that was when he had come up with his plan, to pretend to wish to pawn his own secret so he could get his hands on the book. When he eavesdropped outside the Pickled Trout, that had been just the icing on the cake.

How stupid Joe had been to send the blackmail letter. He had burned all of his bridges in the village and at the same time he had done Jeremiah a great favor. By the time the villagers had gotten rid of Joe it would be too late. Jeremiah would have the Black Book and he would use it to regain his rightful position of power in Pagus Parvus.

If he was honest with himself, in his heart of hearts Jeremiah had never thought it would be so easy to take possession of the Black Book of Secrets. But then who would have thought Joe would surrender it rather than lose his precious frog? Jeremiah was fit to burst with self-congratulation.

As quietly as this delight would allow he hurried inside, unaware that he had omitted to shut the door fully. He was also unaware of the small figure that crept in after him and followed him to the study. This stealthy intruder curled up in the darkest corner and watched and waited. The full moon shone its dusty beams through the window. They lit up the clock on the mantel to show a quarter after three. Jeremiah threw off his coat and dropped it; he pulled off his hat and tossed it aside. With every step he took snow fell off his boots and melted on the rug, leaving dark stains. He held up the prize in triumph, the red ribbon trailing from between its pages.

"I'll show them," he laughed, waving it in the air. "They'll all pay for their treachery."

Jeremiah took himself over to the dying fire and eased himself into one of his very expensive leather chairs. He

glanced at the cover of the book, but couldn't understand it, so he flung it open and laid it flat on his lap. He licked the tip of his stubby forefinger and turned the pages with obvious relish, slowly at first and then more quickly. He tittered, he giggled, he took the Lord's name in vain more than once, stopping every so often to rub his hands together. He did this not in glee, however, but to soothe his burning palms. Saluki's bite, if that is what she had done, was proving to be nearly as irritating as her owner.

"My fortune is made," gloated Jeremiah. "There're secrets in this book I couldn't even have guessed. And not just from Pagus Parvus, from all over. As for Dr. Mouldered! My, my, who'd have thought it!"

With great satisfaction he snapped the book shut and a single page fluttered to the floor to land at his feet. Breathing hard by now, he leaned forward to retrieve it and held it up to the light. Its ragged edge suggested that it had been recently torn from another book. It showed a colorful picture, hand-painted with some skill.

"Frogs?" snorted Jeremiah disdainfully and glanced curiously at the caption. Seconds later he fell back into the chair and let out a tremendous groan.

"What has he done?" he moaned. "The lanky fork-tongued devil, he has duped me."

His hands throbbed and burned. His movements were slowing. A creeping numbness spread up his arms and throughout his body. His chest tightened, his throat swelled.

It was becoming difficult to breathe. But he watched, unable even to express surprise, as the boy emerged from the half-light and came forward.

"Who's there?" Jeremiah stuttered hoarsely.

The boy didn't answer, just stared at the dying man before bending down to pick up the book from the floor.

"Who has done this to you?" whispered the intruder.

Jeremiah's lips moved and silently formed a single word.

The boy shook his head and left.

CHAPTER THIRTY-FIVE

FRAGMENT FROM
THE MEMOIRS OF LUDLOW FITCH

As soon as Jeremiah was gone, I turned on Joe. Even now I still couldn't piece the puzzle together. All I knew was that he had let Jeremiah walk away with his most precious possession.

No, I thought, *my most precious possession, too.*

That book was now part of my very existence. I couldn't stop myself, and blinded by rage and disappointment, I beat upon Joe's chest with my fists.

"Why did you let him take it? You know how he will use it."

Joe shook me off gently and infuriated me with a smile. "Calm down, Ludlow. Don't you understand? This is what we've been waiting for."

He poured another brandy (I had never seen him drink more than one), threw back his head, and swallowed it in one go.

"I have to say the fellow had me worried somewhat. I thought he would have been up here days ago; it would

have saved us a lot of trouble. He has certainly taken his time."

Confused, angry, and burning with questions, I was determined to find the truth.

"You mean you wanted him to do this?"

"It's not what I want," said Joe, "it's what Jeremiah wants. If nothing else he was true to his nature. That man cannot bear others to have what he desires."

"You're talking in riddles again. Just tell me what's really going on. I deserve to know."

"What do you want to know, Ludlow? What is it you think I have kept from you?"

His calm disarmed me. My anger dissipated and I became flustered. "Lots of things. You said you weren't a blackmailer yet you asked Jeremiah for a secret, just like Polly said. Would you have paid him, too?"

Joe looked mildly shocked. "I expected better of you than such an accusation. Jeremiah, for all his faults, deserves a chance, like everyone else, to gain relief from his troubles. Do you think that his innate cruelty prevents him from feeling remorse? I had to give him the opportunity. It is part of what I do."

"The opportunity to do what?"

"To say he was sorry."

"And if he had, what then?"

"Well, if he had told me a secret, then I should have paid him. Rules are rules. Things would have been different, of course; as it is, he has only himself to blame."

I tutted with exasperation. "And just what are these rules you live by?"

He remained silent.

"Who are you, Joe?"

"The truth will come later, I promise you that," he said finally. "What is important now is that you go to retrieve the book."

I laughed sarcastically. "And how am I to do that?"

"You'll find a way, but you'd better hurry. He must be halfway down the hill already."

"You're not coming with me?"

Joe shook his head. "I have played my part. Now it is your turn."

I threw up my hands in frustration, but I didn't waste another second. Whatever else I wanted to say to Joe, it could wait. He was right. I had to get the Black Book back. The secrets of the whole village, and others, were in there. Jeremiah already knew Perigoe's and Horatio's and Obadiah's, but what about everyone else's? There were so many secrets. I realized that until now I had thought of this whole business as a sort of game that Joe and I were playing with the villagers, all of us pitted against Jeremiah Ratchet. But it wasn't a game any longer. It was deadly serious. I had written their confessions and now it was up to me to save them.

So I ran out of the door and down the hill, skidding and slipping and cursing in my head both Jeremiah and Joe, and plagued by terrible doubt. Maybe Job Wright hadn't been so

far off the mark. Maybe Joe was using the villagers and I had been too blind to see it, selfishly hanging on to this new life, so desperate for a real father that I had ignored what was going on under my nose. Was this the punishment for taking what I didn't deserve? But it still didn't make sense.

"It's not about the money," I said to the night. "There has to be another reason."

Jeremiah had already gone inside, but in his haste the latch hadn't caught, so I slipped into the hall and followed his trail of wet footprints to the study. I squatted down just inside the door and watched as he settled in the chair. There was meat pie somewhere close by and the smell made my mouth water.

I didn't know what I was going to do. My heart beat so loudly I thought it would give me away. I could see the top of his head and I could hear pages turning. Soon it would be too late, he would know everything. I heard the book snap shut and saw a page flutter to the floor. He leaned forward to pick it up. He said something, then groaned and fell back into the chair. All I could hear now was his noisy wheezing.

I don't know how long I waited before tiptoeing over. He was so still I wondered if he had fallen asleep. I stood right in front of him. His eyes were open and for a second I expected him to grab me, but he just sat there, a terrible sight to behold. His face was white and his breathing was harsh and rattling. I knew I was looking at a dying man.

"Who's there?" he mumbled and I could hardly hear him.

I bent down and picked up the book from the floor.

"Who has done this to you?" I asked.

Slowly Jeremiah's dry lips formed a silent word.

Joe.

There was nothing else I could do, so I left.

CHAPTER THIRTY-SIX

Fragment from
The Memoirs of Ludlow Fitch

Jeremiah's dying word had shattered my world. When I looked into his eyes I could see no lie. I walked slowly back up the hill and my heart was leaden. I was torn up inside. All this time I had thought Joe was better than the rest of us, better than I could ever hope to be, but in the end he was as bad as my own ma and pa, if not worse; to my knowledge they at least had never willfully killed anyone. Yes, like everyone else, I had wanted Joe to stand up to Jeremiah Ratchet. But I had never thought it would end like this. There was no other way to say it. Joe Zabbidou was a murderer.

But how did he do it?

I went over and over in my head the last meeting between the two of them, searching for clues. There was no weapon and Jeremiah wasn't injured in any way. Perhaps he was poisoned. But how was it administered? It could have been the brandy. But both had drunk from the same bottle. Then maybe it was in the glass.

That was it! Joe had put poison in Jeremiah's glass before pouring the brandy. Jeremiah had drunk it in one gulp and then, presumably to Joe's delight, he had washed it down with more.

Joe was waiting for me by the fire, a glass in his hand, and he looked as if nothing out of the ordinary had happened. He had even straightened out the room.

"Did you get it?"

I handed it over.

"Good work. I knew I could trust you."

I wanted to say something, but I was still too shocked to speak. Then I noticed his satchel on the table. It was buckled and bursting at the seams. A small drawstring bag sat beside it. Icy fear ran in my veins. I found my voice.

"You're not going, are you?"

He put up his hand to silence me.

"Shh," he said. "Listen."

Something was happening outside. I could hear the murmur of voices and the sound of feet breaking through the frozen snow. I crept to the door and looked into the shop. Cloaked shapes moved on the other side of the window with faces like devils lit up in the light of flaming torches. And among them I could see the stooped outline of Obadiah Strang and beside him the tiny figure of Perigoe Leafbinder and beside her the thickness of Horatio Cleaver.

"Come out, Joe Zabbidou," chanted the shadows, a hundred strong, "or we'll burn you out."

At the sight of this demonic throng my legs went weak and I staggered back to Joe in terror. "They're out there, all of them," I hissed. "They've come for us, like Polly said. They're going to kill us."

But Joe stayed where he was and took a long, slow draught of his drink.

"Just be patient," he said. "Just be patient."

"There's no time for patience," I snapped in a panic, clutching at his cloak.

He took me by the wrists and held me away from him. "Not yet."

"Come out, Joe Zabbidou, come out!" The voices swelled into a menacing chorus. Then with a tremendous crash the shopfront window shattered and the counter was sprayed with splintered glass and the room was filled with smoke and the smell of burning oil and the sharp crackle of flames. Outside on the street they were kicking at the door and beating it down with cudgels. The noise was deafening, the smoke black and choking, the heat intensifying.

"Come out, Joe Zabbidou," they cried. "Come out!"

Still he wouldn't move and he wouldn't let go. I tried to pull away, but his grip was like a vice. "Are you going to let me die, too?" I shouted, but he didn't hear me. His head was cocked to one side and he was listening intently.

I began to scream and yell. The abominable cacophony outside rose to an inhuman pitch. Clouds of smoke rolled

into the back room until I could barely see my own hand in front of my face. At last, out of all this madness there came another voice. A shrill voice that carried above the confusion. Polly's voice.

"Ratchet's dead! Jeremiah Ratchet's dead."

Joe released my wrists and raised his arms in triumph above his head.

"*Acta est fabula*," he said. "It is over."

CHAPTER THIRTY SEVEN

Leftovers

Polly had woken in the night but she didn't know why. Now that she was awake, she felt hungry. Certain that Jeremiah would be in bed, she took a candle and crept down the stairs. On her way to the kitchen she noticed that the front door was open and she closed it. So he had gone out after all. "I suppose he'll be back soon enough, drunk as a lord," she muttered. Then she saw the light in the study and went in.

The dinner tray from the previous evening was on the desk, and Polly shook her head in irritation. She hated to see good food go to waste. A slice of pie sat on the plate, untouched. She nibbled at a piece of crust and immediately spat out what she took to be a bit of grit and wrinkled her nose.

"That's one of Horatio Cleaver's pies," she said to herself. The butcher had brought it to the house personally only that evening. She made a mental note to tell Horatio what she thought of it next time she saw him. Then she noticed

damp footprints on the rug that led to the fire, the hat and scarf tossed on the floor.

"Lord above," she exclaimed, hastily wiping any telltale crumbs from her mouth. "Mr. Ratchet, what are you doing here?"

Polly could see the top of his head—instantly identifiable by the shiny bald patch in the middle—above the back of the chair and his remaining hair, gray and white in color, sticking out defiantly over his ears despite daily applications of expensive hair lotion. She rounded the chair cautiously to meet Jeremiah's open-eyed stony gaze of death and screamed.

Nobody would ever claim that Jeremiah Ratchet was an attractive man. He had all the appearance of a toad about to burst. In death he was little changed, just less flexible, sitting stiffly in the chair. In his hand he still had the loose page, held fast between his rigid fingers. Polly wasn't interested in what he had been reading (though she was struck by the beauty of the picture), but she was mesmerized by the expression on his face. His mouth was fixed open in a sort of grimacing yawn and his eyes were unnaturally wide. It was as if he had just been told something truly shocking.

Poor Polly had never encountered a corpse at such close quarters, and it took some moments for her to gather her wits. Once gathered, however, she proved to be a practical girl. With trembling fingers she reached into Jeremiah's waistcoat and found his purse, which she stuffed down the front of her apron. For a moment she beheld poor Jeremiah for the last time. Then she stepped back and hit her foot

against something hard behind her. She looked down to see the coal scuttle.

"Only the flames of hell will warm your cold soul," she mumbled before running out to the street and announcing to the village in her shrill voice:

"Ratchet's dead! Jeremiah Ratchet's dead."

CHAPTER THIRTY-EIGHT

Diagnosis

During his lifetime Jeremiah had successfully kept the villagers at bay; within minutes of his death, however, his house was swarming with them. They ran up and down the stairs, opening and closing doors and pocketing what they could conceal beneath their coats. For one reason or another they all felt they deserved something.

"I heard that his bathtub was pure gold," whispered one as he crammed a polished spittoon into his breast pocket.

"And that he ate only from silver platters and drank from the finest crystal," said his companion, wrenching a fine brass sconce from the wall.

A third man was very busy tapping the stair panels with his hairy knuckles. He was looking for secret passages that led to underground cellars where jewelry and treasure and, more important, ale and wine were said to be stored.

"'Ere 'e is," came the youngest Sourdough's cry from below. "Oooh, 'e's gorn black and blue."

With a great rushing noise the crowd arrived at the study and poured in to gather around Ratchet's chair like water meeting a rock in a stream. It was quite true; Jeremiah's skin had taken on a rather strange mottled hue. This, combined with the yellowish foam at the corners of his mouth and his repulsive grimace, was too much for Lily Weaver. With a deep sigh she swooned and would have fallen to the floor except the crush was so great she remained standing, and came to some moments later supported on all sides by her fellow Pagus Parvians. Then she was lifted up and passed over the sea of heads, as a bottle taken by the tide, only to be dropped unceremoniously into the corridor.

A voice cried out above the hubbub and, with much pushing and shoving and elbowing, Dr. Samuel Mouldered managed to enter the room.

"Thank the 'eavens above yore 'ere," said Elias Sourdough. "Ratchet's kicked the bucket at last."

The room quietened in anticipation of Mouldered's assessment of the case. Few of the villagers were acquainted with the fad of self-diagnosis (with the aid of Dr. Moriarti's *Simplified Medical Dictionary for the Common Man*, available at a small discount from Perigoe Leafbinder's bookshop). They preferred to hear it from the horse's mouth.

Mouldered walked around the chair several times, stroking his sparsely whiskered chin. It was not often he got to hold center stage in this way, and his nerves, tightly wound these past few days, were getting the better of him. Sweat squeezed out of the furrows of his brow and he licked his dry lips with a pale pink tongue. Finally he cleared his throat and announced hoarsely, "I believe that Jeremiah Ratchet has suffered some sort of fit, or apoplexy, of the heart which has caused his untimely death."

The crowd sighed and an air of disappointment was quite apparent. They had been expecting foul play. Certainly it would not have been undeserved.

" 'E looks sort of smothered to me. And 'is 'ands don't look right. Are you sure?"

That Jeremiah might have been smothered was little more than wishful thinking but, upon closer inspection, Mouldered could not deny that his palms were quite red and blistered, as if they had been severely burned.

"I'm sure," he said, with all the conviction of a man who isn't. "Sometimes heart attacks make people's hands, er—" he fumbled in his pockets as if searching for the correct medical term but gave up and finished lamely—"look like this."

Eyebrows were raised, sniggers were barely suppressed, and heads were shaken, but Mouldered refused to say any more and, the excitement over, the villagers shuffled out, jingling and jangling with their hidden spoils. In the silence they left behind them Mouldered closed Jeremiah's eyes with quivering fingers. He took the sheet of paper from his hand, glanced at it briefly, then folded it and was about to pocket it when Perigoe appeared.

"That belongs to Joe," she said. "It's from a book of mine he bought about amphibians."

"Ah, Perigoe," said Mouldered, handing it to her, "then perhaps you could see to it that he gets it."

She nodded and left quickly, clutching a single tatty maroon book under her arm.

Just one? thought Mouldered. *How very restrained.*

CHAPTER THIRTY-NINE

FRAGMENT FROM
THE MEMOIRS OF LUDLOW FITCH

As soon as the crowd heard that Ratchet was dead they had turned tail, one and all, and ran down the hill. Joe went straight through to the shop and began to beat out the flames with an old coat from the window. To be honest, it was more smoke than fire and it didn't take long to put it out. Despite that, the damage was extensive. Everything was charred or blackened with smoke and the acrid smell made breathing quite unpleasant. There was little worth saving. Gradually the air was clearing due to the biting wind that now blew through the broken window and the shattered door. I helped him without knowing why. Eventually Joe stamped out one last stubborn flame and rested, panting from the effort.

"What a dreadful shame, so unnecessary," he murmured. "But I suppose it could have been worse. At least I still have this." He bent down and pulled the wooden leg, miraculously unharmed, from the rubble and went to the back

room. When I looked in he was dressed in cloak and scarf and struggling to force the leg into the satchel.

Suddenly everything was happening far too quickly. I was angry with Joe for the way he behaved, for the murder I was so sure he had committed, but I was frightened, too, because he was leaving.

"Is that it? You're just going to go?"

"There's not much more I can do now," he said. "I have no reason to stay."

"What about the shop?"

"The shop is finished. We can start again somewhere else." He slung the bag over his shoulder and came through, stepping carefully over the wreckage on his way to the door. "You are coming with me?"

How could he be so calm? My heart was racing.

I hesitated. "I don't know if I can."

"Oh." He sounded as if he hadn't considered this and frowned. "I thought you knew we couldn't stay here forever. Perhaps I should have said something before. My work compels me to move on."

"It's not that," I said. "I would have gone anywhere with you but—" I couldn't say it. I felt as if I was choking. We faced each other wordlessly until the silence was gently broken by a soft voice that made us both look up. It was Perigoe.

"Mr. Zabbidou," she said. "Mr. Zabbidou." She came through the remains of the door, and when she saw the destruction she looked distraught. "I want to say sorry," she

whispered. "Everyone wants to say sorry. We know we were wrong to treat you the way we did. We should have trusted you. It was the letter that frightened us all."

"Ah," said Joe, "the letter."

Perigoe looked as if she was about to burst into tears. "It was the oldest Sourdough boy who wrote the letter, blackmailing his own father to line his pockets. He found out that Elias had been to see you and he knew we would blame you. Ruby found another letter he was going to send to Dr. Mouldered. Everyone feels terrible, Mr. Zabbidou. You were right: All we had to do was wait a little longer. Are you a doctor, too? Did you know about his heart?"

I could have laughed out loud. Now they thought Joe was a hero again. What was it then that bothered me so much? Jeremiah had so many enemies he was always going to meet a sticky end one way or the other, so did it really matter how? But I couldn't bear the thought that Joe was involved in such a wretched business. All those times I had worried about having sneaked a look in the Black Book. There were far greater sins being committed than that!

"His heart?" repeated Joe. "Yes, I suspected something was amiss with the fellow."

Perigoe's eyes went to the bag on his shoulder. Her eyelid flickered rapidly and she blushed.

"Are you leaving?"

"Indeed I am. I think Pagus Parvus can do without me now."

A tear squeezed out of the corner of her eye, but she wiped it away quickly and sniffed. "Then I am glad I caught

you. I want to give you something." She handed over a small book. "It doesn't matter anymore, now that Jeremiah's gone. Too many bad memories. I mean, who cares about sheep?"

Joe hesitated. "You do realize what this is worth, don't you?"

Perigoe nodded. "I couldn't take the money. You deserve it, after all you've given us."

"If it is your wish, I accept." Joe tucked the book into his cloak, but not before I managed to catch the title. *The Loneliness of the High Mountain Shepherd.*

"And there's this, too. I nearly forgot. Dr. Mouldered found it. I thought it might be important."

She gave him a piece of paper and he kissed her hand. Then she whispered goodbye and hurried away.

"You see," said Joe as he pocketed the folded page, "inheritance. When I sell the book, the money will keep us going for many months."

"Inheritance?" I scoffed. "You mean you get your money from dead people."

Joe smiled. "I suppose that is close enough to the truth."

"People you have killed."

"I have never killed anyone for money, Ludlow. It is not in my nature."

"You'll be telling me next it's against the rules."

Joe sighed and put down his satchel. "All these weeks you have been such a help to me, Ludlow, and I am immensely grateful. You have been honest and loyal and I know it wasn't easy for you. But more than that, I had thought I saw something in you, something I have been seeking for years. That first night when I found you outside in the snow, you reminded me of myself when I was a young man, and I could see a future for you. That is why I want you to come with me. I have such hopes for your talent. I want us to continue to work together. I can show you the world. Tell me, why won't you come?"

Why not, indeed? Of course I wanted to go, desperately. If he had asked a day ago, even hours ago, I would have had no hesitation. But now things were different. I wasn't sure he was the person I had thought him to be. I wasn't even sure who I was anymore.

"You could have a marvelous future, Ludlow. There is so much I could teach you."

"Like murder?" At last I said it, and the relief was indescribable—as was the fear that came with it.

"Ah," he said and his face lit up knowingly. "I wondered when you would come out with it. Presumably you believe I murdered Jeremiah?"

I nodded slowly. "Can you prove to me that you didn't?"

"I . . ." began Joe, but then another voice hailed us from the shop door. It was Horatio, breathless and sweating from running up the hill.

"I had to come," he said as he crashed through the debris. "I have to tell you, Joe, before you go, I've done something terrible. It wasn't his heart. It was me that did it. I killed him."

Joe took him by the arm and sat him down.

"What is it, Horatio? What do you think you have done?"

"I killed Jeremiah Ratchet. I poisoned his pie and had Polly give it to him. I know I swore I'd never cook up such a dish again but I just had to do something. Dr. Mouldered said you weren't going to help us. I couldn't stand it anymore."

"Listen to me," said Joe, "you mustn't blame yourself. What's done is done. Dr. Mouldered said he had a heart attack and it is best to accept that. Don't say anything about this to anyone, but make sure the remains of the pie are taken away in case someone else eats it. There are plenty who are hungry enough."

"Are you sure, Mr. Zabbidou?" Horatio looked up with red-rimmed eyes.

"Certain. Just get rid of the pie before someone innocent comes to harm."

"I don't know how to thank you, Mr. Zabbidou," said Horatio. "I don't deserve your help."

"The pie," repeated Joe. "Fetch the pie."

As soon as Horatio was gone Joe put his hands on my shoulders and looked me straight in the eye. "So, Ludlow, now do you trust me?"

I was speechless. I had been so certain. "So you didn't do it?" I stammered. I could hardly look at him. "Can you forgive me?" Then a terrible thought struck me. "Do you still want me to come with you?"

Joe laughed. "Ludlow, my dear fellow, of course I do. How could you possibly think otherwise? Come with me now and

I promise if you don't like what you see, and think you cannot live with what you know, then you and I can go our separate ways and our paths need never cross again."

My heart swelled to bursting point with excitement and I grinned so widely I could feel my skin stretching. I wasted no more time. I collected my purse from the fireplace and pulled my cloak tightly around me. But there was still something I had to say.

"I haven't always been honest with you," I began, but Joe shook his head.

"It'll keep," he said. "Now we must go."

We slipped out through the shattered door, carrying no more than we had when we had arrived in the village all those weeks ago. I looked over my shoulder, but the street was empty. A single light shone in Jeremiah's window, but other than that the houses were dark and we left as we came, unseen.

CHAPTER FORTY

FRAGMENT FROM
THE MEMOIRS OF LUDLOW FITCH

We journeyed on foot for two days and two nights. All the time we were climbing and all the time it was snowing. We had no chance to talk. Our efforts were concentrated on plowing through the drifts and fighting against the wind. It was vital that we stayed together. If we had become separated I had no doubt we would have been lost to each other forever. I did not know if we were going north or south, east or west. There was no sun to guide us and no moon at night.

As we traveled I had a chance to think, to mull over the recent past. Although I was elated that Joe had not murdered Jeremiah (and ashamed that I could have accused him of such a thing), I still felt that had Joe not arrived in Pagus Parvus when he did, Jeremiah would probably still be alive. There was also the matter of Joe's "inheritance," as he liked to call it. Joe had said, and I believed him, that he never killed for money. But money and death seemed inextricably linked when he was around.

There were other unanswered questions, of course, and I had come on this trip for those answers, but as the temperature dropped and the snow became thicker, I wondered if I had been so wise. But there was nothing left for me in Pagus Parvus and I soldiered on, trying to stay cheerful. Toward the end of the journey I was so tired I could hardly lift my feet, and Joe carried me on his back, tucked under his cloak, for the last few miles. I could still hear the storm howling, but the steady rhythm of his footfall, even with the limp, sent me into a delicious slumber. I remember very little after that until I woke up again to find that I was stretched out on the ground.

I was lying under my own cloak on a bed of leafy branches on a hard floor. There was no snow, no wind, no chill in the air. I lay for a few minutes unmoving, enjoying the warmth and comfort. I stared up at a ceiling of rock and when I put out my hand I could feel that the floor was sandy. I sat up and looked around cautiously. I was in a low-roofed cave lit by orange-flamed torches jutting out from the walls. The last time I had seen such burning brands, the night Jeremiah died, they had not cast such a comforting light. If I concentrated I could just hear the wind crying outside, but it sounded very far away. There was a fire at my feet, over which hung a blackened kettle. I could smell something familiar bubbling within. Joe was sitting cross-legged on the other side holding out a bowl.

"Soup?"

After we ate it was time to talk. For once Joe seemed happy to answer my questions. He looked different somehow, relaxed, as if he was in a familiar place.

"It is time for the truth," he said. "If we are to continue our journey together, you must trust me. If there is anything you wish to know, now is the time to ask."

Where to begin! I was so nervous I was shaking, but I knew what I wanted to say. I had rehearsed this moment for days. "Tell me your rules."

Joe nodded and began.

"There are only two, both simple, but it is their simplicity that makes them so difficult to follow. I think you know the first."

I did. "You must not change the course of things."

"Exactly. That is not to say I have no influence. The very fact that I arrive in a place affects the future in some way, but wherever I go, each person is responsible for his own actions. Of the two rules, I think this is the harder to obey. I have seen some terrible things, Ludlow, and it makes it so difficult not to interfere. Nigh on every day in Pagus Parvus I was tempted to ignore the rule. The villagers needed my help so badly, but I had to be deaf to their pleas. I don't really know what they wanted me to do—perhaps they wished me to murder Jeremiah"—here he smiled wryly—"but I could only carry on as normal and hope they could wait. To

behave in any other way would have led to disaster. *Dura lex sed lex*. The law is hard but it is the law."

"And the other rule?"

"You are familiar with that one, too. Everyone, no matter who they are, deserves a chance to redeem themselves, to say sorry, to ask for mercy. Even people like Jeremiah Ratchet. You will remember I gave him that opportunity when he came for the book."

I remembered the sight of Jeremiah pleading for help and I shuddered.

"Of course, he didn't really want my help," continued Joe, "but still I had to offer it to him. You were afraid that if he confessed I would use his secret against him. It broke my heart to see your faith in me waver, although I was immensely pleased that you were so concerned for the fate of the villagers. I knew then I hadn't misjudged you. Your loyalty to them is a quality to be admired. We act for the people, Ludlow. Never forget that.

"I will not deny that Jeremiah's own fate was sealed one way or the other when I came to Pagus Parvus, but he killed himself long before I ever turned up: by his selfishness, his avarice, his cruel nature.

"These are the rules, Ludlow, and I live by them regardless."

He looked at me expectantly and I was ready. "The money you used in Pagus Parvus, where did it come from?"

"A dead person, as you suggested, but before you accuse me of foul play let me assure you it was all perfectly legiti-

mate. Before I came to the village I spent some time in a small town near the border. Business was good. In fact, you will find some of their secrets at the beginning of the Black Book. There is an interesting one about a coffin maker . . ."

My heart sank and I flushed bright red and covered my face with my hands. "You knew."

Joe grinned. "Of course I knew. It was written all over your face when I came back."

"Aren't you angry?"

"I was, I suppose, at the time. More with you than with Polly. But at least you started at the beginning."

"We wouldn't have read anymore," I said. "We both felt terrible afterward."

"I'm glad," replied Joe, laughing. "So you should. It would have been easy enough to make you confess, but I thought I should let you live with your guilt. And the book under your cushion—I'm sure to feel that every night was punishment enough. As I said, *Quae nocent docent.*"

The Latin words at the end of the story.

"It means, 'Things that hurt also teach.' "

Now I felt even worse. "So what happened in that small town?" I asked, anxious to know everything.

"After some weeks it came to my attention that the local physician was deliberately poisoning his patients and stealing their money and belongings. After he died the locals rewarded me quite handsomely with a share of his stolen wealth. And then I moved on."

"But how did he die?"

"Not by my hand, I swear it."

"Then how? More poisoned pie?"

Joe laughed. "No, it was an accident, I promise. But let's not dwell on that. There's more important business to attend to. Follow me."

Joe picked up his satchel and crossed the cave to the opposite wall, where I noticed for the first time the entrance to a tunnel. I hesitated at the opening, it was narrow and dark, but Joe had already stepped through, so I took a torch from the wall and ran after him.

CHAPTER FORTY-ONE

Fragment from
The Memoirs of Ludlow Fitch

As we made our way down the rocky tunnel it became narrower and narrower. Joe could no longer stand up straight and I could not walk beside him. Farther down, the air became heavy and thick as if it had not moved for many years. The torch dimmed to an amber glow, and I feared it might go out altogether. I felt and heard living things fly past me, bats perhaps, but I never saw them, just sensed something brushing against my cheeks and catching at my hair.

"Don't worry, Ludlow," called Joe over his shoulder. "You will come to no harm."

Now we were descending. The slope was gentle at first but quickly became steeper, and I had to hold on to the sides of the tunnel to stay upright. The air pressure was increasing all the time and there was a dull ache in my ears. Finally, when I thought I could bear it no longer, the ground leveled off and the tunnel widened again and the roof raised enough for us both to stand erect. Up ahead I could see Joe framed in an archway, his slim figure silhouetted in the yellow light. As soon as I reached him he put his hands over my eyes and guided me the last few feet. I knew when we stepped out of the tunnel because the atmosphere changed and was immediately fresher and cooler. The air was filled with high-pitched moans and wails, and low booms and rumbles that seemed to come and go. My own heartbeat filled my ears.

"Let me see," I whispered. "Let me see."

When Joe took his hands from my eyes I thought that I must be in a dream, that I had stepped from reality into a world that existed only in the imagination, for how else could this be? We stood like tiny insects in an endless hall with an arched roof that was maybe a hundred feet above us. Huge grooved pillars, thicker than ancient tree trunks, reached up to hold aloft the copper ceiling. Light came from shallow dishes of flaming oil that sat upon slender white marble plinths shot through with silver. The walls were dark, made not of rock but from some other material, the nature of which I couldn't determine; and the floor, surely a masterpiece of craftsmanship in itself, was decorated with tiny pieces of colored stone set into the earth.

I stared and stared. I think my mouth was wide open. As I looked around the magnificent room I felt as if I were seeing for the first time. I couldn't take it all in. My eyes flicked from side to side and with every blink I saw something else. The pillars, at first glance smooth, were actually intricately carved. Tiny vines snaked around and upward, and from between the leaves pairs of eyes peeped out. They were so life-like I almost expected them to blink. The floor, when examined closely, was actually a myriad of pictures, each a self-contained scene of rare beauty. Within these I saw monsters and angels, fairies and small folk, scaled creatures of the sea and the air, some hideous, some alluring, all spectacular.

My gaze was drawn in to the area at my feet, just in front of the entrance to the palatial hall. I stood on the edge of a pale mosaic and depicted within were three figures: One sat at a spinning wheel, a second held a measuring rod to the thread, and the third stood over her with a pair of gleaming shears. Their faces were haggard and they seemed to be in dispute.

"Who are these hags?" I asked, for they were truly ugly, and my words echoed around the walls. "Whoooo..."

"The three sister Fates," said Joe. "One spins the thread of life, the other measures it, and the third cuts it off with her shears. They argue constantly as to which sister is the most important of the three."

"The one with the shears?" I ventured.

Joe smiled. "Certainly she is considered the most menacing, but there is no answer, for without one the other two could not exist."

"The three Fates," I murmured. "Why should they be here?"

I stepped a little farther into the hall and realized with a shock that the black walls were not walls at all but the

unmarked spines of books crammed together on shelves that rose to the ceiling.

"Take one," said Joe.

So I ran over and pulled one, with difficulty, so tightly was it held by its neighbors, from the shelf. As soon as I had it in my hands I knew what it was. There were those same golden words on the cover:

Verba Volant Scripta Manent

"Oh, Lord," I gasped in complete amazement. "Is this a book of secrets?"

Joe nodded. I opened it carefully, for it was ancient and the leaves were crumbling into dust. I struggled to read the unfamiliar handwriting. Every page was filled top to bottom, each recording the precious stories of long-dead strangers. I closed it and stood back from the shelves. Joe was watching me closely. Could it be possible . . . ?

"Are they all books of secrets?"

"Yes. Every one. From every corner of the globe."

There must have been thousands. And within each book maybe fifty, a hundred secrets or more. I couldn't begin to understand what this meant. It was a few moments before I could speak again. "Who put them here?"

"I did," said Joe. "And others, of course. You are looking at centuries of confessions, Ludlow. My life's work and that of every other Secret Pawnbroker who ever existed."

"But I thought . . . you mean you're not the only one?"

Joe smiled. "I hope you are not disappointed," he said, "but there have been many of us, and there will be many more. For now the honor goes to me. But I cannot go on forever. Whatever you may think of me, I am still human. I, too, will return to dust one day."

Suddenly I grew nervous. My voice shook, my knees trembled, but I had to ask. "This is where you came, isn't it? When you went away."

Joe nodded. "It is something I have to do. I am responsible in part for this place. In a way this hall is my only home."

"So why have you brought me here?"

"Because it could be your home, too. Soon you will have to make a choice and then, if you do as I think you will do, you need to know all this. Come with me. There is someone I want you to meet."

I followed him, all the time turning my head left and right, up and down, to see more, to take it all in and keep it there. We walked between the pillars to the far end of the hall until we came to a large, dark wood desk with thick, ornately carved legs. It was stacked high with uneven piles of books. As we approached I heard the sound of a chair being pushed back. A man, hidden when seated, stood up and came forward with both arms extended. He wore a long velvet cloak, the color of which changed with every movement he made. His face was concealed beneath a hood, but he pushed it back and I looked into a pair of eyes I had thought never to see again.

"Mr. Jellico?" I managed to gasp just before he gave me a hug so tight I feared it would break my bones.

When he finally released me he patted me on the back and shook my hand over and over. "I'm so pleased to see you again, Ludlow," he said and there was a tear in his eye. "I had no idea what to think. I went away for a few days and when I came back you no longer visited. I thought the worst, of course, that you had met some terrible fate at the hands of your parents, but thank the heavens I was wrong. I could not have forgiven myself if anything had happened to you. You can't know how relieved I am to see it has all worked out in the end. Thanks in part, I'm sure, to my good friend here, Mr. Zabbidou."

I looked from one to the other, completely dumb-founded.

"You do know each other!" I exclaimed. "Joe, why didn't you say?" I couldn't stop shaking my head in disbelief. "But I thought there was only one Secret Pawnbroker."

Mr. Jellico laughed. "I am not a Secret Pawnbroker, nothing so exalted as that. No, I merely look after this place, in a fashion. They call me *Custos,* the Keeper, and this is my realm, *Atrium Arcanorum,* the Hall of Secrets."

"But your shop, in the City?"

"Hmm, yes," he mused, stroking his close-shaven chin. I noticed for once his nails were clean and polished. Even his skin glowed. "It is not easy being in two places at once. I'm sorry I couldn't always be there for you, but as you can see, I have other obligations."

While I reeled from one revelation after another, Joe and Mr. Jellico stepped aside and wandered away down the hall,

deep in conversation. I stood by the desk, dizzy with thinking and seeing. I turned in slow circles and tried to understand. A thousand "What ifs" ran through my head. What if I had never come to Pagus Parvus? What if I had chosen another carriage other than Jeremiah Ratchet's? What if Ma and Pa . . .

I made myself stop. I had to. I could have gone on forever.

It was all supposed to happen exactly as it did, I decided. It wasn't luck, it was meant to be.

Farther down the hall I saw Lembart take the Black Book of Secrets from Joe—the very book in which I had recorded the confessions of Pagus Parvus—and push it onto a shelf. When I looked again I could not tell you where it was. Joe beckoned me over.

"Well, what do you think?" he asked.

"I think this is the most incredible place I have ever seen," I whispered. "It . . . it almost scares me."

"That's what I thought when I first came here," said Mr. Jellico wistfully, "but that was a very long time ago."

"Lembart does a fine job keeping it in order," said Joe.

"I do my best," he said modestly and moved away, leaving us alone.

Joe turned to face me and now his expression was somber. "I have something to give you, Ludlow, if you want it," he said.

He reached under his cloak and handed me a black book, leather-bound with a red ribbon to mark the page, as yet blank inside, but on the cover in the bottom right-hand corner I saw the gold letters:

LF

"A Black Book? Of my own?" I was more than a little dazed.

"It's not an easy life," said Joe thoughtfully. "I think you know that, but it has its own rewards. If you do not wish to pursue it, now is the time to say so."

I couldn't speak, I could only stare with my mouth agape and my eyes fixed. What did all this mean?

"You wouldn't start right now, of course," he continued, "but one day in the future, and I will be here to help until then."

At last I managed to whisper, "Are you asking me to be a Secret Pawnbroker?"

"Not just 'a' but 'the' Secret Pawnbroker," he replied. "Have I chosen well, Ludlow? Do you think you can do it?"

Now I was finding it difficult to breathe. My tongue seemed to be stuck to the roof of my mouth. This was the most important moment in my life and my body was letting me down. I mustered all my energy and inhaled deeply and tried to calm the hammering against my ribs. "But ... but how can I?" I stammered. "I am not ready. What do I know of all this?"

"Enough." He smiled. "As for being ready, well, no one can tell what the three sisters will spin for us, but when the time is right, you'll know."

The three sisters, I thought, and slowly I began to understand why their picture was in the mosaic. This room was not just about secrets, it was about Fate. And Joe, this tall, wild-haired man, was an instrument of Destiny. He was the key to my future. His voice cut into my thoughts.

"As long as you believe you are able," he said, "then there is no reason for it not to happen."

"I believe I am able," I said at last with a little more strength.

Joe patted me on the shoulder. "That is all I wanted to hear," he said. "Now I will ask just one more thing of you."

We walked back to the desk, and I could sense between the two of us an invisible connection that wasn't there before. It gave me confidence and made me hold my head high and my back straight. He sat on one chair and I sat on another. From his satchel he took out the brandy and two glasses. He poured an equal measure into each and handed one to me.

"Drink."

I had to laugh. "Once I thought it might be poisoned," I confessed.

Joe looked at me with great amusement as I sipped from the glass. The burning liquid warmed the back of my throat and made me cough. Joe delved into the bag again and pulled out the ink and the quill. Automatically I reached for them, but he held them back.

"I will write," he said.

I was confused. "But who down here shall tell his secret to us?"

Still holding my book, he opened it on the first page.

"You will, Ludlow," he said. "The first story in your first Black Book will be your own." He looked straight into my eyes and my head filled with singing like angels', and because I thought I might suddenly float away, I wanted to tell him everything.

"It is time for you to give up your secret."

CHAPTER FORTY-TWO

EXTRACT FROM
THE BLACK BOOK OF SECRETS

Ludlow's Confession

My name is Ludlow Fitch and I have a shameful confession. I have carried it with me to Pagus Parvus and now to this deep underground library of secrets. Though I am fearful that you will think less of me, I wish to reveal it, for I can bear it no longer.

You know whence I come, you know what sort of life I led in the City. I am not proud of my past, but neither will I deny it. I did what I had to do to survive.

As the drink took hold of Ma and Pa I realized they would stop at very little in their pursuit of gin. I had never expected, however, that I should become a mere pawn in their selfish games. You can imagine my surprise then when I arrived back one evening to find them lying in wait. As soon as I stepped foot inside the attic room we called home, Ma brought down a chair leg on my skull and I crashed to

the floor. I was hardly alive as they dragged me down the stairs feetfirst, my head bouncing off every step, and when Pa flung me over his shoulder my skull throbbed even more. I don't know how long we walked; I lost track of the turns and corners, and I couldn't read the street names on account of my blurred vision. I knew we were still near the Foedus, her smell was strong in my nostrils, and perhaps I have her to thank for the fact that I remained awake as long as I did. Eventually, however, I succumbed to the terrible throbbing in my brain and I lost consciousness. When I opened my eyes, I was in the basement lair of Barton Gumbroot.

I still hate to think of what he tried to do to me. When I managed to escape onto the street I knew that my life was never going to be the same. The three of them chased me all the way to the river. I could see the Bridge up ahead and I thought if I could just get there, maybe I could find help in one of the taverns. But I was slowing, I couldn't see properly, and I was running out of breath. Then, to my utter horror, Pa caught me.

He grabbed me by the shoulder and spun me around. We both fell in the dirty slush and he jumped on me and clasped his hands around my throat. His strength was superhuman. His desire for money, for gin, made it so, but my desire to live was greater. I reached up and burst his arms apart and at the same time I kneed him in the stomach. He fell sideways and rolled on his back and then the tables were turned. I sat upon his chest and held his arms down over his head.

I looked into his cruel face and saw nothing to stop me. I closed my hands around his scrawny neck and squeezed until he was blue in the face and his eyeballs began to bulge. He writhed and kicked and tried to wrest my hands away. He was unable to speak, but his eyes were begging for mercy and I couldn't ignore their plea. Whatever else he might be, he was still my father. With a shout I let go and stood over him as he wheezed and coughed for breath.

"Why did you do it?" I gasped.

"I'm sorry, son," he croaked in a voice full of remorse and, like a fool, I thought he meant it. Ma and Barton were coming, I could hear them. I turned for no longer than a second and Pa was up again and had his arms tight as a noose around my neck. I elbowed him sharply to make him let go and then I shoved him hard as I could and he stumbled backward down the steep bank.

"No," he cried, "noooo," before landing on his back in the dark waters of the Foedus. I watched in disbelief as she sucked him under in a matter of seconds. I could see his white face, his mouth wide open and bubbling, just below the surface, and then he was gone. "Pa," I whispered and for a second I was rigid with shock. Then I came to my senses and stumbled onto the Bridge, where I saw Jeremiah's carriage just pulling away. With a supreme effort I managed to climb onto the back. As we gathered speed I could still see Ma. She was crying and screaming and Barton was shaking his fist at me and cursing.

I murdered my own father, Joe. Whatever he had done to

me, surely he didn't deserve that. I could have saved him. I could have gone down and dragged him out. I cannot forgive myself. I have dreamed of it every night and always I see his face looking up at me from the water. ✳

Joe put down his quill, laid a sheet of blotting paper between the pages, and closed the book. Tears streamed down Ludlow's cheeks.

"I'm just a filthy murderer," he sobbed. "Why would you want me with you?"

"Ludlow," said Joe softly, "it was never your intention to kill your father. If you were going to, you would have strangled him when you had the chance; instead you pitied him. You don't even know for sure that he's dead."

"I pushed him into the Foedus. No one gets out of that poisonous river alive."

"Maybe your ma and Barton pulled him out. Unless you go back, you'll never know. As for coming with me—I knew what you did. I've always known."

"You knew?" sniffed Ludlow. "How?"

"I don't think you've had a full night's sleep since you came to Pagus Parvus. I have heard you wandering around, I have seen you standing at the window, and I have listened to your nightmares. It wasn't difficult to work out what had happened. Believe me, your story is not the worst to go in a Black Book. But for now it doesn't matter. Let's concentrate on what's ahead, not what has gone before."

Ludlow sat quietly for a moment, and then he asked, "Do you have a secret, Joe?"

He smiled. "I do and it is in the very first Black Book I owned."

"And where is that book?"

"Hmm," he mused. "You'd have to ask Mr. Jellico about that. Though it is so long ago I doubt even he would know which shelf it is on!"

CHAPTER FORTY-THREE

Saluki was croaking loudly in her tank when we emerged, quite breathless, into the upper cave. Joe took her out and stroked her.

"Would you like to hold her?"

"Of course, but will she allow it?"

"Let's find out."

So I held out my quivering hand and Joe placed her gently on my palm. She was as light as a feather. I had never noticed before how delicate she was. Her back was mottled bright red and yellow and her long slender legs were the green of young shoots in the spring, while her underbelly was white with pale blue patches.

"She trusts you," he said simply. I laughed. I had never thought to hold such a beautiful creature in my life. He took her back and carefully placed her in the drawstring bag, and as he did so a piece of paper, the one Perigoe had

given him in the shop, fluttered from under his cloak and landed on the floor.

"What's this?" I asked.

"Read it," he said, and there was a strange look in his eye. I held it up to the dim light and if I had thought I could be surprised no more, then I was to be proved wrong. What I saw and read finally gave me the answer to the ultimate question.

"You clever devil," I said. "So that's how you did it. It wasn't Horatio's pie at all."

"I did it?" he queried and he looked at me with mild irritation. "Are you sure?"

"No, you're right," I exclaimed as I realized what he meant. "You didn't. It's like you said—Jeremiah brought it on himself." And then I realized something else, something far more terrible. "Oh, my Lord," I whispered. "Oh, my Lord."

"What is it, Ludlow?"

"How did you know Saluki trusted me?" I asked slowly. Joe shrugged. *"Fortuna favet fortibus."*

Fortune favors the brave.

My hands were shaking as I gave him back the paper. "Please don't take any more chances," I said. "At least not with me."

"Ah, Ludlow," he said, grinning, "I'm disappointed in you. What is life if not a gamble?"

CHAPTER FORTY-FOUR

Page torn from

Amphibians of the Southern Hemisphere

(Returned to Joe by Perigoe and then given to Ludlow in the cave)

Phyllobates tricolor

This colorful tree frog is a member of the Poison Dart Frog family (Dendrobatidae) and a native of the rain forests of South America. When the creature is under stress, from a predator, for example, it secretes a powerful poison through special pores on its back. This poison causes the skin to burn and blister and seeps into the bloodstream, bringing about rapid muscle and respiratory paralysis and leading inevitably to death. The native Indians of the area tip their arrows with the poison, hence the name Poison Dart. There is no known cure.

If you see one of these frogs, unless you two are well acquainted, it is advisable not to touch it.

CHAPTER FORTY-FIVE

FRAGMENT FROM
THE MEMOIRS OF LUDLOW FITCH

Outside it was impossible to see where we had emerged, even though we stood no more than a few feet away from the entrance. I shielded my eyes from the glare of the snow and looked at Joe. "Where to now?"

"I think we shall go to the City," he said. "There are many there who might benefit from our services."

"Do we have to?" I had no desire as yet to return to that despicable place.

"We are masters of our own destiny, Ludlow," said Joe. "We can go wherever we choose."

"Then let us leave the City for another day."

"Well, as you wish. Though you cannot avoid it forever." Joe turned in the other direction and began to walk.

"Wait," I said. "Just answer me one more question."

"Of course."

"What is so important about the wooden leg?"

"It'll come in useful one day, Ludlow."

"Is it something to do with your limp?"

"That's two questions."

"Please," I begged, but to no avail. Joe looked at me with the hint of a smile and a twinkle in his eye.

"A man must be allowed at least one secret, Ludlow, don't you think?"

CHAPTER FORTY SIX

Loose Ends

Horatio Cleaver never did tell anyone about the poisoned pie. In fact, when he went back to collect it he was both surprised and relieved to see that it had not been touched apart from a piece of crust that had been broken off and, by the looks of it, spat out onto the plate. He concluded then with a clear conscience that Dr. Mouldered's diagnosis had been right.

As for Jeremiah, he was buried in Pagus Parvus cemetery in a grave that was a full nine feet deep. Obadiah had dug with an enthusiasm that was hard to contain. You might have thought that the funeral would have been sparsely attended, but the opposite was true. It seemed that everyone for miles around came to see Ratchet's interment. And, of course, there was little weeping. Indeed, there was a general air of hilarity and jollity, and at the gathering afterward drink flowed freely and laughter rocked the walls of the Pickled Trout.

Jeremiah's grave was robbed only a matter of days after he was buried. The culprits were a little disconcerted by those extra three feet but dug them nonetheless. Upon payment to each of twenty shillings and sixpence Jeremiah ended up on a cold slab in an anatomy school in the City. When the inquisitive surgeon cut into his chest he found a most odd thing: Jeremiah's heart was so small it could fit into a jam pot.

After hearing of its size many eminent physicians and surgeons were curious as to how such a small organ could support the life of such a huge man. Some even wondered whether the ancients had been right all along to attribute the source of life to the liver. It is thought that Jeremiah's heart set back medical progress by at least a decade.

Jeremiah had no family and no will, so it was decided that Ratchet's tenants could claim ownership of their properties. Whether this was lawful or not was hardly a consideration. Sometimes there are advantages to being isolated from the outside world.

As for Polly, with Jeremiah dead and Joe and Ludlow gone, there was little left for her in Pagus Parvus. So a few days later she hitched a ride on Perigoe's trap and took off to the City, still believing it couldn't possibly be as bad as Ludlow made out.

A Note from F. E. Higgins

So there you have it, the tale of Joe Zabbidou and Ludlow Fitch. And let us not forget Saluki, without which frog Destiny could not be fulfilled.

Of course, this is not the end of the story. Where did Ludlow and Joe go? What small village or town or city was next to play host to the Secret Pawnbroker and his apprentice? These questions turned over and over in my head and I knew I had to find the answers. To this end I traveled to a country deep in the heart of the northern mountains until I reached the ancient village of Pachspass. I wonder, does that name excite you as much as it did me when I first came across it? If you say it carefully, it sounds very much like a place we have come to know well.

I rented a tiny attic room in a tall house with small leaded windows that overlook a steep high street. Each night I stand at the window and imagine that I can hear footsteps outside and that I can see a light at the top of the hill. A month has

passed and I am still here, snowbound. Its bright beauty is dazzling but also frustrating, for it prevents the remainder of my journey. As soon as I am able I will be on my way again, unraveling the mystery, and I will take only one thing: the wooden leg. It has not yet yielded its secret to me, but I know that I am closer to finding it now than ever before.

So wish me luck on my journey. I promise whatever I find I will bring it to you as quickly as I can. Until then, as Joe would have said, *Vincit qui patitur.*

F. E. Higgins
Pachspass

Addenda

ON THE BUSINESS OF BODYSNATCHING

Obadiah Strang was not alone in the grisly business of bodysnatching. In his day it was a common problem, to the extent that sometimes guards were paid to watch over the newly buried to ensure they remained underground. The human body was a source of great mystery to people. Although ordinary folk were too busy trying to survive to worry about its secretive workings, there were others, scientists and doctors, who were intrigued by the riddle of bone and flesh, and they knew the only way to find out more was to probe deeper.

There was only so much probing you could do with a live body. For a more thorough investigation you needed a dead one. There were laws: Only the bodies of executed criminals could be used in this sort of research, but it would seem that these were not in sufficient supply to meet demand. Thus emerged the business of bodysnatching. At one time it was possible to make a good living selling wickedly procured

corpses to doctors and surgeons, who would dissect them alone or under the curious gaze of anatomy students.

Jeremiah was shocked when his bodysnatching henchmen suggested that Ludlow would provide a fresh corpse, but they would not have been the only ones to think in such a way. Some years later two fellows, William Burke and William Hare, became infamous for just such a thing. They saw in bodysnatching a marvelous business opportunity, but not for them the hard labor of digging up a corpse. The wily pair decided to bypass the grave altogether and to murder people instead. Their first victim was a lodger in Hare's guesthouse. A case of bed but no breakfast, I suppose.

ON THE BUSINESS OF PIE MAKING

When the Sourdough brothers suggested that Horatio Cleaver put "man meat" in his pies they were joking, but it puts me in mind of another man who was deadly serious about his pies: Sweeney Todd, the infamous cutthroat of Fleet Street.

Sweeney lived in London some years after Horatio was butchering in Pagus Parvus. Abandoned by his parents at an early age, Sweeney was apprenticed to a Mr. John Crook, a cutler by trade who fashioned, among other things, razors. It is highly probable that Crook forced Sweeney to steal for him, not an uncommon arrangement between master and apprentice, so it is not surprising that Sweeney eventually ended up in Newgate Prison. Sweeney had developed a keen

instinct for survival by then and managed to persuade the prison barber, who shaved the prisoners in preparation for execution, to take him on as a soap boy, a perk of which job was the opportunity to pick pockets. When Sweeney emerged from prison he was well equipped with the skills to indulge in the evil inclinations that were to earn him a place in history.

He set up a barbershop in Fleet Street, an insalubrious place in those days, and yielded wholly to his thieving and murderous desires. When you sat in Sweeney's barber chair, by all accounts you sealed your own fate. Its design was such that at the touch of a lever the chair would drop into the basement below, to be replaced by an empty chair that came up. Whether Sweeney slit the throat of his customer and robbed him while he was in the chair, or carried out his crimes after the victim had dropped into the basement, is unclear. What *is* certain is that if you went into his shop there was no guarantee you would come out.

The problem with murder is that inevitably there is a body that requires disposal. As luck would have it, Sweeney's shop was built on the site of an old church complete with underground tunnels and catacombs. One of these tunnels led farther down the street to the basement of his accomplice, a certain Mrs. Lovett. Mrs. Lovett also had a shop on Fleet Street.

A pie shop.

It would appear that she and Sweeney came to a gruesome arrangement that suited them both rather well. Sweeney

solved that problem of the bodies; and as for Mrs. Lovett, well, suffice it to say it was reported at the time that her pies were much sought after on account of their quality and taste.

Perhaps if Sweeney had lived in Pagus Parvus he, too, would have been knocking at Joe's door. Certainly his confession would have put Horatio Cleaver's into the shade.

ON THE BUSINESS OF LIVE BURIAL

You may remember that in the coffin maker's confession, Septimus Stern recalled a case where a young man had been buried alive and discovered too late by his family. One wonders how often this did happen in Ludlow's day—after all, the doctors at the time lacked the medical knowledge or expertise that we have today to determine whether a person really is dead. A certain Count Karnice-Karnicki, alive and kicking in the 1800s, had such little faith in the medical profession that he designed a device to prevent his ever being buried alive. In a similar fashion to the coffin maker, he attached a tube to a coffin and ran it to the surface. If there was any movement after burial, breathing perhaps, the rising and falling of the chest, a flag would be activated above ground and a warning bell would ring. By no means was the count alone in his fear. Around the same time a Mr. Martin Sheets designed his own tomb to include a telephone so he could summon help were he to wake up buried but not yet dead.

ON THE BUSINESS OF TOOTH PULLING

Finally, we cannot finish without mention of Barton Gumbroot, the notorious tooth surgeon of Old Goat's Alley. Tooth rot was a serious problem in Ludlow's day and dentistry was a less sophisticated and more brutal affair than it is now. False teeth were available in a wide range of materials, including hippopotamus and walrus teeth, elephant ivory, and, of course, human teeth. There was also the option of a tooth transplant (as Ludlow found out). It had been discovered that when transplanting a tooth, the fresher the donor tooth the better chance it had of taking root in the receiving gum. Widespread poverty meant there were those willing to surrender teeth for money but, unfortunately for Ludlow, Barton Gumbroot didn't always wait for willing volunteers. Jeremiah had thought to sell corpses' teeth at one stage but, unsurprisingly, such teeth failed to take.

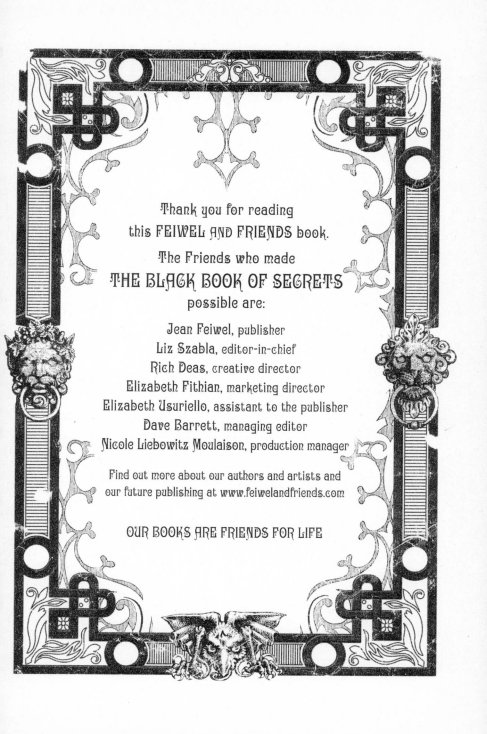

Thank you for reading
this FEIWEL AND FRIENDS book.

The Friends who made
THE BLACK BOOK OF SECRETS
possible are:

Jean Feiwel, publisher
Liz Szabla, editor-in-chief
Rich Deas, creative director
Elizabeth Fithian, marketing director
Elizabeth Usuriello, assistant to the publisher
Dave Barrett, managing editor
Nicole Liebowitz Moulaison, production manager

Find out more about our authors and artists and
our future publishing at www.feiwelandfriends.com

OUR BOOKS ARE FRIENDS FOR LIFE

INTRODUCTION TO QUANTUM THEORY

INTRODUCTION TO

QUANTUM THEORY

HENDRIK F. HAMEKA

PROFESSOR OF CHEMISTRY

UNIVERSITY OF PENNSYLVANIA

HARPER & ROW, PUBLISHERS

NEW YORK EVANSTON LONDON

ILLUSTRATION CREDITS

Fig. 5-7—J. L. Powell and B. Crasemann, "Quantum Mechanics," Addison-Wesley Publishing Company, Inc., Reading, Mass., 1961. Reprinted by permission.

Figs. 8-1, 8-2—Bethe, H. A. und E. E. Salpeter: Quantum Mechanics of one- and two-electron atoms. Berlin-Göttingen-Heidelberg: Springer 1957. Reprinted by permission.

PREFACE

Recently there has been a tendency to shift the teaching of quantum theory to earlier parts of the curriculum. I still remember when quantum mechanics was taught only to graduate students in physics, but now we find courses in the subject during the junior and senior years in physics curricula and the senior and first graduate years in chemistry curricula. The present work was designed to teach quantum theory to either physics or chemistry students at such stages.

The approach is semihistorical. First, it is shown how classical mechanics became inadequate for the explanation of certain experimental findings. This is followed by a discussion of the wave nature of free particles from which the Schrödinger equation is more or less derived. In the historical discussion I felt free to omit certain developments that had no pedagogic value, although they might be important from a historical point of view. I tried to keep the discussion closely linked to physical ideas. Whenever there was a conflict between physical understanding and mathematical rigor, I always decided in favor of the former.

An important consideration in teaching quantum theory at the elementary level is the inadequate mathematical background of the students. In order to understand quantum theory and to apply it, the student must have some knowledge of many branches of mathematics: differential and integral calculus, Fourier analysis, differential equations, vector analysis, complex numbers, matrices and determinants, linear equations and eigenvalue problems, and the theory of special functions. I expect students to be acquainted with elementary differential and integral calculus, but the other mathematical topics listed above are discussed here. Naturally the teacher is free to omit any of them from his discussion if he feels the students are already familiar with them.

I hope the present work can be used for a variety of courses, particularly junior and senior physics courses and senior and first-year graduate chemistry courses. Its length and contents make it suitable for a one-semester course designed as a formal introduction to quantum mechanics. It is also suitable for the first half of a two-semester course in quantum chemistry. In this case, it needs to be supplemented by another text for the second semester. This could be either one of the many books in which wave function determinations of molecules are discussed or my book "Advanced Quantum Chemistry," which contains the applications of quantum theory to electromagnetic and optical properties of molecules.

Because the only prerequisite of the present work is a freshman course in differential and integral calculus, it can be used to teach quantum mechanics to physics or chemistry students at the junior or even the sophomore level.

I wish to express my gratitude to Dr. D. D. Fitts and Dr. D. A. Hutchinson for their many suggestions for improving the manuscript and for numerous discussions on the presentation of quantum theory; to Miss Patricia M. Mullen and Mrs. Mary Hagen for their valuable assistance in typing the manuscript; to Miss Linda K. Landgrebe for her help in making the index; and to Dr. Norah V. Cohan for reading the proofs.

HENDRIK F. HAMEKA

CONTENTS

INTRODUCTION TO QUANTUM THEORY

PRELIMINARIES

1-1 INTRODUCTION

A beginning student usually has more difficulty in learning quantum mechanics than classical mechanics, although the complexities of the two theoretical approaches are not widely different. This difficulty is caused mostly by the fact that everyone is much more familiar with the concepts of classical mechanics than with those of quantum mechanics. For example, a little boy who throws a ball up in the air may be blissfully unaware of the equations of Newtonian mechanics and of Hamilton's equations, but he anticipates their solutions in directing his throw. He knows from experience that he has to use greater force if he wants to throw farther away. If, at a later age, he is informed of Newton's equation

$$\mathbf{F} = m\mathbf{a} \qquad\qquad (1\text{-}1)$$

the expression is in agreement with all his previous experience and therefore is quite acceptable to him. He may not know the acceleration **a** of a particle due to a force **F** is proportional to **F** and inversely proportional to the mass m of the particle, but when he becomes aware of this fundamental equation, he has no difficulty in accepting it.

It is not surprising that, when the structure of the atom was first discovered, scientists expected the particles within the atom to obey the same laws of classical mechanics as did all other systems that they had been able to observe. However, as more experimental information on atomic structure became available, it showed conclusively that classical mechanics was not valid within the atom. In order to explain all these experimental observations in a logical and consistent manner, it became necessary to derive a new mechanics.

Since the evidence of experiments and the authority of leading scientists support the necessity of using quantum mechanics for the description of atomic motion, the beginning student has no choice but to accept this situation. Yet, emotionally he has difficulty in believing a baseball game and an oxygen molecule are governed by different laws of motion, and he clings to the classical concept of electrons orbiting around the nucleus as long as he can. Therefore, before discussing quantum mechanics, we think it is useful to discuss briefly the arguments and experiments that led to the abandonment of classical mechanics for atomic motion. We also discuss some of the main features of classical mechanics so that we will be able to recognize where it differs and where it agrees with quantum mechanics.

1-2 CLASSICAL MECHANICS

The basic equation of classical Newtonian mechanics for a particle in three-dimensional space is Eq. (1-1). This expression contains two vector quantities $\mathbf{F}$ and $\mathbf{a}$ and a scalar quantity m. It may be useful to discuss a few vector properties briefly.

A vector $\mathbf{u}$ may be defined as a directed line segment. It is determined by its three components u_x, u_y, and u_z along the x, y, and z axes (see Fig. 1-1). Therefore, the boldface vector symbol $\mathbf{u}$ actually represents three quantities, which may be denoted by $\mathbf{u} = (u_x, u_y, u_z)$. The direction of $\mathbf{u}$ is determined by the three direction cosines, and its magnitude, which is the length of the line segment and which is denoted by $|\mathbf{u}|$ or u, is given by

length $\rightarrow$
$$u = (u_x{}^2 + u_y{}^2 + u_z{}^2)^{1/2} \tag{1-2}$$

The sum $\mathbf{w}$ of two vectors $\mathbf{u}$ and $\mathbf{v}$

$$\mathbf{w} = \mathbf{u} + \mathbf{v} \tag{1-3}$$

is defined such that each component of $\mathbf{w}$ is the sum of the two corresponding components of $\mathbf{u}$ and $\mathbf{v}$:

sum
$$\begin{aligned} w_x &= u_x + v_x \\ w_y &= u_y + v_y \\ w_z &= u_z + v_z \end{aligned} \tag{1-4}$$

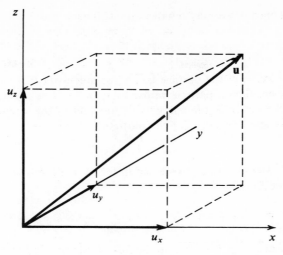

FIG. 1-1

When a vector **u** is a function of a parameter t, that is, each component of **u** is a function of t, then we may define the derivative of **u** with respect to t:

$$\frac{d\mathbf{u}(t)}{dt} = \lim_{\Delta t \to 0} \frac{\mathbf{u}(t + \Delta t) - \mathbf{u}(t)}{\Delta t} \tag{1-5}$$

This definition is again equivalent to the three equations

$$\left(\frac{d\mathbf{u}}{dt}\right)_x = \lim_{\Delta t \to 0} \frac{u_x(t + \Delta t) - u_x(t)}{\Delta t} \quad \text{etc.} \tag{1-6}$$

Let us now return to Eq. (1-1). In classical mechanics the motion of a particle is determined if we know its position **r** as a function of the time t, in other words, the function $\mathbf{r}(t)$. The velocity $\mathbf{v}(t)$ of the particle is defined as

$$\mathbf{v}(t) = \frac{d\mathbf{r}(t)}{dt} \tag{1-7}$$

and the acceleration $\mathbf{a}(t)$, which occurs in Eq. (1-1), is defined as

$$\mathbf{a}(t) = \frac{d\mathbf{v}(t)}{dt} = \frac{d^2\mathbf{r}(t)}{dt^2} \tag{1-8}$$

Closely related to the velocity **v** is the momentum **p** of the particle, which is defined as

$$\mathbf{p} = m\mathbf{v} \tag{1-9}$$

If we introduce **p**, we may rewrite Eq. (1-1) as

$$F = \frac{d\mathbf{p}}{dt} \qquad (1\text{-}10)$$

since the mass m of the particle is not dependent on t.

We now consider a particle whose total energy E is constant in time. In classical mechanics the energy E is the sum of the kinetic energy T and the potential energy V of the particle:

$$E = T + V \qquad (1\text{-}11)$$

The kinetic energy can be expressed in terms of either the velocity **v** or the momentum **p**:

$$T = \frac{1}{2}m(v_x{}^2 + v_y{}^2 + v_z{}^2) = \frac{1}{2m}(p_x{}^2 + p_y{}^2 + p_z{}^2) \qquad (1\text{-}12)$$

The potential energy is related to the force **F** experienced by the particle, since the components of **F** are the derivatives of V with respect to the position coordinates x, y, z:

$$F_x(x,y,z) = -\frac{\partial}{\partial x} V(x,y,z)$$

$$F_y(x,y,z) = -\frac{\partial}{\partial y} V(x,y,z) \qquad (1\text{-}13)$$

$$F_z(x,y,z) = -\frac{\partial}{\partial z} V(x,y,z)$$

Equations (1-13) may be combined into a vector equation

$$\mathbf{F} = -\nabla V(x,y,z) \qquad (1\text{-}14)$$

where the three operators $(\partial/\partial x)$, $(\partial/\partial y)$, and $(\partial/\partial z)$ are symbolically represented by the vector symbol ∇. Each component of **F** is a function of the position coordinates x, y, and z. We write **F**, therefore, as $\mathbf{F}(x,y,z)$, and we call it a *vector field*. The quantity ∇V is called the *gradient* of the function V, so that Eq. (1-14) states that **F** is the negative of the gradient of V. A vector field that can be expressed as the gradient of a function of position is called an *irrotational field*; it should be noted that not all vector fields are irrotational.

Let us now return to Eqs. (1-9) and (1-10). Substitution of Eq. (1-14) into Eq. (1-10) gives the set of equations

$$\frac{\partial p_x}{\partial t} = -\frac{\partial V}{\partial x} \qquad \frac{\partial p_y}{\partial t} = -\frac{\partial V}{\partial y} \qquad \frac{\partial p_z}{\partial t} = -\frac{\partial V}{\partial z} \qquad (1\text{-}15)$$

It follows from Eq. (1-12) that the definition (1-9) may be rewritten as

$$\frac{\partial x}{\partial t} = \frac{\partial T}{\partial p_x} \qquad \frac{\partial y}{\partial t} = \frac{\partial T}{\partial p_y} \qquad \frac{\partial z}{\partial t} = \frac{\partial T}{\partial p_z} \tag{1-16}$$

We next introduce the function

$$H(x,y,z;\, p_x,p_y,p_z) = T(p_x,p_y,p_z) + V(x,y,z) \tag{1-17}$$

which is called the *Hamiltonian function* and which is the energy of the particle written as a function of the three position coordinates x, y, and z and of the momentum components p_x, p_y, and p_z. Since T does not depend on x, y, and z, we have

$$\frac{\partial H}{\partial x} = \frac{\partial V}{\partial x} \qquad \frac{\partial H}{\partial y} = \frac{\partial V}{\partial y} \qquad \frac{\partial H}{\partial z} = \frac{\partial V}{\partial z} \tag{1-18}$$

and since V does not depend on **p**, we have

$$\frac{\partial H}{\partial p_x} = \frac{\partial T}{\partial p_x} \qquad \frac{\partial H}{\partial p_y} = \frac{\partial T}{\partial p_y} \qquad \frac{\partial H}{\partial p_z} = \frac{\partial T}{\partial p_z} \tag{1-19}$$

Hence, Eqs. (1-15) and (1-16) can be reformulated as

$$\frac{\partial x}{\partial t} = \frac{\partial H}{\partial p_x} \qquad \frac{\partial y}{\partial t} = \frac{\partial H}{\partial p_y} \qquad \frac{\partial z}{\partial t} = \frac{\partial H}{\partial p_z}$$

$$\frac{\partial p_x}{\partial t} = -\frac{\partial H}{\partial x} \qquad \frac{\partial p_y}{\partial t} = -\frac{\partial H}{\partial y} \qquad \frac{\partial p_z}{\partial t} = -\frac{\partial H}{\partial z} \tag{1-20}$$

In this way the motion of the particle may be derived mathematically from a single function, the Hamiltonian function H. We note that in Eq. (1-20) the coordinates and momenta have been "paired off": the first pair is p_x and x, the second is p_y and y, and the third is p_z and z. We say that the momentum p_x is conjugate to the coordinate x, etc.

Equations (1-20) are called *Hamilton's equations of motion*. Our derivation is valid only for the set of Cartesian coordinates (x,y,z) in the situation above, but there exists a more comprehensive derivation of Hamilton's equations[1] from which it may be concluded they have a much greater validity than follows from our discussion. Rather than repeat this derivation here, we simply present the results.

[1] See, for example, L. D. Landau and E. M. Lifshitz, "Mechanics," Addison-Wesley Publishing Company, Inc., Reading, Mass., 1960.

In place of the Cartesian coordinates (x,y,z), we introduce a set of new coordinates (q_1,q_2,q_3) that are determined in a certain way by (x,y,z):

$$q_1 = q_1(x,y,z)$$
$$q_2 = q_2(x,y,z) \qquad (1\text{-}21)$$
$$q_3 = q_3(x,y,z)$$

For example, we may wish to use polar, elliptical, or cylindrical coordinates, instead of the Cartesian coordinates (x,y,z). The transformation of Eq. (1-21) also leads to a new set of momenta (p_1,p_2,p_3), so that p_1 is conjugate to q_1, p_2 is conjugate to q_2, etc. It is now possible to construct a Hamiltonian

$$H = H(q_1,q_2,q_3;\, p_1,p_2,p_3) \qquad (1\text{-}22)$$

so that q_i and p_i are determined by the equations

$$\boxed{\frac{\partial q_i}{\partial t} = \frac{\partial H}{\partial p_i} \qquad \frac{\partial p_i}{\partial t} = -\frac{\partial H}{\partial q_i} \qquad i = 1, 2, 3} \qquad (1\text{-}23)$$

This description is also applicable to systems that are determined by N coordinates $(q_1,q_2, \ldots ,q_N)$, with N either smaller or larger than 3. Then, the Hamiltonian is

$$H = H(q_1,q_2, \ldots ,q_N;\, p_1,p_2, \ldots ,p_N) \qquad (1\text{-}24)$$

In the next section we will discuss an example of the solution of Hamilton's equations. Obviously, this solution consists of expressions for $q_i(t)$ and $p_i(t)$ as functions of time. However, each of the Eqs. (1-23) contributes an arbitrary integration constant, so that the solution for an N-coordinate system contains $2N$ undetermined parameters. This result agrees with our experience that we cannot know the exact behavior of a particle in three-dimensional space unless we know its position $\mathbf{r}$ and momentum $\mathbf{p}$ at a certain time t_0. The six quantities $x(t_0)$, $y(t_0)$, $z(t_0)$, $p_x(t_0)$, $p_y(t_0)$, and $p_z(t_0)$ may then be used to determine the six unknown integration constants.

Let us consider, finally, the time dependence of the Hamiltonian. Since the q_i and p_i depend on the time t, the Hamiltonian implicitly depends on t; in addition, it is also possible that H contains t explicitly. We write this as

$$H = H(q_1,q_2, \ldots ,q_N;\, p_1,p_2, \ldots ,p_N;\, t) \qquad (1\text{-}25)$$

The total time derivative of the Hamiltonian is

$$\boxed{\frac{dH}{dt} = \frac{\partial H}{\partial t} + \sum_i \left(\frac{\partial H}{\partial q_i} \frac{\partial q_i}{\partial t} + \frac{\partial H}{\partial p_i} \frac{\partial p_i}{\partial t} \right)} \qquad (1\text{-}26)$$

However, it follows from Eq. (1-23) that the sum is zero, so that

$$\frac{dH}{dt} = \frac{\partial H}{\partial t} \qquad (1\text{-}27)$$

It follows, therefore, that H is time-independent if it does not explicitly depend on t. This result is, of course, required by the law of conservation of energy.

1-3 THE CLASSICAL HARMONIC OSCILLATOR

The harmonic oscillator played a very important role in the theoretical developments at the beginning of this century, since it was an essential part of many of the theories that led to quantum mechanics. It was known at that time that an atom consisted of a nucleus and a certain number of electrons that moved about in the vicinity of the nucleus. Since the exact nature of the electronic motion was not known, theoreticians wished to construct a simple model that would reproduce the essential features of the electronic motion as they were known at that time. The harmonic oscillator fitted these requirements so well that it was often used as a starting point for theories involving electronic motion in atoms, molecules, or crystals.

In one dimension a harmonic oscillator is a particle of mass m, oscillating back and forth around an origin O. At any time it is subject to a force F which tends to move it back toward the origin and which is proportional to the displacement x from the origin:

$$F = -kx \qquad (1\text{-}28)$$

Since

$$F = -\frac{\partial V}{\partial x} \qquad (1\text{-}29)$$

$\rightarrow$ Pot E $Kx = \frac{\partial U}{\partial x}$

it is easily found that the potential energy of the particle is

$$V = \tfrac{1}{2}kx^2 \qquad (1\text{-}30)$$

if we require that $V = 0$ at the point $x = 0$. The Hamiltonian of the one-dimensional harmonic oscillator is, therefore,

$$H(x,p) = \frac{p^2}{2m} + \frac{1}{2}kx^2 \qquad (1\text{-}31)$$

pot

It follows from Hamilton's equations of motion (1-23) that x and p are determined by the equations

$$\frac{\partial x}{\partial t} = \frac{p}{m} \qquad \frac{\partial p}{\partial t} = -kx \qquad (1\text{-}32)$$

$\frac{1}{2}\mu v^2$ $m^2 v^2$

If we differentiate the first Eq. (1-32) with respect to t and eliminate $\partial p/\partial t$ with the second Eq. (1-32), we obtain

$$\frac{\partial^2 x}{\partial t^2} = -\frac{k}{m}x \tag{1-33}$$

It is convenient to introduce the angular frequency

$$\omega = \left(\frac{k}{m}\right)^{1/2} \tag{1-34}$$

so that Eq. (1-33) is written as

$$\ddot{x} + \omega^2 x = 0 \tag{1-35}$$

It is easily verified that the solutions of this differential equation are

$$x = e^{\pm i\omega t} \tag{1-36}$$

so that the general solution for the harmonic oscillator is

$$x(t) = \lambda e^{i\omega t} + \mu e^{-i\omega t} \tag{1-37}$$

The solution contains two undetermined parameters. If we impose the condition that $x(O) = 0$, then we can eliminate one of the parameters, and we obtain the solution

$$x(t) = A \sin \omega t \tag{1-38}$$

The motion of the oscillator is determined by two quantities: ω, which is called the *angular frequency*, and A, which is the *amplitude* of the oscillator. The frequency v of the oscillations, that is, the number of complete cycles of motion that are covered per unit time, is given by

$$\omega = 2\pi v \tag{1-39}$$

It follows from the first Eq. (1-32) that

$$p(t) = Am\omega \cos \omega t \tag{1-40}$$

If this result, together with Eq. (1-38), is substituted into Eq. (1-31), it is found that the Hamiltonian, and consequently the energy, of the system is

$$E = H(x,p) = \tfrac{1}{2}mA^2\omega^2 \tag{1-41}$$

It is obvious that for fixed m and A the energy E is a continuous function of ω that can assume all positive values.

The three-dimensional harmonic oscillator is treated in a manner similar to the one-dimensional case. The Hamiltonian is now

$$H(\mathbf{r},\mathbf{p}) = \frac{1}{2m}(p_x{}^2 + p_y{}^2 + p_z{}^2) + \frac{1}{2}(k_x x^2 + k_y y^2 + k_z z^2) \tag{1-42}$$

Hamilton's equations of motion are

$$\frac{\partial x}{\partial t} = \frac{p_x}{m} \qquad \frac{\partial p_x}{\partial t} = -k_x x$$

$$\frac{\partial y}{\partial t} = \frac{p_y}{m} \qquad \frac{\partial p_y}{\partial t} = -k_y y \qquad (1\text{-}43)$$

$$\frac{\partial z}{\partial t} = \frac{p_z}{m} \qquad \frac{\partial p_z}{\partial t} = -k_z z$$

Each pair of Eqs. (1-43) is identical to Eq. (1-32), and the solutions are easily shown to be

$$x(t) = \lambda_x e^{i\omega_x t} + \mu_x e^{-i\omega_x t}$$

$$y(t) = \lambda_y e^{i\omega_y t} + \mu_y e^{-i\omega_y t} \qquad (1\text{-}44)$$

$$z(t) = \lambda_z e^{i\omega_z t} + \mu_z e^{-i\omega_z t}$$

with
$$\omega_\alpha = \left(\frac{k_\alpha}{m}\right)^{1/2} \qquad \alpha = x, y, z \qquad (1\text{-}45)$$

If, again, we impose the conditions that at $t = 0$ the particle is at the origin, we have

$$x(t) = A_x \sin \omega_x t$$

$$y(t) = A_y \sin \omega_y t \qquad (1\text{-}46)$$

$$z(t) = A_z \sin \omega_z t$$

and the energy of the particle is

$$E = \tfrac{1}{2}m(A_x{}^2\omega_x{}^2 + A_y{}^2\omega_y{}^2 + A_z{}^2\omega_z{}^2) \qquad (1\text{-}47)$$

1-4 THE QUANTIZATION OF THE HARMONIC OSCILLATOR

At the beginning of this century classical Newtonian mechanics was still the basis of every theoretical description of physical and chemical phenomena, as it had been for almost two hundred years. It was generally believed that all fundamental laws of nature were well established and well understood and that it would be only a matter of time before every natural phenomena could be described mathematically in terms of the classical motion of electrons. This optimistic attitude was supported by the work of the great physicist H. A. Lorentz, who set out to explain all electrodynamic and optical phenomena in terms of electronic motion, described, of course, in terms of classical mechanics. The problems that were foremost in the minds of theoreticians at that time were concerned with the nature and properties of the world aether. It was hard for them to foresee that the next few decades would witness the abandonment of classical mechanics for the description of atoms and molecules and a complete revolution of theoretical physics. First, it was shown from the considerations of Lorentz, Poincaré, Einstein, and others that high-speed phenomena could not be adequately described in terms of classical mechanics. Their description was based on entirely new mechanical principles contained in the theory of relativity. Different lines of thought, initiated by Planck, Bohr, Heisenberg, Schrödinger, Dirac, and others, led to the realization that the Newtonian laws of motion also fail when they are applied to atomic phenomena. Here, it was necessary to introduce quantum mechanics.

The first development in the direction of quantum mechanics was due to some inconsistencies in the description of blackbody radiation. Blackbody radiation is an everyday phenomenon that has been observed by anyone who has ever watched an electric heater or kitchen stove. If we watch carefully what happens after an electric heater has been turned on, we first notice some heat radiation. A little later, when the heating element becomes warmer, we notice a red glow that slowly changes to orange, yellow, and white as the temperature of the electric coil increases. This change in color is caused by the change in spectral intensity distribution of the radiation that is produced by the heating coil. Let us imagine that we make an exact measurement of this intensity distribution, the intensity of the emitted light as a function of its wavelength at different temperatures. The result at a given temperature T_1 will look like one of the curves in Fig. 1-2. At a higher temperature T_2 we might measure the

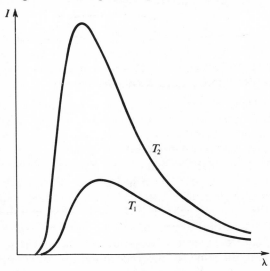

FIG. 1-2

second curve of Fig. 1-2. Our experiments are not very accurate, since we actually measure the sum of the radiation and the light that is reflected by the coil. However, it is relatively easy to eliminate this side effect. For example, we may take a hollow ball of metal with a little hole in it suspended in a heat bath. If the hole is small enough, the light coming out of it is due solely to radiation, since all the reflected light is eliminated in this setup. Many measurements on such systems were performed around the year 1900, and some surprising results emerged.

First of all, it was found that the intensity and intensity distribution of the electromagnetic radiation did not depend on the material of the hollow ball if all the reflected light was eliminated; we may therefore speak of blackbody radiation in a general sense. Apparently the energy density per unit volume of the radiation within the cavity is independent of the wall material, and we should be able to describe it theoretically without considering the properties of the wall at all. It is possible to express this energy density per unit volume of the radiation with frequencies between v and $v + dv$ as $\rho(v,T)\,dv$, and the problem is, first, to derive from the experimental results analytical expressions for the function $\rho(v,T)$ and, second, to give a theoretical justification for these expressions. We may recall that the relation between the frequency v and the wavelength λ of the radiation is

$$c = \lambda v \qquad\qquad V = \text{frequency}$$

(1-48)

if c is the velocity of light.

The first to derive an expression for the function $\rho(v,T)$ was Wien,[1] whose considerations led to

$$\rho(v,T) = a\left(\frac{8\pi v^3}{c^3}\right)\exp\left(\frac{-bv}{T}\right)$$

(1-49)

This result agreed reasonably well with the experimental data at high frequencies, but at low frequencies there were large differences between the experimental curves and Eq. (1-49). A few years later a different expression was derived by Lord Rayleigh,[2] namely,

$$\rho(v,T) = \frac{8\pi v^2}{c^3}\,kT$$

(1-50)

A comparison with experiments showed that this formula was asymptotically correct for low frequencies, but obviously not for high frequencies, since Eq. (1-50) led to infinitively large $\rho(v,T)$ when v tended to infinity. It seemed, therefore, that there were two different expressions for $\rho(v,T)$, Eq. (1-49) being valid at high frequencies and Eq. (1-50) at low frequencies. Naturally there were several attempts to construct an

[1] W. Wien, *Ann. d. Phys.*, **58**: 662 (1896); *Phil. Mag.*, **43**: 214 (1897).
[2] Lord Rayleigh, *Phil. Mag.*, **49**: 539 (1900); *Nature*, **72**: 54, 243 (1905). See also J. H. Jeans, *Phil. Mag.*, **10**: 91 (1905).

expression which would reduce to Eq. (1-50) for small v and which would resemble Eq. (1-49) for large v, but none of these attempts was very successful either from a practical or from a theoretical point of view until Planck directed his attention to this problem.

Planck[1] proposed to derive the theory of blackbody radiation from a model in which the walls of the hollow chamber were covered by an assembly of harmonic oscillators that were in thermal equilibrium with standing electromagnetic radiation waves inside the chamber. In defense of this model, Planck argued that the structure of the chamber walls did not seem to affect the blackbody radiation at all, so that it was permissible to choose a model that made the theory as simple as possible.

The first step of Planck's calculations was concerned with the relation between the energy density $\rho(v,T)$ of the radiation and the average energy U of an oscillator. It followed in a straightforward way from classical electromagnetic theory that this relation was

$$\rho(v,T) = \frac{8\pi v^2}{c^3} U \tag{1-51}$$

Since Planck was an expert on thermodynamics, it was natural for him to study the thermodynamics of the harmonic oscillators and to correlate the results thus obtained with the radiation density by way of Eq. (1-51). Therefore, Planck argued that it was necessary to consider not only the average energy U of an oscillator but also its entropy S. According to thermodynamics these two quantities are related by

$$\frac{dS}{dU} = \frac{1}{T} \tag{1-52}$$

since the volume of the cavity remains constant. Following Planck, we investigate which thermodynamic expressions we may derive from Wien's radiation law (1-49) and from the Rayleigh-Jeans formula (1-50) and how we may link these thermodynamic results together.

It follows from Wien's equation (1-49) and from Eq. (1-51) that

$$U = av \exp\left(\frac{-bv}{T}\right) \tag{1-53}$$

By reversing this formula, we express T in terms of U:

$$\frac{1}{T} = -\frac{1}{bv} \ln \frac{U}{av} \tag{1-54}$$

---

[1] M. K. E. L. Planck, *Verh. d. deutsch. phys. Ges.*, **2**: 202, 929 (1900); *Ann. d. Physik*, **4**: 277 (1901).

and, by substituting this expression into Eq. (1-52), we find

$$\frac{dS}{dU} = -\frac{1}{bv} \ln \frac{U}{av} \tag{1-55}$$

Differentiation with respect to U leads to

$$\frac{d^2S}{dU^2} \propto -\frac{1}{U} = -\frac{a}{b}\frac{1}{U} \tag{1-56}$$

From the Rayleigh-Jeans expression (1-50) we see that $U = kT$, so that

$$\frac{d^2S}{dU^2} \propto -\frac{1}{U^2} = -\frac{k}{U^2} \tag{1-57}$$

We have arrived at two different expressions for the second derivative of the entropy. The first one, Eq. (1-56), is from Wien's equation (1-53) and is valid for large values of v. The second expression (1-57) is from Rayleigh's equation $U = kT$ and is valid for small frequencies. Planck proposed to replace these two asymptotic results (1-56) and (1-57) by the general relation

$$\frac{d^2S}{dU^2} = -\frac{A}{U(\beta + U)} \tag{1-58}$$

For large frequencies we should use Wien's equation (1-53), and we find then that U becomes very small for large v, so that Eq. (1-58) reduces to Eq. (1-56). It appears that for small frequencies β becomes much smaller than U, so that Eq. (1-58) tends asymptotically to Eq. (1-57).

By integrating Eq. (1-58) with respect to U, Planck obtained

$$\frac{dS}{dU} = \frac{1}{T} = \frac{1}{\alpha} \log \frac{\beta + U}{U} \tag{1-59}$$

with α and β undertermined constants, or

$$U = \frac{\beta}{e^{(\alpha/T)} - 1} \tag{1-60}$$

Equation (1-60) describes the temperature dependence of U.

Planck combined Eq. (1-60) with a result which had been obtained previously by Wien[1] and which had been shown to have general validity, namely, that $\rho(v,T)$ must be of the form

$$\rho(v,T) \propto v^3 f\left(\frac{v}{T}\right) \tag{1-61}$$

[1] W. Wien, *Ann. d. Physik*, **52**: 132 (1894).

Together with Eq. (1-60) this relation led to the expressions

$$\rho(v,T) = \frac{8\pi v^3}{c^3} \frac{c_1}{\exp(c_2 v/T) - 1} \tag{1-62}$$

and
$$U = \frac{c_1 v}{\exp(c_2 v/T) - 1} \tag{1-63}$$

where c_1 and c_2 were constants. Equation (1-62) is Planck's radiation law, which found ready acceptance because it showed such an excellent agreement with the experiments.

It should be realized that so far we have not explained the blackbody radiation from first principles but have argued the other way around. We have shown that the experimental data on blackbody radiation are most accurately described analytically if we assume the validity of Eq. (1-63). The difficulty is that it is downright impossible to reconcile Eq. (1-63) with the principles of classical mechanics.

Let us set out to determine from classical theory the average energy of a one-dimensional harmonic oscillator that is in thermal equilibrium with a large number of identical oscillators. It follows from classical statistical mechanics that this average energy $\bar{\varepsilon}(T)$ is determined from

$$\bar{\varepsilon}(T) = \frac{\iint E(x,p) \exp[-E(x,p)/kT] \, dx \, dp}{\iint \exp[-E(x,p)/kT] \, dx \, dp} \tag{1-64}$$

where $E(x,p)$ is the energy of the harmonic oscillator as a function of x and p. We have

$$E(x,p) = H(x,p) = \frac{p^2}{2m} + \frac{1}{2}kx^2 \tag{1-65}$$

according to Eq. (1-31). Substitution of Eq. (1-65) into Eq. (1-64) gives

$$\bar{\varepsilon}(T) = \frac{\int (p^2/2m) \exp(-p^2/2mkT) \, dp}{\int \exp(-p^2/2mkT) \, dp} + \frac{\int (kx^2/2) \exp(-kx^2/2kT) \, dx}{\int \exp(-kx^2/2kT) \, dx} \tag{1-66}$$

This expression contains the two integrals

$$I = \int_0^\infty e^{-ax^2} \, dx \tag{1-67}$$

and
$$J = \int_0^\infty x^2 e^{-ax^2} \, dx \tag{1-68}$$

which occur frequently in statistical mechanics and in the kinetic theory of gases. Since their evaluation is not trivial, we discuss it briefly. The first integral I remains unchanged if we give the variable a different name,

$$I = \int_0^\infty e^{-ay^2}\, dy \tag{1-69}$$

so that we may write

$$I^2 = \int_0^\infty e^{-ax^2}\, dx \int_0^\infty e^{-ay^2}\, dy = \int_0^\infty \int_0^\infty e^{-a(x^2+y^2)}\, dx\, dy \tag{1-70}$$

This integral is evaluated by introducing the polar coordinates

$$\begin{aligned} x &= r \cos \phi \\ y &= r \sin \phi \end{aligned} \tag{1-71}$$

Figure 1-3 shows how two-dimensional space may be divided into volume elements according to Fig. 1-3b instead of Fig. 1-3a. The introduction of polar coordinates leads to

$$I^2 = \int_0^{\pi/2} d\phi \int_0^\infty re^{-ar^2}\, dr = \frac{\pi}{4a} \tag{1-72}$$

or

$$I = \frac{1}{2}\left(\frac{\pi}{a}\right)^{1/2} \tag{1-73}$$

Since

$$J = -\frac{\partial I}{\partial a} \tag{1-74}$$

it follows easily that

$$J = \frac{1}{4}\left(\frac{\pi}{a^3}\right)^{1/2} \tag{1-75}$$

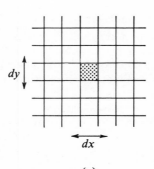

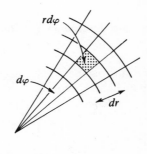

(a)   (b)

FIG. 1-3

Substitution of Eqs. (1-73) and (1-74) into Eq. (1-66) leads to

$$\bar{\varepsilon}(T) = kT \tag{1-76}$$

which is in agreement with the well-known energy equipartition rule that allows for an energy of $\frac{1}{2}kT$ per degree of freedom. The constant k is Boltzmann's constant, which is equal to the gas constant R divided by Avogadro's number N. It is easily shown that for an assembly of three-dimensional harmonic oscillators in thermal equilibrium the average energy of one oscillator is

$$\bar{\varepsilon}(T) = 3kT \tag{1-77}$$

since there are now six degrees of freedom for the motion.

The discrepancy between classical theory and experimental observation is now clear; although the experiments are described by Planck's equation (1-63), the classical theory leads to Eq. (1-76) or (1-77), which are clearly different from Planck's expression.

Planck resolved this discrepancy by making the far-reaching assumption that in the interaction between the radiation field and the harmonic oscillators there was no continuous transfer of energy as in the classical theory, but that the absorption or emission of radiation by an oscillator took place in jumps. This assumption is now regarded as the first step in the direction of quantum mechanics. Planck was able to show how this assumption led to his expression (1-62) for the radiation density. This derivation was later put into simpler form by Lorentz,[1] whose arguments we discuss here.

It follows from classical mechanics that the possible values of the energy $\varepsilon(\omega)$ and their dependence on ω are given by Eq. (1-64). According to Planck's assumption we should instead allow only for a discrete set of energy values

$$\varepsilon(\omega) = \frac{nh\omega}{2\pi} \qquad n = 0, 1, 2, 3, 4, \ldots \tag{1-78}$$

or if we use the frequency v instead of the angular frequency ω,

$$\varepsilon(v) = nhv \tag{1-79}$$

It is not surprising that the proportionality constant h is now universally known as Planck's constant. If we substitute Planck's assumption (1-79) into Eq. (1-65) for the average energy, we obtain

$$\bar{\varepsilon}(T) = \frac{\sum\limits_{0}^{\infty} nhv e^{-nhv/kT}}{\sum\limits_{0}^{\infty} e^{-nhv/kT}} \tag{1-80}$$

[1] H. A. Lorentz, *Phys. Zeits.*, **11**: 1234 (1910).

The denominator S of Eq. (1-80) is a geometrical series, and the sum is

$$S = \sum_0^\infty e^{-nh\nu/kT} = (1 - e^{-h\nu/kT})^{-1} \tag{1-81}$$

since $e^{-h\nu/kT}$ is always smaller than unity. The numerator S' of Eq. (1-80) may be determined from

$$S' = -kT\nu \frac{\partial S}{\partial \nu} = \frac{h\nu e^{-h\nu/kT}}{(1 - e^{-h\nu/kT})^2} \tag{1-82}$$

Hence, we have

$$U = \bar{\varepsilon}(T) = \frac{h\nu e^{-h\nu/kT}}{1 - e^{-h\nu/kT}} = \frac{h\nu}{e^{h\nu/kT} - 1} \tag{1-83}$$

Substitution into Eq. (1-51) leads to Planck's radiation law,

$$\rho(\nu, T) = \frac{8\pi h\nu^3}{c^3} \frac{1}{e^{h\nu/kT} - 1} \tag{1-84}$$

One of the great successes of Planck's theory was the determination of the various constants h, k, and N by comparing Eq. (1-84) with the experimental curves for $\rho(\nu, T)$. Although Planck's proposal that the energy of the harmonic oscillator be allowed to take only the discrete values $nh\nu$ was not compatible with classical mechanics, it was so successful in explaining and predicting experimental facts that it was readily accepted by many scientists.

In 1905 Einstein carried Planck's quantization concept a step further by extending it from the harmonic oscillators and their interaction with radiation to the electromagnetic radiation itself.[1] Einstein studied a cavity filled with monochromatic radiation of frequency ν and of relatively small density. His considerations led to the conclusion that the radiation was quantized into parcels with energy $h\nu$. Consequently, the smallest amount of energy that could be transferred between the radiation and another system would be $h\nu$. Much later (in 1926) G. N. Lewis proposed the name *photon* for one such energy parcel, and this name is still used today.

Einstein applied his considerations to the explanation of the photo-electric effect. Let us consider a metallic surface that is irradiated with monochromatic light of frequency ν. The difference in potential energy for an electron just inside and just outside the metal is called the *work function* and is usually denoted by ϕ_0. Since the smallest energy parcel in the radiation is $h\nu$, the radiation can eject electrons only if

$$h\nu > \phi_0 \tag{1-85}$$

[1] A. Einstein, *Ann. d. Physik*, **17**: 132 (1905); **20**: 199 (1906).

and the kinetic energy T of the ejected electron is

$$T = h\nu - \phi_0 \qquad (1\text{-}86)$$

In this way all aspects of photoelectricity were explained in a very simple and straightforward manner.

Shortly thereafter Einstein[1] used the concept of energy quantization to construct a new theory for the specific heats of solids. According to classical theory every solid should have a specific heat equal to $3R$ per mole at all temperatures. It is true that at high temperatures this result agreed with the experimental data, but at lower temperatures the specific heat of most substances was much less than $3R$, and there was every indication that it tended to zero for $T \to 0$. By applying Planck's quantization concept to the harmonic oscillations within the solid, Einstein derived an expression for the specific heat of a solid that agreed in principle with experiments at all temperatures. A later, more precise theory by Debye[2] led to a theoretical expression for the specific heats of solids that agreed so well with the experiments that even now it is still used to represent some of the experimental results.

We have seen that there was a solid experimental basis to support the concept of energy quantization, in particular, for the harmonic oscillator. However, this concept could in no way be justified from classical mechanics, and therefore it shed some doubt on the general validity of classical Newtonian mechanics. Meanwhile there were developments in different areas of research, namely, the study of atomic structure, which showed up more inconsistencies in the principles of classical mechanics and which led to additional introductions of quantum concepts. We discuss these developments in the following sections.

1-5 PROBLEMS IN THE THEORY OF ATOMIC STRUCTURE

Until the beginning of this century scientific investigators adhered to the healthy principle of believing only what they could see with their own eyes. Circumstances might make it necessary to help their eyes in their task, for example, by using a microscope for the study of very small objects or a telescope for the observation of systems far away. In general, however, they studied systems that could be observed visually one way or another. Around 1900 physicists encountered, for the first time, a system that could not be seen in any way, namely, the atom. The problem of the nature of atomic structure had to be solved by piecing together indirect information, such as scattering data and optical and magnetic atomic properties. Several physicists attempted to guess atomic structure

[1] A. Einstein, *Ann. d. Physik*, **22**: 180, 800 (1907).
[2] P. Debye, *Ann. d. Physik*, **39**: 789 (1912).

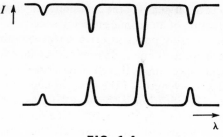

FIG. 1-4

with the aid of the experimental information that was available to them, but it was not until 1911 that the correct model was proposed by Rutherford.[1] According to this model an atom consists of a very small, relatively heavy and positively charged nucleus surrounded by a certain number of negatively charged electrons that orbit around it like the planets around the sun. The diameter of an atom is of the order of 10^{-8} cm, and therefore the angstrom ($1 A = 10^{-8}$ cm) is often used as the unit of length in atomic problems. The nuclear diameter is of the order of 10^{-4} A, its weight is practically equal to the weight of the atom, and its positive atomic charge is Ze. Here Z is the atomic number, which is about half the atomic weight, and the charge of each electron is $-e$. The simplest atom is hydrogen, where there is only one electron orbiting around a nucleus with charge e, which is about two thousand times heavier than the electron. The hydrogen nucleus has a name of its own; it is known as *proton*.

Rutherford's atomic model was consistent with the information that was obtained from various scattering experiments, and it is now universally regarded as the correct description of atomic structure; but many conclusions that could be drawn from it by means of classical mechanics were incompatible with other experimental data. Since these inconsistencies showed up mostly in the field of spectroscopy, we discuss the experimental developments in this area of investigation.

The absorption spectrum of a given sample is measured by placing it in a beam of white light, where the intensity distribution as a function of the wavelength is constant, and by measuring the intensity distribution of the light that has passed through the sample. We can also measure the emission spectrum of the sample; for example, when it is a dilute gas, we can subject it to an electric discharge, and when the discharge causes light emission, we measure the intensity distribution of the emitted light. This is the *emission spectrum* of the sample. Ordinarily the absorption and emission spectrum of the sample are complimentary; this means, as we illustrate in Fig. 1-4, that the valleys of the absorption spectrum (at

[1] E. Rutherford, *Phil. Mag.*, **21**: 669 (1911); **27**: 488 (1914).

the top) correspond to the peaks of the emission spectrum (at the bottom). The remarkable feature of an atomic emission spectrum is that it consists of a series of very narrow peaks at certain wavelengths; we call these *spectral lines*. Each spectral line is determined by its wavelength and its intensity. An atomic spectrum is therefore described by a set of numbers which describe the wavelengths of the spectral lines, and a set of corresponding intensity classifications. The wavelengths can be determined with great accuracy (1 part in 10^7 to 10^8). The intensities, on the other hand, could not be measured very accurately, but this did not matter much, since the intensities never played a very important role in the development of quantum mechanics.

It was only natural that scientists at the beginning of the century attempted to find some rules or regularities for the conglomeration of numbers that constitutes an atomic spectrum. An important success in this direction was achieved by Ritz[1] in 1908. Ritz noted first that we should consider the frequencies v, rather than the wavelengths λ, of the spectral lines. It is then possible to construct a set of terms T_i so that each spectral frequency is the difference of 2 terms

$$v_{ij} = T_j - T_i \tag{1-87}$$

This result is not so trivial as it seems; it means that we need only 10 terms to describe 45 spectral frequencies, 100 terms for 4,950 frequencies, etc., so that it takes considerably fewer terms than frequencies to describe an atomic spectrum.

Much earlier Balmer[2] had discovered that many of the spectral lines of the hydrogen atom could be described with great accuracy by the formula

$$v_n = R_H\left(\frac{1}{4} - \frac{1}{n^2}\right) \tag{1-88}$$

where R_H is known as the Rydberg constant. Eventually this discovery led to the result that for the hydrogen atom the Ritz terms are all described by the expression

$$T_n = \frac{R_H}{n^2} \tag{1-89}$$

The positions of atomic spectral lines are usually described by means of their wave numbers

$$\sigma = \frac{1}{\lambda} = \frac{v}{c} \tag{1-90}$$

which are expressed in terms of cm^{-1}. It should be realized that atomic

[1] W. Ritz, *Phys. Zeits.*, **9**: 521 (1908).
[2] J. J. Balmer, *Basel Verh.*, **7**: 548, 750 (1885).

spectra can be measured with great accuracy; for example, the Rydberg constant R_H for the hydrogen atom is known to be $R_H = 109,677.581$ cm^{-1}.

It is obvious that these spectroscopic observations for the hydrogen atom are incompatible with the Rutherford model if we use classical mechanics as the basis of our theory. Classical theory would always lead to continuous frequency distributions of physical quantities, and therefore it could never lead to discrete spectral lines. As if this inconsistency were not bad enough, even more serious difficulties arise when we combine the Rutherford model with classical mechanics. Let us imagine, according to classical mechanics, that at a certain time the electron occupies a certain orbit around the nucleus, like the earth around the sun. There is an important difference between the electron and the earth, however; the electron has an electric charge, but the earth is neutral. Therefore, it is possible for the earth to remain in a stable orbit, but not for the electron. When the electron moves, its motion is associated with an electromagnetic field, and as a consequence it emits radiation. The emission of radiation causes the electron to lose energy, and therefore it falls back to an orbit of lower energy, which is closer to the nucleus. This process repeats continuously, with the final result that the electron collapses into the nucleus after having emitted radiation of varying frequencies.

Thus, the combination of the concepts of classical mechanics with the Rutherford model leads, not only to discrepancies with the spectroscopic observations, but also to the immediate collapse of the world that we live in. This last prediction is obviously incorrect, as the reader can verify by waiting a few seconds and then looking around.

Since the combination of the Rutherford model and classical mechanics leads to untenable conclusions, the reader may be tempted to assume that the fault lies with the Rutherford model, since there is much more evidence to support the validity of classical mechanics than the Rutherford model. Although this solution may seem tempting, it can never lead to an explanation of all the difficulties. First of all, the existence of discrete spectral lines cannot be explained from classical concepts, whichever atomic model we choose. Obviously, we have to introduce some quantization rules to explain them. Second, there is too much experimental evidence that the hydrogen atom contains a proton and an electron linked together in some kind of stable orbit, and classical mechanics cannot explain this either. We are therefore led to the conclusion that classical mechanics has to be modified in some way before it can be applied to atomic systems.

In the first decade of this century there was an abundance of suggestions on how this purpose could be achieved, some of them correct, some nearly correct, but a good many of them incorrect. The situation became somewhat confusing, and it was the great achievement of Niels Bohr, the Danish physicist, to construct the solution to the problem by discarding the incorrect assumptions and by selecting, combining, and complementing the correct ones. The Bohr theory of the atom is one of the great scientific discoveries of this century, and a good understanding of it is essential to learning quantum mechanics. Before discussing it, however, we have to mention a few more concepts of classical mechanics, in particular angular momentum and central force fields. We do so in the next section and treat the Bohr theory in the section thereafter.

1-6 ANGULAR MOMENTUM AND CENTRAL FORCE FIELD IN CLASSICAL MECHANICS

A quantity that plays a very important role in Bohr's atomic theory is angular momentum $\mathbf{M}$, which is defined as

$$\mathbf{M} = \mathbf{r} \times \mathbf{p} \tag{1-91}$$

for a one-particle system and as

$$\mathbf{M} = \sum_j (\mathbf{r}_j \times \mathbf{p}_j) \tag{1-92}$$

for a many-particle system.

In order to understand these definitions, we have to discuss a little more vector analysis. In Sec. 1-2 we defined the sum of two vectors $\mathbf{u}$ and $\mathbf{v}$. Now we wish to define the product of the two vectors, but we ought to realize that there are two kinds of products. The first product, which is called the *scalar product* or *dot product* of $\mathbf{u}$ and $\mathbf{v}$, is a scalar quantity and is defined as

$$\mathbf{u} \cdot \mathbf{v} = u_x v_x + u_y v_y + u_z v_z = uv \cos \theta_{uv} \tag{1-93}$$

where θ_{uv} is the angle between the vectors $\mathbf{u}$ and $\mathbf{v}$. The second product, which is called the *vector product* or *cross product*, is a vector $\mathbf{w}$ and is defined as

$$\mathbf{w} = \mathbf{u} \times \mathbf{v}$$
$$w_x = u_y v_z - u_z v_y$$
$$w_y = u_z v_x - u_x v_z \tag{1-94}$$
$$w_z = u_x v_y - u_y v_x$$

The direction of $\mathbf{w}$ is perpendicular to the plane formed by the two vectors $\mathbf{u}$ and $\mathbf{v}$, and it points in the direction of motion of a corkscrew being turned from $\mathbf{u}$ to $\mathbf{v}$ (see Fig. 1-5) through the smaller angle.

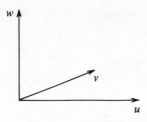

FIG. 1-5

Let us now consider the hydrogen atom according to classical mechanics and investigate the role of the angular momentum. We have two particles: a heavy nucleus with mass M, coordinate $\mathbf{r}_n$, and momentum $\mathbf{p}_n$ and a much lighter electron with mass m, coordinate $\mathbf{r}_e$, and momentum $\mathbf{p}_e$. The potential energy U of this system depends only on the distance $|\mathbf{r}_e - \mathbf{r}_n|$, so that we may write the Hamiltonian as

$$H = \frac{p_e^{\,2}}{2m} + \frac{p_n^{\,2}}{2M} + U(|\mathbf{r}_e - \mathbf{r}_n|) \qquad (1\text{-}95)$$

We begin our discussion by introducing a new set of coordinates. The position $\mathbf{R}$ of the center of gravity of the two-particle system is defined as

$$(m + M)\mathbf{R} = M\mathbf{r}_n + m\mathbf{r}_e \qquad (1\text{-}96)$$

and the relative position of the electron with respect to the nucleus is given by

$$\mathbf{r} = \mathbf{r}_e - \mathbf{r}_n \qquad (1\text{-}97)$$

If we now transform from the coordinates $\mathbf{r}_e$ and $\mathbf{r}_n$ to $\mathbf{r}$ and $\mathbf{R}$, we find that this transformation is given by

$$\mathbf{r}_e = \mathbf{R} + \frac{M}{m + M}\,\mathbf{r}$$

$$\qquad (1\text{-}98)$$

$$\mathbf{r}_n = \mathbf{R} - \frac{m}{m + M}\,\mathbf{r}$$

It may be recalled that the momenta $\mathbf{p}_e$ and $\mathbf{p}_n$ are defined as

$$\mathbf{p}_e = m\,\frac{d\mathbf{r}_e}{dt} \qquad \mathbf{p}_n = M\,\frac{d\mathbf{r}_n}{dt} \qquad (1\text{-}99)$$

We introduce the new momenta

$$\mathbf{P} = (m + M)\,\frac{d\mathbf{R}}{dt} \qquad \mathbf{p} = \mu\,\frac{d\mathbf{r}}{dt} \qquad (1\text{-}100)$$

conjugate to $\mathbf{R}$ and $\mathbf{r}$, respectively, where

$$\mu = \frac{mM}{m + M} \qquad (1\text{-}101)$$

Substitution of Eqs. (1-97)–(1-100) into Eq. (1-95) for the Hamiltonian gives

$$H = \frac{P^2}{2(M + m)} + \frac{p^2}{2\mu} + U(r) \qquad (1\text{-}102)$$

Similarly, it is found that the angular momentum

$$M = (\mathbf{r}_e \times \mathbf{p}_e) + (\mathbf{r}_n \times \mathbf{p}_n) \qquad (1\text{-}103)$$

is transformed into

$$\mathbf{M} = (\mathbf{R} \times \mathbf{P}) + (\mathbf{r} \times \mathbf{p}) \qquad (1\text{-}104)$$

Thus, the Hamiltonian is the sum of a part that depends only on $\mathbf{P}$ and a part that depends only on $\mathbf{r}$ and $\mathbf{p}$. It may be derived from the considerations in Sec. 1-2 that the equations of motion may be separated into two independent sets in that case. The first set describes the motion of the center of gravity. Since the center of gravity moves as a free particle (the potential does not depend on $\mathbf{R}$), there is not much more to say about it.

The interesting part of the problem is the motion of the electron with respect to the nucleus, which may be considered separately. This motion is described by the Hamiltonian

$$H = \frac{p^2}{2\mu} + U(r) \qquad (1\text{-}105)$$

and its angular momentum is

$$\mathbf{M} = \mathbf{r} \times \mathbf{p} \qquad (1\text{-}106)$$

It should be noted that Eq. (1-105) contains the reduced mass μ instead of the electronic mass m. Since M is much larger than m, the difference between m and μ is small, but the difference can still be detected in the spectroscopic experiments, which are so extremely accurate.

Let us now show why the angular momentum is such an important quantity in the present problem. One of its components, for example, the z component, is given by

$$M_z = xp_y - yp_x \qquad (1\text{-}107)$$

whose time derivative is

$$\frac{dM_z}{dt} = p_y \frac{\partial x}{\partial t} - p_x \frac{\partial y}{\partial t} + x \frac{\partial p_y}{\partial t} - y \frac{\partial p_x}{\partial t} \qquad (1\text{-}108)$$

We use Hamilton's equations (1-20) applied to the Hamiltonian (1-105) to replace the time derivatives:

$$\frac{\partial x}{\partial t} = \frac{\partial H}{\partial p_x} = \frac{p_x}{\mu}$$

$$\frac{\partial y}{\partial t} = \frac{\partial H}{\partial p_y} = \frac{p_y}{\mu}$$

$$\frac{\partial p_x}{\partial t} = -\frac{\partial H}{\partial x} = -\frac{x}{r}\frac{\partial U}{\partial r}$$

$$\frac{\partial p_y}{\partial t} = -\frac{\partial H}{\partial y} = -\frac{y}{r}\frac{\partial U}{\partial r}$$

(1-109)

If we substitute these results into Eq. (1-108), we find that

$$\frac{dM_z}{dt} = 0$$

(1-110)

In the same way it may be shown that

$$\frac{dM_x}{dt} = \frac{dM_y}{dt} = 0$$

(1-111)

Consequently, **M** is a constant of the motion and does not depend on time.

The fact that **M** is time-independent enables us to simplify the problem considerably. We take the z axis along the constant **M**, which now becomes

$$M = \mu\left(x\frac{\partial y}{\partial t} - y\frac{\partial x}{\partial t}\right)$$

(1-112)

It follows from the definition (1-106) that **M** is perpendicular to both **r** and **p**, and since **M** is along the z axis, **r** and **p** have to be in the xy plane. Therefore, we may write the time-independent energy E as

$$E = \frac{1}{2}\mu\left[\left(\frac{\partial x}{\partial t}\right)^2 + \left(\frac{\partial y}{\partial t}\right)^2\right] - \frac{e^2}{(x^2 + y^2)^{1/2}}$$

(1-113)

Here, we finally substituted the explicit form for the potential U. Let us now introduce the polar coordinates

$$x = r\cos\phi$$
$$y = r\sin\phi$$

(1-114)

whose time derivatives are

$$\frac{\partial x}{\partial t} = \cos \phi \, \frac{\partial r}{\partial t} - r \sin \phi \, \frac{\partial \phi}{\partial t}$$

$$\frac{\partial y}{\partial t} = \sin \phi \, \frac{\partial r}{\partial t} + r \cos \phi \, \frac{\partial \phi}{\partial t}$$

(1-115)

Substitution of Eqs. (1-114) and (1-115) into Eq. (1-112) for the angular momentum gives

$$M = \mu r^2 \, \frac{\partial \phi}{\partial t}$$

(1-116)

Substitution into Eq. (1-113) for the energy leads to

$$E = \frac{1}{2} \mu \left(\frac{\partial r}{\partial t}\right)^2 + \frac{M^2}{2\mu r^2} - \frac{e^2}{r}$$

(1-117)

It is easily seen that the motion is determined from the two time-independent quantities E and M, even if its mathematical description is not of a very simple form. We may write Eq. (1-117) as

$$\frac{dr}{dt} = \left(\frac{2E}{\mu} - \frac{M^2}{\mu^2 r^2} + \frac{2e^2}{\mu r}\right)^{1/2}$$

(1-118)

This expression may be integrated to yield

$$t = \int \left(\frac{2E}{\mu} - \frac{M^2}{\mu^2 r^2} + \frac{2e^2}{\mu r}\right)^{-1/2} dr + \text{const}$$

(1-119)

which gives the time dependence of r in implicit form.

We also have the two equations

$$d\phi = \frac{M}{\mu r^2} \, dt$$

$$dt = \left(\frac{2E}{\mu} - \frac{M^2}{\mu^2 r^2} + \frac{2e^2}{\mu r}\right)^{-1/2} dr$$

(1-120)

following from Eqs. (1-116) and (1-118). If we substitute one into the other and integrate, we obtain

$$\phi = \int \frac{M}{\mu r^2} \left(\frac{2E}{\mu} - \frac{M^2}{\mu^2 r^2} + \frac{2e^2}{\mu r}\right)^{-1/2} dr + \text{const}$$

(1-121)

This gives ϕ as a function of r, and since r as a function of t is determined from Eq. (1-119), we may derive ϕ as a function of t.

We see that the classical description of the hydrogen atom leads to fairly complicated expressions. Nevertheless, it is not necessary to go into all these mathematical details to understand the more important general conclusions that we reached in our derivation. First, we showed that both **M** and E are time-independent. Second, we derived that the motion is completely determined by the time-independent values of M and E, apart from some integration constants. Third, it followed that in general all values of M and E are possible.

Many of these general conclusions are no longer valid in quantum mechanics.

1-7 BOHR'S THEORY OF ATOMIC STRUCTURE

Bohr's quantum theory of atomic structure was published in a series of papers[1] during the years 1913 to 1915. His theory consisted of a judicious selection of the correct assumptions from the many theoretical suggestions that had been proposed previously, together with some revolutionary new ideas.

Bohr's theory was based on the assumption that Rutherford's atomic model was the correct one. This assumption, of course, is not surprising, since Bohr was a research student of Rutherford's when he began to construct his theory. We saw in Sec. 1-5 that the Rutherford model, when combined with classical mechanics, led to the prediction of atomic collapse. In order to avoid this difficulty, Bohr introduced the hypothesis that an atom could only be in certain stable states, each having a fixed energy and angular momentum, and that the atom did not absorb or emit radiation as long as it remained in one of these stable states. If there were no emission or absorption of radiation when the atom remained in a stable state, he was automatically led to the conclusion that an atomic spectral line was due to the transition from one stable atomic state to another. This idea, that two different atomic states were involved in a spectral transition, had not been thought of before Bohr proposed it; earlier investigators had always assumed that a spectral line involved one atomic state only.

Bohr now made use of the ideas of Planck and Einstein and of Ritz's term scheme and proposed that a spectral transition between two stable states with energies E_k and E_l had a frequency v_{kl} given by

$$h v_{kl} = |E_k - E_l| \tag{1-122}$$

It is important to note that this relation should hold both for absorption and for emission of radiation.

---

[1] N. Bohr, *Phil. Mag.*, **26**: 1, 476, 875 (1913); **27**: 506 (1914); **29**: 332 (1915); **30**: 394 (1915).

The assumptions mentioned so far assure the stability of the atom, and they also explain the connection between spectral transitions and atomic structure. What is left to be explained is the fact that the spectrum is discrete. Apparently, only certain specific energy values are allowed according to Eq. (1-122), and we are reminded of Planck's quantization rules for the harmonic oscillator. However, it was proposed almost simultaneously by Ehrenfest[1] and by Bohr that for atomic systems the angular momentum and not the energy should be taken as the basis for the quantization rules. The specific proposal was

$$M = n\hbar = \frac{nh}{2\pi} \tag{1-123}$$

where n was a positive integer; that is, the angular momentum was a whole multiple of $h/2\pi$. The quantity $h/2\pi$, which often occurs in quantum mechanics, has acquired its own symbol $\hbar$ and is known as the Dirac constant.

Let us now investigate to what quantitative predictions Bohr's assumptions lead. Following Bohr, we assume that the electron moves around the nucleus in a circular orbit of radius r and that the velocity is given by $\mathbf{v} = \boldsymbol{\omega} \times \mathbf{r}$, so that v is time-independent. At any time there is an attractive force e^2/r^2 between the electron and the proton, which must be equal to the centripetal force $\mu v^2/r$ required to keep the electron on the circle. We have, thus,

$$\frac{\mu v^2}{r} = \frac{e^2}{r^2} \tag{1-124}$$

The angular momentum is $\mu v r$ and according to the condition (1-123) we have to satisfy

$$\mu v r = n\hbar \tag{1-125}$$

By combining Eqs. (1-124) and (1-125) we find that

$$v = \frac{e^2}{n\hbar} \qquad r = \frac{n^2\hbar^2}{\mu e^2} \tag{1-126}$$

These expressions describe the stable orbits for the electron. The corresponding energies may be found by substituting these conditions for v and r into the energy expression

$$E = \frac{1}{2}\mu v^2 - \frac{e^2}{r} \tag{1-127}$$

[1] P. Ehrenfest, *Verh. d. deutsch. phys. Ges.*, **15**: 451 (1913).

which gives

$$E_n = -\frac{e^4}{2n^2\hbar^2} \tag{1-128}$$

If we compare this result and Eq. (1-122) with Eq. (1-88) for the Rydberg constant, we find that according to the Bohr theory R_H is given by

$$R_H = \frac{2\pi^2 e^4 \mu}{h^3} \tag{1-129a}$$

or, expressed in terms of cm^{-1}, by

$$R_H = \frac{2\pi^2 e^4 \mu}{ch^3} \tag{1-129b}$$

From the values of the constants that were known at that time, Bohr predicted that $R_H = 108.7 \times 10^3$ cm^{-1}, which agreed remarkably well with the experimental value $R_H = 109.7 \times 10^3$ cm^{-1}.

This prediction of the Rydberg constant gave tremendous support to Bohr's theory. Nevertheless, it should be realized that Bohr's work still left many questions unanswered. For example, the idea of quantization was generally accepted because it led to predictions that agreed with experiment, but no one had offered any real justification for it. Also, it was not easy to understand why there should be stable orbitals for the electrons and why the electrons in these orbitals could not emit or absorb radiation. Bohr pointed out explicitly that we should not try to visualize what happens when an electron jumps from one stable orbital into another while emitting or absorbing light.

However, in spite of all these difficulties there were also grounds for optimism. The development of the theory was moving in the right direction, and there was reason to believe that some new general principles would be found from which all the new assumptions could be explained in a logical way. Two developments led to such a new theory: the work by Heisenberg on uncertainty relations and De Broglie's wave ideas. For the further advancement of quantum mechanics it was necessary that scientists detach themselves from the tendency to visualize the electrons in the atom and to construct models for the electronic motion, because it was exactly this tendency which stood in the way of further progress.

1-8 MATRIX MECHANICS AND WAVE MECHANICS

Around 1925 two new theories were proposed, both of which claimed to explain the Bohr model and the various quantization rules. The first theory, which is now known as matrix mechanics, was formulated by

Born, Heisenberg, and Jordan,[1] following earlier work by Heisenberg.[2] The second approach was initiated with De Broglie's postulates[3] on the wave character of material particles and found its final mathematical formulation in Schrödinger's[4] differential equation. Fortunately, Schrödinger[5] was able to show that his wave mechanics is mathematically equivalent to Heisenberg's matrix mechanics.

Our discussion of quantum mechanics starts with the De Broglie postulates, from which we then justify the Schrödinger equation. After some applications to simple systems, we mention some of the formal mathematics of quantum mechanics involving operators, eigenvalues, eigenfunctions, etc. Matrix mechanics plays a relatively minor role in our treatise, since it is rarely used in calculations on atomic and molecular systems.

Before starting the formal discussion of wave mechanics in the following chapter, we wish to mention a few phenomena in a more general sense in order to prepare the student for the concepts that he will have to get used to. In our opinion the philosophy behind the De Broglie theory is more easily understood if we first mention the Heisenberg uncertainty principle,[6] although Heisenberg derived it a few years later.

Let us imagine that we wish to measure the speed of a car that moves along the highway. We have two checkpoints, separated by a known distance, and we measure the two times that the car passes the first and second checkpoints, respectively. If we divide the known distance by the difference of the two times, we know the velocity with which the car traveled between the two checkpoints. A typical situation would be where the speed of the car is 60 kmph and where the distance between the checkpoints is 50 m; the time difference is then 3 sec. If we have an ordinary watch, then the possible error in each time measurement is 0.1 sec, and the possible error in our velocity measurement is 7 per cent. At the same time there is a margin of 50 m in the position of the car during our measurement. We may conclude from our measurement that the car travels at a velocity between 56 and 64 kmph when it is between two points 50 m apart. If we increase the distance between the checkpoints to 100 m, then the error in the velocity is reduced by a factor of 2, but the uncertainty in the car's position becomes twice as large. If, on the other hand, we want to reduce the uncertainty in the car's position

[1] M. Born and P. Jordan, *Zeits. f. Phys.*, **34**: 858 (1925); M. Born, W. Heisenberg, and P. Jordan, *Zeits. f. Phys.*, **35**: 557 (1926).

[2] W. Heisenberg, *Zeits. f. Phys.*, **33**: 879 (1925).

[3] L. De Broglie, " Thesis," Paris, 1924.

[4] E. Schrödinger, *Ann. d. Physik*, **79**: 361, 489 (1926).

[5] E. Schrödinger, *Ann. d. Physik*, **79**: 734 (1926).

[6] W. Heisenberg, *Zeits. f. Physik*, **43**: 172 (1927).

during our measurement and we take the checkpoints only 25 m apart, then the possible error in our velocity measurement increases to 13 per cent.

When we determine the speed and the position of the car simultaneously, any increase in accuracy of one of the two quantities is accompanied by a decrease in accuracy of the other. If the uncertainty in the measured velocity is denoted by Δv and if the position margin is called Δx, then the situation is mathematically represented by the condition

$$\Delta x \cdot \Delta v > A \qquad (1\text{-}130)$$

The product of the two uncertainties has to be larger than a certain minimum value A.

Obviously we can remove the difficulties in this experiment by using more sophisticated experimental aids. For example, by using electronic devices, we can reduce the error in the time measurements to less than a millisecond, and in principle there is no limit to the accuracy of our measurements.

Let us now consider the motion of an electron in an atom instead of a car on a highway. According to Heisenberg we run into the same difficulties in both cases. If we try to measure the position and the velocity of the particles simultaneously, there will be a lower limit for the product of the uncertainties. The important difference between the two situations is that in the case of the car the lower limit can be made smaller by using better experimental techniques; but in the case of the electron we reach a point beyond which the lower limit cannot be pushed. This is because the electron is so small and its motion so sensitive to outside influences that any experiment that gives us information about the electronic motion also affects the electronic motion. For example, let us imagine that we have an extremely powerful microscope that enables us to see where the electron is at a certain time. This information can be obtained only if the electron scatters light back to our eye through the microscope. This light scattering affects the motion of the electron, and it can change its motion considerably. As a matter of fact, even a single photon can throw the electron off its course. It follows, therefore, that we cannot even look at an electron without influencing its motion.

Guided by these considerations, Heisenberg deduced from his matrix mechanics that, in one dimension, the condition

$$\Delta x \cdot \Delta p > h \qquad (1\text{-}131)$$

has to be satisfied. This means that if we try to determine the position and the momentum of a particle simultaneously, the product of the uncertainties has to be larger than Planck's constant h. In three dimensions these conditions are

$$\Delta x \cdot \Delta p_x > h$$

$$\Delta y \cdot \Delta p_y > h \qquad (1\text{-}132)$$

$$\Delta z \cdot \Delta p_z > h$$

The restriction should be obeyed only for simultaneous determinations of a coordinate and its conjugate momentum. If, for example, we try to measure x and p_y simultaneously, then there is no limitation to the accuracy of the two measurements.

The condition of Eq. (1-132) is known as the *Heisenberg uncertainty principle*. We prove it in the next chapter, but we wish to mention it at this early stage, since it might help us to get a better understanding of the basic principles of quantum mechanics.

If we accept the fact that it is, in principle, impossible to obtain exact experimental information about the coordinates and momenta of a particle, then we should also be aware of this limitation in constructing the theory. One of the consequences of Heisenberg's principle is that the results of classical mechanics, where the exact position and momentum of a particle are predicted as a function of time, can never be verified by experiments. Therefore, we ought to doubt the usefulness of a theoretical description that claims to be more exact than what we can ever hope to measure. We should not forget that all a theory is supposed to do is to explain the experiments and that any predictions that go beyond this become speculations rather than exact theory.

It follows from these considerations that the correct theory of electronic motion should not lead to exact predictions but to probability predictions about the motion of the electron. Let us illustrate this principle by returning to the example of the moving car that we discussed above. It is clear that from the limited information that we obtained from measuring the position and the velocity of the car, we cannot predict exactly where the car is, say, 10 sec later. All we can do is to predict the most probable position of the car, together with the probabilities of finding the car at different positions. Our predictions consist then of a probability pattern instead of a single point. In quantum mechanics the motion of the electron is also predicted in the form of a probability pattern. We see in the next chapter that for electronic motion the probability pattern is constructed by considering wave motion and by combining the functions that represent the various wave motions. Beginning students of quantum mechanics often get confused by this because they get the feeling that we have abandoned the concept of a localized particle and that we have replaced it by a superposition of waves. The truth is that we still have a localized material particle but that we do not know exactly where it is. The probability pattern with which we describe its motion consists of waves, but this does not mean that the particle itself has been transformed into a superposition of waves.

The point to remember is that quantum mechanics recognizes localized particles, as in classical mechanics, but in quantum mechanics the motion of the particles is described by means of probability patterns instead of exact orbits. De Broglie was the first to predict that these probability patterns could be evaluated by connecting them with wave motions, and this concept is taken as the basis of our discussion of quantum mechanics. However, we want to stress again that this does not mean that the electron itself has been changed into a wave, but that the probability patterns with which we predict its motion behave like waves.

P R O B L E M S

1-1 Calculate the products $\mathbf{a} \times (\mathbf{b} \times \mathbf{c})$ and $\mathbf{a} \cdot (\mathbf{b} \times \mathbf{c})$ when $\mathbf{a} = (1,2,3)$, $\mathbf{b} = (-1,2,-1)$, and $\mathbf{c} = (2,1,0)$.

1-2 Express the products $\mathbf{u} \times (\mathbf{v} \times \mathbf{w})$ and $(\mathbf{a} \times \mathbf{b}) \cdot (\mathbf{u} \times \mathbf{v})$ in terms of scalar products only. $v(w \cdot u) - w(v \cdot u)$

1-3 Calculate the vector fields that are obtained as the gradients of the functions $\phi = x^2 + y^2 + z^2$ and $\psi = xyz$. Determine then the scalar that is the dot product of the two gradients.

1-4 Use classical mechanics to determine the motion of two particles in one dimension with an interaction potential $V = \frac{1}{2}k(x_1 - x_2)^2$. It is assumed that the particles are infinitely small and that they can pass each other without interacting. Hints: The Hamiltonian of the system is

$$H = \frac{p_1^2}{2m_1} + \frac{p_2^2}{2m_2} + \frac{1}{2}k(x_1 - x_2)^2$$

Introduce the new coordinates

$$(m_1 + m_2)X = m_1 x_1 + m_2 x_2$$

$$x = x_1 - x_2$$

and momenta

$$P = (m_1 + m_2)\frac{dX}{dt}$$

$$p = \mu \frac{dx}{dt} \qquad \mu = m_1 m_2 (m_1 + m_2)^{-1}$$

1-5   Consider a function $F(q,p)$ of the generalized coordinates q_i and conjugate momenta p_i belonging to a system with the Hamiltonian $H(q,p)$. Prove that

$$\frac{dF}{dt} = \sum_i \left(\frac{\partial F}{\partial q_i} \frac{\partial H}{\partial p_i} - \frac{\partial F}{\partial p_i} \frac{\partial H}{\partial q_i} \right)$$

1-6   Kepler's second law of planetary motion says that in equal times the radius vector of a particle sweeps out equal areas. Prove this.

1-7   Calculate the specific heat of an assembly of a large number of identical harmonic oscillators of frequency ν according to the quantum theory. The result is Einstein's specific heat formula for solids.

1-8   The spectra of H, He$^+$, and Li^{++} can all be represented as $\nu_{n,m} = (Z_x^2 R_x)(n^{-2} - m^{-2})$, where Z_x is the atomic number and R_x is the Rydberg constant of the corresponding nucleus. If the mass ratios between the H, He, and Li nuclei is $1.0080 : 4.0021 : 6.9380$ and the ratio between the electron and proton masses is $1 : 1,836.11$, determine the Rydberg constants for He$^+$ and Li^{++} from $R_H = 109,677.581$ cm^{-1}.

1-9   Determine from Heisenberg's uncertainty principle what the lower limit is for $\Delta x \cdot \Delta v$ for a car of 1,000 kg. Planck's constant is $h = 6.62 \times 10^{-27}$ erg-sec.

1.008

CHAPTER 2

WAVE MECHANICS

2-1 COMPLEX NUMBERS

The numbers that are used to express physical observations are known as *real numbers*; they can be integer, noninteger, positive, negative, zero, etc. We encounter another category of numbers if we take the square root of -1 or if we find the roots of the equations

$$x^2 + 1 = 0 \qquad (2\text{-}1)$$

or

$$x^2 + \alpha^2 = 0 \qquad (2\text{-}2)$$

In order to express the solutions of Eqs. (2-1) and (2-2), we introduce the imaginary unit

$$i = \sqrt{-1} \qquad (2\text{-}3)$$

which enables us to write the roots of Eq. (2-1) as $\pm i$ and those of Eq. (2-2) as $\pm \alpha i$. Every number that can be expressed as the product of a real number and i is known as an *imaginary number*.

It is customary to represent all the real numbers as points on a straight line. We define a point O that corresponds to the number zero and a point E that corresponds to the number one, and now we know exactly which point on the line belongs to a given number and vice versa. In a similar way we can draw a line with two points O for zero and I for i that contains all imaginary numbers. In Fig. 2-1 we draw the two lines

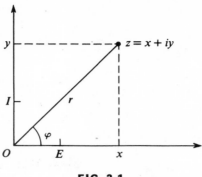

FIG. 2-1

for the real and the imaginary numbers at right angles to each other.

The most general number, which we call a *complex number*, is the sum of a real and an imaginary number, for example,

$$z = x + iy \tag{2-4}$$

Here x and y are real numbers, and z is a complex number. We call x the real part of z and y the imaginary part of z; this is also written as

$$x = \mathscr{R}z$$
$$y = \mathscr{I}z \tag{2-5}$$

It is customary to represent complex numbers as points in a two-dimensional plane, the complex plane. As we show in Fig. 2-1, we obtain the complex plane by taking the real and imaginary lines as the x and y axes of the plane. An arbitrary complex number $x + iy$ has x as its projection on the x axis and y as its projection on the y axis.

We know that the points in a two-dimensional plane can also be represented by the polar coordinates r and ϕ instead of the Cartesian coordinates x and y. The relation is

$$x = r \cos \phi$$
$$y = r \sin \phi \tag{2-6}$$

and if we substitute these relations into Eq. (2-4), we get

$$z = x + iy = r(\cos \phi + i \sin \phi) \tag{2-7}$$

The absolute value, or *modulus*, of the complex number z is defined as the distance between O and the point representing z. In the case of Eq. (2-7) the modulus of z, which is written as $|z|$, is given by

$$|z| = r = (x^2 + y^2)^{1/2} \tag{2-8}$$

The complex conjugate z^* of the number z of Eq. (2-7) is defined as

$$z^* = x - iy \tag{2-9}$$

It is easily verified that

$$zz^* = x^2 + y^2 = |z|^2 \tag{2-10}$$

In wave mechanics we often encounter exponentials where the variable is purely imaginary, that is, $e^{i\phi}$. A very useful property of these exponentials is that they may be expressed as

$$e^{i\phi} = \cos \phi + i \sin \phi \tag{2-11}$$

In order to prove this relation, we observe that the exponential function of an arbitrary variable z is defined as the power series

$$e^z = 1 + z + \frac{z^2}{2!} + \frac{z^3}{3!} + \cdots = \sum_{n=0}^{\infty} \frac{z^n}{n!} \tag{2-12}$$

Substitution of $i\phi$ for z gives

$$e^{i\phi} = \sum_{n=0}^{\infty} \frac{i^n \phi^n}{n!} \tag{2-13}$$

Since i is actually $\sqrt{-1}$, the various powers of i are

$$i^0 = 1$$
$$i^1 = i$$
$$i^2 = -1$$
$$i^3 = -i \tag{2-14}$$
$$i^4 = 1$$
$$i^5 = i \quad \text{etc.}$$

Hence, Eq. (2-13) becomes

$$e^{i\phi} = 1 + i\phi - \frac{\phi^2}{2!} - \frac{i\phi^3}{3!} + \frac{\phi^4}{4!} + \frac{i\phi^5}{5!} - \frac{\phi^6}{6!} - \frac{i\phi^7}{7!} + \cdots$$

$$= \left(1 - \frac{\phi^2}{2!} + \frac{\phi^4}{4!} - \frac{\phi^6}{6!} + \cdots\right) + i\left(\phi - \frac{\phi^3}{3!} + \frac{\phi^5}{5!} - \frac{\phi^7}{7!} + \cdots\right) \tag{2-15}$$

These two series are just the power series expansions for $\cos \phi$ and $\sin \phi$:

$$\cos \phi = 1 - \frac{\phi^2}{2!} + \frac{\phi^4}{4!} - \frac{\phi^6}{6!} + \cdots$$

$$\sin \phi = \phi - \frac{\phi^3}{3!} + \frac{\phi^5}{5!} - \frac{\phi^7}{7!} + \cdots$$

(2-16)

Consequently Eq. (2-11) follows from Eqs. (2-15) and (2-16).

We may use Eq. (2-11) to simplify Eq. (2-7):

$$z = x + iy = r(\cos \phi + i \sin \phi) = re^{i\phi} \qquad (2\text{-}17)$$

We already mentioned that r is known as the modulus of z. We may add that ϕ is called the *argument* of z. The expression of z in terms of r and ϕ is particularly convenient when we consider the product of two complex numbers $z_1 = r_1 \exp(i\phi_1)$ and $z_2 = r_2 \exp(i\phi_2)$. This product is

$$z_1 z_2 = r_1 r_2 e^{\phi_1 + \phi_2} \qquad (2\text{-}18)$$

which is a much simpler expression than if we use x and y.

2-2 WAVES IN ONE DIMENSION

The observation of one-dimensional waves is one of the few experiments that can be performed in a classroom without any special preparation. When we hold the cord of a window shade and move the wrist up and down, the cord exhibits the pattern of a running wave very clearly. The mathematical description of this running wave is an expression for the deviation from equilibrium of each point on the cord as a function of position and time. In deriving this mathematical description we make use of our observations rather than following the correct but more complicated method of solving the differential equation of motion for the cord.

Let us imagine that we take a picture of the cord at a time t_0; the result looks like Fig. 2-2. This is a periodic curve with wavelength λ,

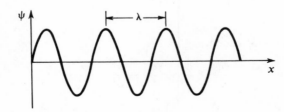

FIG. 2-2

which means that we get the same deviation ψ if we move a distance λ to the right or left:

$$\psi(x \pm \lambda) = \psi(x) \tag{2-19}$$

The best known periodic function is the sine or cosine function, and if we make a careful inspection of our picture, as reproduced in Fig. 2-2, we find that this is indeed a sine or cosine function. The most general function of this kind can be written as

$$\psi(x) = A \sin \left[2\pi(\alpha x + \beta)\right] \tag{2-20a}$$

or $$\psi(x) = A \cos \left[2\pi(\alpha' x + \beta')\right] \tag{2-20b}$$

These two expressions are entirely equivalent because the cosine function (2-20b) can be obtained from Eq. (2-20a) by a judicious selection of the parameters, and vice versa. Without any loss of generality we may consider only Eq. (2-20a).

It is easily seen that the maximum value of the function $\psi(x)$ of Eq. (2-20a) is equal to the parameter A. This parameter is therefore equal to the maximum deviation of any point on the cord from its equilibrium and is known as the *amplitude* of the wave. One of the other parameters, namely α, is related to the quantity λ of Fig. 2-2, which is known as the *wavelength*. It follows from Eq. (2-19) that

$$\alpha\lambda = 2\pi \tag{2-21}$$

Hence, Eq. (2-20a) becomes

$$\psi(x) = A \sin \left[2\pi\left(\frac{x}{\lambda} + \beta\right)\right] \tag{2-22}$$

The parameter β in this expression is known as the *phase constant*. A change in β causes the curve of Fig. 2-2 to shift to the left or to the right, but it does not change the shape of the curve itself.

Now that we have analyzed the shape of the cord at a particular time t_0, we proceed to study the time dependence of the pattern. It follows from our observation that this time dependence is a simple one; we see that the whole pattern moves with a constant velocity v. Let us assume that the pattern moves in the direction of the positive x axis (to the right in Fig. 2-2); in this case v is positive.

We have just mentioned that the horizontal motion of the pattern of Fig. 2-2 is determined only by changes in the phase constant β, and since the time dependence of the wave motion consists solely of such horizontal motion, it follows that the time dependence of the wave function $\psi(x,t)$ must be concentrated in β:

$$\psi(x,t) = A \sin \left[2\pi\left(\frac{x}{\lambda} + \beta(t)\right)\right] \tag{2-23}$$

The wave function ψ represents the deviation from equilibrium of each point on the cord as a function of position and time. Let us now consider the deviation $\psi(x_0, t_0)$ of a point x_0 at a certain time t_0. If we wait a certain amount of time Δt, then the deviation at x_0 changes to the deviation that the point $x_0 - v\Delta t$ had at the time t_0, since the whole pattern moved a distance $v\Delta t$ to the right during the time interval Δt. Hence, we have the condition

$$\psi(x_0,\, t_0 + \Delta t) = \psi(x_0 - v\,\Delta t,\, t_0) \qquad (2\text{-}24)$$

or

$$\psi(x_0, t_0) = \psi(x_0 - v\Delta t,\, t_0 - \Delta t) \qquad (2\text{-}25)$$

This condition is satisfied only if ψ is a function of $(x - vt)$; consequently, it follows from Eq. (2-23) that ψ must be

$$\psi(x,t) = A \sin\left[\frac{2\pi}{\lambda}(x - vt) + \gamma\right] \qquad (2\text{-}26)$$

where γ is again a phase constant, but now it is time-independent.

We would have arrived at essentially the same result if we had started from Eq. (2-20b), containing the cosine instead of the sine function of Eq. (2-20a). We may recall that

$$\cos\alpha = \sin\left(\frac{\pi}{2} - \alpha\right) = \sin\left(\alpha + \frac{\pi}{2}\right) \qquad (2\text{-}27)$$

Therefore, we can change from a sine to a cosine function and vice versa by respectively subtracting or adding an amount $(\pi/2)$ to the phase constant.

At a given time t_0 the position of the cord as a function of the position x is described by the function

$$\psi(x,t_0) = A \sin\left[\frac{2\pi}{\lambda}(x - vt_0) + \gamma\right] \qquad (2\text{-}28)$$

The position of the cord changes as a function of time, but we observe that there is a time $t_0 = T$ when the position of the cord is exactly the same as it was at time t_0. This time T, which is known as the *period* of the oscillation motion, is determined by the condition

$$\psi(x,\, t + T) = \psi(x,t) \qquad (2\text{-}29)$$

which leads to the expression

$$T = \frac{\lambda}{v} \qquad (2\text{-}30)$$

The inverse of the period is known as the *frequency* v of the wave and is given by

$$v = \frac{1}{T} = \frac{v}{\lambda} \qquad (2\text{-}31)$$

Another quantity that is often used in the description of waves is the *wave number* σ, which is the inverse of the wavelength,

$$\sigma = \frac{1}{\lambda} \qquad (2\text{-}32)$$

The function $\psi(x,t)$ of Eq. (2-28) may also be expressed in terms of σ and v:

$$\psi(x,t) = A \sin [2\pi(\sigma x - vt) + \gamma] \qquad (2\text{-}33)$$

2-3 COMPLETE SETS

A mathematical discussion of the properties of waves is based mostly on the branch of applied mathematics known as Fourier analysis. We outline the main features of Fourier analysis without giving rigorous mathematical proofs of the various theorems that are quoted. We also use this opportunity to discuss a few aspects of *approximations in the mean*, since this will prove helpful when we treat eigenfunction expansions at a later stage in this book.

We consider two functions f and g of a real variable x, defined in the interval $a \leqslant x \leqslant b$. The functions may take on complex values. By definition the symbol $\langle f | g \rangle$ stands for

$$\langle f | g \rangle = \int_a^b f^*(x)g(x) \, dx \qquad (2\text{-}34)$$

When the condition

$$\langle f | g \rangle = 0 \qquad (2\text{-}35)$$

is satisfied, we call f and g orthogonal to each other. When

$$\langle f | f \rangle = 1 \qquad (2\text{-}36)$$

we say that f is normalized to unity or just *normalized*. A set of normalized functions $\phi_1, \phi_2, \phi_3, \ldots$, all of which are orthogonal to one another, is called an orthonormal set. We can write this as

$$\langle \phi_n | \phi_m \rangle = \delta_{n,m} \qquad (2\text{-}37)$$

The symbol $\delta_{n,m}$ is known as the Kronecker δ symbol and is equal to unity when $n = m$ and equal to zero when $n \neq m$. The orthonormal set of functions ϕ_n can consist either of a finite or of an infinite number of functions. A simple example of an orthonormal set is the functions

$$\phi_n(x) = (2\pi)^{-1/2} e^{inx} \qquad n = 0, \pm 1, \pm 2, \ldots, \text{etc.} \qquad (2\text{-}38)$$

in the interval $0 \leqslant x \leqslant 2\pi$, since the integral

$$\int_0^{2\pi} \phi_n^*(x)\phi_m(x) \, dx = \frac{1}{2\pi} \int_0^{2\pi} e^{i(m-n)x} \, dx \qquad (2\text{-}39)$$

is zero for $n \neq m$ and unity for $n = m$.

A complete set of functions $u_n(x)$ in the interval $a \leqslant x \leqslant b$ is defined by the property that there exists no other function χ in this interval such that χ is orthogonal to all functions u_n. An example of a complete set is the functions (2-38) for all integer values of n.

The various complete sets of functions that are considered in this book are all orthonormal. In addition, they usually satisfy certain *boundary conditions*, that is, linear relationships between the values of the functions $u_n(x)$ and their derivatives $u_n'(x)$ at the points $x = a$ and $x = b$. For example, in the case of the functions (2-38) we have

$$\phi_n(0) = \phi_n(2\pi)$$

$$\phi_n'(0) = \phi_n'(2\pi) \tag{2-40}$$

for all values of n. It can be shown that a function $f(x)$ that satisfies the same boundary conditions as the functions $u_n(x)$ of a complete set can be expanded as

$$f(x) = \sum_{n=1}^{\infty} c_n u_n(x) \tag{2-41}$$

in the interval $a \leqslant x \leqslant b$.

If we multiply Eq. (2-41) on the left by $u_m^*(x)$ and integrate, we obtain

$$c_m = \langle u_m | f \rangle \tag{2-42}$$

It follows that Eq. (2-41) is equivalent to

$$f(x) = \sum_{n=1}^{\infty} \langle u_n | f \rangle u_n(x) \tag{2-43}$$

Let us now show that Eq. (2-43) is always valid if the $u_n(x)$ form a complete set. If (2-43) were not valid, we would write

$$\chi(x) = f(x) - \sum_{n=1}^{\infty} \langle u_n | f \rangle u_n(x) \tag{2-44}$$

where $\chi(x)$ is not identically zero in the interval $a \leqslant x \leqslant b$. Multiplication on the left by $u_m^*(x)$ and subsequent integration of Eq. (2-44) give then

$$\langle u_m | \chi \rangle = \langle u_m | f \rangle - \langle u_m | f \rangle = 0 \tag{2-45}$$

for all m. This result is inconsistent with the definition of a complete set of functions, and we conclude, therefore, that $\chi(x)$ should be identically zero for $a \leqslant x \leqslant b$ or that Eq. (2-43) is valid.

It follows easily from Eq. (2-41) and from the orthonormality of the functions u_n that

$$\langle f | f \rangle = \sum_{n=1}^{\infty} \sum_{m=1}^{\infty} c_n^* c_m \langle u_n | u_m \rangle$$

$$= \sum_{n=1}^{\infty} \sum_{m=1}^{\infty} c_n^* c_m \delta_{n,m} = \sum_{n=1}^{\infty} c_n c_n^* \qquad (2\text{-}46)$$

According to Eq. (2-10) each of the terms $c_n c_n^*$ that occurs in Eq. (2-46) is a positive number. Therefore, if we truncate the infinite sum on the right side of Eq. (2-46) after a finite number of terms, say N, we find that

$$\sum_{n=1}^{N} c_n c_n^* \leqslant \langle f | f \rangle \qquad (2\text{-}47)$$

This is known as *Bessel's inequality*. Finally it may be deduced from Eqs. (2-46) and (2-47) that

$$\lim_{N \to \infty} \sum_{n=1}^{N} c_n c_n^* = \langle f | f \rangle \qquad (2\text{-}48)$$

This is often used as a criterion for the convergence of expansions in terms of complete sets of functions. If for a given expansion the sum on the left side of Eq. (2-48) converges, we say that the expansion $\sum c_n \phi_n$ converges to f in the mean.

2-4 FOURIER ANALYSIS

Let us now apply these general considerations to Fourier series. A Fourier series is an expansion of a function $f(x)$ in terms of the orthonormal set of functions

$$\phi_n(x) = (2\pi)^{-1/2} e^{inx} \qquad n = 0, \pm 1, \pm 2, \ldots, \text{etc.} \qquad (2\text{-}49)$$

The expansion is written as

$$f(x) = \sum_{n=-\infty}^{\infty} a_n e^{inx} \qquad (2\text{-}50)$$

with

$$a_m = \frac{1}{2\pi} \int_{-\pi}^{\pi} e^{-imt} f(t)\, dt \qquad (2\text{-}51)$$

The expansion of Eq. (2-50) is possible, and the Fourier series is convergent if f is bounded and continuous in the interval $-\pi \leqslant x \leqslant \pi$. Actually f does not even have to be continuous and bounded for the expansion to be possible; it is sufficient if f satisfies the less restrictive set of *Dirichlet's conditions*, which require that f has only a finite number of finite discontinuities and a finite number of minima or maxima in the interval $-\pi \leqslant x \leqslant \pi$. At any rate, most of the functions that we encounter can be expanded as Fourier series in the interval $-\pi \leqslant x \leqslant \pi$.

When the function $f(x)$ is periodic, that is, when it satisfies the condition

$$f(x + 2\pi) = f(x) \tag{2-52}$$

then the Fourier expansion is also valid outside the interval $-\pi < x < \pi$.

These considerations are easily extended to functions of more than one variable, which may be expanded as multiple Fourier series. For example, the function $F(x,y)$ is expanded as

$$F(x,y) = \sum_{m=-\infty}^{\infty} \sum_{n=-\infty}^{\infty} a_{m,n} e^{i(mx+ny)}$$

$$a_{m,n} = \frac{1}{4\pi^2} \int_{-\pi}^{\pi} \int_{-\pi}^{\pi} F(x,y) e^{-i(mx+ny)} \, dx \, dy \tag{2-53}$$

Similar expansions are possible for the functions $F(x,y,z)$, etc.

In the following sections we make extensive use of the Fourier integral theorem, which may be made plausible from the Fourier series expansion. We consider a function $f(y)$, satisfying Dirichlet's conditions in the interval $-\pi \leqslant y \leqslant \pi$, so that it can be expanded as

$$f(y) = \sum_{n=-\infty}^{\infty} a_n e^{iny} \tag{2-54}$$

with the coefficients given by

$$a_n = \frac{1}{2\pi} \int_{-\pi}^{\pi} f(s) e^{-ins} \, ds \tag{2-55}$$

We transform from the variables y and s to x and t by means of

$$ly = \pi x$$

$$ls = \pi t \tag{2-56}$$

so that Eqs. (2-54) and (2-55) become

$$f(x) = \sum_{n=-\infty}^{\infty} a_n \exp\left(\frac{in\pi x}{l}\right)$$

$$a_n = \frac{1}{2l} \int_{-l}^{l} \exp\left(\frac{-in\pi t}{l}\right) f(t) \, dt \tag{2-57}$$

Substitution of the second Eq. (2-57) into the first one gives

$$f(x) = \frac{1}{2l} \sum_{n=-\infty}^{\infty} \int_{-l}^{l} f(t) \exp\left[\frac{in\pi(x-t)}{l}\right] dt \tag{2-58}$$

This expression is valid for the interval $-l \leqslant x \leqslant l$, and it becomes so for all values of x and t if we let l tend to infinity. We introduce the small quantity $\delta = \pi/l$, which tends to zero if l tends to infinity. In terms of δ Eq. (2-58) becomes

$$f(x) = \frac{1}{2\pi} \sum_{n=-\infty}^{\infty} \delta \int_{-l}^{l} f(t) e^{in\delta(x-t)} \, dt \qquad (2\text{-}59)$$

When l tends to infinity, δ tends to zero, and the summation of Eq. (2-59) may be replaced by an integration over a variable we call u. We find then that

$$f(x) = \frac{1}{2\pi} \int_{-\infty}^{\infty} du \int_{-\infty}^{\infty} f(t) e^{-iu(t-x)} \, dt \qquad (2\text{-}60)$$

which is known as the *Fourier integral theorem*.

There are two alternate ways of expressing Eq. (2-60). In the first one we rewrite the equation as two separate steps

$$f(x) = (2\pi)^{-1/2} \int_{-\infty}^{\infty} F(u) e^{iux} \, du$$

$$F(u) = (2\pi)^{-1/2} \int_{-\infty}^{\infty} f(t) e^{-iut} \, dt \qquad (2\text{-}61)$$

The function $F(u)$ here is called the *Fourier transform* of $f(t)$. We see that, if we take the Fourier transform of a function twice, we get the original function back.

The second way of expressing the Fourier integral theorem makes use of the Dirac δ function. The Dirac δ function $\delta(x - x_0)$ is very small for all values of the variable x except when x is close to x_0, where the δ function becomes very large. It is defined by the property

$$f(x_0) = \int f(x)\delta(x - x_0) \, dx \qquad (2\text{-}62)$$

and, consequently,

$$\int \delta(x - x_0) \, dx = 1 \qquad (2\text{-}63)$$

provided x_0 is contained within the limits of integration. Equation (2-63) follows from Eq. (2-62) if we take the function f unity. The specific form of the δ function is not uniquely defined by these conditions, and there are many different ways in which it can be represented.[1] However,

[1] See, for example, H. F. Hameka, "Advanced Quantum Chemistry," Addison-Wesley Publishing Company, Reading, Mass., 1965, p. 267.

it follows from a comparison of Eqs. (2-60) and (2-62) that one of the representations is

$$\delta(x - t) = \frac{1}{2\pi} \int_{-\infty}^{\infty} e^{iu(x-t)} \, du \qquad (2\text{-}64)$$

Finally we wish to point out that the Fourier integral theorem is also valid for functions of more than one variable. For example, if the Fourier transform $F(\lambda,\mu,v)$ of the function $f(u,v,w)$ is given by

$$F(\lambda,\mu,v) = (2\pi)^{-3/2} \int_{-\infty}^{\infty} \int_{-\infty}^{\infty} \int_{-\infty}^{\infty} f(u,v,w) e^{-i(\lambda u + \mu v + vw)} \, du \, dv \, dw \quad (2\text{-}65)$$

then the function $f(x,y,z)$ is determined by

$$f(x,y,z) = (2\pi)^{-3/2} \int_{-\infty}^{\infty} \int_{-\infty}^{\infty} \int_{-\infty}^{\infty} F(\lambda,\mu,v) e^{i(\lambda x + \mu y + vz)} \, d\lambda \, d\mu \, dv \qquad (2\text{-}66)$$

These two equations may also be combined to

$$f(x,y,z) = \frac{1}{(2\pi)^3} \int_{-\infty}^{\infty} \int_{-\infty}^{\infty} \int_{-\infty}^{\infty} \int_{-\infty}^{\infty} \int_{-\infty}^{\infty} \int_{-\infty}^{\infty} f(u,v,w) e^{-i[\lambda(u-x)+\mu(v-y)+v(w-z)]}$$

$$\times \, du \, dv \, dw \, d\lambda \, d\mu \, dv \qquad (2\text{-}67)$$

2-5 WAVES IN THREE DIMENSIONS

Since actual physical phenomena occur in three dimensions rather than in one, we wish to extend our one-dimensional mathematical discussion of Sec. 2-2 to the three-dimensional case. An example of what we wish to consider is the propagation of sound in a gas, which is due to variations in the local density $\rho(x,y,z; t)$. The difference

$$\delta\rho(x,y,z; t) = \rho(x,y,z; t) - \rho \qquad (2\text{-}68)$$

where ρ is the average density, behaves like a three-dimensional wave and is connected with the behavior and propagation of sound. The mathematical representation of $\delta\rho$, that is, a three-dimensional wave, is much more complicated than the one-dimensional case. Therefore, we try to simplify the general case by expressing it as a superposition of simple plane waves. This can be achieved by making use of the Fourier integral theorem of Sec. 2-4, but it requires the introduction of two new concepts, the use of complex wave functions and the superposition of monochromatic waves. We illustrate these ideas first for the one-dimensional case.

In Sec. 2-2 it was shown that the wave function $\psi(x,t)$, which represents the deviation of the cord from its equilibrium position, can be written as

$$\psi(x,t) = A \sin [2\pi(\sigma x - vt) + \gamma] \qquad (2\text{-}69)$$

or
$$\psi(x,t) = A \cos [2\pi(\sigma x - vt) + \gamma] \qquad (2\text{-}70)$$

Let us now consider the expression

$$\phi(x,t) = Ae^{i\gamma}e^{2\pi i(\sigma x - vt)} \tag{2-71}$$

which, according to Eq. (2-11), can also be written as

$$Ae^{2\pi i(\sigma x - vt) + i\gamma} = A\{\cos[2\pi(\sigma x - vt) + \gamma] + i\sin[2\pi(\sigma x - vt) + \gamma]\} \tag{2-72}$$

It is easily verified that Eqs. (2-70) and (2-69) are the real and imaginary parts respectively of the function $\phi(x,t)$ and that the wave motion is completely determined by the function $\phi(x,t)$. We may therefore take the complex function $\phi(x,t)$ as the mathematical representation of the wave motion, although in the examples that were used the observable quantities were all real and not complex. Equation (2-71) can be simplified even further if we allow A to be complex; in this case we can include the phase factor $e^{i\phi}$ in the complex amplitude and write

$$\phi(x,t) = Ae^{2\pi i(\sigma x - vt)} \tag{2-73}$$

as the wave function.

Let us now discuss the superposition of waves in one dimension. For this purpose we again consider the motion of the cord of Sec. 2-2, but now we suppose that instead of one person there are two persons moving the cord up and down at different points. The effect of the action of the first person is described by the wave function

$$\phi_1(x,t) = A_1 \exp[2\pi i(\sigma_1 x - v_1 t)] \tag{2-74}$$

and the second person's actions are represented by

$$\phi_2(x,t) = A_2 \exp[2\pi i(\sigma_2 x - v_2 t)] \tag{2-75}$$

According to the principle of superposition the motion of the cord due to the combined actions of the two persons is described by the function

$$\phi(x,t) = \phi_1(x,t) + \phi_2(x,t)$$
$$= A_1 \exp[2\pi i(\sigma_1 x - v_1 t)] + A_2 \exp[2\pi i(\sigma_2 x - v_2 t)] \tag{2-76}$$

We write this expression in a different form for the case where

$$A_1 = A_2 = A \tag{2-77}$$

by substituting

$$\sigma_1 = \sigma + \sigma' \qquad v_1 = v + v'$$
$$\sigma_2 = \sigma - \sigma' \qquad v_2 = v - v' \tag{2-78}$$

into Eq. (2-76). We obtain

$$\phi(x,t) = Ae^{2\pi i(\sigma x - vt)}[e^{2\pi i(\sigma' x - v't)} + e^{-2\pi i(\sigma' x - v't)}] \tag{2-79}$$

or $\quad\phi(x,t) = 2A\cos[2\pi(\sigma' x - v't)]e^{2\pi i(\sigma x - vt)} \tag{2-80}$

When σ' is much smaller than σ, the position of the cord at a time t_0 is described by the situation in Fig. 2-3. There is a very rapid oscillation described by σ, and the amplitude of this wave varies much more slowly; this variation is determined by σ'. We see that the situation of Fig. 2-3 can be obtained as the sum of two single waves, and we speak here of a superposition of the single waves, leading to the situation of Fig. 2-3.

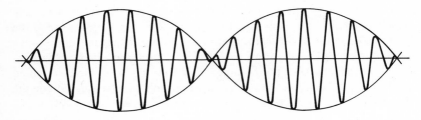

FIG. 2-3

In the same way we may discuss the superposition of three or more waves or even of an infinite number of single waves. The most convenient way to study this situation makes use of the Fourier integral theorem of Eq. (2-61). Let us consider an arbitrary motion of the cord, where the deviations are described by a function $D(x,t)$. The deviation $D(x,0)$ at the time $t = 0$ can be written as

$$D(x,0) = (2\pi)^{-1/2} \int_{-\infty}^{\infty} F(u)e^{iux}\, du \qquad (2\text{-}81)$$

with
$$F(u) = (2\pi)^{-1/2} \int_{-\infty}^{\infty} D(s,0)e^{-ius}\, ds \qquad (2\text{-}82)$$

We write this in a more suitable form by replacing u by $2\pi\sigma$ and by including the factor $\sqrt{2\pi}$ in the function F:

$$D(x,0) = \int_{-\infty}^{\infty} F(\sigma)e^{2\pi i\sigma x}\, d\sigma$$

$$F(\sigma) = \int_{-\infty}^{\infty} D(x,0)e^{-2\pi i\sigma x}\, dx \qquad (2\text{-}83)$$

At the time $t = 0$ we have now expressed $D(x,0)$ as a superposition of an infinite number of single waves. The transformation function $F(\sigma)$, which represents the amplitudes of the single waves, is given by the second Eq. (2-83).

It follows that any arbitrary configuration of the cord at a specific time can be expressed as a superposition of single waves. What we would like to do is to predict the time dependence of $D(x,t)$ from our knowledge of the initial configuration $D(x,0)$, and we wonder how and when this can be achieved. We know that the time dependence of one individual wave is given by

$$e^{2\pi i(\sigma x - vt)} \tag{2-84}$$

and we also know that v is related to σ:

$$v = v(\sigma) \tag{2-85}$$

The dependence of v on σ depends on the properties of the system. For the system of Sec. 2-2 this dependence was of the form

$$v = v\sigma \tag{2-86}$$

but it should be realized that we cannot automatically assume such a simple function with a constant v for waves in general. For example, it might be possible that v depends also on σ or, if we consider different systems, that the function $v(\sigma)$ of Eq. (2-85) is completely different from Eq. (2-86). In general we should allow for all possibilities for the functions $v(\sigma)$, depending on the kind of system that we consider. This function $v(\sigma)$ is known as the *dispersion relation* for the waves in the system that we consider, and it is this function which determines the time dependence of $D(x,t)$. This is easily seen by substituting Eq. (2-84) instead of the time-independent exponential into the first Eq. (2-83), which gives

$$D(x,t) = \int_{-\infty}^{\infty} F(\sigma) \exp\{2\pi i[\sigma x - v(\sigma)t]\}\, d\sigma \tag{2-87}$$

with
$$F(\sigma) = \int_{-\infty}^{\infty} D(x,0)e^{-2\pi i\sigma x}\, dx \tag{2-88}$$

From the configuration $D(x,0)$ at $t = 0$ we can determine the amplitude function $F(\sigma)$ through Eq. (2-88), and if we know the specific form of the dispersion relation $v(\sigma)$, we can predict the time dependence of $D(x,t)$ by means of Eq. (2-87). The motion of the system is thus described as a superposition of single waves, and it is completely determined by the dispersion relation $v(\sigma)$ and by the initial configuration $D(x,0)$.

The advantage of this mathematical description is that it can be extended immediately to the three-dimensional case that we mentioned at the beginning of this section. For the sake of simplicity we use the symbol $\psi(x,y,z; t)$ or $\psi(\mathbf{r};t)$ instead of $\delta\rho$, and we assume that $\psi(\mathbf{r};0)$ is known. We then have

$$\psi(\mathbf{r};0) = \int_{-\infty}^{\infty} A(\sigma_x,\sigma_y,\sigma_z)e^{2\pi i(\sigma_x x + \sigma_y y + \sigma_z z)}\, d\sigma_x\, d\sigma_y\, d\sigma_z$$

$$A(\boldsymbol{\sigma}) = \int_{-\infty}^{\infty} \psi(\mathbf{r};0)e^{-2\pi i(\sigma_x x + \sigma_y y + \sigma_z z)}\, dx\, dy\, dz \tag{2-89}$$

The difference from the one-dimensional case is that now we have three variables $\sigma_x, \sigma_y,$ and σ_z, which form a vector $\boldsymbol{\sigma} = (\sigma_x,\sigma_y,\sigma_z)$, instead of the one variable σ in one dimension. Let us now imagine that we know the three-dimensional dispersion relation

$$v = v(\sigma_x,\sigma_y,\sigma_z) = v(\boldsymbol{\sigma}) \tag{2-90}$$

The time dependence of

$$\psi(\mathbf{r};t) = \int_{-\infty}^{\infty} A(\boldsymbol{\sigma}) \exp \left\{2\pi i[(\boldsymbol{\sigma} \cdot \mathbf{r}) - v(\boldsymbol{\sigma}) \cdot t]\right\} d\boldsymbol{\sigma} \tag{2-91}$$

is completely analogous to the one-dimensional case. Here the function $A(\boldsymbol{\sigma})$ is derived from $\psi(\mathbf{r};0)$ by means of the second Eq. (2-89).

This simple argument, consisting only of Eqs. (2-89) to (2-91), contains the complete mathematical description of waves in three dimensions. We now consider the physical aspects of the situation. It has been shown how in the one-dimensional case we have, in Eq. (2-87), decomposed a complicated wave pattern in terms of single waves, each of which was described by an exponential function. In Eq. (2-91) we have done the same in three dimensions; that is, we have written ψ as a superposition of single waves that are described by the exponentials

$$g = \exp \left\{2\pi i[(\boldsymbol{\sigma} \cdot \mathbf{r}) - v(\boldsymbol{\sigma}) \cdot t]\right\} \tag{2-92}$$

A wave described by the simple function g is called a *plane wave*. In order to appreciate this name we should consider the surfaces of equal phases; these are the surfaces over which g is constant. It is easily verified from Eq. (2-92) that all these surfaces are planes satisfying the equation

$$\sigma_x x + \sigma_y y + \sigma_z z = \text{const} \tag{2-93}$$

All these planes are parallel and they are perpendicular to the vector $\boldsymbol{\sigma}$. This may be understood if we consider the plane of Eq. (2-93), which passes through the origin so that the const is zero. Let us consider a vector between the origin and a point $\mathbf{r}_0$ in this plane. The point (x_0,y_0,z_0) is in the plane when it satisfies the condition

$$\sigma_x x_0 + \sigma_y y_0 + \sigma_z z_0 = 0 \tag{2-94}$$

and this is also the condition that $\mathbf{r}_0$ is perpendicular to $\boldsymbol{\sigma}$.

All planes of equal phases are therefore perpendicular to $\boldsymbol{\sigma}$, and when they move as a function of time, they do so in the direction of propagation $\boldsymbol{\sigma}$. Therefore $\boldsymbol{\sigma}$ gives the direction of propagation of the waves. The velocity of propagation in the $\boldsymbol{\sigma}$ direction is given by

$$v = \frac{v}{\sigma} \tag{2-95}$$

and

$$\sigma = (\sigma_x{}^2 + \sigma_y{}^2 + \sigma_z{}^2)^{1/2} = \lambda^{-1} \tag{2-96}$$

just as in the one-dimensional case. We call σ the *wave vector* of the plane wave; its direction determines the propagation of the wave, and its magnitude is the inverse of the wavelength.

Naturally we could have decomposed ψ in a different way, but since plane waves are so easily visualized, we prefer to write ψ as a superposition of plane waves. This is why Fourier analysis, which describes such superpositions, is so important in wave mechanics.

2-6 DE BROGLIE'S QUANTUM POSTULATE FOR FREE PARTICLES

In 1924 De Broglie[1] suggested that the motion of a free particle is associated with a three-dimensional wave. We have already mentioned that this postulate is best understood if we imagine that the motion of the particle is described by a probability pattern and that this probability pattern is derived from the wave motion. According to De Broglie a free particle, moving with a constant momentum $\mathbf{p}$ and energy E, is associated with a plane wave, determined by a wave vector σ and frequency ν, and the connection between these quantities is given by the relations

$$\mathbf{p} = h\sigma$$
$$E = h\nu \tag{2-97}$$

Here h is Planck's constant. We have seen that for an understanding of the time dependence of such a wave it is essential to know the dispersion relation. This is easily derived, since we know from classical mechanics that

$$E = \frac{p^2}{2m} \tag{2-98}$$

If we substitute Eqs. (2-97) we find that

$$\nu = \frac{h}{2m}(\sigma_x{}^2 + \sigma_y{}^2 + \sigma_z{}^2) \tag{2-99}$$

is the desired dispersion formula. This expression is not relativistically invariant, but throughout this book we limit ourselves to nonrelativistic quantum mechanics.

If we stretch the truth a bit, we may show how De Broglie's postulates lead to Bohr's quantum conditions of Eq. (1-123). Let us consider an electron in a circular orbit around a hydrogen nucleus and moving with a

---

[1] L. De Broglie, " Thesis," Paris, 1924.

constant momentum p. The electron is coupled to a wave whose length λ is given by

$$\lambda = \frac{h}{p} \tag{2-100}$$

The radius of the circle is r and in one complete orbit the electron covers a distance $2\pi r$. It may be understood that the electronic motion is stationary only when this complete orbit is an integer times the wavelength; otherwise the motion pattern would be different in successive orbits. We have, therefore, the condition

$$2\pi r = n\lambda \tag{2-101}$$

or, substituting Eq. (2-100),

$$pr = \frac{nh}{2\pi} \tag{2-102}$$

This is identical to the Bohr condition of Eq. (1-123).

We have seen that a single plane wave may be represented by a wave function

$$g(\mathbf{r};t) = \exp\{2\pi i[(\boldsymbol{\sigma} \cdot \mathbf{r}) - vt]\} \tag{2-103}$$

If we substitute the expressions (2-97) for $\boldsymbol{\sigma}$ and v, we have the motion of a particle that is described by one plane wave. In general we have to represent the motion of a particle by a superposition of plane waves; in this way we obtain wave-mechanical descriptions that bear at least some resemblance to the ideas of classical mechanics. The most general wave motion can be represented as

$$\psi(\mathbf{r};t) = \iiint A(\boldsymbol{\sigma}) \exp\{2\pi i[(\boldsymbol{\sigma} \cdot \mathbf{r}) - v(\boldsymbol{\sigma}) \cdot t]\}\, d\boldsymbol{\sigma} \tag{2-104}$$

with the amplitude function $A(\boldsymbol{\sigma})$ determined by

$$A(\boldsymbol{\sigma}) = \iiint \psi(\mathbf{r};0) \exp[-2\pi i(\boldsymbol{\sigma} \cdot \mathbf{r})]\, d\mathbf{r} \tag{2-105}$$

and the function $v(\boldsymbol{\sigma})$ given by Eq. (2-99). Since the dispersion relation is known, the behavior of the probability pattern of the particle depends entirely on the initial choice of $\psi(\mathbf{r};0)$. We can approach the classical concept of a localized particle moving in a well-defined orbit by choosing $\psi(\mathbf{r};0)$ in such a way that it has a sharp maximum around a point $\mathbf{r}_0$. This assumption leads to a quantum-mechanical description in which, at each time, the position and momentum of the particle can be determined within certain boundaries that are compatible with the

Heisenberg uncertainty relations. Such a superposition of waves that corresponds to approximate localization of the particle is called a *wave packet*. We give a more detailed mathematical description of the properties of wave packets in the following section.

We cannot make any quantitative predictions about the motion of a particle until we have discussed the relation between the wave function ψ and the probability pattern of the particle. Schrödinger[1] was the first to point out the importance of the function

$$\rho(x,y,z; t) = \psi(x,y,z; t) \, \psi^*(x,y,z; t) \tag{2-106}$$

but he related this function to the charge density of the electron. Almost simultaneously Born[2] made the more logical assumption that the function ρ described the probability density for the particle independent of the presence or absence of electric charges. To be more specific, if we take a small volume element $d\tau$ around a point $\mathbf{r}_0$, then the probability P of finding this particle in $d\tau$ at a time t is given by

$$P = \rho(\mathbf{r}_0; t) \, d\tau \tag{2-107}$$

Since the particle must be somewhere in space, it follows that the density function ρ must satisfy the condition

$$\iiint \rho(x,y,z; t) \, dx \, dy \, dz = 1 \tag{2-108}$$

This condition is usually achieved by multiplying ψ with a suitable *normalization constant*.

We should make certain that this normalization constant is time-independent; otherwise the procedure above would not be consistent. In order to prove this time independence, we note that the function $A(\sigma)$ is time-independent, so that we can normalize it to unity by multiplying it with a constant:

$$\int A(\sigma) A^*(\sigma) \, d\sigma = 1 \tag{2-109}$$

The integral (2-108) can now be expressed according to Eq. (2-104):

$$\int \psi(\mathbf{r}; t) \psi^*(\mathbf{r}; t) \, d\mathbf{r} = \iint A(\sigma_1) A^*(\sigma_2) e^{-2\pi i t[\nu(\sigma_1) - \nu(\sigma_2)]} \, d\sigma_1 \, d\sigma_2$$

$$\times \int \exp \{2\pi i[(\sigma_1 - \sigma_2) \cdot \mathbf{r}]\} \, d\mathbf{r} \tag{2-110}$$

---

[1] E. Schrödinger, *Ann. Physik*, **80**: 437, 476 (1926).
[2] M. Born, *Zeits. f. Physik*, **37**: 863 (1926); **38**: 803 (1926).

The last integral is just the representation (2-64) of the δ function, so that we can write

$$\int \psi(\mathbf{r};t)\psi^*(\mathbf{r};t) \, d\mathbf{r} = \iint A(\boldsymbol{\sigma}_1)A^*(\boldsymbol{\sigma}_2)e^{-2\pi i t[v(\sigma_1)-v(\sigma_2)]}\delta(\boldsymbol{\sigma}_1 - \boldsymbol{\sigma}_2) \, d\boldsymbol{\sigma}_1 \, d\boldsymbol{\sigma}_2$$

$$= \int A(\boldsymbol{\sigma})A^*(\boldsymbol{\sigma}) \, d\boldsymbol{\sigma} \tag{2-111}$$

where we have introduced the three-dimensional δ function

$$\delta(\boldsymbol{\sigma}) = \delta(\sigma_x)\delta(\sigma_y)\delta(\sigma_z) \tag{2-112}$$

Since the last integral of Eq. (2-111) is time-independent, the normalization integral for ψ is time-independent also.

Let us now consider the questions of what the most probable position and momentum of the particle are. One way of answering the first question would be to determine the maximum of the function $\rho(\mathbf{r};t)$ as a function of $\mathbf{r}$. However, this procedure is rather tedious, and besides, it is not consistent with other aspects of quantum mechanics. Instead, we define the expectation value $\bar{\mathbf{r}}(t)$ of $\mathbf{r}$ by means of

$$\bar{\mathbf{r}}(t) = \int \psi^*(\mathbf{r};t) \, \mathbf{r} \, \psi(\mathbf{r};t) \, d\mathbf{r} \tag{2-113}$$

and we consider it the average position of the particle at the time t. We can write Eq. (2-113) in a different form if we make use of the Dirac notation:

$$\bar{\mathbf{r}}(t) = \langle \psi(\mathbf{r};t)| \, \mathbf{r} \, |\psi(\mathbf{r};t)\rangle = \int \psi^*(\mathbf{r};t) \, \mathbf{r} \, \psi(\mathbf{r};t) \, d\mathbf{r} \tag{2-114}$$

Obviously this is a shorthand notation for the three equations

$$\bar{x}(t) = \langle \psi(\mathbf{r};t)| \, x \, |\psi(\mathbf{r};t)\rangle$$

$$\bar{y}(t) = \langle \psi(\mathbf{r};t)| \, y \, |\psi(\mathbf{r};t)\rangle \tag{2-115}$$

$$\bar{z}(t) = \langle \psi(\mathbf{r};t)| \, z \, |\psi(\mathbf{r};t)\rangle$$

where all integrations are performed over the three dimensions x, y, and z.

The expectation value $\mathbf{p}$ of the momentum is derived by means of the De Broglie postulates (2-97) from the expectation value $\bar{\boldsymbol{\sigma}}$ of the wave vector, which is defined as

$$\bar{\boldsymbol{\sigma}} = \langle A(\boldsymbol{\sigma})| \, \boldsymbol{\sigma} \, |A(\boldsymbol{\sigma})\rangle = \int A^*(\boldsymbol{\sigma})\boldsymbol{\sigma}A(\boldsymbol{\sigma}) \, d\boldsymbol{\sigma} \tag{2-116}$$

This illustrates that the connection between $\boldsymbol{\sigma}$ and $A(\boldsymbol{\sigma})$ is similar to that between $\mathbf{r}$ and $\psi(\mathbf{r};t)$. In fact, the probability distribution of $\boldsymbol{\sigma}$ depends on

$A(\boldsymbol{\sigma})$ in exactly the same way as the $\mathbf{r}$ probability density depends on $\psi(\mathbf{r};t)$. The components σ_x, σ_y, and σ_z define a three-dimensional space that is known as the *momentum space*. If we define a volume element $d\boldsymbol{\sigma}$ in momentum space around the point $\boldsymbol{\sigma}_0$, then the probability of finding $\boldsymbol{\sigma}$ in this volume element is given by

$$A(\boldsymbol{\sigma}_0)A^*(\boldsymbol{\sigma}_0)\,d\boldsymbol{\sigma} \tag{2-117}$$

in complete analogy to Eq. (2-107). The only difference between the probability patterns of $\mathbf{r}$ and $\boldsymbol{\sigma}$ for a free particle is that the first is time-dependent and the second is not. This is related to one of the principles of classical mechanics that says that a free particle that is not subject to exterior forces has a momentum that is constant in time.

The definitions (2-114) and (2-116) are special cases of more general definitions that state that the expectation values $\bar{f}$ and $\bar{g}$ of a function $f(\mathbf{r})$ of the coordinates and of a function $g(\boldsymbol{\sigma})$ of the wave vector are given by

$$\bar{f} = \langle \psi(\mathbf{r};t)| f(\mathbf{r}) |\psi(\mathbf{r};t)\rangle \tag{2-118}$$

and
$$\bar{g} = \langle A(\boldsymbol{\sigma})| g(\boldsymbol{\sigma}) |A(\boldsymbol{\sigma})\rangle \tag{2-119}$$

respectively. According to these definitions the average square deviation $(\Delta x)^2$ of the coordinate x with respect to the expectation value $\bar{x}$ is given by

$$(\Delta x)^2 = \langle \psi(\mathbf{r};t)| (x - \bar{x})^2 |\psi(\mathbf{r};t)\rangle \tag{2-120}$$

The average square deviation $(\Delta\sigma_x)^2$ of σ_x with respect to $\bar{\sigma}_x$ is similarly defined as

$$(\Delta\sigma_x)^2 = \langle A(\boldsymbol{\sigma})| (\sigma_x - \bar{\sigma}_x)^2 |A(\boldsymbol{\sigma})\rangle \tag{2-121}$$

It is easily verified that Eqs. (2-120) and (2-121) are equivalent to

$$(\Delta x)^2 = \langle \psi(\mathbf{r};t)| x^2 - \bar{x}^2 |\psi(\mathbf{r};t)\rangle \tag{2-122}$$

and
$$(\Delta\sigma_x)^2 = \langle A(\boldsymbol{\sigma})| \sigma_x{}^2 - \bar{\sigma}_x{}^2 |A(\boldsymbol{\sigma})\rangle \tag{2-123}$$

We use these definitions for a more detailed discussion of the properties of wave packets in the next section.

2-7 PROPERTIES OF WAVE PACKETS AND THE UNCERTAINTY PRINCIPLE

The quantum-mechanical analogue of the classical motion of a localized particle is a moving wave packet. Here the wave function has been chosen in such a way that the function $\psi\psi^*$ is very small everywhere except in the vicinity of the point $\mathbf{r}_0$, where it has a sharp maximum. The point $\mathbf{r}_0$ moves with a momentum that is approximately equal to $\mathbf{p}_0$; consequently, the wave vector of the wave packet should be approximately equal to $\boldsymbol{\sigma}_0$ and $h\boldsymbol{\sigma}_0 = \mathbf{p}_0$. We first study a specific example of these wave packets; this will enable us to understand and discuss some of their general properties.

The example that we choose is a one-dimensional wave packet whose wave function $\psi(x;t)$ at $t = 0$ is given by

$$\psi(x;0) = (2\tau)^{1/4} e^{-\pi\tau x^2 + 2\pi i\sigma_0 x} \tag{2-124}$$

It is easily verified from Eqs. (1-67) and (1-73) that this function is normalized to unity. It also follows from Eqs. (1-68) and (1-75) that

$$x_0 = \int_{-\infty}^{\infty} \psi^*(x;0)x\psi(x;0)\,dx = 0 \tag{2-125}$$

and

$$(\Delta x)^2 = \int_{-\infty}^{\infty} \psi^*(x;0)x^2\psi(x;0)\,dx = \frac{1}{4\pi\tau} \tag{2-126}$$

We saw in the previous section that the time dependence of the wave function is determined by first evaluating the amplitude function $A(\sigma)$. According to Eq. (2-89), this function is given by

$$A(\sigma) = \int_{-\infty}^{\infty} \psi(x;0)e^{-2\pi i\sigma x}\,dx \tag{2-127}$$

which in the present case becomes

$$A(\sigma) = (2\tau)^{1/4} \int_{-\infty}^{\infty} e^{-\pi\tau x^2 - 2\pi i(\sigma - \sigma_0)x}\,dx \tag{2-128}$$

This integral is not easily evaluated, but we can write it in the form

$$A(\sigma) = CF(u,p) \tag{2-129}$$

with

$$F(u,p) = \left(\frac{1}{2\pi}\right)^{1/2} \int_{-\infty}^{\infty} e^{-ps^2} e^{ius}\,ds \tag{2-130}$$

This is the Fourier transform of the error function e^{-ps^2} and is well known in the theory of Fourier analysis. We can find its analytic form in any table of Fourier transforms:[1]

$$F(u,p) = \left(\frac{1}{2p}\right)^{1/2} \exp\left(\frac{-u^2}{4p}\right) \tag{2-131}$$

This result is also valid for complex p and u as long as the real part of p

---

[1] For example, I. N. Sneddon, "Fourier Transforms," McGraw-Hill Book Company, Inc., New York, 1951, p. 523.

is positive. By comparing Eqs. (2-128) and (2-129), we find from Eq. (2-131) that

$$A(\sigma) = \left(\frac{2}{\tau}\right)^{1/4} \exp\left[-\frac{\pi(\sigma - \sigma_0)^2}{\tau}\right] \qquad (2\text{-}132)$$

This function is normalized to unity because of Eq. (2-111).

Let us now calculate the expectation values of σ and $(\Delta\sigma)^2$. It is easily verified that

$$\bar{\sigma} = \left(\frac{2}{\tau}\right)^{1/2} \int \sigma \exp\left[-\frac{2\pi(\sigma - \sigma_0)^2}{\tau}\right] d\sigma = \sigma_0 \qquad (2\text{-}133)$$

and

$$(\Delta\sigma)^2 = \left(\frac{2}{\tau}\right)^{1/2} \int (\sigma - \sigma_0)^2 \exp\left[-2\pi(\sigma - \sigma_0)^2\tau\right] d\sigma = \frac{\tau}{4\pi} \qquad (2\text{-}134)$$

The last result is derived from Eqs. (1-68) and (1-75).

Let us now compare the results for Δx and $\Delta\sigma$ from Eqs. (2-126) and (2-134):

$$\Delta x = \frac{\tau^{-1/2}}{\sqrt{4\pi}} \qquad \Delta\sigma = \frac{\tau^{1/2}}{\sqrt{4\pi}} \qquad (2\text{-}135)$$

We can make Δx smaller by increasing τ, and in this way we can reduce the uncertainty in the position of the particle; but this will increase the uncertainty $\Delta\sigma$. If, on the other hand, we decrease τ in order to make $\Delta\sigma$ smaller, then the uncertainty Δx becomes larger. We see that the product

$$\Delta x \cdot \Delta\sigma = \frac{1}{4\pi} \qquad (2\text{-}136)$$

is independent of τ. According to De Broglie's postulates, we have

$$\Delta x \cdot \Delta p = \tfrac{1}{2}\hbar \qquad (2\text{-}137)$$

It can be shown that the wave packet of Eq. (2-124) is that which gives the smallest value for the product $\Delta x \cdot \Delta p$, and consequently this product is always larger than $\tfrac{1}{2}\hbar$. These considerations constitute, therefore, the wave-mechanical proof of the Heisenberg uncertainty relations of Sec. 1-8. Apparently Heisenberg was too generous in his first formulation of the uncertainty relations when the lower limit of $\Delta q_i \cdot \Delta p_i$ was taken to be equal to h; instead, the limit is smaller by a factor 4π. Nevertheless, it is customary in the literature to take h as the lower limit of $\Delta q_i \cdot \Delta p_i$ and to ignore the result above of $\tfrac{1}{2}\hbar$; we are not aware of any reason for this.

We now proceed to determine $\psi(x,t)$. It follows from Eqs. (2-104) and (2-132) that

$$\psi(x;t) = \left(\frac{2}{\tau}\right)^{1/4} \int_{-\infty}^{\infty} \exp\left[-\frac{\pi(\sigma - \sigma_0)^2}{\tau} + 2\pi i\sigma x - \frac{\pi i\hbar\sigma^2}{m}t\right] d\sigma \quad (2\text{-}138)$$

since the dispersion relation $v(\sigma)$ is

$$v = \frac{h\sigma^2}{2m} \tag{2-139}$$

In order to evaluate this integral, we first change to a new integration variable $s = \sigma - \sigma_0$, which gives

$$\psi(x;t) = \left(\frac{2}{\tau}\right)^{1/4} \exp\left[2\pi i\left(\sigma_0 x - \frac{h\sigma_0^2 t}{2m}\right)\right] \int_{-\infty}^{\infty} \exp\left[-\left(\frac{\pi}{\tau} + \frac{\pi i h t}{m}\right)s^2\right]$$

$$\times \exp\left[2\pi i\left(x - \frac{h\sigma_0 t}{m}\right)s\right] ds \tag{2-140}$$

This integral can again be expressed in the form of Eq. (2-129) if we take

$$C = \left(\frac{8\pi^2}{\tau}\right)^{1/4} \exp\left[2\pi i\left(\sigma_0 x - \frac{h\sigma_0^2 t}{2m}\right)\right]$$

$$p = \frac{\pi}{\tau}\left(1 + \frac{ih\tau t}{m}\right) \tag{2-141}$$

$$u = 2\pi\left(x - \frac{h\sigma_0 t}{m}\right)$$

By substitution into Eqs. (2-129) and (2-131) we find that the integral $\psi(x;t)$ is

$$\psi(x,t) = (2\tau)^{1/4}\left(1 + \frac{ih\tau t}{m}\right)^{-1/2} \exp\left[-\pi\tau\left(1 + \frac{ih\tau t}{m}\right)^{-1}\left(x - \frac{h\sigma_0 t}{m}\right)^2\right]$$

$$\times \exp\left[2\pi i\left(\sigma_0 x - \frac{h\sigma_0^2 t}{2m}\right)\right] \tag{2-142}$$

It is also convenient to write the probability density function $\rho(x,t)$, which is

$$\rho(x,t) = (2\tau')^{1/2} \exp\left[-2\pi\tau'(x - v_0 t)^2\right] \tag{2-143}$$

where we have introduced the new parameters

$$\tau' = \tau\left(1 + \frac{h^2\tau^2 t^2}{m^2}\right)^{-1} \qquad v_0 = \frac{h\sigma_0}{m} \tag{2-144}$$

Equations (2-141) and (2-142) give the complete description of the motion of the wave packet defined by Eq. (2-124). It follows from Eq. (2-142) that the expectation value of x as a function of time is given by

$$x(t) = v_0 t \tag{2-145}$$

which is in agreement with classical mechanics. The expectation value $(\Delta x)_t^2$ of $(\Delta x)^2$ as a function of t is given by

$$(\Delta x)_t^2 = \frac{1}{4\pi\tau'} = \frac{1}{4\pi\tau}\left(1 + \frac{h^2\tau^2 t^2}{m^2}\right) \qquad (2\text{-}146)$$

It follows that Δx increases with time, and since $\Delta\sigma$ is time-independent, the product $\Delta x \cdot \Delta\sigma$ also increases as a function of time. Apparently Eq. (2-124) is a very good choice for the wave function at $t = 0$, since at this time the product of the uncertainties Δx and $\Delta\sigma$ is as small as we can ever hope to achieve. However, as times goes on, the uncertainty Δx becomes larger and larger, and eventually there comes a time that Δx is so large that we no longer know where the particle is supposed to be. This means that in quantum mechanics we can only follow the motion of the wave packet for a limited time, after which the accumulated uncertainties become so large that we cannot make any reliable predictions.

This argument can be extended to three dimensions without any difficulties. If we represent the three-dimensional wave function at $t = 0$ as

$$\psi(\mathbf{r};0) = (8\tau_1\tau_2\tau_3)^{1/4}e^{-\pi(\tau_1 x^2 + \tau_2 y^2 + \tau_3 z^2)}e^{2\pi i(\sigma_0 \cdot \mathbf{r})} \qquad (2\text{-}147)$$

then it follows from Eqs. (2-105) and (2-132) that

$$A(\sigma) = \left(\frac{8}{\tau_1\tau_2\tau_3}\right)^{1/4}\exp\left\{-\pi\left[\frac{(\sigma_x - \sigma_{0,x})^2}{\tau_1} + \frac{(\sigma_y - \sigma_{0,y})^2}{\tau_2} + \frac{(\sigma_z - \sigma_{0,z})^2}{\tau_3}\right]\right\} \qquad (2\text{-}148)$$

By analogy to Eq. (2-143) we find

$$\rho(\mathbf{r};t) = (8\tau_1'\tau_2'\tau_3')^{1/2}\exp\{-2\pi[\tau_1'(x - v_{0,x})^2 + \tau_2'(y - v_{0,y})^2 + \tau_3'(z - v_{0,z})^2]\} \qquad (2\text{-}149)$$

with

$$\tau_i' = \tau_i\left(1 + \frac{h^2\tau_i^2 t^2}{m^2}\right)^{-1} \qquad (2\text{-}150)$$

$$m\mathbf{v}_0 = h\sigma_0$$

Obviously all our conclusions for one-dimensional motion are equally valid for each dimension in three-dimensional motion.

We saw in Sec. 2-2 that the propagation of a single wave is described by a velocity $\mathbf{v}$, which is given by

$$v = \frac{v}{\sigma} \qquad (2\text{-}151)$$

This is called the *phase velocity* of the individual waves. A wave packet, constructed as a superposition of waves as described above, has a second velocity $\mathbf{u}$ that is called the *group velocity*. This is the velocity at which the maximum of the function $\psi\psi^*$ moves along, and it is defined as the time derivative of the expectation value $\mathbf{r}(t)$. We show that $\mathbf{u}$ has the same direction as the expectation value of $\boldsymbol{\sigma}$ and that its magnitude is given by

$$u = \frac{dv}{d\sigma} \qquad (2\text{-}152)$$

In order to prove this, let us first investigate how the point $\mathbf{r}(t)$ is characterized from a physical point of view. At $\mathbf{r}(t)$ the function $\psi(\mathbf{r},t)$ has a maximum value, owing to the fact that the various waves from which the wave packet is constructed reinforce each other. They can do this only if they have approximately the same phase, and therefore $\mathbf{r}(t)$ is determined by the condition

$$x_0 \, d\sigma_x + y_0 \, d\sigma_y + z_0 \, d\sigma_z - t_0 \, dv = 0 \qquad (2\text{-}153)$$

At a small time interval dt later, the point $\mathbf{r}(t)$ has moved to $\mathbf{r}_0 + d\mathbf{r}$, and we have

$$(x_0 + dx) \, d\sigma_x + (y_0 + dy) \, d\sigma_y + (z_0 + dz) \, d\sigma_z - (t_0 + dt) \, dv = 0 \qquad (2\text{-}154)$$

If we subtract Eq. (2-153) from Eq. (2-154) and divide by dt, we obtain

$$\frac{dx}{dt} \, d\sigma_x + \frac{dy}{dt} \, d\sigma_y + \frac{dz}{dt} \, d\sigma_z - dv = 0 \qquad (2\text{-}155)$$

From the definition of the group velocity $\mathbf{u}$ we know that the time derivatives in Eq. (2-155) are just the components of the group velocity, so that

$$u_x \, d\sigma_x + u_y \, d\sigma_y + u_z \, d\sigma_z - dv = 0 \qquad (2\text{-}156)$$

The frequency v is a function of $\boldsymbol{\sigma}$, and we have

$$dv = \frac{\partial v}{\partial \sigma_x} \, d\sigma_x + \frac{\partial v}{\partial \sigma_y} \, d\sigma_y + \frac{\partial v}{\partial \sigma_z} \, d\sigma_z \qquad (2\text{-}157)$$

Substitution into Eq. (2-156) gives

$$\left(u_x - \frac{\partial v}{\partial \sigma_x}\right) d\sigma_x + \left(u_y - \frac{\partial v}{\partial \sigma_y}\right) d\sigma_y + \left(u_z - \frac{\partial v}{\partial \sigma_z}\right) d\sigma_z = 0 \qquad (2\text{-}158)$$

Since this equation should be valid for all possible $d\sigma_\alpha$, we find that

$$u_x = \frac{\partial v}{\partial \sigma_x} \qquad u_y = \frac{\partial v}{\partial \sigma_y} \qquad u_z = \frac{\partial v}{\partial \sigma_z} \qquad (2\text{-}159)$$

In most cases v depends only on the modulus σ of $\boldsymbol{\sigma}$. Then we find

$$\frac{\partial v}{\partial \sigma_\alpha} = \frac{dv}{d\sigma} \frac{\sigma_\alpha}{\sigma} \qquad (2\text{-}160)$$

or
$$\mathbf{u} = \frac{1}{\sigma}\frac{dv}{d\sigma}\,\boldsymbol{\sigma} \tag{2-161}$$

by substituting Eq. (2-160) into Eq. (2-159). This means that $\mathbf{u}$ has the same direction as $\boldsymbol{\sigma}$ and that its magnitude is given by Eq. (2-152).

For a free particle, where the dispersion relation is given by (2-140), the group velocity is

$$\mathbf{u} = \frac{\mathbf{p}}{m} \tag{2-162}$$

We see that the motion of a quantum-mechanical wave packet is in every respect equivalent to the classical motion of a localized particle.

PROBLEMS _____

2-1   Find all roots of the equation

$$x^n = i$$

by using Eq. (2-18).

2-2   The function $f(x)$ is defined in the interval $-\pi \leqslant x \leqslant \pi$ as

$$f(x) = 0 \qquad x < 0$$
$$f(x) = \tfrac{1}{2}A \qquad x = 0$$
$$f(x) = A \qquad x > 0$$

Expand $f(x)$ in a Fourier series.

2-3   Prove that the integral

$$\iint f(\mathbf{r}_1)g(\mathbf{r}_2)h(\mathbf{r}_1 - \mathbf{r}_2)\,d\mathbf{r}_1\,d\mathbf{r}_2$$

can also be written as

$$(2\pi)^{-3}\int F(-\boldsymbol{\sigma})G(\boldsymbol{\sigma})H(\boldsymbol{\sigma})\,d\boldsymbol{\sigma}$$

if
$$F(\boldsymbol{\sigma}) = \int f(t)e^{-i\boldsymbol{\sigma}\cdot\mathbf{t}}\,dt$$

$$G(\boldsymbol{\sigma}) = \int g(t)e^{-i\boldsymbol{\sigma}\cdot\mathbf{t}}\,dt$$

$$H(\boldsymbol{\sigma}) = \int h(t)e^{-i\boldsymbol{\sigma}\cdot\mathbf{t}}\,dt$$

This is known as the *Fourier convolution theorem*.

2-4 Determine $\psi(x;t)$ when $\psi(x;0)$ is given by Eq. (2-124) and when the dispersion relation is $\nu = h\sigma/2m$ instead of Eq. (2-139).

2-5 Evaluate the expectation value of $r^2 = x^2 + y^2 + z^2$ of the three-dimensional wave function $\psi(\mathbf{r};0)$ defined by Eq. (2-147).

2-6 If $A(\sigma)$ is real and the origin is chosen so that at $t = 0$ the expectation value of x is zero, show that at later times

$$(\Delta x)^2 = (\Delta x)^2_{t=0} + \frac{(\Delta\sigma)^2 h^2 t^2}{m^2}$$

_____

CHAPTER 3

THE SCHRÖDINGER EQUATION

3-1 THE SCHRÖDINGER EQUATION FOR A FREE PARTICLE

In Chap. 2 we saw that the wave function for a free particle can be written as

$$\psi(\mathbf{r};t) = \int A(\boldsymbol{\sigma})e^{2\pi i\{\boldsymbol{\sigma}\cdot\mathbf{r}-\nu t\}}\,d\boldsymbol{\sigma} \tag{3-1}$$

which is the most general superposition of plane waves of the form

$$g(\mathbf{r};t) = e^{2\pi i\{\boldsymbol{\sigma}\cdot\mathbf{r}-\nu t\}} \tag{3-2}$$

Each of these plane waves has to satisfy the condition that ν and $\boldsymbol{\sigma}$ are related by means of the dispersion formula

$$\nu = \frac{h\sigma^2}{2m} \tag{3-3}$$

We show that each function $g(\mathbf{r};t)$ of Eq. (3-2) that satisfies the condition of Eq. (3-3) is the solution of a specific differential equation. To this end we observe that

$$\frac{1}{2\pi i} \frac{\partial g}{\partial x} = \sigma_x g$$

$$\frac{1}{2\pi i} \frac{\partial g}{\partial y} = \sigma_y g$$

$$\frac{1}{2\pi i} \frac{\partial g}{\partial z} = \sigma_z g \tag{3-4}$$

$$-\frac{1}{2\pi i} \frac{\partial g}{\partial t} = v g$$

and also that

$$-\frac{1}{4\pi^2} \frac{\partial^2 g}{\partial x^2} = \sigma_x^2 g$$

$$-\frac{1}{4\pi^2} \frac{\partial^2 g}{\partial y^2} = \sigma_y^2 g \tag{3-5}$$

$$-\frac{1}{4\pi^2} \frac{\partial^2 g}{\partial z^2} = \sigma_z^2 g$$

If g satisfies the condition of Eq. (3-3), we may write

$$\left[\frac{h}{2m} (\sigma_x^2 + \sigma_y^2 + \sigma_z^2) - v \right] g(\mathbf{r};t) = 0 \tag{3-6}$$

and if we make the substitutions of Eqs. (3-4) and (3-5), this becomes

$$-\frac{h}{8\pi^2 m} \left(\frac{\partial^2}{\partial x^2} + \frac{\partial^2}{\partial y^2} + \frac{\partial^2}{\partial z^2} \right) g + \frac{1}{2\pi i} \frac{\partial g}{\partial t} = 0 \tag{3-7}$$

It follows that every plane wave of the form of Eq. (3-2) whose frequency v and wave vector $\boldsymbol{\sigma}$ are related by the dispersion relation (3-3) satisfies the differential equation (3-7).

Since we can choose arbitrary values for $\sigma_x, \sigma_y,$ and σ_z, Eq. (3-7) has an infinite number of solutions, and as long as v is given by Eq. (3-3), g is a solution of Eq. (3-7). The most general solution of Eq. (3-7) is a linear combination of all the specific solutions of Eq. (3-7). We have already observed that the specific solutions of the differential equation are the functions $g(\mathbf{r};t)$ of Eq. (3-2), where we have a free choice for $\sigma_x, \sigma_y,$ and σ_z. The most general linear combination of these specific solutions is the function (3-1), and therefore $\psi(\mathbf{r};t)$ is the general solution of Eq. (3-7). Any special solution of Eq. (3-7) can be obtained by making a specific choice for the function $A(\boldsymbol{\sigma})$ occurring in Eq. (3-1).

Equation (3-7) can be written in a slightly different way:

$$-\frac{\hbar^2}{2m}\left(\frac{\partial^2}{\partial x^2}+\frac{\partial^2}{\partial y^2}+\frac{\partial^2}{\partial z^2}\right)\psi(\mathbf{r};t) = -\frac{\hbar}{i}\frac{\partial}{\partial t}\psi(\mathbf{r};t) \qquad (3\text{-}8)$$

In this form it is known as the Schrödinger equation for a free particle.

It may be helpful to recall the procedure that led to the formulation of the Schrödinger equation in anticipation of our intention to generalize it for nonfree particles. We started by equating the energy E of the particle with the Hamiltonian as a function of the coordinates and momenta:

$$E = \mathscr{H}(\mathbf{r};\mathbf{p}) \qquad (3\text{-}9)$$

For a free particle the Hamiltonian does not depend on $\mathbf{r}$, but in general, for bound particles, we have to allow for the possibility that $\mathscr{H}$ contains the coordinate $\mathbf{r}$. Let us now combine Eq. (3-9) with De Broglie's postulates; this leads to

$$\mathscr{H}(\mathbf{r};h\boldsymbol{\sigma}) - h\nu = 0 \qquad (3\text{-}10)$$

From this result we derived that

$$[\mathscr{H}(\mathbf{r};h\boldsymbol{\sigma}) - h\nu]g(r;t) = 0 \qquad (3\text{-}11)$$

and we found that we may replace the multiplications by $\boldsymbol{\sigma}$ with differentiations with respect to x, y, and z when g satisfies the dispersion relations. The differential equation (3-8) is therefore derived from

$$\mathscr{H}\left(\mathbf{r};\frac{\hbar}{i}\boldsymbol{\nabla}\right)\psi(\mathbf{r};t) = -\frac{\hbar}{i}\frac{\partial\psi}{\partial t} \qquad (3\text{-}12)$$

The left side of the Schrödinger equation (3-8) is obtained from the Hamiltonian by replacing the vector $\mathbf{p}$ by the three-component operator $-i\hbar\boldsymbol{\nabla}$ with $\boldsymbol{\nabla}$ defined by Eqs. (1-13) and (1-14).

Since every wave function $\psi(\mathbf{r};t)$ of a free particle is a solution of the Schrödinger equation (3-8), we can use this equation to derive a general property for wave functions. We rewrite Eq. (3-8)

$$-\frac{\hbar^2}{2m}\left(\frac{\partial^2}{\partial x^2}+\frac{\partial^2}{\partial y^2}+\frac{\partial^2}{\partial z^2}\right)\psi = -\frac{\hbar}{i}\frac{\partial\psi}{\partial t} \qquad (3\text{-}13)$$

together with its complex conjugate:

$$-\frac{\hbar^2}{2m}\left(\frac{\partial^2}{\partial x^2}+\frac{\partial^2}{\partial y^2}+\frac{\partial^2}{\partial z^2}\right)\psi^* = \frac{\hbar}{i}\frac{\partial\psi^*}{\partial t} \qquad (3\text{-}14)$$

Next we multiply Eq. (3-13) on the left by ψ^* and Eq. (3-14) by ψ, and we subtract the first equation from the second. This gives

$$
\frac{\hbar}{i} \left(\psi \frac{\partial \psi^*}{\partial t} + \psi^* \frac{\partial \psi}{\partial t} \right)
$$

$$
= -\frac{\hbar^2}{2m} \left(\psi \frac{\partial^2 \psi^*}{\partial x^2} - \psi^* \frac{\partial^2 \psi}{\partial x^2} + \psi \frac{\partial^2 \psi^*}{\partial y^2} - \psi^* \frac{\partial^2 \psi}{\partial y^2} + \psi \frac{\partial^2 \psi^*}{\partial z^2} - \psi^* \frac{\partial^2 \psi}{\partial z^2} \right)
$$

$$(3\text{-}15)$$

or

$$
\frac{\partial}{\partial t}(\psi \psi^*) = -\frac{i\hbar}{2m} \left[\frac{\partial}{\partial x} \left(\psi \frac{\partial \psi^*}{\partial x} - \psi^* \frac{\partial \psi}{\partial x} \right) \right.
$$

$$
\left. + \frac{\partial}{\partial y} \left(\psi \frac{\partial \psi^*}{\partial y} - \psi^* \frac{\partial \psi}{\partial y} \right) + \frac{\partial}{\partial z} \left(\psi \frac{\partial \psi^*}{\partial z} - \psi^* \frac{\partial \psi}{\partial z} \right) \right] \quad (3\text{-}16)
$$

We note that the product $\psi \psi^*$ is the probability density function ρ. The right side of Eq. (3-16) can be simplified if we introduce the vector $\mathbf{J}$ with the components

$$
J_x = \frac{i\hbar}{2m} \left(\psi \frac{\partial \psi^*}{\partial x} - \psi^* \frac{\partial \psi}{\partial x} \right)
$$

$$
J_y = \frac{i\hbar}{2m} \left(\psi \frac{\partial \psi^*}{\partial y} - \psi^* \frac{\partial \psi}{\partial y} \right) \quad (3\text{-}17)
$$

$$
J_z = \frac{i\hbar}{2m} \left(\psi \frac{\partial \psi^*}{\partial z} - \psi^* \frac{\partial \psi}{\partial z} \right)
$$

Equation (3-16) is now transformed to

$$
-\frac{\partial \rho}{\partial t} = \frac{\partial J_x}{\partial x} + \frac{\partial J_y}{\partial y} + \frac{\partial J_z}{\partial z} = \nabla \cdot \mathbf{J} \quad (3\text{-}18)
$$

In vector analysis the right side of Eq. (3-18) is known as the *divergence* of the vector $\mathbf{J}$ or div $\mathbf{J}$. We may write, therefore,

$$
\frac{\partial \rho}{\partial t} + \text{div } \mathbf{J} = 0 \quad (3\text{-}19)
$$

The meaning of this equation is best understood if we think of the probability density as a moving gas. At a time t the cube in Fig. 3-1 between the points (x,y,z) and $(x + dx, \; y + dy, \; z + dz)$ contains an amount of gas that is given by $\rho(x,y,z; t)\, dx\, dy\, dz$.

During the time interval dt this amount of gas increases by an amount

$$
\frac{\partial}{\partial t} \rho(x,y,z; t)\, dx\, dy\, dz\, dt \quad (3\text{-}20)
$$

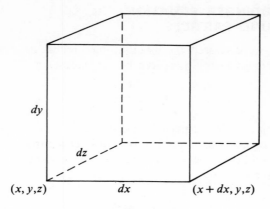

FIG. 3-1

Let us now investigate what causes this increase. Owing to the motion of the gas, we have a transport of gas molecules through all six surfaces of the cube. The motion is described by a vector $\mathbf{J}(x,y,z)$ that is defined so that the transport of gas per unit time through a surface element dS at a point (x_0,y_0,z_0) is given by $J_n(x_0,y_0,z_0)\,dS$. Here J_n is the component of $\mathbf{J}$ perpendicular to dS. According to this definition, the transport of gas into the cube through the left surface is $J_x(x,y,z)\,dy\,dz$. The transport of gas out of the cube through the right surface is $J_x(x + dx, y, z)\,dy\,dz$. The net influx through the two surfaces is given by

$$J_x(x,y,z)\,dy\,dz - J_x(x + dx, y, z)\,dy\,dz = -\frac{\partial J_x(x,y,z)}{\partial x}\,dx\,dy\,dz \qquad (3\text{-}21)$$

We can apply the same argument to the front and rear surfaces and to the upper and lower surfaces of the cube, and we find that the overall transport of gas into the cube is

$$-\left(\frac{\partial J_x}{\partial x} + \frac{\partial J_y}{\partial y} + \frac{\partial J_z}{\partial z}\right) = -\operatorname{div}\mathbf{J} \qquad (3\text{-}22)$$

For a moving gas Eq. (3-19) establishes the fact that the change in density in a small volume element is equal to the net influx of gas into that volume element.

In quantum mechanics ρ is the probability density. In analogy to these considerations, we can define $\mathbf{J}$ as the probability current density. The vector $\mathbf{J}$ represents the transport of probability density, and Eq. (3-19) shows how the change in probability density per unit time is caused by the transport of probability density described by $\mathbf{J}$.

3-2 THE SCHRÖDINGER EQUATION FOR A BOUND PARTICLE

In Sec. 3-1 we discussed the quantum-mechanical description of a free particle, whose energy was given by the expression

$$E = \frac{p^2}{2m} \tag{3-23}$$

This expression describes a particle that moves in a potential field that is everywhere equal to zero. Let us now consider a particle that moves in a potential field that is everywhere equal to a constant U. The energy expression is then

$$E = \frac{p^2}{2m} + U \tag{3-24}$$

The difference between Eqs. (3-23) and (3-24) is caused by a shift of the energy zero point from zero to $-U$, and obviously this should not cause any change in the physical behavior of the particle. We wish to investigate whether this change in energy zero point causes any changes in the wave functions.

Let the wave function $\psi(\mathbf{r};0)$ be known. The amplitude function $A(\boldsymbol{\sigma})$ is then given by

$$A(\boldsymbol{\sigma}) = \int \psi(\mathbf{r};0) e^{-2\pi i (\boldsymbol{\sigma} \cdot \mathbf{r})} \, d\mathbf{r} \tag{3-25}$$

Obviously $A(\boldsymbol{\sigma})$ does not depend on the dispersion relation, and therefore it is independent of the energy zero point. On the other hand, the function $\psi(\mathbf{r};t)$ is given by

$$\psi(\mathbf{r};t) = \int A(\boldsymbol{\sigma}) e^{2\pi i (\boldsymbol{\sigma} \cdot \mathbf{r})} e^{-2\pi i h \sigma^2 t / 2m} \, d\boldsymbol{\sigma} \tag{3-26}$$

The function $\psi'(\mathbf{r};t)$ that we derive from the energy relation (3-24) is

$$\psi'(\mathbf{r};t) = \int A(\boldsymbol{\sigma}) e^{2\pi i (\boldsymbol{\sigma} \cdot \mathbf{r})} e^{-2\pi i U t / h} e^{-2\pi i h \sigma^2 t / 2m} \, d\boldsymbol{\sigma} \tag{3-27}$$

A comparison of Eqs. (3-26) and (3-27) shows that

$$\psi'(\mathbf{r};t) = \psi(\mathbf{r};t) e^{-2\pi i U t / h} \tag{3-28}$$

Although the two functions ψ' and ψ are different, the corresponding probability density functions ρ are identical, and it can be shown that the two sets of expectation values that are derived from ψ and ψ' are identical in every respect. We see that a change in energy zero point changes the wave function by a phase factor of unit modulus but that it does not affect any of our predictions of physical observables.

The functions ψ and ψ', however, satisfy different Schrödinger equations. From Eq. (3-23) we see that ψ is a solution of the Schrödinger equation

$$-\frac{\hbar^2}{2m}\left(\frac{\partial^2}{\partial x^2}+\frac{\partial^2}{\partial y^2}+\frac{\partial^2}{\partial z^2}\right)\psi = -\frac{\hbar}{i}\frac{\partial\psi}{\partial t} \qquad (3\text{-}29)$$

whereas ψ' is a solution of

$$-\frac{\hbar^2}{2m}\left(\frac{\partial^2}{\partial x^2}+\frac{\partial^2}{\partial y^2}+\frac{\partial^2}{\partial z^2}\right)\psi' + U\psi' = -\frac{\hbar}{i}\frac{\partial\psi'}{\partial t} \qquad (3\text{-}30)$$

as follows from Eq. (3-24).

What happens now when the potential field is zero in one part of space, for example, $x < 0$, and the potential is equal to the constant U in the rest of space, $x \geqslant 0$? It seems logical to expect that the wave function is a solution of Eq. (3-29) for $x < 0$ and that it is a solution of Eq. (3-30) for $x \geqslant 0$. In addition we expect the two solutions to match at the plane $x = 0$, so that we impose the condition that both the wave function and its gradient are continuous in every point of the plane $x = 0$.

We can extend this argument to the situation where there are three, four, or more regions of different potential, and finally we can consider the case of an infinite number of regions with different potentials. In particular, we construct a system where space is divided into an infinite number of cubes with dimensions $dx\, dy\, dz$ and where each cube has a different potential. If we number the cubes 1, 2, 3, . . . , etc., and if we denote the potential in the nth cube by U_n, then the wave function is determined by the equation

$$-\frac{\hbar^2}{2m}\left(\frac{\partial^2}{\partial x^2}+\frac{\partial^2}{\partial y^2}+\frac{\partial^2}{\partial z^2}\right)\psi_n + U_n\psi_n = -\frac{\hbar}{i}\frac{\partial\psi_n}{\partial t} \qquad (3\text{-}31)$$

and by the condition that the ψ_n match at the boundaries of the cubes. Since U_n is constant throughout the nth cube, we can introduce the notation

$$U_n = U(\mathbf{r}_n) \qquad (3\text{-}32)$$

where $\mathbf{r}_n$ is a point inside the nth cube.

Let us finally consider the limiting case where the dimensions of each cube tend to zero. The differential equation for the wave function then becomes

$$-\frac{\hbar^2}{2m}\left(\frac{\partial^2}{\partial x^2}+\frac{\partial^2}{\partial y^2}+\frac{\partial^2}{\partial z^2}\right)\psi(\mathbf{r};t) + U(\mathbf{r})\psi(\mathbf{r};t) = -\frac{\hbar}{i}\frac{\partial}{\partial t}\,\psi(\mathbf{r};t) \qquad (3\text{-}33)$$

This is the Schrödinger equation for a particle that moves in a potential field $U(\mathbf{r})$.

We realize fully that this argument does not constitute a rigorous proof for the validity of the Schrödinger equation. On the other hand, we hope that it helps make the Schrödinger equation acceptable to the reader, and we feel that it gives us an idea of how the Schrödinger equation may be related to De Broglie's postulates. The ultimate justification of the Schrödinger equation lies in the fact that all its solutions lead to excellent agreement with observations.

Equation (3-33), known as the *time-dependent* Schrödinger equation, was published in 1926 by Schrödinger.[1] It has an infinite number of specific solutions and a general solution that is a linear combination of all specific solutions. In many cases we are interested in the solutions that describe the *stationary states* of the system, that is, the situations that have specific, well-defined energies. Such a stationary state with an energy E is described by a wave function with a specific frequency v, since $E = hv$. We can write such a wave function $\psi(\mathbf{r};t)$ as

$$\psi(\mathbf{r};t) = \phi(\mathbf{r})e^{-iEt/\hbar} \tag{3-34}$$

where $\phi(\mathbf{r})$ is now time-independent. Substitution of the function of Eq. (3-34) into Eq. (3-33) leads to the following differential equation for ϕ:

$$-\frac{\hbar^2}{2m}\left(\frac{\partial^2}{\partial x^2} + \frac{\partial^2}{\partial y^2} + \frac{\partial^2}{\partial z^2}\right)\phi(\mathbf{r}) + U(\mathbf{r})\phi(\mathbf{r}) = E\phi(\mathbf{r}) \tag{3-35}$$

This is known as the *time-independent* Schrödinger equation[2] for the stationary states of the system. We can introduce a new symbol Δ for the partial differentiations, namely,

$$\Delta = \nabla^2 = \frac{\partial^2}{\partial x^2} + \frac{\partial^2}{\partial y^2} + \frac{\partial^2}{\partial z^2} \tag{3-36}$$

which is known as the *Laplace operator*. The Schrödinger equation may then be written as

$$\left[-\frac{\hbar^2}{2m}\Delta + U(\mathbf{r})\right]\phi(\mathbf{r}) = E\phi(\mathbf{r}) \tag{3-37}$$

Each solution of Eq. (3-37) contains E as a parameter, and since E is a continuous variable, there are an infinite number of solutions. However, many of these solutions are not permissible because of physical requirements. We should realize that a suitable wave function should not only be a solution of the Schrödinger equation, but it should

[1] E. Schrödinger, *Ann. d. Physik*, **81**: 109 (1926).
[2] E. Schrödinger, *Ann. d. Physik*, **79**: 361 (1926).

also describe the behavior of the particle in a realistic way. The latter requirement poses some restrictions on the wave function. Our first condition is that the wave function be continuous and that its gradient be continuous everywhere in space. The second is that it be single-valued everywhere. The third is that it be normalizable; that is, that the integral $\langle \phi | \phi \rangle$ be finite.

It is said that every rule has its exceptions, and we can think of a number of situations where a physically acceptable wave function violates some of the conditions above. However, we think it best to disregard these exceptions for the time being and to postpone their discussion until we have fully appreciated the meaning of the conditions above.

The solutions of the Schrödinger equation (3-37) can be written in the form $\phi(\mathbf{r};E)$, since they contain the continuous variable E as a parameter. In most situations we find that many of these solutions do not satisfy the three conditions that were stated above. Only if we substitute certain specific values $E_1, E_2, E_3, \ldots$, etc., for the parameter E do the corresponding functions $\phi(\mathbf{r};E_1), \phi(\mathbf{r};E_2), \ldots$, etc., satisfy the necessary conditions. We call these values $E_1, E_2, \ldots$, etc., the *energy eigenvalues* of the Schrödinger equation and the functions $\phi_1(\mathbf{r}) = \phi(\mathbf{r};E_1), \phi_2(\mathbf{r}) = \phi(\mathbf{r};E_2), \ldots$, etc., the corresponding *eigenfunctions*. In Sec. 3-3 we discuss a simple example to show how the Schrödinger equation is solved and how its eigenvalues and eigenfunctions are obtained. Once we have acquired some feeling of how this solution is achieved in practice, we proceed to derive some general properties of eigenfunctions and eigenvalues.

3-3 THE QUANTUM-MECHANICAL DESCRIPTION OF A PARTICLE IN A BOX

The simplest quantum-mechanical problem is the particle in a one-dimensional box. This is a particle that moves in a potential field $U(x)$ which is zero for $0 \leqslant x \leqslant a$ and which is infinite elsewhere. This potential is graphically represented in Fig. 3-2, and its algebraic description is

$$U(x) = \infty \qquad x < 0$$
$$U(x) = 0 \qquad 0 \leqslant x \leqslant a \qquad (3\text{-}38)$$
$$U(x) = \infty \qquad x > a$$

The one-dimensional Schrödinger equation is

$$-\frac{\hbar^2}{2m}\frac{\partial^2 \phi}{\partial x^2} + U(x)\phi = E\phi \qquad (3\text{-}39)$$

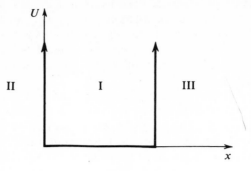

FIG. 3-2

Substitution of Eq. (3-38) leads to the equation

$$-\frac{\hbar^2}{2m}\frac{\partial^2\phi}{\partial x^2} = E\phi \tag{3-40}$$

for region I, where $0 \leqslant x \leqslant a$. In regions II and III we have to substitute ∞ for $U(x)$, and it is easily seen that here the Schrödinger equation can be satisfied only if we take $\phi(x) = 0$. The energy is positive, so that we may write Eq. (3-40) as

$$\frac{\partial^2\phi}{\partial x^2} + k^2\phi = 0 \qquad k^2 = \frac{2mE}{\hbar^2} \tag{3-41}$$

where k is real. At a later stage we give a more detailed discussion of differential equations, but Eq. (3-41) is such a simple equation that we can solve it without much difficulty. It can be verified that the two different functions

$$\phi_1 = e^{ikx} \tag{3-42}$$

and $$\phi_2 = e^{-ikx} \tag{3-43}$$

are solutions of Eq. (3-41). We call these specific solutions. The general solution of Eq. (3-41) is a linear combination of two particular solutions and can be represented as

$$\phi(x) = Ae^{ikx} + Be^{-ikx} \tag{3-44}$$

This function contains three parameters, namely, A, B, and k. Their values are determined by the conditions that we want to impose.

Let us first consider the behavior of the wave function at the point $x = 0$. We know that for $x < 0$ the wave function is zero everywhere, and if we want the wave function to be continuous at the point $x = 0$, we have to require that the function $\phi(x)$ of Eq. (3-44) is also zero at

$x = 0$. We have, therefore,

$$\phi(0) = A + B = 0 \qquad (3\text{-}45)$$

or
$$B = -A \qquad (3\text{-}46)$$

Substitution of this result into Eq. (3-44) leads to elimination of one of the parameters, and we obtain

$$\phi(x) = A(e^{ikx} - e^{-ikx}) = 2iA \sin kx \qquad (3\text{-}47)$$

We may replace the undetermined parameter $2iA$ by C, and hence

$$\phi(x) = C \sin kx \qquad (3\text{-}48)$$

We can now apply the same argument to the point $x = a$ that we applied above to the point $x = 0$. We know that the wave function is zero everywhere for $x > a$, so that we must require that the function $\phi(x)$ of Eq. (3-48) is also zero at $x = a$ in order that the wave function is continuous at the point $x = 0$. The condition is

$$\phi(a) = C \sin ka = 0 \qquad (3\text{-}49)$$

The parameter C must be different from zero; otherwise the wave function would be zero everywhere and could not be normalized. Consequently, we have

$$\sin ka = 0 \qquad (3\text{-}50)$$

whose solutions are

$$ka = n\pi \qquad n = \pm 1, \pm 2, \pm 3, \ldots, \text{etc.} \qquad (3\text{-}51)$$

By substituting this result back into Eq. (3-48), we find that the allowed wave functions are

$$\phi_n(x) = C_n \sin \frac{n\pi x}{a} \qquad (3\text{-}52)$$

The remaining parameter C_n is determined from the normalization condition

$$\int_0^a \phi_n^*(x)\phi_n(x) = 1 \qquad (3\text{-}53)$$

which gives

$$C_n^* C_n \int_0^a \sin^2 \frac{n\pi x}{a} \, dx = 1 \qquad (3\text{-}54)$$

Since the integral in Eq. (3-54) is equal to $\frac{1}{2}a$, the equation for C is

$$C_n C_n^* = \frac{2}{a} \qquad (3\text{-}55)$$

The solution is

$$C_n = \left(\frac{2}{a}\right)^{1/2} e^{i\gamma} \tag{3-56}$$

since Eq. (3-55) determines only the absolute value of C and not its argument. The wave functions are obtained by substituting this value C_n into Eq. (3-52):

$$\phi_n(x) = e^{i\gamma}\left(\frac{2}{a}\right)^{1/2} \sin\frac{n\pi x}{a} \tag{3-57}$$

where γ can take any value. Since the physical significance of the wave function does not depend on γ, it may be seen that ϕ_n and $(-\phi_n)$ are the same wave functions and therefore ϕ_n and ϕ_{-n} can be considered identical. Our final conclusions are thus that the eigenvalues of the particle in a box are given by

$$E_n = \frac{n^2 h^2}{8ma^2} \tag{3-58}$$

according to Eqs. (3-41) and (3-51), and the corresponding eigenfunctions are

$$\phi_n(x) = e^{i\gamma}\left(\frac{2}{a}\right)^{1/2} \sin\frac{n\pi x}{a} \tag{3-59}$$

with $\qquad\qquad n = 1, 2, 3, 4, \ldots, \text{etc.} \tag{3-60}$

It follows that only certain discrete values of the energy lead to permissible wave functions; this situation is typical for bound states.

The observant reader may have noticed that we have been careful to avoid any reference to the continuity of the derivative of the wave function at the points $x = 0$ and $x = a$. Actually these derivatives are not continuous at these points, as is easily verified. However, there is an explanation for this. The potential function $U(x)$ is not only discontinuous at $x = 0$ and $x = a$, but it even has an infinite discontinuity, since the potential jumps from zero to infinity. It can be shown that in such a case the derivative of the wave function does not have to be continuous. Thus, we see that in our first example we already encounter an exception to the rules that were outlined in Sec. 3-2.

3-4 SOME GENERAL PROPERTIES OF EIGENVALUES AND EIGENFUNCTIONS

It is possible to predict some general properties of the eigenvalues and eigenfunctions from a qualitative study of the Schrödinger equation.

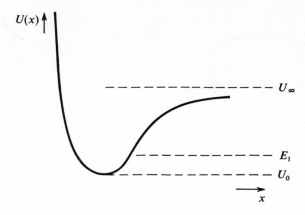

FIG. 3-3

We assume that the potential function $U(x)$ has the general behavior of Fig. 3-3; it tends to infinity for large negative x and to an asymptotic value U_∞ for large positive x. In between it has a minimum value U_0. We write the corresponding one-dimensional Schrödinger equation as

$$\phi'' = \frac{d^2\phi}{dx^2} = \frac{2m(U - E)\phi}{\hbar^2} \tag{3-61}$$

Let us first assume that E has a value that is slightly larger than U_0, for example, the value E_1 of Fig. 3-3. There exists, then, a region of the variable x in which $E > U$. In this region the ratio between ϕ'' and ϕ is negative:

$$\frac{\phi''}{\phi} < 0 \tag{3-62}$$

as follows from Eq. (3-61). We know that in this case the function $\phi(x)$ is concave toward the x axis, as we have symbolically indicated in Fig. 3-4a. We say that such a function behaves in an oscillatory fashion. We can understand this if we imagine that over a small interval U is almost constant, so that we may write

$$\phi'' = -\lambda^2\phi \tag{3-63}$$

This has the solutions $\sin \lambda x$ and $\cos \lambda x$, which are oscillatory functions.

On the left and on the right there are regions where $E < U(x)$, and here we have

$$\frac{\phi''}{\phi} > 0 \tag{3-64}$$

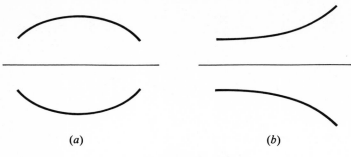

(a)   (b)

FIG. 3-4

In these regions $\phi(x)$ is convex toward the x axis, like the functions we have sketched in Fig. 3-4b. Now, we say that this function behaves in an exponential fashion. We can understand this if we imagine that in a small interval we can write the Schrödinger equation as

$$\phi'' = \mu^2 \phi \qquad (3\text{-}65)$$

which has the solutions $e^{\mu x}$ and $e^{-\mu x}$. We may conclude that $\phi(x)$ behaves in an oscillatory fashion in the regions where $E > U(x)$ and that $\phi(x)$ behaves in an exponential fashion in the regions where $E < U(x)$.

Let us now consider the asymptotic behavior of the wave function $\phi(x)$ for the potential field that we have sketched in Fig. 3-5. We imagine that we know the value of $\phi(P)$ in a point P, together with the derivative

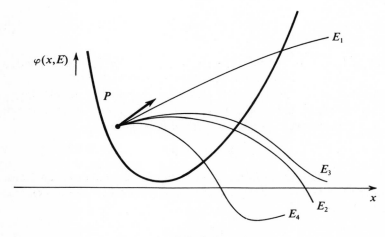

FIG. 3-5

of ϕ, for example, the value and the derivative that we have indicated in Fig. 3-5. Now, we attempt to analyze qualitatively the behavior of $\phi(x)$ at the right side of P. For a value of E that is only slightly larger than the minimum of $U(x)$, for example, E_1, the second derivative of $\phi(x)$ is not large enough to bend $\phi(x)$ very much toward the x axis. In this case $\phi'(x)$ is still positive when we cross over to the area where $\phi(x)$ behaves exponentially, and consequently the asymptotic behavior of $\phi(x)$ for $x \to \infty$ is exponential in x. Since $\phi(x)$ tends to infinity when x tends to infinity, it is not normalizable, and E_1 is therefore not an eigenvalue. For a larger energy, for example, E_2, the second derivative of $\phi(x)$ is so much larger that $\phi(x)$ has bent around to a negative first derivative of $\phi(x)$ when the wave function crosses into the exponential area. Now $\phi(x)$ tends to minus infinity when x tends to infinity, and since $\phi(x)$ cannot be normalized, we conclude that E_2 is not an eigenvalue either.

Since $\phi(x;E)$ is a continuous function of the parameter E and since $\phi(x;E_1)$ tends to plus infinity for $x \to \infty$ and $\phi(x;E_2)$ tends to minus infinity for $x \to \infty$, we argue that there is an energy value E_3 between E_1 and E_2 such that $\phi(x;E_3)$ tends to zero for $x \to \infty$. For this value E_3 it is possible that the wave function can be normalized, and we expect that E_3 is an eigenvalue of the Schrödinger equation. The next eigenvalue is E_4, for which we have indicated the behavior of the wave function in Fig. 3-4. We see that $\phi(x;E_3)$ does not intersect with the $x = 0$ axis, whereas $\phi(x;E_4)$ intersects $x = 0$ once and approaches the $x = 0$ asymptotically from the negative side. In general, the eigenfunction belonging to the lowest eigenvalue has no zero points, or *nodes*; that belonging to the next eigenvalue has one node; and that belonging to the nth eigenvalue has $(n - 1)$ nodes.

Let us now return to the potential field of Fig. 3-3. We again consider a point P in the left region of the potential well, and we assume that $\phi(x)$ has a positive derivative at that point. In the same way as we did for the potential field of Fig. 3-5, we can argue that there is a lowest eigenvalue E_1 with an eigenfunction ϕ_1, a second eigenvalue $E_2, \ldots$, etc. However, there is an important difference between the two cases; the potential field of Fig. 3-5 has an infinite number of discrete eigenvalues, but the situation in Fig. 3-3 contains only a finite number of discrete eigenvalues. In the latter case the wave functions are oscillatory for $x \to \infty$ as soon as $E > U_\infty$, and they are not normalizable in the ordinary sense of the word. All values of $E > U_\infty$ are equally permissible, and we speak of a *continuum* of eigenvalues as opposed to the *discrete spectrum* of Fig. 3-5. We discuss the continuum situation at a later stage. We only mention here that a bound particle usually has a discrete eigenvalue spectrum and that a free particle has a continuous eigenvalue spectrum.

PROBLEMS _____

3-1   The Schrödinger equation for a particle on a circle of radius R is

$$-\frac{\hbar^2}{2mR^2}\frac{\partial^2\psi}{\partial\alpha^2} = E\psi$$

where α is the polar angle. Determine the eigenvalues and eigenfunctions. Hint: The eigenvalues are determined from the condition that the wave function is single-valued.

3-2   The finite potential well is determined by the potential

$$U(x) = 0 \qquad -a \leqslant x \leqslant a$$

$$U(x) = U \qquad \begin{cases} x < -a \\ x > a \end{cases}$$

Derive the algebraic equations that determine the discrete eigenvalues of the system.

3-3   Determine the eigenvalues and eigenfunctions of the system that is described by the potential

$$U(x) = U \qquad -a \leqslant x \leqslant a$$

$$U(x) = 0 \qquad \begin{cases} -2a \leqslant x < -a \\ a < x \leqslant 2a \end{cases}$$

$$U(x) = \infty \qquad \begin{cases} x < -2a \\ x > 2a \end{cases}$$

CHAPTER 4

DIFFERENTIAL EQUATIONS

4-1 INTRODUCTION

An equation that contains a dependent variable u, one or more independent variables $x_1, x_2, \ldots, x_n$, and the derivatives of u with respect to the x_i is called a *differential equation*. When the equation contains more than one independent variable and various partial derivatives, it is called a *partial* differential equation; when there is only one independent variable, we speak of an *ordinary* differential equation. We consider only ordinary differential equations.

Differential equations are classified according to their order and to their degree. Tne order of the equation is equal to the order of the highest derivative in the equation. The degree is equal to the power of the highest derivative in the equation after all fractional powers have been removed. For example,

$$\frac{d^2u}{dx^2} + 5x\left(\frac{du}{dx}\right)^{1/2} + u = x^2 \tag{4-1}$$

is a quadratic, second-order equation.

Obviously there are so many different types of equations that it is impossible to discuss them all. We limit ourselves to those which occur most frequently in quantum-mechanical problems and to a few that give us some general insight. Our first restriction is that we consider only linear equations of the type

$$f_n(x)\frac{d^n u}{dx^n} + f_{n-1}(x)\frac{d^{n-1}u}{dx^{n-1}} + \cdots + f_1(x)\frac{du}{dx} + f_0(x)u = g(x) \quad (4\text{-}2)$$

The most interesting equations of this type are second-order equations. This is because first-order equations can be solved in a straightforward manner according to standard procedures,[1] and equations of higher than second-order cannot be solved analytically. Therefore, we limit ourselves to second-order equations of the type

$$\frac{d^2 u}{dz^2} + p(z)\frac{du}{dz} + q(z)u = 0 \quad (4\text{-}3)$$

The inhomogeneous equations, where the right side is equal to $g(z)$ instead of zero, as in Eq. (4-3), are not discussed here, since they seldom occur in quantum-mechanical problems and since their solutions are customarily derived from the corresponding homogeneous equations.

Finally, we impose some restrictions on the functions $p(z)$ and $q(z)$. First we consider all values of the variable z for which $p(z)$ and $q(z)$ are finite and continuous and have well-defined derivatives; these are called *ordinary* points of the differential equation (4-3). All other points are called *singular* points. Let us now take one such singular point, say c, and let us consider the functions $(z - c)p(z)$ and $(z - c)^2 q(z)$. If both these functions are finite and continuous and if they have well-defined derivatives in c, then we call c a *regular* point of the differential equation; otherwise c is called an *irregular* point. The restriction that we impose is that the differential equation (4-3) has no irregular points in the region where we solve it. If these conditions are satisfied, we can solve Eq. (4-3) according to the method that we outline in Sec. 4-2.

We wish to discuss here a simple example of Eq. (4-3), since we used the results in previous chapters. If $p(z)$ and $q(z)$ are both constants, the equation becomes

$$\frac{d^2 u}{dz^2} + p\frac{du}{dz} + qu = 0 \quad (4\text{-}4)$$

It is easily verified that the function $e^{\lambda z}$ is a solution of this equation if λ satisfies the condition

$$\lambda^2 + p\lambda + q = 0 \quad (4\text{-}5)$$

---

[1] See, for example, H. Margenau and G. M. Murphy, "The Mathematics of Physics and Chemistry," D. Van Nostrand Company, Inc., Princeton, N.J., 1959, p. 33.

In general, this quadratic equation in λ has two different roots λ_1 and λ_2. Equation (4-4) has two solutions $e^{\lambda_1 z}$ and $e^{\lambda_2 z}$. Its general solution $u(z)$ can be written in the form

$$u(z) = A_1 e^{\lambda_1 z} + A_2 e^{\lambda_2 z} \tag{4-6}$$

with A_1 and A_2 arbitrary parameters.

We will see that in general Eq. (4-3) has two different, linearly independent solutions and that its general solution is a linear combination of these two specific solutions. It is to be expected that a second-order differential equation has two undetermined parameters because we get two integration parameters if we integrate twice.

Let us now return to Eq. (4-4) and ask what happens when the two roots λ_1 and λ_2 happen to coincide. In this case the equation is

$$\frac{d^2u}{dz^2} - 2\lambda \frac{du}{dz} + \lambda^2 u = 0 \tag{4-7}$$

We substitute

$$u(z) = v(z)e^{\lambda z} \tag{4-8}$$

and we find that the equation for $v(z)$ is

$$\frac{d^2v}{dz^2} = 0 \tag{4-9}$$

so that
$$u(z) = (Az + B)e^{\lambda z} \tag{4-10}$$

4-2 SERIES EXPANSION METHOD FOR SOLVING DIFFERENTIAL EQUATIONS

It can be shown that the second-order differential equation of Eq. (4-3) can be solved by substituting a power series expansion of $u(z)$ into it if the functions $p(z)$ and $q(z)$ satisfy the conditions that were outlined in Sec. 4-1. If we are interested in the behavior of the solution in the vicinity of a regular point c, we ought to expand in terms of powers of $(z - c)$, but this is not a serious restriction, since it can be shown that the power series expansion represents the solution in other regions also, although the convergence may be slower. We think it may be helpful to discuss first the solution of a specific differential equation by means of the series expansion method to show how it works. As our example we choose the equation

$$x\frac{d^2u}{dx^2} + (c - x)\frac{du}{dx} - au = 0 \tag{4-11}$$

which is well known as the equation for the confluent hypergeometric function.

In order to solve Eq. (4-11), we substitute the power series expansion for $u(x)$:

$$u(x) = x^\rho \sum_{n=0}^{\infty} b_n x^n \qquad (4\text{-}12)$$

The parameter ρ is unknown for the time being, but it is chosen in such a way that the coefficient b_0 is different from zero. Substitution of Eq. (4-12) into Eq. (4-11) gives

$$\sum_{n=0}^{\infty} (n + \rho)(n + \rho + c - 1)b_n x^{n+\rho-1} - \sum_{n=0}^{\infty} (n + \rho + a)b_n x^{n+\rho} = 0 \qquad (4\text{-}13)$$

which we can also write as

$$\rho(\rho + c - 1)b_0 x^{\rho-1} + \sum_{n=0}^{\infty} [(n + \rho + 1)(n + \rho + c)b_{n+1} - (n + \rho + a)b_n]x^{n+\rho} = 0$$
$$(4\text{-}14)$$

The left side of Eq. (4-14) is zero for any value of x, and therefore the coefficient of each power of x must be zero. The lowest power of x is $(\rho - 1)$, and if we equate the corresponding coefficient to zero, we find

$$\rho(\rho + c - 1)b_0 = 0 \qquad (4\text{-}15)$$

Since b_0 is always different from zero, the solutions of this equation are

$$\rho = 0$$
$$\rho = 1 - c \qquad (4\text{-}16)$$

Let us first consider the solution $\rho = 0$. If we substitute this back into Eq. (4-14), we obtain the equation

$$(n + 1)(n + c)b_{n+1} - (n + a)b_n = 0 \qquad (4\text{-}17)$$

or
$$cb_1 = ab_0$$
$$2(c + 1)b_2 = (a + 1)b_1 \qquad (4\text{-}18)$$
$$3(c + 2)b_3 = (a + 2)b_2 \qquad \text{etc.}$$

Since b_0 seems to be an arbitrary parameter, we take it equal to unity and find

$$b_0 = 1 \qquad\qquad b_1 = \frac{a}{c}$$
$$(4\text{-}19)$$
$$b_2 = \frac{a(a + 1)}{1 \cdot 2 \cdot c(c + 1)} \qquad b_3 = \frac{a(a + 1)(a + 2)}{3!\,c(c + 1)(c + 2)} \qquad \text{etc.}$$

The corresponding solution $u_1(x)$ is

$$u_1(x) = 1 + \frac{a}{c}\frac{x}{1!} + \frac{a(a+1)}{c(c+1)}\frac{x^2}{2!} + \frac{a(a+1)(a+2)}{c(c+1)(c+2)}\frac{x^3}{3!} + \cdots \qquad (4\text{-}20)$$

Now we consider the second solution $\rho = 1 - c$. Substitution into Eq. (4-14) gives

$$(n+1)(n+2-c)b'_{n+1} = (n+1+a-c)b'_n \qquad (4\text{-}21)$$

This leads to the solution

$$u_2(x) = x^{1-c} + \frac{1+a-c}{2-c}\frac{x^{2-c}}{1!} + \frac{(1+a-c)(2+a-c)}{(2-c)(3-c)}\frac{x^{3-c}}{2!} + \cdots \qquad (4\text{-}22)$$

The general solution of Eq. (4-11) is thus

$$u(x) = A_1 u_1(x) + A_2 u_2(x) \qquad (4\text{-}23)$$

Now that we have gained some insight into the series expansion method, we outline it in general. For the sake of convenience we take a differential equation that has $x = 0$ as a regular point, and we write it as

$$x^2 \frac{d^2u}{dx^2} + xf(x)\frac{du}{dx} + g(x)u = 0 \qquad (4\text{-}24)$$

The functions $f(x)$ and $g(x)$ are expanded as a power series in x:

$$f(x) = \sum_{n=0}^{\infty} a_n x^n \qquad g(x) = \sum_{n=0}^{\infty} b_n x^n \qquad (4\text{-}25)$$

and we substitute the power series for $u(x)$:

$$u(x) = x^\rho \sum_{n=0}^{\infty} c_n x^n \qquad (4\text{-}26)$$

Again, we substitute Eqs. (4-25) and (4-26) into Eq. (4-24), and we set the various coefficients of $x^{\rho+n}$ equal to zero. The lowest power of x, which is x^ρ, gives

$$(\rho^2 + a_0\rho - \rho + b_0)c_0 = 0 \qquad (4\text{-}27)$$

This is the quadratic equation in ρ, which generally has two different roots ρ_1 and ρ_2. The equations for the higher powers of x lead to relationships between the coefficients c_n that can be solved successively. If we substitute ρ_1 and solve the equations, we obtain the solution $u_1(x)$, and from ρ_2 we derive the solution $u_2(x)$. The final solution $u(x)$ is again a linear combination of $u_1(x)$ and $u_2(x)$.

When the two roots ρ_1 and ρ_2 are equal to each other, this method yields only one specific solution. In this case we have to follow a different procedure in order to derive the second solution. However, this is a rather complicated problem, and since we do not encounter it in our applications in this book, we do not discuss it. Moreover, if $\rho_1 - \rho_2$ is equal to an integer, we may also obtain only one solution by the procedure above.

4-3 DIFFERENTIAL EQUATIONS OF QUANTUM THEORY

Certain types of differential equations occur again and again in physical problems, and as a consequence they have been studied in great detail. The solutions have been obtained in various power series; they have been tabulated, and their properties can be found in the mathematical literature. They are known as *special functions*, such as Bessel functions, Legendre functions, Hermite functions, gamma functions, confluent hypergeometric functions. Three of them, namely, Hermite functions, Legendre functions, and confluent hypergeometric functions, play an important role in quantum-mechanical problems, and we discuss them in the subsequent sections.

There are two ways to derive the properties of special functions. We can start with the differential equation and then derive its solutions. There is another way, which we consider more convenient, namely, to start with the function and then derive its differential equation. The reason for this preference is obvious; it is much easier to derive a differential equation for a given function than the other way around.

Some special functions are defined by means of power series expansion—for example, the confluent hypergeometric function belongs in this category—but many others are defined by means of a generating function $K(z,h)$. This generating function is expanded as a power series in the variable h:

$$K(z,h) = \sum_{n=0}^{\infty} F_n(z)h^n \tag{4-28}$$

and a class of functions $F_n(z)$ is defined in this way. We follow this procedure in our discussion of Hermite and Legendre polynomials.

Our discussion below is limited to those features of special functions which play a role in subsequent quantum-mechanical applications. For a more complete treatment we refer the reader to the mathematical literature.[1]

---

[1] For example, Bateman Manuscript Project, "Higher Transcendental Functions," vols. I, II, III, McGraw-Hill Book Company, Inc., New York, 1953.

4-4 HERMITE POLYNOMIALS

Hermite polynomials can be defined by means of a generating function $K(x,h)$ which has the form

$$K(x,h) = \exp(2hx - h^2) \tag{4-29}$$

Here the variable x can take all real values. We expand $K(x,h)$ as a power series in h:

$$K(x,h) = \sum_{n=0}^{\infty} \frac{H_n(x)}{n!} h^n \tag{4-30}$$

and we define the coefficient $H_n(x)$ as the Hermite polynomial in x of order n.

By differentiating Eq. (4-30) n times with respect to h, we can easily show that

$$H_n(x) = \left[\frac{\partial^n}{\partial h^n} K(x,h) \right]_{h=0} \tag{4-31}$$

We can rewrite this equation in a more useful form by observing that $K(x,h)$ can be represented also as

$$K(x,h) = e^{x^2} e^{-(x-h)^2} \tag{4-32}$$

Consequently, we have

$$H_n(x) = e^{x^2} \left[\frac{\partial^n}{\partial h^n} e^{-(x-h)^2} \right]_{h=0} \tag{4-33}$$

We observe that

$$\frac{\partial^n}{\partial h^n} e^{-(x-h)^2} = (-1)^n \frac{\partial^n}{\partial x^n} e^{-(x-h)^2} \tag{4-34}$$

so that

$$\left[\frac{\partial^n}{\partial h^n} e^{-(x-h)^2} \right]_{h=0} = (-1)^n \left[\frac{\partial^n}{\partial x^n} e^{-(x-h)^2} \right]_{h=0} \tag{4-35}$$

and

$$H_n(x) = (-1)^n e^{x^2} \frac{d^n}{dx^n} e^{-x^2} \tag{4-36}$$

Each function $H_n(x)$ is a polynomial in x, as the name indicates, and the first few polynomials are, according to Eq. (4-36),

$$\begin{aligned} H_0(x) &= 1 \\ H_1(x) &= 2x \\ H_2(x) &= 4x^2 - 2 \\ H_3(x) &= 8x^3 - 12x \end{aligned} \tag{4-37}$$

Hermite polynomials of different order and their derivatives are related to one another by equations that are known as *recurrence relations*. They are derived from the generating function $K(x,h)$ of Eq. (4-29) in combination with Eq. (4-30). If we differentiate $K(x,h)$ with respect to h we find that

$$\frac{\partial K}{\partial h} = -2(h - x)K \tag{4-38}$$

Substitution of Eq. (4-30) gives

$$\sum_{n=0}^{\infty} [H_{n+1}(x) - 2xH_n(x) + 2nH_{n-1}(x)] \frac{h^n}{n!} = 0 \tag{4-39}$$

This expansion is identically zero for all values of h, and therefore each coefficient of the power series expansion must be zero. This leads to our first recurrence relation:

$$H_{n+1}(x) - 2xH_n(x) + 2nH_{n-1}(x) = 0 \tag{4-40}$$

A second recurrence relation is derived in a similar way by differentiating Eq. (4-29) with respect to x:

$$\frac{\partial K}{\partial x} = 2hK \tag{4-41}$$

Substitution of Eq. (4-30) gives

$$\frac{dH_n(x)}{dx} = 2nH_{n-1}(x) \tag{4-42}$$

It can be shown from the properties of the generating function that the functions $H_n(x)e^{-(1/2)x^2}$ form an orthonormal set in the interval from $-\infty$ to $+\infty$. We evaluate the integrals

$$I_{n,m} = \int_{-\infty}^{\infty} H_n(x)H_m(x)e^{-x^2} dx \tag{4-43}$$

by considering the expression

$$e^{-x^2}K(x,h)K(x,k) = e^{-x^2} \sum_{n=0}^{\infty} \sum_{m=0}^{\infty} H_n(x)H_m(x) \frac{h^n k^m}{n!\, m!} \tag{4-44}$$

Integration of both sides of Eq. (4-44) gives

$$\int_{-\infty}^{\infty} K(x,h)K(x,k)e^{-x^2} dx = \sum_{n=0}^{\infty} \sum_{m=0}^{\infty} I_{n,m} \frac{h^n k^m}{n!\, m!} \tag{4-45}$$

The integral on the left is evaluated by substituting Eq. (4-29):

$$\int_{-\infty}^{\infty} K(x,h)K(x,k)e^{-x^2}\,dx = \int_{-\infty}^{\infty} e^{-(x^2-2hx-2kx+h^2+k^2)}\,dx$$

$$= e^{2hk}\int_{-\infty}^{\infty} e^{-(x-h-k)^2}\,d(x-h-k) = e^{2hk}\sqrt{\pi}$$

(4-46)

where we make use of the result of Eq. (1-73). Substitution of this result into Eq. (4-45) gives

$$\sum_{n=0}^{\infty}\sum_{m=0}^{\infty} I_{n,m}\frac{h^n k^m}{n!\,m!} = \sqrt{\pi}e^{2hk} = \sqrt{\pi}\sum_{n=0}^{\infty}\frac{(2hk)^n}{n!}$$

(4-47)

Since this expression is an identity in h and k, it follows that

$$I_{n,m} = 0 \qquad n \neq m$$

$$I_{n,n} = 2^n n!\,\sqrt{\pi}$$

(4-48)

Let us now derive the differential equation that is satisfied by $H_n(x)$. To this end we consider the function

$$w(x) = Ce^{-x^2}$$

(4-49)

and we notice that it satisfies the differential equation

$$\frac{dw}{dx} + 2xw = 0$$

(4-50)

for all values of the arbitrary constant C. We differentiate this expression $(n+1)$ times and obtain

$$\frac{d^{n+2}w}{dx^{n+2}} + 2x\frac{d^{n+1}w}{dx^{n+1}} + 2(n+1)\frac{d^n w}{dx^n} = 0$$

(4-51)

It follows that the function

$$q(x) = \frac{d^n w}{dx^n} = C\frac{d^n}{dx^n}e^{-x^2}$$

(4-52)

satisfies the equation

$$\frac{d^2 q}{dx^2} + 2x\frac{dq}{dx} + 2(n+1)q = 0$$

(4-53)

A comparison of Eqs. (4-36) and (4-52) shows that $H_n(x)$ can be written as

$$H_n(x) = e^{x^2}q(x)$$

(4-54)

if we take the constant C equal to $(-1)^n$. Therefore, if we substitute

$$q(x) = y(x)e^{-x^2} \tag{4-55}$$

into Eq. (4-53), we obtain the differential equation for $H_n(x)$. This substitution leads to

$$\frac{d^2y}{dx^2} - 2x\frac{dy}{dx} + 2ny = 0 \tag{4-56}$$

We have shown that for a nonnegative integer n the Hermite polynomial $H_n(x)$ is a solution of Eq. (4-56), but this covers only a small fraction of the solutions of the differential equations. In the first place Eq. (4-56) also has solutions for noninteger values of n, and second, it has two possible solutions for each value of n. We wish to investigate some properties of all these solutions, and therefore we have to find the general solution of Eq. (4-56). This is achieved by means of the method that we discussed in Sec. 4-2.

We substitute the series expansion for y

$$y = x^\rho \sum_{k=0}^{\infty} a_k x^k \tag{4-57}$$

into Eq. (4-56) and obtain

$$\rho(\rho - 1)a_0 x^{\rho-2} + \rho(\rho + 1)a_1 x^{\rho-1}$$

$$+ \sum_{k=0}^{\infty} [(k + \rho + 1)(k + \rho + 2)a_{k+2} - 2(k + \rho - n)a_k]x^{k+\rho} = 0 \tag{4-58}$$

Since this is an identity in x, we have the following equations:

$$\rho(\rho - 1)a_0 = 0 \tag{4-59a}$$

$$\rho(\rho + 1)a_1 = 0 \tag{4-59b}$$

$$a_{k+2} = \frac{2(k + \rho - n)a_k}{(k + \rho + 1)(k + \rho + 2)} \tag{4-59c}$$

In Sec. 4-2 we mentioned that we should find two different values of ρ, each leading to a different series expansion. In the present case the situation is slightly different because we obtain two different solutions from the one root $\rho = 0$ by taking either $a_0 = 0$ or $a_1 = 0$. These solutions are equivalent to what we obtain by taking $\rho = 0$ and $\rho = 1$.

The first solution is obtained by taking $\rho = 0$, $a_0 = 1$, and $a_1 = 0$. This leads to

$$y_1 = 1 + \frac{2(0 - n)}{2!}x^2 + \frac{2^2(2 - n)(0 - n)}{4!}x^4 + \frac{2^3(4 - n)(2 - n)(0 - n)}{6!}x^6 + \cdots \tag{4-60}$$

The second solution y_2 is obtained by substituting $\rho = 0$, $a_0 = 0$, and $a_1 = 1$ into Eqs. (4-59):

$$y_2 = x + \frac{2(1-n)}{3!}x^3 + \frac{2^2(3-n)(1-n)}{5!}x^5 + \frac{2^3(5-n)(3-n)(1-n)}{7!}x^7 + \cdots$$

$$(4\text{-}61)$$

In general the solutions are infinite power series, but if n is a positive integer, then one of the two solutions reduces to a finite polynomial. We want to know the asymptotic behavior of the solutions for infinite x. This is determined by the values of the coefficients for large k. It follows from Eq. (4-59c) that

$$\lim_{k \to \infty} \frac{a_{k+2}}{a_k} = \frac{2}{k} \qquad (4\text{-}62)$$

We compare this with the power series expansion of the function e^{2x^2}, which is

$$e^{2x^2} = \sum_{m=0}^{\infty} \frac{2^m x^{2m}}{m!} \qquad (4\text{-}63)$$

Here the ratio between two successive coefficients a_k and a_{k+2} is

$$\frac{a_{k+2}}{a_k} = \frac{2}{k+1} \qquad (4\text{-}64)$$

From a comparison of Eqs. (4-62) and (4-64) we conclude that in general both y_1 and y_2 behave asymptotically like e^{2x^2} when x tends to infinity. When n is a nonnegative even integer, y_1 becomes a polynomial, and y_2 behaves asymptotically like e^{2x^2}; and when n is a positive odd integer, y_2 is a polynomial, and y_1 behaves asymptotically like e^{2x^2}. We make use of these general properties of y_1 and y_2 in our quantum-mechanical applications.

4-5 LEGENDRE POLYNOMIALS

From the generating function

$$K(z,h) = (1 - 2zh + h^2)^{-1/2} \qquad (4\text{-}65)$$

we can derive a set of polynomials that are known as Legendre polynomials. It may be assumed without loss of generality that the absolute value of the complex variable z is smaller than a finite number R. If we then assume that h satisfies the condition

$$2R|h| + |h|^2 < 1 \qquad (4\text{-}66)$$

it is possible to expand $K(z,h)$ as a power series in h:

$$K(z,h) = \sum_{n=0}^{\infty} P_n(z)h^n \qquad (4\text{-}67)$$

The Legendre polynomials are defined as the polynomials $P_n(z)$, which are the coefficients of this expansion.

In order to derive explicit expressions for the Legendre polynomials, we first observe that $(1 - x)^{-1/2}$ may be expanded as

$$(1 - x)^{-1/2} = 1 + \frac{1}{2}x + \frac{1}{2}\cdot\frac{3}{2}\frac{x^2}{2!} + \frac{1}{2}\cdot\frac{3}{2}\cdot\frac{5}{2}\frac{x^3}{3!} + \frac{1}{2}\cdot\frac{3}{2}\cdot\frac{5}{2}\cdot\frac{7}{2}\frac{x^4}{4!} + \cdots \qquad (4\text{-}68)$$

if $|x| < 1$. The product $1 \cdot 3 \cdot 5 \cdot 7 \cdots (2n - 1)$ may be written as

$$1 \cdot 3 \cdot 5 \cdot 7 \cdots (2n - 1) = \frac{1 \cdot 2 \cdot 3 \cdot 4 \cdot 5 \cdots 2n}{2^n \cdot 1 \cdot 2 \cdot 3 \cdot 4 \cdots n} = \frac{(2n)!}{2^n n!} \qquad (4\text{-}69)$$

so that Eq. (4-68) may be reduced to

$$(1 - x)^{-1/2} = \sum_{n=0}^{\infty} \frac{(2n)! \, x^n}{2^{2n} \cdot (n!)^2} \qquad (4\text{-}70)$$

The generating function $K(z,h)$ may therefore be expanded as

$$K(z,h) = \sum_{n=0}^{\infty} \frac{(2n)! \, h^n (2z - h)^n}{2^{2n} \cdot (n!)^2} \qquad (4\text{-}71)$$

Let us now expand each product $(2z - h)^n$ as

$$(2z - h)^n = \sum_{m=0}^{n} \frac{(-1)^m n! \, (2z)^{n-m} h^m}{m! \, (n - m)!} \qquad (4\text{-}72)$$

and substitute the result into Eq. (4-71):

$$K(z,h) = \sum_{n=0}^{\infty} \frac{(2n)! \, h^n}{n!} \sum_{m=0}^{n} \frac{(-1)^m h^m z^{n-m}}{2^{n+m} m! \, (n - m)!} \qquad (4\text{-}73)$$

The Legendre polynomial $P_k(z)$ of order k is now obtained from Eq. (4-73) by collecting all terms that contain the factor h^k. These terms are obtained by taking $n = k$ and $m = 0$, $n = k - 1$ and $m = 1$, $n = k - 2$ and $m = 2$, etc. Hence we find $P_k(z)$ by substituting the index $k - r$ for n and the number r for m into Eq. (4-73) and by summing over r instead of over n and m:

$$P_k(z) = \sum_{r=0}^{\alpha} \frac{(-1)^r (2k - 2r)! \, z^{k-2r}}{2^k r! \, (k - r)! \, (k - 2r)!} \qquad (4\text{-}74)$$

The maximum value α that the summation index r can assume is determined by the condition that in Eq. (4-73) $m \leqslant n$. If we substitute r

for m and $k - r$ for n, we find

$$2r \leqslant k \qquad (4\text{-}75)$$

Since r also has to be an integer, it follows that $\alpha = \frac{1}{2}k$ when k is even and $\alpha = \frac{1}{2}(k - 1)$ when k is odd.

We may derive from Eq. (4-74) that the first few Legendre polynomials have the form

$$
\begin{aligned}
P_0(z) &= 1 \\
P_1(z) &= z \\
P_2(z) &= \tfrac{1}{2}(3z^2 - 1) \\
P_3(z) &= \tfrac{1}{2}(5z^3 - 3z) \\
P_4(z) &= \tfrac{1}{8}(35z^4 - 30z^2 + 3) \\
P_5(z) &= \tfrac{1}{8}(63z^5 - 70z^3 + 15z)
\end{aligned}
\qquad (4\text{-}76)
$$

We show that Eq. (4-74) is equivalent to a different expression for $P_k(z)$ which is more concise and which is known as Rodrigues's formula. For this purpose we observe that

$$(z^2 - 1)^k = \sum_{r=0}^{k} \frac{(-1)^r k!\, z^{2k-2r}}{r!\,(k-r)!} \qquad (4\text{-}77)$$

If we differentiate this expression k times, we find that

$$\frac{d^k}{dz^k}(z^2 - 1)^k = \sum_{r=0}^{\alpha} \frac{(-1)^r k!\,(2k - 2r)!\, z^{k-2r}}{r!\,(k-r)!\,(k-2r)!} \qquad (4\text{-}78)$$

A comparison with Eq. (4-74) leads to Rodrigues's formula:

$$P_k(z) = \frac{1}{2^k \cdot k!} \frac{d^k}{dz^k}(z^2 - 1)^k \qquad (4\text{-}79)$$

Let us now derive some of the recurrence formulas for Legendre polynomials of different orders and their derivatives. By differentiating Eq. (4-65) with respect to h, we find that

$$(1 - 2hz + h^2)\frac{\partial K}{\partial h} = (z - h)K \qquad (4\text{-}80)$$

If we now substitute the expansion of Eq. (4-67) into this result, we find that

$$(n + 1)P_{n+1}(z) - (2n + 1)zP_n(z) + nP_{n-1}(z) = 0 \qquad (4\text{-}81)$$

A second recurrence relation is obtained if we differentiate Eq. (4-65) with respect to z and to h. From a comparison of the two results it follows that

$$h \frac{\partial K}{\partial h} = (z - h) \frac{\partial K}{\partial z} \tag{4-82}$$

Substitution of Eq. (4-67) now yields

$$z \frac{dP_n(z)}{dz} - \frac{dP_{n-1}(z)}{dz} = nP_n(z) \tag{4-83}$$

By combining Eqs. (4-81) and (4-83), we derive three additional recurrence formulas

$$P'_{n+1}(z) - zP'_n(z) = (n + 1)P_n(z)$$
$$P'_{n+1}(z) - P'_{n-1}(z) = (2n + 1)P_n(z) \tag{4-84}$$
$$(z^2 - 1)P'_n(z) = nzP_n(z) - nP_{n-1}(z)$$

The differential equation for $P_n(z)$ is easily derived with the aid of Rodrigues's formula. We first consider the function

$$q(z) = C(1 - z^2)^n \tag{4-85}$$

and we observe that it satisfies the equation

$$(1 - z^2) \frac{dq}{dz} + 2nzq = 0 \tag{4-86}$$

for all values of the arbitrary parameter C. Differentiating Eq. (4-86) $(n + 1)$ times gives

$$(1 - z^2) \frac{d^{n+2}q}{dz^{n+2}} - 2z \frac{d^{n+1}q}{dz^{n+1}} + n(n + 1) \frac{d^n q}{dz^n} = 0 \tag{4-87}$$

If we now introduce the function $g(z)$, which is

$$g(z) = C \frac{d^n q}{dz^n} = C'P_n(z) \tag{4-88}$$

according to Eq. (4-79), then we find the required equation

$$(1 - z^2) \frac{d^2 g}{dz^2} - 2z \frac{dg}{dz} + n(n + 1)g = 0 \tag{4-89}$$

for $P_n(z)$.

We know that for a nonnegative integer n the Legendre polynomial $P_n(z)$ is one of the solutions of the equations. Let us now attempt to derive the general solution of Eq. (4-89) for arbitrary values of n. Since the parameter ρ is equal to zero or unity in the present case, we substitute

$$g(z) = \sum_{k=0}^{\infty} a_k z^k \tag{4-90}$$

into Eq. (4-89) and obtain

$$a_{k+2} = \frac{k(k+1) - n(n+1)}{(k+1)(k+2)} a_k = \frac{(k-n)(k+n+1)}{(k+1)(k+2)} a_k \qquad (4\text{-}91)$$

This leads to the following general solution of Eq. (4-89):

$$g(z) = a_0 \left[1 + \frac{(-n)(1+n)}{2!} z^2 + \frac{(-n)(2-n)(1+n)(3+n)}{4!} z^4 + \cdots \right.$$

$$\left. + \frac{(-n)(2-n)(4-n) \cdots (2s-2-n)(n+1)(n+3) \cdots (2s-1+n)}{(2s)!} z^{2s} + \cdots \right]$$

$$+ a_1 z \left[1 + \frac{(1-n)(2+n)}{3!} z^2 + \frac{(1-n)(3-n)(2+n)(4+n)}{5!} z^4 + \cdots \right.$$

$$\left. + \frac{(1-n)(3-n) \cdots (2s-1-n)(2+n)(4+n) \cdots (2s+n)}{(2s+1)!} z^{2s} + \cdots \right] \qquad (4\text{-}92)$$

When n is not an integer, both solutions of Eq. (4-92) have the form of infinite power series in z. In quantum-mechanical problems we are interested in the behavior of the power series for real values of the variable in the interval $-1 \leqslant z \leqslant 1$, and we want to know whether the solutions have any singularities in this interval. This reduces to the question of whether the two power series are convergent for all values of z in the interval $-1 \leqslant z \leqslant 1$. One criterion for this is the limit for $k \to \infty$ of two subsequent terms of each power series. According to Eqs. (4-90) and (4-91) this limit is

$$\lim_{k \to \infty} \frac{a_{k+2} z^{k+2}}{a_k z^k} = \frac{k+1}{k+3} z^2 \qquad (4\text{-}93)$$

When this limit is smaller than unity, the series is convergent; and when it is larger than unity, the series is divergent. We see that the power series is convergent when $|z|^2 < 1$. The problem is that this criterion does not work when $z = \pm 1$ because the limit is exactly equal to unity. However, we can apply more delicate tests[1] for this case, and it appears that the power series diverges for $z = \pm 1$.

In order to obtain a solution of Eq. (4-89) that is finite in the whole interval $-1 \leqslant z \leqslant 1$, we must impose the condition that n is an integer. If n is even, the first solution of Eq. (4-92) becomes a finite polynomial $P_n(z)$ that is finite over the whole interval, and the second solution is infinite for $z = \pm 1$. If n is odd, the second solution becomes $P_n(z)$, and the first solution has singularities for $z = \pm 1$. When n is negative,

[1] Namely, Raabe's test. See T. J. I'A. Bromwich, "An Introduction to the Theory of Infinite Series," Macmillan & Co., Ltd., London, 1959, p. 39.

we obtain nothing new; it is easily seen that Eq. (4-89) remains the same when we replace n by $-n-1$. Therefore, we need only consider positive values of n. We may conclude, therefore, that the only solutions of Eq. (4-89) that are finite everywhere in the interval $-1 \leqslant z \leqslant 1$ are the Legendre polynomials $P_n(z)$. This conclusion is very important in quantum-mechanical applications.

We now show that the Legendre polynomials form an orthogonal set of functions for real values of x in the interval $-1 \leqslant x \leqslant 1$. For this purpose we study the integrals

$$K_{n,m} = \int_{-1}^{1} [(x^2 - 1)^n]_n [(x^2 - 1)^m]_m \, dx \qquad (4\text{-}94)$$

where we have introduced the abbreviation

$$[(x^2 - 1)^n]_n = \frac{d^n}{dx^n} (x^2 - 1)^n \qquad (4\text{-}95)$$

If we subject Eq. (4-94) to a partial integration, we find

$$\int_{-1}^{1} [(x^2 - 1)^n]_n [(x^2 - 1)^m]_m \, dx = \int_{-1}^{1} [(x^2 - 1)^n]_n \frac{d}{dx} [(x^2 - 1)^m]_{m-1} \, dx$$

$$= \{[(x^2 - 1)^n]_n [(x^2 - 1)^m]_{m-1}\}_{-1}^{1}$$

$$\quad - \int_{-1}^{1} [(x^2 - 1)^n]_{n+1} [(x^2 - 1)^m]_{m-1} \, dx$$

$$= - \int_{-1}^{1} [(x^2 - 1)^n]_{n+1} [(x^2 - 1)^m]_{m-1} \, dx \qquad (4\text{-}96)$$

Let us first consider the case where n and m are different. One of the two is then the larger; let it be m. By repeated application of the partial integration above, we transform Eq. (4-94) into

$$\int_{-1}^{1} [(x^2 - 1)^n]_n [(x^2 - 1)^m]_n \, dx = (-1)^m \int_{-1}^{1} [(x^2 - 1)^n]_{n+m} (x^2 - 1)^m \, dx$$

$$(4\text{-}97)$$

If m is larger than n, we have

$$\frac{d^{n+m}}{dx^{n+m}} (x^2 - 1)^n = 0 \qquad (4\text{-}98)$$

so that the right side of Eq. (4-97) is zero, and therefore

$$K_{n,m} = 0 \qquad n \neq m \qquad (4\text{-}99)$$

If m is equal to n, then the procedure above leads to

$$K_{n,n} = (-1)^n \int_{-1}^{1} [(x^2 - 1)^n]_{2n}(x^2 - 1)^n \, dx$$

$$= (2n)! \int_{-1}^{1} (1 - x^2)^n \, dx \qquad (4\text{-}100)$$

We evaluate this integral by introducing the new variable $x = \cos \theta$. This gives

$$K_{n,n} = 2 \cdot (2n)! \int_{0}^{\pi/2} \sin^{2n+1} \theta \, d\theta \qquad (4\text{-}101)$$

This integral can be transformed by a partial integration

$$\int_{0}^{\pi/2} \sin^{2n+1} \theta \, d\theta = - \int_{0}^{\pi/2} \sin^{2n} \theta \, d(\cos \theta) = 2n \int_{0}^{\pi/2} \sin^{2n-1} \theta \cos^2 \theta \, d\theta$$

$$= 2n \int_{0}^{\pi/2} \sin^{2n-1} \theta \, d\theta - 2n \int_{0}^{\pi/2} \sin^{2n+1} \theta \, d\theta \qquad (4\text{-}102)$$

or

$$\int_{0}^{\pi/2} \sin^{2n+1} \theta \, d\theta = \frac{2n}{2n + 1} \int_{0}^{\pi/2} \sin^{2n-1} \theta \, d\theta \qquad (4\text{-}103)$$

Hence

$$K_{n,n} = 2(2n)! \frac{2 \cdot 4 \cdot 6 \cdots \cdot 2n}{1 \cdot 3 \cdot 5 \cdots \cdot (2n + 1)} = \frac{2^{2n+1}(n!)^2}{2n + 1} \qquad (4\text{-}104)$$

From Rodrigues's formula (4-79) we may derive that

$$\int_{-1}^{1} P_n(x) P_m(x) \, dx = 0 \qquad n \neq m$$

$$\int_{-1}^{1} P_n(x) P_n(x) \, dx = \frac{2}{2n + 1} \qquad (4\text{-}105)$$

4-6 SPHERICAL HARMONICS

In addition to Legendre polynomials we will encounter the associated Legendre functions $P_n{}^m(x)$, which are defined as

$$P_n{}^m(x) = (1 - x^2)^{m/2} \frac{d^m}{dx^m} P_n(x) \qquad (4\text{-}106)$$

Here n and m are nonnegative integers, and $n \geq m$. We limit our discussion to the behavior of the functions in the interval $-1 \leq x \leq 1$, since this is the interval that we consider in quantum-mechanical applications. The associated Legendre functions satisfy a differential equation that is derived from Eq. (4-89) for the Legendre functions. If we differentiate this equation m times, we find

$$(1 - x^2)\frac{d^{m+2}g}{dx^{m+2}} - 2x(m+1)\frac{d^{m+1}g}{dx^{m+1}} + (n-m)(n+m+1)\frac{d^m g}{dx^m} = 0 \quad (4\text{-}107)$$

where
$$g = P_n(x) \quad\quad\quad\quad (4\text{-}108)$$

If we introduce the function

$$q(x) = \frac{d^m}{dx^m} g(x) \quad\quad\quad\quad (4\text{-}109)$$

then this function satisfies the equation

$$(1 - x^2)\frac{d^2 q}{dx^2} - 2x(m+1)\frac{dq}{dx} + (n-m)(n+m+1)q = 0 \quad (4\text{-}110)$$

It follows from a comparison of Eqs. (4-106) and (4-109) that the associated Legendre function $P_n{}^m(x)$ is identical to the function $w(x)$ defined as

$$q(x) = (1 - x^2)^{-m/2} w(x) \quad\quad\quad\quad (4\text{-}111)$$

Substitution of Eq. (4-111) into Eq. (4-110) leads, therefore, to the desired differential equation for $P_n{}^m(x)$:

$$(1 - x^2)\frac{d^2 w}{dx^2} - 2x\frac{dw}{dx} + \left[n(n+1) - \frac{m^2}{1-x^2} \right] w = 0 \quad (4\text{-}112)$$

There exist a very large number of recurrence relations between different functions $P_n{}^m(x)$ and their derivatives, and we will not attempt to derive them all. We will derive only the two that we use in our discussion of angular momentum later in the book. One of them will also prove to be useful for the derivation of the integral properties of $P_n{}^m(x)$.

The first recurrence relation is derived from the definition (4-106), which we can also write as

$$P_n{}^{m+1}(x) = (1 - x^2)^{(m+1)/2} \frac{d^{m+1}}{dx^{m+1}} P_n(x) \quad\quad (4\text{-}113)$$

By differentiating Eq. (4-106) once, we find that

$$\frac{dP_n{}^m(x)}{dx} = (1 - x^2)^{m/2} \frac{d^{m+1}}{dx^{m+1}} P_n(x) - mx(1 - x^2)^{(m-2)/2} \frac{d^m}{dx^m} P_n(x) \quad (4\text{-}114)$$

The combination of Eqs. (4-113) and (4-114) leads to

$$P_n{}^{m+1}(x) = (1 - x^2)^{1/2} \frac{dP_n{}^m}{dx} + mx(1 - x^2)^{-1/2} P_n{}^m(x) \quad\quad (4\text{-}115)$$

The second recurrence formula that we are interested in is derived from Eq. (4-107). If we multiply this differential equation by $(1 - x^2)^{m/2}$ we obtain

$$(1 - x^2)^{(m+2)/2} \frac{d^{m+2}}{dx^{m+2}} P_n(x) - \frac{2x(m+1)(1-x^2)^{(m+1)/2}}{(1-x^2)^{1/2}} \frac{d^{m+1}}{dx^{m+1}} P_n(x)$$

$$+ (n - m)(n + m + 1)(1 - x^2)^{m/2} \frac{d^m}{dx^m} P_n(x) = 0 \quad (4\text{-}116)$$

From the definition (4-106) it now follows that

$$P_n^{m+2}(x) - \frac{2(m+1)x}{(1-x^2)^{1/2}} P_n^{m+1}(x) + (n - m)(n + m + 1)P_n^m(x) = 0 \quad (4\text{-}117)$$

If we lower the superscript m by unity, we finally obtain

$$P_n^{m+1}(x) - \frac{2mx}{(1-x^2)^{1/2}} P_n^m(x) + (n + m)(n - m + 1)P_n^{m-1}(x) = 0 \quad (4\text{-}118)$$

The integral properties of the associated Legendre functions are concerned with the integrals

$$I_{n,n'}^m = \int_{-1}^1 P_n^m(x)P_{n'}^m(x)\, dx \quad (4\text{-}119)$$

First, we show that these integrals are zero when $n \neq n'$. From the differential equation (4-112) we can derive the following two equations:

$$P_{n'}^m(1 - x^2) \frac{d^2 P_n^m}{dx^2} - 2xP_{n'}^m \frac{dP_n^m}{dx} + \left[n(n + 1) - \frac{m^2}{1 - x^2} \right] P_n^m P_{n'}^m = 0$$

$$(4\text{-}120)$$

$$P_n^m(1 - x^2) \frac{d^2 P_{n'}^m}{dx^2} - 2xP_n^m \frac{dP_{n'}^m}{dx} + \left[n'(n' + 1) - \frac{m^2}{1 - x^2} \right] P_n^m P_{n'}^m = 0$$

The first of these equations is the differential equation for P_n^m, multiplied by $P_{n'}^m$, and the second is the differential equation for $P_{n'}^m$, multiplied by P_n^m. If we subtract the second equation from the first and integrate, we obtain

$$\int_{-1}^1 \frac{d}{dx} \left\{ (1 - x^2) \left[P_{n'}^m \frac{dP_n^m}{dx} - P_n^m \frac{dP_{n'}^m}{dx} \right] \right\} dx$$

$$+ [n(n + 1) - n'(n' + 1)] \int_{-1}^1 P_n^m P_{n'}^m\, dx = 0 \quad (4\text{-}121)$$

Since the first integral is zero, we find that

$$\int_{-1}^1 P_n^m(x)P_{n'}^m(x)\, dx = 0 \qquad n \neq n' \quad (4\text{-}122)$$

The integral $I_{n,n}^m$ is evaluated from the recurrence formula (4-115). If we square and integrate this expression, we obtain

$$\int_{-1}^{1} [P_n^{m+1}(x)]^2 \, dx = \int_{-1}^{1} (1 - x^2) \left[\frac{dP_n^m}{dx} \right]^2 dx$$

$$+ 2m \int_{-1}^{1} x P_n^m \frac{dP_n^m}{dx} \, dx + m^2 \int_{-1}^{1} \frac{x^2 (P_n^m)^2}{1 - x^2} \, dx \quad (4\text{-}123)$$

By partial integration of the first and second integral on the right side, we obtain

$$\int_{-1}^{1} [P_n^{m+1}(x)]^2 \, dx = - \int_{-1}^{1} P_n^m(x) \frac{d}{dx} \left[(1 - x^2) \frac{dP_n^m}{dx} \right] dx$$

$$- m \int_{-1}^{1} [P_n^m(x)]^2 \, dx + m^2 \int_{-1}^{1} \frac{x^2}{1 - x^2} [P_n^m(x)]^2 \, dx \quad (4\text{-}124)$$

It follows from the differential equation (4-112) that

$$\frac{d}{dx} \left[(1 - x^2) \frac{dP_n^m}{dx} \right] = (1 - x^2) \frac{d^2 P_n^m}{dx^2} - 2x \frac{dP_n^m}{dx}$$

$$= \frac{m^2}{1 - x^2} P_n^m(x) - n(n + 1) P_n^m(x) \quad (4\text{-}125)$$

Substitution of this result into Eq. (4-124) gives

$$\int_{-1}^{1} [P_n^{m+1}(x)]^2 \, dx = [n(n + 1) - m - m^2] \int_{-1}^{1} [P_n^m(x)]^2 \, dx$$

$$= (n - m)(n + m + 1) \int_{-1}^{1} [P_n^m(x)]^2 \, dx \quad (4\text{-}126)$$

If we repeat this procedure a number of times, we find that

$$\int_{-1}^{1} [P_n^m(x)]^2 \, dx = (n - m + 1)(n - m + 2)$$

$$\cdots \cdots (n) \cdot (n + m)(n + m - 1) \cdots \cdots (n + 1) \int_{-1}^{1} [P_n(x)]^2 \, dx \quad (4\text{-}127)$$

Substitution of Eq. (4-105) finally gives

$$\int_{-1}^{1} [P_n^m(x)]^2 \, dx = \frac{(n + m)!}{(n - m)!} \frac{2}{2n + 1} \quad (4\text{-}128)$$

In quantum-mechanical problems we often encounter the functions

$$S_{n,m}(\theta, \phi) = P_n^{|m|}(\cos \theta) e^{im\phi} \quad (4\text{-}129)$$

which are defined for $0 \leqslant \phi \leqslant 2\pi$ and for $0 \leqslant \theta \leqslant \pi$. We assume that they are defined in this way on the surface of a sphere with constant radius. If we integrate the product of two such functions over the surface of the sphere, we can write this integral as

$$\int_0^{2\pi} \int_0^{\pi} S_{n',m'}^* (\theta,\phi)\, S_{n,m} (\theta,\phi) \sin \theta \, d\theta \, d\phi$$

$$= \int_{-1}^{1} P_n^{|m|}(x)\, P_{n'}^{|m'|}(x)\, dx \int_0^{2\pi} e^{i(m-m')\phi}\, d\phi \quad (4\text{-}130)$$

The integral over ϕ is zero if $m \neq m'$, and if $m = m'$, the integral over θ is zero unless $n = n'$. It follows, therefore, from Eq. (4-128) that

$$\int_0^{2\pi} d\phi \int_0^{\pi} S_{n',m'}^*(\theta,\phi) S_{n,m}(\theta,\phi) \sin \theta \, d\theta = \frac{4\pi}{2n+1} \frac{(n+|m|)!}{(n-|m|)!} \delta_{n,n'} \delta_{m,m'} \quad (4\text{-}131)$$

Obviously, the functions

$$Y_{n,m}(\theta,\phi) = \left[\frac{2n+1}{4\pi} \frac{(n-|m|)!}{(n+|m|)!} \right]^{1/2} P_n^{|m|}(\cos \theta) e^{im\phi} \quad (4\text{-}132)$$

form an orthonormal set of functions on the spherical surface. They are known as *spherical harmonics*, and they play an important role in many quantum-mechanical problems.

4-7 CONFLUENT HYPERGEOMETRIC FUNCTIONS

We define the confluent hypergeometric function as

$$\Phi(a,c\,;x) = 1 + \frac{a}{c}\frac{x}{1!} + \frac{a(a+1)}{c(c+1)}\frac{x^2}{2!} + \frac{a(a+1)(a+2)}{c(c+1)(c+2)}\frac{x^3}{3!} + \cdots \quad (4\text{-}133)$$

In the applications where we use $\Phi(a,c\,;x)$, we usually consider x the important variable, and a and c the parameters. It is easily seen that $\Phi(a,c\,;x)$ reduces to a finite polynomial in x when a is a negative integer and that $\Phi(a,c\,;x)$ becomes infinite when c is a negative integer. If we exclude these two possibilities, then $\Phi(a,c\,;x)$ converges for all values of x, and for very large x it behaves asymptotically like e^x.

We showed in Sec. 4-2 that $\Phi(a,c\,;x)$ is a solution of the differential equation

$$x\frac{d^2 y}{dx^2} + (c-x)\frac{dy}{dx} - ay = 0 \quad (4\text{-}134)$$

since this is the differential equation that we discussed as an example of the series expansion method. The second solution, which is expressed in Eq. (4-22), can be written in the form

$$y_2(x) = x^{1-c}\left[1 + \frac{a-c+1}{2-c}\frac{x}{1!} + \frac{(a-c+1)(a-c+2)}{(2-c)(3-c)}\frac{x^2}{2!} + \cdots\right] \quad (4\text{-}135)$$

By comparing this series with Eq. (4-133), we find that this second solution can also be written as

$$y_2(x) = x^{1-c}\Phi(a-c+1, 2-c; x) \quad (4\text{-}136)$$

Let us now derive two additional solutions of Eq. (4-134) by substituting

$$y = e^x w(x) \quad (4\text{-}137)$$

into Eq. (4-134). The equation for $w(x)$ becomes

$$x\frac{d^2w}{dx^2} + (c+x)\frac{dw}{dx} + (c-a)w = 0 \quad (4\text{-}138)$$

If we now introduce the new variable $t = -x$, then the equation

$$t\frac{d^2w}{dt^2} + (c-t)\frac{dw}{dt} - (c-a)w = 0 \quad (4\text{-}139)$$

is again the differential equation for the confluent hypergeometric series. Its two solutions are

$$w_1(t) = \Phi(c-a, c; t)$$
$$w_2(t) = t^{1-c}\Phi(1-a, 2-c; t) \quad (4\text{-}140)$$

If we substitute this back into Eq. (4-137), then we obtain four solutions to the original Eq. (4-134), namely,

$$y_1 = \Phi(a,c; x)$$
$$y_2 = x^{1-c}\Phi(a-c+1, 2-c; x)$$
$$y_3 = e^x\Phi(c-a, c; -x)$$
$$y_4 = x^{1-c}e^x\Phi(1-a, 2-c; -x) \quad (4\text{-}141)$$

We have seen that a second-order differential equation can have only two linearly independent solutions, and therefore we should have two linear relations between the four solutions of Eq. (4-141). From the behavior of the solutions in the vicinity of the point $x = 0$, it follows that y_1 should be proportional to y_3, and y_2 proportional to y_4. By substituting $x = 0$, we see that the proportionality constants should be equal to unity, and we find

$$\Phi(a,c;x) = e^x\Phi(c-a,c;-x) \qquad (4\text{-}142)$$

which is known as *Kummer's transformation*.

There are many more interesting properties of the confluent hypergeometric function, but since we do not need to know them for our quantum-mechanical applications, we refer the reader to the literature[1] for them.

PROBLEMS

4-1 Find the general solution of the equation

$$\frac{d^2y}{dx^2} + 6\frac{dy}{dx} + 9y = 0$$

4-2 Use the series expansion method to derive a solution of the differential equation

$$\frac{d^2y}{dx^2} + \left(-\frac{1}{4} + \frac{k}{x} + \frac{\frac{1}{4} - m^2}{x^2}\right)y = 0$$

4-3 Determine the values of the constants C_n for which the functions

$$g_n(x) = C_n H_n(x)e^{-x^2/2}$$

form an orthonormal set in the interval $-\infty < x < \infty$. Then calculate the integrals

$$\int_{-\infty}^{\infty} g_n(x)\, x g_m(x)\, dx$$

and

$$\int_{-\infty}^{\infty} g_n(x)\frac{d}{dx}g_m(x)\, dx$$

for all possible values of n and m.

4-4 Show that for positive integers n

$$P_n(z) = \sum_{k=0}^{n} \frac{(-1)^k(n+k)!}{(n-k)!\,k!\,k!\,2^{k+1}}[(1-z)^k + (-1)^n(1+z)^k]$$

4-5 Evaluate the integral

$$\int_{-1}^{1} P_{n+1}(x)x^2 P_{n-1}(x)\, dx$$

---

[1] L. J. Slater, "Confluent Hypergeometric Functions," Cambridge University Press, London, 1960.

4-6 Show that for sufficiently small values of $|z|$ and $|h|$ we have

$$\frac{1-h^2}{(1-2hz+h^2)^{3/2}} = \sum_{n=0}^{\infty} (2n+1)h^n P_n(z)$$

4-7 Determine the general solution of Bessel's equation

$$x^2 \frac{d^2y}{dx^2} + x \frac{dy}{dx} + (x^2 - n^2)y = 0$$

by the series expansion method, assuming that n is not an integer.

4-8 Prove that

$$\frac{d}{dx} \Phi(a,c; x) = \frac{a}{c} \Phi(a+1, c+1; x)$$

$$-\frac{\hbar^2}{8\pi^2 m} \frac{\partial^2 \psi}{\partial x^2}$$

$$\frac{\partial^2 \psi}{\partial t^2} = U(x)\phi - E\phi$$

$$= (E - U)\psi$$

SOLUTIONS OF
THE SCHRÖDINGER EQUATION
FOR SIMPLE SYSTEMS

5-1 RECTANGULAR POTENTIAL WELL

We consider a particle of mass m moving in one dimension in the potential field sketched in Fig. 5-1. The algebraic expression for this potential function is

$$V(x) = U \qquad x < 0$$

$$V(x) = 0 \qquad 0 \leqslant x \leqslant a \qquad \qquad \text{(5-1)}$$

$$V(x) = U \qquad x > a$$

In Sec. 3-3 we considered the situation where U is infinite, but now we wish to study the situation where U is finite. The one-dimensional Schrödinger equation can be written in the form

$$\frac{d^2\psi}{dx^2} = -\frac{2m}{\hbar^2}[E - V(x)]\psi \qquad \qquad \text{(5-2)}$$

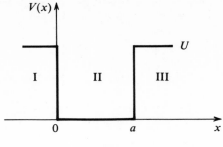

FIG. 5-1

and again we derive its solutions for the different regions I, II, and III, where $x < 0$, $0 \leqslant x \leqslant a$, and $x > a$, respectively. In region II we have $V(x) = 0$, and if we substitute

$$\frac{2mE}{\hbar^2} = \alpha^2 \tag{5-3}$$

then the Schrödinger equation in this region becomes

$$\frac{d^2\psi_{II}}{dx^2} = -\alpha^2\psi_{II} \tag{5-4}$$

We discussed this equation in Sec. 4-1 and found that the general solution is

$$\psi_{II}(x) = A_{II}e^{i\alpha x} + B_{II}e^{-i\alpha x} \tag{5-5}$$

In regions I and III the Schrödinger equation is

$$\frac{d^2\psi}{dx^2} = -\frac{2m}{\hbar^2}(E - U)\psi \tag{5-6}$$

It is useful to distinguish between the two cases $E < U$ and $E > U$. In the first we substitute

$$\frac{2m}{\hbar^2}(E - U) = -\beta^2 \tag{5-7}$$

and we obtain the equation

$$\frac{d^2\psi}{dx^2} = \beta^2\psi \tag{5-8}$$

The solutions are

$$\psi_I(x) = A_Ie^{\beta x} + B_Ie^{-\beta x} \qquad x < 0$$
$$\psi_{III}(x) = A_{III}e^{\beta x} + B_{III}e^{-\beta x} \qquad x > a \tag{5-9}$$

Let us now consider the behavior of the wave function when x tends to plus and minus infinity. When x tends to plus infinity, we have to take $\psi_{\text{III}}(x)$ as the wave function. It is easily seen that the first term of $\psi_{\text{III}}(x)$, namely, $e^{\beta x}$, tends to infinity when x tends to plus infinity. Since we cannot allow this, the constant A_{III} has to be zero. According to the same argument, we find that B_{I} has to be zero, since $e^{-\beta x}$ tends to infinity when x tends to minus infinity. We find, therefore, that for $E < U$ the wave function is

$$\psi(x) = \begin{cases} A_{\text{I}}e^{\beta x} & x < 0 \\ A_{\text{II}}e^{i\alpha x} + B_{\text{II}}e^{-i\alpha x} & 0 \leqslant x \leqslant a \\ B_{\text{III}}e^{-\beta x} & x > a \end{cases} \tag{5-10}$$

The derivatives are

$$\frac{d\psi}{dx} = \begin{cases} \beta A_{\text{I}}e^{\beta x} & x < 0 \\ i\alpha(A_{\text{II}}e^{i\alpha x} - B_{\text{II}}e^{-i\alpha x}) & 0 \leqslant x \leqslant a \\ -\beta B_{\text{III}}e^{-\beta x} & x > a \end{cases} \tag{5-11}$$

We now consider the behavior of $\psi(x)$ and its derivative at the point $x = 0$. The condition that ψ is continuous at $x = 0$ leads to the equation

$$A_{\text{I}} = A_{\text{II}} + B_{\text{II}} \tag{5-12}$$

and the condition that the derivative is continuous at $x = 0$ gives

$$\beta A_{\text{I}} = i\alpha(A_{\text{II}} - B_{\text{II}}) \tag{5-13}$$

The condition that ψ and its derivative are continuous at the point $x = a$ yields the equations

$$A_{\text{II}}e^{i\alpha a} + B_{\text{II}}e^{-i\alpha a} = B_{\text{III}}e^{-\beta a} \tag{5-14}$$

and $\qquad i\alpha(A_{\text{II}}e^{i\alpha a} - B_{\text{II}}e^{-i\alpha a}) = -\beta B_{\text{III}}e^{-\beta a} \tag{5-15}$

From Eqs. (5-12) and (5-13) we find

$$A_{\text{II}} = \frac{1}{2}\left(1 - \frac{i\beta}{\alpha}\right)A_{\text{I}} \qquad B_{\text{II}} = \frac{1}{2}\left(1 + \frac{i\beta}{\alpha}\right)A_{\text{I}} \tag{5-16}$$

Substitution of this result into Eqs. (5-14) and (5-15) gives

$$(\alpha \cos \alpha a + \beta \sin \alpha a)A_{\text{I}} - \alpha e^{-\beta a}B_{\text{III}} = 0 \tag{5-17}$$
$$(\beta \cos \alpha a - \alpha \sin \alpha a)A_{\text{I}} + \beta e^{-\beta a}B_{\text{III}} = 0$$

Elimination of B_{III} yields

$$[2\alpha\beta \cos \alpha a + (\beta^2 - \alpha^2) \sin \alpha a]A_{\text{I}} = 0 \tag{5-18}$$

Hence, the expression

$$2\alpha\beta \cos \alpha a + (\beta^2 - \alpha^2) \sin \alpha a = 0 \tag{5-19}$$

is the equation for the eigenvalues. Equations of this kind are usually solved by graphical methods. For this purpose it is convenient to transform Eq. (5-19) to

$$\cos^2 \alpha a = \left(\frac{\beta^2 - \alpha^2}{\beta^2 + \alpha^2}\right)^2 = \left(1 - \frac{2\alpha^2}{\gamma^2}\right)^2 \tag{5-20}$$

where we have introduced

$$\hbar^2\gamma^2 = 2mU \tag{5-21}$$

Now we plot both the left and right sides of Eq. (5-20) as a function of α, bearing in mind that $\alpha \leqslant \gamma$. The points where the two curves intersect give us the energy eigenvalues (see Fig. 5-2). It may be seen that the

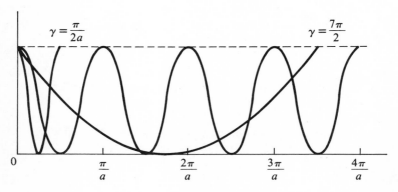

FIG. 5-2

roots depend on the product $a\gamma$. In Fig. 5-2 we sketch the two situations where $a\gamma = \frac{1}{2}\pi$ and $a\gamma = 7\pi/2$. In the first case there are two points of intersection and in the second there are eight, but we should disregard the solutions at $\alpha = 0$, since they do not give acceptable eigenfunctions.

From Eqs. (5-17) and (5-20) we find that

$$B_{III} = e^{\beta a} A_I \tag{5-22}$$

and the complete wave function is therefore

$$\psi(x) = \begin{cases} Ae^{\beta x} & x < 0 \\ A\left[\cos \alpha x + \dfrac{\beta}{\alpha} \sin \alpha x\right] & 0 \leqslant x \leqslant a \\ Ae^{\beta(a-x)} & x > a \end{cases} \tag{5-23}$$

The allowed values of the energy, and hence of α and β, follow from Fig. 5-2.

Let us proceed to consider the situation where $E > U$. Now the Schrödinger equation for regions I and III becomes

$$\frac{d^2\psi}{dx^2} = -\lambda^2\psi \qquad \lambda^2 = \frac{2m}{\hbar^2}(E - U) \tag{5-24}$$

Its general solution is

$$\psi(x) = Ae^{i\lambda x} + Be^{-i\lambda x} \tag{5-25}$$

which we can also write in the form

$$\psi(x) = C \cos \lambda x + D \sin \lambda x \tag{5-26}$$

If we choose the same representation for the solution of Eq. (5-4) in region II, then the complete wave function is

$$\psi_\mathrm{I}(x) = C_\mathrm{I} \cos \lambda x + D_\mathrm{I} \sin \lambda x$$
$$\psi_\mathrm{II}(x) = C_\mathrm{II} \cos \alpha x + D_\mathrm{II} \sin \alpha x \tag{5-27}$$
$$\psi_\mathrm{III}(x) = C_\mathrm{III} \cos \lambda x + D_\mathrm{III} \sin \lambda x$$

and the derivative is

$$\psi_\mathrm{I}'(x) = \lambda(D_\mathrm{I} \cos \lambda x - C_\mathrm{I} \sin \lambda x)$$
$$\psi_\mathrm{II}'(x) = \alpha(D_\mathrm{II} \cos \alpha x - C_\mathrm{II} \sin \alpha x) \tag{5-28}$$
$$\psi_\mathrm{III}'(x) = \lambda(D_\mathrm{III} \cos \lambda x - C_\mathrm{III} \sin \lambda x)$$

From the continuity of ψ and its derivative at the point $x = 0$, we find that

$$C_\mathrm{II} = C_\mathrm{I} = C \qquad D_\mathrm{II} = \frac{\lambda}{\alpha} D_\mathrm{I} = \frac{\lambda}{\alpha} D \tag{5-29}$$

The condition of continuity of ψ and ψ' at the point $x = a$ yields the equations

$$C_\mathrm{II} \cos \alpha a + D_\mathrm{II} \sin \alpha a = C_\mathrm{III} \cos \lambda a + D_\mathrm{III} \sin \lambda a$$
$$\alpha(D_\mathrm{II} \cos \alpha a - C_\mathrm{II} \sin \alpha a) = \lambda(D_\mathrm{III} \cos \lambda a - C_\mathrm{III} \sin \lambda a) \tag{5-30}$$

which lead to the solutions

$$C_\mathrm{III} = \left(\cos \lambda a \cos \alpha a + \frac{\alpha}{\lambda} \sin \lambda a \sin \alpha a\right) C + \left(\frac{\lambda}{\alpha} \cos \lambda a \sin \alpha a - \sin \lambda a \cos \alpha a\right) D$$

$$\tag{5-31}$$

$$D_\mathrm{III} = \left(\sin \lambda a \cos \alpha a - \frac{\alpha}{\lambda} \cos \lambda a \sin \alpha a\right) C + \left(\frac{\lambda}{\alpha} \sin \lambda a \sin \alpha a + \cos \lambda a \cos \alpha a\right) D$$

If we combine the results of Eqs. (5-27), (5-29), and (5-31), we find that the allowed wave functions are

$$\psi_1(x) = \cos \lambda x \qquad x < 0$$

$$= \cos \alpha x \qquad 0 \leqslant x \leqslant a$$

$$= \left(\cos \lambda a \cos \alpha a + \frac{\alpha}{\lambda} \sin \lambda a \sin \alpha a \right) \cos \lambda x$$

$$+ \left(\sin \lambda a \cos \alpha a - \frac{\alpha}{\lambda} \cos \lambda a \sin \alpha a \right) \sin \lambda x \qquad x > a \quad (5\text{-}32)$$

and $\psi_2(x) = \sin \lambda x \qquad x < 0$

$$= \frac{\lambda}{\alpha} \sin \alpha x \qquad 0 \leqslant x \leqslant a$$

$$= \left(\frac{\lambda}{\alpha} \cos \lambda a \sin \alpha a - \sin \lambda a \cos \alpha a \right) \cos \lambda x$$

$$+ \left(\frac{\lambda}{\alpha} \sin \lambda a \sin \alpha a + \cos \lambda a \cos \alpha a \right) \sin \lambda x \qquad x > a \quad (5\text{-}33)$$

It follows that our argument does not lead to any conditions for the energy, and we conclude that all values for E that are larger than U are allowed. The total spectrum of allowed energy values consists, therefore, of a finite number of discrete values of $E \leqslant U$ and of all values of $E > U$. This combination of a discrete spectrum and a continuum occurs frequently in quantum-mechanical problems.

5-2 TUNNELING THROUGH A POTENTIAL BARRIER

The situation described in Fig. 5-3 represents the encounter between a free particle and a potential barrier of height U and length a. The corresponding potential function $V(x)$ is

$$V(x) = \begin{cases} 0 & \text{if} \quad x < 0 \\ U & \text{if} \quad 0 \leqslant x \leqslant a \\ 0 & \text{if} \quad x > a \end{cases} \qquad (5\text{-}34)$$

The classical description of this situation is quite straightforward. If the energy of the free particle is larger than U, then its motion is not essentially affected by the barrier. If its energy is smaller than U, it is totally reflected. The quantum-mechanical theory leads to different

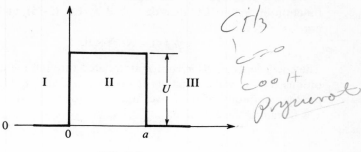

FIG. 5-3

predictions. Here it is found that the particle can pass the barrier even when its energy is smaller than U. This phenomenon is known as *tunneling* and is a quantum-mechanical effect that has found many applications.

Let us consider the Schrödinger equation for the potential function of Eq. (5-34). In regions I and III we may write the Schrödinger equation as

$$\frac{d^2\phi}{dx^2} = -\alpha^2\phi \qquad \alpha^2 = \frac{2mE}{\hbar^2} \tag{5-35}$$

In region II we write it as

$$\frac{d^2\phi}{dx^2} = \lambda^2\phi \qquad \lambda^2 = \frac{2m(U - E)}{\hbar^2} \tag{5-36}$$

when $E \leqslant U$ and as

$$\frac{d^2\phi}{dx^2} = -\mu^2\phi \qquad \mu^2 = \frac{2m(E - U)}{\hbar^2} \tag{5-37}$$

when $E > U$.

The solutions of Eq. (5-35) are $e^{i\alpha x}$ and $e^{-i\alpha x}$. We should realize that these two solutions $e^{i\alpha x}$ and $e^{-i\alpha x}$ describe a particle that moves from left to right or from right to left, respectively. We wish to study the effect of the potential barrier on the motion of a particle that encounters the barrier from the left, and therefore we take the wave function as

$$\phi_{\mathrm{I}}(x) = e^{i\alpha x} + Re^{-i\alpha x} \qquad x < 0$$
$$\phi_{\mathrm{III}}(x) = Te^{i\alpha x} \qquad x > a \tag{5-38}$$

Here $\phi_{\mathrm{III}}(x)$ is the transmitted wave, and the two terms of $\phi_{\mathrm{I}}(x)$ represent the incident and the reflected waves, respectively.

We first consider the case where $E \leqslant U$. The behavior of the wave function in region II is then described by Eq. (5-36), and the solutions are

$$\phi_{\text{II}}(x) = Ae^{\lambda x} + Be^{-\lambda x} \tag{5-39}$$

The coefficients A, B, R, and T are related through the continuity conditions for the wave function at the points x and a. These conditions for the continuity of the wave function and its derivative at the point $x = 0$ lead to the equations

$$1 + R = A + B$$

$$i\alpha(1 - R) = \lambda(A - B) \tag{5-40}$$

The same conditions for the point $x = a$ give

$$Te^{i\alpha a} = Ae^{\lambda a} + Be^{-\lambda a}$$

$$i\alpha Te^{i\alpha a} = \lambda(Ae^{\lambda a} - Be^{-\lambda a}) \tag{5-41}$$

We eliminate A and B from Eqs. (5-40) and (5-41) and obtain

$$(\lambda - i\alpha)R - e^{-\lambda a}e^{i\alpha a}(\lambda + i\alpha)T + (\lambda + i\alpha) = 0$$

$$(\lambda + i\alpha)R - e^{\lambda a}e^{i\alpha a}(\lambda - i\alpha)T + (\lambda - i\alpha) = 0 \tag{5-42}$$

The solution of this equation is

$$R = \frac{(\alpha^2 + \lambda^2)\sinh \lambda a}{(\alpha^2 - \lambda^2)\sinh \lambda a + 2i\lambda\alpha\cosh \lambda a}$$

$$e^{i\alpha a}T = \frac{2i\lambda\alpha}{(\alpha^2 - \lambda^2)\sinh \lambda a + 2i\lambda\alpha\cosh \lambda a} \tag{5-43}$$

The transmission coefficient D of the potential barrier is defined as TT^*. From Eq. (5-43) we find that

$$D = \frac{4\lambda^2\alpha^2}{(\alpha^2 + \lambda^2)^2 \sinh^2 \lambda a + 4\lambda^2\alpha^2} \tag{5-44}$$

since
$$\cosh^2 x - \sinh^2 x = 1 \tag{5-45}$$

When the product λa is much larger than unity, D behaves asymptotically like

$$D \approx 16\gamma(1 - \gamma)e^{-2\lambda a} \qquad \gamma = \frac{E}{U} \tag{5-46}$$

We have already mentioned that according to classical mechanics D is exactly zero, but according to our quantum-mechanical argument it has a finite value given by Eq. (5-44). This phenomenon, is the above mentioned tunneling effect. Since it is predicted only by quantum-mechanical and not by classical arguments, it is called a quantum-mechanical effect by the experimentalists.

Let us now study the situation where $E > U$. The wave function in region II is now determined by Eq. (5-37), which has the solutions

$$\phi_{II}(x) = P \cos \mu x + Q \sin \mu x \qquad (5\text{-}47)$$

The wave function in regions I and III is again given by Eq. (5-38). The conditions for the continuity of the wave function and its derivative at the points $x = 0$ and $x = a$ lead to the equations

$$1 + R = P$$
$$i\alpha(1 - R) = \mu Q \qquad (5\text{-}48)$$

and
$$Te^{i\alpha a} = P \cos \mu a + Q \sin \mu a$$
$$i\alpha Te^{i\alpha a} = \mu(-P \sin \mu a + Q \cos \mu a) \qquad (5\text{-}49)$$

respectively. The solution of these equations is

$$R = \frac{(\alpha^2 - \mu^2) \sin \mu a}{(\alpha^2 + \mu^2) \sin \mu a + 2\alpha\mu i \cos \mu a}$$

$$T = \frac{2\alpha\mu i e^{-i\alpha a}}{(\alpha^2 + \mu^2) \sin \mu a + 2\alpha\mu i \cos \mu a}$$

$$P = \frac{2\alpha(\alpha \sin \mu a + i\mu \cos \mu a)}{(\alpha^2 + \mu^2) \sin \mu a + 2\alpha\mu i \cos \mu a} \qquad (5\text{-}50)$$

$$Q = \frac{2\alpha(-\alpha \cos \mu a + i\mu \sin \mu a)}{(\alpha^2 + \mu^2) \sin \mu a + 2\alpha\mu i \cos \mu a}$$

The transmission coefficient TT^* is now

$$D = \frac{4\alpha^2\mu^2}{(\alpha^2 - \mu^2)^2 \sin^2 \mu a + 4\alpha^2\mu^2} = \frac{4E(E - U)}{U^2 \sin^2 \mu a + 4E(E - U)} \qquad (5\text{-}51)$$

It is easily verified that D approaches unity when E is large compared with U, so that for large energies the particle is not affected by the potential barrier. The possibility that the particle is reflected is given by RR^*, which is

$$RR^* = \frac{U^2 \sin^2 \mu a}{U^2 \sin^2 \mu a + 4E(E - U)} \qquad (5\text{-}52)$$

We see that

$$TT^* + RR^* = 1 \qquad (5\text{-}53)$$

which is in agreement with our expectation that the sum of the probabilities for transmission and for reflection should be equal to unity. For large values of E in comparison with U the reflection coefficient approaches zero. Furthermore, it follows from Eq. (5-52) that the reflection coefficient is zero when

$$\mu a = \frac{[2m(E - U)]^{1/2}a}{\hbar} = n\pi \qquad (5\text{-}54)$$

where n is an integer. In this case there is perfect transmission through the potential barrier.

5-3 PERIODIC POTENTIALS

As an example of a particle moving in a potential field we consider the potential field of Fig. 5-4. Here the potential consists of a set of

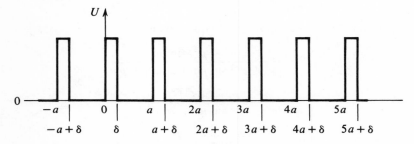

FIG. 5-4

potential barriers of height U and width δ that are equally spaced and separated by distances $(a - \delta)$. This system was used in the early development of solid-state physics as a simple model for the motion of an electron in a metal, and it is known as the *Kronig-Penney model*.[1]

In order to derive the eigenvalues and eigenfunctions for the system, we observe that, in the regions where $V = 0$, we can write the Schrödinger equation as

$$\frac{d^2\phi}{dx^2} = -\lambda^2\phi \qquad \lambda^2 = \frac{2mE}{\hbar^2} \qquad (5\text{-}55)$$

Its solutions are $e^{i\lambda x}$ and $e^{-i\lambda x}$. In the regions where $V = U$, we have to distinguish between the two possibilities that $E < U$ and $E > U$. The most interesting case is the former, where $E < U$, and we restrict our considerations to it. If it is assumed that $E < U$, then we may write

[1] R. de L. Kronig and W. G. Penney, *Proc. Roy. Soc.* (*London*), Ser A: *130*, 499 (1931).

the Schrödinger equation in the regions where $V = U$ as

$$\frac{d^2\phi}{dx^2} = \mu^2\phi \qquad \mu^2 = \frac{2m(U - E)}{\hbar^2} \tag{5-56}$$

Its solutions are $e^{\mu x}$ and $e^{-\mu x}$.

In every region of space we write the wave function as a linear combination of the possible solutions, and the problem that we have to solve is how to choose the coefficients so that the wave function and its derivative are continuous everywhere.

The most convenient approach to this problem is first to study the behavior of the wave function in the vicinity of the kth potential barrier, extending from ka to $ka + \delta$. We have here

$$\phi(x) = a_k e^{i\lambda x} + b_k e^{-i\lambda x} \qquad (k - 1)a + \delta < x < ka$$
$$\phi(x) = c_k e^{\mu x} + d_k e^{-\mu x} \qquad ka \leqslant x \leqslant ka + \delta \tag{5-57}$$
$$\phi(x) = a_{k+1} e^{i\lambda x} + b_{k+1} e^{-i\lambda x} \qquad ka + \delta < x < (k + 1)a$$

for the wave function and

$$\phi'(x) = i\lambda(a_k e^{i\lambda x} - b_k e^{-i\lambda x}) \qquad (k - 1)a + \delta < x < ka$$
$$\phi'(x) = \mu(c_k e^{\mu x} - d_k e^{-\mu x}) \qquad ka \leqslant x \leqslant ka + \delta \tag{5-58}$$
$$\phi'(x) = i\lambda(a_{k+1} e^{i\lambda x} - b_{k+1} e^{-i\lambda x}) \qquad ka + \delta < x < (k + 1)a$$

for the derivative. The conditions that the wave function and its derivative are continuous at the points ka and $ka + \delta$ lead to the equations

$$a_k e^{i\lambda ka} + b_k e^{-i\lambda ka} = c_k e^{\mu ka} + d_k e^{-\mu ka}$$
$$i\lambda(a_k e^{i\lambda ka} - b_k e^{-i\lambda ka}) = \mu(c_k e^{\mu ka} - d_k e^{-\mu ka})$$
$$a_{k+1} e^{i\lambda(ka+\delta)} + b_{k+1} e^{-i\lambda(ka+\delta)} = c_k e^{\mu(ka+\delta)} + d_k e^{-\mu(ka+\delta)} \tag{5-59}$$
$$i\lambda[a_{k+1} e^{i\lambda(ka+\delta)} - b_{k+1} e^{-i\lambda(ka+\delta)}] = \mu[c_k e^{\mu(ka+\delta)} - d_k e^{-\mu(ka+\delta)}]$$

In order to solve these equations, we substitute

$$a_k = e^{-i\lambda ka}\rho^k A \qquad c_k = e^{-\mu ka}\rho^k C$$
$$b_k = e^{i\lambda ka}\rho^k B \qquad d_k = e^{\mu ka}\rho^k D \tag{5-60}$$

into Eq. (5-59). We then obtain

$$A + B = C + D$$
$$i\lambda(A - B) = \mu(C - D)$$
$$\rho[e^{-i\lambda(a-\delta)}A + e^{i\lambda(a-\delta)}B] = Ce^{\mu\delta} + De^{-\mu\delta} \tag{5-61}$$
$$i\lambda\rho[e^{-i\lambda(a-\delta)}A - e^{i\lambda(a-\delta)}B] = \mu(Ce^{\mu\delta} - De^{-\mu\delta})$$

These equations are independent of k, so that they are the same for each potential barrier. Consequently, if we find a set of values of ρ,

A, B, C, and D for which Eq. (5-61) is satisfied, then the wave function and its derivative are continuous everywhere.

In order to solve Eq. (5-61), we write its second pair of equations as

$$\rho[(A + B)\cos\gamma - i(A - B)\sin\gamma] = Ce^{\mu\delta} + De^{-\mu\delta}$$

$$i\lambda\rho[(A - B)\cos\gamma - i(A + B)\sin\gamma] = \mu(Ce^{\mu\delta} - De^{-\mu\delta}) \tag{5-62}$$

where we have introduced the abbreviation

$$\gamma = \lambda(a - \delta) \tag{5-63}$$

If we now eliminate A and B by means of the first pair of Eqs. (5-61), then we obtain

$$(\lambda\rho\cos\gamma - \lambda\cosh\mu\delta)(C + D) - (\mu\rho\sin\gamma + \lambda\sinh\mu\delta)(C - D) = 0$$

$$(\lambda\rho\sin\gamma - \mu\sinh\mu\delta)(C + D) + (\mu\rho\cos\gamma - \mu\cosh\mu\delta)(C - D) = 0 \tag{5-64}$$

These equations have solutions only when they are proportional to each other, that is, when the following condition is satisfied:

$$\lambda\mu(\rho^2 + 1) = 2\lambda\mu\rho\cos\gamma\cosh\mu\delta + (\mu^2 - \lambda^2)\rho\sin\gamma\sinh\mu\delta \tag{5-65}$$

Let us first consider the possible values for the parameter ρ. It is easily verified that for $|\rho| > 1$ the wave function tends to infinity when k tends to infinity, so that this is not allowed. If $|\rho| < 1$, then the wave function becomes infinite when k tends to minus infinity, so that this is not allowed either. Consequently $|\rho|$ has to be equal to unity, and we write it as

$$\rho = e^{i\sigma a} \tag{5-66}$$

If we substitute this into Eq. (5-65), we obtain

$$\cos\sigma a = \cos\lambda(a - \delta)\cosh\mu\delta + \frac{\mu^2 - \lambda^2}{2\lambda\mu}\sin\lambda(a - \delta)\sinh\mu\delta \tag{5-67}$$

as the condition for the energy eigenvalues.

Equation (5-67) can be solved graphically, but we prefer to simplify our model before attempting its solution. We let the height U of the potential barrier become very large, and at the same time we let δ become very small in such a way that the product $U\delta$ remains finite. This finite product is defined as

$$P = \frac{mU\delta}{\hbar^2} \tag{5-68}$$

In the limiting case where $U \to \infty$, $\delta \to 0$, $U\delta \to (\hbar^2 P/m)$ Eq. (5-67) becomes

$$\cos\sigma a = \cos\lambda a + \frac{P}{\lambda}\sin\lambda a \tag{5-69}$$

In Fig. 5-5 we plot the right side of this equation as a function of λa for

a certain value of *Pa*. An important feature of Eq. (5-69) now is that
it has solutions only for those values of λa where the right side of the

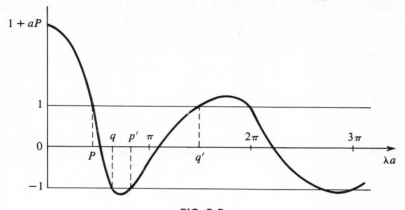

FIG. 5-5

equation has values between minus unity and plus unity, since the left
side of the equation has to stay within those limits. It follows, therefore,
from Fig. 5-4 that the lowest eigenvalue occurs when $a\lambda = p$, the projection of the point where the curve intersects with the 1 axis. This
lowest eigenvalue corresponds to the value $\sigma = 0$. All energy values
between the points p and q are allowed, but at the point q, which is the
projection of the intersection with the -1 axis, we enter a region of forbidden energy values. The region between the points p' and q' leads
again to allowed energy values, etc. The energy eigenvalues depend on
σ, and in Fig. 5-6 we have a typical plot of λ versus σ. We see that there

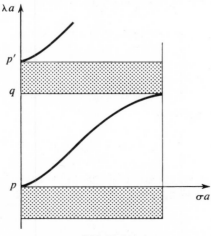

FIG. 5-6

are certain regions that contain a continuum of allowed energy values, and these regions are separated by finite regions that contain no eigenvalues. In a situation like this we speak of energy bands, which are the eigenvalue regions, and of energy gaps, which are the remaining energy regions. This band structure plays a very important role in the theory of solids.

5-4 THE HARMONIC OSCILLATOR

A particle moving in a one-dimensional quadratic potential field with a minimum is called a harmonic oscillator. If we take the minimum of the potential as the zero point for the energy and the position of the minimum as the origin of the coordinate system, then we can write the potential function as

$$V(x) = \tfrac{1}{2}kx^2 \tag{5-70}$$

where k is the force constant. The Schrödinger equation is

$$-\frac{\hbar^2}{2m}\frac{d^2\phi}{dx^2} + \frac{1}{2}kx^2\phi = E\phi \tag{5-71}$$

We introduce a new parameter

$$\varepsilon = \frac{2mE}{\hbar^2} \tag{5-72}$$

so that the equation becomes

$$\frac{d^2\phi}{dx^2} + \left(\varepsilon - \frac{km}{\hbar^2}x^2\right)\phi = 0 \tag{5-73}$$

Now we change from the variable x to a new variable y by way of the transformation

$$x = \sqrt{\alpha}y \qquad \alpha^2 = \frac{\hbar^2}{km} \tag{5-74}$$

The equation then becomes

$$\frac{d^2\phi}{dy^2} + (\alpha\varepsilon - y^2)\phi = 0 \tag{5-75}$$

In order to solve an equation of this kind, it is often useful to determine the asymptotic behavior of its solution first. We consider the function

$$g(y) = e^{\pm(1/2)y^2} \tag{5-76}$$

which has a second derivative

$$g''(y) = (y^2 \pm 1)e^{\pm (1/2)y^2} \tag{5-77}$$

The differential equation for g is therefore

$$g'' - (\pm 1 + y^2)g = 0 \tag{5-78}$$

For very large values of y the term ± 1 in Eq. (5-78) becomes negligible, as does the term $\alpha\varepsilon$ in Eq. (5-75), so that Eqs. (5-75) and (5-78) become identical for large values of y. We may therefore conclude that for large values of y the solutions of Eq. (5-75) behave asymptotically like $\exp(\pm \frac{1}{2}y^2)$. The solution that behaves like $\exp(\frac{1}{2}y^2)$ is unsuitable, since it tends to infinity when y tends to plus or minus infinity. Consequently the desired solution of Eq. (5-75) behaves asymptotically like $\exp(-\frac{1}{2}y^2)$, and in order to solve the equation, we substitute

$$\phi(y) = w(y)e^{-(1/2)y^2} \tag{5-79}$$

into Eq. (5-75). The differential equation for $w(y)$ then is

$$\frac{d^2w}{dy^2} - 2y\frac{dw}{dy} + (\alpha\varepsilon - 1)w = 0 \tag{5-80}$$

Let us compare this with Eq. (4-56) for the Hermite polynomial $H_n(y)$, which is

$$\frac{d^2w}{dy^2} - 2y\frac{dw}{dy} + 2nw = 0 \tag{5-81}$$

Equations (5-80) and (5-81) become identical if we take

$$\alpha\varepsilon - 1 = 2n \tag{5-82}$$

We saw in Sec. 4-4 that for integer nonnegative values of n one of the two solutions of Eq. (5-81) is a Hermite polynomial $H_n(y)$. The other solution and all solutions for noninteger values of n behave asymptotically like $\exp(y^2)$, and they are not allowed, since they would cause the wave function $\phi(y)$ to behave asymptotically like $\exp(\frac{1}{2}y^2)$, according to Eq. (5-79). We find, therefore, that we obtain acceptable solutions of the Schrödinger equation if we impose the condition

$$\alpha\varepsilon = 2n + 1 \qquad n = 0, 1, 2, 3, 4, \ldots, \text{etc.} \tag{5-83}$$

The energy eigenvalues are therefore

$$E_n = (n + \tfrac{1}{2})\hbar\omega \qquad n = 0, 1, 2, \ldots, \text{etc.} \tag{5-84}$$

according to Eqs. (5-72), (5-74), and (5-83). Here we have introduced the angular frequency

$$\omega = \left(\frac{k}{m}\right)^{1/2} \tag{5-85}$$

It follows from Eq. (5-79) and from the considerations above that the corresponding eigenfunctions are

$$\phi_n = C_n H_n(y) e^{-(1/2)y^2} \qquad y = (\alpha)^{-(1/2)} x \qquad (5\text{-}86)$$

The normalization constants C_n are determined from the condition

$$C_n C_n^* \int_{-\infty}^{\infty} H_n(y) H_n(y) e^{-y^2} dx = C_n C_n^* \sqrt{\alpha} \int_{-\infty}^{\infty} H_n(y) H_n(y) e^{-y^2} dy = 1 \quad (5\text{-}87)$$

The value of the integral is reported in Eq. (4-48), and substitution leads to

$$C_n C_n^* \sqrt{\alpha} 2^n n! \sqrt{\pi} = 1 \qquad (5\text{-}88)$$

or $\qquad\qquad C_n = (\pi\alpha)^{-1/4}(2^n \cdot n!)^{-1/2} \qquad (5\text{-}89)$

In Eq. (4-37) we reported the explicit forms of some of the Hermite polynomials. We use these expressions to plot the normalized eigenfunctions versus the variable y in Fig. 5-7 for some of the lower eigenvalues.

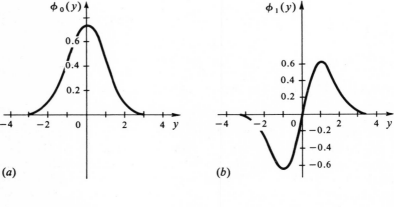

(a) (b)

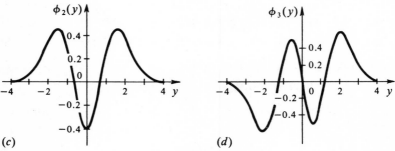

(c) (d)

FIG. 5-7

It follows from Fig. 5-7 that the eigenfunctions are either symmetric or antisymmetric in the coordinate. We will show that this is true in general as long as the potential function is symmetric in x, that is,

$$V(x) = V(-x) \tag{5-90}$$

We write the Schrödinger equation as

$$\left[-\frac{\hbar^2}{2m} \frac{d^2}{dx^2} + V(x) \right] \phi(x) = E\phi(x) \tag{5-91}$$

Let us now consider an eigenvalue E_n that has one and only one corresponding eigenfunction $\phi_n(x)$. We then have

$$\left[-\frac{\hbar^2}{2m} \frac{d^2}{dx^2} + V(x) \right] \phi_n(x) = E_n \phi_n(x) \tag{5-92}$$

and also

$$\left[-\frac{\hbar^2}{2m} \frac{d^2}{dx^2} + V(-x) \right] \phi_n(-x) = E_n \phi_n(-x) \tag{5-93}$$

Because of Eq. (5-90) we can also write Eq. (5-93) as

$$\left[-\frac{\hbar^2}{2m} \frac{d^2}{dx^2} + V(x) \right] \phi_n(-x) = E_n \phi_n(-x) \tag{5-94}$$

Let us now compare Eqs. (5-92) and (5-94). It follows that not only $\phi_n(x)$ but also $\phi_n(-x)$ is an eigenfunction belonging to E_n. However, since E_n can have only one eigenfunction, $\phi_n(x)$ and $\phi_n(-x)$ must be proportional to each other, or

$$\phi_n(-x) = \rho \phi_n(x) \tag{5-95}$$

If we apply Eq. (5-95) twice, we find that

$$\phi_n(-x) = \rho \phi_n(x) = \rho^2 \phi_n(-x) \tag{5-96}$$

or

$$\rho^2 = 1 \tag{5-97}$$

Obviously $\rho = \pm 1$, so that there are two possibilities, namely,

$$\phi_n(x) = \phi_n(-x) \tag{5-98}$$

or

$$\phi_n(x) = -\phi_n(-x) \tag{5-99}$$

In the first case we call $\phi_n(x)$ symmetric in x, and in the second case $\phi_n(x)$ is antisymmetric in x.

Finally, we wish to evaluate the quantities

$$(x)_{n,m} = \langle \phi_n(x) | \, x \, | \phi_m(x) \rangle \tag{5-100}$$

and

$$(\delta)_{n,m} = \langle \phi_n(x) | \frac{d}{dx} | \phi_m(x) \rangle \tag{5-101}$$

since we need to know them in subsequent applications. We write Eq. (5-100) as

$$(x)_{n,m} = C_n C_m \int_{-\infty}^{\infty} H_n(y) x H_m(y) e^{-y^2} dx$$

$$= \left(\frac{\pi}{\alpha} 2^{n+m} \cdot n! \cdot m!\right)^{-1/2} \int_{-\infty}^{\infty} H_n(y) y H_m(y) e^{-y^2} dy \qquad (5\text{-}102)$$

According to Eq. (4-40), we have

$$y H_m(y) = m H_{m-1}(y) + \tfrac{1}{2} H_{m+1}(y) \qquad (5\text{-}103)$$

Substitution into Eq. (5-102) gives

$$(x)_{n,m} = \left(\frac{\pi}{\alpha} \cdot 2^{n+m} \cdot n! \, m!\right)^{-1/2} \left(m I_{n,m-1} + \tfrac{1}{2} I_{n,m+1}\right)$$

with
$$I_{n,m} = \int_{-\infty}^{\infty} H_n(y) H_m(y) e^{-y^2} dy = (2^n \cdot n! \, \sqrt{\pi}) \delta_{n,m} \qquad (5\text{-}104)$$

We obtain

$$(x)_{n,n+1} = \left[\frac{1}{2} \alpha(n+1)\right]^{1/2}$$

$$(x)_{n,n-1} = \left(\frac{1}{2} \alpha n\right)^{1/2} \qquad (5\text{-}105)$$

$$(x)_{n,m} = 0 \quad \text{if} \quad m \neq n \pm 1$$

Equation (5-101) can be written as

$$(\delta)_{n,m} = C_n C_m \int_{-\infty}^{\infty} H_n(y) e^{-(1/2)y^2} \frac{d}{dy} [H_m(y) e^{-(1/2)y^2}] dy$$

$$= C_n C_m \int_{-\infty}^{\infty} [H_n(y) H_m'(y) - H_n(y) y H_m(y)] e^{-y^2} dy \qquad (5\text{-}106)$$

Substitution of the recurrence Eqs. (4-40) and (4-42) gives

$$(\delta)_{n,m} = (\pi\alpha \cdot 2^{n+m} \cdot n! \, m!)^{-1/2} (m I_{n,m-1} - \tfrac{1}{2} I_{n,m+1}) \qquad (5\text{-}107)$$

It follows from Eq. (5-104) that

$$(\delta)_{n,n+1} = \left(\frac{n+1}{2\alpha}\right)^{1/2}$$

$$(\delta)_{n,n-1} = -\left(\frac{n}{2\alpha}\right)^{1/2} \qquad (5\text{-}108)$$

$$(\delta)_{n,m} = 0 \quad \text{if} \quad m \neq n \pm 1$$

5-5 THE RIGID ROTOR

We define a rigid rotor as two particles of masses m_1 and m_2 which are connected by a rigid weightless rod of length R and which move in a potential field that is everywhere zero. We impose the restriction that the center of gravity of the system has to remain at rest. It is convenient to make use of the results that we obtained in Sec. 1-6 in order to derive the Hamiltonian. According to Eq. (1-102) the Hamiltonian of two particles moving in a potential field $V(\mathbf{r}) = 0$ can be written as

$$H = \frac{P^2}{2(m_1 + m_2)} + \frac{p^2}{2\mu} \tag{5-109}$$

where

$$\mu = \frac{m_1 m_2}{m_1 + m_2} \tag{5-110}$$

Here $\mathbf{P}$ is the momentum of the center of gravity, and $\mathbf{p}$ is associated with the relative motion of the particles; in Sec. 1-6 it was defined as

$$\mathbf{p} = \mu \frac{d\mathbf{r}}{dt} \qquad \mathbf{r} = \mathbf{r}_1 - \mathbf{r}_2 \tag{5-111}$$

if $\mathbf{r}_1$ and $\mathbf{r}_2$ are the positions of the two particles, respectively.

It follows that the motion of two particles, moving in a zero potential field in such a way that their center of gravity remains at rest, is described by a Schrödinger equation

$$-\frac{\hbar^2}{2\mu}\left(\frac{\partial^2}{\partial x^2} + \frac{\partial^2}{\partial y^2} + \frac{\partial^2}{\partial z^2}\right)\psi(x,y,z) = E\psi(x,y,z) \tag{5-112}$$

Before we consider the restriction that the distance r has to remain equal to R, we transform Eq. (5-112) to the polar coordinates (r,θ,ϕ), which are defined as

$$x = r \sin\theta \cos\phi$$
$$y = r \sin\theta \sin\phi \tag{5-113}$$
$$z = r \cos\theta$$

This transformation is discussed in Appendix A, and the result is given by Eq. (A-15). Substitution into Eq. (5-112) gives

$$\left(\frac{\partial^2}{\partial r^2} + \frac{2}{r}\frac{\partial}{\partial r} + \frac{1}{r^2}\frac{\partial^2}{\partial\theta^2} + \frac{\cos\theta}{r^2\sin\theta}\frac{\partial}{\partial\theta} + \frac{1}{r^2\sin^2\theta}\frac{\partial^2}{\partial\phi^2}\right)\psi(r,\theta,\phi) + \frac{2\mu E}{\hbar^2}\psi(r,\theta,\phi) = 0$$

$$\tag{5-114}$$

Now we impose the restriction that r has to be equal to a constant R.

We may then omit the differentiations with respect to r and replace r by R in the other terms. This gives

$$\left(\frac{\partial^2}{\partial\theta^2} + \frac{\cos\theta}{\sin\theta}\frac{\partial}{\partial\theta} + \frac{1}{\sin^2\theta}\frac{\partial^2}{\partial\phi^2}\right)\psi(\theta,\phi) + \lambda\psi(\theta,\phi) = 0 \qquad (5\text{-}115)$$

with

$$\lambda = \frac{2\mu R^2 E}{\hbar^2} \qquad (5\text{-}116)$$

This is the Schrödinger equation for the rigid rotor, which we take as the starting point for our considerations.

In order to solve Eq. (5-115) we write the function $\psi(\theta,\phi)$ in the form

$$\psi(\theta,\phi) = f(\theta)g(\phi) \qquad (5\text{-}117)$$

Substitution into Eq. (5-115) gives

$$\frac{1}{f(\theta)}\left(\frac{\partial^2}{\partial\theta^2} + \frac{\cos\theta}{\sin\theta}\frac{\partial}{\partial\theta}\right)f(\theta) + \frac{1}{g(\phi)\sin^2\theta}\frac{\partial^2 g}{\partial\phi^2} + \lambda = 0 \qquad (5\text{-}118)$$

which can be separated to

$$\frac{d^2 g}{d\phi^2} = -m^2 g(\phi) \qquad (5\text{-}119a)$$

$$\frac{d^2 f}{d\theta^2} + \frac{\cos\theta}{\sin\theta}\frac{df}{d\theta} + \left(\lambda - \frac{m^2}{\sin^2\theta}\right)f(\theta) = 0 \qquad (5\text{-}119b)$$

Here m is an arbitrary real parameter.

The solutions of Eq. (5-119a) can all be written in the form

$$g(\phi) = e^{im\phi} \qquad (5\text{-}120)$$

if we let m take both positive and negative values. Let us now investigate for which values of m we obtain acceptable wave functions. We mentioned in Sec. (3-2) that the general conditions for the wave functions are that they and their derivatives are everywhere finite, continuous, and single-valued. The essential condition that we have to worry about in the present situation is that $g(\phi)$ is single-valued. It may be seen that the sets of polar coordinates (θ,ϕ) and $(\theta, \phi + 2\pi)$ represent the same orientation of the rigid rotor, and if we wish the wave function to be single-valued, we have to impose the condition

$$g(\phi) = g(\phi + 2\pi) \qquad (5\text{-}121)$$

or

$$e^{2\pi im\phi} = 1 \qquad (5\text{-}122)$$

It follows that the allowed values of m are

$$m = 0, \pm 1, \pm 2, \pm 3, \ldots, \text{etc.} \qquad (5\text{-}123)$$

Let us now consider the differential equation (5-119b), with m given by Eq. (5-123). We introduce the new variable

$$s = \cos\theta \tag{5-124}$$

and observe that

$$\frac{df}{d\theta} = -\sin\theta\,\frac{df}{ds}$$

$$\frac{d^2f}{d\theta^2} = \sin^2\theta\,\frac{d^2f}{ds^2} - \cos\theta\,\frac{df}{ds} \tag{5-125}$$

Equation (5-119b) then becomes

$$(1 - s^2)\frac{d^2f}{ds^2} - 2s\frac{df}{ds} + \left(\lambda - \frac{m^2}{1 - s^2}\right)f = 0 \tag{5-126}$$

We notice that this is identical to the differential equation (4-112) for the associated Legendre polynomials $P_n{}^m(x)$:

$$(1 - x^2)\frac{d^2w}{dx^2} - 2x\frac{dw}{dx} + \left[n(n + 1) - \frac{m^2}{1 - x^2}\right]w = 0 \tag{5-127}$$

if we take

$$\lambda = n(n + 1) \tag{5-128}$$

If we take m equal to zero, then Eq. (5-127) reduces to the differential equation (4-89) for the Legendre polynomials. We showed in Sec. 4-5 that the solutions of Eq. (4-89) are usually infinite for $x = \pm 1$. It can be shown in a similar way that for $m \neq 0$ the solutions of Eq. (5-127) are usually infinite for $x = \pm 1$ and that, only if n is a nonnegative integer and $n \geqslant |m|$, one of the two solutions, namely, $P_n{}^{|m|}(x)$, is finite for $x = \pm 1$. Hence, the condition that the wave function is acceptable is given by Eq. (5-128), with n a nonnegative integer and $n \geqslant |m|$. The energy eigenvalues of the system are obtained by combining Eqs. (5-116) and (5-128):

$$E_n = n(n + 1)\frac{\hbar^2}{2\mu R^2} \qquad n = 0, 1, 2, 3, \ldots, \text{etc.} \tag{5-129}$$

The corresponding eigenfunctions are

$$\psi_{n,m}(\theta,\phi) = P_n^{|m|}(\cos\theta)e^{im\phi} = Y_{n,m}(\theta,\phi) \quad m = -n, -n + 1, \ldots, -1, 0, 1, 2, \ldots n, \tag{5-130}$$

where the functions $Y_{n,m}(\theta,\phi)$ are the spherical harmonics that were defined in Eq. (4-132). They are orthonormal functions on the surface of a sphere.

We see that there is more than one eigenfunction corresponding to an eigenvalue; to be exact the eigenvalue E_n has $(2n + 1)$ eigenfunctions. We speak here of a degeneracy or a $(2n + 1)$-fold degenerate eigenvalue. The consequences of degeneracies are discussed in greater detail in Chap. 7.

It should be mentioned here that the eigenvalues and eigenfunctions of the rigid rotor are the same as those of the angular momentum operator M^2. As such they play a very important role in the quantum theory of atomic systems, and the results above will prove to be useful when we discuss the hydrogen atom in Chap. 8.

PROBLEMS _____

5-1   Consider a particle of mass m moving in a potential field $V(x)$ that is defined as

$$V(x) = 0 \qquad x < 0$$
$$V(x) = U \qquad x \geqslant 0$$

Assume that the particle is coming from the left with an energy $E < U$. Determine the reflection coefficient for the particle. (The reflection coefficient is defined analogously to the one of Sec. 5-2.)

5-2   Determine the eigenvalues and eigenfunctions of the two-dimensional rigid rotor. This is the system composed of two particles of masses m_1 and m_2, connected by a rigid weightless rod of length R, and moving in two dimensions such that the center of gravity of the system remains at rest.

5-3   Calculate the expectation value of (x^2) as a function of n, where x is the coordinate, for the various states n of a harmonic oscillator.

5-4   If $\psi_n(x)$ is the eigenfunction of the nth state of a harmonic oscillator and if it is zero for the values $x = x_1, x = x_2, \ldots, x_n$, evaluate $\Sigma_i x_i^2$.

5-5   Calculate the transmission coefficient for tunneling of an electron through a rectangular potential barrier with a height of 1 ev and a width of 1 A when the electron has successive energy values 0.1, 0.5, and 0.9 ev. Perform the same calculation for a proton and compare.

5-6   Evaluate the five lowest rotational energies ($n = 1, 2, 3, 4, 5$) for the molecules H_2, HF, and F_2. (Hint: Treat the molecules as rigid rotors and neglect the masses of the electrons.)

5-7   To a first approximation we may represent the vibrational motion of a diatomic molecule AB as a harmonic oscillator. The oscillations are described by a displacement coordinate $q = R - R_0$, where R is the internuclear distance and R_0 its equilibrium value, and by a reduced mass $\mu_{AB} = m_A m_B (m_A + m_B)^{-1}$, where m_A and m_B are the nuclear masses. It has been found experimentally that the energy differences between the vibrational ground states and first excited states for H_2, HF, and O_2 are 4,395 cm^{-1}, 4,738 cm^{-1} and 1,580 cm^{-1} respectively. Calculate, for each of these molecules, the force constant k of the harmonic motion and the root-mean-square deviation from equilibrium, that is, the square root of the expectation value of q^2, for the ground state of the harmonic oscillator.

CHAPTER 6

MATRICES AND DETERMINANTS

6-1 PERMUTATIONS

Let us consider the set of numbers $(1,2,3,4, \ldots ,N)$ arranged in a monotonic increasing sequence. Any other sequence, for example, $(n_1,n_2,n_3, \ldots ,n_N)$, of these numbers is called a *permutation* of the original sequence. The operator that leads to the change from the original sequence $(1,2,3, \ldots ,N)$ to the permuted sequence $(n_1,n_2, \ldots ,n_N)$ is called a *permutation operator P*, and we write

$$(n_1,n_2,n_3, \ldots ,n_N) = P(1,2,3,4, \ldots ,N) \qquad (6\text{-}1)$$

The specific nature of P is determined by the two sequences that occur on the left and right. In the case that these two sequences are identical, P is called the *identity permutation P_0*.

A permutation operator can be described by means of its cycles. Let us illustrate this by writing a permuted sequence of nine numbers under its original sequence:

$$\begin{array}{ccccccccc} 1 & 2 & 3 & 4 & 5 & 6 & 7 & 8 & 9 \\ 8 & 3 & 1 & 7 & 2 & 6 & 9 & 5 & 4 \end{array} \qquad (6\text{-}2)$$

In order to describe this permutation, we start with the number 1 of the upper sequence, and we note that in the lower sequence its place has been taken by the number 8. We now look at this number 8 in the upper sequence, and we find number 5 below it. Under number 5 we find number 2; under number 2, number 3; and under number 3, we find our starting point, number 1. We write this succession of replacements as the cycle (1,8,5,2,3). The first number that does not occur in this cycle is 4, and we take this as the starting point of a second cycle, which is (4,7,9). Finally, we have number 6, which has remained in the same position. We denote this degenerate cycle by (6). The permutation (6-2) can thus be represented as (1,8,5,2,3) (4,7,9) (6), that is, as three cycles of five, three, and one elements, respectively.

Each permutation can also be obtained by a succession of pairwise interchanges. As an example we show in (6-3) how the lower sequence of (6-2) is obtained from the upper sequence in this way. On each line we have underlined the two elements that we have interchanged to obtain the subsequent line:

$$
\begin{array}{ccccccccc}
\underline{1} & 2 & 3 & 4 & 5 & 6 & 7 & \underline{8} & 9 \\
8 & 2 & 3 & 4 & \underline{5} & 6 & 7 & \underline{1} & 9 \\
8 & \underline{2} & 3 & 4 & \underline{1} & 6 & 7 & 5 & 9 \\
8 & \underline{1} & 3 & 4 & \underline{2} & 6 & 7 & 5 & 9 \\
8 & 3 & 1 & \underline{4} & 2 & 6 & \underline{7} & 5 & 9 \\
8 & 3 & 1 & \underline{7} & 2 & 6 & \underline{4} & 5 & 9 \\
8 & 3 & 1 & 7 & 2 & 6 & \underline{9} & 5 & \underline{4} \\
\end{array}
\qquad (6\text{-}3)
$$

Obviously we could also have obtained this result by means of a different succession of pairwise interchanges. In each case the total number of interchanges can vary but not its parity; for example, the permutation (6-2) can be obtained only by an even number of interchanges. It is therefore possible to use this number of interchanges as a criterion for the division of permutations into even and odd permutations. If a permutation can be achieved by an even number of pairwise interchanges, it is called even, and if it is achieved by an odd number of interchanges, it is called odd. In this connection we introduce the symbol δ_P, which is equal to plus unity when P is even and minus unity when P is odd. It is easily shown that for a permutation P of N elements that can be represented by C cycles δ_P is given by

$$
\delta_P = (-1)^{N+C} \qquad (6\text{-}4)
$$

In this discussion we have taken a sequence of numbers as the basis for our argument, but we can consider permutations of any other set of quantities. In general, we speak of the elements of a permutation. Often we consider permutations of a set of variables $q_1, q_2, \ldots, q_N$ of a function Ψ. As an example we take a function Ψ of four variables q_1, q_2, q_3, and q_4. A permutation of the variables, in general, leads to a different function. For instance, if P is described by

$$P = (13)(24) \tag{6-5}$$

then

$$P\Psi(q_1,q_2,q_3,q_4) = \Psi(q_3,q_4,q_1,q_2) \tag{6-6}$$

Any function $\Psi(q_1,q_2,\ldots,q_N)$ that satisfies the condition

$$\Psi(q_1,q_2,\ldots,q_N) = P\Psi(q_1,q_2,\ldots,q_N) \tag{6-7}$$

is called *symmetric* with respect to permutations. If the function satisfies the condition

$$\Psi(q_1,q_2,\ldots,q_N) = P\delta_P\Psi(q_1,q_2,\ldots,q_N) \tag{6-8}$$

then it is called *antisymmetric* with respect to permutations. Equation (6-8) means that Ψ remains unchanged if its variables are subjected to an even permutation and that Ψ changes sign if it is subjected to an odd permutation.

An arbitrary function $\psi(q_1,q_2,\ldots,q_N)$ is in general neither symmetric nor antisymmetric with respect to permutations. However, we can construct a symmetric function Φ from it by taking

$$\Phi = \sum_P P\psi(q_1,q_2,\ldots,q_N) \tag{6-9}$$

and an antisymmetric function Ψ by

$$\Psi = \sum_P P\delta_P\psi(q_1,q_2,\ldots,q_N) \tag{6-10}$$

The summations in Eqs. (6-9) and (6-10) are to be taken over all possible permutations, including the identity permutation.

Finally, we derive the total number $S(N)$ of possible permutations for N elements. If there is only one element, then the only possible permutation is the identity permutation, so that

$$S(1) = 1 \tag{6-11}$$

For a system of two elements there are two permutations, namely, the identity permutation and the exchange of the two elements, and therefore

$$S(2) = 2 \tag{6-12}$$

The general expression for $S(N)$ can be obtained by deriving a relation between $S(N)$ and $S(N + 1)$. Let us consider a particular permutation of N numbers that is described by a particular sequence

$$n_1 n_2 n_3 n_4 \cdots n_N \tag{6-13}$$

of the numbers. If we now try to fit an additional number $(N + 1)$ into this sequence, then we see that there are $(N + 1)$ different ways of doing this, and each of these arrangements leads to a different permutation for the $(N + 1)$ numbers. We find that an arbitrary permutation of N elements gives $(N + 1)$ different permutations for $(N + 1)$ elements, and therefore

$$S(N + 1) = (N + 1)S(N) \tag{6-14}$$

From Eqs. (6-11), (6-12), and (6-14) it is easily found that

$$S(N) = 1 \cdot 2 \cdot 3 \cdot 4 \cdot \cdots \cdot N = N! \tag{6-15}$$

6-2 MATRICES

A matrix is defined as a two-dimensional, rectangular array of numbers or functions. It is customarily represented as

$$\begin{bmatrix} a_{1,1} & a_{1,2} & a_{1,3} & \cdots & \cdots & \cdots & a_{1,N} \\ a_{2,1} & a_{2,2} & a_{2,3} & \cdots & \cdots & \cdots & a_{2,N} \\ a_{3,1} & a_{3,2} & a_{3,3} & \cdots & \cdots & \cdots & a_{3,N} \\ \cdots & \cdots & \cdots & \cdots & \cdots & \cdots & \cdots \\ \cdots & \cdots & \cdots & \cdots & \cdots & \cdots & \cdots \\ a_{M,1} & a_{M,2} & a_{M,3} & \cdots & \cdots & \cdots & a_{M,N} \end{bmatrix} \tag{6-16}$$

or, briefly, as

$$[a_{i,j}] \quad \begin{matrix} i = 1, 2, 3, \ldots, M \\ j = 1, 2, 3, \ldots, N \end{matrix} \tag{6-17}$$

All elements that are on the same horizontal line are said to form a *row* and all elements that are on the same vertical line are said to form a *column*. The mth row of the matrix (6-16) is composed of the elements $(a_{m,1}, a_{m,2}, a_{m,3}, \ldots, a_{m,N})$ and the nth column is $(a_{1,n}, a_{2,n}, a_{3,n}, \ldots, a_{M,n})$. The sum of two matrices $[a_{i,j}]$ and $[b_{i,j}]$ is defined as

$$[c_{i,j}] = [a_{i,j}] + [b_{i,j}] \tag{6-18}$$

where each element $c_{i,j}$ is the sum of the corresponding two elements $a_{i,j}$ and $b_{i,j}$:

$$c_{i,j} = a_{i,j} + b_{i,j} \tag{6-19}$$

This definition is logical only if the dimensions of the matrices $[a_{i,j}]$ and $[b_{i,j}]$ are the same or, as the mathematicians say, if they are conformable for addition or subtraction. We conclude, therefore, that two matrices can be added or subtracted only if they are conformable for addition or subtraction. It is easily verified from the definition that

$$[a_{i,j}] + [b_{i,j}] = [b_{i,j}] + [a_{i,j}] \tag{6-20}$$

The product matrix $[u_{i,j}]$ of two matrices $[a_{i,j}]$ and $[b_{i,j}]$

$$[u_{i,j}] = [a_{i,j}] \times [b_{i,j}] \tag{6-21}$$

is defined in such a way that the elements $u_{i,j}$ are given by

$$u_{i,j} = \sum_k a_{i,k} \cdot b_{k,j} \tag{6-22}$$

It follows from this definition that $u_{i,j}$ is obtained by taking the ith row of the first matrix and the jth column of the second matrix, by multiplication of the corresponding elements, and finally by summation. This procedure can be followed only if the rows of the first matrix and the columns of the second matrix are of equal length, that is, if the horizontal dimension of the first matrix and the vertical dimension of the second matrix are equal or if they are conformable for multiplication. An example of the multiplication of two matrices is

$$\begin{bmatrix} 1 & 0 & 3 & 4 \\ 2 & 1 & 0 & 1 \end{bmatrix} \times \begin{bmatrix} 3 & 0 \\ 1 & 2 \\ 0 & 5 \\ 1 & 3 \end{bmatrix} = \begin{bmatrix} 7 & 27 \\ 8 & 5 \end{bmatrix} \tag{6-23}$$

It follows from the definitions (6-21) and (6-22) that, in general,

$$[a_{i,j}] \times [b_{i,j}] \neq [b_{i,j}] \times [a_{i,j}] \tag{6-24}$$

For example, if we change the order of multiplication of the two matrices of Eq. (6-23), we obtain

$$\begin{bmatrix} 3 & 0 \\ 1 & 2 \\ 0 & 5 \\ 1 & 3 \end{bmatrix} \times \begin{bmatrix} 1 & 0 & 3 & 4 \\ 2 & 1 & 0 & 1 \end{bmatrix} = \begin{bmatrix} 3 & 0 & 9 & 12 \\ 5 & 2 & 3 & 6 \\ 10 & 5 & 0 & 5 \\ 7 & 3 & 3 & 7 \end{bmatrix} \tag{6-25}$$

which is quite different from Eq. (6-23).

A vector $\mathbf{v} = (v_x, v_y, v_z)$ can also be written in the form of a matrix. We can do this in two different ways, namely, as

$$\mathbf{v} = [v_x \quad v_y \quad v_z] \tag{6-26}$$

or as

$$\mathbf{v} = \begin{bmatrix} v_x \\ v_y \\ v_z \end{bmatrix} \tag{6-27}$$

The quantities in Eqs. (6-26) and (6-27) are called a *row vector* and a *column vector* respectively. In these definitions we do not have to restrict ourselves to three-dimensional vectors. In general we have row vectors and column vectors of order N. The word "order" is used to describe the dimensions of a matrix, and in general we say that a matrix of m rows and n columns is of order "m by n." If the matrix is square and has n rows and n columns, we call it a square matrix of order n. The matrix (6-26) is of order "1 by 3," and the matrix (6-27) is of order "3 by 1"; but in the case of row or column vectors this is usually abbreviated as above.

The inner product of two vectors **u** and **v**, each of order N, can be written in matrix form as

$$\mathbf{u} \cdot \mathbf{v} = [u_1 \quad u_2 \quad \cdots \quad u_N] \times \begin{bmatrix} v_1 \\ v_2 \\ \cdots \\ \cdots \\ v_N \end{bmatrix} \tag{6-28}$$

Let us now consider some properties and definitions of *square matrices*. If we multiply a column vector **u** of order N by a square matrix $[a_{i,j}]$ of the same order, we obtain another column vector **v**:

$$\begin{bmatrix} a_{1,1} & a_{1,2} & \cdots & \cdots & a_{1,N} \\ a_{2,1} & a_{2,2} & \cdots & \cdots & a_{2,N} \\ \cdots & \cdots & \cdots & \cdots & \cdots \\ \cdots & \cdots & \cdots & \cdots & \cdots \\ a_{N,1} & a_{N,2} & \cdots & \cdots & a_{N,N} \end{bmatrix} \times \begin{bmatrix} u_1 \\ u_2 \\ \cdots \\ \cdots \\ u_N \end{bmatrix} = \begin{bmatrix} v_1 \\ v_2 \\ \cdots \\ \cdots \\ v_N \end{bmatrix} \tag{6-29}$$

The elements of **v** are given by

$$v_k = \sum_i a_{k,i} u_i \tag{6-30}$$

and we see that Eq. (6-29) represents a linear transformation between two vectors of order N.

There are various types of square matrices whose elements have certain properties, and we will define some of these types. The *identity matrix* is defined as

$$\begin{bmatrix} 1 & 0 & 0 & \cdots & \cdots & 0 \\ 0 & 1 & 0 & \cdots & \cdots & 0 \\ 0 & 0 & 1 & \cdots & \cdots & 0 \\ \cdots & \cdots & \cdots & \cdots & \cdots & \cdots \\ \cdots & \cdots & \cdots & \cdots & \cdots & \cdots \\ 0 & 0 & 0 & \cdots & \cdots & 1 \end{bmatrix} \tag{6-31}$$

and its elements are given by

$$a_{i,j} = \delta_{i,j} \tag{6-32}$$

The elements $a_{i,i}$ are defined as the diagonal of the matrix, and in the identity matrix all diagonal elements are equal to unity and all off-diagonal elements are equal to zero. A *diagonal matrix* is defined by

$$a_{i,j} = a_i \delta_{i,j} \qquad (6\text{-}33)$$

Here all off-diagonal elements are again zero, but the diagonal elements can now be different from one another.

A *symmetric matrix* has elements that satisfy the condition

$$a_{i,j} = a_{j,i} \qquad (6\text{-}34)$$

If

$$a_{i,j} = -a_{j,i} \qquad (6\text{-}35)$$

we speak of a *skew-symmetric matrix*. In this case we have

$$a_{i,i} = -a_{i,i} \qquad (6\text{-}36)$$

and it follows that the diagonal elements of a skew-symmetric matrix are all zero. The elements of a matrix can, in general, be complex quantities, but if they are all real or imaginary, we have a *real* or an *imaginary matrix*, respectively. A very important type of matrix in quantum mechanics is the *Hermitian matrix*, which is defined by the property

$$a_{i,j} = a_{j,i}^* \qquad (6\text{-}37)$$

Finally, we have the *unitary matrix*, which is defined by

$$\sum_k a_{i,k} a_{j,k}^* = \delta_{i,j}$$
$$\sum_k a_{k,i} a_{k,j}^* = \delta_{i,j} \qquad (6\text{-}38)$$

Here the rows form a mutually orthogonal set of unit vectors, and the same is true of the columns. A coordinate transformation that results from a rotation of the coordinate axes is described by a unitary transformation.

Let us now consider two square matrices $[a_{i,j}]$ and $[b_{i,j}]$ of the same order N and the possible relations between them. If

$$b_{i,j} = a_{j,i} \qquad (6\text{-}39)$$

we call $[b_{i,j}]$ the transpose of $[a_{i,j}]$. If the matrix $[b_{i,j}]$ is denoted by the symbol **B** and the matrix $[a_{i,j}]$ by the symbol **A**, as often done in the mathematical literature, then we can use the notation

$$\mathbf{B} = \tilde{\mathbf{A}} \qquad (6\text{-}40)$$

in order to describe **B** as the transpose of **A**. If the elements of **B** are the complex conjugates of the elements of **A**,

$$b_{i,j} = a_{i,j}^* \qquad (6\text{-}41)$$

then we say that the matrix **B** is the complex conjugate of **A**. The notation for this is

$$B = A^* \tag{6-42}$$

We call **B** the *associate matrix* of **A**, or

$$B = A^\dagger \tag{6-43}$$

when their elements are related by

$$b_{i,j} = a_{j,i}^* \tag{6-44}$$

It is easily seen that

$$A^\dagger = (\tilde{A})^* \tag{6-45}$$

We saw in Eq. (6-24) that, in general, the product of two matrices **A** and **B** depends on the order of multiplication. However, if the matrices satisfy the condition

$$A \times B = B \times A \tag{6-46}$$

then we say that they *commute*. Similarly, **A** and **B** *anticommute* when

$$A \times B = -B \times A \tag{6-47}$$

If

$$A \times B = I \tag{6-48}$$

where **I** is an identity matrix, then **B** is the inverse of **A**, which is written as

$$B = (A)^{-1} \tag{6-49}$$

It can be shown that for a unitary matrix **U** we have

$$U \times U^\dagger = U^\dagger \times U = I \tag{6-50}$$

If **U** has the elements $u_{i,j}$, then $U^\dagger$ has the elements $u_{j,i}^*$, and Eq. (6-50) states that

$$\sum_k u_{i,k} u_{j,k}^* = \delta_{i,j} \tag{6-51}$$

$$\sum_k u_{k,i}^* u_{k,j} = \delta_{i,j} \tag{6-52}$$

which is identical to Eq. (6-38).

6-3 DETERMINANTS

Let us consider an arbitrary square matrix of order N:

$$A = \begin{bmatrix} a_{1,1} & a_{1,2} & a_{1,3} & \cdots & \cdots & a_{1,N} \\ a_{2,1} & a_{2,2} & a_{2,3} & \cdots & \cdots & a_{2,N} \\ a_{3,1} & a_{3,2} & a_{3,3} & \cdots & \cdots & a_{3,N} \\ \cdots & \cdots & \cdots & \cdots & \cdots & \cdots \\ \cdots & \cdots & \cdots & \cdots & \cdots & \cdots \\ a_{N,1} & a_{N,2} & a_{N,3} & \cdots & \cdots & a_{N,N} \end{bmatrix} \tag{6-53}$$

By following a rather complex procedure, which will shortly be outlined, we can derive a number A from this matrix, and this number is known as the *determinant* corresponding to the matrix. We write this as

$$A = \begin{vmatrix} a_{1,1} & a_{1,2} & \cdots & \cdots & a_{1,N} \\ a_{2,1} & a_{2,2} & \cdots & \cdots & a_{2,N} \\ \cdots & \cdots & \cdots & \cdots & \cdots \\ \cdots & \cdots & \cdots & \cdots & \cdots \\ a_{N,1} & a_{N,2} & \cdots & \cdots & a_{N,N} \end{vmatrix} \tag{6-54}$$

Often we do not take the trouble of evaluating the number A; instead we discuss its features from the array of numbers (6-54) by making use of the properties of determinants. We should remember that a determinant is always a single number even when it is represented as an array of numbers.

In order to evaluate A, we first select one element of each row of the matrix in such a way that each column is represented by one and only one element. A group of such elements is

$$(a_{1,n_1}; \quad a_{2,n_2}; \quad a_{3,n_3}; \quad \cdots; \quad a_{N,n_N}) \tag{6-55}$$

The second indices of the elements $(n_1, n_2, n_3, \ldots, n_N)$ are one of the permutations of the numbers $(1,2,3,\ldots,N)$. All possible groups of the type of Eq. (6-55) are obtained by taking all possible permutations of the N numbers; their number is $N!$ according to Eq. (6-15). The determinant A is now defined as

$$A = \sum_P \delta_P P(n_1, n_2, \ldots, n_N) a_{1,n_1} \cdot a_{2,n_2} \cdot a_{3,n_3} \cdot \cdots \cdot a_{N,n_N} \tag{6-56}$$

where the permutations have to be taken with respect to the natural order $(1,2,3,\ldots,N)$. This means that we have to take all possible groups of the type of Eq. (6-55), and in each group we take the product of the elements and the corresponding δ_P (unity when P is even and minus unity when P is odd) and, finally, add all $N!$ terms.

According to this definition the determinants of order two and three are obtained as

$$\begin{vmatrix} a_{1,1} & a_{1,2} \\ a_{2,1} & a_{2,2} \end{vmatrix} = a_{1,1}a_{2,2} - a_{1,2}a_{2,1} \tag{6-57}$$

and

$$\begin{vmatrix} a_{1,1} & a_{1,2} & a_{1,3} \\ a_{2,1} & a_{2,2} & a_{2,3} \\ a_{3,1} & a_{3,2} & a_{3,3} \end{vmatrix} = a_{1,1}a_{2,2}a_{3,3} + a_{1,2}a_{2,3}a_{3,1}$$
$$+ a_{1,3}a_{2,1}a_{3,2} - a_{1,3}a_{2,2}a_{3,1}$$
$$- a_{1,1}a_{2,3}a_{3,2} - a_{1,2}a_{2,1}a_{3,3} \tag{6-58}$$

A determinant of order four has 24 terms, and it becomes impractical to evaluate it directly. We will see that there are less laborious methods for evaluating determinants of higher order.

It can be derived from the definition (6-56) that the exchange of two rows in Eq. (6-54) leads to a determinant value of $-A$. The exchange leads to the same group of products as in Eq. (6-56), but each δ_P changes sign as a result of the exchange, hence the minus sign. Since the definition of the determinant is symmetric in the columns and rows, we also obtain $-A$ if we exchange two columns. It follows, therefore, that a determinant is zero when two of its rows or two of its columns are identical. In addition, we have seen that a determinant remains unchanged if we transpose the matrix from which it is derived.

Let us now set out to derive some properties of determinants that are helpful in their evaluation. We start by considering the determinant

$$A = \begin{vmatrix} a_{1,1} & a_{1,2} & \cdots & a_{1,k} & \cdots & a_{1,N} \\ a_{2,1} & a_{2,2} & \cdots & a_{2,k} & \cdots & a_{2,N} \\ a_{3,1} & a_{3,2} & \cdots & a_{3,k} & \cdots & a_{3,N} \\ \cdots & \cdots & \cdots & \cdots & \cdots & \cdots \\ \cdots & \cdots & \cdots & \cdots & \cdots & \cdots \\ a_{N,1} & a_{N,2} & \cdots & a_{N,k} & \cdots & a_{N,N} \end{vmatrix} \tag{6-59}$$

where k is an arbitrary column. It is easily seen that

$$\lambda A = \begin{vmatrix} a_{1,1} & a_{1,2} & \cdots & \lambda a_{1,k} & \cdots & a_{1,N} \\ a_{2,1} & a_{2,2} & \cdots & \lambda a_{2,k} & \cdots & a_{2,N} \\ a_{3,1} & a_{3,2} & \cdots & \lambda a_{3,k} & \cdots & a_{3,N} \\ \cdots & \cdots & \cdots & \cdots & \cdots & \cdots \\ \cdots & \cdots & \cdots & \cdots & \cdots & \cdots \\ a_{N,1} & a_{N,2} & \cdots & \lambda a_{N,k} & \cdots & a_{N,N} \end{vmatrix} \tag{6-60}$$

since each product in Eq. (6-56) acquires a factor λ. It follows, therefore, that a determinant is not only zero when two of its columns or rows are identical but also when their elements are proportional to each other.

Let us now consider a second determinant A'

$$A' = \begin{vmatrix} a_{1,1} & a_{1,2} & \cdots & a'_{1,k} & \cdots & a_{1,N} \\ a_{2,1} & a_{2,2} & \cdots & a'_{2,k} & \cdots & a_{2,N} \\ a_{3,1} & a_{3,2} & \cdots & a'_{3,k} & \cdots & a_{3,N} \\ \cdots & \cdots & \cdots & \cdots & \cdots & \cdots \\ \cdots & \cdots & \cdots & \cdots & \cdots & \cdots \\ a_{N,1} & a_{N,2} & \cdots & a'_{N,k} & \cdots & a_{N,N} \end{vmatrix} \tag{6-61}$$

which differs from A only in its kth column. It again follows from the definition (6-56) that

$$A + \lambda A' = \begin{vmatrix} a_{1,1} & a_{1,2} & \cdots & (a_{1,k} + \lambda a'_{1,k}) & \cdots & a_{1,N} \\ a_{2,1} & a_{2,2} & \cdots & (a_{2,k} + \lambda a'_{2,k}) & \cdots & a_{2,N} \\ a_{3,1} & a_{3,2} & \cdots & (a_{3,k} + \lambda a'_{3,k}) & \cdots & a_{3,N} \\ \cdots & \cdots & \cdots & \cdots & \cdots & \cdots \\ \cdots & \cdots & \cdots & \cdots & \cdots & \cdots \\ a_{N,1} & a_{N,2} & \cdots & (a_{N,k} + \lambda a'_{N,k}) & \cdots & a_{N,N} \end{vmatrix} \qquad (6\text{-}62)$$

We now take the column $a'_{i,k}$ equal to another column $a_{i,l}$. Then $A' = 0$, since two of its columns are identical. Consequently

$$A = \begin{vmatrix} a_{1,1} & a_{1,2} & \cdots & a_{1,k} + \lambda a_{1,l} & \cdots & a_{1,N} \\ a_{2,1} & a_{2,2} & \cdots & a_{2,k} + \lambda a_{2,l} & \cdots & a_{2,N} \\ a_{3,1} & a_{3,2} & \cdots & a_{3,k} + \lambda a_{3,l} & \cdots & a_{3,N} \\ \cdots & \cdots & \cdots & \cdots & \cdots & \cdots \\ \cdots & \cdots & \cdots & \cdots & \cdots & \cdots \\ a_{N,1} & a_{N,2} & \cdots & a_{N,k} + \lambda a_{N,l} & \cdots & a_{N,N} \end{vmatrix} \qquad (6\text{-}63)$$

We see that a determinant remains unchanged if we add one of its columns, multiplied by an arbitrary parameter λ, to another column. Since this procedure can be repeated a number of times, we conclude that a determinant remains unchanged if we add an arbitrary linear combination of a number of columns or rows to another column or row, respectively.

Let us next consider the expansion of a determinant along one of its rows and columns. For this purpose we first define the minors and cofactors of the elements of the determinant (6-53). The minor of the element $a_{i,j}$ of A is defined as the determinant that is obtained by deleting the ith row and jth column of A. The cofactor of $a_{i,j}$, which we denote by $A_{i,j}$, is the minor of $a_{i,j}$ multiplied by $(-1)^{i+j}$. It can now be shown that

$$A = \sum_j a_{i,j} A_{i,j} = \sum_i a_{i,j} A_{i,j} \qquad (6\text{-}64)$$

This is known as the *expansion* of the determinant along its ith row or along its jth column, respectively.

In order to prove Eq. (6-64), we start from the definition (6-56), and we first consider the expansion of A along the first row. We select all terms that contain the element $a_{1,1}$, and we note that in each of these terms we have chosen an element from the first column and the first row so that none of the other elements can belong to the first row and the first column. According to the definition (6-56) the sum of the terms containing $a_{1,1}$ can be represented as

$$a_{1,1} \sum_P \delta_P P(n_2, n_3, \ldots, n_N) a_{2,n_2} \cdot a_{3,n_3} \cdots a_{N,n_N} = a_{1,1} A_{1,1} \qquad (6\text{-}65)$$

Next we consider all terms that contain the element $a_{1,j}$. We can evaluate their sum by moving the jth column of the determinant to the left side of the determinant, since we may then use Eq. (6-65). This move is achieved by first exchanging column j with column $(j-1)$, then exchanging column $(j-1)$ with column $(j-2)$, etc., until the original column j has become the first column. As a result of these interchanges the determinant should be multiplied by a factor $(-1)^{j-1}$. If we now apply Eq. (6-65) to this new determinant, we find that for the original determinant the sum of the terms that contain $a_{1,j}$ is given by

$$a_{1,j}(-1)^{j-1}\sum_P \delta_P P(n_1,\ldots,n_{j-1},n_{j+1},\ldots,n_N)a_{1,n_1}\cdots$$

$$a_{j-1,n_{j-1}}\cdots a_{j+1,n_{j+1}}\cdots a_{N,n_N} = a_{1,j}A_{1,j} \quad (6\text{-}66)$$

The value of A is now obtained by summing Eq. (6-66) over all values of j:

$$A = \sum_{j=1}^{N} a_{1,j}A_{1,j} \quad (6\text{-}67)$$

The expansion along the ith row can be described if we move the ith row to the top of the determinant by first exchanging rows i and $i-1$, then exchanging rows $i-1$ and $i-2$, etc. We then find from Eq. (6-66) that

$$(-1)^{i-1}A = \sum_{j=1}^{N} a_{i,j}(-1)^{i-1}A_{i,j} \quad (6\text{-}68)$$

or

$$A = \sum_j a_{i,j}A_{i,j} \quad (6\text{-}69)$$

The second Eq. (6-64) is easily derived from Eq. (6-69) if we take the transpose of the matrix **A**, since this leaves the determinant unchanged. We now consider the determinant

$$\begin{vmatrix} a_{1,1} & a_{1,2} & \cdots & \cdots & a_{1,j-1} & a_{1,k} & a_{1,j+1} & \cdots & a_{1,N} \\ a_{2,1} & a_{2,2} & \cdots & \cdots & a_{2,j-1} & a_{2,k} & a_{2,j+1} & \cdots & a_{2,N} \\ a_{3,1} & a_{3,2} & \cdots & \cdots & a_{3,j-1} & a_{3,k} & a_{3,j+1} & \cdots & a_{3,N} \\ \cdots & \cdots & \cdots & \cdots & \cdots & \cdots & \cdots & \cdots & \cdots \\ \cdots & \cdots & \cdots & \cdots & \cdots & \cdots & \cdots & \cdots & \cdots \\ a_{N,1} & a_{N,2} & \cdots & \cdots & a_{N,j-1} & a_{N,k} & a_{N,j+1} & \cdots & a_{N,N} \end{vmatrix} = 0 \quad (6\text{-}70)$$

which is obtained from Eq. (6-53) by replacing column j by one of the other columns k. This determinant (6-70) is equal to zero, since two of its columns are identical. If we expand along the jth column, we get

$$\sum_i a_{i,k}A_{i,j} = 0 \quad j \neq k \quad (6\text{-}71)$$

where the cofactors $A_{i,j}$ are identical to the cofactors of the determinant (6-53). Combination of Eqs. (6-64) and (6-71) yields, finally,

$$\sum_i a_{i,j} A_{i,k} = A\delta_{j,k}$$

$$\sum_i a_{j,i} A_{k,i} = A\delta_{j,k}$$

(6-72)

We can use Eq. (6-72) to construct the inverse of a square matrix $[a_{i,j}]$. We define the matrix $[b_{i,j}]$ by means of

$$b_{i,j} = \frac{A_{j,i}}{A}$$

(6-73)

Since the elements of the product matrix

$$[c_{i,j}] = [a_{i,j}] \times [b_{i,j}]$$

(6-74)

are

$$c_{i,j} = \sum_k a_{i,k} b_{k,j} = \frac{1}{A} \sum_k a_{i,k} A_{j,k} = \delta_{i,j}$$

(6-75)

it follows that **B** is the inverse of **A**.

It may be useful to illustrate the evaluation of some simple determinants by making use of the properties above. The determinant

$$D_5 = \begin{vmatrix} x & 1 & 0 & 0 & 0 \\ 1 & x & 1 & 0 & 0 \\ 0 & 1 & x & 1 & 0 \\ 0 & 0 & 1 & x & 1 \\ 0 & 0 & 0 & 1 & x \end{vmatrix}$$

(6-76)

can be expanded along its first row:

$$D_5 = x\begin{vmatrix} x & 1 & 0 & 0 \\ 1 & x & 1 & 0 \\ 0 & 1 & x & 1 \\ 0 & 0 & 1 & x \end{vmatrix} - \begin{vmatrix} 1 & 1 & 0 & 0 \\ 0 & x & 1 & 0 \\ 0 & 1 & x & 1 \\ 0 & 0 & 1 & x \end{vmatrix}$$

(6-77)

Expansion of the two determinants of Eq. (6-77) along their first column gives

$$D_5 = x^2\begin{vmatrix} x & 1 & 0 \\ 1 & x & 1 \\ 0 & 1 & x \end{vmatrix} - x\begin{vmatrix} 1 & 0 & 0 \\ 1 & x & 1 \\ 0 & 1 & x \end{vmatrix} - \begin{vmatrix} x & 1 & 0 \\ 1 & x & 1 \\ 0 & 1 & x \end{vmatrix}$$

(6-78)

From Eq. (6-58) we find

$$\begin{vmatrix} x & 1 & 0 \\ 1 & x & 1 \\ 0 & 1 & x \end{vmatrix} = x^3 - 2x \qquad \begin{vmatrix} 1 & 0 & 0 \\ 1 & x & 1 \\ 0 & 1 & x \end{vmatrix} = x^2 - 1$$

(6-79)

Hence, we have

$$D_5 = (x^2 - 1)(x^3 - 2x) - x(x^2 - 1) = x(x^2 - 1)(x^2 - 3) \qquad (6\text{-}80)$$

The following is an example of the evaluation of a determinant by adding rows and columns together and subsequent expansion:

$$\begin{vmatrix} 1 & 2 & 3 & 4 & 0 \\ 0 & 1 & 3 & -1 & 2 \\ -1 & 4 & 3 & 2 & 1 \\ 0 & 0 & 2 & 1 & 1 \\ 1 & 2 & 3 & 4 & 1 \end{vmatrix} = \begin{vmatrix} 1 & 2 & 3 & 4 & 0 \\ 0 & 1 & 3 & -1 & 2 \\ 0 & 6 & 6 & 6 & 1 \\ 0 & 0 & 2 & 1 & 1 \\ 0 & 0 & 0 & 0 & 1 \end{vmatrix}$$

$$= \begin{vmatrix} 1 & 3 & -1 & 2 \\ 6 & 6 & 6 & 1 \\ 0 & 2 & 1 & 1 \\ 0 & 0 & 0 & 1 \end{vmatrix} = \begin{vmatrix} 1 & 3 & -1 \\ 6 & 6 & 6 \\ 0 & 2 & 1 \end{vmatrix} = \begin{vmatrix} 1 & 2 & -2 \\ 6 & 0 & 0 \\ 0 & 2 & 1 \end{vmatrix}$$

$$= -6 \begin{vmatrix} 2 & -2 \\ 2 & 1 \end{vmatrix} = -36 \qquad (6\text{-}81)$$

Finally we wish to show that the determinant of a product matrix is equal to the product of the determinants of the original matrices. We consider two matrices $[a_{i,j}]$ and $[b_{i,j}]$, both of order N, and their product matrix $[c_{i,j}]$, which is defined by

$$c_{i,j} = \sum_k a_{i,k} b_{k,j} \qquad (6\text{-}82)$$

The corresponding determinants are A, B, and C respectively. From the definition of a determinant it follows that

$$\begin{vmatrix} a_{1,1} & a_{1,2} & \cdots & \cdots & a_{1,N} & 0 & 0 & \cdots & \cdots & 0 \\ a_{2,1} & a_{2,2} & \cdots & \cdots & a_{2,N} & 0 & 0 & \cdots & \cdots & 0 \\ \cdots & \cdots & \cdots & \cdots & \cdots & \cdots & \cdots & \cdots & \cdots & \cdots \\ \cdots & \cdots & \cdots & \cdots & \cdots & \cdots & \cdots & \cdots & \cdots & \cdots \\ a_{N,1} & a_{N,2} & \cdots & \cdots & a_{N,N} & 0 & 0 & \cdots & \cdots & 0 \\ -1 & 0 & \cdots & \cdots & 0 & b_{1,1} & b_{1,2} & \cdots & \cdots & b_{1,N} \\ 0 & -1 & \cdots & \cdots & 0 & b_{2,1} & b_{2,2} & \cdots & \cdots & b_{2,N} \\ \cdots & \cdots & \cdots & \cdots & \cdots & \cdots & \cdots & \cdots & \cdots & \cdots \\ \cdots & \cdots & \cdots & \cdots & \cdots & \cdots & \cdots & \cdots & \cdots & \cdots \\ 0 & 0 & \cdots & \cdots & -1 & b_{N,1} & b_{N,2} & \cdots & \cdots & b_{N,N} \end{vmatrix} = AB \qquad (6\text{-}83)$$

We add the first column, multiplied by a factor $b_{1,1}$, to the $(N + 1)$st column; then we add the second column, multiplied by a factor $b_{2,1}$, to the $(N + 1)$st column; etc. In general, we add the jth column $(1 \leqslant j$

$\leq N$), multiplied by a factor $b_{j,1}$, to the $(N+1)$st column. We obtain

$$
\begin{vmatrix}
a_{1,1} & a_{1,2} & \cdots & \cdots & a_{1,N} & c_{1,1} & 0 & \cdots & \cdots & 0 \\
a_{2,1} & a_{2,2} & \cdots & \cdots & a_{2,N} & c_{2,1} & 0 & \cdots & \cdots & 0 \\
\cdots & \cdots & \cdots & \cdots & \cdots & \cdots & \cdots & \cdots & \cdots & \cdots \\
\cdots & \cdots & \cdots & \cdots & \cdots & \cdots & \cdots & \cdots & \cdots & \cdots \\
a_{N,1} & a_{N,2} & \cdots & \cdots & a_{N,N} & c_{N,1} & 0 & \cdots & \cdots & 0 \\
-1 & 0 & \cdots & \cdots & 0 & 0 & b_{1,2} & \cdots & \cdots & b_{1,N} \\
0 & -1 & \cdots & \cdots & 0 & 0 & b_{2,2} & \cdots & \cdots & b_{2,N} \\
\cdots & \cdots & \cdots & \cdots & \cdots & \cdots & \cdots & \cdots & \cdots & \cdots \\
\cdots & \cdots & \cdots & \cdots & \cdots & \cdots & \cdots & \cdots & \cdots & \cdots \\
0 & 0 & \cdots & \cdots & -1 & 0 & b_{N,2} & \cdots & \cdots & b_{N,N}
\end{vmatrix} = AB \quad (6\text{-}84)
$$

We treat all columns $N+1$, $N+2$, $N+3$, $\ldots$, $2N$ in this way. For example, we add the first column, multiplied by a factor $b_{1,k}$, to column $N+k$, the second column, multiplied by a factor $b_{2,k}$, to column $N+k$, etc. This procedure gives

$$
\begin{vmatrix}
a_{1,1} & a_{1,2} & \cdots & \cdots & a_{1,N} & c_{1,1} & c_{1,2} & \cdots & \cdots & c_{1,N} \\
a_{2,1} & a_{2,2} & \cdots & \cdots & a_{2,N} & c_{2,1} & c_{2,2} & \cdots & \cdots & c_{2,N} \\
\cdots & \cdots & \cdots & \cdots & \cdots & \cdots & \cdots & \cdots & \cdots & \cdots \\
\cdots & \cdots & \cdots & \cdots & \cdots & \cdots & \cdots & \cdots & \cdots & \cdots \\
a_{N,1} & a_{N,2} & \cdots & \cdots & a_{N,N} & c_{N,1} & c_{N,2} & \cdots & \cdots & c_{N,N} \\
-1 & 0 & \cdots & \cdots & 0 & 0 & 0 & \cdots & \cdots & 0 \\
0 & -1 & \cdots & \cdots & 0 & 0 & 0 & \cdots & \cdots & 0 \\
\cdots & \cdots & \cdots & \cdots & \cdots & \cdots & \cdots & \cdots & \cdots & \cdots \\
\cdots & \cdots & \cdots & \cdots & \cdots & \cdots & \cdots & \cdots & \cdots & \cdots \\
0 & 0 & \cdots & \cdots & -1 & 0 & 0 & \cdots & \cdots & 0
\end{vmatrix} = AB \quad (6\text{-}85)
$$

It is easily seen now that the determinant on the left side of Eq. (6-85) is equal to C, so that

$$ AB = C \quad (6\text{-}86) $$

which is what we wished to prove.

6-4 HOMOGENEOUS LINEAR EQUATIONS

The equations

$$
a_{1,1}x_1 + a_{1,2}x_2 + a_{1,3}x_3 + \cdots + a_{1,N}x_N = \lambda_1
$$
$$
a_{2,1}x_1 + a_{2,2}x_2 + a_{2,3}x_3 + \cdots + a_{2,N}x_N = \lambda_2
$$
$$
\cdot \quad \cdot \quad \cdot \quad \cdot \quad \cdot \quad \cdot \quad \cdot \quad \cdot \quad \cdot \quad \cdot \quad \cdot \quad \cdot \quad \cdot \quad \cdot \quad \cdot \quad (6\text{-}87)
$$
$$
a_{M,1}x_1 + a_{M,2}x_2 + a_{M,3}x_3 + \cdots + a_{M,N}x_N = \lambda_M
$$

form a set of M linear equations in the N unknowns x_i. We speak of homogeneous equations if all the λ_i are equal to zero; otherwise we have a set of inhomogeneous equations. In dealing with linear equations, there are a number of different cases to be considered, depending on the relative magnitudes of N and M and whether the equations are homogeneous or inhomogeneous. We start with the homogeneous equations where the number of equations is equal to the number of variables:

$$\sum_{j=1}^{N} a_{i,j} x_j = 0 \qquad i = 1, 2, 3, \ldots, N \tag{6-88}$$

Before attempting to solve these equations, let us first discuss what we consider by its solution. First we note that, if we take every variable x_j equal to zero, we obtain a solution for every type of homogeneous equation. This is known as the *zero solution*, but we discount it, since it is trivial and generally of no use to us. Let us now imagine that we have obtained a specific solution $(x'_1, x'_2, x'_3, \ldots, x'_N)$ of a homogeneous equation. It is easily verified that $(\rho x'_1, \rho x'_2, \ldots, \rho x'_N)$ is also a solution if ρ is an arbitrary nonzero parameter. What counts, however, is the ratio between the variables x_j, so that we should look upon (x'_j) and $(\rho x'_j)$ as a single solution of the equations. In general we count only solutions that are linearly independent; that is, we consider that we have s independent solutions $(x_j{}^1), (x_j{}^2), \ldots, (x_j{}^s)$ if there exists no relationship

$$\sum_{\alpha} \rho_{\alpha} x_j{}^{\alpha} = 0 \qquad j = 1, 2, \ldots, N \tag{6-89}$$

between the solutions. Naturally, if we have s linearly independent solutions, then each linear combination of them is also a solution of the equations. We have then actually $(\infty)^s$ solutions, but we count them only as s solutions.

We return now to Eqs. (6-88). Apparently these equations are completely determined by the matrix $[a_{i,j}]$ of the coefficients, and we can therefore derive the solutions from this matrix only. We first show that the equations have no solution other than the zero solution if the determinant A, belonging to the matrix $[a_{i,j}]$, is different from zero. If we multiply the first Eq. (6-88) by $A_{1,1}$, the second by $A_{2,1}$, etc., and then add them, we obtain

$$\sum_{j} a_{j,1} A_{j,1} x_1 + \sum_{j} a_{j,2} A_{j,1} x_2 + \cdots + \sum_{j} a_{j,N} A_{j,1} x_N = 0 \tag{6-90}$$

or, according to Eq. (6-72),

$$A x_1 = 0 \tag{6-91}$$

Since A is different from zero, $x_1 = 0$. In the same way we prove that every $x_j = 0$, and since we discount the zero solution, we conclude that the equations have no solution if A is different from zero.

If $A = 0$ we have, according to Eq. (6-72),

$$\sum_j a_{i,j} A_{k,j} = 0 \qquad i = 1, 2, 3, \ldots, N \tag{6-92}$$

Hence, $$x_j = A_{k,j} \tag{6-93}$$

is a solution of the equations. We see that we can obtain a valid solution of the equations if at least one of the cofactors $A_{i,j}$ is different from zero.

At first sight it seems as if we have obtained N different solutions, but this is not true. We will prove that each solution is either zero or proportional to the others if at least one of the $A_{k,j}$ is different from zero. Let us assume that $A_{1,1}$ is different from zero. Then we omit the first Eq. (6-88), and we write the others as

$$a_{2,2}x_2 + a_{2,3}x_3 + \cdots + a_{2,N}x_N = -a_{2,1}x_1$$

$$a_{3,2}x_2 + a_{3,3}x_3 + \cdots + a_{3,N}x_N = -a_{3,1}x_1 \tag{6-94}$$

$$\cdot \quad \cdot \quad \cdot \quad \cdot \quad \cdot \quad \cdot \quad \cdot \quad \cdot \quad \cdot \quad \cdot \quad \cdot \quad \cdot \quad \cdot \quad \cdot$$

$$a_{N,2}x_2 + a_{N,3}x_3 + \cdots + a_{N,N}x_N = -a_{N,1}x_1$$

The coefficients on the left sides of Eq. (6-94) form a matrix $[b_{i,j}]$ with $b_{i,j} = a_{i-1,j-1}$. We denote the cofactors of $b_{i,j}$ by $B_{i,j}$. Let us now multiply the first Eq. (6-94) by $B_{1,1}$, the second Eq. (6-94) by $B_{2,1}$, etc., and add all the equations. The result is

$$-Bx_2 = x_1(a_{2,1}B_{1,1} + a_{3,1}B_{2,1} + a_{4,1}B_{3,1} + \cdots + a_{N,1}B_{N-1,1}) \tag{6-95}$$

We observe that the expression between parentheses on the right side of Eq. (6-95) can be written as

$$\begin{vmatrix} a_{2,1} & a_{2,3} & a_{2,4} & \cdots & a_{2,N} \\ a_{3,1} & a_{3,3} & a_{3,4} & \cdots & a_{3,N} \\ \cdots & \cdots & \cdots & \cdots & \cdots \\ a_{N,1} & a_{N,3} & a_{N,4} & \cdots & a_{N,N} \end{vmatrix} = -A_{1,2} \tag{6-96}$$

and that $B = A_{1,1}$, where $A_{i,j}$ are cofactors of the determinant $|a_{i,j}|$. We thus have

$$A_{1,1}x_2 = A_{1,2}x_1 \tag{6-97}$$

for all values of x_2 and x_1 that satisfy Eqs. (6-94). However, all solutions of Eqs. (6-88) satisfy also Eqs. (6-94), and according to Eq. (6-93) we have

$$A_{1,1}A_{k,2} = A_{1,2}A_{k,1} \tag{6-98}$$

or if $A_{1,2}$ and $A_{1,1}$ are both different from zero,

$$\frac{A_{k,1}}{A_{1,1}} = \frac{A_{k,2}}{A_{1,2}} \qquad (6\text{-}99)$$

Along the same lines we can prove that

$$\frac{A_{k,1}}{A_{1,1}} = \frac{A_{k,2}}{A_{1,2}} = \frac{A_{k,3}}{A_{1,3}} \cdots = \frac{A_{k,N}}{A_{1,N}} \qquad (6\text{-}100)$$

If any of the $A_{1,i}$ is zero, then it follows from Eq. (6-98) or its analogue that the corresponding $A_{k,i}$ is also zero. It follows, therefore, that Eq. (6-93) represents only one solution for the N homogeneous equations with N unknowns.

The reader may wonder what happens when all cofactors $A_{i,j}$ are zero, but we bypass this question for the time being and instead consider first the case of N homogeneous equations with $(N + 1)$ variables:

$$a_{1,1}x_1 + a_{1,2}x_2 + a_{1,3}x_3 + \cdots + a_{1,N}x_N + a_{1,N+1}x_{N+1} = 0$$

$$a_{2,1}x_1 + a_{2,2}x_2 + a_{2,3}x_3 + \cdots + a_{2,N}x_N + a_{2,N+1}x_{N+1} = 0$$

$$\cdot \quad \cdot \quad \cdot \quad \cdot \quad \cdot \quad \cdot \quad \cdot \quad \cdot \quad \cdot \quad \cdot \quad \cdot \quad \cdot \quad \cdot \quad \cdot \quad \cdot \quad \cdot \quad \cdot \quad \cdot \quad \cdot \quad \cdot$$

$$a_{N,1}x_1 + a_{N,2}x_2 + a_{N,3}x_3 + \cdots + a_{N,N}x_N + a_{N,N+1}x_{N+1} = 0$$

$$(6\text{-}101)$$

This case is easily transformed to the previous situation if we add an additional equation, for example, if we write the first equation twice. We then obtain $(N + 1)$ equations with $(N + 1)$ unknowns, and the solution can be written as the cofactor of the first row, since the determinant of the coefficients is zero. The solution of Eq. (6-101) is therefore obtained as follows. First we write the matrix of the coefficients:

$$\begin{bmatrix} a_{1,1} & a_{1,2} & \cdots & \cdots & a_{1,N+1} \\ a_{2,1} & a_{2,2} & \cdots & \cdots & a_{2,N+1} \\ \cdots & \cdots & \cdots & \cdots & \cdots \\ a_{N,1} & a_{N,2} & \cdots & \cdots & a_{N,N+1} \end{bmatrix} \qquad (6\text{-}102)$$

We then define Δ_n as the determinant corresponding to the square matrix of order N, which we obtain by deleting the nth column from the matrix (6-102). The solution of Eq. (6-101) is now

$$x_n = (-1)^{n-1}\Delta_n \qquad (6\text{-}103)$$

This method is known as *Cramer's rule*, and it assumes that at least one of the determinants Δ_n is different from zero.

We will not derive the solution of every type of homogeneous equation in detail, but we will state some general rules. For this purpose it is useful to introduce the concept of the *rank* of a matrix. If we consider an arbitrary rectangular matrix of N columns and M rows, then we can construct square matrices by deleting a certain number of columns and rows from the original matrix. If the largest such matrix that has a non-zero determinant is of the Rth order, then we say that the original $N \times M$ matrix has the rank R. It is easily seen that the largest possible value of R is equal to N if $N \leqslant M$ and equal to M when $M \leqslant N$. The general rule is that M linear homogeneous equations in N unknowns have $(N - R)$ linearly independent solutions if R is the rank of the matrix of the coefficients. As we have mentioned, it is not our intention to prove this general rule, but it is easily verified that it applies to the cases discussed above.

6-5 INHOMOGENEOUS LINEAR EQUATIONS

The solution of a set of inhomogeneous equations can, in general, be derived by making use of the theory of homogeneous equations. As an example we take the case of N equations with N unknowns:

$$a_{1,1}x_1 + a_{1,2}x_2 + \cdots + a_{1,N}x_N + \lambda_1 = 0$$

$$a_{2,1}x_1 + a_{2,2}x_2 + \cdots + a_{2,N}x_N + \lambda_2 = 0$$

$$\cdot \quad \cdot \quad \cdot \quad \cdot \quad \cdot \quad \cdot \quad \cdot \quad \cdot \quad \cdot \quad \cdot \quad \cdot \quad \cdot \quad \cdot$$

$$a_{N,1}x_1 + a_{N,2}x_2 + \cdots + a_{N,N}x_N + \lambda_N = 0$$

$$(6\text{-}104)$$

The solution is obtained by considering the set of homogeneous equations

$$a_{1,1}x_1 + a_{1,2}x_2 + \cdots + a_{1,N}x_N + \lambda_1 y = 0$$

$$a_{2,1}x_2 + a_{2,2}x_2 + \cdots + a_{2,N}x_N + \lambda_2 y = 0$$

$$\cdot \quad \cdot \quad \cdot \quad \cdot \quad \cdot \quad \cdot \quad \cdot \quad \cdot \quad \cdot \quad \cdot \quad \cdot \quad \cdot \quad \cdot$$

$$a_{N,1}x_1 + a_{N,2}x_2 + \cdots + a_{N,N}x_N + \lambda_N y = 0$$

$$(6\text{-}105)$$

The rank of the matrix **M**

$$\mathbf{M} = \begin{bmatrix} \lambda_1 & a_{1,1} & a_{1,2} & \cdots & a_{1,N} \\ \lambda_2 & a_{2,1} & a_{2,2} & \cdots & a_{2,N} \\ \cdots & \cdots & \cdots & \cdots & \cdots \\ \lambda_N & a_{N,1} & a_{N,2} & \cdots & a_{N,N} \end{bmatrix}$$

$$(6\text{-}106)$$

is always smaller than $N + 1$, so that Eqs. (6-105) always have at least one solution. If the rank R_M of $\mathbf{M}$ is N, then the solution is, according to Eq. (6-103),

$$y = \begin{vmatrix} a_{1,1} & a_{1,2} & \cdots & a_{1,N} \\ a_{2,1} & a_{2,2} & \cdots & a_{2,N} \\ \cdots & \cdots & \cdots & \cdots \\ a_{N,1} & a_{N,2} & \cdots & a_{N,N} \end{vmatrix} = \Delta \tag{6-107}$$

and

$$x_n = -\Delta_n \tag{6-108}$$

where Δ_n is obtained from Δ by replacing its nth column by the column λ_i. Since only the ratio of the unknowns is determined by Eqs. (6-105), we now find the solution of the inhomogeneous equations (6-104) by setting y equal to unity. Hence, the solution of Eq. (6-104) is

$$x_n = -\frac{\Delta_n}{\Delta} \tag{6-109}$$

This procedure leads to the solution of the set of inhomogeneous equations as long as Δ is different from zero. If $\Delta = 0$, then the inhomogeneous equations have no solution, and we call them *inconsistent*. An example of such a case is

$$x + y = 1$$
$$2x + 2y = 3 \tag{6-110}$$

It is easily seen that these two equations are not consistent with one another, and it is therefore impossible to find a solution for them.

We will finally state the general rule for establishing the number of possible solutions for a set of k linear, inhomogeneous equations in N unknowns

$$a_{1,1}x_1 + a_{1,2}x_2 + \cdots + a_{1,N}x_N + \lambda_1 = 0$$

$$a_{2,1}x_1 + a_{2,2}x_2 + \cdots + a_{2,N}x_N + \lambda_2 = 0$$

$$\cdots \cdots \cdots \cdots \cdots \cdots \cdots \cdots \tag{6-111}$$

$$a_{k,1}x_1 + a_{k,2}x_2 + \cdots + a_{k,N}x_N + \lambda_k = 0$$

We write the two matrices

$$\mathbf{M} = \begin{bmatrix} a_{1,1} & a_{1,2} & \cdots & \cdots & a_{1,N} & \lambda_1 \\ a_{2,1} & a_{2,2} & \cdots & \cdots & a_{2,N} & \lambda_2 \\ \cdots & \cdots & \cdots & \cdots & \cdots & \cdots \\ a_{k,1} & a_{k,2} & \cdots & \cdots & a_{k,N} & \lambda_k \end{bmatrix} \tag{6-112}$$

and

$$\mathbf{A} = \begin{bmatrix} a_{1,1} & a_{1,2} & \cdots & \cdots & a_{1,N} \\ a_{2,1} & a_{2,2} & \cdots & \cdots & a_{2,N} \\ \cdots & \cdots & \cdots & \cdots & \cdots \\ a_{k,1} & a_{k,2} & \cdots & \cdots & a_{k,N} \end{bmatrix} \tag{6-113}$$

and we denote their ranks by R_M and R_A, respectively. Equations (6-111) are inconsistent and have, therefore, no solutions if $R_M > R_A$. If $R_M = R_A$, then the number of solutions is given by $N - R_A + 1$.

6-6 EIGENVALUE PROBLEMS

We consider the set of N homogeneous linear equations in N unknowns

$$(a_{1,1} - \lambda)x_1 + a_{1,2}x_2 + a_{1,3}x_3 + \cdots + a_{1,N}x_N = 0$$

$$a_{2,1}x_1 + (a_{2,2} - \lambda)x_2 + a_{2,3}x_3 + \cdots + a_{2,N}x_N = 0$$

$$a_{3,1}x_1 + a_{3,2}x_2 + (a_{3,3} - \lambda)x_3 + \cdots + a_{3,N}x_N = 0 \qquad (6\text{-}114)$$

$$\cdot \quad \cdot \quad \cdot \quad \cdot \quad \cdot \quad \cdot \quad \cdot \quad \cdot \quad \cdot \quad \cdot \quad \cdot \quad \cdot \quad \cdot \quad \cdot \quad \cdot \quad \cdot$$

$$a_{N,1}x_1 + a_{N,2}x_2 + a_{N,3}x_3 + \cdots + (a_{N,N} - \lambda)x_N = 0$$

where λ is an undetermined parameter, and we ask for which values of λ this system has nonzero solutions and what these solutions are. Any value λ_n for which Eq. (6-114) has a solution is called an *eigenvalue*, and the corresponding solution $(x_1{}^n, x_2{}^n, \ldots, x_N{}^n)$ is called an *eigenvector*. The entire problem is known as the eigenvalue problem of the matrix $[a_{i,j}]$.

From the considerations of Sec. 6-4 it is easily seen how we can solve an eigenvalue problem. A set of N homogeneous equations has solutions only when the determinant of the coefficients is zero, and the eigenvalues of Eq. (6-114) are therefore derived from the equation

$$|a_{i,j} - \lambda\delta_{i,j}| = 0 \qquad (6\text{-}115)$$

This is a polynomial of the Nth degree in λ, and we can write it as

$$(\lambda - \lambda_1)(\lambda - \lambda_2) \cdots (\lambda - \lambda_n) \cdots (\lambda - \lambda_N) = 0 \qquad (6\text{-}116)$$

where the λ_n are its roots. If all λ_n are different, then we have N single roots. If one or more of the λ_n are equal, for example, if the root λ_k occurs as a factor $(\lambda - \lambda_k)^r$, then we call λ_k a multiple root and its multiplicity is r.

It can be shown that, if λ_n is a single root of Eq. (6-115), then the matrix

$$[a_{i,j} - \lambda_n\delta_{i,j}] \qquad (6\text{-}117)$$

has the rank $(N - 1)$. Equations (6-114) have, then, one solution $(x_i{}^n)$ corresponding to λ_n. By making use of the rules of matrix multiplication, we can write this situation as

$$\begin{bmatrix} a_{1,1} - \lambda_n & a_{1,2} & \cdots & a_{1,N} \\ a_{2,1} & a_{2,2} - \lambda_n & \cdots & a_{2,N} \\ \cdots & \cdots & \cdots & \cdots \\ a_{N,1} & a_{N,2} & \cdots & a_{N,N} - \lambda_n \end{bmatrix} \begin{bmatrix} x_1{}^n \\ x_2{}^n \\ \cdots \\ x_N{}^n \end{bmatrix} = \begin{bmatrix} 0 \\ 0 \\ \cdots \\ 0 \end{bmatrix} \tag{6-118}$$

or as
$$[a_{i,j}]\mathbf{x}^n = \lambda_n \mathbf{x}^n \tag{6-119}$$

We call λ_n a nondegenerate eigenvalue of the matrix $\mathbf{A}$ and $\mathbf{x}^n$ its corresponding eigenvector.

If λ_m is a multiple root of Eq. (6-115) and its multiplicity is r, then it can be shown that the matrix

$$[a_{i,j} - \lambda_m \delta_{i,j}] \tag{6-120}$$

has the rank $N - r$. Hence the substitution of λ_m into Eqs. (6-114) leads to r different, linearly independent solutions $\mathbf{x}^{m,\delta}$, each of which satisfies the equation

$$[a_{i,j}]\mathbf{x}^{m,\delta} = \lambda_m \mathbf{x}^{m,\delta} \qquad \delta = 1, 2, \ldots, r \tag{6-121}$$

We now say that λ_m is an r-fold degenerate eigenvalue of the matrix $\mathbf{A}$, since it has r different eigenvectors. Each linear combination of $\mathbf{x}^{m,\delta}$ is also an eigenvector of λ_m.

The evaluation of the eigenvalues and eigenvectors of a large matrix by means of the direct approach that we outlined above can be very laborious. It is therefore not surprising that various alternate methods for solving eigenvalue problems have been suggested. Nowadays these methods usually involve the use of an electronic computer, and very few scientists endeavor the solution of an eigenvalue problem of any matrix that is larger than 3×3 without using the computer. We first discuss some general properties of eigenvalues and eigenfunctions, and then, in Sec. 6-7, we outline some of the principles that are at the basis of the computer programs. We limit ourselves only to eigenvalue problems of Hermitian matrices, since practically all matrices that we encounter in quantum-mechanical eigenvalue problems are Hermitian. We may recall from Eq. (6-37) that such a Hermitian matrix is defined by

$$a_{i,j} = a_{j,i}^* \qquad \mathbf{A} = \mathbf{A}^\dagger \tag{6-122}$$

We will first show that the eigenvalues of a Hermitian matrix are all real. If $\mathbf{A}$ is a Hermitian matrix, λ_n is one of its eigenvalues, and $\mathbf{x}^n$ the corresponding eigenvector, written as a column vector, then we have the equation

$$\mathbf{A}\mathbf{x}^n = \lambda_n \mathbf{x}^n \tag{6-123}$$

Since $\mathbf{x}^n$ is defined as a column vector, the transpose of $\mathbf{x}^n$, $\tilde{\mathbf{x}}^n$, is the row vector

$$\tilde{\mathbf{x}}^n = [x_1{}^n \quad x_2{}^n \quad x_3{}^n \quad \cdots \quad x_N{}^n] \tag{6-124}$$

It is easily verified that

$$(\tilde{\mathbf{x}}^n)^* \cdot \mathbf{x}^n = \sum_k (x_k{}^n)^* \cdot x_k{}^n = N_n \tag{6-125}$$

where N_n is a positive real number. We have, therefore,

$$(\mathbf{x}^n)^\dagger \mathbf{A} \mathbf{x}^n = \lambda_n N_n \tag{6-126}$$

The complex conjugate of this equation is

$$\tilde{\mathbf{x}}^n \mathbf{A}^* (\mathbf{x}^n)^* = \lambda_n^* N_n \tag{6-127}$$

It follows from the definition of matrix multiplication that

$$(\widetilde{\mathbf{A} \cdot \mathbf{B} \cdot \mathbf{C}}) = \tilde{\mathbf{C}} \cdot \tilde{\mathbf{B}} \cdot \tilde{\mathbf{A}} \tag{6-128}$$

Hence, we can write Eq. (6-127) as

$$\lambda_n^* N_n = \tilde{\mathbf{x}}^n \mathbf{A}^* (\mathbf{x}^n)^* = (\tilde{\mathbf{x}}^n)^* \tilde{\mathbf{A}}^* \mathbf{x}^n = (\mathbf{x}^n)^\dagger \mathbf{A}^\dagger \mathbf{x}^n \tag{6-129}$$

or, since $\mathbf{A}$ is Hermitian, as

$$(\mathbf{x}^n)^\dagger \mathbf{A} \mathbf{x}^n = \lambda_n^* N_n \tag{6-130}$$

Subtraction of Eq. (6-130) from Eq. (6-126) gives

$$(\lambda_n - \lambda_n^*) N_n = 0 \tag{6-131}$$

and it follows, therefore, that λ_n is real.

Two N-dimensional vectors $\mathbf{u}$ and $\mathbf{v}$ are defined to be orthogonal if

$$\sum_k u_k^* v_k = 0 \tag{6-132}$$

We can also write this definition in the matrix notation

$$\mathbf{u}^\dagger \cdot \mathbf{v} = 0 \tag{6-133}$$

if we take $\mathbf{u}$ and $\mathbf{v}$ as column vectors. We will now prove that the two eigenvectors $\mathbf{x}^m$ and $\mathbf{x}^n$ of a Hermitian matrix $\mathbf{A}$ are orthogonal if they belong to different eigenvalues λ_m and λ_n, respectively.

Since $\mathbf{x}^m$ and $\mathbf{x}^n$ are eigenvectors, they satisfy the equations

$$\mathbf{A} \mathbf{x}^n = \lambda_n \mathbf{x}^n \tag{6-134}$$

and
$$\mathbf{A}^* (\mathbf{x}^m)^* = \lambda_m (\mathbf{x}^m)^* \tag{6-135}$$

We multiply Eq. (6-134) on the left by $(\mathbf{x}^m)^\dagger$ and Eq. (6-135) by $\tilde{\mathbf{x}}^n$. This gives

$$(\mathbf{x}^m)^\dagger \cdot \mathbf{A} \cdot \mathbf{x}^n = \lambda_n(\mathbf{x}^m)^\dagger \cdot (\mathbf{x}^n)$$
$$(\tilde{\mathbf{x}}^n) \cdot \mathbf{A}^* \cdot (\mathbf{x}^m)^* = \lambda_m(\tilde{\mathbf{x}}^n) \cdot (\mathbf{x}^m)^* \tag{6-136}$$

The second equation can also be written as

$$(\mathbf{x}^m)^\dagger \cdot \mathbf{A} \cdot (\mathbf{x}^n) = \lambda_m(\mathbf{x}^m)^\dagger \cdot (\mathbf{x}^n) \tag{6-137}$$

and if we subtract it from the first Eq. (6-136), we obtain

$$(\mathbf{x}^m)^\dagger \cdot (\mathbf{x}^n) = 0 \tag{6-138}$$

since λ_m and λ_n are different.

Two different eigenvectors that belong to the same eigenvalue do not have to be orthogonal, but by choosing suitable linear combinations of degenerate eigenvectors, we can make them orthogonal. It is always possible, therefore, to obtain the eigenvectors of a Hermitian matrix as an orthonormal set of vectors.

6-7 DIAGONALIZATION OF HERMITIAN MATRICES

Two matrices $\mathbf{B}$ and $\mathbf{A}$ are connected by a *similarity transformation* if $\mathbf{B}$ can be written as

$$\mathbf{B} = \mathbf{M}^{-1}\mathbf{A}\mathbf{M} \tag{6-139}$$

If $\mathbf{M}$ is unitary, that is, if

$$\mathbf{B} = \mathbf{U}^{-1}\mathbf{A}\mathbf{U} = \mathbf{U}^\dagger\mathbf{A}\mathbf{U} \tag{6-140}$$

then we speak of a *unitary transformation*. If we start with an arbitrary matrix $\mathbf{A}$, then the problem of finding a unitary matrix $\mathbf{U}$ so that the transformed matrix $\mathbf{B}$ is diagonal is called the diagonalization of the matrix $\mathbf{A}$.

If $\mathbf{A}$ is a Hermitian matrix $\mathbf{H}$, then it is always possible to diagonalize it. Let λ_n be the eigenvalues of $\mathbf{H}$ and $\mathbf{x}^n$ its eigenvectors, which have been selected in such a way that they form an orthonormal set. We allow for degeneracies so that several of the eigenvalues λ_n can be equal to one another. We now construct a matrix $\mathbf{U}$ as

$$\mathbf{U} = \begin{bmatrix} x_1^1 & x_1^2 & \cdots & x_1^N \\ x_2^1 & x_2^2 & \cdots & x_2^N \\ \cdots & \cdots & \cdots & \cdots \\ x_N^1 & x_N^2 & \cdots & x_N^N \end{bmatrix} \tag{6-141}$$

It is easily verified that

$$AU = \begin{bmatrix} \lambda_1 x_1^{\ 1} & \lambda_2 x_1^{\ 2} & \cdots & \lambda_N x_1^{\ N} \\ \lambda_1 x_2^{\ 1} & \lambda_2 x_2^{\ 2} & \cdots & \lambda_N x_2^{\ N} \\ \cdots & \cdots & \cdots & \cdots \\ \lambda_1 x_N^{\ 1} & \lambda_2 x_N^{\ 2} & \cdots & \lambda_N x_N^{\ N} \end{bmatrix} \tag{6-142}$$

and

$$U^\dagger AU = \begin{bmatrix} \lambda_1 & 0 & 0 & \cdots & \cdots & 0 \\ 0 & \lambda_2 & 0 & \cdots & \cdots & 0 \\ 0 & 0 & \lambda_3 & \cdots & \cdots & 0 \\ \cdots & \cdots & \cdots & \cdots & \cdots & \cdots \\ \cdots & \cdots & \cdots & \cdots & \cdots & \cdots \\ 0 & 0 & 0 & \cdots & \cdots & \lambda_N \end{bmatrix} \tag{6-143}$$

since the eigenvectors are orthonormal. We see that we can diagonalize **A** if we know its eigenvalues and eigenvectors.

On the other hand, the eigenvalues and eigenvectors of **A** are easily derived from the unitary matrix by which **A** is diagonalized. Let us first show that the two matrices **A** and $(U^\dagger \cdot A \cdot U)$ have the same eigenvalues. The eigenvalues of **A** are obtained as the roots of the determinant

$$|A - \lambda I| \tag{6-144}$$

written in the form of a polynomial. We have now

$$|A - \lambda I| = |U^\dagger| \, |A - \lambda I| \, |U| = |U^\dagger AU - \lambda U^\dagger I U| = |U^\dagger AU - \lambda I| \tag{6-145}$$

The two polynomials are the same, and they have the same roots; consequently, **A** and $(U^\dagger \cdot A \cdot U)$ have the same eigenvalues.

Although the eigenvectors of **A** and $U^\dagger \cdot A \cdot U$ are not the same, they are easily derived from each other. The eigenvalues and eigenvectors of **A** satisfy the equations

$$Ax^n = \lambda_n x^n \tag{6-146}$$

We introduce a new set of vectors y^n that are derived from the x^n by means of the transformation

$$x^n = Uy^n \tag{6-147}$$

where **U** is a unitary matrix. Substitution into Eq. (6-146) gives

$$AUy^n = \lambda_n Uy^n \tag{6-148}$$

and multiplication on the left by $U^\dagger$ yields

$$(U^\dagger AU)y^n = \lambda_n y^n \tag{6-149}$$

We conclude that **A** and $(U^\dagger AU)$ have the same eigenvalues and that their eigenvectors are related to each other through Eq. (6-147).

Let us imagine that we have found a unitary transformation **U** that diagonalizes the matrix **A**:

$$\mathbf{U}^\dagger\mathbf{A}\mathbf{U} = [b_i\delta_{i,j}] \tag{6-150}$$

The eigenvalues and eigenvectors of $[b_i\delta_{i,j}]$ are easily obtained. It follows immediately from Eq. (6-114) that the eigenvalues are $\lambda_n = b_n$ and that the eigenvectors are

$$y_i^n = \delta_{n,i} \tag{6-151}$$

By making use of Eq. (6-147), we obtain the eigenvectors of **A**. The eigenvalues of **A** are λ_n, since they are the same as for **B**. It follows, therefore, that the diagonalization of a matrix and finding its eigenvalues and eigenfunctions are equivalent problems.

It is now possible to show that two matrices **A** and **B** must commute if they have the same set of eigenvectors. In this case, they are both diagonalized by the same unitary transformation **U**:

$$\mathbf{U}^\dagger\mathbf{A}\mathbf{U} = [a_i\delta_{i,j}]$$
$$\mathbf{U}^\dagger\mathbf{B}\mathbf{U} = [b_i\delta_{i,j}] \tag{6-152}$$

Two diagonal matrices always commute so that

$$(\mathbf{U}^\dagger\mathbf{A}\mathbf{U})(\mathbf{U}^\dagger\mathbf{B}\mathbf{U}) = (\mathbf{U}^\dagger\mathbf{B}\mathbf{U})(\mathbf{U}^\dagger\mathbf{A}\mathbf{U}) \tag{6-153}$$

or

$$\mathbf{U}^\dagger\mathbf{A}\mathbf{B}\mathbf{U} = \mathbf{U}^\dagger\mathbf{B}\mathbf{A}\mathbf{U} \tag{6-154}$$

It follows, therefore, that **A** and **B** commute. It can also be shown that there exists a unitary transformation that diagonalizes both **A** and **B** if they commute.

Most computer programs for obtaining the eigenvalues and eigenvectors of a Hermitian matrix **H** are based on the diagonalization of **H**. A customary procedure for the case that **H** is real is the following. We first scan **H** and determine the off-diagonal element $h_{m,n}$ with the largest absolute value $|h_{m,n}|$. Now we subject **H** to a unitary transformation defined by a matrix $\mathbf{U}_1$:

$$\mathbf{H}^1 = \mathbf{U}_1^\dagger\mathbf{H}\mathbf{U}_1$$

$$\mathbf{U}_1 = \begin{bmatrix} 1 & 0 & \cdots & 0 & \cdots & 0 & \cdots & 0 \\ 0 & 1 & \cdots & 0 & \cdots & 0 & \cdots & 0 \\ \cdots & \cdots & \cdots & \cdots & \cdots & \cdots & \cdots & \cdots \\ \cdots & \cdots & \cdots & \cos\phi & \cdots & -\sin\phi & \cdots & 0 \\ \cdots & \cdots & \cdots & \cdots & \cdots & \cdots & \cdots & \cdots \\ \cdots & \cdots & \cdots & \sin\phi & \cdots & \cos\phi & \cdots & \cdots \\ \cdots & \cdots & \cdots & \cdots & \cdots & \cdots & \cdots & \cdots \\ 0 & 0 & \cdots & 0 & \cdots & 0 & \cdots & 1 \end{bmatrix} \begin{matrix} \\ \\ \\ \leftarrow m \\ \\ \leftarrow n \\ \\ \\ \end{matrix} \tag{6-155}$$

$$\begin{matrix} \uparrow & \uparrow \\ m & n \end{matrix}$$

U_1 is the identity matrix, except for columns m and n and rows m and n, where the elements are defined as

$$U_{m,m} = \cos \phi \qquad U_{m,n} = -\sin \phi$$
$$U_{n,m} = \sin \phi \qquad U_{n,n} = \cos \phi$$

(6-156)

We select ϕ in such a way that

$$h^1_{m,n} = h^1_{n,m} = 0$$

(6-157)

It can be shown that such a transformation does not increase the other off-diagonal elements to any great extent.

We now repeat this procedure for $\mathbf{H}^1$ by making a unitary transformation with a matrix $\mathbf{U}_2$:

$$\mathbf{H}^2 = \mathbf{U}_2^\dagger \mathbf{H}^1 \mathbf{U}_2 = \mathbf{U}_2^\dagger \mathbf{U}_1^\dagger \mathbf{H} \mathbf{U}_1 \mathbf{U}_2$$

(6-158)

Since the product of two unitary matrices is also unitary, we obtain $\mathbf{H}^2$ from $\mathbf{H}$ by a unitary transformation. We keep repeating this procedure until we have obtained a matrix $\mathbf{H}^v$ that is diagonal to within the accuracy that we desire. This can be written as

$$\mathbf{H}^v = \mathbf{U}^\dagger \mathbf{H} \mathbf{U}$$
$$\mathbf{U} = \mathbf{U}_1 \cdot \mathbf{U}_2 \cdot \mathbf{U}_3 \cdot \cdots \cdot \mathbf{U}_v$$

(6-159)

The eigenvalues of $\mathbf{H}$ are now obtained as the diagonal elements of $\mathbf{H}_v$, and the eigenvectors can be derived from $\mathbf{U}$.

PROBLEMS

6-1 Prove that

$$\begin{vmatrix} 0 & 1 & 1 & 1 \\ 1 & 0 & z^2 & y^2 \\ 1 & z^2 & 0 & x^2 \\ 1 & y^2 & x^2 & 0 \end{vmatrix} = (x^2 - y^2 - z^2)^2 - 4y^2z^2$$

6-2 Calculate the determinant

$$\begin{vmatrix} x & 1 & 0 & 0 & 0 & 1 \\ 1 & x & 1 & 0 & 0 & 0 \\ 0 & 1 & x & 1 & 0 & 0 \\ 0 & 0 & 1 & x & 1 & 0 \\ 0 & 0 & 0 & 1 & x & 1 \\ 1 & 0 & 0 & 0 & 1 & x \end{vmatrix}$$

6-3 Determine the matrix $U^\dagger AU$ if

$$A = \begin{vmatrix} a_{1,1} & a_{1,2} & a_{1,3} \\ a_{2,1} & a_{2,2} & a_{2,3} \\ a_{3,1} & a_{3,2} & a_{3,3} \end{vmatrix} \qquad U = \begin{vmatrix} \cos\phi & 0 & \sin\phi \\ 0 & 1 & 0 \\ -\sin\phi & 0 & \cos\phi \end{vmatrix}$$

6-4 Determine the values of λ for which the following set of equations has a solution, and determine each solution:

$$\lambda x + y + u = 0$$
$$\lambda y + z = 0$$
$$x - u = 0$$
$$y - z = 0$$

6-5 Find the values of λ for which the following set of equations has solutions, and find each solution:

$$\lambda x + y + u = 0$$
$$x + \lambda y + z = 0$$
$$y + \lambda z + u = 0$$
$$x + z + \lambda u = 0$$

6-6 Determine the inverse of the matrix

$$\begin{bmatrix} (\cos\alpha\cos\gamma - \sin\alpha\cos\beta\sin\gamma) & (\sin\alpha\cos\gamma + \cos\alpha\cos\beta\sin\gamma) & \sin\beta\sin\gamma \\ (\cos\alpha\sin\gamma + \sin\alpha\cos\beta\cos\gamma) & (-\sin\alpha\sin\gamma + \cos\alpha\cos\beta\cos\gamma) & -\sin\beta\cos\gamma \\ \sin\alpha\sin\beta & \cos\alpha\sin\beta & \cos\beta \end{bmatrix}$$

and show that it is unitary.

6-7 Derive the eigenvalues and eigenvectors of the matrix

$$\begin{bmatrix} a & b & 0 & 0 & 0 & b \\ b & a & b & 0 & 0 & 0 \\ 0 & b & a & b & 0 & 0 \\ 0 & 0 & b & a & b & 0 \\ 0 & 0 & 0 & b & a & b \\ b & 0 & 0 & 0 & b & a \end{bmatrix}$$

and the matrix

$$\begin{bmatrix} a & b & 0 & 0 \\ b & a & b & 0 \\ 0 & b & a & b \\ 0 & 0 & b & a \end{bmatrix}$$

6-8 Solve the equations

$$3x - 2y \qquad\qquad = 7$$
$$2y + 2z + u = 5$$
$$x - 2y - 3z - 2u = -1$$
$$y + z + u = 6$$

6-9   Take the square of the matrix

$$\mathbf{M} = \begin{bmatrix} a & b & 0 & 0 & 0 \\ b & a & b & 0 & 0 \\ 0 & b & a & b & 0 \\ 0 & 0 & b & a & b \\ 0 & 0 & 0 & b & a \end{bmatrix}$$

and determine the eigenvalues and eigenvectors of both $\mathbf{M}$ and $\mathbf{M}^2$.

CHAPTER **7**

———————

THE SCHRÖDINGER EQUATION AS AN EIGENVALUE PROBLEM

7-1 OPERATORS

A procedure that transforms a given function f into a different function g can be represented as

$$g = \Omega f \qquad (7\text{-}1)$$

where Ω is called an operator.

In quantum mechanics we encounter mostly multiplicative and differential operators. For example, multiplication of f by a function h, which we write as

$$g = hf \qquad (7\text{-}2)$$

can also be written in the operator representation of Eq. (7-1) if we take the operator Ω equal to h. If g is obtained as the derivative of f,

$$g = \frac{\partial f}{\partial x} \qquad (7\text{-}3)$$

then we have to take

$$\Omega = \frac{\partial}{\partial x} \tag{7-4}$$

We have already introduced the Laplace operator

$$\Delta = \frac{\partial^2}{\partial x^2} + \frac{\partial^2}{\partial y^2} + \frac{\partial^2}{\partial z^2} \tag{7-5}$$

Obviously, we have

$$\Delta f = \frac{\partial^2 f}{\partial x^2} + \frac{\partial^2 f}{\partial y^2} + \frac{\partial^2 f}{\partial z^2} \tag{7-6}$$

These examples are all linear operators, which are defined by the property

$$\Omega(af_1 + bf_2) = a\Omega f_1 + b\Omega f_2 \tag{7-7}$$

Not all operators are linear. If we take the function g of Eq. (7-1) as the square of f, we can write this in operator language as

$$g = \text{sq}\, f \tag{7-8}$$

In general

$$\text{sq}\, (f_1 + f_2) \neq \text{sq}\, f_1 + \text{sq}\, f_2 \tag{7-9}$$

and it follows from the definition (7-7) that the operator sq is nonlinear. Throughout this book we limit our considerations to linear operators. We assume, therefore, that all operators that we encounter satisfy Eq. (7-7).

The sum Ω of two operators Ω_1 and Ω_2 is defined by

$$\Omega f = \Omega_1 f + \Omega_2 f \tag{7-10}$$

Similarly, we define the product

$$\Lambda = \Omega_1 \Omega_2 \tag{7-11}$$

by

$$\Lambda f = \Omega_1 \Omega_2 f = \Omega_1 (\Omega_2 f) \tag{7-12}$$

It is easily verified that

$$\Omega_1 + \Omega_2 = \Omega_2 + \Omega_1 \tag{7-13}$$

is always valid, but often

$$\Omega_1 \Omega_2 \neq \Omega_2 \Omega_1 \tag{7-14}$$

If we take

$$\Omega_1 = x \qquad \Omega_2 = \frac{\partial}{\partial x} \qquad (7\text{-}15)$$

then

$$\Omega_1 \Omega_2 f = x \frac{\partial f}{\partial x} \qquad (7\text{-}16)$$

and

$$\Omega_2 \Omega_1 f = \frac{\partial}{\partial x}(xf) = x \frac{\partial f}{\partial x} + f \qquad (7\text{-}17)$$

This is an example of the inequality (7-14). On the other hand, if we take

$$\Omega_1 = \frac{\partial}{\partial x} \qquad \Omega_2 = \frac{\partial}{\partial y} \qquad (7\text{-}18)$$

then

$$\frac{\partial}{\partial x}\left(\frac{\partial f}{\partial y}\right) = \frac{\partial}{\partial y}\left(\frac{\partial f}{\partial x}\right) \qquad (7\text{-}19)$$

so that

$$\Omega_1 \Omega_2 = \Omega_2 \Omega_1 \qquad (7\text{-}20)$$

We say that two operators Ω_1 and Ω_2 commute when they satisfy Eq. (7-20). The commutator $[\Omega_1, \Omega_2]$ of the two operators is defined as

$$[\Omega_1, \Omega_2] = \Omega_1 \Omega_2 - \Omega_2 \Omega_1 \qquad (7\text{-}21)$$

Obviously the commutator is equal to zero when the two operators commute.

The complex conjugate Ω^* of an operator Ω is defined by

$$(\Omega f)^* = \Omega^* f^* \qquad (7\text{-}22)$$

An operator is defined to be Hermitian if for any two functions f and g it satisfies the condition

$$\int f \Omega g \, dq = \int g \Omega^* f \, dq \qquad (7\text{-}23)$$

Here the integration is performed over all variables that occur in both functions and in the operator. It will be seen that Hermitian operators play a very important role in quantum mechanics.

It is convenient to introduce a new notation for the integrals of Eq. (7-23). We define

$$\langle f | \Omega | g \rangle = \int f^* \Omega g \, dq \qquad (7\text{-}24)$$

The advantage of this notation is that we do not have to write out all the integration variables. In our new notation we find that Ω is Hermitian if

$$\langle f | \Omega | g \rangle = \langle g^* | \Omega^* | f^* \rangle = \langle g | \Omega | f \rangle^* \qquad (7\text{-}25)$$

It is interesting to let an operator Ω work on the functions ϕ_n of a complete set

$$g_n = \Omega\phi_n \tag{7-26}$$

The result can now be expanded in terms of the complete set

$$g_n = \sum_m a_{n,m}\phi_m \tag{7-27}$$

so that we have

$$\Omega\phi_n = \sum_m a_{n,m}\phi_m \tag{7-28}$$

In Chap. 2, where we discussed the properties of complete sets of functions, we mentioned that usually the functions are orthonormal:

$$\langle \phi_n | \phi_m \rangle = \delta_{n,m} \tag{7-29}$$

and we assume that this is the case here. If we multiply Eq. (7-28) on the left by ϕ_k^* and integrate, we obtain

$$a_{n,k} = \langle \phi_k | \Omega | \phi_n \rangle = \Omega_{k,n} \tag{7-30}$$

The effect of Ω on any of the functions ϕ_n can thus be described as

$$\Omega\phi_n = \sum_k \Omega_{k,n}\phi_k \tag{7-31}$$

In this way we have represented the operator as a matrix of infinite order.

If we take a different complete set of functions ψ_n as a starting point, we obtain

$$\Omega\psi_n = \sum_k \Omega'_{k,n}\psi_k$$
$$\Omega'_{k,n} = \langle \psi_k | \Omega | \psi_n \rangle \tag{7-32}$$

This gives a different matrix of infinite order as the representation of the operator. In general there is an infinite number of ways in which we can describe the operator by way of a matrix. All these matrices can have different elements, but certain essential characteristics of the operator are contained in every matrix, and certain matrix representations are often useful for deriving some properties of the operator.

Some of the procedures in Sec. 2-3, where we discussed Fourier transforms, can also be expressed in terms of operators. For instance, in Eq. (2-61) we introduced the Fourier transform $F(u)$ of a function $f(t)$ by means of

$$F(u) = (2\pi)^{-1/2} \int_{-\infty}^{\infty} e^{-iut} f(t)\, dt \tag{7-33}$$

Since this describes a specific procedure for deriving a function F from a function f, we can also represent this procedure as

$$F = \Lambda f \qquad (7\text{-}34)$$

The operator Λ is defined here by

$$F(x) = \int_{-\infty}^{\infty} \Lambda(x;x')f(x')\, dx'$$
$$\Lambda(x;x') = (2\pi)^{-1/2} e^{-ixx'} \qquad (7\text{-}35)$$

This is an example of an integral representation of an operator. It can be shown that many operators may be described in this fashion.

The unit operator Ω_E describes the multiplication of a function by unity and is defined by

$$f = \Omega_E f \qquad (7\text{-}36)$$

The integral representation of this operator can be written as

$$f(x) = \int_{-\infty}^{\infty} \Omega_E(x,x')f(x')\, dx' \qquad (7\text{-}37)$$

and if we compare this with Eq. (2-62)

$$f(x) = \int_{-\infty}^{\infty} \delta(x - x')f(x')\, dx' \qquad (7\text{-}38)$$

we conclude that

$$\Omega_E(x,x') = \delta(x - x') \qquad (7\text{-}39)$$

In operator language, therefore, we may call the Dirac δ function the *integral representation* of the unit operator. From the δ function we can also derive the integral representation of the differential operator

$$D = \frac{\partial}{\partial x} \qquad (7\text{-}40)$$

This integral representation is defined by

$$\frac{\partial f}{\partial x} = \int_{-\infty}^{\infty} D(x,x')f(x')\, dx' \qquad (7\text{-}41)$$

From Eq. (7-38) we see that

$$\frac{\partial f(x)}{\partial x} = \int_{-\infty}^{\infty} \delta(x - x')\frac{\partial f(x')}{\partial x'}\, dx' \qquad (7\text{-}42)$$

Integration by parts gives

$$\frac{\partial f(x)}{\partial x} = \delta(x - x')f(x') \bigg|_{-\infty}^{\infty} - \int_{-\infty}^{\infty} \left[\frac{\partial}{\partial x'} \delta(x - x') \right] f(x')\, dx'$$

$$= \int_{-\infty}^{\infty} \left[\frac{\partial}{\partial x} \delta(x - x') \right] f(x')\, dx' = \int_{-\infty}^{\infty} \delta'(x - x')f(x')\, dx' \quad (7\text{-}43)$$

By comparing Eqs. (7-41) and (7-43) we find that

$$\delta'(x - x') = D(x,x') \qquad (7\text{-}44)$$

so that the derivative of the δ function is the integral representation of the operator D.

7-2 EIGENVALUES AND EIGENFUNCTIONS OF OPERATORS

We have seen that a given operator Λ, when working on an arbitrary function f, usually produces a completely different function g. However, there usually exists a set of functions f_n for which the result of the operation is proportional to the original function:

$$\Lambda f_n = \lambda_n f_n \qquad (7\text{-}45)$$

We call λ_n an eigenvalue of the operator Λ and f_n its corresponding eigenfunction. An eigenvalue is called nondegenerate when it has only one eigenfunction; otherwise we call it degenerate. When there are s different, linearly independent eigenfunctions $f_{k,s}$, all belonging to the same eigenvalue λ_k, then we call λ_k an s-fold degenerate eigenvalue.

It is easily seen that the Schrödinger equation

$$-\frac{\hbar^2}{2m}\left(\frac{\partial^2}{\partial x^2} + \frac{\partial^2}{\partial y^2} + \frac{\partial^2}{\partial z^2}\right)\psi + V(x,y,z)\psi = E\psi \qquad (7\text{-}46)$$

can also be written as an eigenvalue problem. If we take the Hamiltonian operator H as

$$H = -\frac{\hbar^2}{2m}\left(\frac{\partial^2}{\partial x^2} + \frac{\partial^2}{\partial y^2} + \frac{\partial^2}{\partial z^2}\right) + V(x,y,z) \qquad (7\text{-}47)$$

then we can write the time-independent Schrödinger equation as

$$H\psi = E\psi \qquad (7\text{-}48)$$

The solutions are given by

$$H\psi_n = E_n\psi_n \qquad (7\text{-}49)$$

and we see that E_n and ψ_n are eigenvalues and eigenfunctions, respectively, of the operator H.

From a mathematician's point of view the one-dimensional Schrödinger equation can be regarded as a special case of a Sturm-Liouville
equation. This is a second-order differential equation over an interval
$a \leqslant x \leqslant b$ where the solutions are restricted by the condition that they
have certain prescribed values at the boundaries $x = a$ and $x = b$. In
the case of the harmonic oscillator the boundary conditions are that
the solution is zero for x approaching plus or minus infinity. It is useful
to know that all these different problems are related to one another,
since it enables us to describe the same system from different mathematical approaches.

In quantum mechanics Hermitian operators play an important role,
since in the formal presentation of the subject a basic assumption is
that every observable can be represented by a Hermitian operator. We
briefly discuss some properties of the eigenvalues and eigenfunctions
of Hermitian operators.

It is easily shown that the eigenvalues h_n of a Hermitian operator H
are all real. We write

$$H\psi_n = h_n\psi_n \tag{7-50}$$

Multiplication on the left by ψ_n^* and subsequent integration give

$$\langle\psi_n| H |\psi_n\rangle = h_n\langle\psi_n|\psi_n\rangle \tag{7-51}$$

The complex conjugate of this equation is

$$\langle\psi_n| H |\psi_n\rangle^* = h_n^*\langle\psi_n|\psi_n\rangle^* \tag{7-52}$$

Since H is Hermitian, we can also write this as

$$\langle\psi_n| H |\psi_n\rangle = h_n^*\langle\psi_n|\psi_n\rangle \tag{7-53}$$

It now follows from Eqs. (7-51) and (7-53) that

$$h_n = h_n^* \tag{7-54}$$

which means that the eigenvalue is real.

Two eigenfunctions ψ_n and ψ_m that belong to two different eigenvalues h_n and h_m, respectively, of a Hermitian operator H are orthogonal. We prove this by first writing the two equations

$$H\psi_n = h_n\psi_n$$
$$(H\psi_m)^* = h_m\psi_m^* \tag{7-55}$$

Multiplication of these equations on the left by ψ_m^* and by ψ_n, respectively, and subsequent integration give

$$\langle\psi_m| H |\psi_n\rangle = h_n\langle\psi_m|\psi_n\rangle$$
$$\langle\psi_n| H |\psi_m\rangle^* = h_m\langle\psi_n|\psi_m\rangle^* \tag{7-56}$$

Since H is Hermitian, we can also write the second Eq. (7-56) as

$$\langle \psi_m | H | \psi_n \rangle = h_m \langle \psi_m | \psi_n \rangle \qquad (7\text{-}57)$$

If we subtract this from the first Eq. (7-56), we obtain

$$(h_n - h_m)\langle \psi_m | \psi_n \rangle = 0 \qquad (7\text{-}58)$$

and it follows that ψ_n and ψ_m are orthogonal if h_n and h_m are different.

If the eigenvalue h_n is degenerate, then its eigenfunctions are not necessarily orthogonal. However, by taking suitable linear combinations we can obtain a new set of orthogonal functions. Let us imagine that h_n is s-fold degenerate and that originally its eigenfunctions are $\psi_{n,1}, \psi_{n,2}, \ldots, \psi_{n,s}$. As a first step we now construct a new set of eigenfunctions

$$\psi'_{n,1} = \psi_{n,1}$$

$$\psi'_{n,2} = \langle \psi_{n,1} | \psi_{n,1} \rangle \psi_{n,2} - \langle \psi_{n,1} | \psi_{n,2} \rangle \psi_{n,1}$$

$$\cdots \qquad\qquad\qquad\qquad\qquad\qquad (7\text{-}59)$$

$$\psi'_{n,s} = \langle \psi_{n,1} | \psi_{n,1} \rangle \psi_{n,s} - \langle \psi_{n,1} | \psi_{n,s} \rangle \psi_{n,1}$$

The functions $\psi'_{n,2}, \psi'_{n,3}, \ldots, \psi'_{n,s}$ and each linear combination of them are now orthogonal to $\psi'_{n,1}$. We now repeat this procedure with the functions $\psi'_{n,2}, \psi'_{n,3}, \ldots, \psi'_{n,s}$, and we construct a new set of functions $\psi''_{n,3}, \psi''_{n,4}, \ldots, \psi''_{n,s}$ that are orthogonal to $\psi''_{n,2}$. Repeated applications of these transformations lead to a new orthogonal set of eigenfunctions $\phi_{n,1}, \phi_{n,2}, \ldots, \phi_{n,s}$ of the eigenvalue h_n. Thus we see that we can select a completely orthogonal set of eigenfunctions of the operator H. If, finally, we normalize every eigenfunction to unity, we obtain an orthonormal set of functions.

The reader may have detected some similarities between these derivations and the discussion in Chap. 6 of the eigenvalues and eigenvectors of a Hermitian matrix. This is not surprising, since the two problems are analogous to each other and we can transform the eigenvalue problem of an operator into an eigenvalue problem of a matrix.

Let us take an arbitrary complete set of functions ϕ_n as the basis for our considerations, and let us consider the eigenvalue problem

$$\Omega \psi = \lambda \psi \qquad (7\text{-}60)$$

We denote the eigenvalues by λ_n and the corresponding eigenfunctions by ψ_n. Every function ψ can be expanded in terms of our complete set

$$\psi = \sum_k c_k \phi_k \qquad (7\text{-}61)$$

and if we substitute this expansion into Eq. (7-60), the eigenvalue problem becomes

$$\sum_k c_k \Omega \phi_k = \lambda \sum_k c_k \phi_k \qquad (7\text{-}62)$$

The problem is now to determine the coefficients c_k in such a way that the function ψ is an eigenfunction of Ω. We multiply Eq. (7-62) on the left by ϕ_m and integrate. This gives

$$\sum_k \Omega_{m,k} c_k = \lambda c_m$$

$$\Omega_{m,k} = \langle \phi_m | \Omega | \phi_k \rangle \qquad (7\text{-}63)$$

For the sake of simplicity we assume that Ω is a Hermitian operator. Then we have

$$\Omega_{m,k} = \langle \phi_m | \Omega | \phi_k \rangle = \langle \phi_k | \Omega | \phi_m \rangle^* = \Omega_{k,m}^* \qquad (7\text{-}64)$$

and we see that the matrix $\Omega_{m,k}$ is also Hermitian. It follows that a Hermitian operator is represented by a Hermitian matrix.

A comparison of Eqs. (7-60) and (7-63) shows that we have transformed the eigenvalue problem (7-60) of a Hermitian operator into the eigenvalue problem (7-63) of an infinite Hermitian matrix, and the two problems are therefore equivalent. Since $\Omega_{m,k}$ is Hermitian, there exists a unitary transformation, defined by a matrix $[u_{k,n}]$, that diagonalizes the matrix Ω:

$$\sum_m \sum_k u_{l,m}^\dagger \Omega_{m,k} u_{k,n} = \lambda_n \delta_{l,n} \qquad (7\text{-}65)$$

Let us now multiply these equations by $u_{i,l}$ and sum over l:

$$\sum_l \sum_m \sum_k u_{i,l} u_{l,m}^\dagger \Omega_{m,k} u_{k,n} = \lambda_n \sum_l u_{i,l} \delta_{l,n} \qquad (7\text{-}66)$$

Since U is unitary, we have

$$\sum_l u_{i,l} u_{m,l}^* = \sum_l u_{i,l} u_{l,m}^\dagger = \delta_{i,m} \qquad (7\text{-}67)$$

so that we may rewrite Eq. (7-66) as

$$\sum_m \sum_k \delta_{i,m} \Omega_{m,k} u_{k,n} = \lambda_n u_{i,n} \qquad (7\text{-}68)$$

or

$$\sum_k \Omega_{i,k} u_{k,n} = \lambda_n u_{i,n} \qquad (7\text{-}69)$$

By comparing this expression with Eq. (7-63), we may deduce that λ_n is an eigenvalue of Ω and that the corresponding eigenvector is

$$\mathbf{u}_n = (u_{1,n}, u_{2,n}, u_{3,n}, \dots) \qquad (7\text{-}70)$$

It follows, therefore, that λ_n is also an eigenvalue of the operator Ω and that the corresponding eigenfunction is

$$\psi_n = \sum_k u_{k,n}\phi_k \tag{7-71}$$

In general different operators have different eigenvalues and eigenfunctions, but commuting Hermitian operators have the same eigenfunctions. In order to prove this statement, we consider two commuting Hermitian operators Ω and Λ,

$$\Omega\Lambda = \Lambda\Omega \tag{7-72}$$

Their eigenvalues are ω_n and λ_n, and the corresponding eigenfunctions are w_n and u_n:

$$\Lambda u_n = \lambda_n u_n$$
$$\Omega w_n = \omega_n w_n \tag{7-73}$$

First we show that for a nondegenerate eigenvalue λ_n of Λ the corresponding eigenfunction u_n is also an eigenfunction of Ω. We have

$$\Lambda(\Omega u_n) = \Omega\Lambda u_n = \Omega\lambda_n u_n = \lambda_n(\Omega u_n) \tag{7-74}$$

Hence (Ωu_n) is also an eigenfunction of Λ belonging to λ_n. Since λ_n is nondegenerate, there is only one eigenfunction, so that (Ωu_n) and u_n have to be proportional:

$$\Omega u_n = \sigma_n u_n \tag{7-75}$$

Consequently, u_n is an eigenfunction of both Λ and Ω.

If λ_n is degenerate, the situation becomes more complicated. We assume that the degeneracy is s-fold and that $u_{n,1}, u_{n,2}, u_{n,3}, \cdots, u_{n,s}$ are a set of linearly independent eigenfunctions belonging to λ_n. Again, we can write

$$\Lambda(\Omega u_{n,i}) = \Omega\Lambda u_{n,i} = \Omega\lambda_n u_{n,i} = \lambda_n(\Omega u_{n,i}) \tag{7-76}$$

for an arbitrary eigenfunction $u_{n,i}$. It follows again that $(\Omega u_{n,i})$ is an eigenfunction of Λ, belonging to λ_n, but this time we may conclude only that $(\Omega u_{n,i})$ is a linear combination of the $u_{n,j}$:

$$\Omega u_{n,i} = \sum_j c_{i,j} u_{n,j} \tag{7-77}$$

We assume that the $u_{n,i}$ are orthonormal, so that multiplication on the left by $u_{n,k}$ and subsequent integration give

$$c_{i,k} = \Omega_{k,i} = \langle u_{n,k}| \Omega |u_{n,i}\rangle \tag{7-78}$$

It follows, therefore, that

$$\Omega u_{n,i} = \sum_k \Omega_{k,i} u_{n,k} \tag{7-79}$$

where $[\Omega_{k,i}]$ is a Hermitian matrix of order s.

Apparently, the functions $u_{n,i}$ are not necessarily eigenfunctions of Ω. However, let us attempt to find a new set of functions

$$v_j = \sum b_{j,i} u_{n,i} \tag{7-80}$$

such that the v_j are eigenfunctions of Ω. The functions v must then satisfy the condition

$$\Omega v = \sum_i b_i \Omega u_{n,i} = \sigma v = \sigma \sum_i b_i u_{n,i} \tag{7-81}$$

Multiplication on the left by $u_{n,j}$ and subsequent integration give

$$\sum_i \Omega_{j,i} b_i = \sigma b_j \tag{7-82}$$

This is an eigenvalue problem of a finite Hermitian matrix of order s, and it can always be solved. Let its eigenvalues be σ_k and the corresponding eigenvectors $b_{k,j}$. Then the σ_k are also eigenvalues of Ω, and the corresponding eigenfunctions are

$$v_k = \sum_j b_{k,j} u_{n,j} \tag{7-83}$$

The functions v_k are also eigenfunctions of the operator Λ, belonging to the eigenvalue λ_n, and they are therefore eigenfunctions of both Ω and Λ. It may be concluded that two commuting Hermitian operators always have a set of common eigenfunctions.

7-3 EIGENFUNCTION EXPANSIONS

In Sec. 2-3 we discussed the expansion of a function in terms of a complete set of functions. Now we want to consider the special case of the expansion of an arbitrary function in terms of the complete set of eigenfunctions of a Hermitian operator. The crucial question here is whether such a set of eigenfunctions constitutes a complete set in the sense that we defined in Sec. 2-3. It is not easy to answer this question for the general case, but a number of special situations have been investigated in great detail.[1] The results of these studies give us sufficient grounds to assume that in general the eigenfunctions of a Hermitian operator form a complete set. This means that an arbitrary function that satisfies the same boundary conditions as the eigenfunctions can be expanded in terms of them and that this expansion is convergent in the mean.

[1] E. C. Titchmarsh, "Eigenfunction Expansions Associated with Second-order Differential Equations," Oxford University Press, London, part I, 1946, and part II. 1958.

The situation is quite straightforward if the eigenvalues from which we derive the eigenfunctions form a denumerable set, as in the case of the harmonic oscillator. If we call the operator Λ, the eigenvalues λ_n, and the eigenfunctions ϕ_n, then we can expand a function f as

$$f = \sum_n c_n \phi_n \tag{7-84}$$

We assume that Λ is Hermitian and that the ϕ_n have been chosen to be orthonormal. Then it is easily found that

$$c_n = \langle \phi_n | f \rangle \tag{7-85}$$

so that

$$f = \sum_n \langle \phi_n | f \rangle \phi_n \tag{7-86}$$

We have assumed that the set ϕ_n is complete, which implies that the expansion (7-86) is allowed and is convergent in the mean.

The problem becomes much more interesting when the eigenvalue spectrum contains both a discrete part and a continuum. Here we must be aware of the difficulties in normalizing the wave functions. We will study this problem for a simple one-dimensional example, namely, the eigenvalues of the one-dimensional Hamiltonian H whose potential function $U(x)$ is given by Fig. 7-1. The function $U(x)$ tends to infinity

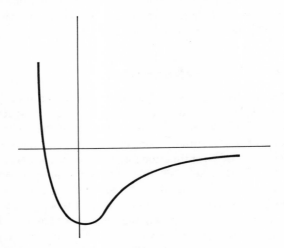

FIG. 7-1

for $x \to -\infty$ and asymptotically to zero for $x \to \infty$. It has a minimum value U_0 for $x = 0$. The operator H has a set of eigenvalues E_n with corresponding eigenfunctions $\phi_n(x)$ for $E \leqslant 0$, and it also has a set of eigenfunctions $\phi(x;E)$ for $E > 0$. All positive values of E are allowed, and since there is a wave function belonging to each positive value of E, we write these functions as $\phi(x;E)$.

We suspect that an arbitrary function $\psi(x)$, which tends to zero for $x \to -\infty$, can be expanded as

$$\psi(x) = \sum_n \gamma_n \phi_n(x) + \int_0^\infty \gamma(E)\phi(x;E)\, dE \qquad (7\text{-}87)$$

We wish to investigate whether such an expansion is allowed and how the functions $\phi(x;E)$ ought to be normalized.

In order to answer these questions, we consider the eigenvalues and eigenfunctions of the operator H'

$$H' = T + V(x) \qquad (7\text{-}88)$$

where we define

$$\begin{aligned} V(x) &= U(x) & x \leqslant a \\ V(x) &= \infty & x > a \end{aligned} \qquad (7\text{-}89)$$

We take a to be a very large but finite number. The eigenvalue spectrum of H' is now discrete, and we denote the eigenvalues by ε_n and the eigenfunctions by $\tilde{\phi}_n(x)$. For positive eigenvalues, $\varepsilon_n > 0$, it will prove to be convenient to write the corresponding eigenfunctions as $\tilde{\phi}(x;\varepsilon_n)$. We will assume that, in the case that a tends to infinity,

$$\lim_{a \to \infty} \varepsilon_n = E_n$$

$$\lim_{a \to \infty} \tilde{\phi}_n(x) = \phi_n(x) \qquad (7\text{-}90)$$

$$\lim_{a \to \infty} \tilde{\phi}(x;\varepsilon_n) = \phi(x;E)$$

Any function $\psi(x)$ which is defined for $x \leqslant a$ and which is zero for $x = a$ can now be expanded as

$$\psi(x) = \sum_n c_n \tilde{\phi}_n(x) + \sum_k c_k \tilde{\phi}(x;\varepsilon_k) \qquad (7\text{-}91)$$

where the first summation is to be performed over all states with negative (or zero) eigenvalues and the second summation over all states with positive eigenvalues. We assume that the functions $\tilde{\phi}_n(x)$ are normalized to unity. The $\tilde{\phi}(x;\varepsilon_k)$ do not have to be normalized; therefore we introduce the quantities

$$N(a;\varepsilon) = \int_{-\infty}^a \tilde{\phi}(x;\varepsilon)\tilde{\phi}^*(x;\varepsilon)\, dx \qquad (7\text{-}92)$$

We also define

$$c(a;\varepsilon) = \int_{-\infty}^a \tilde{\phi}^*(x;\varepsilon)\psi(x)\, dx \qquad (7\text{-}93)$$

The expansion (7-91) can now be written as

$$\psi(x) = \sum_n c_n \tilde{\phi}_n(x) + \sum_k \frac{c(a;\varepsilon_k)\tilde{\phi}(x;\varepsilon_k)}{N(a;\varepsilon_k)} \tag{7-94}$$

with
$$c_n = \langle \tilde{\phi}_n(x) | \psi(x) \rangle \tag{7-95}$$

Let us now investigate what happens to Eq. (7-94) when a tends to infinity. The first sum offers no difficulties. We have already assumed that

$$\lim_{a \to \infty} \tilde{\phi}_n(x) = \phi_n(x) \tag{7-96}$$

and therefore we have

$$\lim_{a \to \infty} c_n = \gamma_n \tag{7-97}$$

The second sum becomes an integral in the limiting case, but we have to study the detailed dependence on a of all quantities involved before we can determine this sum. When a is large, the wave function $\tilde{\phi}(x;\varepsilon_k)$ takes the form

$$\tilde{\phi}(x;\varepsilon_k) = A_k \sin\left[\frac{(2m\varepsilon_k)^{1/2}x}{\hbar} + \alpha_k\right] \tag{7-98}$$

for large values of x. Here A is the amplitude and α a phase factor. For large values of a the normalization function $N(a;\varepsilon_k)$ behaves asymptotically like

$$N(a;\varepsilon_k) \simeq \tfrac{1}{2}A_k^2 a \tag{7-99}$$

The values of the energy eigenvalues are determined by the condition that the wave function is zero for $x = a$. For large values of a we may deduce from Eq. (7-98) that this condition is

$$(2m\varepsilon_k)^{1/2}a + \alpha_k\hbar = kh\pi \tag{7-100}$$

with k a positive integer. The difference $\Delta\varepsilon_k$ between ε_{k+1} and ε_k can be obtained as

$$\Delta\varepsilon_k = \frac{(2m\varepsilon_k)^{1/2}\hbar\pi}{ma} \tag{7-101}$$

when k is sufficiently large. We now rewrite Eq. (7-94) as

$$\psi(x) = \sum_n c_n \tilde{\phi}_n(x) + \sum_k \frac{c(a;\varepsilon_k)}{N(a;\varepsilon_k)\Delta\varepsilon_k} \tilde{\phi}(x;\varepsilon_k)\Delta\varepsilon_k \tag{7-102}$$

It follows now from Eqs. (7-99) and (7-101) that the product $N(a;\varepsilon_k)\Delta\varepsilon_k$ tends to a finite limit when a tends to infinity:

$$\lim_{a \to \infty} N(a;\varepsilon_k)\Delta\varepsilon_k = \frac{A_k^2(2m\varepsilon_k)^{1/2}\hbar\pi}{2m} \tag{7-103}$$

We are still free to choose the normalizing factor A, and we do so in such a way that the limit (7-103) becomes unity. It follows now that in the limit for a tending to infinity the expansion (7-102) becomes

$$\psi(x) = \sum_n \gamma_n \phi_n(x) + \int_0^\infty \gamma(E)\phi(x;E)\, dE \qquad (7\text{-}104)$$

with
$$\gamma_n = \langle \phi_n(x) \,|\, \psi(x) \rangle$$

$$\gamma(E) = \int_{-\infty}^\infty \phi^*(x;E)\psi(x)\, dx \qquad (7\text{-}105)$$

From this expansion we can derive an orthogonality relation for the functions $\phi(x;E)$. We choose $\psi_0(x)$ orthogonal to the eigenfunctions $\phi_n(x)$ of the discrete states, and we obtain

$$\psi_0(x) = \int_0^\infty \gamma(E)\phi(x;E)\, dE \qquad (7\text{-}106)$$

If we substitute this back into the second Eq. (7-105), we obtain

$$\gamma(E) = \int_{-\infty}^\infty \gamma(E')\, dE' \int_{-\infty}^\infty \phi^*(x;E)\phi(x;E')\, dx \qquad (7\text{-}107)$$

Let us now compare this with Eq. (7-38), which we rewrite as

$$\gamma(E) = \int_{-\infty}^\infty \delta(E - E')\gamma(E')\, dE' \qquad (7\text{-}108)$$

Obviously it may be concluded that

$$\int_{-\infty}^\infty \phi^*(x;E)\phi(x;E')\, dx = \delta(E - E') \qquad (7\text{-}109)$$

This is known as the improper orthogonality of continuum eigenfunctions.

PROBLEMS _____

7-1 Write the operators for x, y, z, p_x, p_y, and p_z, and derive the commutators between all pairs of these operators. Do the same for M^2, M_x, M_y, and M_z, where **M** is the angular momentum.

7-2 Show that $\Delta, p_x, p_y,$ and p_z are Hermitian operators for normalizable functions.

7-3 Show that
$$[x^n, p_x] = i\hbar n x^{n-1}$$
if n is a positive integer.

8

THE HYDROGEN ATOM

8-1 THE CENTRAL FORCE FIELD

The hydrogen atom is a special case of a particle of mass μ in a three-dimensional central force field. A central force field is characterized by a potential function that depends only on the distance between the particle and the origin. If we employ polar coordinates (r,θ,ϕ), then V does not depend on the angles θ and ϕ. It is a function of r only, and we write it as $V(r)$. The Hamiltonian is

$$H = -\frac{\hbar^2}{2\mu}\Delta + V(r) = -\frac{\hbar^2}{2\mu}\left(\frac{\partial^2}{\partial x^2} + \frac{\partial^2}{\partial y^2} + \frac{\partial^2}{\partial z^2}\right) + V(r) \qquad (8\text{-}1)$$

and the Schrödinger equation is

$$\left[\Delta + \frac{2\mu}{\hbar^2}(E - V)\right]\Psi(r,\theta,\phi) = 0 \qquad (8\text{-}2)$$

The problem is most conveniently discussed by introducing the polar coordinates (r,θ,ϕ), which are defined as

$$x = r \sin\theta \cos\phi$$
$$y = r \sin\theta \sin\phi \qquad (8\text{-}3)$$
$$z = r \cos\theta$$

We showed in Appendix A that the Laplace operator Δ, when expressed in polar coordinates, takes the form

$$\Delta = \frac{\partial^2}{\partial r^2} + \frac{2}{r}\frac{\partial}{\partial r} + \frac{1}{r^2}\frac{\partial^2}{\partial \theta^2} + \frac{\cos\theta}{r^2 \sin\theta}\frac{\partial}{\partial \theta} + \frac{1}{r^2 \sin^2\theta}\frac{\partial^2}{\partial \phi^2} \qquad (8\text{-}4)$$

The Schrödinger equation (8-2) becomes, therefore,

$$\left[\frac{\partial^2}{\partial r^2} + \frac{2}{r}\frac{\partial}{\partial r} + \frac{1}{r^2}\frac{\partial^2}{\partial \theta^2} + \frac{\cos\theta}{r^2 \sin\theta}\frac{\partial}{\partial \theta} + \frac{1}{r^2 \sin^2\theta}\frac{\partial^2}{\partial \phi^2}\right]\Psi(r,\theta,\phi)$$

$$= \frac{2\mu}{\hbar^2}[V(r) - E]\Psi(r,\theta,\phi) \qquad (8\text{-}5)$$

We take this equation as the basis of our discussion.

The solution of Eq. (8-5) is obtained by substituting

$$\Psi(r,\theta,\phi) = g(r)\psi(\theta,\phi) \qquad (8\text{-}6)$$

It is easily verified that the two equations

$$\left[\frac{\partial^2}{\partial \theta^2} + \frac{\cos\theta}{\sin\theta}\frac{\partial}{\partial \theta} + \frac{1}{\sin^2\theta}\frac{\partial^2}{\partial \phi^2}\right]\psi(\theta,\phi) + \lambda\psi(\theta,\phi) = 0 \qquad (8\text{-}7)$$

and

$$\left[\frac{\partial^2}{\partial r^2} + \frac{2}{r}\frac{\partial}{\partial r} - \frac{\lambda}{r^2} + \frac{2\mu E}{\hbar^2} - \frac{2\mu V(r)}{\hbar^2}\right]g(r) = 0 \qquad (8\text{-}8)$$

are equivalent to Eq. (8-5).

We have already discussed Eq. (8-7), since it is identical to Eq. (5-115) for the rigid rotor. Its eigenvalues are reported in Eq. (5-128) as

$$\lambda = l(l+1) \qquad l = 0, 1, 2, 3, \ldots \qquad (8\text{-}9)$$

and the corresponding eigenfunctions are

$$\psi_{l,m}(\theta,\phi) = Y_{l,m}(\theta,\phi) \qquad m = 0, \pm 1, \pm 2, \ldots, \pm l \qquad (8\text{-}10)$$

according to Eq. (5-130). Here $Y_{l,m}$ are the spherical harmonics, defined in Eq. (4-132):

$$Y_{l,m}(\theta,\phi) = \left[\frac{2l+1}{4\pi}\frac{(l-|m|)!}{(l+|m|)!}\right]^{1/2} P_l^{|m|}(\cos\theta)e^{im\phi} \qquad (8\text{-}11)$$

which form an orthonormal set of functions on a sphere.

We find, therefore, that the eigenfunctions for a particle in a central force field are

$$\Psi_{l,m}(r,\theta,\phi) = g_l(r)Y_{l,m}(\theta,\phi) \qquad (8\text{-}12)$$

where the functions $g_l(r)$ and the eigenvalues are to be determined from the equation

$$\frac{d^2 g_l}{dr^2} + \frac{2}{r} \frac{dg_l}{dr} - \left[\frac{l(l+1)}{r^2} + \frac{2\mu}{\hbar^2} \{V(r) - E\} \right] g_l = 0 \qquad (8\text{-}13)$$

We discuss the hydrogen atom as a special case of this general situation.

8-2 THE HYDROGEN ATOM

All hydrogenlike atoms consist of a nucleus with mass m_n and charge Ze and of an electron with mass m_e and charge $(-e)$. Their Hamiltonian is

$$H = \frac{p_n^2}{2m_n} + \frac{p_e^2}{2m_e} - \frac{Ze^2}{|\mathbf{r}_e - \mathbf{r}_n|} \qquad (8\text{-}14)$$

Here $\mathbf{r}_n$ and $\mathbf{r}_e$ are the coordinates and $\mathbf{p}_n$ and $\mathbf{p}_e$ the momenta of the nucleus and the electron, respectively. In Sec. 1-6 we saw that we should introduce the new coordinates

$$\mathbf{R} = \frac{m_n \mathbf{r}_n + m_e \mathbf{r}_e}{m_n + m_e} \qquad \mathbf{r} = \mathbf{r}_e - \mathbf{r}_n \qquad (8\text{-}15)$$

and the corresponding momenta

$$\mathbf{P} = M\dot{\mathbf{R}} \qquad \mathbf{p} = \mu\dot{\mathbf{r}}$$

$$M = m_n + m_e \qquad \mu = \frac{m_n m_e}{m_n + m_e} \qquad (8\text{-}16)$$

The transformed Hamiltonian becomes, then,

$$H = \frac{P^2}{2M} + \frac{p^2}{2\mu} - \frac{Ze^2}{r} \qquad (8\text{-}17)$$

This may be separated into the motion of the center of gravity $\mathbf{R}$, which behaves like a free particle and is of no further interest to us, and the motion of the electron with respect to the nucleus, which is described by the coordinate $\mathbf{r}$. The latter is represented by the Hamiltonian

$$H = -\frac{\hbar^2}{2\mu} \Delta - \frac{Ze^2}{r} \qquad (8\text{-}18)$$

and we see that this is a special case of a particle in a central force field with

$$V(r) = -\frac{Ze^2}{r} \qquad (8\text{-}19)$$

The situation is therefore described by Eqs. (8-12) and (8-13), and the differential equation for $g_l(r)$ is

$$\frac{d^2g_l}{dr^2} + \frac{2}{r}\frac{dg_l}{dr} + \left[\frac{2\mu E}{\hbar^2} + \frac{2\mu Ze^2}{\hbar^2 r} - \frac{l(l+1)}{r^2}\right]g_l = 0 \qquad (8\text{-}20)$$

Let us first consider the discrete states, where E is negative. We may then introduce a new eigenvalue parameter ρ by means of

$$E = -\frac{\mu Z^2 e^4}{2\hbar^2 \rho^2} \qquad (8\text{-}21)$$

The equation becomes, then,

$$\frac{d^2g_l}{dr^2} + \frac{2}{r}\frac{dg_l}{dr} + \left[-\frac{\mu^2 Z^2 e^4}{\hbar^4 \rho^2} + \frac{2\mu Ze^2}{\hbar^2 r} - \frac{l(l+1)}{r^2}\right]g_l = 0 \qquad (8\text{-}22)$$

Next we introduce a new variable x by substituting

$$r = \frac{\rho\hbar^2}{2\mu Ze^2}\,x \qquad (8\text{-}23)$$

We then obtain

$$\frac{d^2g_l}{dx^2} + \frac{2}{x}\frac{dg_l}{dx} + \left[-\frac{1}{4} + \frac{\rho}{x} - \frac{l(l+1)}{x^2}\right]g_l = 0 \qquad (8\text{-}24)$$

For very large x this expression approaches the equation

$$\frac{d^2g_l}{dx^2} - \frac{1}{4}g_l = 0, \qquad (8\text{-}25)$$

which has the solutions $e^{(x/2)}$ and $e^{-(x/2)}$. The first solution leads to unnormalizable eigenfunctions and is ruled out. The second describes the asymptotic behavior of g_l, and we substitute, therefore,

$$g_l = w(x)e^{-(1/2)x} \qquad (8\text{-}26)$$

in order to solve Eq. (8-24). We then obtain

$$\frac{d^2w}{dx^2} + \left(\frac{2}{x} - 1\right)\frac{dw}{dx} + \left(\frac{\rho - 1}{x} - \frac{l(l+1)}{x^2}\right)w = 0 \qquad (8\text{-}27)$$

We solve this equation by means of the series expansion method of Sec. 4-2, and then we substitute

$$w(x) = x^\alpha \sum_{n=0}^{\infty} a_n x^n \qquad (8\text{-}28)$$

and we find that the characteristic equation for α is

$$\alpha^2 + \alpha - l(l+1) = 0 \qquad (8\text{-}29)$$

The two solutions are

$$\alpha_1 = l$$

$$\alpha_2 = -l - 1$$

(8-30)

The second root α_2 leads to a function $w(x)$ which is infinite for $x = 0$ and which is therefore inadmissible as an eigenfunction. The other root α_1 leads to a solution that we derive by substituting

$$w(x) = x^l u(x)$$

(8-31)

The differential equation for $u(x)$ is now obtained as

$$x \frac{d^2u}{dx^2} + (2l + 2 - x) \frac{du}{dx} + (\rho - l - 1)u = 0$$

(8-32)

We have already discussed this equation, since it is identical to the differential equation (4-134)

$$x \frac{d^2u}{dx^2} + (c - x) \frac{du}{dx} - au = 0$$

(8-33)

for the confluent hypergeometric series $\Phi(a,c; x)$. In our problem we have to substitute

$$a = l + 1 - \rho$$

$$c = 2l + 2$$

(8-34)

and it follows from Sec. 4-7 that the two solutions of Eq. (8-32) are

$$u_1(x) = \Phi(l + 1 - \rho, 2l + 2; x)$$

$$u_2(x) = x^{-2l-1}\Phi(-l - \rho, -2; x)$$

(8-35)

The second solution has a singularity at $x = 0$, and it can be ruled out immediately. The first is the series

$$\Phi(a,c; x) = 1 + \frac{a}{c}\frac{x}{1!} + \frac{a(a + 1)}{c(c + 1)}\frac{x^2}{2!} + \frac{a(a + 1)(a + 2)}{c(c + 1)(c + 2)}\frac{x^3}{3!} + \cdots$$

(8-36)

and in general it behaves asymptotically as e^x for large x. This leads to unnormalizable eigenfunctions, and it follows that in general the solution $\Phi(l + 1 - \rho, 2l + 2; x)$ does not produce acceptable wave functions.

We obtain an acceptable wave function only if we see to it that the infinite series (8-36) is reduced to a finite polynomial. This can be achieved by taking a equal to a negative integer $-\nu$. The eigenvalues are therefore determined from the condition

$$l + 1 - \rho = -\nu \qquad \nu = 0, 1, 2, 3, \ldots$$

(8-37)

or

$$\rho = \nu + l + 1 \qquad \nu = 0, 1, 2, 3, \ldots$$

(8-38)

The corresponding eigenfunctions $g_{l,v}(r)$ are

$$g_{l,v}(x) = x^l e^{-(1/2)x}\Phi(-v, 2l + 2; x)$$

$$x = \frac{2\mu Ze^2}{(v + l + 1)\hbar^2} r$$

(8-39)

The complete set of eigenfunctions $\Psi_{v,l,m}(r,\theta,\phi)$ of the hydrogen atom are now obtained by combining Eqs. (8-12) and (8-39)

$$\Psi_{v,l,m}(r,\theta,\phi) = g_{l,v}(x)Y_{l,m}(\theta,\phi)$$

(8-40)

where the allowed values for v, l and m are

$$v = 0, 1, 2, 3, \ldots$$

$$l = 0, 1, 2, 3, \ldots$$

(8-41)

$$m = 0, \pm 1, \pm 2, \pm 3, \ldots, \pm l$$

This set of indices is known as the *quantum numbers,* describing the states of the hydrogen atom.

Although these quantum numbers describe all eigenfunctions of the hydrogen atom, it is customary to use a different set. We can write

$$\rho = n \qquad n = l + 1, l + 2, l + 3, \ldots$$

$$l = 0, 1, 2, 3, 4, \ldots$$

(8-42)

The condition here is that $n \geqslant l + 1$, but this can also be satisfied by taking

$$n = 1, 2, 3, 4, \ldots$$

$$l = 0, 1, 2, 3, \ldots, n - 1$$

(8-43)

$$m = 0, \pm 1, \pm 2, \ldots, \pm l$$

Now the energy eigenvalues are, according to Eq. (8-21),

$$E_n = -\frac{\mu Z^2 e^4}{2\hbar^2} \frac{1}{n^2}$$

(8-44)

and the corresponding eigenfunctions are

$$\Psi_{n,l,m}(r,\theta,\phi) = x^l e^{-(1/2)x}\Phi(l + 1 - n, 2l + 2; x)Y_{l,m}(\theta,\phi)$$

$$x = \frac{2\mu Ze^2}{n\hbar^2} r$$

(8-45)

The allowed values of the quantum numbers are prescribed by Eq. (8-43).

8-3 THE BEHAVIOR OF THE HYDROGEN EIGENFUNCTIONS

It is useful to gain some insight into the general properties of the eigenfunctions and eigenvalues of the hydrogenlike atoms. We use Eqs. (8-44) and (8-45) as a starting point for deriving these properties. The considerations of Sec. 8-2 are valid for the series of atoms H, He$^+$, Li^{++}, etc., and we can put the results on a common basis by introducing the proper units of length and energy.

To avoid carrying too many numerical factors in atomic calculations, it is convenient to make use of the atomic units introduced by Hartree. The units of length and energy are defined as

$$a_0 = \frac{\hbar^2}{m_e e^2} \qquad \varepsilon_0 = 2R_\infty \qquad R_\infty = \frac{e^2}{2a_0} \tag{8-46}$$

Here a_0 is called the *Bohr radius*, and its magnitude is $a_0 = 5.2917 \times 10^{-9}$ cm. The quantity R_∞ is known as the *Rydberg constant* for infinite mass, and its magnitude is 109,727.3 cm^{-1}; the energy unit ε_0 expressed in terms of electron volts is $\varepsilon_0 = 27.21$ ev.

In order to describe a specific atom A, consisting of a nucleus, with mass m_A and charge $Z_A e$, and of one electron, we introduce the quantities

$$a_A = \frac{\hbar^2}{\mu_A Z_A e^2} = \frac{m_A + m_e}{Z_A m_A} a_0 \tag{8-47}$$

and
$$\varepsilon_A = \frac{Z_A e^2}{a_A} = \frac{Z_A{}^2 m_A}{m_A + m_e} \varepsilon_0 \tag{8-48}$$

as units of length and energy, respectively. We also introduce the Rydberg constant R_A for atom A,

$$\varepsilon_A = 2Z_A{}^2 R_A \qquad R_A = \frac{m_A R_\infty}{m_A + m_e} \tag{8-49}$$

We see that R_A approaches R_∞ when m_A tends to infinity; this is why the notation R_∞ is used.

In terms of these units a_A and ε_A of length and energy the energy eigenvalues of an arbitrary atom A can be written as

$$E_n = -\frac{1}{2n^2} \tag{8-50}$$

The eigenvalue depends only on n, and since the other quantum numbers l and m can take the values

$$l = 0, 1, 2, 3, \ldots, n - 1$$
$$m = 0, \pm 1, \pm 2, \ldots, \pm l \tag{8-51}$$

for a given n value, E_n is generally degenerate. The order ρ_n of the degeneracy is derived by observing that there are $2l + 1$ possible values of m for each value of l, so that

$$\rho_n = 1 + 3 + 5 + \cdots + (2n - 1) = n^2 \qquad (8\text{-}52)$$

Each stationary state of the hydrogen atom is determined by the quantum numbers n, l, and m, but we usually describe them by means of a different notation, which is due to the old spectroscopic theories. First we look at the quantum number l, and if $l = 0$, we speak of an s state; for $l = 1$ we have a p state; $l = 2$ is a d state; $l = 3$ an f state; $l = 4$ a g state; etc. The value of n is given by writing it in front of these letters. The lowest states of the hydrogen atom are given thus in Table 8-1.

TABLE 8–1

$n = 1$	$l = 0$	$1s$
$n = 2$	$l = 0$	$2s$
$n = 2$	$l = 1$	$2p$
$n = 3$	$l = 0$	$3s$
$n = 3$	$l = 1$	$3p$
$n = 3$	$l = 2$	$3d$
etc.		

The values of m are indicated by adding subscripts. For example, the $2p$ states are written as $2p_1$, $2p_0$, and $2p_{-1}$ for $m = 1$, $m = 0$, and $m = -1$, respectively.

It is useful to know all wave functions for the states given in Table 8-1, since these functions play a role in many chemical problems. If we express r in terms of the unit a_A, then the radial wave functions are, according to Eq. (8-39),

$$g_{l,n}(r) = r^l \exp\left(-\frac{r}{n}\right) \Phi\left(l + 1 - n,\ 2l + 2;\ \frac{2r}{n}\right) \qquad (8\text{-}53)$$

It follows from the definition of the confluent hypergeometric series that

$$g_{0,1}(r) = A_{0,1} e^{-r}$$

$$g_{0,2}(r) = A_{0,2}(1 - \tfrac{1}{2}r)e^{-(1/2)r}$$

$$g_{1,2}(r) = A_{1,2} r e^{-(1/2)r}$$

$$g_{0,3}(r) = A_{0,3}\left(1 - \frac{2r}{3} + \frac{2r^2}{27}\right)e^{-(1/3)r} \qquad (8\text{-}54)$$

$$g_{1,3}(r) = A_{1,3} r\left(1 - \frac{r}{6}\right)e^{-(1/3)r}$$

$$g_{2,3}(r) = A_{2,3} r^2 e^{-(1/3)r}$$

The $A_{l,n}$ are normalization constants, which are determined by the condition

$$\int_0^\infty \{g_{l,n}(r)\}^2 r^2 \, dr = 1 \tag{8-55}$$

The normalized functions are therefore

$$g_{0,1}(r) = 2e^{-r}$$

$$g_{0,2}(r) = \frac{1}{2\sqrt{2}}(r-2)e^{-(1/2)r}$$

$$g_{1,2}(r) = \frac{1}{2\sqrt{6}}re^{-(1/2)r}$$

$$g_{0,3}(r) = \frac{2}{81\sqrt{3}}(2r^2 - 18r + 27)e^{-(1/3)r} \tag{8-56}$$

$$g_{1,3}(r) = \frac{2\sqrt{2}}{81\sqrt{3}}(r^2 - 6r)e^{-(1/3)r}$$

$$g_{2,3}(r) = \frac{2\sqrt{2}}{81\sqrt{15}}r^2 e^{-(1/3)r}$$

The orthonormal spherical harmonics $Y_{l,m}(\theta,\phi)$ are, according to Eq. (4-132),

$$Y_{0,0}(\theta,\phi) = \frac{1}{\sqrt{4\pi}}$$

$$Y_{1,0}(\theta,\phi) = \left(\frac{3}{4\pi}\right)^{1/2}\cos\theta$$

$$Y_{1,1}(\theta,\phi) = \left(\frac{3}{8\pi}\right)^{1/2}\sin\theta\, e^{i\phi}$$

$$Y_{1,-1}(\theta,\phi) = Y_{1,1}^*(\theta,\phi)$$

$$Y_{2,0}(\theta,\phi) = \frac{1}{2}\left(\frac{5}{4\pi}\right)^{1/2}(3\cos^2\theta - 1) \tag{8-57}$$

$$Y_{2,1}(\theta,\phi) = \left(\frac{15}{8\pi}\right)^{1/2}\sin\theta\cos\theta\, e^{i\phi}$$

$$Y_{2,2}(\theta,\phi) = \left(\frac{15}{32\pi}\right)^{1/2}\sin^2\theta\, e^{2i\phi}$$

$$Y_{2,-1}(\theta,\phi) = Y_{2,1}^*(\theta,\phi)$$

$$Y_{2,-2}(\theta,\phi) = Y_{2,2}^*(\theta,\phi)$$

We can now construct the orthonormal eigenfunctions for the states described in Table 8-1. The s states are all nondegenerate, and we have

$$\psi(1s) = \frac{1}{\sqrt{\pi}} e^{-r}$$

$$\psi(2s) = \frac{1}{4\sqrt{2\pi}} (r - 2)e^{-(1/2)r} \tag{8-58}$$

$$\psi(3s) = \frac{1}{81\sqrt{3\pi}} (2r^2 - 18r + 27)e^{-(1/3)r}$$

Each p state is three-fold degenerate, and the wave functions for the $2p$ and $3p$ states are

$$\psi(2p_1) = \frac{1}{8\sqrt{\pi}} r \sin\theta\, e^{i\phi}e^{-(1/2)r}$$

$$\psi(2p_0) = \frac{1}{4\sqrt{2\pi}} r \cos\theta\, e^{-(1/2)r}$$

$$\psi(2p_{-1}) = \frac{1}{8\sqrt{\pi}} r \sin\theta\, e^{-i\phi}e^{-(1/2)r}$$

$$\psi(3p_1) = \frac{1}{81\sqrt{\pi}} (r^2 - 6r) \sin\theta\, e^{i\phi}e^{-(1/3)r} \tag{8-59}$$

$$\psi(3p_0) = \frac{\sqrt{2}}{81\sqrt{\pi}} (r^2 - 6r) \cos\theta\, e^{-(1/3)r}$$

$$\psi(3p_{-1}) = \frac{1}{81\sqrt{\pi}} (r^2 - 6r) \sin\theta\, e^{-i\phi}e^{-(1/3)r}$$

The five-fold degenerate $3d$ state has the eigenfunctions

$$\psi(3d_2) = \frac{1}{81\sqrt{4\pi}} r^2 \sin^2\theta\, e^{2i\phi}e^{-(1/3)r}$$

$$\psi(3d_1) = \frac{1}{81\sqrt{\pi}} r^2 \sin\theta \cos\theta\, e^{i\phi}e^{-(1/3)r}$$

$$\psi(3d_0) = \frac{1}{81\sqrt{6\pi}} r^2(3\cos^2\theta - 1)e^{-(1/3)r} \tag{8-60}$$

$$\psi(3d_{-1}) = \frac{1}{81\sqrt{\pi}} r^2 \sin\theta \cos\theta\, e^{-i\phi}e^{-(1/3)r}$$

$$\psi(3d_{-2}) = \frac{1}{81\sqrt{4\pi}} r^2 \sin^2\theta\, e^{-2i\phi}e^{-(1/3)r}$$

We have already mentioned that a set of degenerate eigenfunctions may be replaced by a different set, which is obtained by taking linear combinations of the first set. Consequently we may represent the hydrogen wave functions in a different way. It follows from Eq. (8-59) that $\psi(2p_0)$ can also be written as

$$\psi(2p_0) = \frac{1}{4\sqrt{2\pi}} ze^{-(1/2)r} \qquad (8\text{-}61)$$

and we often find it denoted by $\psi(2p_z)$. By taking the sum and the difference of $\psi(2p_1)$ and $\psi(2p_{-1})$, we can obtain the functions $\psi(2p_x)$ and $\psi(2p_y)$, and we may replace the set of eigenfunctions $\psi(2p_m)$ of Eq. (8-59) by

$$\psi(2p_x) = \frac{1}{4\sqrt{2\pi}} xe^{-(1/2)r}$$

$$\psi(2p_y) = \frac{1}{4\sqrt{2\pi}} ye^{-(1/2)r} \qquad (8\text{-}62)$$

$$\psi(2p_z) = \frac{1}{4\sqrt{2\pi}} ze^{-(1/2)r}$$

By the same method we may replace the $3p$ eigenfunctions of Eq. (8-59) by the set

$$\psi(3p_x) = \frac{\sqrt{2}}{81\sqrt{\pi}} (r - 6)xe^{-(1/3)r}$$

$$\psi(3p_y) = \frac{\sqrt{2}}{81\sqrt{\pi}} (r - 6)ye^{-(1/3)r} \qquad (8\text{-}63)$$

$$\psi(3p_z) = \frac{\sqrt{2}}{81\sqrt{\pi}} (r - 6)ze^{-(1/3)r}$$

Often we also find a different set of $3d$ functions instead of the $\psi(3d_m)$ of Eq. (8-60), namely,

$$\psi(3d_{zz}) = \frac{1}{81\sqrt{6\pi}} (r^2 - 3z^2)e^{-(1/3)r}$$

$$\psi(3d_{xz}) = \frac{\sqrt{2}}{81\sqrt{\pi}} xze^{-(1/3)r}$$

$$\psi(3d_{yz}) = \frac{\sqrt{2}}{81\sqrt{\pi}} yze^{-(1/3)r} \qquad (8\text{-}64)$$

$$\psi(3d_{xy}) = \frac{\sqrt{2}}{81\sqrt{\pi}} xye^{-(1/3)r}$$

$$\psi(3d_{x^2-y^2}) = \frac{1}{81\sqrt{2\pi}} (x^2 - y^2)e^{-(1/3)r}$$

It is convenient to express the probability density functions for these states in terms of polar coordinates. If we define $P(r,\theta,\phi)\, dr\, d\theta\, d\phi$ as the probability that the polar coordinates of the electron are between r and $r + dr$, θ and $\theta + d\theta$, and ϕ and $\phi + d\phi$, then we have

$$P(r,\theta,\phi) = \psi\psi^* r^2 \sin\theta \qquad (8\text{-}65)$$

For a state (n,l,m) we can write this as

$$P_{n,l,m} = [g_{l,n}(r)]^2 r^2 Y_{l,m}(\theta,\phi) Y_{l,m}^*(\theta,\phi) \sin\theta \qquad (8\text{-}66)$$

that is, as the product of a radial function

$$R_{n,l} = [g_{l,n}(r)]^2 r^2 \qquad (8\text{-}67)$$

and an angular function

$$F(\Omega) = Y_{l,m}(\theta,\phi) Y_{l,m}^*(\theta,\phi) \sin\theta \qquad (8\text{-}68)$$

For the s states the angular distribution function is a constant, and we only have to consider the radial distribution functions, which we plot in Fig. 8-1. It may be useful to know that the expectation value of r, that is, the integral

$$(r)_n = \int [g_{0,n}(r)]^2 r^3\, dr \qquad (8\text{-}69)$$

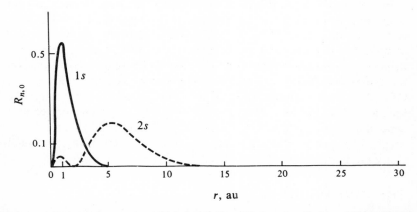

FIG. 8-1   Radial distribution functions $R_{n,l}$ (2) for the (1s) and (2s) functions.

has the value

$$(r_s)_n = \frac{3n^2}{2} \tag{8-70}$$

It follows, thus, that the average distance between the electron and the nucleus increases with increasing values of the quantum number n.

The radial distribution functions for the $2p$ and $3p$ states are plotted in Fig. 8-2. Now the expectation values of r are

$$(r_p)'_n = \frac{3n^2}{2} - 1 \tag{8-71}$$

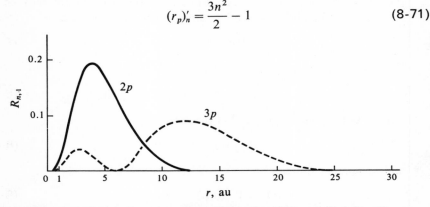

FIG. 8-2   Radial distribution functions $R_{n,l}$ (2) for the (2p) and (3p) functions.

However, the angular distribution function now plays a very important role. For example, $\psi(2p_z)$ is zero in the xy plane, and for any given r it has a maximum value on the z axis. We may therefore say that $\psi(2p_z)$ is directed along the z axis. In the same way we find that $\psi(2p_x)$ and $\psi(2p_y)$ are directed along the x axis and y axis, respectively.

In the case of the $3d$ functions the angular distribution is much more interesting than the radial dependence. It is easily verified that $\psi(3d_{xy})$ is zero in the planes $x = 0$ and $y = 0$ and that the planes $x = \pm y$ contain the relative maxima. The function $\psi(3d_{x^2-y^2})$ has the same behavior if we rotate $45°$ around the z axis, and here the maxima are on the planes $x = 0$ and $y = 0$, and the wave function is zero when $x = \pm y$. Obviously, the functions $\psi(3d_{xz})$ and $\psi(3d_{yz})$ behave similarly. The function $\psi(3d_{zz})$ is zero when $3 \cos^2 \theta = 1$, that is, on the surface of a cone making an angle of $27\frac{1}{2}°$ with the z axis and passing through the origin. The relative maxima of the function are in the plane $z = 0$ and along the z axis.

8-4 THE CONTINUUM

When $E > 0$, all energy values lead to allowed, unnormalizable wave functions that behave in an oscillatory fashion. The analytical form of these functions is easily derived from Eqs. (8-44) and (8-45) if we realize that n should now assume purely imaginary values. For positive energy values we introduce the parameter

$$\lambda^2 = \frac{\mu Z^2 e^4}{2\hbar^2 \varepsilon} \tag{8-72}$$

and the variable

$$x = -\frac{2\mu Z e^2}{\hbar^2}\frac{ir}{\lambda} \tag{8-73}$$

The eigenfunctions are then

$$\Psi_{l,m}(r,\theta,\phi; \varepsilon) = x^l e^{-(1/2)x}\Phi(l + 1 - i\lambda, 2l + 2; x)Y_{l,m}(\theta,\phi) \tag{8-74}$$

Whenever we expand a function in terms of the hydrogen-atom eigenfunctions, the continuum eigenfunctions must be included in the expansion. Otherwise, the continuum functions play only a minor role in atomic problems. They occur only in the theory of scattering, which is not discussed in this book. For an extensive discussion of the properties of the hydrogen continuum functions we refer the reader to the book by Bethe and Salpeter.[1]

P R O B L E M S

8-1 The Rydberg constant for hydrogen is

$$R_{\rm H} = 109,677.58 \text{ cm}^{-1}.$$

Use this value to determine the lowest excitation energy $E_{2s} - E_{1s}$ of the ions He$^+$, Li^{++}, and Be^{+++}. Evaluate also the expectation value of r^2 for the $1s$ states of these atoms from the value

$$a_0 = \frac{\hbar^2}{me^2} = 5.2917 \times 10^{-9} \text{ cm}$$

where m is the electron mass.

8-2 Consider a particle of mass m in a spherical box, where $V(r) = 0$ if $r \leqslant R$ and $V(r) = \infty$ if $r > R$. Calculate the energy eigenvalues and the eigenfunctions for the case that the angular quantum number l is equal to zero.

8-3 The eigenvalues and eigenfunctions of the three-dimensional harmonic oscillator

$$V(r) = \frac{1}{2}k(x^2 + y^2 + z^2) = \frac{1}{2}kr^2$$

[1] H. A. Bethe and E. E. Salpeter, "Quantum Mechanics of One- and Two-electron Atoms," Springer-Verlag, Berlin, 1957.

are easily obtained by separating the Hamiltonian into an x-dependent, a y-dependent, and a z-dependent part. Show that the same results are obtained if we follow the procedure of Sec. 8-1, where we use polar coordinates.

8-4 Derive the detailed analytical expression for the normalized wave functions for the states $4s$, $4p$, $4d$, and $4f$ of the hydrogen atom.

CHAPTER 9

ANGULAR
MOMENTUM

9-1 COMMUTATOR RELATIONS

We saw in Sec. 1-6 that the angular-momentum vector **M** is defined in classical mechanics as

$$\mathbf{M} = \mathbf{r} \times \mathbf{p} \qquad (9\text{-}1)$$

In quantum mechanics we represent the three components of this vector as the operators

$$M_x = -i\hbar\left(y\,\frac{\partial}{\partial z} - z\,\frac{\partial}{\partial y}\right)$$

$$M_y = -i\hbar\left(z\,\frac{\partial}{\partial x} - x\,\frac{\partial}{\partial z}\right) \qquad (9\text{-}2)$$

$$M_z = -i\hbar\left(x\,\frac{\partial}{\partial y} - y\,\frac{\partial}{\partial x}\right)$$

Here we follow the usual procedure of replacing **p** by $-i\hbar\nabla$. The operator

185

M^2 is defined as

$$M^2 = M_x^2 + M_y^2 + M_z^2 \qquad (9\text{-}3)$$

where the M_α are the operators defined by Eq. (9-2).

In certain cases the operators M_α and M^2 commute with the Hamiltonian operator H, and then a knowledge of the eigenfunctions of the angular momentum can be very useful. In particular, we obtain a better insight into the properties of a particle in a central force field, like the hydrogen atom, if we include the angular momentum in our considerations. Let us therefore study first the commutators between the Hamiltonian and the angular momentum.

It is easily verified that the Laplace operator

$$\Delta = \frac{\partial^2}{\partial x^2} + \frac{\partial^2}{\partial y^2} + \frac{\partial^2}{\partial z^2} \qquad (9\text{-}4)$$

commutes with each component M_α of the angular momentum

$$[M_x, \Delta] = [M_y, \Delta] = [M_z, \Delta] = 0 \qquad (9\text{-}5)$$

Since we have, for two arbitrary operators Ω and Λ,

$$[\Omega^2, \Lambda] = \Omega[\Omega, \Lambda] + [\Omega, \Lambda]\Omega \qquad (9\text{-}6)$$

if follows from Eq. (9-5) that also

$$[M^2, \Delta] = 0 \qquad (9\text{-}7)$$

In the same way it may be derived that

$$[M_x, V(r)] = [M_y, V(r)] = [M_z, V(r)] = [M^2, V(r)] = 0 \qquad (9\text{-}8)$$

and it follows that for a particle in a central force field

$$[M_\alpha, H] = [M^2, H] = 0 \qquad (9\text{-}9)$$

We have seen that two commuting operators have a set of eigenfunctions in common, and a knowledge of the eigenfunctions of M_α and M^2 can supply us, therefore, with useful information about the eigenfunctions of H.

Let us now derive the commutator relations between the various components M_α. We have

$$[M_x, M_y] = (i\hbar)^2 \left[\left(y\frac{\partial}{\partial z} - z\frac{\partial}{\partial y} \right)\left(z\frac{\partial}{\partial x} - x\frac{\partial}{\partial z} \right) - \left(z\frac{\partial}{\partial x} - x\frac{\partial}{\partial z} \right)\left(y\frac{\partial}{\partial z} - z\frac{\partial}{\partial y} \right) \right]$$

$$= (i\hbar)^2 \left(y\frac{\partial}{\partial x} - x\frac{\partial}{\partial y} \right) = i\hbar M_z \qquad (9\text{-}10)$$

Therefore, we find

$$[M_x, M_y] = i\hbar M_z$$

$$[M_y, M_z] = i\hbar M_x \tag{9-11}$$

$$[M_z, M_x] = i\hbar M_y$$

Obviously we also have

$$[M_x, M_x] = [M_y, M_y] = [M_z, M_z] = 0 \tag{9-12}$$

We can now use Eq. (9-6) to derive that

$$[M^2, M_x] = M_x[M_x, M_x] + [M_x, M_x]M_x + M_y[M_y, M_x]$$

$$+ [M_y, M_x]M_y + M_z[M_z, M_x] + [M_z, M_x]M_z = 0 \tag{9-13}$$

Hence, we see that

$$[M^2, M_\alpha] = 0 \qquad \alpha = x, y, z \tag{9-14}$$

We see that the operators M^2 and M_x have a set of common eigenfunctions and also the operators M^2 and M_y or M^2 and M_z. However, M_x and M_y do not commute, and they do not have the same eigenfunctions. We find, therefore, that an eigenfunction of one of the operators M_α is also an eigenfunction of M^2, but it is not an eigenfunction of a different component M_β. We can construct a common set of eigenfunctions for the pair of commuting operators M^2 and M_x, for the pair M^2 and M_y, or for the pair M^2 and M_z, but the three sets of eigenfunctions are different because of Eq. (9-11). Usually we take the pair of operators M^2 and M_z as the basis of our considerations, since this is the simplest from a mathematical point of view, but it is equally possible to take one of the other pairs.

9-2 THE EIGENVALUES AND EIGENFUNCTIONS

The eigenvalues and eigenfunctions of the angular momentum are best derived by introducing polar coordinates (r, θ, ϕ). We find then

$$M_x = i\hbar \left(\sin \phi \, \frac{\partial}{\partial \theta} + \cot \theta \cos \phi \, \frac{\partial}{\partial \phi} \right)$$

$$M_y = i\hbar \left(-\cos \phi \, \frac{\partial}{\partial \theta} + \cot \theta \sin \phi \, \frac{\partial}{\partial \phi} \right) \tag{9-15}$$

$$M_z = -i\hbar \, \frac{\partial}{\partial \phi}$$

and subsequently

$$M^2 = -\hbar^2 \left(\frac{\partial^2}{\partial \theta^2} + \frac{\cos \theta}{\sin \theta} \frac{\partial}{\partial \theta} + \frac{1}{\sin^2 \theta} \frac{\partial^2}{\partial \phi^2} \right) \qquad (9\text{-}16)$$

The eigenvalue problem of the operator M^2 can be written in the form

$$\left(\frac{\partial^2}{\partial \theta^2} + \frac{\cos \theta}{\sin \theta} \frac{\partial}{\partial \theta} + \frac{1}{\sin^2 \theta} \frac{\partial^2}{\partial \phi^2} \right) \psi(\theta,\phi) + \lambda \psi(\theta,\phi) = 0 \qquad (9\text{-}17)$$

and we see that this is a differential equation that we have already encountered twice. It is identical to Eq. (5-115) for the rigid rotor and also to Eq. (8-7) for a particle in a central field. We have seen that the eigenvalues are obtained for

$$\lambda = l(l + 1) \qquad l = 0, 1, 2, 3, \ldots \qquad (9\text{-}18)$$

and that the corresponding eigenfunctions are

$$Y_{l,m}(\theta,\phi) = \left[\frac{2l + 1}{4\pi} \frac{(l - |m|)!}{(l + |m|)!} \right]^{1/2} P_l^{|m|}(\cos \theta) e^{im\phi} \qquad (9\text{-}19)$$

By combining Eqs. (9-16) and (9-17), we find that

$$M^2 Y_{l,m}(\theta,\phi) = l(l + 1)\hbar^2 Y_{l,m}(\theta,\phi) \qquad (9\text{-}20)$$

describes the eigenvalues and eigenfunctions of M^2. The allowed values of the quantum number m are

$$m = -l, -l + 1, \ldots, 0, \ldots, l - 1, l \qquad (9\text{-}21)$$

Each eigenvalue of M^2 is therefore $(2l + 1)$-fold degenerate.

The eigenfunctions of M_x, M_y, and M_z are all obtained as linear combinations

$$\sum_{m=-l}^{l} a_m Y_{l,m}(\theta,\phi) \qquad (9\text{-}22)$$

since the M_α commute with M^2. The derivation of the eigenfunctions of M_x and M_y is rather complicated, and we will discuss their properties by means of the matrix representations that we are going to derive. The eigenfunctions of M_z have a simple form, and we will determine them directly. The corresponding equation

$$M_z f(\phi) = m\hbar f(\phi) \qquad (9\text{-}23)$$

has the form

$$i \frac{\partial f}{\partial \phi} = mf \qquad (9\text{-}24)$$

The solutions of this equation are obtained as

$$f(\phi) = e^{im\phi} \tag{9-25}$$

and from the condition that $f(\phi)$ is single-valued we derive that

$$m = 0, \pm 1, \pm 2, \pm 3, \ldots \tag{9-26}$$

It follows, therefore, that each function $Y_{l,m}(\theta,\phi)$ is also an eigenfunction of M_z and that its eigenvalues are given by

$$M_z Y_{l,m}(\theta,\phi) = m\hbar Y_{l,m}(\theta,\phi) \tag{9-27}$$

Let us now return to the hydrogen atom, where the eigenfunctions are, according to Eq. (8-45),

$$\Psi_{n,l,m}(r,\theta,\phi) = r^l e^{-(r/n)} \Phi\left(l + 1 - n, 2l + 2; \frac{2r}{n}\right) Y_{l,m}(\theta,\phi) \tag{9-28}$$

It may now be seen that

$$H\Psi_{n,l,m}(r,\theta,\phi) = \left(-\frac{1}{2n^2}\right)\Psi_{n,l,m}(r,\theta,\phi)$$

$$M^2\Psi_{n,l,m}(r,\theta,\phi) = l(l + 1)\hbar^2 \Psi_{n,l,m}(r,\theta,\phi) \tag{9-29}$$

$$M_z\Psi_{n,l,m}(r,\theta,\phi) = m\hbar\Psi_{n,l,m}(r,\theta,\phi)$$

Since

$$[H,M^2] = 0$$

$$[H,M_z] = 0 \tag{9-30}$$

$$[M^2,M_z] = 0$$

the three operators have a set of eigenfunctions in common, and the functions $\Psi_{n,l,m}$ are eigenfunctions of all three operators. The quantum number n labels the eigenvalue of H, the quantum number l refers to M^2, and the quantum number m to M_z.

It is easily seen now why we prefer to choose M_z rather than M_x or M_y as the operator to be considered. The spherical harmonics $Y_{l,m}(\theta,\phi)$ are already eigenfunctions of M_z, whereas the eigenfunctions of M_x or M_y are linear combinations of the $Y_{l,m}(\theta,\phi)$. Although this does not make any difference in principle, the choice of M_z has the practical advantage of mathematical simplicity.

9-3 THE MATRIX REPRESENTATION OF THE ANGULAR-MOMENTUM OPERATORS

We have already mentioned that we wish to study the properties of the eigenfunctions of M_x and M_y by means of their matrix representations rather than attempt an analytical derivation. Let us therefore set out to derive these matrix representations.

Since the three operators M_α all commute with M^2, we have

$$M_x Y_{l,m}(\theta,\phi) = \hbar \sum_{m'=-l}^{l} a_{m,m'}^l Y_{l,m'}(\theta,\phi)$$

$$M_y Y_{l,m}(\theta,\phi) = \hbar \sum_{m'=-l}^{l} b_{m,m'}^l Y_{l,m'}(\theta,\phi) \qquad \text{(9-31)}$$

$$M_z Y_{l,m}(\theta,\phi) = \hbar \sum_{m'=-l}^{l} c_{m,m'}^l Y_{l,m'}(\theta,\phi)$$

where

$$\hbar a_{m,m'}^l = \langle Y_{l,m'}| M_x |Y_{l,m}\rangle$$

$$\hbar b_{m,m'}^l = \langle Y_{l,m'}| M_y |Y_{l,m}\rangle \qquad \text{(9-32)}$$

$$\hbar c_{m,m'}^l = \langle Y_{l,m'}| M_z |Y_{l,m}\rangle$$

The matrix $[c_{m,m'}^l]$ is easily derived, since it follows immediately from Eq. (9-27) that

$$[c_{m,m'}^l] = \begin{bmatrix} -l & 0 & 0 & \cdots & \cdots & 0 & 0 \\ 0 & -l+1 & 0 & \cdots & \cdots & 0 & 0 \\ 0 & 0 & -l+2 & \cdots & \cdots & 0 & 0 \\ \cdots & \cdots & \cdots & \cdots & \cdots & \cdots & \cdots \\ \cdots & \cdots & \cdots & \cdots & \cdots & \cdots & \cdots \\ 0 & 0 & 0 & \cdots & \cdots & l-1 & 0 \\ 0 & 0 & 0 & \cdots & \cdots & 0 & l \end{bmatrix} \qquad \text{(9-33)}$$

The derivation of the other two matrices is considerably more complicated. It is convenient to introduce the new operators M_1 and M_{-1}, which are defined as

$$M_1 = M_x + iM_y$$

$$M_{-1} = M_x - iM_y \qquad \text{(9-34)}$$

From Eq. (9-15) we derive that

$$M_1 = \hbar e^{i\phi}\left(\frac{\partial}{\partial\theta} + i \cot\theta \frac{\partial}{\partial\phi}\right)$$

$$M_{-1} = \hbar e^{-i\phi}\left(-\frac{\partial}{\partial\theta} + i \cot\theta \frac{\partial}{\partial\phi}\right) \qquad \text{(9-35)}$$

First we consider only M_1, since the properties of M_{-1} may then be derived by taking into account that

$$M_{-1}M_1 = M^2 - M_z^2 - \hbar M_z \qquad \text{(9-36)}$$

We modify Eq. (9-35) by introducing a new variable

$$s = \cos\theta \qquad (9\text{-}37)$$

which gives

$$M_1 = \hbar e^{i\phi}\left[-(1-s^2)^{1/2}\frac{\partial}{\partial s} + \frac{is}{(1-s^2)^{1/2}}\frac{\partial}{\partial\phi}\right] \qquad (9\text{-}38)$$

The crucial question now is what the result is of

$$M_1 Y_{l,m}(s,\phi) = ? \qquad (9\text{-}39)$$

One of the recurrence relations of Sec. 4-6 is Eq. (4-115), which states that

$$\left[(1-s^2)^{1/2}\frac{d}{ds} + \frac{ms}{(1-s^2)^{1/2}}\right]P_l^m(s) = P_l^{m+1}(s) \qquad m \geqslant 0 \qquad (9\text{-}40)$$

Since we can write

$$M_1 Y_{l,m}(s,\phi) = -\hbar e^{i(m+1)\phi}\left[\frac{2l+1}{4\pi}\frac{(l-m)!}{(l+m)!}\right]^{1/2}$$

$$\times \left[(1-s^2)^{1/2}\frac{d}{ds} + \frac{ms}{(1-s^2)^{1/2}}\right]P_l^m(s) \qquad (9\text{-}41)$$

when $m \geqslant 0$, it follows that

$$M_1 Y_{l,m}(s,\phi) = -\hbar\left[\frac{2l+1}{4\pi}\frac{(l-m)!}{(l+m)!}\right]^{1/2}e^{i(m+1)\phi}P_l^{m+1}(s) \qquad (9\text{-}42)$$

if $m \geqslant 0$. According to the definition

$$Y_{l,m+1}(s,\phi) = \left[\frac{2l+1}{4\pi}\frac{(l-m-1)!}{(l+m+1)!}\right]^{1/2}e^{i(m+1)\phi}P_l^{m+1}(s) \qquad (9\text{-}43)$$

for $m \geqslant 0$, we see that

$$M_1 Y_{l,m}(s,\phi) = -\hbar[l(l+1) - m(m+1)]^{1/2}Y_{l,m+1}(s,\phi) \qquad m \geqslant 0 \qquad (9\text{-}44)$$

When $m < 0$, say $m = -v$, where v is a positive integer, then the analogue of Eq. (9-41) is

$$M_1 Y_{l,m}(s,\phi) = -\hbar e^{i(m+1)\phi}\left[\frac{2l+1}{4\pi}\frac{(l-v)!}{(l+v)!}\right]^{1/2}$$

$$\times \left[(1-s^2)^{1/2}\frac{d}{ds} - \frac{vs}{(1-s^2)^{1/2}}\right]P_l^v(s) \qquad (9\text{-}45)$$

Now the recurrence formula (9-40) cannot be used, since there is a different sign. However, we can write it in the form

$$\left[(1-s^2)^{1/2}\frac{d}{ds} - \frac{vs}{(1-s^2)^{1/2}}\right]P_l^v(s) = -\frac{2vs}{(1-s^2)^{1/2}}P_l^v(s) + P_l^{v+1}(s) \qquad (9\text{-}46)$$

and, if we apply this to Eq. (9-45), we obtain

$$M_1 Y_{l,m}(\theta,\phi) = \hbar e^{i(m+1)\phi} \left[\frac{2l+1}{4\pi} \frac{(l-v)!}{(l+v)!} \right]^{1/2} \left[\frac{2vs}{(1-s^2)^{1/2}} P_l^v(s) - P_l^{v+1}(s) \right]$$
$$(9\text{-}47)$$

This can be simplified by using the recurrence formula (4-118), which states that

$$\frac{2vs}{(1-s^2)^{1/2}} P_l^v(s) - P_l^{v+1}(s) = (l+v)(l-v+1)P_l^{v-1}(s) \qquad (9\text{-}48)$$

The result is

$$M_1 Y_{l,m}(\theta,\phi) = \hbar e^{i(m+1)\phi} \left[\frac{2l+1}{4\pi} \frac{(l-v)!}{(l+v)!} \right]^{1/2} (l+v)(l-v+1)P_l^{v-1}(s) \quad (9\text{-}49)$$

For negative values of m, where $v = |m|$, the spherical harmonics are defined as

$$Y_{l,m+1} = \left[\frac{2l+1}{4\pi} \frac{(l-v+1)!}{(l+v-1)!} \right]^{1/2} e^{i(m+1)\phi} P_l^{v-1}(s) \qquad (9\text{-}50)$$

It follows, therefore, that

$$M_1 Y_{l,m}(\theta,\phi) = \hbar [l(l+1) - m(m+1)]^{1/2} Y_{l,m+1}(\theta,\phi) \qquad m < 0 \qquad (9\text{-}51)$$

Combination of Eqs. (9-45) and (9-51) gives

$$M_1 Y_{l,m}(\theta,\phi) = -\hbar [l(l+1) - m(m+1)]^{1/2} Y_{l,m+1}(\theta,\phi) \qquad m \geqslant 0$$
$$M_1 Y_{l,m}(\theta,\phi) = \hbar [l(l+1) - m(m+1)]^{1/2} Y_{l,m+1}(\theta,\phi) \qquad m < 0$$
$$(9\text{-}52)$$

In order to determine the effect of M_{-1}, we operate on the left of Eq. (9-52) by M_{-1}, and we find

$$M_{-1} Y_{l,m+1}(\theta,\phi) = -\frac{1}{\hbar} [l(l+1) - m(m+1)]^{-1/2} M_{-1} M_1 Y_{l,m}(\theta,\phi) \qquad m \geqslant 0$$
$$(9\text{-}53)$$

$$M_{-1} Y_{l,m+1}(\theta,\phi) = \frac{1}{\hbar} [l(l+1) - m(m+1)]^{-1/2} M_{-1} M_1 Y_{l,m}(\theta,\phi) \qquad m < 0$$

According to Eq. (9-36) we now have

$$(M_{-1} M_1) Y_{l,m}(\theta,\phi) = \hbar^2 [l(l+1) - m^2 - m] Y_{l,m}(\theta,\phi) \qquad (9\text{-}54)$$

so that
$$M_{-1} Y_{l,m+1} = -\hbar [l(l+1) - m(m+1)]^{1/2} Y_{l,m} \qquad m \geqslant 0$$
$$(9\text{-}55)$$
$$M_{-1} Y_{l,m+1} = \hbar [l(l+1) - m(m+1)]^{1/2} Y_{l,m} \qquad m < 0$$

or $\quad M_{-1}Y_{l,m} = -\hbar[l(l+1) - m(m-1)]^{1/2}Y_{l,m-1} \qquad m \geqslant 0$

$\qquad M_{-1}Y_{l,m} = \hbar[l(l+1) - m(m-1)]^{1/2}Y_{l,m-1} \qquad m < 0$

(9-56)

For mathematical convenience we introduce a new set of basis functions $Y'_{l,m}$ that are defined as

$$Y'_{l,m} = (-1)^m Y_{l,m} \qquad m \geqslant 0$$

$$Y'_{l,m} = Y_{l,m} \qquad m < 0$$

(9-57)

Now we can combine the two pairs of Eqs. (9-52) and (9-56) into the single equations

$$M_1 Y'_{l,m} = \hbar[l(l+1) - m(m+1)]^{1/2}Y'_{l,m+1}$$

$$M_{-1}Y'_{l,m} = \hbar[l(l+1) - m(m-1)]^{1/2}Y'_{l,m-1}$$

(9-58)

which are now valid for all possible values of m.

By adding and subtracting the two Eqs. (9-58), we obtain, finally,

$$M_x Y'_{l,m} = \tfrac{1}{2}\hbar\{[l(l+1) - m(m+1)]^{1/2}Y'_{l,m+1} + [l(l+1) - m(m-1)]^{1/2}Y'_{l,m-1}\}$$

(9-59)

$$M_y Y'_{l,m} = \tfrac{1}{2}\hbar i\{-[l(l+1) - m(m+1)]^{1/2}Y'_{l,m+1} + [l(l+1) - m(m-1)]^{1/2}Y'_{l,m-1}\}$$

By comparison with Eq. (9-31) we find that the matrices $[a^l_{i,j}]$ and $[b^l_{i,j}]$ that represent M_x and M_y are given by

$$a^l_{m,m+1} = \tfrac{1}{2}[(l+m+1)(l-m)]^{1/2}$$

$$a^l_{m,m-1} = \tfrac{1}{2}[(l+m)(l-m+1)]^{1/2}$$

$$a^l_{m,m'} = 0 \qquad m' \neq m \pm 1$$

(9-60)

and by $\qquad b^l_{m,m+1} = -\tfrac{1}{2}i[(l+m+1)(l-m)]^{1/2}$

$$b^l_{m,m-1} = \tfrac{1}{2}i[(l+m)(l-m+1)]^{1/2}$$

$$b^l_{m,m'} = 0 \qquad m' \neq m \pm 1$$

(9-61)

It may be recalled from Eq. (9-33) that the matrix $[c^l_{m,m'}]$, representing M_z, is given by

$$c^l_{m,m'} = m\delta_{m,m'}$$

(9-62)

The matrices of the three operators are usually presented in such a way that the variable m takes the values $m = l, l-1, l-2, \ldots, 0, -1, \ldots, -l$, that is, in descending order. Also, if we recall the rules of matrix multiplication and the definition of the matrix representation of an operator, we see that we ought to take the transpose of the matrices

A, B, and **C.** We find, then, that the matrix representations are, for $(M_x/\hbar)$,

$$\begin{bmatrix} 0 & \frac{1}{2}\sqrt{2l \cdot 1} & 0 & \cdots & \cdots & 0 & 0 \\ \frac{1}{2}\sqrt{2l \cdot 1} & 0 & \frac{1}{2}\sqrt{(2l-1) \cdot 2} & \cdots & \cdots & 0 & 0 \\ 0 & \frac{1}{2}\sqrt{(2l-1) \cdot 2} & 0 & \cdots & \cdots & 0 & 0 \\ \cdots & \cdots & \cdots & \cdots & \cdots & \cdots & \cdots \\ \cdots & \cdots & \cdots & \cdots & \cdots & \cdots & \cdots \\ 0 & 0 & 0 & \cdots & \cdots & 0 & \frac{1}{2}\sqrt{1 \cdot 2l} \\ 0 & 0 & 0 & \cdots & \cdots & \frac{1}{2}\sqrt{1 \cdot 2l} & 0 \end{bmatrix}$$

(9-63)

for $(M_y/\hbar)$,

$$\begin{bmatrix} 0 & -\frac{1}{2}i\sqrt{2l \cdot 1} & 0 & \cdots & \cdots & 0 & 0 \\ \frac{1}{2}i\sqrt{2l \cdot 1} & 0 & -\frac{1}{2}i\sqrt{(2l-1) \cdot 2} & \cdots & \cdots & 0 & 0 \\ 0 & \frac{1}{2}i\sqrt{(2l-1) \cdot 2} & 0 & \cdots & \cdots & 0 & 0 \\ \cdots & \cdots & \cdots & \cdots & \cdots & \cdots & \cdots \\ \cdots & \cdots & \cdots & \cdots & \cdots & \cdots & \cdots \\ 0 & 0 & 0 & \cdots & \cdots & 0 & -\frac{1}{2}i\sqrt{1 \cdot 2l} \\ 0 & 0 & 0 & \cdots & \cdots & \frac{1}{2}i\sqrt{1 \cdot 2l} & 0 \end{bmatrix}$$

(9-64)

and for $(M_z/\hbar)$,

$$\begin{bmatrix} l & 0 & 0 & \cdots & \cdots & 0 & 0 \\ 0 & l-1 & 0 & \cdots & \cdots & 0 & 0 \\ 0 & 0 & l-2 & \cdots & \cdots & 0 & 0 \\ \cdots & \cdots & \cdots & \cdots & \cdots & \cdots & \cdots \\ \cdots & \cdots & \cdots & \cdots & \cdots & \cdots & \cdots \\ 0 & 0 & 0 & \cdots & \cdots & -l+1 & 0 \\ 0 & 0 & 0 & \cdots & \cdots & 0 & -l \end{bmatrix}$$

(9-65)

9-4 TRANSFORMATION THEORY

Although we do not intend to discuss transformation theory in any great detail, we wish to illustrate some of its aspects by treating some simple examples of the theory of angular momentum. In Sec. 9-3 we used the set of functions $Y'_{l,m}$ as the basis of our considerations because it was so convenient from a mathematical point of view. In addition, we found that the matrix for (M_z) was diagonal when we used the $Y'_{l,m}$.

However, from a physical point of view there is no compelling reason for preferring one basis set over another. We might equally well choose a set of functions for which M_x is diagonal. We expect that in this situation the matrix for M_x assumes the same form as the matrix for M_z in the old representation. Let us study this problem for the simple case where $l = 1$.

If $l = 1$ and if we express the angular momentum in terms of $\hbar$, then the matrix for M_x becomes

$$[M_x] = \begin{bmatrix} 0 & \frac{1}{2}\sqrt{2} & 0 \\ \frac{1}{2}\sqrt{2} & 0 & \frac{1}{2}\sqrt{2} \\ 0 & \frac{1}{2}\sqrt{2} & 0 \end{bmatrix} \tag{9-66}$$

Its eigenvalues are determined from the equation

$$\begin{vmatrix} -\lambda & \frac{1}{2}\sqrt{2} & 0 \\ \frac{1}{2}\sqrt{2} & -\lambda & \frac{1}{2}\sqrt{2} \\ 0 & \frac{1}{2}\sqrt{2} & -\lambda \end{vmatrix} = -\lambda^3 + \lambda = 0 \tag{9-67}$$

The three eigenvalues are $\lambda_1 = 1, \lambda_2 = 0, \lambda_3 = -1$, as we anticipated. The corresponding eigenvectors are

$$\lambda_1 = 1 \qquad \mathbf{u}_1 = (\tfrac{1}{2}, \tfrac{1}{2}\sqrt{2}, \tfrac{1}{2})$$

$$\lambda_2 = 0 \qquad \mathbf{u}_2 = (\tfrac{1}{2}\sqrt{2}, 0, -\tfrac{1}{2}\sqrt{2}) \tag{9-68}$$

$$\lambda_3 = -1 \qquad \mathbf{u}_3 = (\tfrac{1}{2}, -\tfrac{1}{2}\sqrt{2}, \tfrac{1}{2})$$

Hence the matrix $[M_x]$ is diagonal if we take the set

$$\psi_1 = \tfrac{1}{2}Y'_{1,1} + \tfrac{1}{2}\sqrt{2}Y'_{1,0} + \tfrac{1}{2}Y'_{1,-1}$$

$$\psi_2 = \tfrac{1}{2}\sqrt{2}Y'_{1,1} - \tfrac{1}{2}\sqrt{2}Y'_{1,-1} \tag{9-69}$$

$$\psi_3 = \tfrac{1}{2}Y'_{1,1} - \tfrac{1}{2}\sqrt{2}Y'_{1,0} + \tfrac{1}{2}Y'_{1,-1}$$

as our basis functions.

It is easily verified that

$$M_z\psi_1 = \tfrac{1}{2}\sqrt{2}\psi_2$$

$$M_z\psi_2 = \tfrac{1}{2}\sqrt{2}(\psi_1 + \psi_3) \tag{9-70}$$

$$M_z\psi_3 = \tfrac{1}{2}\sqrt{2}\psi_2$$

so that the new matrix for M_z becomes

$$[M_z'] = \begin{bmatrix} 0 & \tfrac{1}{2}\sqrt{2} & 0 \\ \tfrac{1}{2}\sqrt{2} & 0 & \tfrac{1}{2}\sqrt{2} \\ 0 & \tfrac{1}{2}\sqrt{2} & 0 \end{bmatrix} \qquad (9\text{-}71)$$

We see that a change in basis set affects the matrices but not the eigenvalues of the operators. This is easily seen if we realize that a change in basis causes the matrices to be subjected to a unitary transformation. In the case above, this transformation is given by the matrix

$$\mathbf{U} = \begin{bmatrix} \tfrac{1}{2} & -\tfrac{1}{2}\sqrt{2} & \tfrac{1}{2} \\ \tfrac{1}{2}\sqrt{2} & 0 & -\tfrac{1}{2}\sqrt{2} \\ \tfrac{1}{2} & \tfrac{1}{2}\sqrt{2} & \tfrac{1}{2} \end{bmatrix} \qquad (9\text{-}72)$$

It can be verified that

$$\mathbf{U}^\dagger [M_y] \mathbf{U} = \begin{bmatrix} 0 & -\tfrac{1}{2}i\sqrt{2} & 0 \\ \tfrac{1}{2}i\sqrt{2} & 0 & -\tfrac{1}{2}i\sqrt{2} \\ 0 & \tfrac{1}{2}i\sqrt{2} & 0 \end{bmatrix} \qquad (9\text{-}73)$$

and the matrix for M_y is the same in both representations.

In general we can change from one representation to another as we wish. These transformations are not restricted to angular-momentum operators but can be used for any operator. A detailed discussion of transformation theory may be found in Kramers's book.[1]

PROBLEMS

9-1   The component of the angular momentum in a certain direction may be represented by the operator

$$M_p = \alpha M_x + \beta M_y + \gamma M_z$$

where α, β, and γ are direction cosines. Derive the eigenvalues and eigenfunctions of M_p for the case in which $l = 1$.

9-2   Calculate the eigenvalues and eigenfunctions of the operator M_x for $l = 2$.

9-3   Determine $M_{-1} Y_{l,m}$ directly from the properties of the spherical harmonics.

[1] H. A. Kramers, "Quantum Mechanics," chap. 4, North-Holland Publishing Company, Amsterdam, 1937.

CHAPTER **10**

PERTURBATION THEORY

10-1 PERTURBATION THEORY FOR A NONDEGENERATE STATE

The goal of perturbation theory is to derive the eigenvalues and eigenfunctions of an operator H if those of another operator H_0 are known. It is assumed here that H_0 is close to H; usually we write this as

$$H = H_0 + \lambda H' \qquad (10\text{-}1)$$

where λ is a scaling parameter that is much smaller than unity. We do not attempt to specify how small λ should be in order that perturbation theory is applicable. Usually this question is resolved by practical considerations. If the expansions in terms of λ that we are going to use converge to our satisfaction, then we conclude that λ is sufficiently small; otherwise it is not.

We denote the known eigenvalues and eigenfunctions of H_0 by ε_n and ϕ_n, respectively:

$$H_0\phi_n = \varepsilon_n\phi_n \qquad (10\text{-}2)$$

and the unknown eigenvalues and eigenfunctions of H by E_n and ψ_n:

$$H\psi_n = E_n\psi_n \qquad (10\text{-}3)$$

The basic assumption of Rayleigh-Schrödinger perturbation theory is now that we can expand E_n and ψ_n as

$$E_n = \varepsilon_n + \sum_{k=1}^{\infty} \lambda^k E_{n,k}$$

$$\psi_n = \phi_n + \sum_{k=1}^{\infty} \lambda^k \psi_{n,k} \tag{10-4}$$

Here we bypass all complications that arise if the eigenvalue spectra of H and H_0 are different. For the time being we also assume that the particular state for which we evaluate the perturbation has a non-degenerate eigenvalue.

Substitution of the series expansions (10-4) into the Schrödinger equation (10-3) gives

$$\left(H_0 + \lambda H' - \varepsilon_n - \sum_{k=1}^{\infty} \lambda^k E_{n,k} \right) \left(\phi_n + \sum_{k=1}^{\infty} \lambda^k \psi_{n,k} \right) = 0 \tag{10-5}$$

We now set the coefficients of successive powers of λ equal to zero in order to obtain successive approximations to ψ_n and E_n. The first equation of this kind is

$$(H_0 - \varepsilon_n)\phi_n = 0 \tag{10-6}$$

This equation is always satisfied because ε_n is an eigenvalue of H_0 and ϕ_n its corresponding eigenfunction. The second equation is

$$(H_0 - \varepsilon_n)\psi_{n,1} + (H' - E_{n,1})\phi_n = 0 \tag{10-7}$$

The third equation is

$$(H_0 - \varepsilon_n)\psi_{n,2} + (H' - E_{n,1})\psi_{n,1} - E_{n,2}\phi_n = 0 \tag{10-8}$$

The general equation is

$$(H_0 - \varepsilon_n)\psi_{n,k} + (H' - E_{n,1})\psi_{n,k-1} - E_{n,2}\psi_{n,k-2} \cdots - E_{n,k-1}\psi_{n,1} - E_{n,k}\phi_n = 0 \tag{10-9}$$

Let us now attempt to solve these equations successively, starting with Eq. (10-7). If we multiply on the left by ϕ_n^* and integrate, we obtain

$$\langle \phi_n | H_0 - \varepsilon_n | \psi_{n,1} \rangle + \langle \phi_n | H' - E_{n,1} | \phi_n \rangle = 0 \tag{10-10}$$

Since we suppose H_0 to be Hermitian, we have

$$\langle \phi_n | H_0 - \varepsilon_n | \psi_{n,1} \rangle = \langle \psi_{n,1} | H_0 - \varepsilon_n | \phi_n \rangle^* = 0 \tag{10-11}$$

because of Eq. (10-2). We find, therefore,

$$E_{n,1} = \langle \phi_n | H' | \phi_n \rangle \tag{10-12}$$

if we assume that the ϕ_n form an orthonormal set.

Now that we have derived an expression for $E_{n,1}$, we write Eq. (10-7) as

$$(H_0 - \varepsilon_n)\psi_{n,1} = (E_{n,1} - H')\phi_n \qquad (10\text{-}13)$$

Since we know all the quantities on the right side of the equation, this is an inhomogeneous differential equation in $\psi_{n,1}$ only. The corresponding homogeneous equation is

$$(H_0 - \varepsilon_n)\psi = 0 \qquad (10\text{-}14)$$

and we already know that its solution is ϕ_n. According to the theory of inhomogeneous differential equations, we write the general solution of Eq. (10-13) as

$$\psi_{n,1} = \psi_{n,1}^0 + \alpha\phi_n \qquad (10\text{-}15)$$

where $\psi_{n,1}^0$ is a specific solution of Eq. (10-13) and α is an arbitrary parameter. It is now convenient to choose α in such a way that $\psi_{n,1}$ is orthogonal to ϕ_n

$$\langle \psi_{n,1} \mid \phi_n \rangle = 0 \qquad (10\text{-}16)$$

The specific form of $\psi_{n,1}$ obviously depends on H_0 and H', so that we cannot derive the general solution. However, let us assume that we have obtained a solution $\psi_{n,1}$ of Eq. (10-13) that is orthogonal to ϕ_n, and let us proceed to Eq. (10-8). Again we multiply on the left by ϕ_n^* and integrate, and we now find that

$$E_{n,2} = \langle \phi_n | H' | \psi_{n,1} \rangle \qquad (10\text{-}17)$$

We now write Eq. (10-8) as

$$(H_0 - \varepsilon_n)\psi_{n,2} = (E_{n,1} - H')\psi_{n,1} + E_{n,2}\phi_n \qquad (10\text{-}18)$$

and we observe that all quantities on the right are known. Again we solve the differential equation in $\psi_{n,2}$, and we impose the condition that

$$\langle \psi_{n,2} \mid \phi_n \rangle = 0 \qquad (10\text{-}19)$$

In this way $\psi_{n,2}$ is uniquely determined.

In general, we find that

$$E_{n,k} = \langle \phi_n | H' | \psi_{n,k-1} \rangle \qquad (10\text{-}20)$$

if we see to it that all functions $\psi_{n,1}, \psi_{n,2}, \psi_{n,3}, \ldots, \psi_{n,k-1}$ are orthogonal to ϕ_n.

In Sec. 10-2 we discuss a simple example of this method. We trust that this example will familiarize the reader with the procedures to be followed.

10-2 THE HARMONIC OSCILLATOR IN AN ELECTRIC FIELD

We apply the approach above to the evaluation of the ground-state energy and eigenfunction of the harmonic oscillator in an electric field F. The Schrödinger equation for this system is

$$-\frac{\hbar^2}{2m}\frac{d^2\psi}{dx^2} + \frac{1}{2}kx^2\psi - eFx\psi = E\psi \tag{10-21}$$

From the considerations in Sec. 5-4 it is clear that the problem is considerably simplified if we introduce the quantity $\sqrt{\alpha}$ as the unit of length, where

$$\alpha = \left(\frac{\hbar^2}{km}\right)^{1/2} \tag{10-22}$$

and the quantity $(\hbar^2/2m\alpha)$ as the unit of energy. The equation then becomes

$$\left(-\frac{d^2}{dx^2} + x^2\right)\psi - \frac{2eF}{k\sqrt{\alpha}}x\psi = E\psi \tag{10-23}$$

If we now introduce the perturbation parameter μ, we can write this as

$$(H_0 + \mu H')\psi = E\psi$$

$$H_0 = -\frac{d^2}{dx^2} + x^2$$

$$H' = -2x \tag{10-24}$$

$$\mu = \frac{eF}{k\sqrt{\alpha}}$$

The eigenvalues and eigenfunctions of the operator H_0 were obtained in Sec. 5-4, where we discussed the harmonic oscillator. They are

$$\varepsilon_n = 2n + 1 \qquad \phi_n = \frac{H_n(x)e^{-(1/2)x^2}}{(\sqrt{\pi}\,2^n n!)^{1/2}} \tag{10-25}$$

Let us set out to calculate the perturbation to the ground state $n = 0$. Here we have

$$\varepsilon_0 = 1 \qquad \phi_0 = (\pi)^{-1/4}e^{-(1/2)x^2} \tag{10-26}$$

First we calculate the energy correction $E_{0,1}$ by means of Eq. (10-12). We find

$$E_{0,1} = \langle\phi_0|\,H'\,|\phi_0\rangle = -\frac{2}{\sqrt{\pi}}\int_{-\infty}^{\infty} xe^{-x^2}\,dx = 0 \tag{10-27}$$

Next we evaluate the first-order correction term $\psi_{0,1}$ of the wave function. According to Eq. (10-13) we have to solve the equation

$$(H_0 - \varepsilon_0)\psi_{0,1} = -H'\phi_0 \tag{10-28}$$

or, substituting Eqs. (10-24) and (10-26),

$$\left(-\frac{d^2}{dx^2} + x^2 - 1\right)\psi_{0,1} = \frac{2x}{(\pi)^{1/4}} e^{-(1/2)x^2} \tag{10-29}$$

It follows from Eq. (10-25) that the function $xe^{-(1/2)x^2}$ is an eigenfunction of H_0 belonging to the eigenvalue ε_1. We substitute, therefore,

$$\psi_{0,1} = axe^{-(1/2)x^2} \tag{10-30}$$

into Eq. (10-29) and obtain

$$2axe^{-(1/2)x^2} = 2x(\pi)^{-1/4}e^{-(1/2)x^2} \tag{10-31}$$

Hence, the solution is

$$\psi_{0,1} = (\pi)^{-1/4}xe^{-(1/2)x^2} \tag{10-32}$$

and it is easily verified that this function is orthogonal to ϕ_0.

The next energy correction $E_{0,2}$ is obtained by using Eq. (10-17):

$$E_{0,2} = \langle\phi_0| H' |\psi_{0,1}\rangle = -\frac{2}{\sqrt{\pi}} \int_{-\infty}^{\infty} x^2 e^{-x^2} \, dx = -1 \tag{10-33}$$

We now proceed to evaluate $\psi_{0,2}$ from Eq. (10-18), which becomes, in this case,

$$\left(-\frac{d^2}{dx^2} + x^2 - 1\right)\psi_{0,2} = (2x^2 - 1)\frac{e^{-(1/2)x^2}}{(\pi)^{1/4}} \tag{10-34}$$

We note that the right side of this equation is proportional to $H_2(x)e^{-(1/2)x^2}$, so that we substitute

$$\psi_{0,2} = b(2x^2 - 1)e^{-(1/2)x^2}(\pi)^{-1/4} \tag{10-35}$$

into Eq. (10-34). We find that

$$4b = 1 \tag{10-36}$$

so that

$$\psi_{0,2} = \tfrac{1}{4}(\pi)^{-1/4}(2x^2 - 1)e^{-(1/2)x^2} \tag{10-37}$$

The third-order energy is

$$E_{0,3} = \langle\phi_0| H' |\psi_{0,2}\rangle = 0 \tag{10-38}$$

because ϕ_0 and $\psi_{0,2}$ are both symmetric in x and H' is antisymmetric in x.

Summarizing the above results, we see that

$$E_0 = 1 - \mu^2 + \cdots$$
$$\psi_0 = (\pi)^{-1/4} e^{-(1/2)x^2} [1 + \mu x + \mu^2 (\tfrac{1}{2} x^2 - \tfrac{1}{4}) + \cdots] \tag{10-39}$$

These results can be verified, since it is possible to solve Eq. (10-24) exactly. If we write the equation as

$$\left[-\frac{d^2}{dx^2} + (x - \mu)^2 - \mu^2 \right] \psi = E\psi \tag{10-40}$$

then we can transform it to the Schrödinger equation for the harmonic oscillator

$$\left(-\frac{d^2}{dz^2} + z^2 \right) \psi(z) = E' \psi(z) \tag{10-41}$$

if we substitute

$$z = x - \mu \qquad E' = E + \mu^2 \tag{10-42}$$

The energy and eigenfunction of the ground state are therefore

$$E_0 = 1 - \mu^2$$
$$\psi_0 = (\pi)^{-1/4} \exp\left[-\tfrac{1}{2}(x - \mu)^2 \right] \tag{10-43}$$

which agrees with the results from our perturbation treatment.

10-3 PERTURBATION EXPANSIONS

Although the separation of the Hamiltonian according to Eq. (10-1) is always possible, we often find it convenient to use a different expansion instead:

$$H = H_0 + \lambda H^{(1)} + \lambda^2 H^{(2)} + \lambda^3 H^{(3)} + \cdots \tag{10-44}$$

Here each successive term is supposed to be an order of magnitude smaller than its predecessor, and λ is again a scaling parameter. An example is an electron in a potential field $V(r)$ that moves in a homogeneous magnetic field **H**. Here the Hamiltonian is

$$H = \frac{p^2}{2m} + V(r) - \frac{e}{2mc} (\mathbf{M} \cdot \mathbf{H}) + \frac{e^2}{8mc^2} [H^2 r^2 - (\mathbf{H} \cdot \mathbf{r})^2] \tag{10-45}$$

If we take the magnetic field here as the scaling parameter, then we see that the first two terms constitute H_0, the third term $\lambda H^{(1)}$, and the last term $\lambda^2 H^{(2)}$.

The perturbation equations now have a slightly different form from the expressions in Sec. 10-1. If we denote the eigenvalues and eigen-functions of H_0 again by ε_n and ϕ_n, respectively, and expand the eigen-values and eigenfunctions of H as

$$E_n = \varepsilon_n + \sum_{k=1}^{\infty} \lambda^k E_{n,k}$$

$$\psi_n = \phi_n + \sum_{k=1}^{\infty} \lambda^k \psi_{n,k}$$

(10-46)

then the analogue of Eq. (10-5) is

$$\left(H_0 + \sum_{k=1}^{\infty} \lambda^k H^{(k)} - \varepsilon_n - \sum_{k=1}^{\infty} \lambda^k E_{n,k}\right)\left(\phi_n + \sum_{k=1}^{\infty} \lambda^k \psi_{n,k}\right) = 0 \qquad (10\text{-}47)$$

The first four perturbation equations are now

$$(H_0 - \varepsilon_n)\phi_n = 0 \tag{10-48a}$$

$$(H_0 - \varepsilon_n)\psi_{n,1} = -(H^{(1)} - E_{n,1})\phi_n \tag{10-48b}$$

$$(H_0 - \varepsilon_n)\psi_{n,2} = -(H^{(1)} - E_{n,1})\psi_{n,1} - (H^{(2)} - E_{n,2})\phi_n \tag{10-48c}$$

$$(H_0 - \varepsilon_n)\psi_{n,3} = -(H^{(1)} - E_{n,1})\psi_{n,2} - (H^{(2)} - E_{n,2})\psi_{n,1} - (H^{(3)} - E_{n,3})\phi_n \tag{10-48d}$$

If H_0 is Hermitian and if we take the $\psi_{n,k}$ to be orthogonal to ϕ_n, we obtain

$$E_{n,1} = \langle\phi_n|H^{(1)}|\phi_n\rangle$$

$$E_{n,2} = \langle\phi_n|H^{(2)}|\phi_n\rangle + \langle\phi_n|H^{(1)}|\psi_{n,1}\rangle \qquad (10\text{-}49)$$

$$E_{n,3} = \langle\phi_n|H^{(3)}|\phi_n\rangle + \langle\phi_n|H^{(2)}|\psi_{n,1}\rangle + \langle\phi_n|H^{(1)}|\psi_{n,2}\rangle$$

by multiplying Eq. (10-48) on the left by ϕ_n^* and subsequent integration.

In addition to the methods that we discussed in Sec. 10-2 there exists another procedure for determining the functions $\psi_{n,k}$. This approach is based on the expansion of the $\psi_{n,k}$ in terms of the complete set of eigen-functions ϕ_k. We will show how $\psi_{n,1}$ and $\psi_{n,2}$ are obtained in this way. Again it is assumed that the state n is nondegenerate.

We expand $\psi_{n,1}$ as

$$\psi_{n,1} = \sum_{k \neq n} a_k \phi_k \tag{10-50}$$

where we may exclude the term $a_n\phi_n$, since $\psi_{n,1}$ has to be orthogonal to ϕ_n. It should be realized that this expansion should also be extended over the possible continuum states, as we discussed in Sec. 7-4. We assume that the continuum states are included in our summation sign.

Substitution of this expansion into Eq. (10-48b) gives

$$\sum_{k \neq n} a_k (H_0 - \varepsilon_n)\phi_k = -(H^{(1)} - E_{n,1})\phi_n \qquad (10\text{-}51)$$

Multiplication on the left by ϕ_m^* ($m \neq n$) and subsequent integration yield

$$a_m(\varepsilon_m - \varepsilon_n) = -\langle \phi_m | H^{(1)} | \phi_n \rangle \qquad (10\text{-}52)$$

which we abbreviate to

$$a_m = -\frac{H_{m,n}^{(1)}}{\varepsilon_m - \varepsilon_n} \qquad (10\text{-}53)$$

Hence $\psi_{n,1}$ is obtained as

$$\psi_{n,1} = -\sum_{k \neq n} \frac{H_{k,n}^{(1)}}{\varepsilon_k - \varepsilon_n} \phi_k \qquad (10\text{-}54)$$

By substituting this expression into Eq. (10-49), we derive an analytical expression for $E_{n,2}$:

$$E_{n,2} = H_{n,n}^{(2)} - \sum_{k \neq n} \frac{H_{n,k}^{(1)} H_{k,n}^{(1)}}{\varepsilon_k - \varepsilon_n} \qquad (10\text{-}55)$$

containing only the known eigenvalues and eigenfunctions of H_0.

In the same way we can substitute the expansion

$$\psi_{n,2} = \sum_{k \neq n} b_k \phi_k \qquad (10\text{-}56)$$

into Eq. (10-48c), and we find

$$(\varepsilon_k - \varepsilon_n)b_k = -\langle \phi_k | H^{(1)} | \psi_{n,1} \rangle + E_{n,1}\langle \phi_k | \psi_{n,1} \rangle - H_{k,n}^{(2)} \qquad (10\text{-}57)$$

or

$$b_k = \frac{-1}{\varepsilon_k - \varepsilon_n}\left[H_{k,n}^{(2)} + \frac{H_{n,n}^{(1)} H_{k,n}^{(1)}}{\varepsilon_k - \varepsilon_n} + \sum_{m \neq n} \frac{H_{k,m}^{(1)} H_{m,n}^{(1)}}{\varepsilon_m - \varepsilon_n} \right] \qquad (10\text{-}58)$$

We see that the correction terms $E_{n,k}$ and $\psi_{n,k}$ to the eigenvalues and eigenfunctions become increasingly more complicated as we proceed to higher orders. It is generally impractical to consider terms beyond the second-order correction to the energy and beyond the first order to the wave function. The basic assumption of perturbation theory is that λ is so small that the various expansions in terms of λ are rapidly convergent. If the convergence is so slow that we should consider higher orders, then we should not have applied perturbation theory in the first place, but instead we should have looked for different approximate methods to solve our problem.

At first sight it seems that the perturbation treatment of the present section is easier to apply than the method that we developed in Sec.

10-1. In our present description we obtain the $E_{n,k}$ and $\psi_{n,k}$ in closed form, expressed in a straightforward way in terms of a set of integrals that can all be evaluated in principle. In Sec. 10-1 we had to solve a set of differential equations. However, in practice there is little difference between the two approaches. We should realize that in Sec. 10-1 we needed to know only the ground-state wave function in order to evaluate the perturbation of the ground state. In the present section we must know the eigenfunctions of all states, and although we know them in principle, this is not quite the same as writing them all down, evaluating an infinite number of integrals, and adding up all terms. In practice only the method of Sec. 10-1 leads to exact perturbation results. The description in this section can be used for purely formal theoretical descriptions and also to obtain rough estimates of perturbation effects without much computational effort.

The latter estimates are obtained by utilizing an interesting summation theorem. If Ω and Λ are two operators, f and g two functions, and ϕ_n a complete set of functions, then we have

$$\sum_n \langle f| \Omega |\phi_n\rangle\langle\phi_n| \Lambda |g\rangle = \langle f| \Omega\Lambda |g\rangle \qquad (10\text{-}59)$$

We can prove this by expanding the function Λg in terms of the ϕ_n:

$$\Lambda g = \sum a_n\phi_n$$
$$a_n = \langle\phi_n| \Lambda |g\rangle \qquad (10\text{-}60)$$

If we now operate on both sides of the first Eq. (10-60) by Ω, we find

$$\Omega\Lambda g = \sum_n \Omega\phi_n\langle\phi_n| \Lambda |g\rangle \qquad (10\text{-}61)$$

Multiplication on the left by f^* and integration then lead to Eq. (10-59).

As an example, we consider the perturbation of a hydrogen atom in its ground state by a homogeneous electric field F. By using atomic units throughout, we write the Hamiltonian as

$$H = H_0 + FH'$$

$$H_0 = -\frac{1}{2}\Delta - \frac{1}{r} \qquad (10\text{-}62)$$

$$H' = -z$$

We will show later, in Sec. 10-5, that

$$E_0 = \varepsilon_0 + E_{0,1}F + E_{0,2}F^2 + \cdots$$
$$E_{0,1} = 0 \qquad (10\text{-}63)$$
$$E_{0,2} = -\tfrac{9}{3}$$

Let us now try to estimate these energy corrections from Eqs. (10-55) and (10-59). It follows easily that $E_{0,1} = 0$, whereas $E_{0,2}$ is given by

$$E_{0,2} = - \sum_{k \neq 0} \frac{\langle \phi_0| H' |\phi_k\rangle \langle \phi_k| H' |\phi_0\rangle}{\varepsilon_k - \varepsilon_0} \qquad (10\text{-}64)$$

where we have to sum over all excited states of the hydrogen atom. We note that every term of the infinite series is positive, and we replace the sum by

$$\sum_{k \neq 0} \frac{\langle \phi_0| H' |\phi_k\rangle \langle \phi_k| H' |\phi_0\rangle}{\varepsilon_k - \varepsilon_0} = \frac{1}{\Delta E} \sum_{k} \langle \phi_0| H' |\phi_k\rangle \langle \phi_k| H' |\phi_0\rangle \qquad (10\text{-}65)$$

We call ΔE here the *effective average excitation energy*. Although we do not know its exact value, we expect from our physical intuition that its value lies between the first excitation energy and the ionization energy of the hydrogen atom, that is,

$$\tfrac{3}{8} < \Delta E < \tfrac{1}{2} \qquad (10\text{-}66)$$

The sum on the right side of Eq. (10-65) can now be evaluated by making use of the summation theorem (10-59):

$$\sum_{k} \langle \phi_0| H' |\phi_k\rangle \langle \phi_k| H' |\phi_0\rangle = \langle \phi_0| (H')^2 |\phi_0\rangle = 1 \qquad (10\text{-}67)$$

We predict, therefore, that

$$-2 < E_{0,2} < - \tfrac{8}{3} \qquad (10\text{-}68)$$

which is in agreement with Eq. (10-63).

10-4 PERTURBATION THEORY FOR A DEGENERATE STATE

It is easier to discuss the perturbations of degenerate states on the basis of the variational principle that we discuss in Chap. 11, but we feel obliged to discuss the theory also from the point of view of perturbation theory. Again we start with a Hamiltonian H that can be expanded as

$$H = H_0 + \lambda H^{(1)} + \lambda^2 H^{(2)} + \cdots \qquad (10\text{-}69)$$

We denote the eigenvalues of H_0 by ε_k, and we assume that ε_0 is an s-fold degenerate eigenvalue with the orthonormal eigenfunctions $\phi_{0,1}, \phi_{0,2}, \phi_{0,3}, \ldots, \phi_{0,s}$. Naturally any linear combination of the functions $\phi_{0,i}$ is also an eigenfunction of H_0 belonging to ε_0.

We now assume that the operator H has one or more eigenvalues E_0 that differ from ε_0 by an amount that is of the order of magnitude of λ.

Each of these eigenvalues can then be expanded as a power series in λ, and a typical term of this kind is

$$E_0 = \varepsilon_0 + \lambda E_0' + \lambda^2 E_0'' + \cdots \qquad (10\text{-}70)$$

The corresponding eigenfunction can be written as

$$\psi_0 = \Psi_0 + \lambda \psi_0' + \lambda^2 \psi_0'' + \cdots \qquad (10\text{-}71)$$

where Ψ_0 is a linear combination of the $\phi_{0,i}$:

$$\Psi_0 = \sum_i c_i \phi_{0,i} \qquad (10\text{-}72)$$

Our perturbation equations can be derived by considering the coefficients of successive powers of λ in the equation

$$[(H_0 - \varepsilon_0) + \lambda(H^{(1)} - E_0') + \lambda^2(H^{(2)} - E_0'') + \cdots][\Psi_0 + \lambda \psi_0' + \lambda^2 \psi_0'' + \cdots] = 0$$

$$(10\text{-}73)$$

The perturbation equation of order zero is

$$(H_0 - \varepsilon_0)\Psi_0 = 0 \qquad (10\text{-}74)$$

and is always satisfied. The first-order perturbation equation is

$$(H_0 - \varepsilon_0)\psi_0' + (H^{(1)} - E_0')\Psi_0 = 0 \qquad (10\text{-}75)$$

Let us first set out to determine E_0'. We multiply Eq. (10-75) on the left by $\phi_{0,j}^*$, and we integrate. Since H_0 is Hermitian, we obtain

$$\langle \phi_{0,j} | H^{(1)} | \Psi_0 \rangle - E_0' \langle \phi_{0,j} | \Psi_0 \rangle = 0 \qquad (10\text{-}76)$$

If we now substitute Eq. (10-72) for Ψ_0, we obtain the following set of equations for the unknown coefficients c_i and for E_0':

$$\sum_i H_{j,i}^{(1)} c_i - E_0' c_j = 0 \qquad j = 1, 2, 3, \ldots, s \qquad (10\text{-}77)$$

where $$H_{j,i}^{(1)} = \langle \phi_{0,j} | H^{(1)} | \phi_{0,i} \rangle \qquad (10\text{-}78)$$

We recognize this as the eigenvalue problem of the matrix $[H_{j,i}^{(1)}]$. Let the eigenvalues of this matrix be $E_{0,1}', E_{0,2}', \ldots, E_{0,s}'$ and the corresponding eigenvectors $\mathbf{c}^k$. Then the first-order approximation to the eigenvalues close to ε_0 is

$$E_{0,k} = \varepsilon_0 + \lambda E_{0,k}' \qquad k = 1, 2, \ldots, s \qquad (10\text{-}79)$$

and the corresponding eigenfunctions, in zero-order approximation, are

$$\psi_{0,k} = \Psi_{0,k} = \sum_i c_i^k \phi_{0,i} \qquad (10\text{-}80)$$

There are now two different situations to be considered. In the first case none of the eigenvalues $E_{0,k}'$ is degenerate, and in the second there are one or more degeneracies. We do not discuss the second case here, since it will be dealt with in Chap. 11. Therefore, it is assumed that none of the eigenvalues $E'_{0,k}$ of the matrix $[H^{(1)}_{i,j}]$ is degenerate.

In order to determine the higher-order perturbation corrections, we employ now the expansions

$$E_{0,k} = \varepsilon_0 + \lambda E'_{0,k} + \lambda^2 E''_{0,k} + \cdots$$
$$\psi_{0,k} = \Psi_{0,k} + \lambda \psi'_{0,k} + \lambda^2 \psi''_{0,k} + \cdots \tag{10-81}$$

instead of Eqs. (10-70) and (10-71). After substituting these new expansions into the Schrödinger equation, we obtain, for the first-order perturbation equation,

$$(H_0 - \varepsilon_0)\psi'_{0,k} + (H^{(1)} - E'_{0,k})\Psi_{0,k} = 0 \tag{10-82}$$

For the unknown function $\psi'_{0,k}$ we substitute the expansion

$$\psi'_{0,k} = \sum_{n \neq 0} a_{k,n}\phi_n + \sum_{l \neq k} b_{k,l}\Psi_{0,l} \tag{10-83}$$

We have assumed that the functions $\phi_{0,i}$ form an orthonormal set, and consequently the $\Psi_{0,k}$ are also orthonormal. For convenience sake, we now assume that $\psi'_{0,k}$ is orthogonal to $\Psi_{0,k}$, and we omit, therefore, the term $l = k$ in the second summation of Eq. (10-83). The result of the substitution is

$$\sum_{n \neq 0} a_{k,n}(H_0 - \varepsilon_0)\phi_n + \sum_{l \neq k} b_{k,l}(H_0 - \varepsilon_0)\Psi_{0,l} + (H^{(1)} - E'_{0,k})\Psi_{0,k} = 0 \quad \tag{10-84}$$

By multiplying on the left by ϕ_m^* and integrating, we find that

$$(\varepsilon_m - \varepsilon_0)a_{k,m} + \langle \phi_m | H^{(1)} |\Psi_{0,k}\rangle = 0 \tag{10-85}$$

or

$$a_{k,m} = -\frac{\langle \phi_m | H^{(1)} |\Psi_{0,k}\rangle}{\varepsilon_m - \varepsilon_0} \tag{10-86}$$

It is not possible to derive the values for the expansion coefficients $b_{k,l}$ from Eq. (10-82), and we proceed, therefore, to the next perturbation equation.

By substituting the expansions (10-81) into the Schrödinger equation, we find that the second perturbation equation for the state $(0,k)$ is

$$(H^{(0)} - \varepsilon_0)\psi''_{0,k} + (H^{(1)} - E'_{0,k})\psi'_{0,k} + (H^{(2)} - E''_{0,k})\Psi_{0,k} = 0 \quad \tag{10-87}$$

First, we multiply this equation on the left by $\Psi^*_{0,l}$, where $l \neq k$, and integrate to give

$$\langle \Psi_{0,l}| H^{(1)} - E'_{0,k} |\psi'_{0,k}\rangle + \langle \Psi_{0,l}| H^{(2)} |\Psi_{0,k}\rangle = 0 \tag{10-88}$$

Next, we substitute the expansion (10-83) for $\psi'_{0,k}$ and obtain

$$\sum_{n\neq 0} \langle \Psi_{0,l}| H^{(1)} |\phi_n\rangle a_{k,n} + \sum_{j\neq k} \langle \Psi_{0,l}| H^{(1)} - E'_{0,k} |\Psi_{0,j}\rangle b_{k,j} + \langle \Psi_{0,l}| H^{(2)} |\Psi_{0,k}\rangle = 0$$

$$(10\text{-}89)$$

Since $\qquad\qquad \langle \Psi_{0,l}| H^{(1)} |\Psi_{0,j}\rangle = E'_{0,l}\delta_{l,j}$ $\qquad\qquad\qquad$ (10-90)

we find that

$$(E'_{0,l} - E'_{0,k})b_{k,l} = -\langle \Psi_{0,l}| H^{(2)} |\Psi_{0,k}\rangle - \sum_{n\neq 0} \langle \Psi_{0,l}| H^{(1)} |\phi_n\rangle a_{k,n} \quad (10\text{-}91)$$

or, using Eq. (10-86),

$$b_{k,l} = -\frac{\langle \Psi_{0,l}| H^{(2)} |\Psi_{0,k}\rangle}{E'_{0,l} - E'_{0,k}} + \sum_{n\neq 0} \frac{\langle \Psi_{0,l}| H^{(1)} |\phi_n\rangle\langle \phi_n| H^{(1)} |\Psi_{0,k}\rangle}{(\varepsilon_n - \varepsilon_0)(E'_{0,l} - E'_{0,k})} \quad (10\text{-}92)$$

The function $\psi'_{0,k}$ is now completely determined by Eqs. (10-83), (10-86), and (10-92).

The second-order energy correction $E''_{0,k}$ may be derived by multiplying Eq. (10-87) on the left by $\Psi^*_{0,k}$ and by subsequent integration:

$$E''_{0,k} = \langle \Psi_{0,k}| H^{(2)} |\Psi_{0,k}\rangle + \langle \Psi_{0,k}| H^{(1)} - E'_{0,k} |\psi'_{0,k}\rangle \quad (10\text{-}93)$$

If we replace $\psi'_{0,k}$ by the expansion (10-83), we find that

$$E''_{0,k} = \langle \Psi_{0,k}| H^{(2)} |\Psi_{0,k}\rangle + \sum_{n\neq 0} \langle \Psi_{0,k}| H^{(1)} |\phi_n\rangle a_{k,n} \quad (10\text{-}94)$$

or $\quad E''_{0,k} = \langle \Psi_{0,k}| H^{(2)} |\Psi_{0,k}\rangle - \sum_{n\neq 0} \frac{\langle \Psi_{0,k}| H^{(1)} |\phi_n\rangle\langle \phi_n| H^{(1)} |\Psi_{0,k}\rangle}{\varepsilon_n - \varepsilon_0} \quad (10\text{-}95)$

10-5 MODERN DEVELOPMENTS IN PERTURBATION THEORY

What we have discussed so far is known as the Rayleigh-Schrödinger perturbation theory. A similar approach is the Brillouin-Wigner perturbation theory, but we postpone its discussion until Chap. 11, since it is most conveniently derived from the variational principle. Both methods lead to formal solutions for the perturbation equations, and at first sight it seems that our discussion has covered all possibilities of perturbation theory. However, if we seek to obtain numerical results for practical problems, then we realize very soon that the discussion above leaves many questions in perturbation theory unanswered. As we have already pointed out, although we know all the eigenvalues and eigenfunctions of the operator H_0 exactly, we have to evaluate and sum an infinite number of integrals in order to obtain the energy corrections. Often the continuum states contribute significantly, and it becomes impractical to evaluate, for example, the term E_2''. Frequently we encounter even worse difficulties, since we only know approximately what the eigenvalues and eigenfunctions of the unperturbed system are. Consequently, perturbation theory is a dynamic area for research at the moment, and there have been many interesting developments in it beyond the formal theory that we discussed above.

A good survey of recent advances in perturbation theory can be found in the review article by Hirschfelder, Byers Brown, and Epstein.[1] It would lead us too far beyond the scope of this book to mention all modern developments in perturbation theory, but we wish to discuss a technique that has recently been developed and successfully applied by Dalgarno and his coworkers.

The Dalgarno perturbation method is directed toward solving Eq. (10-7) for the state 0, which is

$$(H_0 - \varepsilon_0)\psi_{0,1} + (H' - E_{0,1})\phi_0 = 0 \qquad (10\text{-}96)$$

It is assumed that the perturbation function $\psi_{0,1}$ can be written as

$$\psi_{0,1} = F\phi_0 \qquad (10\text{-}97)$$

where F is a scalar function of the variables that occur in H. This assumption is not always valid, but it is true in many cases, and then it leads to a convenient solution method for Eq. (10-96). The first term of the equation can now be represented as

$$(H_0 - \varepsilon_0)F\phi_0 = (H_0F - FH_0)\phi_0 = [H_0,F]\phi_0 \qquad (10\text{-}98)$$

We write the second term as

$$(H' - E_{0,1})\phi_0 = (H' - \langle\phi_0|H'|\phi_0\rangle)\phi_0 = V\phi_0 \qquad (10\text{-}99)$$

where the operator V is now known. Equation (10-96) becomes, then,

$$[H_0,F]\phi_0 + V\phi_0 = 0 \qquad (10\text{-}100)$$

The operator H_0 generally has the form

$$H_0 = -\tfrac{1}{2}\sum_i \nabla_i^2 + U \qquad (10\text{-}101)$$

where the subscript i can be equal to x in one-dimensional problems, equal to x and y in two dimensions, and to x, y, and z in three dimensions. Since U and F commute, we can replace Eq. (10-100) by

$$\sum_i [\nabla_i^2,F]\phi_0 = 2V\phi_0 \qquad (10\text{-}102)$$

[1] J. O. Hirschfelder, W. Byers Brown, and S. T. Epstein, Recent Developments in Perturbation Theory, in "Advances in Quantum Chemistry," vol. I, Academic Press Inc., New York, 1964.

It may seem strange to the reader, but in practice we often encounter the difficulty that we do not know what H_0 is in our perturbation problems. These are situations where we know an approximate eigenfunction ϕ_0 of a Hamiltonian H and where we wish to improve the accuracy of the eigenfunction by means of perturbation theory. Since ϕ_0 is an approximate eigenfunction of H, there must be another Hamiltonian H_0, close to H, of which ϕ_0 is an eigenfunction, but often it is not possible to determine H_0. In situations of this type the Dalgarno perturbation method has the great advantage that we do not have to know H_0. It is easily seen that

$$(H_0 - \langle \phi_0 | H_0 | \phi_0 \rangle)\phi_0 = 0 \tag{10-103}$$

If we combine this with Eq. (10-99) we find that V can also be defined by

$$V\phi_0 = (H - \langle \phi_0 | H | \phi_0 \rangle)\phi_0 \tag{10-104}$$

so that it depends on the total Hamiltonian H only.

Usually Eq. (10-102) is written in a slightly different form when F may be assumed to be real. If we multiply on the left by ϕ_0^*, we obtain

$$\sum_i \left(\phi_0^* \phi_0 \frac{\partial^2 F}{\partial r_i^2} + 2\phi_0^* \frac{\partial \phi_0}{\partial r_i} \frac{\partial F}{\partial r_i} \right) = 2\phi_0^* V \phi_0 \tag{10-105}$$

The complex conjugate of Eq. (10-105) is

$$\sum_i \left(\phi_0 \phi_0^* \frac{\partial^2 F}{\partial r_i^2} + 2\phi_0 \frac{\partial \phi_0^*}{\partial r_i} \frac{\partial F}{\partial r_i} \right) = 2\phi_0 V^* \phi_0^* \tag{10-106}$$

if F is real. Addition of the two equations gives

$$\sum_i \mathbf{\nabla}_i \cdot (\phi_0^* \phi_0 \mathbf{\nabla}_i F) = \phi_0^* V \phi_0 + \phi_0 V^* \phi_0^* \tag{10-107}$$

If ϕ_0 and V are also real, this reduces to

$$\sum_i \mathbf{\nabla}_i \cdot (\phi_0^2 \mathbf{\nabla}_i F) = 2\phi_0 V \phi_0 \tag{10-108}$$

In order to illustrate this technique, we apply it to the Stark effect of the ground state of the hydrogen atom. Here the total Hamiltonian is

$$H = -\frac{1}{2}\Delta - \frac{1}{r} - \lambda z \tag{10-109}$$

if we use atomic units throughout and if we denote the electric field strength by λ. Consequently

$$H' = -z \tag{10-110}$$

We know that the ground-state wave function of the hydrogen atom is

$$\phi_0 = (\pi)^{-1/2} e^{-r} \tag{10-111}$$

It easily follows that

$$E_{0,1} = \langle \phi_0 | H' | \phi_0 \rangle = 0 \tag{10-112}$$

so that $V = H'$. If we substitute Eqs. (10-110) to (10-112) into Eq. (10-108), we find that the differential equation for F is

$$e^{2r} \sum_i \frac{\partial}{\partial r_i} \left(e^{-2r} \frac{\partial F}{\partial r_i} \right) = -2z \tag{10-113}$$

or

$$-\Delta F + \frac{2}{r} \left(x \frac{\partial F}{\partial x} + y \frac{\partial F}{\partial y} + z \frac{\partial F}{\partial z} \right) = 2z \tag{10-114}$$

We observe that

$$\Delta(z) = 0 \qquad \Delta(zr) = \frac{4z}{r} \tag{10-115}$$

and also that

$$\Omega(z) = \frac{z}{r} \qquad \Omega(zr) = 2z \tag{10-116}$$

if we introduce the operator

$$\Omega = \frac{1}{r} \left(x \frac{\partial}{\partial x} + y \frac{\partial}{\partial y} + z \frac{\partial}{\partial z} \right) \tag{10-117}$$

Hence, we substitute

$$F = az + bzr \tag{10-118}$$

into Eq. (10-114), and we find

$$(2a - 4b) \frac{z}{r} + 4bz = 2z \tag{10-119}$$

This equation is satisfied if $a = 1$, $b = \frac{1}{2}$ and the solution of Eq. (10-114) is

$$F = z(1 + \frac{1}{2}r) \tag{10-120}$$

It follows from Eq. (10-17) that $E_{0,2}$ can be written as

$$E_{0,2} = \langle \phi_0 | H' | F\phi_0 \rangle \tag{10-121}$$

and we find

$$E_{0,2} = -\frac{9}{4} \tag{10-122}$$

This is the result that we used in Eq. (10-63).

In one-dimensional problems we can often integrate Eq. (10-108) directly. If the wave function $\phi_0(x)$ is defined in the interval $a \leqslant x \leqslant b$ and if the boundary conditions for the wave function ϕ_0 are

$$\phi_0(a) = \phi_0(b) = 0 \qquad \phi_0'(a) = \phi_0'(b) = 0 \tag{10-123}$$

then the same boundary conditions are valid for the perturbed function, so that

$$\phi_0(a)F(a) = \phi_0(b)F(b) = 0 \qquad [\phi_0(a)]^2 F'(a) = [\phi_0(b)]^2 F'(b) = 0 \qquad (10\text{-}124)$$

Equation (10-108) is now

$$\frac{d}{dx}\left(\phi_0^2 \frac{dF}{dx}\right) = 2\phi_0 V \phi_0 \qquad (10\text{-}125)$$

and if we integrate once, we find

$$\frac{dF}{dx} = \frac{2}{\phi_0^2}\int_a^x \phi_0(y)V(y)\phi_0(y)\,dy \qquad (10\text{-}126)$$

A second integration gives

$$F(x) = F(a) + 2\int_a^x [\phi_0(z)]^{-2}\,dz \int_a^z \phi_0(y)V(y)\phi_0(y)\,dy \qquad (10\text{-}127)$$

However, this procedure is valid only when the function ϕ_0 has no nodes in the interval $a \leqslant x \leqslant b$, and this means it is applicable to the ground state only. Once we have determined F, it is relatively easy to determine $E_{0,2}$.

The energy correction $E_{0,3}$ can also be derived from ϕ_0, F, and V. We have, in this case,

$$E_{0,3} = \langle \phi_0 | FVF | \phi_0 \rangle = \tfrac{1}{2} \sum_i \langle F^2 | \nabla_i \cdot | \phi_0^2 \, \nabla_i F \rangle$$
$$= -\sum_i \langle \phi_0 | F | (\nabla_i F \cdot \nabla_i F)\phi_0 \rangle \qquad (10\text{-}128)$$

The proof of these expressions may be found in the above-mentioned review by Hirschfelder and others. We do not attempt to reproduce it here.

PROBLEMS

10-1 Calculate the second-order energy correction due to a magnetic field of a hydrogen atom in its ground state. If we take the magnetic field **H** along the z axis, the total Hamiltonian of the system is given by

$$H = -\frac{\hbar^2}{2m}\Delta - \frac{e}{2mc}HM_z + \frac{e^2}{8mc^2}H^2(x^2 + y^2)$$

10-2 Derive the expressions for $E_{n,3}$ and $\psi_{n,2}$ in terms of the eigenvalues and eigenfunctions of the unperturbed system if the state is nondegenerate.

10-3 Evaluate the corrections to the energy and eigenfunction of the ground state of the hydrogen atom due to a point charge e located at a large distance R from the nucleus on the z axis. (Hint: The perturbation potential $V = e(R^2 + r^2 - 2Rr \cos \theta)^{-1/2}$ can be expanded as

$$V = \frac{e}{R} \sum_n \left(\frac{r}{R}\right)^n P_n (\cos \theta)$$

Treat R^{-1} now as the perturbation parameter.)

10-4 Derive the second-order perturbation of a homogeneous electric field on the ground state of a harmonic oscillator by means of the Dalgarno perturbation theory.

10-5 Derive the second-order perturbation of a homogeneous electric field on the ground state of a particle in a one-dimentional box by means of the Dalgarno perturbation theory.

10-6 Evaluate the first- and second-order energy corrections to the ground state of the harmonic oscillator due to a perturbation $V = \alpha x^3$. It suffices if the result is obtained in the form of an infinite sum.

THE VARIATION THEOREM

11-1 DEFINITION

The theorem that is discussed in the present section shows the equivalence of the eigenvalue problems involving operators and those involving matrices. It has been used to derive procedures that lead to approximations to eigenvalues and eigenfunctions of a given operator. The theorems that are discussed in Sec. 11-2 predict upper and lower bounds for the smallest eigenvalue of a given operator. It is customary to use the name *variation theorem* to describe all these theorems, although this is somewhat confusing.

Let us first investigate what is meant by an infinitesimal variation of a function f of a number of variables. As an example, we take the function

$$f(x) = (a_1 + a_2 x) \exp\left(-\frac{a_3 x^2}{(a_4 + a_5 x^2)^{1/2}}\right) \qquad (11\text{-}1)$$

If any of the parameters a_k is varied by a small amount δa_k, then we get a slightly different function $f(x) + \delta f(x)$, and we can write

$$\delta f = \sum_k \frac{\partial f}{\partial a_k} \delta a_k \qquad (11\text{-}2)$$

However, there are many more ways of obtaining a slightly different function. For example, if we replace the term a_3x^2 by $a_3x^2 + \delta a_6$, we also get a new function $f + \delta f$. In general, there are an infinite number of ways to get a different function $f + \delta f$. We can imagine that we expand the function $f(x)$ in terms of a complete set of functions ϕ_n:

$$f(x) = \sum_n c_n \phi_n(x) \tag{11-3}$$

If we replace any of the coefficients c_n by $c_n + \delta c_n$, then we obtain a variation of the function $f(x)$ by an amount δf. Hence, if we talk about all possible variations δf of a function f, we should recognize that there are an infinite number of them.

We now consider a Hermitian operator H and an arbitrary function f, and we construct the two integrals

$$E = \langle f | H | f \rangle \qquad S = \langle f | f \rangle \tag{11-4}$$

An arbitrary variation δf in the function f leads to a variation δE in E and a variation δS in S:

$$\delta E = \langle \delta f | H | f \rangle + \langle f | H | \delta f \rangle$$
$$\delta S = \langle \delta f | f \rangle + \langle f | \delta f \rangle \tag{11-5}$$

Instead of considering all possible variations δf, we want to restrict ourselves to those variations $\delta f'$ for which $\delta S = 0$. It is not difficult to derive a general expression for these variations $\delta f'$. Let δf_1 be a variation for which

$$\langle \delta f_1 | f \rangle + \langle f | \delta f_1 \rangle \neq 0 \tag{11-6}$$

Then we have, in general,

$$\delta f' = \delta f - \alpha \delta f_1$$
$$\alpha = \frac{\langle \delta f | f \rangle + \langle f | \delta f \rangle}{\langle \delta f_1 | f \rangle + \langle f | \delta f_1 \rangle} \tag{11-7}$$

if δf is an arbitrary variation. It is important to recognize that α is real.

We now impose the condition that $\delta E = 0$ for all possible variations $\delta f'$. We find

$$\langle \delta f - \alpha \delta f_1 | H | f \rangle + \langle f | H | \delta f - \alpha \delta f_1 \rangle = 0 \tag{11-8}$$

We can also write this as

$$[\langle \delta f | H | f \rangle + \langle f | H | \delta f \rangle] - \lambda [\langle \delta f | f \rangle + \langle f | \delta f \rangle] = 0 \tag{11-9}$$

if we define the real number λ as

$$\lambda = \frac{\langle \delta f_1 | H | f \rangle + \langle f | H | \delta f_1 \rangle}{\langle \delta f_1 | f \rangle + \langle f | \delta f_1 \rangle} \tag{11-10}$$

This number is the same for all possible variations δf. Since H is Hermitian and λ is real, we write Eq. (11-9) as

$$\mathscr{R}\langle \delta f | H - \lambda | f \rangle = 0 \tag{11-11}$$

This equation can be satisfied for all possible variations δf only if

$$(H - \lambda)f = 0 \tag{11-12}$$

which means that f is an eigenfunction of H with eigenvalue λ. We find, thus, that f is an eigenfunction of H if $\delta E = 0$ for all variations $\delta f'$ that satisfy the restraint $\delta S = 0$.

The reader may recognize this derivation as a variational problem with an auxiliary restraint. Our parameter λ is actually the Lagrangian multiplier that is used in solving this kind of problem. We did not make use of the calculus of variations, since some readers may not be familiar with it.

The variation theorem above is in every respect equivalent to the matrix representation of the Schrödinger equation that we discussed in Chap. 7. If we have a complete set of functions ϕ_n, then any function f can be expanded as

$$f = \sum_n c_n \phi_n \tag{11-13}$$

and any variation δf in f is obtained by varying the expansion coefficients c_n. The integrals E and S can now be reduced to

$$E = \langle f | H | f \rangle = \sum_n \sum_m c_n c_m^* H_{m,n}$$

$$S = \langle f | f \rangle = \sum_n \sum_m c_n c_m^* S_{m,n} \tag{11-14}$$

if

$$H_{m,n} = \langle \phi_m | H | \phi_n \rangle = H_{n,m}^*$$

$$S_{m,n} = \langle \phi_m | \phi_n \rangle = \delta_{m,n} \tag{11-15}$$

The variational problem is

$$\delta E - \lambda \, \delta S = \delta \sum_n \sum_m c_n c_m^* (H_{m,n} - \lambda \, \delta_{m,n}) = 0 \tag{11-16}$$

The variation is zero if the derivatives with respect to the parameters c_n are zero. If we differentiate Eq. (11-16) with respect to the real and imaginary parts of c_n, we find that the variational problem is equivalent to the sets of equations

$$\sum_m (H_{n,m} - \lambda \, \delta_{n,m}) c_m = 0$$

$$\sum_m (H_{m,n} - \lambda \, \delta_{m,n}) c_m^* = 0 \tag{11-17}$$

The second set is the complex conjugate of the first set, and we can disregard it. The first set of equations represents the eigenvalue problem of the matrix $[H_{n,m}]$.

It follows that, in principle, the variation theorem above does not teach us anything that we did not know before. However, we can regard it as a starting point for deriving several useful approaches to solve the Schrödinger equation approximately. In practice, we may attempt to approximate some of the eigenfunctions of H by the expansions

$$f_N(x) = \sum_{n=1}^{N} c_n \phi_n(x) \tag{11-18}$$

where $\phi_1, \phi_2, \ldots, \phi_N$ are the first N fuctions of the complete set of functions ϕ_n. We construct the integrals

$$E_N = \langle f_N | H | f_N \rangle \qquad S_N = \langle f_N | f_N \rangle \tag{11-19}$$

and we solve the variational problem

$$\delta E_N - \lambda \delta S_N = 0 \tag{11-20}$$

This supplies us with N eigenvalues of the matrix $[H_{m,n}]$ of order N and their corresponding eigenvectors. If N tends to infinity, then in the limit we obtain the exact eigenvalues and eigenfunctions of H. The interesting question is how the eigenvalues and eigenvectors of Eq. (11-20) for finite N compare with the true eigenvalues and eigenvectors of the infinite matrix. This problem has attracted a good deal of attention, and it has led to some useful theorems concerning upper and lower bounds of eigenvalues, which we discuss in Sec. 11-2.

11-2 UPPER AND LOWER BOUNDS OF EIGENVALUES

One of the most useful theorems in quantum theory is the following. Let H be a Hermitian operator with the eigenvalues ε_n and the corresponding eigenfunctions ϕ_n, and let ε_1 be the smallest of the eigenvalues. Then, if f is an arbitrary function, we have

$$\frac{\langle f | H | f \rangle}{\langle f | f \rangle} \geqslant \varepsilon_1 \tag{11-21}$$

The equality in Eq. (11-21) holds only when f is identical to ϕ_1. In order to prove this inequality, we imagine that f is expanded in terms of the ϕ_n:

$$f = \sum c_n \phi_n \tag{11-22}$$

It may then be derived that

$$\langle f | H - \varepsilon_1 | f \rangle = \sum_n \sum_m c_n c_m^* \langle \phi_m | H - \varepsilon_1 | \phi_n \rangle = \sum_n \sum_m c_m^* c_n (\varepsilon_n - \varepsilon_1) \delta_{m,n}$$

$$= \sum_n c_n c_n^* (\varepsilon_n - \varepsilon_1) \tag{11-23}$$

The result is positive or zero, since every term in the infinite series is nonnegative. Hence, we have

$$\langle f | H - \varepsilon_1 | f \rangle \geqslant 0 \tag{11-24}$$

or $$\langle f | H | f \rangle \geqslant \varepsilon_1 \langle f | f \rangle \tag{11-25}$$

In practice this theorem has proved to be very useful for deriving approximate eigenvalues and eigenfunctions for the ground states of various systems. Especially in quantum chemistry it has been widely applied, and in reading some books on molecular orbital calculations, one gets the impression that it has almost replaced the Schrödinger equation as the basic equation of quantum theory. We assume that we have a Hermitian operator H and that we have a rough idea of what its ground state eigenfunction ϕ_1 looks like. We now construct a function $\Phi(x; s_1, s_2, \ldots, s_N)$ that contains, in addition to the particle coordinates, which we symbolically denote by x, a number of arbitrary parameters s_i. The expectation value

$$E(s_1, s_2, \ldots, s_N) = \frac{\langle \Phi | H | \Phi \rangle}{\langle \Phi | \Phi \rangle} \tag{11-26}$$

is then always larger than or equal to the lowest eigenvalue ε_1 of H. We now determine the set of values s_i^0 for which $E(s_1, s_2, \ldots, s_N)$ has a minimum by solving the equations

$$\frac{\partial E(s_1, s_2, \ldots, s_N)}{\partial s_i} = 0 \tag{11-27}$$

The energy $E_0 = E(s_1^0, s_2^0, \ldots, s_N^0)$ and the function $\Phi_0 = \Phi(x; s_1^0, s_2^0, \ldots, s_N^0)$ are then the best possible approximation to ε_1 and its eigenfunction ϕ_1 that can be obtained from the function Φ.

The essential feature of this procedure is the choice of the function Φ, and this choice is a matter of physical or chemical intuition. In many cases this is a difficult decision to make, but sometimes the choice is obvious. As an example, we discuss the harmonic oscillator in a homogeneous electric field. This problem was treated in Chap. 10 from the point of view of perturbation theory.

According to Eq. (10-24) we can represent the Hamiltonian of a harmonic oscillator in an homogeneous electric field **F** as

$$H = -\frac{d^2}{dx^2} + x^2 - 2\mu x \qquad (11\text{-}28)$$

if we introduce the proper units. Since the ground-state wave function in the absence of a magnetic field is $\exp(-\frac{1}{2}x^2)$, we take our variational function as

$$\Phi = (1 + sx)e^{-(1/2)x^2} \qquad (11\text{-}29)$$

It is easily verified that

$$\langle \Phi | \Phi \rangle = \int_{-\infty}^{\infty} e^{-x^2}\, dx + s^2 \int_{-\infty}^{\infty} x^2 e^{-x^2}\, dx = \sqrt{\pi}\left(1 + \frac{1}{2}s^2\right) \qquad (11\text{-}30)$$

From Eq. (10-25) we derive that

$$\left(-\frac{d^2}{dx^2} + x^2\right)e^{-(1/2)x^2} = e^{-(1/2)x^2} \qquad (11\text{-}31)$$

$$\left(-\frac{d^2}{dx^2} + x^2\right)xe^{-(1/2)x^2} = 3xe^{-(1/2)x^2}$$

Hence

$$\langle \Phi | H | \Phi \rangle = \int_{-\infty}^{\infty} (1 + sx)(1 - 2\mu x)e^{-x^2}\, dx + s\int_{-\infty}^{\infty} (1 + sx)(3 - 2\mu x)xe^{-x^2}\, dx$$

$$= \int_{-\infty}^{\infty} e^{-x^2}\, dx + (3s^2 - 4\mu s)\int_{-\infty}^{\infty} x^2 e^{-x^2}\, dx$$

$$= \frac{1}{2}\sqrt{\pi}(2 + 3s^2 - 4\mu s) \qquad (11\text{-}32)$$

We obtain, therefore,

$$E(s) = \frac{\langle \Phi | H | \Phi \rangle}{\langle \Phi | \Phi \rangle} = \frac{2 + 3s^2 - 4\mu s}{2 + s^2} \qquad (11\text{-}33)$$

This has a minimum for

$$s^0 = \frac{1}{\mu}(\sqrt{1 + 2\mu^2} - 1) \qquad (11\text{-}34)$$

and the minimum is

$$E(s^0) = \frac{(3 + 6\mu^2) - (3 + 2\mu^2)\sqrt{1 + 2\mu^2}}{1 + 2\mu^2 - \sqrt{1 + 2\mu^2}}$$

For small values of μ we can expand $E(s^0)$ as

$$E(s^0) \simeq \frac{\mu^2 - \frac{1}{2}\mu^4}{\mu^2 + \frac{1}{2}\mu^4} \simeq 1 - \mu^2 \qquad (11\text{-}35)$$

and $\Phi(s^0)$ as

$$\Phi(s^0) \simeq (1 + \mu x)e^{-(1/2)x^2} \tag{11-36}$$

These results are in agreement with Eq. (10-39).

From the inequality (11-21) we can also make some predictions about the results of a variational treatment with a limited set of functions as a basis. Let H be a Hermitian operator with eigenvalues ε_n and corresponding eigenfunctions u_n, and let $\psi_1, \psi_2, \ldots, \psi_n, \ldots$, etc., be a complete set of functions. Now we construct the integrals

$$H_N = \langle g_N | H | g_N \rangle$$
$$S_N = \langle g_N | g_N \rangle \tag{11-37}$$

where g_N is the expansion

$$g_N = \sum_{n=1}^{N} c_n^N \psi_n \tag{11-38}$$

The solution of the variational problem

$$\delta(H_N - \lambda S_N) = 0 \tag{11-39}$$

consists now of a set of N eigenvalues $\lambda_1^N, \lambda_2^N, \ldots, \lambda_N^N$ with a corresponding set of eigenvectors $\mathbf{a}_k^N$ from which we can construct the functions

$$f_k^N = \sum_{n=1}^{N} a_{k,n}^N \psi_n \tag{11-40}$$

We assume that the eigenvalues λ_k and also the eigenvalues ε_n are arranged in ascending order, so that

$$\lambda_1^N \leqslant \lambda_2^N \leqslant \lambda_3^N \leqslant \lambda_4^N \leqslant \cdots \leqslant \lambda_N^N$$
$$\varepsilon_1 \leqslant \varepsilon_2 \leqslant \varepsilon_3 \leqslant \varepsilon_4 \leqslant \cdots \tag{11-41}$$

It may be derived from Eq. (11-21) that always

$$\lambda_1^N \geqslant \varepsilon_1 \tag{11-42}$$

Furthermore, we found in Sec. 11-1 that

$$\lim_{N \to \infty} \lambda_1^N = \varepsilon_1 \tag{11-43}$$

It has also been shown[1] that for the other eigenvalues we have the inequalities

$$\lambda_2^N \geqslant \varepsilon_2, \lambda_3^N \geqslant \varepsilon_3, \ldots, \lambda_N^N \geqslant \varepsilon_N \tag{11-44}$$

[1] J. K. L. MacDonald, *Phys. Rev.*, 43: 830 (1933).

The proof is rather complicated, and we do not attempt to reproduce it here.

It seems reasonable to conclude from the relations above that the difference between λ_k^N and ε_k becomes smaller with increasing N. However, it is quite another matter to predict exactly what the magnitudes of these differences are. This question has been studied extensively, but the results of these investigations cannot be expressed in any simple form.

Heretofore we have made predictions only about the upper bounds of the eigenvalues. There are also some theorems that are concerned with the lower bounds. In general, they are not very useful, and consequently they are little known. As an illustration we derive one of them. If the function f is again given by Eq. (11-22), then it follows readily that

$$\langle f|(H - \varepsilon_1)(H - \varepsilon_2)|f\rangle = \sum_n \sum_m c_n^* c_m \langle \phi_n|(H - \varepsilon_1)(H - \varepsilon_2)|\phi_m\rangle$$

$$= \sum_n (\varepsilon_n - \varepsilon_1)(\varepsilon_n - \varepsilon_2)c_n c_n^* \geqslant 0 \qquad (11\text{-}45)$$

or $\qquad \langle f|H^2|f\rangle - (\varepsilon_1 + \varepsilon_2)\langle f|H|f\rangle + \varepsilon_1 \varepsilon_2 \langle f|f\rangle \geqslant 0 \qquad (11\text{-}46)$

We can write this as

$$\varepsilon_1[\langle f|H|f\rangle - \varepsilon_2\langle f|f\rangle] \leqslant [\langle f|H^2|f\rangle - \varepsilon_2\langle f|H|f\rangle] \qquad (11\text{-}47)$$

Presumably f is a reasonably good approximation to the ground-state eigenfunction of H, so that we may assume that

$$\langle f|H|f\rangle < \langle f|f\rangle \varepsilon_2 \qquad (11\text{-}48)$$

We then find that

$$\varepsilon_1 \geqslant \frac{\varepsilon_2\langle f|H|f\rangle - \langle f|H^2|f\rangle}{\varepsilon_2\langle f|f\rangle - \langle f|H|f\rangle} \qquad (11\text{-}49)$$

If we combine this with Eq. (11-21), we obtain

$$\frac{\varepsilon_2\langle f|H|f\rangle - \langle f|H^2|f\rangle}{\varepsilon_2\langle f|f\rangle - \langle f|H|f\rangle} \leqslant \varepsilon_1 \leqslant \frac{\langle f|H|f\rangle}{\langle f|f\rangle} \qquad (11\text{-}50)$$

and we have obtained both an upper and a lower bound for ε_1. In practice, however, it is rather difficult to evaluate the lower bound, and predictions of lower bounds have not proved to be very useful.

From Eq. (11-21) we can also derive some interesting inequalities that are useful in perturbation calculations. In Sec. 10-1 we derived that the first-order perturbation correction $\psi_{0,1}$ to the unperturbed eigenfunction ϕ_0 is determined by the equation

$$(H_0 - \varepsilon_0)\psi_{0,1} + (H' - E_{0,1})\phi_0 = 0 \qquad (11\text{-}51)$$

and that the energy corrections $E_{0,1}$ and $E_{0,2}$ are given by

$$E_{0,1} = \langle \phi_0 | H' | \phi_0 \rangle$$
$$E_{0,2} = \langle \phi_0 | H' - E_{0,1} | \psi_{0,1} \rangle$$

(11-52)

Let us now imagine that we know H_0, ϕ_0, and ε_0 exactly and we wish to evaluate $E_{0,2}$, but we are unable to solve the differential equation (11-51). For situations like this, Hylleraas[1] devised an interesting variational approach that is based on the inequality

$$E_{0,2} \leqslant \langle g | H_0 - \varepsilon_0 | g \rangle + \langle g | H' - E_{0,1} | \phi_0 \rangle + \langle \phi_0 | H' - E_{0,1} | g \rangle$$

(11-53)

where g is an arbitrary function. In order to prove Eq. (11-53), we transform its right side with the aid of Eq. (11-51):

$$\langle g | H_0 - \varepsilon_0 | g \rangle + \langle g | H' - E_{0,1} | \phi_0 \rangle + \langle \phi_0 | H' - E_{0,1} | g \rangle$$
$$= \langle g | H_0 - \varepsilon_0 | g \rangle - \langle g | H_0 - \varepsilon_0 | \psi_{0,1} \rangle - \langle \psi_{0,1} | H_0 - \varepsilon_0 | g \rangle$$
$$+ \langle \psi_{0,1} | H_0 - \varepsilon_0 | \psi_{0,1} \rangle - \langle \psi_{0,1} | H_0 - \varepsilon_0 | \psi_{0,1} \rangle$$
$$= \langle g - \psi_{0,1} | H_0 - \varepsilon_0 | g - \psi_{0,1} \rangle - \langle \psi_{0,1} | H_0 - \varepsilon_0 | \psi_{0,1} \rangle \quad \text{(11-54)}$$

Since
$$E_{0,2} = - \langle \psi_{0,1} | H_0 - \varepsilon_0 | \psi_{0,1} \rangle$$
(11-55)

we have

$$\langle g | H_0 - \varepsilon_0 | g \rangle + \langle g | H' - E_{0,1} | \phi_0 \rangle + \langle \phi_0 | H' - E_{0,1} | g \rangle$$
$$= E_{0,2} + \langle g - \psi_{0,1} | H_0 - \varepsilon_0 | g - \psi_{0,1} \rangle \quad \text{(11-56)}$$

It follows from Eq. (11-21) that

$$\langle g - \psi_{0,1} | H_0 - \varepsilon_0 | g - \psi_{0,1} \rangle \geqslant 0$$
(11-57)

and therefore we have proved the inequality (11-53). Thus, we can obtain approximate results for perturbation calculations by means of variational methods.

From Eq. (11-55) it also follows that

$$E_{0,2} \leqslant 0$$
(11-58)

which is an obvious but still interesting inequality.

11-3 CONNECTIONS BETWEEN PERTURBATION THEORY AND THE VARIATION THEOREM

Most of the results that were derived in Chap. 10 on perturbation theory can also be obtained by starting from the variation theorem of

[1] E. A. Hylleraas, *Zeits. f. Physik*, **65**: 209 (1930).

Sec. 11-1. In many cases it becomes a matter of taste whether one wants to use a perturbation approach or a variational approach to solve a specific problem. Personally we tend to favor the latter because of its greater flexibility, but many scientists prefer the former, since this enables them to estimate the magnitudes of possible errors. The perturbation results that we derive from the variation theorem are usually known as the Brillouin-Wigner perturbation method, as opposed to the Rayleigh-Schrödinger theory of Chap. 10. The differences between the two theories are relatively minor, and the two methods can easily be transformed into one another. We distinguish between them because they are directed toward slightly different purposes.

Again we seek to determine the eigenvalues and eigenfunctions of an operator H that can be seperated into

$$H = H_0 + H' \tag{11-59}$$

We assume that we know the eigenvalues ε_n and the corresponding eigenfunctions ϕ_n of H_0. If we make use of the variation theorem of Sec. 11-1, we can reduce our problem to

$$\delta[\langle f| H |f \rangle - E\langle f | f \rangle] = 0 \tag{11-60}$$

As our trial function f we take the expansion

$$f = \sum_n c_n \phi_n \tag{11-61}$$

in terms of the complete set of eigenfunctions of H_0. The eigenvalues of H are the roots of the equation

$$|H_{n,m} - E\delta_{n,m}| = 0 \tag{11-62}$$

and the corresponding eigenfunctions are obtained by solving the equations

$$\sum_m (H_{n,m} - E\delta_{n,m})c_m = 0 \tag{11-63}$$

Here we have to substitute for E one of the roots of Eq. (11-62).

Let us now consider a nondegenerate state 0 of H_0 for which

$$|H_{n,0}| \ll |\varepsilon_n - \varepsilon_0| \tag{11-64}$$

for all values of n. It may then be expected that H has an eigenvalue E_0, close to ε_0, so that

$$|E_0 - \varepsilon_0| \ll |\varepsilon_n - \varepsilon_0| \tag{11-65}$$

The corresponding eigenfunction f_0 can be written as

$$f_0 = \sum a_n \phi_n \tag{11-66}$$

It follows from Eq. (11-63) that the coefficients a_n are the solutions of the equations

$$\sum_m (H_{n,m} - E_0\delta_{n,m})a_m = 0 \tag{11-67}$$

Since

$$H_{n,m} = \varepsilon_n\,\delta_{n,m} + H'_{n,m}$$
$$H'_{n,m} = \langle \phi_n| H' |\phi_m\rangle \tag{11-68}$$

we can also write these equations as

$$\sum_m [H'_{n,m} + (\varepsilon_n - E_0)\,\delta_{n,m}]a_m = 0 \tag{11-69}$$

Let us first seperate this set of equations into the equation where $n = 0$

$$(H'_{0,0} + \varepsilon_0 - E_0)a_0 = - \sum_{m\neq 0} H'_{0,m}a_m \tag{11-70}$$

and into the set where $n \neq 0$, which we can write as

$$(H'_{n,n} + \varepsilon_n - E_0)a_n = - H'_{n,0}a_0 - \sum_{m\neq n\neq 0} H'_{n,m}a_m \tag{11-71}$$

Obviously we may anticipate that

$$E_0 \simeq \varepsilon_0 + H'_{0,0}$$
$$a_0 \simeq 1$$
$$|a_n| \ll 1 \qquad n \neq 0 \tag{11-72}$$

We may therefore divide Eq. (11-70) and (11-71) by a_0 and introduce the new variables

$$b_n = \frac{a_n}{a_0} \qquad n \neq 0 \tag{11-73}$$

In addition, we define

$$U_n = H'_{n,n} + \varepsilon_n$$
$$U_0 = H'_{0,0} + \varepsilon_0 \tag{11-74}$$

We now obtain

$$E_0 = U_0 + \sum_n H'_{0,n}\, b_n \tag{11-75}$$

where the b_n are determined by the equations

$$b_n = - \frac{H'_{n,0}}{U_n - E_0} - \sum_{m\neq n} \frac{H'_{n,m}}{U_n - E_0} b_m \tag{11-76}$$

These equations can now be solved by iteration. The first-order approximation is

$$b_n \simeq - \frac{H'_{n,0}}{U_n - E_0} \tag{11-77}$$

which gives

$$E_0 \simeq U_0 - \sum_n \frac{H'_{0,n} H'_{n,0}}{U_n - E_0} \simeq U_0 - \sum_n \frac{H'_{0,n} H'_{n,0}}{U_n - U_0} \qquad (11\text{-}78)$$

The second-order approximate solution is obtained by substituting the first-order approximation (11-77) into the right side of Eq. (11-76):

$$b_n \simeq -\frac{H'_{n,0}}{U_n - E_0} + \sum_{m \neq n} \frac{H'_{n,m} H'_{m,0}}{(U_n - E_0)(U_m - E_0)} \qquad (11\text{-}79)$$

and by substituting Eq. (11-78) for E_0. We may simplify this by expanding

$$\frac{1}{U_n - E_0} \simeq \frac{1}{U_n - U_0} - \frac{1}{(U_n - U_0)^2} \sum_k \frac{H'_{0,k} H'_{k,0}}{U_k - U_0} \qquad (11\text{-}80)$$

In this fashion we obtain the successive perturbation terms in a straightforward manner. In our opinion this approach has another great advantage compared with the perturbation theory of Chap. 10; namely, we do not need to know what H_0 is. It is easily verified that the treatment above is also valid if we consider only the matrix elements $H_{n,m}$ of H. If we define

$$U_n = \langle \phi_n | H | \phi_n \rangle$$
$$H_{n,m} = \langle \phi_n | H | \phi_m \rangle \qquad (11\text{-}81)$$

and if

$$|H_{n,m}| \ll |U_n - U_0| \qquad (11\text{-}82)$$

then we can obtain the perturbation equations

$$E_0 = U_0 + \sum_n H_{0,n} b_n$$
$$b_n = -\frac{H_{n,0}}{U_n - E_0} - \sum_{m \neq n} \frac{H_{n,m}}{U_n - E_0} b_m \qquad (11\text{-}83)$$

by exactly the same arguments that we used in the derivation of Eqs. (11-75) and (11-76). Since the two sets of perturbation equations are identical if we replace $H'_{n,m}$ by $H_{n,m}$ everywhere, their results are also identical if we make the same substitution. Elsewhere[1] we have studied by means of the variational perturbation method above, the situation where the complete set of functions ϕ_n are not orthonormal, and we have derived the second-order perturbation corrections.

Let us study, finally, the perturbation theory for degenerate or near-degenerate states. We again consider the Hamiltonian (11-59), but now

[1] H. F. Hameka, "Advanced Quantum Chemistry," Addison-Wesley Publishing Company, Inc., Reading, Mass., 1965.

we assume that H_0 has a finite set of eigenvalues $\varepsilon_1, \varepsilon_2, \ldots, \varepsilon_N$ that are grouped closely together so that their differences are of the order of magnitude of the $H_{k,l}$. We denote these eigenvalues by the subscripts k or l. The other eigenvalues, for which we use subscripts n or m, are seperated from the ε_k by larger energy differences so that

$$|\varepsilon_n - \varepsilon_k| \gg H'_{n,k} \tag{11-84}$$

If we again expand the eigenfunctions of H in terms of the orthonormal set of eigenfunctions ϕ_k and ϕ_n of H_0

$$f = \sum_k c_k \phi_k + \sum_n c_n \phi_n \tag{11-85}$$

then the equations for the expansion coefficients are

$$\sum_{l=1}^{N} (H_{k,l} - E\delta_{k,l})c_l + \sum_{n=N+1}^{\infty} H_{k,n}c_n = 0 \qquad k = 1, 2, \ldots, N$$

$$\sum_{k=1}^{N} H_{n,k}c_k + \sum_{m=N+1}^{\infty} (H_{n,m} - E\delta_{n,m})c_m = 0 \qquad n = N+1, N+2, \ldots \tag{11-86}$$

These equations have a solution if E is taken as one of the eigenvalues of H. Let us now assume that E is approximately equal to one of the ε_k. In this case we write the second Eq. (11-86) as

$$\sum_{k=1}^{N} H_{n,k}c_k + (H_{n,n} - E)c_n = -\sum_{m \neq n} H_{n,m}c_m \tag{11-87}$$

To a first approximation we may neglect the right side of this equation. We find, then,

$$c_n \simeq -\sum_{k=1}^{N} \frac{H_{n,k}c_k}{H_{n,n} - E} \tag{11-88}$$

or if we denote the average of $\varepsilon_1, \varepsilon_2, \ldots, \varepsilon_N$ by λ,

$$c_n \simeq -\sum_{k=1}^{N} \frac{H_{n,k}c_k}{H_{n,n} - \lambda} \tag{11-89}$$

If we substitute this back into the first Eq. (11-86), we obtain

$$\sum_{l=1}^{N} (H_{k,l} - E\delta_{k,l})c_l - \sum_{l=1}^{N} \sum_{n=N+1}^{\infty} \frac{H_{k,n}H_{n,l}}{H_{n,n} - \lambda} c_l = 0 \tag{11-90}$$

which we can also write as

$$\sum_{l=1}^{N} (\Omega_{k,l} - E\delta_{k,l})c_l = 0 \tag{11-91}$$

with

$$\Omega_{k,l} = H_{k,l} - \sum_{n=N+1}^{\infty} \frac{H_{k,n}H_{n,l}}{H_{n,n} - \lambda} \tag{11-92}$$

If we now solve the secular equation

$$|\Omega_{k,l} - E\delta_{k,l}| = 0 \tag{11-93}$$

then its eigenvalues $\tilde{E}_1, \tilde{E}_2, \ldots, \tilde{E}_N$ are equal to the eigenvalues E_k to a second-order approximation. If $\mathbf{c}^k$ is the eigenvector belonging to $\tilde{E}_k$, then the function

$$f_k = \sum_{l=1}^{N} c_l^{k} \left[\phi_l - \sum_n \frac{H_{n,l}\phi_n}{H_{n,n} - \tilde{E}_k} \right] \tag{11-94}$$

is an eigenfunction of H, belonging to E_k, to a first approximation.

This procedure is comparable with what we discussed in Sec. (10-4). The main difference is that there we first solved the secular equation for the near-degenerate states and then mixed in the higher states, whereas here the two procedures are reversed. The type of problem determines which of the two methods is to be preferred.

In general it is hard to say which of the two approaches, the straight-forward perturbation theory of Chap. 10 or the variation-perturbation method of the present chapter, is the more convenient one. Personally we are inclined to favor the variation-perturbation approach, but many theoreticians are of a different opinion.

PROBLEMS

11-1 Calculate the ground-state energy of a hydrogen atom in a homogeneous electric field $\mathbf{F}$ along the z axis from the variational function

$$f = a\psi(1s) + b\psi(2p_z) + c\psi(3p_z)$$

11-2 Determine the best possible value of the ground-state energy of the hydrogen atom that can be obtained from the variational function

$$f = e^{-\alpha r^2}$$

11-3 We expand the eigenfunctions of the Hermitian operator H in terms of a complete set of functions ϕ_n:

$$f = \sum_n a_n \phi_n$$

The functions ϕ_n are not orthonormal, but they satisfy the conditions

$$\langle \phi_n | \phi_n \rangle = 1 + \rho_n \lambda^2$$

$$\langle \phi_n | \phi_m \rangle = \rho_{n,m} \lambda$$

where λ is much smaller than unity. Furthermore, we have

$$\langle \phi_n | H | \phi_n \rangle = \varepsilon_n + h_n \lambda^2$$

$$\langle \phi_n | H | \phi_m \rangle = h_{n,m} \lambda$$

Determine the lowest eigenvalue E_0 of H, accurate to within second powers of λ, from the variation function f.

11-4 Show that for a nondegenerate state the third-order energy corrections according to both the Brillouin-Wigner and the Rayleigh-Schrödinger theories are identical.

CHAPTER 12

TWO-ELECTRON SYSTEMS

12-1 ELECTRON SPIN

The motion of an electron around a nucleus has often been likened to the planetary motion of the earth around the sun. We know that the earth not only describes an orbit around the sun, but it also performs a diurnal rotation around its north-south axis. Hence, if this analogue between electronic and terrestial motion is extended further, then we might speculate whether an electron could somehow exhibit a similar rotation around an axis. The first question to arise, then, is how such a rotation could be detected experimentally. In classical mechanics the rotation of a rigid body, such as the earth, is always associated with an angular momentum $\mathbf{M}$ directed along the axis of rotation. When the rotating body has a net electric charge, then it also has a magnetic moment $\boldsymbol{\mu}$, which is proportional to $\mathbf{M}$. Since these magnetic moments interact with one another and also with the orbital motion of the electrons, we might expect these interactions to have some effect on the energy levels and therefore on the spectra of atomic or molecular systems. In particular, they might play a role in the Zeeman effect, that is, the splitting of spectral lines due to the presence of a homogeneous magnetic field.

It is quite possible that considerations such as these were contributary to the formulation of the electron-spin hypothesis by Goudsmit and Uhlenbeck.[1] This hypothesis consists of two parts. The first part states that all electrons rotate and that each rotation is associated with an angular momentum $\mathbf{M}$ that has the constant value $|\mathbf{M}| = \frac{1}{2}\hbar$. The second part states that the magnetic moment μ due to this rotation is proportional to $\mathbf{M}$ and that the ratio is determined by

$$\mu = - \frac{e}{mc} \mathbf{M} \tag{12-1}$$

Nowadays we use the name *electron spin* for this rotational motion, and we speak of the *spinning electron*.

Goudsmit and Uhlenbeck were young graduate students when they advanced their hypothesis. They were well acquainted with atomic spectra and their interpretation, and they recognized that the electron-spin assumption allowed for an accurate and straightforward explanation of the fine structure of alkalilike spectra and of the anomalous Zeeman effect. However, it was not at all easy to reconcile their ideas with classical electromagnetic theory. We are tempted to compare the electron-spin assumption with Planck's quantum hypothesis. In both situations we encounter a bold assumption which offers a reasonable explanation of experimental data but which was not entirely justified until some later time.

We have discussed the non-quantum-mechanical theory of the spinning electron elsewhere.[2] It appears that relativistic effects play an important role, and therefore we limit our discussion here to some of the results without any derivations.

In classical electromagnetic theory, for an electron that describes an orbit around a nucleus the ratio of its magnetic moment μ_0 to its angular momentum M_0 is given by

$$\mu_0 = - \frac{e}{2mc} M_0 \tag{12-2}$$

It is important to note that this differs by a factor 2 from the ratio (12-1). Uhlenbeck and Goudsmit showed that for a uniformly rotating spherical charge shell the ratio between μ and $\mathbf{M}$ was indeed given by Eq. (12-1), but this result is not very useful. First, it is no longer valid when the charge shell is not spherical, and, second, it fails to explain

---

[1] G. E. Uhlenbeck and S. Goudsmit, *Naturwiss.*,**13**: 953 (1925); *Nature*, **117**: 264 (1926).

[2] H. F. Hameka, "Advanced Quantum Chemistry," chap. 3, Addison-Wesley Publishing Company, Inc., Reading, Mass., 1965.

how the magnetic moment of the electron spin can be of the same order of magnitude as the orbital magnetic moment.

A second difficulty arises if we attempt to evaluate the energy of a spinning electron with the spin angular momentum **M** that moves with a velocity **v** in an electromagnetic field, described by the electric and magnetic field vectors **F** and **H**, respectively. According to classical electromagnetic theory this energy is given by

$$E = \frac{e}{mc}\left\{\mathbf{M}\cdot\left(\mathbf{H} + \frac{1}{c}\,[\mathbf{F}\times\mathbf{v}]\right)\right\} \tag{12-3}$$

if we use Eq. (12-1). On the other hand, the interpretation of the experiments seems to require that this energy is

$$E = \frac{e}{mc}\left\{\mathbf{M}\cdot\left(\mathbf{H} + \frac{1}{2c}\,[\mathbf{F}\times\mathbf{v}]\right)\right\} \tag{12-4}$$

where the term containing the electric-field vector differs by a factor 2 from Eq. (12-3).

All these difficulties were removed when the motion of a spinning electron in an electromagnetic field was studied with the aid of relativity theory.[1] First of all Thomas showed that Eq. (12-3) was correct only if we observe the system from the position of the moving electron. To an observer who is stationed at the nucleus it seems as if the electron has an additional precession, which is known as the *Thomas precession*, and this causes the factor $\frac{1}{2}$ to appear in the energy expression (12-4). This factor is therefore known as the *Thomas factor*. Finally it follows from relativity theory that the ratio between the magnetic moment and angular momentum of the electron spin must be given by Eq. (12-1), since the theory would otherwise not be relativistically invariant.

We see that ultimately all the assumptions that were made by Goudsmit and Uhlenbeck were consistent with electromagnetic theory as long as relativistic effects were taken into account. We may add that the necessity of including the electron spin in quantum theory was shown a few years later by Dirac.[2] We should realize that the Schrödinger equation is not invariant with respect to relativistic transformations, and therefore it cannot be correct from a relativistic point of view. In order to remedy this situation, Dirac introduced a new set of basic quantum-mechanical equations, which are relativistically invariant and which reduce to the Schrödinger equation when relativistic effects become negligible. It was found that the spin properties were automatically

---

[1] L. H. Thomas, *Nature*, **117**: 514 (1926); *Phil. Mag.*, **3**: 1 (1927). See also H. A. Kramers, *Physica*, **1**: 825 (1934).

[2] P. A. M. Dirac, *Proc. Roy. Soc.*, *Ser A*, **117**: 610 (1928); *Ser A*, **118**: 351 (1928).

contained in the Dirac theory. We feel that the Dirac equations go beyond the scope of our book, and they are therefore not discussed.

12-2 THE QUANTUM-MECHANICAL DESCRIPTION OF THE SPIN

If we want to avoid the Dirac theory, then the most convenient way of describing the spin quantum-mechanically is by analogy with the orbital angular momentum. In Chap. 9 we saw that the eigenvalues and eigenfunctions of the operator M^2, which is the square of the angular momentum operator **M**, are given by

$$M^2 Y'_{l,m} = l(l+1)\hbar^2 Y'_{l,m}$$

$$Y'_{l,m} = (-1)^m Y_{l,m} \qquad m \geqslant 0 \qquad (12\text{-}5)$$

$$Y'_{l,m} = Y_{l,m} \qquad m < 0$$

The functions $Y'_{l,m}$ are also eigenfunctions of the operator M_z, since

$$M_z Y'_{l,m} = m\hbar Y'_{l,m} \qquad |m| \leqslant l \qquad (12\text{-}6)$$

We note that in quantum theory there is a difference between the magnitude M of **M** and the maximum projection of **M** along the z axis. From Eq. (12-5) we predict that

$$M = \hbar \sqrt{l(l+1)} \qquad (12\text{-}7)$$

whereas it follows from Eq. (12-6) that the maximum value of M_z is equal to $\hbar l$. This difference is due to the Heisenberg uncertainty principle.

In order to derive the quantum-mechanical description of the electron spin, we ought to modify the first hypothesis of Goudsmit and Uhlenbeck somewhat. If we introduce the customary notation **S** for the spin angular momentum, then we should require that the maximum value of the projection of **S** in any given direction is $\frac{1}{2}\hbar$ rather than that the value of S is equal to $\frac{1}{2}\hbar$.

Formally, we can now construct a quantum-mechanical description of the electron spin that is in every respect equivalent to the theory of the angular momentum if we take the quantum number l equal to $\frac{1}{2}$. At first this may seem strange, since the essential condition for the eigenvalues of M^2 was that the quantum numbers were all integers. We showed that for noninteger l the functions $Y_{l,m}$ become infinite for $\theta = 0$ and $\theta = \pi$. However, as long as we limit ourselves to the matrix representation of the angular momentum, there is really no need to know the eigenfunctions. The matrix description is concerned only with the transformation properties of the eigenfunctions, and the specific analytical form of these functions is actually immaterial. There is no compelling reason why we cannot consider the transformation properties of functions $Y'_{l,m}$ with $l = \frac{1}{2}$.

If we are not concerned with the specific form of the functions $Y'_{l,m}$, we can easily derive the transformation properties for such functions with half-integer quantum numbers. First we note that, if $l = \frac{1}{2}$, the other quantum number m can assume the values $m = \pm\frac{1}{2}$ when we adhere to the condition $|m| \leqslant l$. Our basis set of functions consists, therefore, of

$$\alpha = Y'_{1/2,1/2} \qquad \beta = Y_{1/2,-1/2} \tag{12-8}$$

From Eq. (12-5) it follows that

$$S^2\alpha = \tfrac{3}{4}\hbar^2\alpha \qquad S^2\beta = \tfrac{3}{4}\hbar^2\beta \tag{12-9}$$

The effect of the operators S_x, S_y, and S_z on α and β can be derived from the results of Chap. 9. We derive from Eq. (9-59) that

$$\begin{aligned} S_x\alpha &= \tfrac{1}{2}\hbar\beta & S_y\alpha &= \tfrac{1}{2}i\hbar\beta \\ S_x\beta &= \tfrac{1}{2}\hbar\alpha & S_y\beta &= -\tfrac{1}{2}i\hbar\beta \end{aligned} \tag{12-10}$$

and from Eq. (12-6) that

$$S_z\alpha = \tfrac{1}{2}\hbar\alpha \qquad S_z\beta = -\tfrac{1}{2}\hbar\beta \tag{12-11}$$

In this way we obtain a formal quantum-mechanical description of the electron spin, at the basis of which are the two spin functions α and β. In this approach the operators S_x, S_y, and S_z can be represented as the matrices

$$S_x = \frac{\hbar}{2}\begin{bmatrix} 0 & 1 \\ 1 & 0 \end{bmatrix} \qquad S_y = \frac{\hbar}{2}\begin{bmatrix} 0 & -i \\ i & 0 \end{bmatrix} \qquad S_z = \frac{\hbar}{2}\begin{bmatrix} 1 & 0 \\ 0 & -1 \end{bmatrix} \tag{12-12}$$

and the spin functions α and β as the column vectors

$$\alpha = \begin{bmatrix} 1 \\ 0 \end{bmatrix} \qquad \beta = \begin{bmatrix} 0 \\ 1 \end{bmatrix} \tag{12-13}$$

In this formal matrix representation of the electron spin the form of the basis functions has become completely immaterial, and we do not have to worry about it any more. Moreover, the conclusions that can be drawn from it are in complete agreement with the experiments. Let us consider, for example, a spinning electron in the presence of a homogeneous magnetic field H directed along the z axis. According to Eq. (12-4) the Hamiltonian for this system is

$$H_s = \frac{e}{mc} H S_z \tag{12-14}$$

It follows immediately from Eq. (12-11) that the eigenvalues and eigenfunctions of this operator are given by

$$H_s\alpha = \frac{e\hbar H}{2mc}\,\alpha \qquad H_s\beta = -\frac{e\hbar H}{2mc}\,\beta \qquad (12\text{-}15)$$

The separation ΔE between the two energy levels is

$$\Delta E = \frac{e\hbar H}{mc} = 2\mu_0 H \qquad (12\text{-}16)$$

The quantity

$$\mu_0 = \frac{e\hbar}{2mc} \qquad (12\text{-}17)$$

is known as the *Bohr magneton*. This result is in complete agreement with the experiments.

The description above was first presented by Pauli,[1] and the matrices (12-12) are known as the *Pauli matrices*. Although it contains several features that can only be explained from relativity theory, it is known as the *nonrelativistic spin theory*, as opposed to the relativistic Dirac theory.

Let us now investigate how the wave function of a bound particle ought to be represented if we include the spin in our considerations. In general we ought to expand the wave function in terms of all possible spin states. In the case of an electron we are fortunate that there are only two spin states, characterized by the functions α and β, so that the general wave function $\psi(x,y,z;\,s)$ can always be written as

$$\psi(x,y,z;\,s) = \psi_+(x,y,z)\alpha + \psi_-(x,y,z)\beta \qquad (12\text{-}18)$$

The function $\psi(x,y,z;\,s)$ is an eigenfunction of the complete Hamiltonian H of the system, which is a sum of a large number of contributions $H_0, H_1, H_2, \ldots$, etc., if we wish to consider all relativistic contributions and all spin energies. We have derived these various contributions elsewhere,[2] and we found that they are in general extremely small as compared with the main term

$$H_0 = -\frac{h^2}{2m}\Delta + V(\mathbf{r}) \qquad (12\text{-}19)$$

To a first approximation we may therefore neglect all other contributions to H. In this case ψ_+ and ψ_- should be one and the same eigenfunction of the operator H_0. The only effect of our introduction of the spin is

[1] W. Pauli, *Zeits, f. Physik*, **43**: 601 (1927).
[2] Hameka, *op. cit.*

to make every nondegenerate eigenvalue of H_0 two-fold degenerate and to double the degree of degeneracy of the other levels.

It would lead us too far to consider in detail the effects of the other contributions to the Hamiltonian, since it would be pointless to consider one of them without the others. For a complete discussion of the relativistic theory of a hydrogen atom in the presence of external fields, we refer the reader to the book by Bethe and Salpeter.[1]

12-3 THE PAULI EXCLUSION PRINCIPLE

Before we go into many-particle systems, it may be helpful to recall briefly how we construct the Schrödinger equation for one electron moving in a potential field $V(\mathbf{r})$. From the Hamiltonian function

$$H = T + V = \frac{1}{2m}(p_x{}^2 + p_y{}^2 + p_z{}^2) + V(\mathbf{r}) \qquad (12\text{-}20)$$

we construct the Hamiltonian operator

$$H = -\frac{\hbar^2}{2m}\left(\frac{\partial^2}{\partial x^2} + \frac{\partial^2}{\partial y^2} + \frac{\partial^2}{\partial z^2}\right) + V(\mathbf{r}) \qquad (12\text{-}21)$$

by replacing $\mathbf{p}$ by $(-i\hbar\nabla)$ everywhere. The time-independent Schrödinger equation is then obtained as the eigenvalue problem

$$H\psi = \varepsilon\psi \qquad (12\text{-}22)$$

and its solutions are ε_n and ψ_n

$$H\psi_n = \varepsilon_n\psi_n$$

We have not discussed the time-dependent Schrödinger equation

$$H\phi = i\hbar\frac{\partial\phi}{\partial t} \qquad (12\text{-}23)$$

at any great length, but it is easily verified that its general solution is

$$\phi = \sum_n a_n\psi_n \exp\frac{\varepsilon_n t}{i\hbar} \qquad (12\text{-}24)$$

The Schrödinger equation for a many-particle system is constructed by following the same procedure exactly. For example, the Hamiltonian function of a helium atom is

$$H = \frac{1}{2m}(p_1{}^2 + p_2{}^2) - \frac{2e^2}{r_1} - \frac{2e^2}{r_2} + \frac{e^2}{r_{12}} \qquad (12\text{-}25)$$

---

[1] H. A. Bethe and E. E. Salpeter, "Quantum Mechanics of One- and Two-electron Atoms," Springer-Verlag, Berlin, 1957.

after we eliminate the motion of the center of gravity. We replace $\mathbf{p}_1$ by $(-i\hbar\nabla_1)$ and $\mathbf{p}_2$ by $(-i\hbar\nabla_2)$, and we obtain the Hamiltonian operator

$$H = -\frac{\hbar}{2m}\left(\frac{\partial^2}{\partial x_1^2} + \frac{\partial^2}{\partial y_1^2} + \frac{\partial^2}{\partial z_1^2} + \frac{\partial^2}{\partial x_2^2} + \frac{\partial^2}{\partial y_2^2} + \frac{\partial^2}{\partial z_2^2}\right) - \frac{2e^2}{r_1} - \frac{2e^2}{r_2} + \frac{e^2}{r_{12}}$$

(12-26)

If we use atomic units of length and energy, this operator may be simplified to

$$H = -\frac{1}{2}(\Delta_1 + \Delta_2) - \frac{2}{r_1} - \frac{2}{r_2} + \frac{1}{r_{12}}$$

(12-27)

The Schrödinger equation for the helium atom is therefore

$$-\frac{1}{2}(\Delta_1 + \Delta_2)\Psi - \left(\frac{2}{r_1} + \frac{2}{r_2} - \frac{1}{r_{12}}\right)\Psi = E\Psi$$

(12-28)

The Hamiltonian for an atom or ion with nuclear charge Ze and with N electrons is obtained as

$$H = -\frac{1}{2}\sum_{j=1}^{N}\Delta_j - Z\sum_{j=1}^{N}\frac{1}{r_j} + \sum_{j>k}\frac{1}{r_{jk}}$$

(12-29)

A molecule containing s nuclei with charges $Z_\alpha e$ and masses M_α, and N electrons, is represented by a Hamiltonian

$$H = -\sum_{\alpha=1}^{s}\frac{\hbar^2}{2M_\alpha}\left(\frac{\partial^2}{\partial X_\alpha^2} + \frac{\partial^2}{\partial Y_\alpha^2} + \frac{\partial^2}{\partial Z_\alpha^2}\right) - \sum_{j=1}^{N}\frac{\hbar^2}{2m}\left(\frac{\partial^2}{\partial x_j^2} + \frac{\partial^2}{\partial y_j^2} + \frac{\partial^2}{\partial z_j^2}\right)$$

$$-\sum_{j=1}^{N}\sum_{\alpha=1}^{s}\frac{Z_\alpha e^2}{r_{j,\alpha}} + \sum_{j>k}\frac{e^2}{r_{j,k}} + \sum_{\alpha>\beta}\frac{Z_\alpha Z_\beta e^2}{R_{\alpha,\beta}}$$

(12-30)

Here $\mathbf{r}_j = (x_j, y_j, z_j)$ and $\mathbf{R}_\alpha = (X_\alpha, Y_\alpha, Z_\alpha)$ are the coordinates of electron j and nucleus α, respectively, and the other quantities are defined as

$$r_{j,\alpha} = |\mathbf{r}_j - \mathbf{R}_\alpha|$$

$$r_{j,k} = |\mathbf{r}_k - \mathbf{r}_j|$$

(12-31)

$$R_{\alpha,\beta} = |\mathbf{R}_\beta - \mathbf{R}_\alpha|$$

Let us now consider a system that contains N electrons only, for example, the system that is described by the Hamiltonian (12-29). Since the electrons all play exactly the same role, the Hamiltonian remains unchanged if we permute any of the electrons. We can write this as

$$[H,P] = 0$$

(12-32)

Let ε_n be one of the eigenvalues of H and ψ_n a corresponding eigenfunction, so that

$$H\psi_n = \varepsilon_n\psi_n \tag{12-33}$$

It follows that we also have

$$P(H\psi_n) = P(\varepsilon_n\,\psi_n) \tag{12-34}$$

where the operator P represents an arbitrary permutation of the N electrons. It now follows from Eq. (12-32) that we can also write this as

$$H(P\psi_n) = \varepsilon_n(P\psi_n) \tag{12-35}$$

since H and P commute. It follows that not only ψ_n but also the functions $(P\psi_n)$ are eigenfunctions of H belonging to ε_n. If all these functions are different, the eigenvalue ε_n is $(N!)$-fold degenerate.

The experiments clearly indicate that degeneracies of so large an order do not usually occur in N-electron systems and the conclusion above is therefore incorrect. It is not possible to resolve this discrepancy by making use of the quantum theory that we have discussed so far, and we have to introduce an additional basic assumption in quantum mechanics if we want our predictions for N-electron systems to be compatible with the experimental observation. This basic assumption can be derived from the Pauli exclusion principle,[1] which states that two electrons in a central field can never be in states that have the same four quantum numbers. Expressing this in more general form, we require that the wave function ψ_n is antisymmetric with respect to permutations of the electron coordinates. Hence, the only solutions of the Schrödinger equation that give physically acceptable eigenfunctions are those which satisfy the condition

$$P\Psi_n = \delta_P\Psi_n \tag{12-36}$$

The result of this restriction is that only one particular linear combination of the $N!$ functions $(P\psi_n)$ is an acceptable eigenfunction. If ψ_n is already antisymmetric, then all functions $(P\psi_n)$ are the same eigenfunctions. If ψ_n is not antisymmetric, then we can use it as a basis for the construction of an antisymmetric function Ψ_n if we take

$$\Psi_n = (N!)^{-1/2}\sum_P P\delta_P\psi_n \tag{12-37}$$

Here the summation is to be taken over all possible permutations, including the identity permutation. If ψ_n is symmetric with respect to any of the electron permutations, then it is impossible to construct an

[1] W. Pauli, *Zeits. f. Physik*, **31**: 765 (1925).

antisymmetric eigenfunction from it because the procedure of Eq. (12-37) would lead to zero for Ψ_n. We must conclude, therefore, that such symmetric functions ψ_n are inadmissible at all times. It may be seen that this conclusion is identical to the original formulation of the Pauli exclusion principle, since any atomic state in which two electrons have the same set of quantum numbers would be represented by a symmetric wave function, and such states cannot exist.

In applying the exclusion principle, we should be aware that the permutations refer not only to the space coordinates of the electrons but also to the spin coordinates. The four quantum numbers that we mentioned before refer to the eigenvalues of the operators H, M^2, M_z, and S_z for each individual electron. We will see that the description of atomic states by means of quantum numbers for the individual electrons is not rigorous, and the original formulation of the Pauli principle has only limited validity.

The general exclusion principle is not restricted to electrons alone; it is valid for any system that contains one or more groups of identical particles. It requires that the wave function of such a system be either symmetric or antisymmetric with respect to any permutation of the coordinates of a group of identical particles. The function should be symmetric if the particles in question have integer spin, and antisymmetric if the particles have half-integer spin.

It may be helpful if we make a few comments on this general formulation of the exclusion principle. We have discussed only the quantum theory of the electron spin in which we took the quantum number l equal to $\frac{1}{2}$ and then made use of the matrix representation of the angular-momentum operators. A number of other particles, namely, the neutron, the proton, the nuclei H^3, He^3, C^{13}, N^{15}, etc., can be treated in the same manner, and we say that all these particles have spin $\frac{1}{2}$. However, there are some nuclei, such as H^2, Li^6, N^{14}, in which we obtain a satisfactory description of the spin properties only if we take the quantum number l equal to 1. These particles are said to have spin 1. Certain nuclei, for example, C^{12}, have no spin whatsoever, and we say that they have spin 0. If we look through a table of nuclear properties of the elements, we see that many different spins occur in nature; some notable cases are O^{17} and Al^{27}, which have spin $\frac{5}{2}$, V^{50} with spin 6, and Ge^{73} with spin $\frac{9}{2}$. The permutation properties of the wave function depend only on whether the spins of the particles are integer or half-integer and not on the magnitudes of the spin.

As an example of the exclusion principle, let us compare the situation for the three molecules H_2, HD, and D_2. If we denote the space and spin coordinates for the two nuclei symbolically by a and b and for the two electrons by 1 and 2, then we can write any wave function of the molecules as $\Psi(1,2; a,b)$. Since the electrons have spin $\frac{1}{2}$, the symmetry condition for all three molecules is that

$$\Psi(2,1; a,b) = -\Psi(1,2; a,b) \qquad (12\text{-}38)$$

A proton also has spin $\frac{1}{2}$, so that for the H_2 molecule the wave function must satisfy also the condition

$$\Psi(1,2; b,a) = -\Psi(1,2; a,b) \qquad (12\text{-}39)$$

A deuteron has spin 1, and therefore we have, for the D_2 molecule, the condition

$$\Psi(1,2; b,a) = \Psi(1,2; a,b) \qquad (12\text{-}40)$$

In the HD molecule the two nuclei are different, and the two functions $\Psi(1,2; a,b)$ and $\Psi(1,2; b,a)$ are not related in any way.

The permutation properties of the wave functions are also decisive in determining the type of statistics that the particles obey. Particles with integer spin are distributed according to the Bose-Einstein expression, and particles with half-integer spin follow Fermi-Dirac statistics. This is discussed in detail in any book on statistical mechanics.[1]

12-4 TWO-ELECTRON SYSTEMS

It is not easy to give a general and accurate description of the properties of the wave functions of N-electron systems, and we will restrict ourselves first to a two-electron system. To a first approximation we may write the Hamiltonian of such a system as

$$H_0 = -\frac{\hbar^2}{2m}(\Delta_1 + \Delta_2) + V(\mathbf{r}_1,\mathbf{r}_2) \qquad (12\text{-}41)$$

An acceptable eigenfunction of a two-electron system must satisfy two conditions: (1) it must be an eigenfunction, and (2) it must be antisymmetric with respect to a permutation of the two sets of electronic coordinates.

The wave function should also contain the spin variables of the two electrons. It is convenient to study first the dependence on the spin variables before going into the dependence on the space coordinates $\mathbf{r}_1$ and $\mathbf{r}_2$ of the wave function. We have seen that for a one-electron system there are two possible states for the spin, namely, α and β. For a two-electron system there are four possible spin states, namely, $\alpha_1\alpha_2$, $\alpha_1\beta_2$, $\beta_1\alpha_2$, and $\beta_1\beta_2$. The notation is self-explanatory; for example, the symbol

---

[1] See, for example, R. C. Tolman, "The Principles of Statistical Mechanics," Oxford University Press, London, 1938.

$\alpha_1\beta_2$ refers to the situation in which electron 1 is in spin state α and electron 2 is in spin state β. Any wave function Ψ_n of the system can now be represented by the general expression

$$\Psi_n = \psi_{n,++}(\mathbf{r}_1,\mathbf{r}_2)\alpha_1\alpha_2 + \psi_{n,+-}(\mathbf{r}_1,\mathbf{r}_2)\alpha_1\beta_2 + \psi_{n,-+}(\mathbf{r}_1,\mathbf{r}_2)\beta_1\alpha_2 + \psi_{n,--}(\mathbf{r}_1,\mathbf{r}_2)\beta_1\beta_2$$

$$(12\text{-}42)$$

Let us now make use of the exclusion principle and impose the condition

$$P\Psi_n = -\Psi_n \qquad (12\text{-}43)$$

It follows from Eq. (12-42) that

$$P\Psi_n = \psi_{n,++}(\mathbf{r}_2,\mathbf{r}_1)\alpha_1\alpha_2 + \psi_{n,+-}(\mathbf{r}_2,\mathbf{r}_1)\beta_1\alpha_2 + \psi_{n,-+}(\mathbf{r}_2,\mathbf{r}_1)\alpha_1\beta_2 + \psi_{n,--}(\mathbf{r}_2,\mathbf{r}_1)\beta_1\beta_2$$

$$(12\text{-}44)$$

The condition (12-43) can be broken down into the following set of requirements:

$$\psi_{n,++}(\mathbf{r}_1,\mathbf{r}_2) = -\psi_{n,++}(\mathbf{r}_2,\mathbf{r}_1)$$
$$\psi_{n,+-}(\mathbf{r}_1,\mathbf{r}_2) = -\psi_{n,-+}(\mathbf{r}_2,\mathbf{r}_1)$$
$$\psi_{n,-+}(\mathbf{r}_1,\mathbf{r}_2) = -\psi_{n,+-}(\mathbf{r}_2,\mathbf{r}_1)$$
$$\psi_{n,--}(\mathbf{r}_1,\mathbf{r}_2) = -\psi_{n,--}(\mathbf{r}_2,\mathbf{r}_1)$$

$$(12\text{-}45)$$

It follows that both $\psi_{n,++}$ and $\psi_{n,--}$ must be antisymmetric, and we introduce, therefore, the new notation

$$a_{n,1}(1,2) = \psi_{n,++}(\mathbf{r}_1,\mathbf{r}_2)$$
$$a_{n,-1}(1,2) = \psi_{n,--}(\mathbf{r}_1,\mathbf{r}_2)$$

$$(12\text{-}46)$$

The other two functions $\psi_{n,+-}(\mathbf{r}_1,\mathbf{r}_2)$ and $\psi_{n,-+}(\mathbf{r}_1,\mathbf{r}_2)$ can be combined to form an antisymmetric function

$$a_{n,0}(1,2) = 2^{-1/2}[\psi_{n,+-}(\mathbf{r}_1,\mathbf{r}_2) + \psi_{n,-+}(\mathbf{r}_1,\mathbf{r}_2)] \qquad (12\text{-}47)$$

and a symmetric function

$$s_n(1,2) = 2^{-1/2}[\psi_{n,+-}(\mathbf{r}_1,\mathbf{r}_2) - \psi_{n,-+}(\mathbf{r}_1,\mathbf{r}_2)] \qquad (12\text{-}48)$$

If we substitute all these results back into Eq. (12-42), we find that Ψ_n can be written as

$$\Psi_n = {}^3\Psi_n + {}^1\Psi_n \qquad (12\text{-}49)$$

where

$${}^3\Psi_n = a_{n,1}(1,2)\,{}^3\zeta_1(1,2) + a_{n,0}(1,2)\,{}^3\zeta_0(1,2) + a_{n,-1}(1,2)\,{}^3\zeta_{-1}(1,2) \qquad (12\text{-}50)$$

and

$$\qquad\qquad {}^1\Psi_n = s_n(1,2)\,{}^1\zeta(1,2) \qquad (12\text{-}51)$$

Here we have introduced the new set of spin functions

$$
\begin{aligned}
{}^3\zeta_1(1,2) &= \alpha_1\alpha_2 \\
{}^3\zeta_0(1,2) &= 2^{-1/2}(\alpha_1\beta_2 + \beta_1\alpha_2) \\
{}^3\zeta_{-1}(1,2) &= \beta_1\beta_2 \\
{}^1\zeta(1,2) &= 2^{-1/2}(\alpha_1\beta_2 - \beta_1\alpha_2)
\end{aligned}
\tag{12-52}
$$

Let us first study the properties of these spin functions. If we introduce the new operators

$$
\mathbf{S} = \mathbf{S}_1 + \mathbf{S}_2
$$
$$
S^2 = (\mathbf{S}_1 + \mathbf{S}_2)^2 = S_1{}^2 + S_2{}^2 + 2\mathbf{S}_1 \cdot \mathbf{S}_2
\tag{12-53}
$$

then it is easily verified that

$$
S^2\,{}^3\zeta_m(1,2) = 2\hbar^2\,{}^3\zeta_m(1,2)
$$
$$
S_z\,{}^3\zeta_m(1,2) = m\hbar\,{}^3\zeta_m(1,2) \qquad m = 1, 0, -1
\tag{12-54}
$$

and

$$
S^2\,{}^1\zeta(1,2) = 0
$$
$$
S_z\,{}^1\zeta(1,2) = 0
\tag{12-55}
$$

All four spin functions of Eq. (12-52) are therefore eigenfunctions of both operators S^2 and S_z. The three functions ${}^3\zeta_m$ have the same transformation properties with respect to $\mathbf{S}$ as the functions $Y_{l,m}'$ of Chap. 9 have with respect to $\mathbf{M}$ if we take the quantum number l equal to unity.

The behavior of the spin functions can be understood on the basis of a simple physical picture. If we take the direction of the first spin as the quantization axis for the second spin, then there are two possibilities: the second spin can point in either the same or the opposite direction of the first spin. In the first case the total spin of the system is equal to unity; it can have three possible orientations in any given direction, so that we have a three-fold degeneracy. We speak, therefore, of a *triplet state*. In the second case the total spin is zero. Since there is no degeneracy, we call this a *singlet state*.

Let us now proceed to the properties of the orbital functions $a_{n,m}$ and s_n. If we impose the condition that Ψ_n is an eigenfunction of the operator (12-41)

$$
H_0\Psi_n = \lambda_n\Psi_n
\tag{12-56}
$$

and we substitute Eq. (12-49), we find that

$$
\begin{aligned}
H_0 a_{n,1} &= \lambda_n a_{n,1} \\
H_0 a_{n,0} &= \lambda_n a_{n,0} \\
H_0 a_{n,-1} &= \lambda_n a_{n,-1} \\
H_0 s_n &= \lambda_n s_n
\end{aligned}
\tag{12-57}
$$

In general we do not expect the eigenvalue λ_n to be four-fold degenerate; at least for atomic systems there is little evidence that this occurs ordinarily. Therefore, we may assume that in most cases the three functions $a_{n,m}$ are proportional to one another, so that the triplet function $^3\Psi_n$ can be represented as

$$^3\Psi_n = a_n(1,2) \,^3\zeta(1,2)$$

$$^3\zeta(1,2) = c_1 \,^3\zeta_1(1,2) + c_0 \,^3\zeta_0(1,2) + c_{-1} \,^3\zeta_{-1}(1,2) \tag{12-58}$$

The spin function $^3\zeta(1,2)$ is an arbitrary linear combination of the three spin functions $^3\zeta_m$.

There cannot exist any linear relation between the functions $a_n(1,2)$ and $s_n(1,2)$, since the first function is antisymmetric and the second function is symmetric with respect to permutations. At the same time it is extremely unlikely that the two functions $a_n(1,2)$ and $s_n(1,2)$ are eigenfunctions with the same eigenvalue; to be specific, we are not aware of any situation in which this has ever been observed. We must, therefore, conclude that the eigenfunction of λ_n is either $a_n(1,2)$ or $s_n(1,2)$. The eigenvalues and eigenfunctions of H_0 can therefore be separated into two groups: the eigenvalues $^1\lambda_n$, which have the eigenfunctions $s_n(1,2)$, and the eigenvalues $^3\lambda_n$, which have the eigenfunctions $a_n(1,2)$. The final eigenfunctions which contain the spin variables and which satisfy the exclusion principle are obtained as

$$H_0 \,^1\Psi_n = \,^1\lambda_n \,^1\Psi_n \qquad\qquad ^1\Psi_n = s_n(1,2) \,^1\zeta(1,2)$$

$$H_0 \,^3\Psi_{k,m} = \,^3\lambda_k \,^3\Psi_{k,m} \qquad ^3\Psi_{k,m} = a_k(1,2) \,^3\zeta_m(1,2) \tag{12-59}$$

The spin multiplicity is usually denoted by a superscript on the left side of the wave function. The symbol is 1 for a singlet state, since there is no degeneracy, and it is 3 for a triplet state, because this state is three-fold degenerate.

The spin magnetic moments interact with each other and with the electromagnetic field due to the electrons and the nuclei. These interaction energies are described by a spin Hamiltonian H_s. In this discussion we have disregarded all the effects of the spin Hamiltonian H_s on the energy levels and on the eigenfunctions. For two-electron systems this is a reasonable approximation, since the changes in energy due to this operator are of the order of 1 to 10 cm^{-1}, whereas the energy eigenvalues of H_0 are of the order of a few hundred thousand cm^{-1}. However, it can be seen that indirectly the spin can have a very large effect on the energy, since the nature of the spin function determines whether the orbital function is symmetric or antisymmetric in the electron coordinates. For example, if we construct approximate atomic eigenfunctions for the helium atom, starting from a set of one-electron functions, then the energy difference between a singlet and a triplet state, constructed from the same pair of one-electron functions, can amount to 10^4 cm^{-1} or more. This is the reason that the spin functions should always be considered when we construct atomic or molecular wave functions.

We may recall that our final set of eigenfunctions, as described by Eq. (12-59), are all eigenfunctions of the operators S^2 and S_z. This is generally true for the proper eigenfunctions of N-electron systems, and it is often convenient to impose this condition to start with when deriving the proper eigenfunctions.

12-5 THE HELIUM ATOM

According to Sec. 12-4 the eigenfunctions of the helium atom are

$$^1\Psi_n = s_n(\mathbf{r}_1,\mathbf{r}_2) \, ^1\zeta(1,2)$$
$$^3\Psi_{k,m} = a_k(\mathbf{r}_1,\mathbf{r}_2) \, ^3\zeta_m(1,2)$$

(12-60)

where the orbital functions s_n and a_k are eigenfunctions of the Hamiltonian

$$H_0 = -\frac{1}{2}(\Delta_1 + \Delta_2) - \frac{2}{r_1} - \frac{2}{r_2} + \frac{1}{r_{12}}$$

(12-61)

Here we have introduced atomic units of length and energy. No exact solutions of the corresponding Schrödinger equation have ever been found, and we must limit ourselves to the derivation of approximate eigenfunctions. The customary approach uses the variation theorem, starting with a trial function that contains a number of parameters. Obviously, the results will become more accurate if we use more complex trial functions with an increasing number of parameters. We first investigate a few simple functions and then indicate how to modify the functions in order to obtain more accurate results.

In general, it may be expected that the functions s_n and a_k depend on the coordinates of both electrons in some complicated way, but as a first approximation we choose them separable in the electron coordinates. This means that s_n can be written as

$$s_n(\mathbf{r}_1,\mathbf{r}_2) = f_n(\mathbf{r}_1)f_n(\mathbf{r}_2)$$

(12-62)

or

$$s_n(\mathbf{r}_1,\mathbf{r}_2) = f_n(\mathbf{r}_1)g_n(\mathbf{r}_2) + g_n(\mathbf{r}_1)f_n(\mathbf{r}_2)$$

(12-63)

and that $a_k(\mathbf{r}_1,\mathbf{r}_2)$ is approximated as

$$a_k(\mathbf{r}_1,\mathbf{r}_2) = f_k(\mathbf{r}_1)g_k(\mathbf{r}_2) - g_k(\mathbf{r}_1)f_k(\mathbf{r}_2)$$

(12-64)

These approximations are the basis of the Hartree-Fock equations, which we discuss in Chap. 13.

Let us now make an educated guess as to the approximate form of the functions f_k and g_k. Let us imagine for a moment that the term r_{12}^{-1} in the Hamiltonian (12-61) is absent. In this case the Schrödinger equation would be separable into the two sets of electron coordinates, and the functions f and g would be hydrogenlike wave functions with a nuclear charge $Z = 2$. The lowest eigenstate of the helium atom would be obtained by placing two electrons with opposite spins in a $(1s)$ state, which we might denote as the $(1s)^2$ state. In the same way we would obtain a singlet $(1s)(2s)$ state, a triplet $(1s)(2s)$ state, etc. In this approximation each helium state can be constructed from two hydrogenlike states. We know that this approximation is not quite correct, but at least it gives us a starting point for our attempts to construct approximate wave functions. Also, it indicates clearly that the ground state of the helium atom ought to be a singlet state and that we should approximate its wave function as

$$s_0(\mathbf{r}_1, \mathbf{r}_2) = f_0(\mathbf{r}_1) f_0(\mathbf{r}_2) \qquad (12\text{-}65)$$

Of course, it is not permissible to neglect the term r_{12}^{-1}, but at least we can think of a crude way to estimate how its presence might affect the hydrogenlike wave function. If we think of one of the two electrons as moving in the potential field of the nucleus and of the other electron and if we assume that the charge cloud of the second electron is spherically symmetric, then we can use classical electrostatic theory to get a rough idea what this potential field looks like. Let $\delta(r)$ be the fraction of the probability density of the second electron that is contained in a sphere of radius r around the nucleus; then the first electron experiences a potential

$$V(r) = -\frac{2 - \delta(r)}{r} \qquad (12\text{-}66)$$

at a distance r from the nucleus. It is clear that $\delta(r)$ is zero for $r = 0$ and $\delta(r)$ is unity when r tends to infinity, so that $V(r)$ varies between $(-2/r)$ close to the nucleus and $(-1/r)$ at great distances. On the average the first electron experiences, therefore, a potential

$$V(r) = -\frac{Z}{r} \qquad 1 < Z < 2 \qquad (12\text{-}67)$$

Accordingly, we approximate $f_0(\mathbf{r})$ as

$$f_0(\mathbf{r}) \simeq e^{-Zr} \qquad (12\text{-}68)$$

where Z is a number between 1 and 2 that we will try to determine by means of the variation theorem.

Our normalized trial function is

$$s_0(1,2) = \frac{Z^3}{\pi} e^{-Zr_1} \cdot e^{-Zr_2} \tag{12-69}$$

and we wish to evaluate the expectation value

$$E(Z) = \langle s_0(1,2)| H_0 |s_0(1,2)\rangle \tag{12-70}$$

as a function of the parameter Z. We observe first that

$$\left(-\frac{\Delta_1}{2} - \frac{Z}{r_1}\right) e^{-Zr_1} = -\frac{Z^2}{2} e^{-Zr_1} \tag{12-71}$$

so that we may simplify $E(Z)$ to

$$E(Z) = -Z^2 + (2Z - 4)\langle s_0| r_1^{-1} |s_0\rangle + \langle s_0| r_{12}^{-1} |s_0\rangle \tag{12-72}$$

It is easily found that

$$\langle s_0| r_1^{-1} |s_0\rangle = Z \tag{12-73}$$

The other integral can be transformed to

$$\langle s_0| r_{12}^{-1} |s_0\rangle = \frac{Z}{32\pi^2} \iint \frac{e^{-r_1} e^{-r_2}}{r_{12}} \, d\mathbf{r}_1 \, d\mathbf{r}_2 \tag{12-74}$$

This is just the integral J that is evaluated in Appendix B, and if we substitute the result $(B\text{-}24)$, we find that

$$\langle s_0| r_{12}^{-1} |s_0\rangle = \tfrac{5}{8}Z \tag{12-75}$$

Substitution of Eqs. (12-73) and (12-75) into the expression (12-72) for $E(Z)$ gives

$$E(Z) = Z^2 - \tfrac{27}{8}Z = (Z - \tfrac{27}{16})^2 - \tfrac{729}{256} \tag{12-76}$$

It follows that the energy has a minimum for $Z = 1.6875$ and that the minimum is $E(Z_0) = -2.8477$ au. The experimental value is $E_{exp} = -2.90372$ au, so that the agreement is not too bad.

Let us now investigate how to obtain more accurate energies for the ground state of the helium atom. Our first thought is to use more elaborate trial functions $f_0(\mathbf{r})$, for example,

$$f_0(\mathbf{r}) \simeq (1 + ar)e^{-Zr} \tag{12-77}$$

but this approach has its limitations. It has been shown that, as long as we stay within the approximation (12-65), the best possible energy value that can be obtained is $E_0 = -2.8617$ au. This result is obtained by means of the Hartree-Fock method that we discuss in Chap. 13. This is not a significant improvement over the result that was obtained from the simple variation function (12-68). If we wish to get better results, we must therefore abandon the approximation (12-65).

Since the ground state of the helium atom has zero angular momentum, it may be shown that its wave function $s_0(\mathbf{r}_1,\mathbf{r}_2)$ is a function only of r_1, r_2, and r_{12}:

$$s_0(\mathbf{r}_1,\mathbf{r}_2) = \psi(r_1,r_2,r_{12}) \qquad (12\text{-}78)$$

It is obvious that the wave function must contain the variable r_{12}, since the repulsion term $r_{12}{}^{-1}$ in the Hamiltonian (12-61) has the effect of keeping the electrons away from each other. Somehow this behavior should be reflected in the wave functions.

There are two different ways to include the electron repulsion in the variational trial functions. The first one is straightforward; it consists of the expansion of $\psi(r_1,r_2,r_{12})$ as a power series in r_1, r_2, r_{12}. This method was applied as early as 1929 by Hylleraas,[1] and it led to satisfactory results. In all these expansions it is customary to introduce the new set of variables

$$s = r_1 + r_2 \qquad t = r_1 - r_2 \qquad u = r_{12} \qquad (12\text{-}79)$$

Hylleraas's calculation was based on the trial function

$$\psi = e^{-Zs} \sum_k \sum_l \sum_m a_{k,l,m} s^k t^{2l} u^m \qquad (12\text{-}80)$$

There are practical limitations as to how far this expansion can be extended. Hylleraas restricted his calculation to a six-term trial function, and he obtained an excellent result, $E = -2.90324$.

More recently Kinoshita[2] observed that the Hylleraas expansion (12-80) can never lead to the correct eigenfunction for the helium atom. As a more suitable trial function he proposed, therefore,

$$\psi = e^{-Zs} \sum_{l=0}^{\infty} \sum_{m=0}^{\infty} \sum_{n=0}^{\infty} c_{l,m,n} s^{l-m} u^{m-2n} t^{2n} \qquad (12\text{-}81)$$

From a 38-term function of this type Kinoshita predicted an energy value $E = -2.9037225$ au.

The reader might wonder what the practical use of such elaborate calculations is. In this way the nonrelativistic ground-state energy of the helium atom can be determined to within an accuracy of a fraction of a cm^{-1}. The experimental ground-state energy, which can be measured with a similar accuracy, is the sum of the nonrelativistic and the relativistic energies. From a comparison between Kinoshita's result and the

[1] E. A. Hylleraas, *Zeits. f. Physik*, **54**: 347 (1929).
[2] T. Kinoshita, *Phys. Rev.*, **105**: 1490 (1957).

experimental value we may derive the relativistic contribution to the ground-state energies with an accuracy of about 0.2 per cent. In this way several aspects of relativity theory and quantum-field theory could be verified.

At the present time calculations of this type are performed with the aid of high-speed computers. Recently they have been extended to trial functions that contain more than 1,000 adjustable parameters. In this way the wave functions of the helium atom can be derived to any degree of accuracy that may be desired.

The second method for including electron repulsion in the wave function is based on what is called *configuration interaction*. In the case of the helium atom it is considerably less effective than the other approach, but it has the advantage that it can be more conveniently extended to other atoms and also to molecules. We illustrate it by considering the trial function

$$s_0(\mathbf{r}_1, \mathbf{r}_2) = Ae^{-Z(r_1+r_2)} + B(e^{-Z_1 r_1}e^{-Z_2 r_2} + e^{-Z_2 r_1}e^{-Z_1 r_2}) \qquad (12\text{-}82)$$

This function does not contain r_{12} explicitly, but by choosing the parameters Z_1 and Z_2, we can see to it that the second term of Eq. (12-82) represents a situation in which the two electrons are kept apart. For example, if we take $Z_1 = 2$ and $Z_2 = 1$, then one of the two electrons is much closer to the nucleus than the other, and on the average the two electrons will be much further apart than in the first term. We can extend this expansion by including terms of the type $(1s)$ $(2s)$, $(2s)^2$, $(2p)^2$, etc., but the energies that are obtained in this way are usually much less accurate than Kinoshita's value. On the other hand, this approach of expanding the wave function as a linear combination of a number of configurations can supply us with a useful tool for improving wave functions of complex atoms.

PROBLEMS

12-1 Derive the eigenfunctions, containing the spin, that are consistent with the exclusion principle for a three-electron system.

12-2 Perform a variational treatment for the ground state of the He atom from the trial function

$$s_0(1,2) = e^{-Zr_1}e^{-Z'r_2} + e^{-Z'r_1}e^{-Zr_2}$$

Determine the energy minimum and the values of Z and Z' for which this minimum occurs.

12-3 Determine the energy eigenvalues and eigenfunctions of a triplet state in a magnetic field **H** in an arbitrary direction. The Hamiltonian for this system is

$$H_s = \frac{eh}{mc} \mathbf{S} \cdot \mathbf{M}$$

where $\mathbf{S} = \mathbf{S}_1 + \mathbf{S}_2$.

12-4 Determine the ground-state energy of the He atom by means of the variation theorem from the wave function

$$s_0(1,2) = e^{-Zr_1} e^{-Zr_2} (1 + ar_{12})$$

(Hint: The integrals containing r_{12} can be evaluated by using the Fourier convolution theorem of Appendix C.)

CHAPTER **13**
————————

ATOMS

13-1 INTRODUCTION

A complex atom or ion consists of N electrons and a nucleus with charge Ze. The main contribution H_0 to its Hamiltonian is

$$H_0 = -\frac{\hbar^2}{2m} \sum_{j=1}^{N} \Delta_j - \sum_{j=1}^{N} \frac{Ze^2}{r_j} + \sum_{i>j} \frac{e^2}{r_{ij}} \tag{13-1}$$

The complete Hamiltonian H contains, in addition to H_0, the spin Hamiltonian H_s and several relativistic contributions, but these are not considered here.

It is essentially impossible to derive the exact eigenvalues and eigenfunctions of H_0, so that we have to resort again to approximate methods. Fortunately, we have a rough idea of what the atomic wave functions ought to look like. We are helped here by the experimental information from atomic spectra and from chemical properties and by the results that we have discussed for the helium spectrum. The most important feature of atomic structure, which we take as a starting point for our theoretical discussion, is that the individual electrons can be identified by sets of hydrogenlike quantum numbers. It may be recalled that our first approximation to the ground-state wave function of the helium atom was the function

$$s_0(1,2) = \left(\frac{Z^3}{\pi}\right)e^{-Zr_1} \cdot e^{-Zr_2} \tag{13-2}$$

We argued that in the ground state each of the two electrons moves in an effective potential $(-Ze^2/r)$. The eigenvalues and eigenfunctions that correspond to this potential are characterized by the hydrogen quantum numbers n, l, and m with the lowest eigenvalue described as $(1s)$. According to this simplified model the ground state of the helium atom is obtained by placing both electrons in a $(1s)$ state, which we denote by $(1s)^2$. Because of the Pauli exclusion principle the two electrons must have opposite spins in the configuration $(1s)^2$. Thus we conclude that in its ground state the helium atom has a singlet $(1s)^2$ configuration. We do not intend to discuss atomic excited states in any detail, but it is easily seen that the helium atom can have the configurations $(1s)(2s)$, $(1s)(3s)$, $(1s)(2p)$, $(1s)(3p)$, . . . , etc., in its excited states.

Let us now use the same approximate approach to describe the ground state of the Li atom. Here we have three electrons, and because of the Pauli principle, it is not permissible to place all three electrons in a $(1s)$ state. The lowest atomic states must therefore have the configurations $(1s)^2(2s)$ or $(1s)^2(2p)$ where the two $(1s)$ electrons have opposite spins. It now follows from the atomic spectra and from general physical considerations that in this approximate model the energies of the states (ns) are always lower than the energies of the states (np). Consequently the ground state of the Li atom has the configuration $(1s)^2(2s)$, and the first excited state has the configuration $(1s)^2(2p)$.

By means of a similar argument we derive that the ground-state configuration of the Be atom is $(1s)^2(2s)^2$, etc. We list the ground-state configurations of the first 36 elements in Table 13-1. We have already mentioned that the (ns) states have lower energies than the (np) states; similarly we may derive from the atomic spectra that the (np) states have lower energies than the (nd) states, etc. For more complex atoms this effect becomes very pronounced, and we see that the $(4s)$ states have, in general, lower energies than the $(3d)$ states, the $(5s)$ states have lower energies than the $(4f)$ states, etc. It should be realized that this crude description cannot account for the more subtle effects in atomic spectra; for example, the $(1s)^2(2s)^2(2p)^2$ configuration of the carbon atom is highly degenerate, and we expect that there are a number of atomic states that all have the same configuration. However, for the time being we do not consider these complications, and we discuss only atoms with closed-shell ground states. These are states with the configuration

$(a)^2(b)^2(c)^2 \cdots (n)^2$, in which each one-electron state is doubly occupied by a pair of electrons with antiparallel spins.

TABLE 13–1 Ground-state Configurations

1.	H $(1s)$	19.	K	$\ldots (3s)^2(3p)^6(4s)$
2.	He $(1s)^2$	20.	Ca	$\ldots (3s)^2(3p)^6(4s)^2$
3.	Li $(1s)^2(2s)$	21.	Sc	$\ldots (3s)^2(3p)^6(3d)(4s)^2$
4.	Be $(1s)^2(2s)^2$	22.	Ti	$\ldots (3s)^2(3p)^6(3d)^2(4s)^2$
5.	B $(1s)^2(2s)^2(2p)$	23.	V	$\ldots (3s)^2(3p)^6(3d)^3(4s)^2$
6.	C $\ldots (2s)^2(2p)^2$	24.	Cr	$\ldots (3s)^2(3p)^6(3d)^5(4s)$
7.	N $\ldots (2s)^2(2p)^3$	25.	Mn	$\ldots (3s)^2(3p)^6(3d)^5(4s)^2$
8.	O $\ldots (2s)^2(2p)^4$	26.	Fe	$\ldots (3s)^2(3p)^6(3d)^6(4s)^2$
9.	F $\ldots (2s)^2(2p)^5$	27.	Co	$\ldots (3s)^2(3p)^6(3d)^7(4s)^2$
10.	Ne $\ldots (2s)^2(2p)^6$	28.	Ni	$\ldots (3s)^2(3p)^6(3d)^8(4s)^2$
11.	Na $\ldots (2s)^2(2p)^6(3s)$	29.	Cu	$\ldots (3s)^2(3p)^6(3d)^{10}(4s)$
12.	Mg $\ldots (2s)^2(2p)^6(3s)^2$	30.	Zn	$\ldots (3s)^2(3p)^6(3d)^{10}(4s)^2$
13.	Al $\ldots (3s)^2(3p)$	31.	Ga	$\ldots (4s)^2(4p)$
14.	Si $\ldots (3s)^2(3p)^2$	32.	Ge	$\ldots (4s)^2(4p)^2$
15.	P $\ldots (3s)^2(3p)^3$	33.	As	$\ldots (4s)^2(4p)^3$
16.	S $\ldots (3s)^2(3p)^4$	34.	Se	$\ldots (4s)^2(4p)^4$
17.	Cl $\ldots (3s)^2(3p)^5$	35.	Br	$\ldots (4s)^2(4p)^5$
18.	Ar $\ldots (3s)^2(3p)^6$	36.	Kr	$\ldots (4s)^2(4p)^6$

Our assumption is that the solution of the Schrödinger equation

$$H_0\Psi_0 = E_0\Psi_0 \tag{13-3}$$

can be approximated by a product of one-electron functions

$$\Psi_0 = \phi_1(1)\phi_1(2)\phi_2(3)\phi_2(4)\phi_3(5)\phi_3(6) \cdots \phi_N(2N-1)\phi_N(2N) \tag{13-4}$$

Let us use this product as a starting point for the construction of the proper antisymmetrical atomic eigenfunction containing the spin variables. We limit our discussion to closed-shell ground states only. We have seen that for a two-electron system the desired eigenfunction takes the form

$$\Psi_0 = \phi_1(1)\phi_1(2)[\alpha(1)\beta(2) - \beta(1)\alpha(2)] \tag{13-5}$$

It is easily verified that for an N-electron system we should take the function

$$\Psi_0 = \sum_P P\delta_P[\phi_1(1)\alpha(1)\phi_1(2)\beta(2)\phi_2(3)\alpha(3)\phi_2(4)\beta(4) \cdots$$
$$\phi_N(2N-1)\alpha(2N-1)\phi_N(2N)\beta(2N)] \tag{13-6}$$

where the summation is to be performed over all permutations of the electrons. It was observed by Slater[1] that this expression can also be written as a determinant, namely,

$$\Psi_0 = \begin{vmatrix} \phi_1(1)\alpha(1) & \phi_1(1)\beta(1) & \cdots & \cdots & \phi_N(1)\alpha(1) & \phi_N(1)\beta(1) \\ \phi_1(2)\alpha(2) & \phi_1(2)\beta(2) & \cdots & \cdots & \phi_N(2)\alpha(2) & \phi_N(2)\beta(2) \\ \cdots & \cdots & \cdots & \cdots & \cdots & \cdots \\ \cdots & \cdots & \cdots & \cdots & \cdots & \cdots \\ \phi_1(2N-1)\alpha(2N-1) & \phi_1(2N-1)\beta(2N-1) & \cdots & \cdots & \phi_N(2_N-1)\alpha(2_N-1) & \phi_N(2N-1)\beta(2N-1) \\ \phi_1(2N)\alpha(2N) & \phi_1(2N)\beta(2N) & \cdots & \cdots & \phi_N(2N)\alpha(2N) & \phi_N(2N)\beta(2N) \end{vmatrix}$$

$$(13\text{-}7)$$

Determinants of the type of (13-7) are therefore known as *Slater determinants*.

We saw in Chap. 6 that a determinant remains unchanged if we add a linear combination of some columns to a different column. It follows, therefore, that the functions ϕ_k do not necessarily have to be orthogonal, and any nonorthogonality effects cancel out automatically if we evaluate the determinant. On the other hand, if the functions ϕ_k are not orthogonal, we can always transform the determinant in such a way that it is reexpressed in terms of an orthogonal set of functions ϕ_k', as long as the original functions ϕ_k are linearly independent. In practice it is more convenient to work with orthonormal sets of functions ϕ_k, and since we can always express the Slater determinant in terms of an orthonormal set of functions, it is assumed throughout this chapter that the ϕ_k form an orthonormal set. In this case we have

$$\langle \Psi_0 | \Psi_0 \rangle = (2N)! \qquad (13\text{-}8)$$

for the function Ψ_0 of Eq. (13-7), since the determinant is constructed from $(2N)!$ products. The normalized function Ψ_0 should therefore be written as

$$\Psi_0 = [(2N)!]^{-1/2} \sum_P P\delta_P \left[\prod_{k=1}^{N} \phi_k(2k-1)\phi_k(2k)\alpha(2k-1)\beta(2k) \right] \qquad (13\text{-}9)$$

13-2 SLATER ORBITALS

In many cases it is useful to have a rough idea about the form of the functions ϕ_k that occur in a Slater determinant. For example, we saw

[1] J. C. Slater, *Phys. Rev.*, 34: 1293 (1929).

in Chap. 12 that in the case of the He atom we approximated the function ϕ_1 as

$$\phi_1 = \left(\frac{Z^3}{\pi}\right)^{1/2} e^{-Zr} \tag{13-10}$$

By making use of the variation theorem, we found that the lowest energy is obtained for $Z = 1.6875$. From similar considerations we can also derive approximate one-electron functions for more complex atoms.

We may recall that the physical reasoning that we used in constructing the function (13-10) was that each electron moves in the potential field of the nucleus and of the second electron. We argued that the effect of the repulsion by the second electron may be roughly represented as a shielding of the nuclear charge 2 by an amount σ due to the fraction of the charge cloud of the second electron that is situated between the nucleus and the first electron. In the case of the helium atom it was found that $\sigma = 2 - Z = 0.3125$.

We can use the same arguments for the construction of the one-electron functions, or *orbitals*, as they are called, for more complex atoms. For example, in the case of neon, which has the configuration $(1s)^2(2s)^2(2p)^6$, we can use the approximations

$$\phi(1s) = \left(\frac{Z_1^3}{\pi}\right)^{1/2} e^{-Z_1 r}$$

$$\phi(2s) = \left(\frac{Z_2^3}{32\pi}\right)^{1/2} (Z_2 r - 2) \exp\left(-\frac{1}{2}Z_2 r\right) \tag{13-11}$$

$$\phi(2p_\alpha) = \left(\frac{Z_3^5}{32\pi}\right)^{1/2} r_\alpha \exp\left(-\frac{1}{2}Z_3 r\right)$$

and determine the values of Z_1, Z_2, and Z_3 by means of the variation theorem. A calculation of this type was performed by Zener[1] for the carbon atom, in which case Z_1 is very close to the nuclear charge 6, whereas Z_2 and Z_3 are close to 3. Shortly thereafter, Slater[2] proposed some very simple algebraic rules for estimating the values of the effective nuclear charges that are obtained in this way. First, however, it was pointed out by Slater that instead of the exact hydrogenlike wave functions we may just as well take the simplified functions

$$\phi_{n,l,m}(r,\theta,\phi) = r^n \exp\left(\frac{-Z'r}{n}\right) Y_{l,m}(\theta,\phi) \tag{13-12}$$

as the basis for our approximate description. In the case of the hydrogen

[1] C. Zener, *Phys. Rev.*, **36**: 51 (1930).
[2] J. C. Slater, *Phys. Rev.*, **36**: 97 (1930).

atom the exact eigenfunctions $\psi_{n,l,m}(r,\theta,\phi)$ have the advantage of being orthogonal to one another, but this advantage disappears if we substitute different nuclear charges in the different states. The functions $\phi_{n,l,m}(r,\theta,\phi)$, which are now generally known as *Slater orbitals*, form just as satisfactory a basis set for describing atomic states as the exact hydrogen eigenfunctions $\psi_{n,l,m}(r,\theta,\phi)$, and since the Slater orbitals are easier to deal with than the $\psi_{n,l,m}$, we might as well use them.

In order to estimate the effective nuclear charges Z' we write them as

$$Z' = Z - \sigma \qquad (13\text{-}13)$$

where Z is the exact nuclear charge and σ represents the shielding of the nucleus by the other electrons. The value of σ depends on the state of the electron that we are concerned with and on the states of the other electrons that are present in the atom. According to Slater's rules, σ is obtained as a sum of the shielding contributions of these other electrons. These contributions are:

1. Nothing from any electron that has a principal quantum number n that is higher than the one that we consider
2. An amount 0.35 from each electron that has the same principal quantum number as the electron that we consider, except that when we consider a $(1s)$ electron, the contribution from the other $(1s)$ electron is 0.30
3. An amount 0.85 from each electron that has a principal quantum number n that is 1 less than the quantum number of the electron that we consider if the latter is an s or a p electron and an amount 1.00 from each electron whose principal quantum number is less by 1 than the electron that we consider if the latter is in a $d, f,$ or g state
4. An amount 1.00 from each electron with a principal quantum number that is less by 2 or more than the quantum number of the electron considered

We illustrate these rules for the sulfur atom. According to Table 13-1 the atomic configuration here is $(1s)^2(2s)^2(2p)^6(3s)^2(3p)^4$, and the nuclear charge is 16. The effective nuclear charges Z' for the various electrons are

$$Z'(1s) = 16 - 0.30 = 15.70$$

$$Z'(2s) = 16 - 7 \times 0.35 - 2 \times 0.85 = 11.85$$

$$Z'(2p) = Z'(2s) = 11.85 \qquad (13\text{-}14)$$

$$Z'(3s) = 16 - 2 \times 1 - 8 \times 0.85 - 5 \times 0.35 = 5.45$$

$$Z'(3p) = Z'(3s) = 5.45$$

For the helium atom Slater's rules predict an effective nuclear charge $Z' = 1.70$, which is reasonably close to the value $Z' = 1.6875$ that we obtained in Chap. 12 from the variation theorem.

These Slater orbitals have found wide applicability in atomic and molecular problems. They are obviously very convenient for performing crude order-of-magnitude calculations for atomic properties. They are also useful in more precise theoretical work. We will see that in some methods for deriving more accurate atomic wave functions we make use of iterative procedures in which we start with approximate orbitals that are transformed progressively into more and more accurate orbitals. Here the Slater orbitals supply us with a convenient starting point for the iterative process.

13-3 THE HARTREE-FOCK EQUATIONS

Once we have made the approximation of writing the atomic eigenfunctions as antisymmetrized products of one-electron functions, we can try to determine the best possible eigenfunctions that are consistent with this approximation. By making use of the variation theorem, we can derive a set of differential equations for the orbitals that are known as the Hartree-Fock equations.[1] These equations depend on the spin multiplicity of the atomic state that we are concerned with and also on the orbital degeneracy. We limit our discussion to the simplest possible case, namely, a singlet, closed-shell, ground state, where the atomic wave function is approximated as

$$\Psi = [(2N)!]^{-1/2} \sum_P P \, \delta_P \left[\prod_{k=1}^{N} \phi_k(2k-1)\alpha(2k-1)\phi_k(2k)\beta(2k) \right] \quad (13\text{-}15)$$

The first step in our derivation is to express the energy expectation value

$$E = \langle \Psi | H_0 | \Psi \rangle \quad (13\text{-}16)$$

and the overlap integral

$$S = \langle \Psi | \Psi \rangle \quad (13\text{-}17)$$

in terms of the one-electron orbitals ϕ_k. Here H_0 is the Hamiltonian of Eq. (13-1). It is convenient to write H_0 as a sum of one- and two-electron contributions:

$$H_0 = \sum_{j=1}^{N} G(j) + \sum_{i>j} \Omega(i,j) \quad (13\text{-}18)$$

where

$$G(j) = -\frac{\hbar^2}{2m} \Delta_j - \frac{Ze^2}{r_j}$$

$$\Omega(i,j) = \frac{e^2}{r_{ij}} \quad (13\text{-}19)$$

[1] D. R. Hartree, *Proc. Cambridge Phil. Soc.*, **24**: 89 (1927); V. Fock, *Zeits. f. Phys.*, **61**: 126 (1930).

We mentioned in Sec. 13-2 that it is always possible to write the Slater determinant Ψ in such a way that the orbitals ϕ_k form an orthonormal set

$$\langle \phi_k | \phi_l \rangle = \delta_{k,l} \tag{13-20}$$

Since this greatly facilitates the computations, we assume that this condition (13-20) is satisfied.

It is easily proved that the overlap integral S is now equal to unity. According to Eq. (13-17) S is given by

$$S = [(2N)!]^{-1} \langle \sum_P P \, \delta_P \left[\prod_{k=1}^{N} \phi_k(2k-1)\alpha(2k-1)\phi_k(2k)\beta(2k) \right] |$$

$$| \sum_P P \, \delta_P \left[\prod_{k=1}^{N} \phi_k(2k-1)\alpha(2k-1)\phi_k(2k)\beta(2k) \right] \rangle \tag{13-21}$$

which we can also write as

$$S = \langle \sum_P P \, \delta_P \left[\prod_{k=1}^{N} \phi_k(2k-1)\alpha(2k-1)\phi_k(2k)\beta(2k) \right] |$$

$$| \prod_{k=1}^{N} \phi_k(2k-1)\alpha(2k-1)\phi_k(2k)\beta(2k) \rangle \tag{13-22}$$

We consider first the contribution from the identity permutation, which is

$$\langle \prod_{k=1}^{N} \phi_k(2k-1)\alpha(2k-1)\phi_k(2k)\beta(2k) | \prod_{k=1}^{N} \phi_k(2k-1)\alpha(2k-1)\phi_k(2k)\beta(2k) \rangle = 1 \tag{13-23}$$

Here each set of electron coordinates occurs in the same functions on the left and on the right, and the result is unity because of Eq. (13-20). For any other permutation, different from the identity permutation, there are at least two "misfits," where for one set of electron coordinates the functions on the left and on the right differ either in the orbital part or in the spin part. Because of the orthogonality of the orbitals ϕ_k and of the spin functions α and β, the contribution from any one of these permutations is zero. Hence S is equal to unity.

We use the same technique to evaluate E. First we write E as a sum of two terms

$$E = E_1 + E_2 \tag{13-24}$$

which are defined as

$$E_1 = \langle \Psi | \sum_j G(j) | \Psi \rangle \tag{13-25}$$

and

$$E_2 = \langle \Psi | \sum_{i>j} \Omega(i,j) | \Psi \rangle \tag{13-26}$$

We observe first that E_1 can be written as

$$E_1 = \left\langle \sum_P P \, \delta_P \left[\prod_{k=1}^{N} \phi_k(2k-1)\bar{\phi}_k(2k) \right] \Big| \sum_j G(j) \Big| \prod_{k=1}^{N} \phi_k(2k-1)\bar{\phi}_k(2k) \right\rangle \quad \text{(13-27)}$$

where we have introduced the abbreviations

$$\phi_k = \phi_k \alpha \qquad \bar{\phi}_k = \phi_k \beta \quad \text{(13-28)}$$

Again we consider first the diagonal term of the Slater determinant, which gives

$$E_1' = \left\langle \prod_{k=1}^{N} \phi_k(2k-1)\bar{\phi}_k(2k) \Big| \sum_j G(j) \Big| \prod_{k=1}^{N} \phi_k(2k-1)\bar{\phi}_k(2k) \right\rangle$$

$$= \sum_{k=1}^{N} [\langle \phi_k| G |\phi_k \rangle + \langle \bar{\phi}_k| G |\bar{\phi}_k \rangle] = 2 \sum_{k=1}^{N} G_k \quad \text{(13-29)}$$

$$G_k = \langle \phi_k(i)| G(i) |\phi_k(i) \rangle$$

Each of the other permutations creates at least two "misfits"; that is, there are at least two sets of electronic coordinates that occur in different functions on the left and right sides of the operators in Eq. (13-27). Since each term of the operator depends only on one set of electronic coordinates, the contributions of all these other permutations are zero. Our final result is therefore

$$E_1 = 2 \sum_{k=1}^{N} G_k \quad \text{(13-30)}$$

The other energy term E_2 can be written as

$$E_2 = \left\langle \sum_P P \, \delta_P \left[\prod_{k=1}^{N} \phi_k(2k-1)\bar{\phi}_k(2k) \right] \Big| \sum_{i>j} \Omega(i,j) \Big| \prod_{k=1}^{N} \phi_k(2k-1)\bar{\phi}_k(2k) \right\rangle \quad \text{(13-31)}$$

Here the contribution from the diagonal term is

$$E_2' = \left\langle \prod_{k=1}^{N} \phi_k(2k-1)\bar{\phi}_k(2k) \Big| \sum_{i>j} \Omega(i,j) \Big| \prod_{k=1}^{N} \phi_k(2k-1)\bar{\phi}_k(2k) \right\rangle \quad \text{(13-32)}$$

If we define the integrals $J_{k,l}$ as

$$J_{k,l} = \langle \phi_k(i)\phi_l(j)| \Omega(i,j) |\phi_k(i)\phi_l(j) \rangle \quad \text{(13-33)}$$

then it is easily verified that E_2' can be expressed as

$$E_2' = \sum_{k=1}^{N} \left(J_{k,k} + 2 \sum_{l \neq k} J_{k,l} \right) \quad \text{(13-34)}$$

Let us now determine the contributions to E_2' from the other permutations. First we consider the permutations that correspond to a pairwise interchange of two sets of electron coordinates. It may be seen that these permutations give rise to two "misfits" in the expression for E_2. If the permutation involves a pair of electrons in which one electron has an even subscript and the other an odd subscript, then the discrepancy is located in the spin functions, and the result of the integration is zero. On the other hand, if the permutation involves a pair of electrons whose subscripts are both even or both odd, then the discrepancy is located in the orbital functions. In the present case the operator is a sum of two-electron terms, so that for each pair of "misfits" that is restricted to the orbital functions only, there exists one term in the Hamiltonian that gives a nonzero contribution. For example, if the permutation consists of an interchange of electrons $2k$ and $2l$, then its contribution to E_2 is

$$E_2(k,l) = -\langle \bar{\phi}_l(2k)\bar{\phi}_k(2l)|\,\Omega(2k,2l)\,|\bar{\phi}_k(2k)\bar{\phi}_l(2l)\rangle \qquad (13\text{-}35)$$

It may be deduced that the sum of all these contributions to E_2 can be written in the form

$$E_2'' = -\sum_{k=1}^{N}\sum_{l\neq k} K_{k,l} \qquad (13\text{-}36)$$

if we define

$$K_{k,l} = \langle \phi_l(i)\phi_k(j)|\,\Omega(i,j)\,|\phi_k(i)\phi_l(j)\rangle \qquad (13\text{-}37)$$

It is easily verified that

$$K_{k,l} = K_{l,k} \qquad (13\text{-}38)$$

since the operator is symmetric in i and j.

The contributions to E_2 of all other permutations, which go beyond a simple pairwise interchange of two electrons, are all zero. These permutations give rise to at least three "misfits," and since each term in the Hamiltonian depends only on two sets of electron coordinates, we find that the integrations all give zero. The total result for E_2 is obtained by adding Eqs. (13-34) and (13-36):

$$E_2 = \sum_{k=1}^{N}\left[J_{k,k} + \sum_{l\neq k}(2J_{k,l} - K_{k,l})\right] \qquad (13\text{-}39)$$

We can write this in a slightly different form. Since

$$J_{k,k} = K_{k,k} \qquad (13\text{-}40)$$

we may add a term $J_{k,k}$ to Eq. (13-39) if at the same time we also subtract a term $K_{k,k}$. The result becomes, then,

$$E_2 = \sum_{k=1}^{N}\sum_{l=1}^{N}(2J_{k,l} - K_{k,l}) \qquad (13\text{-}41)$$

The total expectation value E is now obtained as the sum of E_1 and E_2:

$$E = 2\sum_{k=1}^{N}\left[G_k + \sum_{l=1}^{N}(J_{k,l} - \tfrac{1}{2}K_{k,l})\right] \qquad (13\text{-}42)$$

We now impose the condition that E remains invariant under arbitrary small variations $\delta\phi_k$ in any of the orbitals ϕ_k, with the auxiliary condition that the change in ϕ_k does not affect the orthonormality of the one-electron orbitals. Let us first determine the change δE_k in E due to the variation $\delta\phi_k^*$. According to Eq. (13-42) we have

$$\delta E_k = 2\left(\delta G_k + \delta J_{k,k} + 2\sum_{l\neq k}\delta J_{k,l} - \tfrac{1}{2}\delta K_{k,k} - \sum_{l\neq k}\delta K_{k,l}\right) \quad (13\text{-}43)$$

Here, the variations in the Coulomb integrals are

$$\delta J_{k,k} = 2\langle\delta\phi_k(i)\phi_k(j)|\,\Omega(i,j)\,|\phi_k(i)\phi_k(j)\rangle$$
$$\delta J_{k,l} = \langle\delta\phi_k(i)\phi_l(j)|\,\Omega(i,j)\,|\phi_k(i)\phi_l(j)\rangle \quad (13\text{-}44)$$

the variations in the exchange integrals are

$$\delta K_{k,k} = 2\langle\delta\phi_k(i)\phi_k(j)|\,\Omega(i,j)\,|\phi_k(i)\phi_k(j)\rangle$$
$$\delta K_{k,l} = \langle\delta\phi_k(i)\phi_l(j)|\,\Omega(i,j)\,|\phi_l(i)\phi_k(j)\rangle \quad (13\text{-}45)$$

and δG_k is

$$\delta G_k = \langle\delta\phi_k(i)|\,G(i)\,|\phi_k(i)\rangle \quad (13\text{-}46)$$

We now introduce the Coulomb operator $J_n(i)$ and the exchange operator $K_n(i)$. The Coulomb operator is defined as

$$J_n(i) = \int \phi_n^*(j)\Omega(i,j)\phi_n(j)\,d\mathbf{r}_j \quad (13\text{-}47)$$

and the exchange operator as

$$K_n(i)\psi(i) = \left[\int \phi_n^*(j)\Omega(i,j)\psi(j)\,d\mathbf{r}_j\right]\phi_n(i) \quad (13\text{-}48)$$

Substitution of Eq. (13-47) into Eq. (13-44) gives

$$\delta J_{k,k} = 2\langle\delta\phi_k(i)|\,J_k(i)\,|\phi_k(i)\rangle$$
$$\delta J_{k,l} = \langle\delta\phi_k(i)|\,J_l(i)\,|\phi_k(i)\rangle \quad (13\text{-}49)$$

and substitution of Eqs. (13-48) into Eq. (13-45) gives

$$\delta K_{k,k} = 2\langle\delta\phi_k(i)|\,K_k(i)\,|\phi_k(i)\rangle$$
$$\delta K_{k,l} = \langle\delta\phi_k(i)|\,K_l(i)\,|\phi_k(i)\rangle \quad (13\text{-}50)$$

It follows from Eqs. (13-46), (13-49), and (13-50) that Eq. (13-43) can be transformed to

$$\delta E_k = 2\langle\delta\phi_k(i)|\,G(i) + \sum_l[2J_l(i) - K_l(i)]\,|\phi_k(i)\rangle \quad (13\text{-}51)$$

It is customary to introduce the Hartree-Fock Hamiltonian operator F, which is defined as

$$F = G + \sum_l (2J_l - K_l) \tag{13-52}$$

This enables us to rewrite Eq. (13-51) as

$$\delta E_k = 2\langle \delta\phi_k | F | \phi_k \rangle \tag{13-53}$$

We should remember that the one-electron operator F contains the one-electron orbitals ϕ_k that we seek to determine. In the derivation above we have required that the orthonormality of the orbitals is not affected by the changes in ϕ_k, so that we imposed the conditions

$$\langle \delta\phi_k | \phi_l \rangle = 0 \qquad l = 1, 2, \ldots, N \tag{13-54}$$

It follows from our discussion in Sec. 11-1 that the variational problem $\delta E_k = 0$ with the auxiliary restraints (13-54) leads to

$$\delta E_k - 2\sum_l \lambda_{k,l}\delta_{k,l} = 0 \tag{13-55}$$

where $\lambda_{k,l}$ are a set of N Lagrangian multipliers. Substitution of Eqs. (13-53) and (13-54) into Eq. (13-55) gives

$$2\langle \delta\phi_k | F - \sum_l \lambda_{k,l} | \phi_l \rangle = 0 \tag{13-56}$$

The electronic orbitals ϕ_k must therefore satisfy the equations

$$F\phi_k = \sum_l \lambda_{k,l} \phi_l \tag{13-57}$$

These are the Hartree-Fock equations for the orbitals ϕ_k.

The solution of these equations is not easy, since the operators depend on the solutions and since Eq. (13-57) represents a set of N coupled differential equations. Usually we can transform the set of functions ϕ_k by means of a unitary transformation, so that the matrix $\lambda_{k,l}$ becomes diagonal, and in this case the equations reduce to

$$F\phi_k = \lambda_k \phi_k \tag{13-58}$$

The customary approach to the solution of these equations is by way of iterative procedures. We start with a set of approximate orbitals and use them to construct the operator J. We then solve the equations, and in this way we obtain a new, improved set of orbitals. We now construct a new set of operators from this solution and solve the equations again. We keep repeating this procedure until the solutions of the equations are identical to the orbitals that we have used for the construction of the operators. In this case we say that the orbitals are self-consistent. Hence, the name *self-consistent field theory* is used for the Hartree-Fock method.

It is not possible, in general, to solve the Hartree-Fock equations, but for atomic systems their solutions have been derived by means of numerical methods. In this case, we know the angular dependence of the orbitals ϕ_k, so that we have to derive only the radial parts $R_k(r)$. We reduce the Hartree-Fock equations to a set of one-dimensional differential equations, which can be solved numerically. We refer the reader to Hartree's book[1] for a detailed discussion of the reduction of the equations into radial form and of the various numerical solution methods.

13-4 FINAL REMARKS

We wish to point out that we have only touched briefly on the theory of atomic structure. We have been concerned only with atomic ground states that are nondegenerate and can be represented as closed shells. In the theory of atomic spectra the excited states are of equal importance, since we are interested in transitions between different states. Much information can also be obtained by studying the effects of electromagnetic fields on the atomic energy levels. However, we feel that all these topics fall outside the range of this book, and we refer the interested reader to the extensive literature in this area.[2]

[1] D. R. Hartree, "The Calculation of Atomic Structures," John Wiley & Sons, Inc., New York, 1957.

[2] See, for example, G. Herzberg, "Atomic Spectra and Atomic Structure," Dover Publications, Inc., New York, 1944, for an elementary discussion, and A. Sommerfeld, "Atomic Structure and Spectral Lines," Methuen, London, 1934, and E. U. Condon and G. H. Shortley, "The Theory of Atomic Spectra," Cambridge University Press, London, 1935, for more sophisticated treatments.

APPENDIX A THE TRANSFORMATION OF THE LAPLACE OPERATOR INTO POLAR COORDINATES

We wish to transform the Laplace operator

$$\Delta = \frac{\partial^2}{\partial x^2} + \frac{\partial^2}{\partial y^2} + \frac{\partial^2}{\partial z^2} \tag{A-1}$$

into polar coordinates (r,θ,ϕ), which are defined as

$$x = r \sin \theta \cos \phi$$
$$y = r \sin \theta \sin \phi \tag{A-2}$$
$$z = r \cos \theta$$

We perform this transformation in two steps, the first given by

$$x = \rho \cos \phi$$
$$y = \rho \sin \phi \tag{A-3}$$

We have

$$\frac{\partial f}{\partial \rho} = \frac{\partial x}{\partial \rho} \frac{\partial f}{\partial x} + \frac{\partial y}{\partial \rho} \frac{\partial f}{\partial y}$$

$$\frac{\partial f}{\partial \phi} = \frac{\partial x}{\partial \phi} \frac{\partial f}{\partial x} + \frac{\partial y}{\partial \phi} \frac{\partial f}{\partial y} \tag{A-4}$$

or

$$\frac{\partial f}{\partial \rho} = \cos \phi \frac{\partial f}{\partial x} + \sin \phi \frac{\partial f}{\partial y}$$

$$\frac{\partial f}{\partial \phi} = -\rho \sin \phi \frac{\partial f}{\partial x} + \rho \cos \phi \frac{\partial f}{\partial y} \tag{A-5}$$

263

From these equations we derive

$$\frac{\partial f}{\partial x} = \cos \phi \, \frac{\partial f}{\partial \rho} - \frac{\sin \phi}{\rho} \, \frac{\partial f}{\partial \phi}$$

$$\frac{\partial f}{\partial y} = \sin \phi \, \frac{\partial f}{\partial \rho} + \frac{\cos \phi}{\rho} \, \frac{\partial f}{\partial \phi}$$

(A-6)

In the same way, we obtain for the second derivatives

$$\frac{\partial^2 f}{\partial x^2} = \cos^2 \phi \, \frac{\partial^2 f}{\partial \rho^2} - \frac{2 \sin \phi \cos \phi}{\rho} \, \frac{\partial^2 f}{\partial \rho \, \partial \phi}$$

$$+ \frac{\sin^2 \phi}{\rho^2} \, \frac{\partial^2 f}{\partial \phi^2} + \frac{\sin^2 \phi}{\rho} \, \frac{\partial f}{\partial \rho} + \frac{2 \sin \phi \cos \phi}{\rho^2} \, \frac{\partial f}{\partial \phi}$$

$$\frac{\partial^2 f}{\partial y^2} = \sin^2 \phi \, \frac{\partial^2 f}{\partial \rho^2} + \frac{2 \sin \phi \cos \phi}{\rho} \, \frac{\partial^2 f}{\partial \rho \, \partial \phi}$$

$$+ \frac{\cos^2 \phi}{\rho^2} \, \frac{\partial^2 f}{\partial \phi^2} + \frac{\cos^2 \phi}{\rho} \, \frac{\partial f}{\partial \rho} - \frac{2 \sin \phi \cos \phi}{\rho^2} \, \frac{\partial f}{\partial \phi}$$

(A-7)

Addition of these two equations gives

$$\frac{\partial^2 f}{\partial x^2} + \frac{\partial^2 f}{\partial y^2} = \frac{\partial^2 f}{\partial \rho^2} + \frac{1}{\rho} \, \frac{\partial f}{\partial \rho} + \frac{1}{\rho^2} \, \frac{\partial^2 f}{\partial \phi^2}$$

(A-8)

The Laplace operator Δ of Eq. (A-1) can now be written as

$$\Delta = \frac{\partial^2}{\partial \rho^2} + \frac{\partial^2}{\partial z^2} + \frac{1}{\rho} \, \frac{\partial}{\partial \rho} + \frac{1}{\rho^2} \, \frac{\partial^2}{\partial \phi^2}$$

(A-9)

The second step of our transformation is

$$z = r \cos \theta$$

$$\rho = r \sin \theta$$

(A-10)

By analogy to Eq. (A-8) we find

$$\frac{\partial^2}{\partial \rho^2} + \frac{\partial^2}{\partial z^2} = \frac{\partial^2}{\partial r^2} + \frac{1}{r} \, \frac{\partial}{\partial r} + \frac{1}{r^2} \, \frac{\partial^2}{\partial \theta^2}$$

(A-11)

Similarly, we derive from the second Eq. (A-6) that

$$\frac{\partial}{\partial \rho} = \sin \theta \, \frac{\partial}{\partial r} + \frac{\cos \theta}{r} \, \frac{\partial}{\partial \theta}$$

(A-12)

Consequently, we have

$$\frac{1}{\rho} \, \frac{\partial}{\partial \rho} = \frac{1}{r} \, \frac{\partial}{\partial r} + \frac{\cos \theta}{r^2 \sin \theta} \, \frac{\partial}{\partial \theta}$$

(A-13)

In addition, we have

$$\frac{1}{\rho^2}\frac{\partial^2}{\partial\phi^2} = \frac{1}{r^2\sin^2\theta}\frac{\partial^2}{\partial\phi^2} \qquad\text{(A-14)}$$

Substitution of Eqs. (A-1), (A-13), and (A-14) into Eq. (A-9) gives, finally,

$$\Delta = \frac{\partial^2}{\partial r^2} + \frac{2}{r}\frac{\partial}{\partial r} + \frac{1}{r^2}\frac{\partial^2}{\partial\theta^2} + \frac{\cos\theta}{r^2\sin\theta}\frac{\partial}{\partial\theta} + \frac{1}{r^2\sin^2 v}\frac{\partial^2}{\partial\phi^2} \qquad\text{(A-15)}$$

APPENDIX B THE EXPANSION OF r_{12}^{-1}

In atomic calculations we often encounter integrals of the type

$$I = \iint f(\mathbf{r}_1) r_{12}^{-1} g(\mathbf{r}_2)\, d\mathbf{r}_1\, d\mathbf{r}_2 \qquad\text{(B-1)}$$

where
$$r_{12} = |\mathbf{r}_1 - \mathbf{r}_2| \qquad\text{(B-2)}$$

These integrals can often be evaluated rigorously by introducing the two sets of polar coordinates (r_1,θ_1,ϕ_1) and (r_2,θ_2,ϕ_2) and by expanding r_{12} as a power series in r_1 and r_2. The specific form of this series expansion can be derived from the theory of spherical harmonics, as discussed in Secs. 4-5 and 4-6.

According to the cosine rule we can express r_{12} as

$$r_{12} = (r_1^2 + r_2^2 - 2r_1 r_2 \cos\theta_{12})^{1/2} \qquad\text{(B-3)}$$

if θ_{12} is the angle between $\mathbf{r}_1$ and $\mathbf{r}_2$. Let R and r now be the greater and the smaller of r_1 and r_2; then we have

$$\frac{1}{r_{12}} = \frac{1}{R}(1 - 2h\cos\theta_{12} + h^2)^{-1/2} \qquad h = \frac{r}{R} \qquad\text{(B-4)}$$

This function is just the generating function (4-65) for the Legendre polynomials so that we may expand

$$\frac{1}{r_{12}} = \frac{1}{R}\sum_{n=0}^{\infty}\left(\frac{r}{R}\right)^n P_n(\cos\theta_{12}) \qquad\text{(B-5)}$$

The problem now is to express $P_n(\cos\theta_{12})$ in terms of the angles θ_1, θ_2, ϕ_1, and ϕ_2. Let us consider the coordinate systems in Fig. B-1. We denote the polar angles with respect to XYZ by θ and ϕ. We also consider the rotated coordinate system $X'Y'Z'$, and we denote the polar

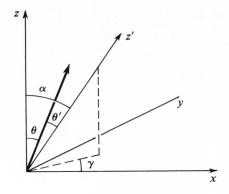

FIG. B-1

angles with respect to $X'Y'Z'$ by θ' and ϕ'. The direction of the z' axis with respect to XYZ is determined by the angles α and γ. Our problem now is to express $P_n(\cos\theta')$ in terms of θ, ϕ, α, and γ.

We saw in Sec. 5-5 that $P_n(\cos\theta')$ is an eigenfunction of the rigid rotor belonging to the $(2n+1)$-fold degenerate eigenvalue E_n in the coordinate system $X'Y'Z'$. The complete set of eigenfunctions belonging to this eigenvalue is given by

$$\psi'_{n,m} = P_n^{|m|}(\cos\theta')e^{im\phi'} \tag{B-6}$$

In the coordinate system XYZ the eigenfunctions belonging to E_n are

$$\psi_{n,m} = P_n^{|m|}(\cos\theta)e^{im\phi} \tag{B-7}$$

The two sets of eigenfunctions (B-6) and (B-7) must be equivalent, and consequently each function $\psi'_{n,m}$ can be written as a linear combination of the functions $\psi_{n,m}$ of the other set, and vice versa. We have, therefore,

$$P_n(\cos\theta') = \sum_{m=-n}^{n} A_m P_n^{|m|}(\cos\theta)e^{im\phi} \tag{B-8}$$

and also
$$P_n^{|m|}(\cos\theta)e^{-im\phi} = \sum_{l=-n}^{n} B_{m,l}P_n^{|l|}(\cos\theta')e^{il\phi'} \tag{B-9}$$

The second expansion is valid for all possible values of θ and ϕ, and it holds, therefore, if $\theta = \alpha$ and $\phi = \gamma$ also. In this case, however, θ' becomes equal to zero, and $\cos\theta'$ becomes equal to unity. It follows from the definition of the associated Legendre polynomials that

$$P_n^{|l|}(1) = 0 \qquad l \neq 0 \tag{B-10}$$

and from the definition of the Legendre polynomials that

$$P_n(1) = 1 \tag{B-11}$$

We find, therefore, that

$$B_{m,0} = P_n^{|m|}(\cos \alpha)e^{-im\gamma} \qquad \text{(B-12)}$$

Let us now return to the first expansion (B-8). Because of the orthogonality of the spherical harmonics we can derive that

$$2\pi A_m \int_0^\pi [P_n^{|m|}(\cos \theta)]^2 \sin \theta \, d\theta = \int_0^\pi\int_0^{2\pi} P_n(\cos \theta')P_n^{|m|}(\cos \theta)e^{-im\phi} \sin \theta \, d\theta \, d\phi$$

$$\text{(B-13)}$$

or, making use of Eq. (4-128),

$$A_m = \frac{2n + 1}{4\pi} \frac{(n - |m|)!}{(n + |m|)!} \int_0^{2\pi} e^{-im\phi} \, d\phi \int_0^\pi P_n(\cos \theta')P_n^{|m|}(\cos \theta) \sin \theta \, d\theta \quad \text{(B-14)}$$

Instead of integrating over θ and ϕ, we may also integrate over θ' and ϕ', and if we substitute the expansion (B-9), we obtain

$$A_m = \frac{2n + 1}{4\pi} \frac{(n - |m|)!}{(n + |m|)!} \sum_{l=-n}^{n} B_{m,l} \int_0^{2\pi} e^{il\phi'} \, d\phi' \int_{-1}^1 P_n(s)P_n^{|l|}(s) \, ds \quad \text{(B-15)}$$

The result is

$$A_m = \frac{(n - |m|)!}{(n + |m|)!} B_{m,0} = \frac{(n - |m|)!}{(n + |m|)!} P_n^{|m|}(\cos \alpha)e^{-im\gamma} \qquad \text{(B-16)}$$

and the expansion for $P_n(\cos \theta')$ is obtained as

$$P_n(\cos \theta') = \sum_{m=-n}^{n} \frac{(n - |m|)!}{(n + |m|)!} P_n^{|m|}(\cos \theta)P_n^{|m|}(\cos \alpha)e^{im(\phi - \gamma)} \qquad \text{(B-17)}$$

If this is substituted into Eq. (B-5), we obtain, finally,

$$\frac{1}{r_{12}} = \frac{1}{R} \sum_{n=0}^{\infty} \left(\frac{r}{R}\right)^n \sum_{m=-n}^{n} \frac{(n - |m|)!}{(n + |m|)!} P_n^{|m|}(\cos \theta_1)P_n^{|m|}(\cos \theta_2)e^{im(\phi_1 - \phi_2)} \quad \text{(B-18)}$$

As an illustration of this expansion let us calculate the integral

$$J = \iint \frac{e^{-r_1}e^{-r_2}}{r_{12}} \, d\mathbf{r}_1 \, d\mathbf{r}_2 \qquad \text{(B-19)}$$

If we introduce polar coordinates and substitute Eq. (B-18), we can write the integral as

$$J = \sum_{n=0}^{\infty} \iint \frac{r_1^2 e^{-r_1} r_2^2 e^{-r_2}}{R} \left(\frac{r}{R}\right)^n \, dr_1 \, dr_2 \sum_{m=-n}^{n} \frac{(n - |m|)!}{(n + |m|)!} \iint P_n^{|m|}(\cos \theta_1)$$

$$\times P_n^{|m|}(\cos \theta_2) \sin \theta_1 \sin \theta_2 \, d\theta_1 \, d\theta_2 \iint e^{im(\phi_1 - \phi_2)} \, d\phi_1 \, d\phi_2 \quad \text{(B-20)}$$

First we integrate over the angles ϕ_1 and ϕ_2, and we find that the result is zero if $m \neq 0$ and that it is $4\pi^2$ if $m = 0$. Hence

$$J = 4\pi^2 \sum_{n=0}^{\infty} \iint \frac{r_1{}^2 e^{-r_1} r_2{}^2 e^{-r_2}}{R} \left(\frac{r}{R}\right)^n dr_1 \, dr_2 \int_{-1}^{1} P_n(s_1) \, ds_1 \int_{-1}^{1} P_n(s_2) \, ds_2 \tag{B-21}$$

The next integration over s_1 and s_2 reduces J to

$$J = 16\pi^2 \iint \frac{r_1{}^2 e^{-r_1} r_2{}^2 e^{-r_2}}{R} \, dr_1 \, dr_2 \tag{B-22}$$

Since R is the larger of r_1 and r_2, we have

$$J = 16\pi^2 \left[\int_0^{\infty} r_1 e^{-r_1} \, dr_1 \int_0^{r_1} r_2{}^2 e^{-r_2} \, dr_2 + \int_0^{\infty} r_1{}^2 e^{-r_1} \, dr_1 \int_{r_1}^{\infty} r_2 e^{-r_2} \, dr_2 \right] \tag{B-23}$$

The integrals are easily evaluated by integrating by parts, and the result is

$$J = 20\pi^2 \tag{B-24}$$

We make use of this result in Sec. 12-5.

APPENDIX C THE FOURIER CONVOLUTION THEOREM

Integrals of the type

$$I = \iint f(\mathbf{r}_1) h(\mathbf{r}_{12}) g(\mathbf{r}_2) \, d\mathbf{r}_1 \, d\mathbf{r}_2 \tag{C-1}$$

where
$$\mathbf{r}_{12} = \mathbf{r}_2 - \mathbf{r}_1 \tag{C-2}$$

can also be evaluated with the aid of the Fourier convolution theorem. It follows from the Fourier integral theorem (2-67) that the functions f, g, and h can be represented as

$$f(\mathbf{r}_1) = \frac{1}{(2\pi)^3} \int F(\mathbf{k}) e^{i\mathbf{k} \cdot \mathbf{r}_1} \, d\mathbf{k}$$

$$g(\mathbf{r}_2) = \frac{1}{(2\pi)^3} \int G(\mathbf{k}) e^{i\mathbf{k} \cdot \mathbf{r}_2} \, d\mathbf{k} \tag{C-3}$$

$$h(\mathbf{r}_{12}) = \frac{1}{(2\pi)^3} \int H(\mathbf{k}) e^{i\mathbf{k} \cdot \mathbf{r}_2} e^{-i\mathbf{k} \cdot \mathbf{r}_1} \, d\mathbf{k}$$

if we define the Fourier transforms F, G, and H as

$$F(\mathbf{k}) = \int f(\mathbf{r})e^{-i\mathbf{r}\cdot\mathbf{k}}\, d\mathbf{r}$$

$$G(\mathbf{k}) = \int g(\mathbf{r})e^{-i\mathbf{r}\cdot\mathbf{k}}\, d\mathbf{r} \qquad \text{(C-4)}$$

$$H(\mathbf{k}) = \int h(\mathbf{r})e^{-i\mathbf{r}\cdot\mathbf{k}}\, d\mathbf{r}$$

If we now substitute Eq. (C-3) into Eq. (C-1), we can write I as

$$I = \frac{1}{(2\pi)^9} \iiint\!\!\iint F(\mathbf{k}_1)e^{i\mathbf{k}_1\cdot\mathbf{r}_1}G(\mathbf{k}_2)e^{i\mathbf{k}_2\cdot\mathbf{r}_2}H(\mathbf{k}_3)e^{i\mathbf{k}_3\cdot\mathbf{r}_2}e^{-i\mathbf{k}_3\cdot\mathbf{r}_1}\, d\mathbf{k}_1\, d\mathbf{k}_2\, d\mathbf{k}_3\, d\mathbf{r}_1\, d\mathbf{r}_2$$

$$\text{(C-5)}$$

We may transform this by changing the order of integration

$$I = \frac{1}{(2\pi)^9} \iiint F(\mathbf{k}_1)G(\mathbf{k}_2)H(\mathbf{k}_3)\, d\mathbf{k}_1\, d\mathbf{k}_2\, d\mathbf{k}_3$$

$$\times \int \exp\left[i\mathbf{r}_1\cdot(\mathbf{k}_1 - \mathbf{k}_3)\right] d\mathbf{r}_1 \int \exp\left[i\mathbf{r}_2\cdot(\mathbf{k}_2 + \mathbf{k}_3)\right] d\mathbf{r}_2 \quad \text{(C-6)}$$

According to Eq. (2-64) we now have

$$\int \exp\left[i\mathbf{r}_1\cdot(\mathbf{k}_1 - \mathbf{k}_3)\right] d\mathbf{r}_1 = (2\pi)^3\delta(\mathbf{k}_1 - \mathbf{k}_3)$$

$$\text{(C-7)}$$

$$\int \exp\left[i\mathbf{r}_2\cdot(\mathbf{k}_2 + \mathbf{k}_3)\right] d\mathbf{r}_2 = (2\pi)^3\delta(\mathbf{k}_2 + \mathbf{k}_3)$$

so that I can be reduced to

$$I = \frac{1}{(2\pi)^3} \iiint F(\mathbf{k}_1)H(\mathbf{k}_3)G(\mathbf{k}_2)\delta(\mathbf{k}_1 - \mathbf{k}_3)\delta(\mathbf{k}_2 + \mathbf{k}_3)\, d\mathbf{k}_1\, d\mathbf{k}_2\, d\mathbf{k}_3 \qquad \text{(C-8)}$$

or
$$I = \frac{1}{(2\pi)^3} \int F(\mathbf{k})H(\mathbf{k})G(-\mathbf{k})\, d\mathbf{k} \qquad \text{(C-9)}$$

The net result is that we have reduced the six-dimensional integration of Eq. (C-1) to four three-dimensional integrations.

Let us illustrate this method by calculating the same integral

$$J = \iint e^{-r_1}r_{12}^{-1}e^{-r_2}\, d\mathbf{r}_1\, d\mathbf{r}_2 \qquad \text{(C-10)}$$

that we evaluated in Appendix B. We have here

$$f(\mathbf{r}) = g(\mathbf{r}) = e^{-r}$$
$$h(\mathbf{r}) = r^{-1} \qquad \text{(C-11)}$$

The Fourier transforms are

$$F(\mathbf{k}) = \int e^{-r} e^{-i\mathbf{r} \cdot \mathbf{k}} \, d\mathbf{r}$$

$$H(\mathbf{k}) = \int r^{-1} e^{-i\mathbf{r} \cdot \mathbf{k}} \, d\mathbf{r}$$

(C-12)

We evaluate both integrals by introducing polar coordinates (r,θ,ϕ) with respect to the vector $\mathbf{k}$. This leads to

$$F(\mathbf{k}) = 2\pi \int_0^\infty r^2 e^{-r} \, dr \int_{-1}^1 e^{-irks} \, ds = \frac{4\pi}{k} \int_0^\infty r e^{-r} \sin kr \, dr$$

$$H(\mathbf{k}) = 2\pi \int_0^\infty r \, dr \int_{-1}^1 e^{-irks} \, ds = \frac{4\pi}{k} \int_0^\infty \sin kr \, dr$$

(C-13)

The first integral can be found in an integral table,[1] namely,

$$\int_0^\infty r e^{-r} \sin kr \, dr = \frac{2k}{(1 + k^2)^2}$$

(C-14)

The second integral can be evaluated by means of an integration in the complex plane

$$\int_0^\infty \sin kr \, dr = \frac{1}{k} \int_0^\infty \sin x \, dx = \frac{1}{k}$$

(C-15)

We obtain, therefore,

$$F(\mathbf{k}) = G(\mathbf{k}) = \frac{8\pi}{(1 + k^2)^2}$$

$$H(\mathbf{k}) = \frac{4\pi}{k^2}$$

(C-16)

If we substitute this in Eq. (C-9), we find that the integral J is obtained as

$$J = 32 \int \frac{d\mathbf{k}}{k^2 (1 + k^2)^4} = 128\pi \int_0^\infty \frac{dk}{(1 + k^2)^4}$$

(C-17)

Again, we find in an integral table[2] that

$$\int_0^\infty \frac{dk}{(1 + k^2)^4} = \frac{5\pi}{32}$$

so that

$$J = 20\pi^2$$

in agreement with Eq. (B-24).

[1] See, for example, I. M. Ryshik and I. S. Gradstein, "Tables of Series, Products and Integrals," p. 180, VEB Deutscher Verlag der Wissenschaften, Berlin, 1963.
[2] *Ibid.*, p. 144.

This method is particularly useful for the evaluation of those integrals in which the function $h(\mathbf{r}_{12})$ has a more complicated form, since there the expansion method of Appendix B is no longer convenient.

INDEX